A GRIM AND SUNKEN VOW

ALSO BY ASHLEY SHUTTLEWORTH

A Dark and Hollow Star
A Cruel and Fated Light

Book Three in the HOLLOW STAR *Saga*

A GRIM AND SUNKEN VOW

ASHLEY SHUTTLEWORTH

Margaret K. McElderry Books

NEW YORK · LONDON · TORONTO · SYDNEY · NEW DELHI

MARGARET K. McELDERRY BOOKS

An imprint of Simon & Schuster Children's Publishing Division

1230 Avenue of the Americas, New York, New York 10020

Text © 2023 by Ashley Shuttleworth

Jacket illustration © 2023 by Mélanie Delon

Jacket design by Greg Stadnyk © 2023 by Simon & Schuster, Inc.

MARGARET K. McELDERRY BOOKS is a trademark of Simon & Schuster, Inc.

For information about special discounts for bulk purchases, please contact Simon & Schuster Special Sales at 1-866-506-1949 or business@simonandschuster.com.

The Simon & Schuster Speakers Bureau can bring authors to your live event. For more information or to book an event, contact the Simon & Schuster Speakers Bureau at 1-866-248-3049 or visit our website at www.simonspeakers.com.

Interior design by Hilary Zarycky

The text for this book was set in Adobe Garamond Pro.

Manufactured in the United States of America

First Edition

2 4 6 8 10 9 7 5 3 1

Library of Congress Cataloging-in-Publication Data

Names: Shuttleworth, Ashley, author.

Title: A grim and sunken vow / Ashley Shuttleworth.

Description: First edition. | New York : Margaret K. McElderry, 2023. | Series: The Hollow Star saga ; 3 | Audience: Ages 14 up. | Audience: Grades 9 up. | Summary: Arlo and her friends must decide how far they are willing to go to depose a cruel ruler.

Identifiers: LCCN 2023009019 (print) | LCCN 2023009020 (ebook) | ISBN 9781665918770 (hardcover) | ISBN 9781665918794 (ebook)

Subjects: CYAC: Fairies—Fiction. | Alchemy—Fiction. | Fantasy. | LCGFT: Fantasy fiction. | Novels.

Classification: LCC PZ7.1.S51834 Gr 2023 (print) | LCC PZ7.1.S51834 (ebook) | DDC [Fic]—dc23

LC record available at https://lccn.loc.gov/2023009019

LC ebook record available at https://lccn.loc.gov/2023009020

For Nyx.
Every joy I took in writing this book
was because of you.

AUTHOR'S NOTE

This book is a work that comes from an incredibly personal place; it is also a work that features fairly heavy subject matter that may be difficult to engage with/potentially triggering for some readers. It is vitally important that we destigmatize the discussion of mental health, depression, and suicide—especially among our youth. While books are one of the safest spaces we have in which to talk about these very real and serious issues, it is also crucial that you, the reader, be fully aware of and consenting to that exploration. As such, please be advised of the content warnings listed below, provided for your discretion.

Content warnings: anger, arson, blood/gore (moderate), depression, grief (loss of sister/mother/father/family members), murder, murder of minors, parental abuse/neglect, psychopathy, psychological manipulation, self-harm (past, minor description), suicide (past, off-page), suicidal ideation, child trafficking (moderate description), torture, torture of minor, violence (semi-graphic)

A GRIM AND SUNKEN VOW

Alecto

The Immortal Realm of Cosmos—The Road to Farewell

ALECTO HAD NEVER BEEN one for words. Her emotions tended toward physical displays to make themselves known. As such, she had nothing to offer the competitive tradition of inventing names for the mountain that kept the Starpool.

Alecto had never been one for words, and even less so now—now that her heart lay in shattered pieces at the bottom of her soul. But poetic tongues called the mountain many things in attempt to do what she could not: to define that indescribable mixture of despair and peace evoked by the mere sight of Sorrow Spire . . .

End of Worlds . . .

The Hail and Farewell.

> *Does it eat at you, Alecto?*
> *The guilt of what you've done?*
> *You are—and have always been—a monster.*

"Alecto—I asked you what you're doing."

Alecto dropped her eyes to her hands.

She wasn't supposed to be here off duty, up in the Realm of Cosmos that was home to more "wholesome" things than Furies. She wasn't supposed to be doing any of this at all. Tisiphone's death had been self-Destruction, chosen and acted upon without the Divine Council's *blessing*. It was weakness in their eyes, and in the eyes of the people—weakness and abhorrent disgrace, and none who "sullied" immortal dignity in such a way as her sister had done were permitted funerary honors.

Does it eat at you, sister?

But immortal dignity could go fuck itself.

Does it bother you at all?

So too could honor, and the Divine Council, and Megaera hissing like an angry goose behind her.

It should, Alecto.
This is all your fault—only you can make it right.

Make it right—that one refrain was a constant on Alecto's mind.

That refrain called to her, taunted her, drove her on in a voice that mocked Tisiphone's. The rational part of her knew this voice was in her head, knew her sister hadn't thought these things, would never have said these things, certainly wasn't saying them now. The rational part of her knew that the glimpses she could swear she caught of her sister in the corners of her vision weren't real. Tisiphone's stark face wasn't actually watching her, wasn't waiting for Alecto to make it right. . . .

"Alecto! I am speaking to you."

A hand gripped her shoulder.

Alecto hated when people touched her without her permission. But she spun regardless to meet her sister's icy anger.

What was she doing, Megaera wanted to know. It was plainly obvious. Here on the pale gold cobblestone that composed the Road to Farewell—the street that cut directly through the Cosmic Realm's central district of magnificent, ornate temples and wound its way to the seven hundred thousand steps that led up to the Starpool's summit—there was no mistaking Alecto's intentions. Not dressed as she was in simple white robes, her long hair shorn short, a milk-white candle clasped between her noticeably trembling hands. . . .

The Divine Council thought they could forbid her from giving Tisiphone the funeral she deserved? Ridiculous—she couldn't care at all about the opinion of others, and she'd done this numerous times before, for people who mattered less than a fraction of what Tisiphone meant to her.

When immortals decided their time was over, that their lives and goals were sufficiently fulfilled, they could apply for Destruction. If granted, their funerals became celebrations, and all considered family and friend were invited to gather on the Road to Farewell to walk with them to their valiant ends.

The motions were all so familiar.

Tisiphone meant everything to Alecto.

And none of the scandalized glances and glares from the early-morning temple-goers who stopped to whisper and gawk at her mattered a damn—so why did Alecto tremble?

Shoulder still in hand, Megaera gave her a rough shake, as though she could dispel Alecto's foolishness by force. "You will cut this out immediately and return with me home. I understand you're grieving, Sister. We all grieve for this tragic loss. But what you're doing right now is wholly obscene—"

Obscene?

She was being obscene for wanting to mark her sister's passing with a funeral?

"Pull yourself together, Alecto. Remember yourself; you're an Erinys—"

Pull yourself together, Tisiphone! Remember yourself; you're an Erinys!

We need you out there; I need you out there. Not shut away in your room moping.

Keep it up, and they're going to strip you of your position. I heard them talking—keep it up, Siph, and you really will be the pathetic thing they're all out there calling you—

Alecto flinched to hear the same words she'd hurled at Tisiphone thrown back in her face.

Make it right!

Squeezing her eyes shut, she tried to block the memory of Tisiphone standing on the Starpool's ledge, water-gray eyes full of hopeless misery as they peered at Alecto through the mess of her coral-red hair. . . .

You monster.

Of the horrible, awful, *monstrous* way Alecto had treated her sister the night before that shattering moment; the mounting frustration with herself for being unable to fix what had crushed the last of Tisiphone's hope; the suffocating fear that she would watch Tisiphone waste away in that deities-damned bedroom, unable to do anything about that, too, just like she'd been powerless to stop the Divine Council from ordering Tisiphone replaced in the role she'd worked so hard to earn.

All over a mortal boy who'd broken her heart—as though a broken heart were some trivial injury so easily recovered from, Alecto had foolishly let herself believe. . . .

She recently discovered how devastating a broken heart truly was.

Smack.

Startled, Alecto opened her eyes.

"I'm speaking to you—you *will* listen."

She stared down at her stinging fingers, where Megaera had just slapped her.

The crowd that had gathered to watch Alecto's humiliation gasped in delight. Immortalkind so loved dramatics, and what better than the chastisement of this miserable display of sorrow? Her people, who went to such lengths to conceal things like grief, believing it was something to be weathered only in private. Her people, who looked at her right now like she was an embarrassment to all they stood for.

And Alecto didn't care.

Not about that.

She did care, though, that the candle she'd been holding now lay swatted from her clasp, extinguished and broken in two on the road's stone.

Something about the sight of it . . . the fragile wax body in fractured pieces under the callous cruelty of someone who'd once claimed to love her—damn it; *damn it*, she'd said such awful, ruthless things to Tisiphone, had treated her just like Megaera had this candle, and now Tisiphone was *gone*.

All because of her.

Now Alecto's lips trembled as well.

Her eyes welled up with watery heat. . . .

She bent down and tried to recover the remains of her candle. Her shaking hands dropped the pieces several times, and Megaera . . . instead of helping, lifted a merciless heel—

"No! Please don't—" she cried out in anguish.

But the plea fell on unhearing ears.

That heel came down and ground one of the errant halves of wax into the unyielding road.

No.

Why couldn't Megaera let her have this—just this? That candle was an important part of the ceremony; she needed it, couldn't complete the funeral without it. White robes, clipped hair, lit candle, song— these were the elements that defined this tradition, and Tisiphone deserved every one of them.

"Go home, Alecto," Megaera ordered, her steel eyes flashing. "Before you disgrace us even furth—*urgh*."

Something had happened.

Alecto couldn't really see.

Her eyes were hot, her face was wet, and her hands refused to stop trembling. Megaera's shadow shrank aside to make way for another, and all Alecto could focus on in the moment was the candle.

Snow white, freshly molded—not *her* pulverized candle, but a new one, held out before her face and pinched between two very long, very adamantine claw-tipped fingers. . . .

Alecto's sight traveled past the pristine wax.

It took in the long body and crooked limbs crouched before her . . . the gunmetal-black hair . . . poison for eyes. . . . How was, why was, *what was* . . .

"Lethe?"

Lethe rolled those too-green eyes as though it should be very obvious why he'd come to her rescue.

Like they'd ever been close.

Like he'd ever been nice to her or once displayed that he even knew what compassion was, let alone how to extend it to others. And yet he was here, doing . . . exactly that, by the looks of things, with his deities-damned candle.

The candle he proceeded next to shove into her hands.

Grabbing her much like Megaera had done, he hauled her back to her feet. She had just enough time between this and the next moment to note other things now, like the fact that Lethe was also dressed in white, which he'd *never* before adorned for any occasion or passing.

That there behind him was Vesper pushing xis way through the parting crowd, hastily righting xis own white robes xe'd clearly thrown on in a hurry.

Yue behind xim, in white that draped flawlessly as porcelain around his slender form.

Eris, behind Yue, in white that fit with militaristic precision.

The Wild Hunt . . . they'd come to join Tisiphone's Procession.

Alecto felt like crying anew.

"Sorry we're late," Vesper apologized gently, as though xe'd been expected. Reaching into xis pocket, xe fished out a candle of xis own and handed two more back to Yue and Eris. Then they all settled into place behind Alecto, her steadfast friends—her family . . . the only ones left who mattered.

Darling of Immortal Society, the greatest Flame
to ever burn.
How wonderful it must be to be loved . . .
As you always insisted you loved me.
But if that were true, you wouldn't have killed me.
If that were true, you'd make this right—

"You think this pathetic funeral is going to change anything, Alecto? You think this makes what Tisiphone did any better?"

Megaera stood livid. Black-ice hair and steel-gray eyes—everything about her glinted threat. She wasn't afraid of the Wild Hunt as most everyone else here was, but even she wouldn't pit herself against Lethe. So there she stood, enraged but unable to act upon it, unable to interfere any further, though something inside Alecto had recovered enough to wish she would try. Because . . .

What *Tisiphone* did?

Better?

Alecto's fury ignited in an instant.

She felt it flood through her, a scalding-hot wave that flushed the grief from her veins until all that was left was *BetterBetterBetter-Better—you think this makes what Tisiphone did better?*

As though their sister had been the one to do something wrong.

Before Alecto could say or do anything, Lethe spun her around to face the mountain they would make for in the looming distance, the Starpool into which they'd drop their lit candles to serve as "guidance" for Tisiphone's soul—not that Destruction left anything of it to guide, but even immortals needed the scant few comforts they allowed themselves.

Better.

Make it right.

Alecto's fingers stopped their shaking. Her tears began to subside. She was no good with words, but words weren't needed at all for this *thing* welling up inside her that she would soon come to know as true, unfettered rage.

Make it right.

"Sing, goddess," Lethe purred against her ear before drawing back to release her.

And Alecto would—the song she'd sing, the rage she'd scream . . . she'd make this better, make it right, the only way she could now. But for everyone who looked at *what Tisiphone did* as weakness, wrong, in need of forgiveness . . .

Megaera.

The Divine Council.

Their Goddess Mother . . .

For them, she'd make it so much worse.

CHAPTER 1

Celadon

~⌒~

The Luminous Palace—Throne Room, Present Day

NUMB.

This was all Celadon could feel right now, standing in the throne room of the woman who'd only just hours ago violently murdered his family in front of him.

Between the sound of Arlo's screams . . . the dull thud of his father dropping dead to the floor . . . the overwhelming scent of blood hanging thick in the ballroom . . .

This entire night would haunt him forever.

In the ballroom, he hadn't wanted to look at the contorted, mangled corpses of people he'd known all his life—his family, the Verdant Guard, Lords Lekan and Morayo—now speared on iron tree roots, dangling overhead like broken marionettes. But the alternative, the sight that had absorbed the other half of the room right after the massacre . . . it wasn't much better.

Because there, in the center of yet another damned array, lay a young ironborn servant, strangely silent and still, as Councillor Briar Sylvain—the vile traitor he turned out to be—cracked open the poor boy's chest and tore out the stone that resided in the place of a heart.

The same Councillor Briar Sylvain who had tried to reject Arlo's status as fae, despite the fact that he was apparently ironborn himself and highly skilled at the illegal alchemical magic that he'd claimed so vehemently to hate. Councillor Briar Sylvain, who'd been so happy to use that power he'd been Weighed as having no inheritance of, a proper sidhe fae according to what would have been wiped-clean records of his status after his coming of age, all at *her* behest.

Her—the woman who now, only hours after her brutal, bloody coup, sat perfectly poised on her throne, in a room of crystal and stained glass and vibrant yellow gemwork, of dazzling radiance, even though morning was still a few hours off.

Immaculate.

Brilliant.

Flawlessly composed . . .

And all around the room—deities help him—the whispers had already begun.

"Look at his hair . . ."

". . . his eyes . . ."

"Do you think he was in on it?"

"Do you think he knew all along what she planned to do?"

Celadon wanted to curl in on himself. He wanted to run, to scream. To turn around and grab the gossiping bastards behind him and shake them until they remembered that he'd just lost most of his entire family tonight, damn it all—couldn't they spare him a *moment* to grieve that without having to listen to their asinine thoughts on the matter? But . . .

"It's unnatural; he shouldn't exist."

Numb.

"Do you see the way he glows with her radiance?"

Celadon couldn't do anything but stand in place, eyes forward, so very *numb* down to his core. His russet hair now blazing Lysterne copper . . . one eye the vibrant, verdant jade of Spring, the other the freezing electric blue of Summer . . . Radiance in his skin, a brighter, purer light than the royal twilight glow of UnSeelie fae blood.

They were right—he *shouldn't* exist. . . .

He knew just as well as anyone that a union between Heads of Courts was strictly forbidden. The Seasons didn't mix—*wouldn't* mix. Forcing them together was said to result in such a catastrophic, unstable concoction of powers that if the child didn't simply combust to ash at birth, their minds would undoubtedly warp with age, their bodies rebel with time, and the magic too great for flesh-and-bone confines would build and build until it broke free by any means possible—at the expense of everything around it.

He shouldn't exist.

But here he stood, gathered along the wall with a handful of others who'd been summoned to witness their next High Sovereign's Crowning, and Celadon felt like a stranger to himself—and to the rest of the world, because come sunrise, he was sure he'd be cast as the fallen idol who'd conspired with a murderous queen to steal his own father's throne.

How long they let him live, if his own body didn't betray him first, was entirely dependent on what *that woman* was able to defend him against.

Riadne Lysterne, Seelie Queen of Summer.

His *mother*.

Hells.

"Don't listen to them, Your Highness," said a voice under breath beside him, low-pitched but firm.

Theodore Reynolds—he looked awful right now, wrecked. They all did, the lot of them. Tired, haggard, terrified, speckled and stained with blood and dust and shards of glass. Last night seemed to have aged him by years: bags under his usually bright, warm brown eyes and a tightness to his expression. But beneath it all . . . a composure Celadon envied right now. As though somehow last night hadn't been the worst he'd ever had to endure—and sure, it had been Celadon's family who'd borne the brunt of Riadne's wrath, but where the rest of the room stood in fear of her, Celadon was struck with the impression that Theodore was merely wary.

And what did that mean? Celadon wondered.

The prince had been fast by his side this entire time, but Celadon assumed that was out of guilt for the part he'd played in the night's events by kidnapping Celadon, or perhaps an attempt to assuage whatever trouble he might be in with Riadne for failing to keep Celadon out of the ballroom during his family's slaughter.

Numb.

Celadon wanted to be angry with Theodore too. If Theodore hadn't drugged him under Riadne's orders and pulled him from the ballroom at such a critical time—the price of securing his own family's survival, which Celadon could understand—he might have been able to prevent what *he'd* lost in result, might have been able to talk Riadne down from her rage unleashed. He might have been able to save his family too, if it weren't for the boy beside him.

Might-haves, could-haves, maybes—they plagued him, but all Celadon could feel right now was numb.

"Don't give them an inch of space in your head, Celadon. They aren't worth it."

Celadon looked on, Theodore's fervent advice flowing in one ear and very much out the other.

More than anything, Celadon wished Arlo were here, but he hadn't seen her so far at all.

He looked on at his mother. At the boy beside her, seated on a lesser throne—exhausted too, pale, the picture of grimness, his electric-blue eyes puffy with recently shed tears and barely restrained fury.

Vehan Lysterne . . . his younger brother.

Numb, numb, numb, *numb*—

"The door—look!"

"They're here!"

A creaking at the end of the room drew everyone's attention to Celadon's left. Carved ivory doors, two fully grown bull trolls in height, swung open, and at the sound, the room's collective tension sharpened.

Riadne sat straighter in her golden seat.

The whispers stopped.

Breath cowered in the backs of throats.

Those who weren't fastened in place by this moment's monumentality shriveled up on themselves and shrank toward the walls, instinct driving them back from the source of centuries of cruelty and subjugation.

Celadon didn't blame either reaction.

Were he capable of feeling any sort of emotion at all right now, he was sure he'd be similarly gripped by awe. It wasn't every day, after all, that the gods were granted permission to descend from their immortal keep to visit the realm of mortals—certainly not one of the Western Great Three and, only under one specific occasion, all Three of them together.

This was that occasion.

"Blessed light!" exclaimed a breathy voice in the crowd behind Celadon.

Gasps broke out once more around the room as, one by one, its occupants realized their visitors had been toying with them and hadn't entered through any door but were already in fact here.

The group Celadon stood with skittered back even farther, hands over their hearts and mouths, eyes wide in alarm and disbelief both. Only he and Theodore remained unflinching, through foolishness or bravery, Celadon couldn't say, but what—or rather, *who*—had appeared at his immediate right utterly transfixed him.

"Cosmin," he exclaimed in breathless astonishment, face growing warm for what he'd just blurted, because the man beside him . . .

Wavy, unbound hair, moonstone white in certain slants, black as inky night in others; eyes like the void of black holes. There, in robes of black rot and stark bone, cosmic dust and melting stars, stood Cosmin, Lord of Death and Night.

He was so tall that Celadon had to tilt his head to meet the god's unnerving gaze, and the fact alone that Lord Cosmin was looking at him . . . *acknowledging* him—this god in particular, who was symbol of night and to whom UnSeelie Spring had paid their worship . . .

Celadon couldn't explain it.

13

How quickly he went from numb to overwhelmed—had to blink his eyes against the sudden stinging rush of emotions, this small but oh-so-significant gesture showing Celadon that, no matter who his mother was, he was still considered a child of night.

Cosmin tilted his chin a fraction down at Celadon—a nod that didn't go unnoticed by those around them, judging by the rustling of background movement. Then, as wordlessly as he'd appeared, he strode forward for Mother Tellis, who bloomed like a flower from a pool of greenery that had fountained to life at the room's cleared center.

Mother Tellis was a beautiful, robust woman robed in clinging moss and live butterflies, with wings fluttering where they fixed themselves in place. She had earthen-brown hair and gray-stone eyes, a fox's ears and tail. She never appeared exactly the same way twice, in neither dress nor form, Celadon remembered learning. But she was unmistakable no matter her presentation.

Spring *sang* inside Celadon to simply behold her . . .

And all at once, his emotions spilled over.

Unable to be contained any longer, his magic burst from him in an outpour of verdant foliage and blossoming flowers—life, the Gift of his Season that marked him as his Court's successor.

A Gift that, until this very moment, Celadon had never displayed a hint of.

Another thing his father's magic had worked so hard to conceal in him, it seemed, undoubtedly owing to the amount of attention the Courts had already fastened on him in his youth. But if he'd been a verified contender for the throne, their watch of him would have been much sharper.

And there they were again—the whispers.

Celadon couldn't reel the Gift in, couldn't stamp out the flowers quickly enough, just as the folk behind him could no longer contain their gossip.

"Radiance and Life both?"

"This doesn't bode well, mark my words . . ."

"Wasn't there Autumn in the High King's blood? His mother, the late Queen Iris—wasn't she born of an Autumn prince?"

"And Winter runs in Queen Riadne's thanks to her late father. . . ."

Celadon tried to block out the voices, but they were speaking into existence his own fears. What would they do if it turned out that Celadon had inherited a Gift from all four Seasons? What would they do if they genuinely started to believe he might use these powers against their Courts?

"Riadne Lysterne."

Silence tightened its grip on the room with the arrival of the third and final of their Great guests.

They heard her before they saw her.

Light drew inward, gathering up in a ball behind Riadne's throne. It spoke volumes about her character, Celadon supposed, that Riadne didn't startle, didn't gasp or shriek or any of the other displays of alarm that scorched through the room like a quick bolt of lightning.

No, Riadne sat as tall and poised as ever, with the barest curl at the edge of her mouth. . . . The queen wasn't afraid, far from it. The look she wore was one of triumph and satisfaction.

Her goals achieved at long last.

Slowly, the ball of light behind her took shape, until out from the throne's shadow—and dragging that only spot of darkness in the room like a cloak behind her—stepped Urielle, Lady of the Elements, of the Light that Seelie Summer worshipped, and so it would be up to Urielle to bestow Riadne's blood-soaked Bone Crown.

In her own time, and no doubt aware that this entire room watched her as she walked, Urielle made her way down the throne's dais to join her siblings. Undefinable—as though each of the goddess's features was immediately erased from memory as soon as beheld—all Celadon could say about her was that she was easily the most formidable of all Three, a being of flame and water and air, of shadows and light and earth and stone, all of it twisting and teeming together. And she looked nothing like her daughter, Nausicaä, save the same self-assured, fiery countenance in which she conducted herself.

Once Urielle reached her siblings, she turned—in great leisure—back to the throne. No one had spoken this entire time, not even Riadne, though she'd been addressed. The two women occupied their respective spaces with firm command, and Celadon couldn't help but wonder what each was thinking.

This ceremony was more or less for show, and Riadne's actions were far from scandalous to these gods—Cosmin would likely deem them *commendable*. But power would always test itself against a foreign source, and Celadon wouldn't go so far as to call them equals, but a goddess wouldn't square herself against a mortal the way this one was doing if she truly thought they posed no danger.

And if even a goddess felt threatened by their new High Queen . . .

"Riadne Lysterne." It was Mother Tellis who now spoke, regality ringing in her gentle tone.

The ceremony was underway.

Celadon felt ill.

"Your defeat of the UnSeelie Spring High King, Azurean Lazuli-Viridian, has afforded you great opportunity," Lord Cosmin continued where Tellis left off, his alto-pitched voice deathly calm and cool; Celadon was sure he wasn't the only one to shiver at hearing it.

"Responsibility, too," said Tellis.

Now it was Urielle's turn to speak, and with all the severity of ice. "The choice is simple, and yours alone to make, as it was for all who came before you. The Crown you have won is yours for keeping—so, too, is it yours to return. Name any immortal you wish—bestow upon *them* the Crown's heavy burden—and you will be free of this object that has been the center of much grief, harm, and bloodshed in your realm. Free to reimagine your mortal Courts in any shape you so desire, greater than what the distraction of power narrows one's focus to create."

She took a pause.

Her eyes flashed in what Celadon could read only as a dare.

Riadne said nothing, the room held fast to its breathless intensity, and Urielle continued on.

"Take, instead, the Crown for your own, and it will grant you status, control, and strength beyond your mortal ken. Yours will be as divinity, a power that even titans seek to possess, but this magic, this grandeur, dear queen . . . it comes at a price. A price you will pay in the currency of *time*—your time, your very essence. The lives after death that are owed your kind will be denied to you, dwindled down to this one alone. The Crown will be yours, as will you belong to it, in grave as in life, and so we ask, Riadne Lysterne—"

"What will you choose?"

"Power . . . or freedom?"

"Will you accept the Crown you've won or return it whence it came?"

Celadon hadn't been alive for Azurean's Crowning. This was an entirely new experience to him. But he'd learned enough about these events to know that normally they didn't take place until a week after the previous High Sovereign's death—not mere hours later—and only after a funeral and period of mourning was observed, which his father certainly hadn't been afforded.

They weren't cloistered affairs either.

Only those who'd survived the Solstice's carnage had been "permitted" to attend—forced, when it was supposed to be optional and open to any of the royal families and fae aristocracy.

He also knew that every successful Challenger was presented the option to return the Bone Crown—to the Great Three holding current dominion over the Immortal Realm or to new blood of their choosing, displacing Cosmin in his lordship over Night. It would free the Courts of the Crown's hold over them and its wearer from its cruel toll. To Celadon, who'd been unable to do anything but watch as this power decayed his father from the inside out . . . Were it him in this position, he'd be tempted to hand it back to Cosmin and be done.

Tempted . . . but in giving the Bone Crown back to the Immortal Realm, they might as well tear up the peace treaty between them for how effective it would be in enforcing their separation.

The choice wasn't Celadon's, though. And Riadne hadn't schemed and murdered and spurned tradition to get to this point just to hand back her coveted prize. So it was to no one's surprise, least of all his, that she replied, "I accept."

The words rang clear.

Tellis waved a hand, and in her grasp appeared the Crown— bleached-white antler bone, twisted into a modest circlet; such a plain and unassuming thing, this trinket that had become the heart of sidhe fae corruption.

Lord Cosmin waved a hand as well, and night splashed out behind him like a gash in the air. From it stepped four black-robed figures Celadon was intimately familiar with—the Wild Hunt in full ceremonial attire, armed with their glinting adamantine weapons.

Eris, Yue, Vesper . . . Lethe.

Celadon looked quickly away when that poison-green gaze cut from Riadne to him, watching instead as Urielle bade Riadne to rise from her throne with a nod of her chin. And as she did, the whole room watched, breath locked tight in their chests as the Seelie Queen of Light and Summer proceeded to make her descent for the Great Three, the glass shards that comprised her gown now clean of Azurean's blood, but Celadon could still see it there in his mind's eye, vibrant blue and fresh as it had been when first spilled.

Riadne strode forward, the click of her heels echoing around the room, and as she moved, Tellis transferred the Bone Crown to Urielle. Riadne positioned herself before the Goddess of the Elements, but unlike all her predecessors, and again unlike their well-established tradition, she didn't bend her knee.

There was no bow.

There was no curtsy.

Riadne stood just as tall and commanding as she'd sat on her throne, arctic-blue gaze sparking-bright. A moment passed in which Celadon knew they all wondered the same thing: Would Urielle strike her down for this defiance?

But the gods held no power here—Riadne's display was an embarrassing reminder to them of this fact. All Urielle could do in the face of it was lift the Bone Crown, as easy as though this slight hadn't bothered her at all, and place it on Riadne's head. Then taking a step back, she fell to *her* knee, as custom dictated, Tellis and Cosmin following suit, the Wild Hunt behind them.

"High Queen," Urielle declared in a loud, formal greeting, folding her hand over her heart. In unison, the rest of the room deferred now too. Vehan stood from his throne to kneel, but Celadon was hesitant, very aware of the eyes that were on him, waiting to see what he would do. Yet defiance at this moment might cost him the little he had left to protect, so reluctantly Celadon too bowed, submitting along with everyone else to their new High Sovereign, Riadne Lysterne, first Crowned High Queen of the Eight Great Courts.

"High Queen, do you wish to renew the contract of peace between our Immortal and Mortal Realms, in all its current conditions?"

Riadne considered Urielle's question long enough that Celadon's gaze snapped up from the ground.

His wasn't the only to do so—Riadne couldn't seriously be considering a renegotiation with the Immortal Realm on the one thing protecting them from even worse cruelty than her own. . . .

"For now," Riadne replied at last in a cut-glass, succinct tone.

Cosmin—she *was*.

There was that feeling of nausea again.

Urielle stood in a singular, swift, fluid motion, quicker than she'd done anything this evening. Tellis and Cosmin rose as well. One by one, the Hunters fanned out and around the group, stalking the throne room to their place behind Riadne's seat. Vehan glared down at Lethe all the while, but Lethe ignored him entirely—his attention tracked Celadon, and Celadon only.

Why, Celadon had no idea, except that it couldn't mean anything good.

Lethe almost looked . . . bewildered, Celadon would describe it, as though something about Celadon's appearance or magical aura unmasked by Azurean's passing surprised the Hunter. But surely Lethe had known? Lethe knew everything, more or less.

"For now," Urielle echoed, and was that amusement in her voice? Celadon snapped his attention from Lethe back to the goddess, but Urielle wicked out of existence in the next moment with nothing but a ribbon of smoke curling in her wake to signal she'd been there at all.

Tellis withered back into her pool of lush greenery, which shriveled down to a lone, dead leaf.

Celadon turned his gaze to Lord Cosmin.

The first to arrive, the last to leave, the god stood a moment longer than the rest, his gaze shifting from Riadne to the Hunters beyond—one in particular, it seemed: Lethe. And as though following Lethe's line of sight like a tangible thread, he tracked the invisible trail of the Hunter's focus back to Celadon.

Unsure what to do with the god's returned attention, Celadon nodded.

Whether this was the right thing to do or not, Cosmin took his leave now too, dissolving into a cloud of ash that took its time to settle.

Once it did, and only then, Riadne squared herself to the room. "Rise," she bade, firm and loud and clear.

The room rose to their feet.

"The Courts summon before them Nausicaä Kraken. Theodore Reynolds. Vehan Lysterne. And Celadon Fleur-Viridian. And Arlo Jarsdel."

Arlo . . .

Celadon's heart picked up pace in his chest. He hadn't been allowed to see his cousin since they'd all been pulled and ushered from the ballroom. Guards had whisked her off somewhere—they'd *all* been separated, though the one who'd tried to peel Nausicaä from her stricken girlfriend's side had had his arm broken in a swift snap behind his back, and none of the others felt it was worth the death her steely eyes promised to make any further attempt.

He wanted to see Arlo so badly it hurt.

Just *one* of his family, alive, tangible, not a ghost haunting the backs of his eyelids. Someone he loved who loved him back—he didn't realize how much he needed Arlo's surety beside him until just now with the numbness beginning to recede and everything all at once rushing in.

As Celadon moved to the center of the room with Theodore trailing behind in tense silence, his gaze scoured the room yet again for sign of his missing cousin.

For the familiar flash of red, now so close to his bright new Lysterne copper.

He couldn't find her.

But then . . .

Whispers—Celadon turned to the open door, to the scene that seemed to spook the room almost as much as the arrival of the Great Three had.

Massive, tattered wings spread wide and cupped around his cousin like a protective shell; tall and frighteningly skeletal, her mouth a wide gash of gruesome teeth, her metallic eyes molten hot, hair spilling like white flame, and black razor talons for nails—*this* was Nausicaä. This was the Fury in her terrible, true form, the monster this entire realm feared.

The Dark Star . . . and still it was Arlo who scared him most at this moment.

Arlo, contained in Nausicaä's fierce protection as she walked in through the ivory doors. Arlo, who looked . . . nothing like herself right now, a void to Celadon's numbness, a corpse bride in her bloodied black ballgown.

She made her way to the center of the room, took her place beside

Celadon without once even acknowledging he was there. Her gaze was fixed on Riadne, but what she felt, what she thought—even Celadon couldn't say at all. His cousin, his dearest friend, sister in all ways that mattered, she moved like a hollow shell.

"Arlo?" he murmured, in an attempt to draw her attention to him.

No reaction—he looked to Nausicaä, who shook her head at him in a minute movement, like her own attempts to elicit a response had failed in the exact same way.

Did Arlo . . . blame him?

Did she also think he'd been in on this with Riadne? No; everyone else, anyone else, they could all think whatever they wanted about him, but *Arlo* couldn't . . . not Arlo. . . .

Cutting into the crescendo of Celadon's panic, Riadne spoke again. "To those I've permitted witness of the beginning of our reform, I wish to make a few of my intentions *abundantly* clear."

The room refocused itself on the High Queen. No one moved, save to quickly reposition themselves with a better view of the scene before them.

"Vehan Lysterne, step forward."

Vehan did as commanded.

Stiff. Still. Vibrating with anger.

Celadon hadn't had time yet to catch up on everything that had gone on this night, but Aurelian's suspicious absence and the prince's *sparking* outrage that verged on mania suggested Riadne had at least attempted to make good on more than one of her violent threats this past evening—and *no*, please, he couldn't be responsible for Aurelian's death too. . . .

"My son," said Riadne, in what might almost be a gentle tone for her. "You are the prince of this Court. You were born to it. You were raised by it. You are Seelie Summer by blood and right. Renew this morning your vow of allegiance to me and your people, and you will remain our Crown High Prince. You will be this throne's successor; no other."

Not Celadon, in other words, as would have no doubt been the mass concern once it spread to the Courts what had happened while they'd been asleep, that Celadon might try to make a play for Vehan's birthright too.

Vehan, meanwhile, remained silent.

Unmoving.

For a whole, eternal minute, he stood as defiant as his mother had been in Urielle's face. Would he abdicate? Would he turn his back on her after all these years of living under her strict control?

A subtle shift—Vehan lowered himself to his knees with all the air of crumbling defeat, incapable to his very core of disobedience. But Celadon was willing to bet the gaze he tucked out of view still burned.

In the brief period of time he'd spent with Vehan, Celadon knew how much this Court and its people meant to him. But Aurelian had meant more, plain and simple—had meant *everything*. It was clear by the tremors that racked his younger brother's body, the way he seemed to be doing his all to just hold himself together. And if Aurelian was really gone . . .

"I swear myself to the Seelie Summer Court. I accept the role of its Crown High Prince."

"Done," Riadne said, and in her next breath, "Celadon Fleur-Viridian, Arlo Jarsdel—step forward."

Arlo moved on automatic out of the semi-enclosure of Nausicaä's wings and slotted herself into place on Vehan's left with no sign of hesitation . . . or any real conscious decision to do so.

And that concerned him.

It was fully possible that Arlo was simply too overwhelmed right now. But Celadon couldn't shake the feeling that something was wrong. With Riadne's Magnetic Gift of mesmerization and the added support of her new High Status, of course Arlo would be quick to comply to the queen's summons, regardless of the situation, but something about this . . . something about *Arlo* felt . . . different.

Had Riadne *bound* Arlo in some way? What had occurred when

Celadon had been smuggled away? Damn it, *damn it*, he'd already failed her so greatly. . . .

Please don't blame me, he begged in silence as he stepped forward too, falling into place on Vehan's right. *I didn't want any of this.*

"Celadon."

He could feel the room's attention grow hotter on his back. This was what they'd been waiting for, this first interaction between mother and son, with everything between them out in the open. This was where they'd learn their "truth"—warped and twisted into what they wanted to hear, because nothing that happened this morning would absolve him of their suspicion, nor of the guilt in his heart that, want it or not, he'd allowed it all to happen.

Drawing himself to full height and squaring his shoulders, Celadon relied on the scraps of composure he had left and matched Riadne's electric gaze. "Mother," he greeted mildly.

The room began to buzz with whispers.

Riadne looked back at him.

It was hard to say with what expression, but there was a sort of starvation behind those eyes that made him wonder, however briefly, what it must have been like to watch the child she might actually have wanted grow up without knowing who she really was to him.

"Celadon Cornelius Viridian," Riadne began again, and it wouldn't have escaped anyone that Reseda's surname had been omitted. "In exchange for your knee and your own vows of loyalty, you will henceforth be granted all rights and privileges of the Lysterne family name. High Prince still, and my recognized, legitimate son by our late High King Azurean's blood. Swear to me your allegiance, Celadon, and as natural heir and eldest living Viridian royal marked by Spring's Crowning Gift, it will be my decree as High Queen that *you* continue your father's great legacy as Head of UnSeelie Spring."

. . . Head of UnSeelie Spring?

Riadne wanted . . . to make him *king*?

Celadon's mind reeled—he should have seen this coming. Of

course she'd do this. Of course it would serve her to have her own puppets on the other thrones. But Celadon's entire family had just been wiped from his life like a stain, and Arlo wouldn't look at him, and Celadon hadn't been groomed in the least like his sister Cerelia had been her whole life to fill such an intimidating and difficult role . . . like *Elyas* had been too—hells, Elyas! Where was his nephew? Was he all right?

Too caught up in his internalized shock, his brain heard the conversation move on, but nothing in him registered the words that were spoken.

"All that's required to pass this motion is the acceptance of one other Viridian." Riadne turned her gaze on Arlo. "Arlo Jarsdel. I asked you this night to make a willing choice—to pledge me your allegiance; to bind yourself and your power to me."

Celadon felt frost clench around his heart.

She really had. Riadne really had done something to trap Arlo here, to secure her compliance, and Celadon hadn't been able to protect her at all, as he'd promised he always would.

"You chose to accept, and already that magic has cemented its pact between us, your place here as my *guest.*"

Guest—the term was laughable. If Arlo had sworn herself to Riadne in any shape or form, even just a nod of compliance to a request of services, then Arlo was little better than a captive. And now he understood why Nausicaä hadn't whisked her away from all this the moment she appeared in the ballroom last night. With even a nod from Arlo, and until Riadne set her terms of the contract between them, magic wouldn't let her leave.

"You made your choice, but you will confirm it now again before witness in spoken vow—our oldest and most powerful of magics. Arlo Jarsdel"—the way Riadne grinned around his cousin's name . . . she'd won: absolutely everything she'd wanted, Riadne had won in mere hours, and Celadon had never felt such hopelessness in his life—"do you swear me your allegiance, your compliance, your service and all skill?"

Arlo looked up at the queen's glinting gaze, into an expression that older, braver, grittier warriors would have cowered before to see directed at them. "I do," she replied. Steady. Lifeless, as everything else about her.

"Do you, as blood of the Viridian line, accept High Prince Celadon as UnSeelie Spring's king?"

"Sure," Arlo agreed.

While it lacked proper etiquette and any feeling or thought, it was apparently good enough for Riadne. His mother turned her gaze back to Celadon, and with it, every pair of eyes returned to him as well. "Your answer, Celadon," she prompted, a curl of amusement beneath her words, because who would be so foolish as to reject so much for so little?

Celadon drew a breath—released it slowly through his nose.

He bowed his head. "I accept," he said, as graciously as he could around his broken heart, and in an elegant sweep, bent himself to one knee. "Thank you, Your Highness."

So many people he'd failed last night . . .

If this was the only way to protect what was left to him, so be it.

Let them think this was what he'd been after all along. Let them think he was content to play into his mother's hand. Let them think him a monster—if Riadne wanted to dole out even a *sliver* of power right now, he'd take it.

"Done." She sealed it as she had with Vehan before carrying on just as quickly. "Theodore Reynolds and the Dark Star, Nausicaä Kraken—I summon you next before me."

The pang of a memory shot through him of the last time someone had dared to summon Nausicaä to do anything.

His father.

Nausicaä had blown off his demands for days before Arlo had cornered her at the Faerie Ring and given her incentive to cooperate. She hadn't been too happy about it then, and she didn't seem any happier now. But Nausicaä stepped up to Arlo's side, because even a deadly, immortal Fury knew when to pick her battles—and no doubt she was wary of doing something that put Arlo's life in danger.

Taking the room by muffled surprise, Riadne reached a hand over her shoulder and pulled out the gold, glass, and jeweled sword she'd used to slay Celadon's father. Wielding her weapon like a scepter, she slammed the point of it to the ground.

The strike reverberated like a crack of lightning, startling all but Arlo and the ever-unflappable Nausicaä.

Riadne waited until she was sure she had everyone's fear and focus alike.

Sweeping the room with a piercing glance, she returned her attention to the five before her, but her words were for all to hear.

"The both of you wish to remain in my good graces. Theodore—traitor and spy—you may be bound to another master, but *I'm* the one who keeps your parents, Eurora and Mavren. You can rest assured that for now they are unharmed; how long they remain this way, however . . ."

She trailed off in her open threat, switching then to her next target.

"Nausicaä—law unto yourself, an immortal cat among pixie mortals. How long has it been since you've had anyone to care about other than yourself?"

A glance at Arlo—another quirk of amusement.

Nausicaä *glared* at the Seelie Summer High Queen hotly enough that Riadne resumed.

"One wishes to remain steadfast at true love's side. One wishes to keep his family alive. *I* wish for your bended knee—and in exchange, I'll allow you to stay. Of course, you'll have to serve some purpose to me; this is a palace, not an orphanage for pitiful children. But I think I have just the thing. . . . I could use, after all, a well-trained assassin."

Oh . . . no.

Celadon might not be operating at full faculty right now, but he could see where this was going. Riadne Lysterne, who'd been playing her dangerous games for so long, of course she wouldn't relent in them now. Did she even know how to?

Nausicaä . . . Theodore . . . Riadne had already given her sport away in her taunt—she could use, after all, *a* well-trained assassin.

"Oh, but you know, I've only really the need for one. . . ."

And there it was.

"So, I think we can make this a *challenge,* hmm? A little bit of fun. . . ."

Celadon swallowed.

How?

How on earth would this be a challenge? For Theodore, surely—such unfair odds in pitting him against an immortal Fury—and damn Riadne all over again for her twisted, cruel games, that boy didn't deserve this.

Theodore was . . . well, he was Celadon's friend.

His friend, and Riadne was going to *crush* him.

His friend, and she was going to use Nausicaä to do so.

"The two of you will have until the Autumn Equinox to bring me the heart of the most fearsome monster you can find. The winner gets to stay on in my employ; the loser gets death—or banishment in your case, my dear," she amended to Nausicaä. "Until then, you will serve me both, and it matters very much how well you do that; if I start to suspect either of you might not be up to the task, I'll simply choose neither and do away with you altogether."

No.

Celadon wanted to shout at them to stop. To not accept. To cut their losses and turn away now. He wanted to warn them not to do this. They weren't unintelligent; they had to know what Riadne intended in issuing this task so specifically.

Don't agree to this; it's a trap and you know it—but how could they refuse?

It was Theodore who sank to his knee first. Folding his hand over his heart, he bowed his head and answered Riadne with "I accept."

Riadne said nothing.

Her gaze slid to Nausicaä, a fine brow quirking in question: *And you?*

The second ticked into seconds ticked into a full minute in which nothing happened. Then, with a rippling gust, Nausicaä's wings retracted in on themselves. Her height shrank to its usual six feet. Her appearance morphed back into what Celadon better recognized: a beautiful teenage girl in the two-piece black suit she'd worn for the ball, left open to no undershirt, only her bright red bra.

Without comment, without reply, with only a glance at Arlo, who wouldn't look back at *her* either, Nausicaä sank to her knees as well.

And that was enough.

"Briar Sylvain!" Riadne rounded immediately on the gathered crowd, who'd been wisely quiet through this whole exchange, though they'd have much to gossip about afterward. The fae and folk who'd been spared Riadne's wrath . . . but at what cost? Celadon wondered. What had they paid to secure this . . . and what would Riadne collect later as recompense?

With a rustle of movement, Councillor Sylvain emerged from the audience.

All stepped aside to admit him forward, and Celadon had finally lifted his head now that Riadne no longer watched him to regard the man who shared a heavy portion of responsibility for the past night's tragedy.

"High Majesty Riadne," Councillor Sylvain exalted, pushing his way between Celadon and Theodore to drop himself to his knees at her feet. "My queen."

Lifting his cupped hands, Sylvain presented the gleaming red stone he'd pulled from the servant boy's chest hours before.

He *adored* her—it made Celadon want to throw up to hear such sycophantic worship in his voice.

"Briar Sylvain," Riadne repeated, plucking the stone from his grasp and holding it up to her examination. Her tone had worn down to a far gentler caress now, even more than it had on Vehan. "I owe you tremendous gratitude for what you've helped make possible. Your service all these years . . ."

"My queen, it is *I* who is grateful!" Councillor Sylvain lifted his head from his scraping bow. Celadon couldn't see his face, but he could hear quite clearly the passion in his voice. "I have served you happily, will continue to serve you with unparalleled devotion. The stone I created for you this night is but one of many I can arm you with—all seven that you desire will be yours, and once the Courts are under your complete control, you and I, with their own magic pitted against them, can truly stamp out all this *impurity* together, purge our ranks of infection, and restore the sidhe fae to their glorious—"

A titter of laughter sounded from the dais.

Celadon couldn't peel his eyes away from Riadne's face, as she transferred her attention from her stone to Sylvain, but he didn't need to look to know the wicked delight had come from Lethe.

"Stamp out impurity . . ."

"Yes, my queen. That . . . that *is* the aim? The faerie and ironborn blood polluting our Great Courts . . . that's what you—"

"What I *what*?"

That gentle tone had frozen over deadly.

Clearly, Councillor Sylvain had been misled, used—and it served him right.

Fae were good at wording their promises to serve their own aims; Riadne was best, and whatever she'd said to convince Sylvain to work for her, he'd very obviously been tricked.

What Celadon wouldn't give to see the shock on the Councillor's face right now.

And then, too quickly for Celadon to comprehend, Riadne raised her sword. The blade of it sang as it sliced through the air, and as sudden as a blink, Celadon *could* see the look he'd been imagining— severed from his neck, Sylvain's head rolled to Celadon's knee and stopped, a trail of purplish-blue blood in its wake.

"Unfortunate that you failed to press for clarification, Councillor. Your service has, again, been greatly appreciated, but I have no intentions of *stamping out impurity*—quite the opposite, in fact. How am I to pursue my ends with alchemy a criminal offense?" Riadne lifted her gaze again to the crowd, who all took a step back in response, like she might swing her blade at them next . . . and really, she could.

Riadne was already wholly unstable. With the Crown on her head . . . she was only going to get so much worse.

"A demonstration for the gathered powers: every single one of you is alive until I decide it no longer suits me for that to be so. Remember this in the coming days. You are all dismissed—now *go*."

Yes, Riadne was unstable. And it was her blood that ran through Celadon's veins.

How long . . . ?

How long, Celadon wondered, before his body gave out under magic it couldn't handle? How long until that Crown morphed Riadne's cruelty into the Courts' worst nightmare?

How long did he have to save the people he loved from the foolish mistake he'd let come to pass?

"Vehan and Celadon—you two remain. I wish to speak further with you both."

The surface was on fire, and Lethe wanted to see.

He wasn't the only one; so many of his people had been drawn to the spectacle, an entire ship set roaring ablaze while a handful of other ships looked on. Mer floated at varying levels of closeness to those wooden underbellies, in gossiping groups and solitary curiosity both. The heat of the flames was such that Lethe could feel its warmth begin to sink through the temperate water along with bits of wooden debris, which meant it wasn't only gawkers in congregation tonight but gatherers, too, darting around to snatch up precious building materials.

This wasn't a wholly uncommon occurrence.

Fire had long been a marvel to them, a big part of what had first lured the merfolk to land, but ships catching flame did happen with enough regularity—by conflict or stormy weather—that a crowd this size, this vibrant with excitement, meant only one thing: this wasn't just a burning but a *sacrifice*, and Lethe . . . he only wanted to see.

The Moon loved best the stories he brought it of things it could view only from afar.

"Your Highness, wait!"

"Prince Lethe!"

"Little brother, please—oh, *please* be careful!"

In and out Lethe wove; up and up and around he darted—too young, they said. He was *too young* to join tonight's "festivities." The mer liked to turn these rare occasions into their own brand of tribute to the sea, reveling in the warmth and light, whipped into a frenzy by the blood that seeped through the water, and feasting on the flesh and bone that fell to them from above. It was a long-standing tradition not meant for fingerlings like him, even those of royal blood—but Lethe hadn't slipped his guard of sisters and given them chase all the way from the palace just to watch what *his* people got up to in these affairs.

The Moon had heard enough about that.

Lethe wanted to see.

He wanted to *know*.

It was one of the things that had brought them together when Lethe had been just a minnow. When he'd first snuck away to the surface, where he wasn't meant to be, and encountered the moonlight, heard its gentle voice in his head.

A surprise to them both; neither had expected it.

The voice had spoken to him more out of its own loneliness than any real expectation of a return reply. Mortal ears weren't supposed to be able to register the speech of Celestials—the Sun and Moon and Constellations, cosmic beings of great importance even to immortals, all with life cycles of their own.

The Moon hadn't known Lethe could hear it, hadn't known about his own immortal ties, and Lethe—who'd never before conversed with a Celestial—hadn't anticipated one ever turning its attention to a realm that couldn't understand it.

His initial reaction had been wariness. The Moon, though—with a voice so young Lethe surmised they were around the same age—had been ecstatic.

Had been so *bored*, it told him, and it wasn't long before they realized their shared fascination.

He and the Moon—they had so many questions about human culture, and any time Lethe's sisters couldn't provide an answer to what he asked (which was increasingly often, almost always now), they'd laugh and ruffle his hair, tell him to put such things from his mind, because humans would never really be their concern. He couldn't tell them he wanted to know because the Moon had asked.

He wasn't supposed to go to the surface; he shouldn't know the Moon at all.

What *those Above* got up to was of little consequence to them, they liked to tell him—little consequence to *him*, they added; Lethe, future King of the Seas.

"Little brother, please—you mustn't!" Princess Esthe's melodic voice cut through the water after him.

The mer were all siblings to him, brothers, sisters, but Esthe was the only one related by blood. Older by nearly two entire decades, she wasn't first in line for their mother's throne only because she hadn't been born with the Pull, the Gift unique to the sea's chosen heir, and them alone.

The Gift that gave its bearer command over the water's tides.

It was Lethe who'd inherited the Pull from Queen Alanthe. Pathetic as his control of the Gift currently was—he was only eleven years old, nowhere near out of childhood by his people's measure of such things, and therefore far too young to muster anything worthy of note—the moment he'd been born, a ripple had burst out across the sea, felt clear and wide by the saltwater mer of his kingdom.

Lethe was their future king—their first king, for never before had this Gift manifested in a male of the sea's royal family. Never before had the sea's royal family given birth to a male heir at all.

"You mustn't," Princess Esthe continued to scold after him. "Mother forbade this, Lethe! Please don't make me report it to her. . . ."

It pained him to disobey his sister—any of them, but Esthe especially.

He adored his siblings, was adored by them. They were fierce warriors and caregivers both, his teachers and protectors. Males of their kind weren't permitted at the palace, so it was only his sisters and otherwise-gendered siblings that Lethe made any true friendships with, but Esthe . . . she'd always meant the most.

Tonight was important, though.

Tonight, Lethe had to put other things first.

Tonight, he was sure to acquire knowledge neither the Moon

nor their people had ever before possessed. Why the humans performed these sacrifices, what they gained from such things, who they chose, who they sacrificed *to*—anything gleaned would be valuable. Few thought much of those Above, but the mer had been enticed to land . . . eventually, those Above might be enticed below, as well.

It would be smart to learn as much about them as Lethe could before that point. Never mind that he was barely out of infancy; never mind that his mother had forbidden trips to the surface until he was grown enough to protect himself.

Smart . . . and it would make the Moon, his best and only real friend, so happy. . . .

In and out Lethe wove; up and up and around he darted. Pleas followed as he swam—startled greetings, laughter and coos of "hello, brother" and shouts of "good luck" as he passed—his moon-white hair streaming behind him, the cascade of his pearlescent silver tail glinting in the watery slants of firelight.

It took mer years to prepare for life on land. Learning how to split their tail into legs was only a sliver of what they needed to master in order to survive the venture. Lethe stole away to the surface more than anyone knew—more the closer he grew to the Moon, just as bright and pale as he was, when all his other siblings flashed colorful fins and hair similar to the tropical fish of their home.

He wasn't a prince for nothing, wasn't inquisitive for nothing. A fast study, he'd always been called, so it didn't take him long to figure survival out on his own, enough at least that he was able to shake his stupor quickly when he finally broke through the surface into chaos—into sounds and vibrancy and crystal clarity, vivid flame, and fragrant air.

"Your Highness!" a voice gasped in delighted shock, the sound of it so cut-glass *loud* above the surface that it made Lethe wince a little to hear it. "Little brother, good evening—are you . . . are you supposed to be up here? Where's Sister Esthe? Does she know you're—"

It was one of his siblings, their head bobbing just above the water too, seafoam-and-teal hair spread in a pool around them like a swirling film.

There were others scattered about as well. None paid him any attention; most lurked below the ships where it was far safer, but his siblings of the palace were their best trained warriors and certainly wouldn't let something as dull as risk keep them from satiating their own curiosity tonight.

And there, above it all, the cool and familiar face of his friend, bright and full and unusually large.

Hello, Lethe. It spoke its greeting in his mind the way it always did—warmer than its cool light suggested, as elegant and careful as the brush of swaying seaweed against his skin. But tonight, there was the extra swell of unrestrained excitement in its voice.

Hello, Patron of Lonely Things, Lethe pressed warmly back, using the title the Moon had jokingly introduced itself as when they'd first made acquaintance.

Swallowing back a bubble of laughter, he pushed aside the desire to preen a little that the Moon was so excited because of him.

He loved the Moon.

He loved the Moon perhaps as much as he loved Esthe, for the Moon . . . it seemed to understand him, and Lethe understood it— trapped up there, forever gazing down at a world it would never get to walk through and touch.

How curious it was about what went on beneath its watch, as curious as Lethe, and some nights he would anchor himself to a rock, bob in the water, spend hours trading stories with it, all the things they'd like to know and the things Lethe vowed to answer for them both. . . .

He gave his sibling a curt nod and swam on before anyone thought to stop him.

He needed to be fast.

Before Esthe and the others could catch up to him and corral him back to the palace.

Cutting through the dark waves gilded fiery orange, Lethe made for the school of ships sitting a safe distance opposite the one that currently burned. Even for a mer, Lethe was a strong swimmer. Not so much as a ripple shuddered in his wake as he moved toward the lead ship.

For undoubtedly *this* was where he'd find it—his answers, his story for the Moon that would make it glow oh so happy.

All he needed was a glimpse—a brief listening-in.

He'd scale the ship's hull, keep out of sight, and spend a few moments on observation, and as soon as he learned all he could worth sharing, he'd drop back to the water unscathed, uncaught, perfectly safe.

Everyone would be watching the fire; no one would be watching out for spying little merboys.

Moonlight glinted off the waves as though guiding him along the safest course. In no time at all, as quietly as he'd moved through the water, Lethe touched the wooden hull and bobbed a moment upright. Pressed as close to the ship as possible, as low down in the water as he could keep with his head still above it, he focused his magic just as he'd practiced alone in his room for months a few years back.

Slowly, his fin began to part. His lower body began to separate into two halves.

Slowly, a bit like knives shredding him to ribbons, his tail remade itself into silvery-scaled legs, his fin into feet. A bit warped, these newly fashioned limbs of his. They reminded him a little of driftwood—and that was due to lack of training; real practice with a real mentor would smooth that out for him later. For now this crude but effective self-taught method took mere seconds—he was good at it even without a formal teacher, another impressive feat he pridefully noted to balance out his underwhelming grasp of the Pull.

Be careful, Lethe, the Moon pressed in warning. *This burning is something of significance. The gods have been invoked—do not draw their attention.*

I'm always careful, Lethe thought back, perhaps a touch arrogantly.

The gods don't scare me. He could practically feel the burst of fond exasperation through whatever magic connected them.

It would all be okay. He wasn't there to interfere, would give no cause to draw anyone's attention at all.

But now would come the true test of his skill.

A time or two he'd heaved himself up onto the rocks to converse with the Moon, but never before had Lethe dared to fully utilize these bizarre human appendages to carry himself around.

Claw-tipped fingers sinking sure into the wood, Lethe pulled himself upward. His feet were clumsy. Easier by far than trying to get his fin to do this, but the *effort* it took his brain to have to constantly tell his feet what to do—exhausting.

How humans went about like this, he would never understand.

Up the side of the ship he climbed, clumsily but true, and blessedly silent in comparison to the shouting and reveling and music on the other ships behind, the crackling wood and roar of flames of the dying ship at front.

When he reached the railing, he paused.

This ship was quiet, with only one conversation to overhear, but much too far from where Lethe hung to pick out anything substantial with everything else going on. Inching a little farther up along the rail, he finally dared to peek up over his fingers enough to gauge if anyone was close.

Thankfully, they weren't.

Revealed to Lethe was the ship's deck, lanterns here and there to light it with pools of soft, orange light. Men stood about, some filthy and sweating, others in much finer garb and far better composure, but all alike in grips of what could be described only as a fearful, stricken hush.

Every pair of eyes was trained forward, but not on the burning across the way. No, what captivated their attention was what drew Lethe's, too.

A man, standing apart from the rest.

This one's robes were the most splendid of all, white and turquoise, decorated in gold, pearls, and sapphires, and paired against bangles and rings and numerous necklaces was an elegant crown atop his head. He could be no one other than a king. And with the waves and fish and tridents embroidered on his clothing . . . the *Atlantean* king, Lethe recalled from his personal studies of nearby Above regions.

King Atlas.

Standing directly opposite him was . . .

Lethe reeled back in shock, nearly losing his grip on the rail and dropping to the sea.

"—an honor," he overhead King Atlas saying, "that you have answered the prayers of a human, yourself in the flesh, no less."

You could have mentioned it was him, Lethe huffed at the Moon, then rolled his eyes at the answering swell of sheepish apology.

Hair that flashed white in one angle, black as the glittering night sky in others. Eyes deeper, darker, than the void of the sea's great chasms. In robes of black rot and stark bone, cosmic dust and melting stars, stood Cosmin, Lord of Death and Night himself—and not at all who Lethe had expected to encounter here.

The gods had been invoked, indeed.

Lord Cosmin.

Lethe's *father.*

But why?

King Atlas had said it himself—he was a *human* mortal, had his own pantheon of gods to whom he could pray. Why and how he even knew of one of the folk's greatest deities was a baffling mystery.

"You appeal for my favor, human king," Cosmin replied, low and cool and steady in a voice smooth as the scales of Lethe's tail. "A great deal of life was sacrificed this evening for it."

King Atlas stood tall. Lethe had heard tell of even other gods who couldn't claim that much bravery in Cosmin's presence. Lethe could barely bring himself to look him in the eye the whole two occasions

39

they'd met since his birth, in which his father had said very little to him.

"We weren't sure how much it would take for what we need . . . Forgive me, I know not what to call you—I've never before consorted with the barbarian faerie gods."

Cosmin regarded him, expression bland and fathomless. "Call me whatever you wish," he said after a protracted pause. "In death you learn no life is worth more than another's, and titles are as easily lost as won. Speak, King Atlas. The eldest sons of your twelve Great Houses burn before you—on what do you spend such precious payment?"

"On a son of my own, Lord Cosmin."

Almost without conscious effort, Lethe pulled himself closer. Shifting was slow; though the railing was handsome and polished to a sleek shine, his hands disliked the feel of dry things and seemed to fight against him moving.

"A son for the greatest kingdom known to man. A son for the people, who will one day turn to father himself, charged with care for each of them. Not I, but *we*, Atlantis united, spend this worthy sacrifice on our future. You are the first to answer our prayers. Our own gods spurned us. Perhaps the faerie ones are better deserving of worship within our walls."

Twelve sons for the price of one?

Could this king produce none of his own, then?

The mer birthed so few sons themselves; Lethe had been a bargain, a deal made between his mother and Lord Cosmin, both who desired an heir for different reasons, none of which they'd sufficiently illuminated to him beyond the want of a child.

Twelve deaths seemed like a waste, and *he* wouldn't have dared to appeal to Lord Cosmin's time for aid in this matter, besides—Lord Cosmin's was the realm of death alone. Tellis, goddess of fertility, would be the better bet here, but King Atlas . . . Lethe's information told him he was a shrewd man well-known for his intelligence, and Lethe had to concede it wasn't a terrible idea asking Death to skip his house rather than inviting in fragile life with no protection when gods could spin a prayer any way they desired, and just as quickly steal that life away.

"Twelve sons for the price of one," Lord Cosmin replied, echoing Lethe's astonishment with a genuine flicker of surprise on his marble-perfect face. "A son you wish to secure for the future of your people."

"A son who will help our kingdom's legend last throughout the rest of time," King Atlas added in clarification, because oh, but he'd been taught well by *someone* to mind the way he phrased his requests. "My wife's attempts so far to provide such an heir have been fruitless; the wife before her as well. It is, perhaps, that no woman in Atlantis is in possession of a womb great enough to bear this task, and so it's to the gods I turn for assistance. Will you grant me what I seek, O Faerie Lord of the starry heavens?"

It was no small ask.

Perhaps his own gods had spurned him because a request like that required *more* in payment.

But Cosmin replied, "Very well," and in response, King Atlas straightened.

Lethe couldn't see his face from this angle, but undoubtedly that stiffness was shock. Because very rarely did the Great Three answer the folk's prayers themselves, and this one in particular . . . Perhaps Lord Cosmin was simply amused. Perhaps he suspected Atlas would be some future asset in his pocket, or merely that Atlas wouldn't stop at twelve sons on a burning ship to get what he wanted.

But "very well"?

How many prayers had Lord Cosmin ignored in his time, only to grant this one with the bid of two words?

Void-black eyes slid past the king and locked firmly onto Lethe's gaze, and another shock of surprise shot down his spine—followed quickly by unspooling dread that froze Lethe in place.

Lord Cosmin . . . he knew Lethe was there.

41

Lethe! He heard the Moon in his head, frantic and urgent in its plea. *Lethe, drop back to the water!*

"You wish for a son of stock to secure Atlantis's place in legend." Lord Cosmin spoke to Atlas, but not once did his eyes leave Lethe's.

Those eyes watched Lethe the entire time, too black, too deeply mired in something that might have been sorrow? Regret? Apology? Lethe couldn't place the expression exactly, and similarly couldn't move for it. He was immobilized, unable to heed the Moon's direction despite how loudly his own instinct to do just that screamed alongside the Moon's panic.

"You offer, in exchange, the lives and futures of twelve young men. Fate has ordained this, has instructed my attendance. I am but her servant, so very well, King Atlas—I accept . . . and deliver what's due."

No sooner had he spoken those heavy words than Cosmin vanished, dissolving into ash that scattered on the swell of a passing breeze.

I accept, and deliver.

Lethe! The Moon fairly sobbed.

But it was Cosmin's proclamation that rang in Lethe's ears well after the god who'd spoken it was gone.

They meant something, those words. The look on Lord Cosmin's face before he left, the hint of remorse that pulled at his speech, as though he'd known he'd been meant to yield a son tonight, but not until now did he realize which one.

It meant something . . . the way he'd been watching Lethe as he spoke . . .

And it was too late to work it all out.

A flash of moonlight glinted off metal—Lethe couldn't recover from his shock in time, and the Moon couldn't do much to protect him all the way up in its realm as it was. But still it tried to buy Lethe time. . . .

Someone nearby yelped in pain as that glint left him momentarily sightless.

And there was more shouting now, more than just the caution in his head, more than what issued from the ships beyond. His siblings, his sisters—their *shrieking*; the sea below—*wailing*.

More glinting light, but not enough; hands wrapped themselves under Lethe's arms and hauled him up over the rail.

"What do we have here?"

Lethe struggled.

The sea churned in violent outrage.

He tried to use his Pull to call to it, to free himself, to coax a wave to swell up and swallow the ship entire into the sea, or at the very least upset the man holding him into tumbling overboard . . . but nothing happened. The water didn't respond beyond a pitiful slap against the hull.

No doubt some of his sisters had gone to fetch his mother; the rest of his siblings gathered to his rescue—he could hear shouts of the men now too, calling for harpoons and spears and anything they could get their hands on to fend off what seeped from the sea's deadly depths.

None of it would be in time.

"What is it?" barked King Atlas. "Toss it back and be done. The sea begins to rage—we've angered Poseidon with what we've done tonight. It's time to return home!"

Yes, throw him back, release him!

"But Lord Atlas—it's a *boy!*"

"A boy . . ." It broke out in whispered disbelief, spreading like the fire in that half-consumed ship beyond. It was followed by the reverent addition of "I accept, and deliver what's due."

A son.

King Atlas paused.

With wary eyes he regarded Lethe, took a step closer to him. Skepticism was clear in his expression, a small distaste as though he'd have much preferred this son he was due be one that shared his blood . . . but curiosity, too. Interest. A boy, hanging off the edge of his ship all the way out here where boys shouldn't be, and who was Atlas to argue with the gods that chose to grant wishes?

He'd be a fool to turn Lethe away.

And Lethe could see it—the very moment his fate was sealed in the resignation that steeled the king's expression. Fight drained from Lethe's limbs entirely as soon as their gazes met, and his destiny locked into place, trapping him in its clutches, powerless to escape.

"I accept, and deliver," Atlas echoed. Then added, "Bring him here."

CHAPTER 2

Aurelian

~⌒~

AURELIAN LEANED AGAINST THE far wall of an office he might have found impressive under any other circumstance.

It was located in the upper portion of a busy tavern; the wall opposite him and the entrance was consumed by an enormous obsidian fireplace. Warmth danced in its glassy reflection, spilled out into a richly stained mahogany room accented with blackwood furniture—bookshelves lined to bursting with thick, leather-bound tomes; cabinets of glittering trinkets, and jeweled and golden treasures; divans and cushions upholstered in demask gold and opulent, bloodred silks.

It was the handsome desk stationed directly in front of that unnecessarily large fireplace that commanded the room, and if it weren't for her gleaming attire, the woman seated behind it might have been completely blacked out by the haloing glow of light at her back.

Melora, Lethe had greeted upon their arrival.

Aurelian's gaze had no problem cutting through the obstructing glare to assess a beautiful woman, tall and shapely, wearing gold as though armor had been melted and poured down the swell of her breast and around the flare of her wide hips. Beneath the metal clung a skintight dress made of something pearlescent that gleamed like scales, and she was adorned with so much jewelry—bangles and necklaces and piercings and rings, all of ruby encrusted with yet more gold—that she could rival a dragon's hoard, everything in stark contrast against the deepest umber of her flawless skin.

Melora looked . . . unreal in her perfection, sat in her high-backed wooden chair with all the regality of a queen on her throne. But it wasn't Aurelian she studied back, or the unlikely collection of company Lethe had brought before her tonight. It was Lethe himself, the blood-fire red of her gaze locked steady with the poison green of his.

"It's done, then?"

Lethe inclined his head with an overabundance of flourish.

Aurelian couldn't see his face, but he could hear the curl of crass amusement in his tone when he replied, "The High King is dead. Riadne's Crowning should be underway as we speak. Long live our new High *Queen*."

Elyas, tucked against his mother's side, issued a sound in the back of his throat that made Aurelian's heart constrict to hear. He'd been too young to attend the Solstice, thank the gods for that much, and Elexa—as Aurelian had pieced together—had been too anxious about leaving his side to accompany her husband. She'd stayed with her son, and if she hadn't, she would have been dead alongside the Viridian royals.

Whatever Lethe's aims truly were, whoever's side he was truly on (if anyone's at all), and how anything that had happened this past night actually served him, he and Lethe had been the ones to retrieve Elyas and Elexa at the Palace of Spring before Riadne could send anyone to capture them. It had been their last stop in the whirlwind handful of hours since Lethe had whisked him away from the Solstice party, before leading the lot of them here to the Hiraeth—the forest that was the very life-vein of magic, sealed to any save those still connected to the Wild.

Rory Jarsdel, Nikos Chorley, Elyas and Elexa Viridian, and Aurelian Bessel—an odd troupe they made up. Whatever Lethe was after in drawing them all together, Aurelian couldn't begin to guess the full extent of it. But he'd overheard enough information between his own kidnapping and all their stops along the way here to piece together something of the bigger picture.

"Time to remember who you are, last but one Flamel . . ."

*". . . if you can find it within your mortal pride to set
aside petty differences, the Assistance might actually be useful for
once . . ."*

*"She is coming for your little Springling prince. By all
means stay here, but if you do, neither of you will outlast the
night . . . I doubt even the coming hour."*

"Very well." Melora spoke, breaking Aurelian from his memories of the night up to now. Delicately she set the long-stem cigarette holder she'd been pulling drags from throughout this meeting on an obsidian tray beside her. Rising then from her seat, she uncoiled with all the elegance of a great serpent. "So it begins. And this, I assume, is to be our fighting chance? Two fugitive royals, a long-forgotten alchemist, a tired vigilante, and . . . a lesidhe boy."

Lethe wheeled around so quickly his Hunter's robe fanned around him.

Facing Aurelian now, he grinned, and it was Aurelian's instinct to glare back, because like hells if they thought he would play along nicely in all this shadowy business. He had no damned idea what he was doing here, why he hadn't been allowed to go back to Vehan yet, and even just the *thought* of Vehan . . . how far he'd been torn from his prince's side, what danger Vehan was in right now with Aurelian nowhere near to protect him . . .

A lurch in his chest—a flutter of panic that wrenched his heart over a series of misfired beats, so profoundly that Aurelian almost gasped aloud.

"You'll thank me soon for the lesidhe boy," was Lethe's cryptic reply. "He's going to be a most useful general once he comes into himself." Then, tilting his head back enough to meet Melora's stern expression, he raised a hand in farewell and added, "Your requested seeds to grow your army, my illustrious *Madam*. The rest is up to you. Now, if you'll excuse me, it seems we've reached the point in our

High Queen's Crowning where I must make an appearance. My lord Cosmin summons—play nicely, now. . . ."

And he was gone.

Seeds to grow your army . . .

Your most useful general . . .

Aurelian's glare transferred to Melora, but before he could make any demand of her to explain what the hells was going on—

"Riadne Lysterne killed my grandfather?"

Elyas stepped forward.

He squared his jaw.

Aurelian's attention shifted to him, this boy who was so much like Celadon in certain angles, save all that starlight-white hair. Eleven years old—Elyas was just a child, but he looked so much older at this moment, standing tall in a room of grown adults discussing what sounded like war.

Melora transferred her burning gaze to the young Viridian prince as well. She said nothing, merely considered him, but that didn't deter Elyas in the least.

"During the Solstice—where my father was too, and aunt and uncle and grandmother and . . . and Arlo. And—"

"You wish to know what's happened to your family."

Cut off mid–floundering speech, Elyas kept his mouth open a moment longer, as though weighing how best to respond. In the next moment, it closed, and Elyas nodded curtly.

Drawing herself fully upright, Melora wound around her desk to stand before them. She had a way of moving that was pure, swaying grace, and at the same time . . . *careful,* as though her mass weighed heavier, her body wider, than appeared to the eye.

Melora was more than the face she presented, but Aurelian had known *that* from the moment they arrived. There was something terrible in her magic, an enormity, a great antiquity that betrayed that while she might not be immortal like Lethe, formidable like called to formidable like.

She was no mere faerie or fae.

"Lethe has told you nothing, I'm sure," she sighed. "That's his

48

prerogative—we should count ourselves lucky he's invested this much of his attention in our matters. But I'm sure it hasn't escaped your notice where you are?"

"The Goblin Market," Elyas replied, his tone betraying nothing of what he felt about that fact.

Melora nodded. "The original, where it fled when the Courts formed and fae chose to center *themselves* as the source of their own power, with their Sovereigns as their core. It's grown in population over the last couple of years, because the Wild knows—it's sensed for some time—the rot that's begun to root itself in our realm. The Goblin Market has always been a sanctuary, but now more so than ever with philosopher's stones being created and the Sins being powered anew. Their dark forces already begin to infect the lands, eating away at its fringes like mold."

She had a melodic voice, whoever this woman was. Something in the back of Aurelian's mind attached familiarity to this situation—he couldn't quite pin what sparked the embers of recognition, whether it was her name, her appearance, or her residence, but Lethe didn't strike him as the sort who made "friends" with insignificant people.

Melora had to be *someone*—the question was, who?

"Soon," she continued, ignorant to Aurelian's musing, "this Market might be the realm's only refuge, but of course you haven't noticed any of this yet. Court fae have grown so detached from the nature that once nurtured them. For the time being, your cloistered existence protects your kind, but not for long. Your grandfather, Prince Elyas, the late High King Azurean, has fallen to the very woman behind this stirring evil—your grandfather and, my condolences, young prince, nearly the whole of your Viridian family too."

Aurelian's heart gave another painful lurch.

No.

He'd been right all along. *The woman behind this stirring evil* was none other than Riadne; she *had* been involved—somehow or other—in all the horrific deaths of late, just as he'd been suspecting.

Lethe had fed him only enough information when he'd stolen Aurelian away from the Solstice party to confirm Riadne had indeed plotted to execute her revenge that night. What that revenge was he hadn't bothered to elucidate. All Aurelian had been given was the vague threat that a great deal of blood would be spilled, and his had been meant to join it, and perhaps he should stop asking asinine questions and let them continue with their busy night if he wanted to save his dark-haired prince from the perilous heart of his mother's endgame.

Hearing now what Riadne had done . . . seeing the impact of those words on Elyas's stricken face—it *froze* him, the dread that rushed through his veins sudden as a bursting dam. Celadon . . . Arlo . . . if anything had happened to them . . . He'd never actually *lost* someone who mattered to him before, not beyond mere acquaintance at least. He'd been so consumed with his own predicament, with keeping Vehan alive in addition, that it hadn't even occurred to him . . . *Celadon and Arlo* . . . somehow or another, they'd gone and made themselves important to him too.

They couldn't be gone.

He *refused* to accept that.

"Please," said a voice that hadn't spoken all evening.

Raw, rough around the English-accented edges, Rory Jarsdel had already known a significant amount of trauma this night, what with Lethe lifting the magic he'd woven to lock away Rory's memories. Forced to relive *everything* he'd been made to forget in the span of minutes—everything he'd done and been before he'd given up what conversation hinted had been his life and love and *truth* as one of the last living members of the Flamel family line—Rory looked . . . tired.

Rory *Flamel* . . . which meant Arlo was . . .

"Please . . . my daughter. My wife?"

Aurelian looked between Rory and Melora, heart hammering in his chest. He knew exactly nothing about Arlo's family history, but it didn't require anything deeper than a glance at the man across the room to see how much he loved them, his daughter . . . his wife. . . . If

Melora named Arlo among the dead, that far-too-trusting and good-hearted girl, *his friend*—

The anger, he could feel it building. . . .

"I think, perhaps, this would work best if I showed you." Melora reached behind her to pluck an object from her desk. She held out to them a small glass orb, clear as a droplet of water, that Lethe had tossed to her the moment he'd waltzed through her office door. "The enormity of what I have to tell you all, how truly dire our situation is—it will be graphic. I would recommend the young prince and his mother step outside."

"I'm not going anywhere," Elyas growled, his mother clasping his shoulders firmly. Though she was pale and trembling slightly, no less resolution shone in her eyes. "I want to see—"

"You do not," Melora interjected, but did nothing to force Elyas into the hall outside her door. "None of you do, but this is only the beginning of what's to occur, and it won't do any of you any good to go forward from this in ignorance. You have to know."

Did Aurelian wish to see?

No, he really didn't.

He already knew. He was well acquainted with Riadne's vicious-ness, had no desire to bear witness to whatever she'd done to the people she hated most in this world—was certain it would haunt him to do so. But there he stood regardless, unable to move, unable to voice any objection, trapped by the gnawing that grew in his chest. No one else took a step toward the office door either, to leave.

Melora looked each of them in the eye, lingering a moment on every gaze. "I apologize for this necessity."

And carefully squeezed her hand.

The orb popped, like it really had been water ready to burst. But it poured from her palm in far more than the trickle its size suggested. It poured, and it poured, forming a pool at her feet of swirling colors that spread across the floor.

As the pool grew—across the wooden planks, up the walls around

51

them, closing overhead—the office washed away, the colors painting them into a different scene altogether. Mahogany gave way to broken glass. Cabinets morphed into uprooted iron trees. In an instant, Aurelian was plunged back into the Luminous Palace's Grand Ballroom, suspended in time, one cruelly preserved moment in history—but the place looked nothing like how he'd left it.

No more than handfuls of folk remained of the hundreds of invited guests—all but a few cowered at the base of the staircase Aurelian had descended with Celadon only hours ago.

The trees that had been beautiful, gleaming gold stood tarnished, warped, their roots snaking across the broken glass floor, several of them suspended in the air. When Aurelian looked up to see what they dangled, his immediate reaction was to cut that gaze back; to close his eyes; to will away the image burned into his mind of the contorted bodies of the Viridian royal family, of the Verdant Guards that had tried to protect them, of Lord Lekan and High Lord Morayo . . . they hung now in place of where cherry blossoms once bloomed.

Elexa gasped, holding her son's head to keep his gaze from traveling upward too, keeping it firmly on what was in front of them instead, though that wasn't any better—Councillor Briar Sylvain, bent over the body of the serving boy Aurelian had bumped into earlier that evening, the one with the strange hollowness to him, the red glowing eyes . . . Sylvain, frozen with the boy's chest rent in horrific two, his ribs pried open, and held aloft in bloody hands over the gaping cavity was the ruby-bright stone the Councillor had wrenched free.

Riadne stood just across the way, on the outskirts of the array that *had* been the same as what was etched on Vehan's chest—damn it, *damn it*! He'd known all along, been right all along. Aurelian could have prevented all of this . . . but he hadn't.

And there she was.

Bone Crown clutched so tightly in her hands that the points pierced through her skin; her own sapphire blood trickling down her fingers to mix with the High King's life that was splashed up the entire front of her dress.

Riadne, triumphant . . . High Queen at long last.

The impossible, gnawing, seething *anger* that had been building inside him ever since Riadne had revealed what she intended for both him and her son . . .

He almost couldn't keep grasp of it right now.

His body shook with the rags of all the effort he had left to keep from igniting with the rage that scorched the edges of his vision.

"Riadne Lysterne has been rejuvenating the Sins one by one, using carefully groomed alchemists to pull them from subjects she primed long ago for this very purpose," Melora explained, turning to sweep a hand out at the *evil* before them. "She seeks to resurrect Ruin, a titan so formidable they've been kept under careful guard and lock since the deities rose to power. Only with the Sins brought together can that lock be broken, and summoning them alone . . . It's a complicated process, I'm informed. Requires far more than the most advanced alchemy to see it through. Only a child's heart can be made into a stone, you see, as children are the most mutable, most adaptable to change, have yet to be affected in any significant way by outside influence. The heart must then be strong enough to withstand the magic that calls the Sins forth. If it isn't, they succumb to it and die; if it is, they're open to the Sin's choosing for whomever they deem their most favorable host."

Aurelian and Vehan had worked out a great deal of what Melora so readily revealed to them now, but here he was, finally learning the answers they'd been after for *so long*, and Aurelian could barely listen.

Anger pulsed so loud in his ears. . . .

He was so stuck on Vehan, his prince, his boyfriend, the love of his whole, cursed life—Vehan, frozen in his struggle against the guards holding him back from his mother. Vehan, alive, for now, and *furious* . . .

He was so stuck on Arlo—oh gods, she was all right. Or rather, she too was alive. All right looked very much the opposite of her current well-being, and the way she stood, alone save Nausicaä behind her on the middle landing of that staircase . . . Even if she hadn't been a moment in time preserved by magic, there was something about the way she held herself that hinted she'd been just as dead-eyed and unresponsive in real time.

Aurelian couldn't . . . he couldn't imagine . . .

He'd met Arlo's mother barely weeks ago, had *gamed* with her at Arlo's bedside while her daughter recovered from near-fatal poisoning. Thalo Viridian-Verdell . . . she hung in the branches above his head as well.

This was his fault.

Oh gods, *this was all his fault!*

His search became frantic now—two people he cared about were safe, but where was the third? And the fourth, because Theodore, damn it all, he mattered too. . . .

There—he spotted him. Finally. Thank goodness. Theodore, standing apart from the group as though he'd been somewhere else moments prior, had only just returned to this nightmare unfolding. Theodore . . . alive, shock etched clear across his face as he tried with no real effort to hold someone back . . . a young man with copper hair and mismatched eyes. . . .

He almost looked like Celadon.

He almost looked like *Vehan.*

He *definitely* looked like Riadne. This was . . . what was . . .

Melora's voice stole over the wiped-blank slate of Aurelian's thoughts. "Alchemy," she continued on, "is then required to pull free that Sin and stone united. In order to do so, a price must be paid. Tonight, it was Lust freed into the world. Briar Sylvain paid in what he loved most to make that happen—his pride. His false identity as a full-blooded sidhe fae was sacrificed to his *achievement*, his ironborn heritage revealed to the world. Riadne will claim his life, if she hasn't already; in order for her to gain control of the Sin, the former possessor must die. Once she has it, it won't matter that she didn't summon it forth. Its Gift will still belong to her. Each Sin grants one."

"How do you know any of this?"

It was Nikos Chorley who spoke, peeling his focus from Rory's tight, upturned face to growl at Melora. "We've known each other for many years, *Melora*, kept each other's secrets. What have you been keeping from *us*?"

A crack of emotion finally showed on Melora's face. She raised her hands in a placating gesture. "Peace, old friend. I am far from clean of blood, you well know that, but this I've had no part in. It's once again Lethe we have to thank for this intimate knowledge. He made it clear how much better it would serve my ambitions to be aligned with him rather than Riadne. A queen who seeks control of all can hardly be trusted to share power, to leave her allies alone to theirs. No, Lethe brought me in on this the exact same way he brought the rest of you, and—"

"And you trust him, do you?" Aurelian retorted, returning to himself at last to glare down their mysterious host—though apparently not so mysterious to Nikos.

Melora's lip curled over her teeth, but the hand she raised wasn't to deliver any sort of punishment for his impertinence. She snapped her fingers, and the scene around them burst once more into watercolors that ran together, melting away from the walls like they were swirling down some unseen drain.

Once the room was again Melora's office, the ballroom nothing but the clear orb droplet it had come from, Elexa dissolved into tears. Rory stepped forward to comfort her, wrapping an arm around her shoulder, his own face white as death, eyes red with his own unshed grief—the Viridians . . . awful as they'd no doubt been to him, they'd been his family, too.

Aurelian had forgotten.

So much of this pain is all my fault.

He shouldn't have been so slow to warn them, should have tried harder to make Vehan listen. Riadne had never made it secret to him who she really was because he'd been meant to die in that ballroom too, and Lethe, for whatever reason, had gone against that wish to spare him.

Why?

Why *him*? Who was Aurelian that he should get this second chance at life and not someone like Arlo's mother, a far more useful general than he could ever be?

"No matter what Riadne *believes* she'll be able to do once all seven stones are collected . . . Ruin is destruction, plain and simple. They will heed her order only until the Sins burn through her life, and once they do, the titan even our mysterious benefactor speaks of in wary terms will be freed. Ruin will stop at nothing to devour this world, to tear it apart at the seams until your precious Courts fall, and their pieces are consumed, and our only hope then will be turning to the gods for help—our immortal tyrants, returned at last. We stand quite literally against *everything* in trying to stop this end. I don't question why Lethe has betrayed his ilk for our gain; I question why he thinks you, lesidhe boy, will be any help to me."

Aurelian understood the sentiment.

He opened his mouth—to bite back with what, he didn't know, only that he still couldn't regain control over the anger that made him tremble—but was once again interrupted before he could find out what it would have him say.

"You're building an army."

Elyas stood, white in the face, but determined. Aurelian was sure the boy hadn't needed to look to know how gruesome an end his family had met. Eleven years old . . . but Melora was starting to come around to him, Aurelian could tell that, too. She eyed him with a hotter fire that could be only interest.

"I am. Our new High Queen has the Bone Crown, three of the Seven Sins, and the Immortal Realm's grudge on her side. If we have any hope of standing against that, we'll need an army, and soon. Because soon *she'll* have all *she* needs to summon Wrath, last of the

Sins—and the army Wrath gifts her . . . We'll need everything we can muster just to contend with it."

"I'm going to fight."

The corner of Melora's mouth quirked in amusement. "I should hope so, young prince," she sniffed, but there was no missing the relief that flickered across her expression, which said clearly that she wanted all the help she could get. "Your connections will be most useful. Many will want to gather around the last of the tragic Viridians. Already there is a task I would set you to—an Autumn prince of your High Grandfather's bloodline who'd be more amendable to meeting with someone closer to his age, status, and relation."

This was all his fault—like hells was Aurelian letting this young boy sign himself away to . . . whoever this was, not unprotected. Celadon was alive, was still in Aurelian's debt to protect Vehan and his family, all trapped within Riadne's walls. Least he could do in return was protect Celadon's young nephew with every *fiber* of his being. "I'm going too."

Melora turned a much harder eye on him. "A wise decision," she replied after a prolonged moment. "It may just prove your usefulness to me, incline me to see what a god finds so *valuable* in you that he'd put you up for the role of general."

A . . . god?

Did she mean Lethe?

Were all Hunters considered more than just standard immortal, or did Lethe occupy a status the rest of them were unaware of?

"And you owe me a debt—several, I'd say. That goblin fire in the desert . . . the lost sales in all the commotion you lot caused in my arena—"

The . . . goblin fire?

Lost sales . . .

Wait a moment.

"I wish to go with them too, Melora."

Rory stepped forward, polite as he'd been all evening, so much like his daughter that Aurelian felt his guilt ratchet up all over again, but that had to take a back seat for now to the puzzle his brain had just pieced together.

"I'm sorry, Rory. You've only just returned to us—but I need you for another purpose. Already Riadne gathers talented alchemists to aid in her efforts, and we could use with one of our own nestled in that viper's nest. I would beg your aid as well, Nikos; people trust your efforts where they mistrust mine and would be quicker to join our united cause if it was, indeed, united. And, Elexa, love, I do hate to ask it as you've suffered a great upset tonight, but there are so many here in need of such a talented healer and empath as you—your Spring Gifts would be most appreciated, if you could spare their use."

Rory nodded resolutely. Nikos grunted. Elexa inclined her head graciously—it was Aurelian who burst away from the wall to cut Melora off once more. Because the anger . . . It wouldn't let this go, not now, not when he'd figured out at last who this was before him.

"Wait a moment."

The room turned to him.

"You *know*." He stood incredulous.

Nikos knew her.

Rory knew her.

Elexa seemed to know her too—and none of them had run, had warned him, had done anything to prepare him or Elyas for what, for *who*, they'd just signed themselves over to. "You know who she is, and you're helping her?"

Melora . . .

"You mean we know she's the Madam, head of the Grim Brotherhood," Rory hedged. Damn him for that soft tone. For his mannerism. For everything about him that reminded Aurelian of Arlo, a girl who'd been nothing but good to him, to Vehan—

"My boy—"

"I'm not *your boy*," Aurelian spat, tensing up on himself, furious now with the way he'd just spoken to Arlo's very well-meaning and definitely hurting father. And yet he couldn't help himself. He was afraid—the Madam.

He was so impossibly angry.

The *Grim Queen.*

The head of the magical community's most dangerous mafia, and they'd just sworn themselves to one of her tasks. . . .

Rory raised his hands in a show of peace, like Aurelian might spool and flee at any moment.

He couldn't.

He'd just sworn himself to a woman who was easily as deadly as Riadne, as cruel and scheming and—

"Yes, you *will* refer to me as Madam," Melora—the Madam—cut in. Her voice was stern, but it lacked the sharpness it probably should have worn, given who she was. The things she'd been responsible for in her very long lifetime . . . "And under normal circumstances, I'd be tempted to punish your continuous interruptions, boy, but I'm not without a heart entirely, and you've had a difficult night. Rest and food—I'm a gracious host, and the Goblin Market is now your home. Take the day to indulge in both; come tomorrow's nightfall, should you condescend to side with the only help and protection you're going to find right now, I'll expect you back here for a more civilized briefing."

Aurelian looked around the room, shocked to his core.

The Grim Fucking Queen.

He'd been pushed and pulled around for years, by Riadne, then Lethe, and now . . . no one but him seemed to realize they'd just jumped out of the lightning storm into the fire. One vicious mistress traded for another. . . .

A hand slipped into his own, small and smooth and warm.

Looking down, he found Elyas beside him, already tugging Aurelian toward the door. "Come on," Elyas urged gently.

Damn it . . . Aurelian blinked back the heat that stung his eyes.

Celadon . . . Arlo . . . they were too much like each other in their

damned big hearts, and Aurelian's hesitation to make Vehan understand, no matter the cost, what his mother would do . . . it had *broken*
them.

But here was Elyas, a boy who'd just lost everything, family and
home alike, extending Aurelian comfort instead. "You can bunk with
me, Aurelian. We can rest together. It'll be all right, you'll see."

There were tears on Elyas's face as he spoke, and a look as though
he was working hard to hold back as many as he could.

It was the least Aurelian could do to follow him into the hall before
anyone else could spot them too.

CHAPTER 3

Vehan

VEHAN REMAINED KNEELING BEFORE his mother as the room filtered out behind him. Head bent, gaze fixed on the coagulating pool of bluish amethyst that oozed from the neck of Councillor Sylvain's severed head, he tried very hard to collect himself; to temper the anger burning inside him; to hold on to what little was left of his composure.

What had happened during the Solstice . . . the sound of Arlo screaming for her mother . . . the lifeless bodies of the Viridian royal family and their closest allies strung up like grotesque trophies over the battleground of Riadne's rage . . .

So much seethed inside Vehan—confusion, guilt, and grief, all of it twisted and writhing around a glowing core of hottest anger.

He'd been unable to even *look* at Arlo here in the throne room, the shell of a girl who'd done so much to help him, had treated his mother with trust and respect where everyone else hesitated.

And Celadon.

Where the hells did he even begin with Celadon Cornelius Fleur-Viridian, who wasn't only a Viridian, it seemed. His entire family had been murdered in front of him—horribly, cruelly—but Riadne Lysterne hadn't left him an orphan, because lo! Surprise! Celadon, as it happened, wasn't the late Queen Reseda's son at all but actually the secret love child of Vehan's own mother and the late High King.

Making Celadon Cornelius Fleur-Viridian-Lysterne his Urielle-damned brother.

What the actual fuck was he supposed to do about that?

His brother.

His brother, whom he'd had a *romantic crush on for years*, because no one had bothered to let Vehan in on this secret, and all his mother had ever done was shake her head at his fanboying.

Celadon was his *brother*.

Vehan couldn't actually comprehend that right now. The person kneeling beside him was a complete stranger to him, and every time Vehan's brain kicked up the unhelpful reminder that he'd had some pretty explicit wet dreams about the—well, he supposed Celadon was still High Prince, good for him—Vehan wanted to be sick all over the floor.

And all of this—*all of this*—was just a distraction.

Because the thing he struggled the most with right now . . . what currently ate away at every instinct of self-preservation, balled up like poison in his chest, left him breathless and trembling and immobilized with fear . . .

Aurelian was gone.

He hadn't seen his boyfriend all evening, and no one would tell him where he was.

His mother had barely acknowledged Vehan's existence since this night took its turn from dreamscape to horror, let alone responded to what he'd *begged* to know. No one would tell him a thing about Aurelian's fate, and Vehan couldn't decide if it made him feel better or worse that he hadn't been able to spot him among the casualties in the ballroom. But his mother would not put him off any longer.

This anger, this fear, this guilt and uselessness that gutted him from the inside out . . . She was going to tell him, and *now*—he'd make sure of that.

But first Vehan had to calm himself down. His mother might currently be just as much a stranger to him as Celadon, but he knew who she was on a fundamental level, and who she was wouldn't yield to him in the slightest if his heart won out over his manners.

A shadow fell over them.

Vehan looked up at last, right into his mother's face.

Riadne stood even closer now, peering down at both her sons. They both, no doubt, understood what she wanted of them, but it was Celadon who was quicker to rise—not overly eager, but with far more grace than the brittle frost settling into Vehan's very soul permitted him to move.

They shared a look, mother and long-separated son.

What did Celadon think about all of this? Vehan wondered idly.

How long had he known who Riadne was to him, who Vehan was? Vehan could read just as little on his face as he could his mother's—*their* mother's—and Urielle, but the resemblance between them . . . now that the extra bit of High King Azurean had been scrubbed away, it was striking just how much Celadon looked like the woman who birthed him.

All the signs . . . they'd been there the whole time.

Celadon's poise, his intelligence, his cunning for Court politics and competence when it came to playing their games . . . UnSeelie faction qualities, they'd all assumed, but no—this was the son Riadne Lysterne could be *proud* of, a boy after her own design.

Riadne leaned forward, and in response, Celadon and Vehan both stiffened.

Whatever either had been expecting, Vehan was further stunned as, instead of punishment or threat or words at all, Riadne lifted her arms.

And wrapped them around her elder son.

Celadon looked . . . even less sure of what to do with himself than Vehan did at the moment. He stood in Riadne's embrace with eyes blown wide, arms limp at his sides. Vehan could count on one hand the number of times in his life his mother had ever hugged *him*, so he understood the shock of the experience, but Riadne looked far from insulted when she pulled back, Celadon's shoulders still clutched in her hands.

"My sons . . . together at last."

What sort of person was Vehan that after everything she'd done, it

63

still broke his heart a little to imagine how hard it must have been for his mother to watch from a distance as her own child she very much wanted grew up in someone else's family.

"There is much you wish to say to me, Celadon," she continued in a voice Vehan didn't recognize at all for how much genuine feeling had been packed into it. "And much you deserve to hear from me. For what it's worth, I *am* sorry. Your father was a great man."

Celadon merely looked at her.

"Time enough for that conversation later, though," she then declared in a slightly brighter tone, as though nothing about this entire situation were off. Stepping back, she folded her hands gracefully in front of her, the picture of a regal queen once more. "My son, High Prince and Head of UnSeelie Spring—I'm very proud of you, you know. You'll do well in this position. And don't worry, you have *me* now; I'll teach you everything you need to know about ruling a Court. My doors will always be open to you. In fact, I expect to see you often for dinner. But first, a show of strength—you *must* return home and establish your throne. The less time your people have to form conjectures, the easier this whole transition will be."

That Riadne could stand there talking with a boy whose family she'd just committed alarming violence against with all the ease and amiability of discussing the mild weather was, of everything that had happened so far, perhaps the most obvious sign that his mother wasn't *well*.

"And you, Vehan—"

"Where's Aurelian?" The words came out in a growl, so sudden that they caught even Vehan off guard. He hadn't meant to reply at all, but she'd startled him by switching her attention to him so quickly, enough to blurt out the question sitting heaviest on his tongue.

So be it.

The damage was already done.

Riadne raised a delicate brow. Celadon's impertinence might get a pass—she possessed that much compassion, at least. But it was clear she expected much better of Vehan, who hadn't just lost a father and mother and two out of three of his siblings.

He hadn't meant to start things off this way, but anger had a will of its own, and damn this entire situation; damn his mother too if she'd done something to the boy he loved.

"What did you do to Aurelian? *Answer me*," Vehan demanded, drawing himself taller, looking his mother square in the eye. "You've been ignoring me all night, and Aurelian's been missing since—"

"Oh, for *goodness'* sake, you ridiculous child—he's just a boy! There are countless others in this Court who'd be more than happy to have your attentions, but from the time the two of you met, you've been insufferably obsessed with stunning mediocrity. Aurelian is fine! Or he's dead—by Mab, it shouldn't matter. All I can tell you is that I had no part in his disappearance, but I assure you, if he'd remained in that ballroom last night, I would have. You can thank Lethe for absconding somewhere with the little fool, I'm sure, but if you think that puts him in any greater safety . . ." She snorted. "Aurelian has been nothing but a *weakness* to you from the very—"

"How many times have I told you, when you kept pressing and pressing for me to choose someone else? When you basically tied me to Theodore without my permission. How many more times do I have to say it before you understand? I *LOVE* HIM—"

CRACK.

Riadne had been so quick that Vehan couldn't comprehend what had happened until it was done.

One moment, electric heat was flaring hot in his veins, his Radiant Gift glaring brighter with his temper.

He loved Aurelian.

He had *always* loved Aurelian.

From the very first moment they'd met. And the days afterward he'd spent in tears, when his mother had pulled him away to return home, and Vehan just couldn't bear the awful breaking inside him at the separation.

Why couldn't his mother let him have anything good in his life? She didn't care about him at all, fine, but did she actually *loathe* him? To deny him so vehemently that care from anyone else?

One moment, Vehan had been angry—the next, stunned.

Staring at the wall to his right.

His cheek stung where his mother had stricken him, not simply with her hand but with her raw electric power too. His nerves sang with the pain of it, enough that if he'd been anyone other than a Seelie Summer fae, she'd have probably fried the side of his face.

But before he could work the smarting and stiffness from his jaw, decide whether she'd intended the extra force or not, Riadne's hand darted out once more and snatched his chin in a viselike grip.

"Love means *nothing*," she hissed at him, and Vehan . . . couldn't recognize this person at all.

Something flickered across his mother's face—a flinch, perhaps, like whatever truth she guarded in her heart had called her out in this profound lie. Love did not mean nothing, not even to Riadne Lysterne, but the way she glared down at him . . . She looked so unhinged in her wide-eyed insistence otherwise that Vehan found himself unable to—*afraid* to—argue back.

It was Celadon who broke the tension. "Mother, forgive him. It's been a long night. We're all a little tired right now and not thinking clearly."

A moment ticked by . . .

Followed by two . . .

Riadne released Vehan's face and withdrew into herself for a moment. By the time she'd fully reeled back to straight, she'd recovered her composure. "I'll hear nothing further about Aurelian Bessel," she resumed in deathly calm. "You'll have better things to occupy yourself with soon enough. You're going to need strengthening for what's to come, my love. Training in body and power. Your heart as it currently is won't be able to serve as the vessel for Ruin—much like the Sins, it requires *iron* to give it an anchor in this world. An issue

66

easily rectified, I'm sure—there's nothing I haven't been able to do yet—but it won't matter if you yourself aren't—"

"*You* put this brand on my chest?" Vehan interrupted, his voice pitched just as dangerously as his mother's.

He'd known all along, deep down. He'd *known* she'd been responsible for this . . . for everything, from the very beginning, but he hadn't wanted to believe it—had given himself every desperate excuse to look the other way despite all the warning signs. But for the first time since Vehan had started asking about this scar burned into his skin, Riadne actually gave him an answer.

The answer.

The answer he'd been dreading to hear, and *already knew*.

"Of course I did. Or rather, I had it done—to you, and dozens of others. I won't expect you to understand yet, darling—"

"Good, because I don't."

"But you'll see, in the end. Everything I've done, I've done it for the three of us."

One more than the others, though.

And Vehan had reached his limit.

"Excuse me, I need to be . . . anywhere else but here right now."

It was the rudest he'd ever allowed himself to be in his mother's presence, and he didn't care. Without waiting for her dismissal, Vehan turned his back on her and stormed from the throne room.

Celadon followed close behind, and that only served to irritate Vehan further, for reasons he couldn't figure out right now. He didn't need *looking after*; Celadon could take a . . .

He stopped in his tracks.

There, just a few paces up the hall, a man with gunmetal-black hair and acid for eyes stood leaning against the marble wall. He existed in this glittering, bright space like a void, dressed in deepest black and biting silvers, and the way he grinned—not at Vehan, but at Celadon behind him; the fascination in his stare . . .

"Take me to Aurelian," Vehan demanded.

"Try again, sweetheart," Lethe purred, but there was no amusement in the promise of swift dismemberment that soured the Hunter's expression, now turned on him like a weapon. "I think you've forgotten who you're talking to."

"Take me to Aurelian!" Vehan bellowed, launching forward to grab at Lethe by the front of his robes.

It was a fool's attempt—Lethe snatched him up immediately; wrenched his arm painfully behind his back; pinned him to the floor with a knee to the base of his neck, and all the Hunter would need to do was apply a little more pressure to snap it. . . .

"I'd appreciate it if everyone stopped trying to murder what's left of my family tonight."

Vehan could *feel* Lethe's gaze peel off the back of his head. It was pretty much the only thing he could feel over blinding pain and frustration, tears of both welling up in his eyes.

All he wanted was to see Aurelian. . . .

He didn't need *Celadon's* protection.

"Yes, I expect you do." A long, eternal moment later, the pressure at the top of Vehan's spine lessened and the shooting agony up his arm began to ease into the tingling of returned blood flow. Lethe released him, lifting himself from Vehan's crumpled body to step gracefully over it. "Are you—"

"—going to ask if I'm all right?" Celadon countered, dryness in his voice.

Vehan couldn't see Lethe's face, but his posture contorted enough that he could imagine the look of disgust the Hunter had just pulled. "Perhaps I should have let you die too."

"Yes . . . your book. I almost forgot."

"My *what?*"

A modicum of victory—Lethe actually sounded thrown by that last statement, even if Vehan didn't understand it either. It was nothing to the tension that tightened his posture, however, when Celadon reached into a fold in his robes, extracted a small black book, and tossed it unceremoniously to the Hunter.

"Your book," Celadon repeated tonelessly. "The one you've been crossing out my name in? Whatever for, I don't care right now. What does concern me is if you know, in your comings and goings, whether my nephew is okay?"

Damn it—of course. The family of the previous Sovereign had a full moon's cycle after the new Sovereign's Crowning to present themselves and swear their fealty, no hard feelings. Elyas Viridian . . . not only was he an heir to the throne with his already budding verdant Gift of Life, but as a direct blood descendant of both the UnSeelie Spring's previous king and queen, there'd be no small gathering in Elyas's corner supporting him as the true successor.

If Elyas didn't present himself to Riadne soon and declare himself loyal . . . Before last night, Vehan would have refused to believe she'd put a Hunter's assassination Mark out on an innocent young child. But now . . .

Lethe shrugged.

His reply was a little *too* light, as if he were still stuck on the mysterious book Celadon had mentioned. "The boy's alive. I stored him away in the same place as your lesidhe lover, Your Newly Higher Highness," he added over his shoulder to Vehan. "Though after that pathetic display, I'm thinking I might just—"

"Thank you." Celadon bowed to him, so suddenly and deeply that he might as well have prostrated himself on the floor at Lethe's feet. "Thank you . . . for saving them."

Lethe's focus recentered on Celadon.

Again, Vehan couldn't see his expression, but he could tell by his posture—his weight pouring languidly to his left hip, arms crossing over his chest—that Lethe was at the very least bemused.

"*Hmmm*—to think what so many folk would give to be in my place right now."

Celadon sighed, unfurled himself back to standing. He eyed Lethe warily, just as lost as Vehan about what to make of . . . not quite flirting, but there was definitely the promise of some sort of interest in that comment. Wholly inappropriate, given everything at hand, but Lethe existed in his own realm of morality. "I'm in your debt," Celadon murmured, not without feeling, however soft.

"Oh, I definitely know that."

"Would you take him?"

A beat of silence passed in which Vehan was pretty sure Lethe was trying to work out whether he'd just been offered *Vehan* as payment for services rendered.

"To Aurelian," Celadon clarified. "To Elyas. You've done so much for me and my family tonight alone, but if I could ask just one more thing of your generosity . . . if you could take Vehan to check on—"

"The continued High Prince confuses me for a taxi."

They stood there staring at each other for a long, tense moment. Finally recovered from the worst of his pain—his face still hurt, his arm now too, and the anger, the fear, the guilt, the uselessness gnawed ever away at his stomach—Vehan collected himself from the floor and rose to standing too.

Lethe's words sounded like a rejection, but there he remained, as though waiting for Celadon to sweeten the request; as though knowing that he would. So Vehan hesitated, holding himself back from begging, because it seemed to him there was only one person right now Lethe wanted to hear that sort of thing from, for whatever reason.

"No, I think I understand you quite clearly," Celadon replied, in clipped brevity. "And I can't tell you how *little* capacity I have for this right now. Please take my brother to check on my friend and nephew. When he's returned here to his palace, you're welcome to come find me at mine, where you can tell me all about the things people would do to see me at their feet, you, I suppose, included. Excuse me."

If Vehan hadn't been reeling enough already, Celadon's *very* bold and fairly suggestive dismissal would have made him splutter. He had been open enough about his demi-asexuality. Celadon might not take interest in people that particular way, not without a great deal of time and connection between them, but it didn't mean he was clueless to how very much so many people wanted *him*, regardless. And neither, apparently, did it mean he didn't know exactly how to weaponize that want against them.

If the High Prince felt any embarrassment or shame over . . . what Vehan understood to be an offer to *sleep* with Lethe in exchange for a favor, he didn't show it. He merely turned on his heels and strode off down the hall in the opposite direction, leaving Vehan to deal with whatever aftermath his dramatic departure incurred.

Lethe swept around to face Vehan.

Though Lethe's was completely unreadable, the sudden lock of their gazes made Vehan's back stiffen, pain ricocheting down his spine all over again from where he'd been pinned.

Vehan opened his mouth, whether to tack on an apology or plead his case once more, he had no idea and wouldn't find out—because in a few long strides, the Hunter that frightened Vehan more than any of the others combined stalked back to him, snatched him up by the front of *his* robes, and snarled in his face, "You have one hour."

Hunters weren't supposed to be able to transport themselves in and out of folk abodes, but the palace of their Sovereign had always been the exception. Sure enough, there was that telltale darkness pooling at their feet like tar, spreading and rising up in a great wave around them to crash back down over their heads.

Vehan *hated* teleporting around this way, this cold, almost wriggling sensation like night and death combined.

In an instant, he was . . . elsewhere.

One moment, in the Luminous Palace, the next . . . trees rose all around him, bending and warped.

He'd been here before—the charged air sparking with magic . . . the ground that seemed to swell and deflate like working lungs. . . . This was the *Hiraeth*, albeit a part he hadn't been to the first time. And thank goodness for that. He didn't think he had it in him right now to

71

contend with the Sleeping Hollow the goblin gang that had worked for Hieronymus Aurum had chased him into.

"One hour," Lethe reminded him, tugging on the back of Vehan's shirt to redirect his focus.

Vehan turned.

Behind him—now in front—was revealed a wide stretch of wooden posts nearly as tall as the surrounding forest. Crudely bound together with weathered rope, the posts formed a fence, lanterns dotted along its length holding soft greenish flames cupped in their glass. Every time the breeze stirred, it sent their hinges creaking, an eerie sound with nothing else but forest ambience for background.

"Once we're in—"

"Where are we?" Vehan asked, his curiosity beyond his control.

Lethe drew a steadying breath. "The Goblin Market. Once we're in—"

"Like . . . the *real* Goblin Market? The one that supposedly vanished when the—"

"When the sidhe fae colonized the majority of the Wild for their Courts, yes, the *real* Goblin Market," Lethe snapped, rounding on Vehan so ferociously that he took a small step in retreat. "If you interrupt me one more time, I'll bring that lesidhe toy of yours your tongue and leave the rest of you out here for the Shriekers. *Once we're inside*, it's straight to the tavern. One hour, and then I'm leaving—without you, if you're late."

When it was apparent Lethe had finished speaking, Vehan finally dared to clarify: "Are you . . . not coming with me?" He didn't know which answer to hope for. It struck him this was the sanest and easiest Lethe had ever conversed with him, but he was still . . . frightening. Unstable. Perhaps not a villain entirely, but certainly not a good person, and on that note, Celadon was *far* out of his league if Lethe really was interested in trying to strike something up there. . . .

Lethe snorted.

That was all the answer Vehan was to get, too, because the Hunter strode up to the wooden fence and placed his long-fingered, starlight-pale hand on one of the posts.

For a moment . . . nothing.

Vehan watched and, when another nothing moment passed, took a step forward for closer inspection—maybe something was going on that he couldn't see from so far back?

But then a ripple passed over the fence, like some invisible force field shifting to give way to something else: a gate. Branches shot out from the separating posts, weaving together to form a door that fell instantly open to them once completed.

"Those branches would have snatched us up if the Market decided to reject us, just so you know," Lethe informed him in bright tones, as though delighted by the concept. "They would have plucked us from the earth and pulled us apart at the seams like dolls."

Like the Viridians had been by Vehan's mother . . . The curiosity that had budded inside him began to wilt at the memory.

"You aren't welcome here, High Prince *Lysterne*. Hunters aren't welcome here either. But . . ." He grinned, not at Vehan but upward at the two burly goblins suddenly exposed, with wicked knives and fitted leather armor, matching glowers angled down at them.

Hunters weren't welcome here—yes, Vehan knew that. The Goblin Market had always existed in a safe space for the Wild folk, where immortal blood wasn't permitted unless by express invitation.

Which meant Lethe had exactly that. From whom, Vehan could only guess, and right now he was too preoccupied to care. Because the gate had opened and through it they'd passed, and revealed to him was . . . impossible to describe.

Like stepping into something straight out of a human-spun fairy tale, Vehan couldn't shake the weird feeling of both *home* and complete, foreign detachment.

This place was how they'd all lived, once upon a time—fae and faeries alike.

Though definitely modernized, it was currently a sleepy storybook village of mossy cabins and vine-tangled treehouses, and hill forts covered in vibrant toadstools. Every roof was a different, charming color. Smoke streamed in whimsical rainbow clouds from chimneys stacked to preposterous angles. A stone path marked the way from the gate's fortified entrance, where twin watchtowers loomed on either side of them to survey the beyond, and a redbrick barracks hut stirred with early-morning activity.

Dawn had just begun to lift itself over the horizon.

With it, the scent of fresh breads and hot porridges, frying eggs and cured meats, fragrant teas and bold coffees began to fill the air.

Vehan's stomach rumbled loudly, reminding him it had been a while since he'd been able to eat anything. But there was no pausing for breakfast. Lethe led him through the Market with very little interest in what unfolded around them, and when Vehan remembered what he was here for—who he was here for—he sped just a little faster on his tail.

They passed shops and vending stalls, apothecaries and pubs. A bathhouse. A school. This Market seemed to have everything, as though folk didn't just visit it for shopping, or vacation here for a break from the world's iron, but *lived* here all year-round.

The Wild folk—this was their territory; a space reserved for the faeries and lesidhe.

As they journeyed toward an enormous tavern, with its bloodred roof and gold accents and towering lanterns carved into the likeness of dragons spitting flame, positioned in the center of the Market like its focal point, Vehan hadn't spotted a single sidhe fae.

"One hour," Lethe reminded as they crossed a bridge over a sprawling pond of shimmery gold and pure white koi and continued up the path that led to the tavern's entrance.

"One hour," he reminded again as they passed through the already busy main floor, where folk sat with their food and drink, and a young faerie man with a stag's great antlers plucked at notes of a song he'd composed on his lute.

"One hour," he snapped when they reached the second landing and stopped in front of a firmly closed door. "One hour, and then our welcome wears out. You will be downstairs before then, or I leave without you." He rapped once on the plain plank of wood before them, then without so much as a glance at Vehan, he whisked himself back down the hall, glittering robes trailing in a stream of night at his heels.

The door pulled open.

Vehan could only stare.

Mouth agape, his plea of *please, I'm here to see Aurelian Bessel* caught on the end of his tongue, Vehan could only stare at the boy he hadn't realized until just this moment how deeply it would unravel him to lose.

The boy stared back.

Vehan had to look half-dead, completely exhausted and pale, his Solstice makeup smudged and smeared all over his face, his elegant robes wrinkled and askew.

"Vehan?" The boy whispered his name in both worship and disbelief, like it was the sweetest word; like he'd been just as terrified he'd lost Vehan too last night, and like seeing him here now had been an improbable hope he hadn't dared let get too high.

There was so much Vehan wanted to say.

So much he wanted to ask.

"What are you . . . ? *How* are you . . . ? Elyas just fell asleep."

What was he doing here? As though Vehan wouldn't follow this boy to the ends of the earth and whatever lay beyond.

"Okay," Vehan replied, completely overwhelmed by this moment.

Everything had changed in the span of hours. His entire life, his view of his mother, his status as High Prince. He'd really thought he'd lost the boy in front of him, the person he loved most in this world. It had always been him, *would* always be him. . . .

"Aurelian . . ."

Whatever spell had been holding them back broke at the utterance of Aurelian's name.

And Aurelian gasped—a desperate sound that perhaps shocked Vehan more than anything else this evening. Not once, in all the time he'd known Aurelian, had he ever seen him break down into a genuine, heart-wrenching cry.

"I'm s-so sorry." Aurelian reached for Vehan and hauled him in close, fastening deceptively strong arms around his torso and burying his face deep in the crook of Vehan's neck. "I'm so sorry. I'm so *sorry*," he rasped, over and over, shaking and crying . . . like somehow any of this had been his fault.

Vehan lifted his arms as well and wrapped them around Aurelian's shoulders.

He pressed his face against his hair, breathed him in, that faint but woodsy, fallen-leaves scent that clung to him, unique to his boyfriend.

"I just wanted things to be okay. . . ."

"They will be," Vehan vowed, and he would make sure of it. He'd let Aurelian shoulder the truth of everything for far too long on his own—no more. None of this was Aurelian's fault, and Vehan was going to make things *right* again if it was the last thing he did. He would be the son his mother wanted, keep her happy and focused closer to home, not here in the Market, where Vehan's heart was stowed. Aurelian had done enough; it was now Vehan's turn to contend with the enormity that was Riadne Lysterne. "Everything's going to be okay. I swear it, Rel. We'll make it through this."

Together—he and Aurelian, Nausicaä and Arlo, Celadon and Theo, they were going to make it through this, all six of them . . . together. Let his mother do her absolute worst.

CHAPTER 4

Arlo

S LEEP . . .

"Your allegiance, Arlo.
"You, and your little die, and all that alchemy you
just wished on yourself.
"I demand all three . . ."

Sleep.

". . . and in exchange . . . I will spare one of your
family tonight.
"I will even let you choose."

Sleep!
Numb.
Arlo felt . . . numb.

Exhausted? Maybe. Definitely light-headed, the air molasses thick against her every movement, the ground rising and falling out beneath each step like trying to cross ocean waves on foot.

She walked with no real awareness of her surroundings.

As though it had short-circuited the moment her mother had been impaled on that iron tree root, her brain could operate only in a feedback loop of words that were at once significant and completely meaningless.

"I wish I possessed enough skill and knowledge in
alchemy to be able to remove
the array etched on Vehan Lysterne's chest."

"Speak the name of who you wish to save.
Decline, and I will kill
every single one of them."

"Arlo—survive."

Sleep!

The words tried to make her feel other things.

Things that made her heart stutter, her lungs clench, her stomach roil. Things she couldn't handle right now, and so she pushed them down—down below the numbness. All her *ExhaustionGuilt-AgonyANGER—*

"Arlo—survive."

SLEEP.

"Arlo?"

Arlo's feet came to a stop.

She emerged from her thoughts to register a door planted before her—two doors, twins; beautiful, tall, and arching, leafed with gold and inlaid with yellow jewels, carved with Seelie Summer symbols of bolts of lightning and gleaming suns . . .

Doors that led to the Grand Ballroom.

"Arlo, let's . . . go back to your room, okay? Let's get washed and . . . and changed and . . . maybe some food? Some sleep? Whatever you want, Red, but just . . . let's not be *here*—"

Arlo pushed the doors open.

It was funny—*was* it funny? It was certainly something, that they gave way so easily to her fingertips. That hell should yield itself to a nothing eighteen-year-old girl. That rather than run the opposite way, as far as she could from this unbearable nightmare, instead she stepped inside.

Broken glass . . . uprooted iron . . . sapphire blood and gore . . .

Arlo's brain refused to catalogue the ballroom with any coherence.

There was absolute silence save for the memory of iron creaking, of bone snapping, of people running and screaming in terror. There was darkness save for the memory of the blinding red light as Councillor Sylvain pulled an ironborn's heart from their chest and held it aloft as a newly made philosopher's stone.

Steely dawn peeked through hollow archways, casting shadows like even more ghosts around the cavernous—*QuietStillDeathly*— room. Arlo picked her way around jagged slabs of floor, jutting up around solid roots as thick as pythons that snaked this way and that across her path.

To the center of the room, she waded through the carnage—the bloody heap of ironborn remains; the pieces of her family that had been severed and detached from bodies that now hung like amorphous wraiths in the gloom.

Once again her feet stopped moving.

Arlo came to a halt and looked up.

> *"You're not at all your mother's daughter, you*
> *know—how ashamed she'd be."*
> *"Celadon."*
> *"MOTHER . . . WHAT HAVE YOU DONE?"*

ExhaustionGuiltAgonyANGER—
SLEEPSLEEPSLEEP!

"Arlo?"

Arlo closed her eyes.

She closed them against the noise that wouldn't leave her ears, the stillness that pressed in all around her, the too much and too little feeling inside. Bending to her knees, she pictured an array in her mind—an unconscious effort. A reaching for something without any real awareness of doing so, and the way it sprang so readily to her use . . . she didn't have the energy or care to examine it right now. All that mattered was that she'd called, and the magic in her had answered with a picture in her head, some distant memory of an array she could almost say she'd seen before. Arlo could see it clearly and precisely, as though she'd always known how to do this. All the equations that balanced the science, the symbols that measured out the magic—she carved her array in the ballroom floor, and as it glowed to life there, she willed her alchemy to wind the iron roots back into the ground and deposit their Viridian captives gently on the floor, and the world outside her head responded to match.

Azurean, Reseda, Cerelia, Serulian, *Thalo* . . . one by one, the UnSeelie Spring royal family members were released to her; Lord Lekan and High Lord Morayo, and the Verdant Guards who'd stood by their High King's side. . . . One by one, the roots shrank back to the earth.

She'd never done alchemy like this before.

How surprising—was it surprising? It was certainly . . . something. To discover it wasn't that hard.

But it did leave her tired. Or had she already been tired to begin with? Had she simply been tired her entire life?

Movement pinged in her periphery.

Nausicaä—two of her, phasing in and out of her own image, one a formidable, winged goddess . . . the other a more familiar blond human girl, as though Arlo's brain couldn't sort out which version of her was the current one she saw. Regardless, Nausicaä had set herself to work. She'd gathered up the wayward rest of Arlo's family, the pieces and limbs that had wandered off and were in need of herding back to their owners.

Thank you.

Had she said the words aloud? Had that been inside her head or without? Hmm . . . she was tired, but Arlo couldn't rest, couldn't sleep, not until her family was given rest themselves.

Because Riadne hadn't cremated them.

This was all really foul of tradition.

More movement—Nausicaä reeled upright, wings flaring wide like a king cobra hissing a threat to whoever approached . . . but quickly she relented. Blond locks and metal eyes and hard curves once again, Nausicaä watched carefully as Celadon crossed the ballroom to stand in front of Arlo.

He looked so pale.

Two different people too. Incongruous images meshed over one another, Riadne and Azurean, but also still her Celadon.

Arlo reached out a hand to plant it against his heart.

Still hers.

Nausicaä resumed her collection. Celadon looked down at Arlo in something like relief, like his whole world might fly apart and him with it, and it was Arlo's hand alone keeping him tethered.

"Celadon."

"Arlo—survive."

"And if I'm wrong about trusting her . . .
at least I'll have the power
to put things right."

Put things right . . .

Hand dropping from Celadon's chest, she peeled away from him, moving to the nearest Viridian.

Reseda.

With two fingers, Arlo closed the UnSeelie Queen of Spring's sightless eyes and muttered the funeral prayer more traditionally uttered by the High Priests of their old religion, but Arlo would have to do in their stead.

On to the next. Celadon hadn't been able to finish the prayer himself, collapsed on his father's chest in tears. With a brush of her fingers through his copper-bright hair—new but still family, still *him*—Arlo wove the High King's farewell too, then moved on to the next. On to the next. Every fallen member of UnSeelie Spring's Court, until at last . . .

"Arlo—survive."

"From hence in peace, Thalo Viridian-Verdell Jarsdel—the stars await your return. Until we meet again," Arlo prayed, in a voice too thick for such delicate words, "may Darkness keep you." And even though they'd never spoken about it—so many things they'd never said, would never now get to share—Arlo knew her mother's beliefs, and added, "May Mab embrace you."

Her vision swam.

Leaning over her mother's body, she pressed a kiss to her forehead and added, "I'm sorry, Mom. I'm so sorry." Tears spilled over, streaked down her face; emotion choked her breath. "I'm so sorry. I'll make this right—and I won't ever, *ever* use that die again."

The die Luck had given her . . . the one responsible for all this death.

The one she'd used to make her foolish wish and play right into Riadne's plans.

Arlo had killed her mother. It was up to her to make this right.

It was hard to move bodies in a ballgown, she discovered. She already carried the entire weight of the Viridians' tragic fate on her shoulders. If she'd listened to Nausicaä back in the garden earlier that night when she'd warned Arlo against spending a wish on increasing her alchemy prowess for Riadne's gain . . . if she'd listened to *everyone* who told her not to trust the queen of Seelie Summer . . . if she'd been able to stand up to Riadne at all, if she'd said Thalo's name instead of Celadon's when forced to choose between which loved one to keep . . . This was all on Arlo.

It was hard to move bodies in a ballgown, but at least it was lighter than the crushing *ExhaustionGuiltAgonyAngerAngerANGERANGER* beginning to break through their numb confines. . . .

Out into the Courtyard she carried her burden, one body painstakingly by one.

Nausicaä helped, and Celadon too, once he recovered enough to stand.

Others turned up as the dawn became morning and slipped into day—Vehan, Theodore, all four of the Wild Hunt, strangely even Lethe included. Not many . . . Riadne Lysterne appeared on the ballroom staircase at one point to watch. The onlookers peeking through the doors and gathered on the sidelines might have been disappointed that she merely looked on, a handful of long minutes, before turning away and leaving, permitting the Viridians their meager funeral without argument or immediate punishment.

Maybe she would have punished Arlo if she'd thought it would achieve anything.

Maybe she would still.

Arlo ignored her when she arrived and ignored her when she left. She kept her focus on transferring her family out into the Courtyard. The Viridians, the Guards, Lord Lekan and Lord Morayo, they all deserved better than to be bidden their last farewell in the backyard of the woman who'd killed them, but this . . . was the best she could do.

She hoped they'd forgive her.

Which they probably wouldn't—they were dead because of what her choices had allowed to happen. This was all her fault. *All hers.* But she hoped just the same . . . that they'd at least get to rest when she didn't think *she* ever would again.

It took the entire day to wipe down the bodies. To wrap them in the sheer curtains pulled from windows around the palace. To build the pyre on which they'd burn to the dust that would return them to the stars, and by the end of it, Arlo was tired.

Exhausted.

Filthy.

No less angry.

SleepSleepSleep pulled viciously at her consciousness.

Nausicaä stood beside her, Celadon too, both of them hand in hand with Arlo as though anchoring her to the earth, which might fall away if they didn't.

Night poured over the sky anew by the time they were able to light up the pyre with Nausicaä's fire.

Arlo watched as the flames grew high. She watched as they burned her mother to ash and released her soul back to Fate, and when she could watch no more, Arlo turned again for the ballroom.

She crossed back over the glassy floor.

To the staircase, and the sword Thalo had there flung, embedded point down in the debris like a legend her brain couldn't currently recall. When she reached the hilt, she tugged it free as easily as though it had been waiting for her to claim it.

Her mother's sword.

Thalo had been a legend of her own to their people by this blade. Arlo wasn't worthy of wielding it, but she couldn't, *wouldn't* leave it here.

"Let me take you to bed, Arlo."

It was harder than ever to keep up with events now.

Arlo's eyes had grown so heavy, her fatigue so dire, but that was Nausicaä who'd spoken, and Arlo felt herself nod. She followed her girlfriend out into the hall again and on and on and up to a bedroom that wasn't Arlo's, would never be Arlo's—except it *was* home now, she supposed. Riadne had trapped her here with a promise to serve, and she doubted very much she'd be allowed to leave any time soon.

Problems for later.

Information for later.

In a fog Arlo moved to her closet and stuffed that sword she was so completely unworthy of even looking at in the back behind her clothing. Like a hollow shell, she went next to her bedside table, yanked open the drawer, threw her die to the back of it too, and closed it away with a slam.

Never again.

She then allowed Nausicaä to lead her to the bathroom, let her free Arlo from her dress. With a warm cloth and a great amount of care, Nausicaä washed as much dirt and dust and blood from the exposed bits of Arlo's skin as she could, then wrapped her up in something soft, while Arlo watched it all like looking in on someone else's life.

"Stay, please?" Arlo heard herself ask in such a pathetic voice when Nausicaä finally directed her to bed. Pathetic, but . . .

A knock at the door.

Softer voices.

Nausicaä's weight dipped the side of her bed, followed by another's on her opposite. Spring rain and cedarwood and a newer, gingery scent like Riadne's and Vehan's, but it was Celadon's now too, and he was still hers, and it was *him* crawling into bed alongside her, like they were little kids again and everything was as it should be.

Arlo had no memory of falling asleep tucked up between her girlfriend and her cousin. The world had filtered to black like water spiraling down a drain. One moment Arlo had been sinking with it—the next . . .

"Hello, Arlo Cyan Jarsdel."

Her eyes fluttered open.

The room that greeted her sight was wholly unfamiliar to her. She'd never seen it before, this quiet, stone-gray temple crumbling to time.

Moss and weeds and vines ate away at it; rain and snow and sun had worn it down to smooth and weathered and faded. Bluebells and snowdrops and crocuses popped through various cracks in the floor, and there was a hint of warmth in the otherwise cool air that smelled like damp earth and melted wax—a hint of spring that made something in Arlo's chest settle.

It took her a moment to remember that someone had spoken her name.

Gaze sliding back forward, she considered the person who stood before her, barely more than a few steps away. Red hair like wildfire . . . bright eyes hard as jade . . . It was a delayed response, but surprise bubbled at last to the surface, followed more quickly by confusion.

"Uh . . ." was Arlo's ineloquent reply. The person before her was *her*, Arlo—a little bit wilder and a lot bit more attractive, something about the way magic glowed beneath her skin and highlighted every feature, every ample curve, giving this version of her much more life and energy.

"Hello?" she finally managed to return.

It wasn't *all* that shocking, she supposed. Given what had just occurred, strange and vivid dreams should almost be an expected reaction for the next little while. However real this felt, and at the same time foreign, the more she tried to suppress her emotions in her waking hours, the weirder her nights were bound to become.

"There's no need to be afraid, Arlo."

"I'm . . . not," she said, and found she actually meant it.

At the moment, she wasn't afraid at all. She wasn't distressed, or upset, or anything like she should be feeling . . . only calm. Not in a negative, repressed way like earlier. With all this magic in the air, it felt like standing in the Hiraeth had felt when Nausicaä had taken her to meet Vehan and Aurelian for the first time at the Assistance's headquarters.

The other Arlo gave a benign nod.

She was oddly dressed, Arlo noted. Never had *she* personally worn or even seen this outfit in her life, this gown of something that wasn't fabric but more like pearly soft glitter that held itself together in shape and shifted fluidly with each of Other Arlo's movements.

"I'm glad to hear it. We've known each other our entire lives, after all."

Arlo looked up from the dress. "We have?"

"Of course. I am Magic, and *you* have made a wish of me."

A minute ticked by . . . ticked into another. . . . It threaded itself together, eventually, the meaning behind Other Arlo's words. They were *Magic*, the primordial entity in the flesh, or rather, in Arlo's flesh—Arlo, who'd used the die Luck had given her to spend one of the four wishes she'd been allotted on asking for greater skill in alchemy—skill to remove Vehan's array from his chest.

That deities-damned wish . . .

If only Arlo hadn't made it, things might have been so different—she might still have her mother right now, for instance.

"Perhaps," Magic replied to Arlo's unspoken thoughts, compassion warm in their voice. "Perhaps it would have resulted in the same at the end of a different path. Regardless, the wish has been made, and so it cannot be undone. I apologize for the extra fatigue you've been feeling—that is in part my work. What you've requested of me requires our meeting, and I cannot take form like this outside of mortal dreams, where all is possible."

Wrapping her arms around her middle—Arlo might be in the clutches of dreaming, but reality was creeping in, the gravity of her situation, of what she'd done . . . of what she'd lost—Arlo eyed Magic with a touch of apprehension. "What do you mean?" What she'd requested . . . "Don't I already have better alchemy?"

Vaguely she recalled what she'd done in the ballroom, the array she'd never used before that had carved in her mind regardless, and thinking on it now, she had just assumed at the moment that it was her ill-bought wish that had made it real.

Magic folded their hands in front of them. "Oh yes, you do. You have no idea how great your power truly is. But what you performed earlier was no result of your wish. That strength was already in your possession."

Already in her possession?

"There is such potential inside you, Arlo, the likes of which this realm hasn't known for quite some time. Yours is the alchemy of legend, reborn of the very first to ever achieve immortality by mortal means. The things you are capable of . . . You wished for alchemic ability to dissolve your friend's array, but this I cannot grant, for you already possess the knowledge of what must be done to rescue Vehan Lysterne from his mother's designs."

Arlo stared.

A wasted wish, then . . . a wasted choice. . . . Riadne *knew* Arlo would pick Celadon. Somehow she'd known, and still she said nothing, let Arlo believe he was in danger of dying that night too because Celadon was a Viridian, and Arlo hadn't known he was a Lysterne as well.

"Arlo—survive."

A wasted wish and a wasted choice.

"You're angry."

"You don't make sense," Arlo countered hotly.

"And I won't, not until you locate the one who locked away the memory of who you really are." Magic sighed, unfolded their hands, stepped close enough to Arlo to take hers, and held them in palms that seeped tingling warmth up her arms. "I will do what I can. I will make it so that when you do remember, your mastery of this art will be even easier, incomparable to all who came before. I will bestow upon you the pieces that your knowledge is missing, but first, before this can come into effect, you must find a way to dispel the magic that guards the pieces already there. For it *is* magic . . . the sort I have no consent to unweave."

She didn't understand at all.

Her entire life had been accounted for, uneventful until now.

Who could have possibly stolen memories from her? *Why?* She'd only ever been Arlo, just Arlo, and despite all the other things people said she was these days, she still felt only that.

Just Arlo.

"Could I . . . wish for them returned?" she asked in a small voice. Magic might be her mirrored reflection, but they stood somehow taller, surer than she did. And she *hurt.* . . . There was something about Magic that made her want to throw herself at them like a child hiding in her mother's skirts.

A mother Arlo no longer had . . . and never would again.

"You could—to disastrous effect. The one who requested this wipe performed knew what they were doing, what to ask for, how to word it. As I said, I do not have consent to break this magic—forcing my hand, going against it, returning your memories in any way other than what was outlined, would cause tremendous harm. To yourself. To others . . ."

Arlo flinched.

She'd done enough harm already with a callous wish and had no desire to do so again in any way.

Magic squeezed her hands. "There is always a price." The warmth that spread up her limbs flared with a fizzle of soothing heat. Already their image began to shift, their face no longer recognizably hers but indefinable and many. "Find the one who put the block there, Arlo. Complete the conditions for its natural removal. Once you remember who you are, the rest will unfold—your power will be restored, and greater."

"I don't want greatness," she heard herself say. "I just want things to go back to the way they were. I'm scared. . . ."

The temple grew brighter around them, sunlight eating away at Arlo's periphery. She was waking, she noted distantly; soon she'd be returned to the harsh reality that felt more unreal to her than this dream, and she didn't want to go. She wanted to stay here, where it was warm and safe and *calm* . . . where no one else had to die because of her.

"Change is difficult," Magic replied, their glittering body sifting apart to a cloud of shimmering dust. "But it happens to us all, whether we want it or not. You are great, Arlo Jarsdel, and yes, you are scared. But only those who have known fear can be considered brave."

Heroes went through so much hardship.

Heroes were the stuff of tragedies.

After all she'd done to prevent this, how far she'd tried to flee from Fate, she still had wound up back where she started—hero after all?

"Ah, but does it not take bravery to be the villain, too?" There was something in the way Magic said this . . . some hidden amusement, a hint of possibility that Arlo just . . . couldn't chase right now. Stored away for later consideration.

"Something to think about . . . in what's to come. Farewell, dear girl, and if I may—good luck in whatever role you choose; I can't wait to see what you'll do this second time around."

Hands slotted themselves under Lethe's arms, hauled him up from the training arena's dusty earth where exhaustion had collapsed him.

I will find a way to free you, Lethe.

How long had he been on land now? The days were growing harder to track, blending one into the next, an unrelenting stream of dust and glaring sunlight, bruises and broken bones.

Whatever I must do, whoever I must ask for help, I will find a way to your rescue.

There was a constant prickling up and down his legs like thousands of pins in his skin. His hair had begun to change its color. The water called to him in increasing panic.

He'd been gone too long, that much he knew, that much he could *feel*, and if he didn't return home soon, he'd lose his fin for good—his sanity not far behind. But finding his way out of here unaided . . . This kingdom was built like ripples around a glorious, golden palace and grounds; ten rings of land—ten districts, each with its own function, all contained within the bounds of a stone wall at Atlantis's outer limits, tall as the greatest tidal wave the sea could crash against it. This place . . . Lethe hadn't seen much more of Atlantis than this cursed arena and the barracks where he was kept, all here in the soldiers' Third District.

He had no real idea where he was.

What he knew of the rest of Atlantis was whispers and gossip traded at night between lads who missed their homes too. *Lethe* missed home—how long had he been gone, and perhaps more importantly, why hadn't anyone come to rescue him yet? No one but the Moon.

Whatever I must do . . . I'm so sorry, Lethe, this is all my fault—

Hush, Lethe pressed back through whatever it was that bound them. So much weaker during the day, when the Moon could exist only as an imprint in the sky, but no matter what, his friend hadn't abandoned him. Patron of the lonely, indeed, the Moon stayed constant with him through this all.

Some days, that was the only thing keeping him hopeful.

This isn't your fault, but yes, if there's someone you could speak to who could inform my mother of where I am . . . My father isn't the only immortal she pays sacrifice to. You could try Luck—

I will—I have! I've asked any who will listen to intervene, and no one wishes to go against what Fate's ordained. But I will keep trying! Again, and again, and oh . . . I wish I could be of any actual use to you. I wish I could do more than beg others to your aid. I would do anything to help you, Lethe . . . my friend. . . .

The Moon was too young to do anything but plead for help from others. Just like Lethe, it hadn't come fully into its own powers yet. With every UnSeelie faction to power and all the realm's water to govern, it didn't have anything extra to spare for Lethe's plight—doing so would mean chaos; devastation; possibly even the Moon's untimely death, to be stretched so thin too soon.

And Lethe wouldn't risk the Moon for anything, not even this, though the Moon had offered on several occasions now to try.

"Pick up your feet, you useless creature."

"A little fucking siren girl, this one. All you do is mope around . . . good for nothing. The king was cheated, if you ask me. He never should have put his trust in a barbarian god."

No help was coming.

The immortals had forsaken him.

His siblings had witnessed his abduction firsthand, and not even they had shown sign of rescue effort. Perhaps it was easier for them to wish Lethe luck in his new life, his questions and curiosities out of their hair, no longer their problem. . . . A new son could always be bought, as apparently the gods were happy to trade in.

"If you don't use those disgusting legs of yours, we're going to *drag* you by them," snarled one of the men who held Lethe captive.

Get your hands off him . . . The Moon seethed at his abusers.

Lethe merely attempted to comply.

It wasn't so easy, not with his body screaming in pain day in and day out from the sunrise-to-sunset exercises they had him doing. The grappling, the wrestling, the running, the obstacle courses . . . all of this on top of misshapen limbs that weren't yet used to their new form, aching to be stuck like this for so long on little food and even less sleep . . . his instructors taking their every frustration and fear out on him—Lethe, the merboy traded for twelve *proper* sons who would have been so much better a choice for their king, they liked to remind him.

He just wanted to go home.

"*Oof,*" Lethe grunted, tripping over his feet to plant chin-first on the stony earth. The familiar saltiness of warm blood filled his mouth, spraying the ground when he cried out as the two men made good on their promise to take him by the ankles.

"Enough with your fucking squealing, piglet—"

"I'm almost happy it can't speak, you know?" He imitated what Lethe supposed was *him*, issuing several piercing shrieks that weren't at all flattering—noise that had been more or less all he could produce at first, still unused to speech on land when they'd dragged him here all those nights ago. Now he simply chose to hold his tongue. Words were for those who deserved them—for the Moon, however infrequently he could sneak out of bed to visit his only remaining sympathy in the world. "A fucking rock is more intelligent conversation. Can't imagine what we'd have to listen to if he knew how to string two words together."

Sorrow, rage, disgust, Lethe felt everything the Moon could barely repress through their bond.

He didn't have much energy for it, but he tried to press back with soothing reassurance that he was okay. He didn't have much energy for it, but it pained him worse than anything else to be the cause of the Moon's distress. So Lethe struggled as best he could to free himself from this indignity; embarrassment lit his face, a splotchy sapphire that never failed to earn him the wrong sort of attention here.

The two soldiers who'd fetched him from the arena dragged him through the streets, over the bridge that spanned the moat between the Third and Second Districts, then on and over the bridge that connected the Second to First—the palace grounds. All the while people stopped what they were doing to stare; to giggle and point and laugh meanly as the bare scraps of cloth he was given to conceal delicate human genitalia bunched up and were torn askew; to witness as the ground sliced and scraped Lethe's skin, tougher than the ordinary human variety but not impervious to damage altogether.

He coughed on dust, spluttered on the bumps and dips that jostled the breath from his lungs.

Someone threw a rotting vegetable at him, because why not, when Lethe had learned so far that what the common Atlantean people loved above all else was entertainment at any cost. Others joined in— one even emptied his bladder in Lethe's direction, which the Moon took so poorly that Lethe choked on that swell of fury too, and the soldiers took special care to wade him through it all, so that by the time they arrived at King Atlas's marble-and-gilt-and-jewel abode, Lethe both looked and smelled as pitiful as they thought of him.

"The king requested his *son*," one of the men said, dropping Lethe at last at the feet of two other soldiers standing guard outside a rather ordinary, closed door.

One of them raised a heavy brow. "That's a son, is it?"

All four of them looked Lethe over, battered and bruised on the tiled floor, filthy and reeking, practically naked save the cloth tangled around his hips.

His sunburnt and flaking pale skin stretched tighter than ever over protruding ribs; moonlight-pearl hair, stringy with grime, had begun the inevitable darkening to a grayish black at the roots—a mer act of self-preservation, to dampen their vibrancy when instinct deemed their environment overly hostile; poison-bright eyes and shark-sharp teeth that, despite everything, bared themselves in trembling out-rage. . . .

He was eleven years old—nearly a man by this culture's standards, but still a child by all. Another thing Lethe had learned, though, in the unfathomable span of time he'd been hostage here was that age mattered very little; strength, everything.

The door behind the soldiers opened.

Lethe hadn't seen King Atlas since that ill-fated night on the ship he would give anything to go back to and this time heed the Moon's warning to retreat. Atlas stood here now, though, in far simpler attire than before, a short chiton tunic of marble white hemmed in blue, his head full of boar-black hair curling around a golden crown, eyes the deep color of farming soil. Atlas was a man of hard lines and proud features and solid muscle, and it was easy to see why he commanded respect from his people. But while he possessed the warrior's phy-sique, he held himself with the delicate regality of a god.

Perhaps he saw himself as one?

All that mattered right now to Lethe was that the dark threat on his brow wasn't directed at *him* but at the soldiers.

"What's this, then?"

"Prince Zeuxis, O Atlas. As you requested."

Zeuxis.

They'd taken everything from him that night on the ship when Lord Cosmin offered him up to their prayers. Let them try to take his name, as well. Lethe wouldn't answer to it, to them at all, not a single word, until *Zeuxis* died and Lethe was free.

"The delivery leaves something to be desired. This is how you treat a prince?"

"When he earns the title," said one of the soldiers who'd dragged him here—if they couldn't be bothered to learn Lethe's name, he

95

wouldn't learn any of theirs, either—"he'll earn better treatment."

It surprised Lethe that common men could be so bold with the one who ruled them. Alanthe, his mother, wouldn't have permitted such disrespect from her subjects, and no one would have *dared* lay a hand on him as they'd done here. Was this human culture or something specific to Atlantis? Regardless, King Atlas waved his hand at the comment and stepped aside, clearing the way for the soldiers to haul Lethe roughly back to his feet and push him forward.

He stumbled over the threshold, fell to his hands and knees inside the room.

It was much cooler in here, a blessing to his baking skin, which had never known this much sunlight in his life, let alone in the span of days. Cooler, and damp—the stone beneath his palms was slick, and a brininess clung to the air that Lethe drank down in great breaths. His wide eyes were meant for the gloom, and they adjusted quickly when the door creaked closed behind him and latched shut, locking him in with Atlas, away from his tormentors.

A bit of the ringing in his head subsided.

To be out of the sun, out of the heat, out of the glaring brightness . . . Salt welled up in his eyes. He balled his fists on the ground. He hadn't had a chance to make his plea to the king yet, had been taken from the ship and brought straight to the training camp, where they kicked him around, and when they weren't screaming at him to speak their language, they were shouting, cursing, threatening him to move faster, hit harder, run farther, *be stronger.* . . .

King Atlas . . . he had to be a reasonable man.

He had to see that Lethe wasn't meant to make his kingdom a legend.

King Atlas would let him go back to the sea—what use would Lethe be to him, after all, kept up here to turn siren?

The room was lit only by a few candles on a desk and a torch on the opposite wall. Lethe could see just fine in the dark, but he'd yet to find the energy to lift his head, could only watch King Atlas's feet as the man came and knelt before him, a cloth in hand that made Lethe flinch when it was pressed against the side of his face.

He'd known so little kindness here that this one small gesture made the salt in his eyes spill over. "Please," he creaked out. Their language was still new to him, hard to force into the shape of sound, but Lethe had always been a quick study. . . . "P-please, I—"

"You look thirsty, my son."

King Atlas wiped away the dirt, the urine, the tears. He took Lethe's chin in bejeweled fingers and tilted it upward so that their eyes could meet. "Would you like some water?"

Lethe nodded. "*Please.* Yes, please."

The king rose and circled back around him to the table against the wall, just behind Lethe's view. Lethe, meanwhile, reeled himself upright, sniffled a little. He wiped away the rest of his tears on the back of his hand and arranged his weight to settle a little more comfortably on his knees.

A drink of water, and then—a negotiation.

King Atlas was a reasonable man; Lethe had to believe this. If words alone couldn't persuade him to let Lethe go, the promise of reward might. There had to be better sons out there for him, and with all of the sea looking out for such, surely it wouldn't take long to present him a better replacement.

This nightmare would be over soon, and once it was, Lethe would never—

He gasped, doubling back over on all fours.

For a moment, he couldn't make sense of what had happened. Ice engulfed him from behind, froze the air in his chest. It was a whole minute before he realized the cold was water pitched from a bucket straight at his back—one bucket, then another.

"You want a *drink?*" King Atlas seethed. "You spineless, sorry excuse for a boy!"

Ringed fingers dug deep into the back of Lethe's head, wound tight around his hair, and yanked him upright, holding him like a sad, wriggling worm on a hook. Again Lethe cried out; his hands scrambled to the wrist that held him at such a painful angle.

"You want to go home, I imagine."

Lethe struggled, but Atlas was stronger.

He shook him until Lethe couldn't help but comply, to still and catch a proper look at what this room contained. The dampness on the floor . . . the brininess in the air . . . at the far end of the room were siblings—sisters. A whole heap of them, his family, warriors sent from the sea to fetch him because Lethe hadn't been forgotten after all—his people had heard and heeded the Moon's pleas—but his sisters . . . his *sisters*!

Carved up and pieced apart, flayed of scales, soiled and defiled . . . Lethe . . . he *hated*.

He'd never felt so much hate in his life as he did at this moment, hanging limply from King Atlas's grip, staring blankly at the mound of mer carcasses bleeding sapphire across the floor.

Hate . . . and with no means to make the ones responsible feel its burn.

"You want to go home? *This* is your home. Your demon gods seek to make a fool of me. They hope to see my legend turned a joke by their gift. You useless child, there is a man somewhere underneath all your sniveling softness, and if I have to break you apart completely to reveal him, I'll do just that. The gods will find no fools here."

Throwing him to the ground, Atlas took a step back.

Lethe could only collapse on the stone, his legs completely unable to hold him aloft now, his energy entirely sapped by the sight of his sisters . . . dead.

Esthe . . . *please*, she couldn't be among them . . . not her. . . .

"Please . . ."

The king turned back for his table. Lethe heard him sift through its contents, pluck something heavy from its wooden surface, judging by the scrape of it, and long by the leathery slither. "Enough, my son.

That's enough tears. There's a man to be made, and it starts with a simple but crucial question."

Pain burst like stars across Lethe's vision.

His sunburnt back screamed like flame.

"What sort of man do you wish to be, Zeuxis: With me or against me? Hero to the people of Atlantis, or . . . their *villain?*"

The force with which Atlas whipped him sliced his already raw skin to shreds, made Lethe vomit on the floor.

"Tsk, tsk, tsk . . . I see we have our work cut out for us."

His back flared with vicious heat once more. . . .

CHAPTER 5

Nausicaä

T HIS BLOWS." VESPER POUTED, dragging a twig through the forest detritus strewn around xis boots. "I was lied to; I want a refund; this club freaking sucks."

Folding her arms over her chest, Nausicaä eyed the youngest member of the Wild Hunt. Balanced on xis haunches, xe looked so utterly dejected that she might have laughed if their situation were even a little different. "Pretty sure all they advertised in the pamphlet was fresh air and exercise," she pointed out, "both of which we just had, so . . ."

"It's so *boring.* I want to kill something."

"I mean . . . you could probably kill *him.*" Nausicaä nudged the man they'd captured with her foot—russet-haired, green-eyed, definitely old even by sidhe fae standards, but not so old that he hadn't been able to give them a bit of sport in chasing him down. Another distant Viridian royal who'd failed to present himself to Riadne and swear fealty in the month they'd been allotted. Nearly a whole of that time frame had now passed since the Crowning, and here she was, dragging another of Arlo's family to their Luminous grave.

Bound and lying prone on the ground, as soon as Nausicaä's boot met his thigh, he resumed his angry writhing, his ragged demands to let him go or kill him here and now—*take me not to that witch of a queen. I'll never recognize her as mine!*

"He seems pretty down for it."

"It's not the same," Vesper sighed, lifting ximself to xis feet. "Where's the glory in picking off weak, defenseless fae?"

Their Viridian captive growled at the insinuation that he was no threat to them, and really, Nausicaä was kind of impressed with the guy. There weren't many people who could hold on to bravery like this in the face of the Dark Star and her Wild cohort, but perhaps not so surprising of this one—he had, after all, chosen treason in refusing to acknowledge Riadne as the true, succeeding High Queen, a woman who was quickly hacking her way through the entirety of his family tree.

Points where points were due, she supposed.

The soft thud of solid weight dropping to the earth behind them heralded Yue's descent at last from the trees where all three of them had been previously keeping in wait. "You're both children."

"Well, you have sex with this child," Vesper replied in a deeply supercilious tone to xis boyfriend's comment. "So that makes *you* a pervert."

Ignoring his partner with practiced ease, Yue stalked between them, pulling a long black sash from the folds of his cloak. Bending down, he proceeded to fix it across their captive's mouth, muffling his outrage to indecipherable noise that . . . wasn't much better, to be perfectly honest, but Nausicaä wasn't here to kink-shame Yue's tastes.

She watched through a mixture of emotions, none of which she allowed to show on her face.

This was . . . hard.

She understood perfectly where Vesper was coming from. Hunting down an old fae man, chasing him through some random forest in the Canadian backwoods, didn't make her feel powerful—it made her feel cheap.

There was no pride in this, even if the man had been so close to escaping them, to reaching the portal that would have let him slip between here and the Hiraeth. Undoubtedly it would have spat him out close enough to the Goblin Market, where neither she nor the Hunters could touch him without invite.

He'd almost made it.

Nausicaä had been tempted to let it happen.

But letting it happen meant pissing off the Mortal Realm's new and cruelly volatile High Queen. Normally, Nausicaä would be happy to give that two fat middle fingers and carry on with whatever she wanted, but it wasn't . . . it wasn't just Nausicaä anymore.

Pissing off Riadne meant putting *Arlo* in danger of her foul mood.

Pissing off Riadne meant risking expulsion from the palace; from Arlo's side, where Nausicaä couldn't watch over her, out for her, the girl she cared for more than anyone, who was far from okay right now, no matter how many times Arlo reassured in that flat, dismissive tone of hers that she was.

It wasn't like Nausicaä could just whisk her away from this all, be damned—Arlo was tied to Riadne's service and had been since Riadne had tricked her into contract during the Solstice. Even if she hadn't, Nausicaä knew Arlo wouldn't have left with her in the brief chance they would have had to escape the ballroom where Arlo had stood *screaming* before falling to stricken nothingness. The only word she'd spoken to Nausicaä all that evening had been a firm, resounding *no* when Nausicaä had tried to at least tug her out of the ballroom, away from danger.

But there was no leaving. Arlo refused to abandon her family, both alive and slain.

And Nausicaä refused to leave her—despite how obviously Arlo had taken to trying to push Nausicaä away, for her own damned noble intentions most likely, and out of fear that she might lose Nausicaä, too. But like hells was Nausicaä going anywhere, not with all of Arlo's defensive walls of late. Not with Arlo withdrawing into herself. Not with Nausicaä growing terrified, more and more every day, that Arlo might be inching closer to the same ledge Tisiphone had been pushed to.

And this was all just fucking *hard*.

Wild—that something finally meant more to Nausicaä than herself, after over a hundred years of purposeful selfishness and self-indulgence, of keeping everything and everyone out. And here it was. Her walls obliterated, heart laid bare, everything cold and callous and untouchable she'd worked so hard to craft in herself undone by another red-haired girl whose safety was ultimately out of her hands. But damn it, she had to *try.* . . .

Pissing off Riadne meant putting Arlo in danger, but not pissing her off meant hurting the girl she loved. This old man . . . he was Arlo's blood.

Hopefully he'd been shit to her like all the rest of her family—it would make what she had to do now a little easier.

"Also, we aren't supposed to kill anything tied to Fate," Yue added in reminder, rising once more and turning to glare between them. "We do not take lives unmarked for Fate's death; we collect only that which has already ended, and those without ties—the lower creatures of this world. These are the rules. It has been this way since time immemorial."

Vesper tapped a finger to xis chin. "But I mean, where's the line between *lower creature* and fae? And by whose perspective? Because, like, I'm pretty sure I'm higher up on the food chain now, which means fae would technically—"

"This isn't up for debate," Yue warned, his violet eyes narrowing on Vesper as though suspecting xis line of question for attempted persuasion, like winning this argument with him changed anything. "I don't make the rules. Fae are not animals, Vesper—they are not prey marked for death at birth—no matter your low opinion of their threat to you."

"This is all very true," Nausicaä interjected. It spoke to how frustrated they *all* were by the degradation they'd been put through for so long that even Vesper, a gentle soul by immortal standards, was feeling the itch of Hunter bloodlust. "But I'm going to point out—the rules? Actually pretty lax. For instance, this guy here has been marked for death by Riadne, the same person we're bound to serve, and the one who sent us out to play fetch. *Technically* that's permission to engage, because *technically* it's just us acting as her method of execution. We could totally kill him or anyone else without repercussion so long as Riadne tells us to."

"It behooves me to remind you that (a) she did *not* tell us to, and (b) you were expelled from the Immortal Realm for reckless observation of the Law, so perhaps we won't be taking any advice from—"

"Quiet, pervert," said Nausicaä, throwing her palm in his face.

Vesper snickered.

"Let's just get this over with, okay? We were sent to track down . . . gosh, I really did forget your name already. . . ." She trailed off, looking down at the man, who glared back up at her, as though he hadn't appreciated their mockery of his situation one bit, the three of them standing over him, crassly debating the semantics of who was allowed to take his life.

Arlo's family . . .

Nausicaä had been sent to round up so many of them in the past few weeks and lead them back to their new High Queen like little sacrificial lambs to slaughter.

Each time she had to face Arlo after, see the knowing in her girlfriend's eyes, because of course Arlo *knew* what Riadne had her doing, and of course she cared, even if most of these deities-damned fae had been awful to her. Each time . . .

Nausicaä had been labeled a monster a good deal of her life, but this was the first time in a long while she truly felt like one.

Not since the initial days of her banishment—when her rage began to morph into depression, and all she could see was the blood on her hands—had she really *believed* what gossip said about her.

"Doesn't matter." She shook herself out of her thoughts, her worries, and the trauma of a past she couldn't change and apparently couldn't escape, either. "We have what we came for; it's time to go back. Riadne's expecting us."

Vesper rose to standing. "It's weird that Azurean's gone," xe mumbled, more to ximself, but loud enough to be heard nonetheless. "Eris and Yue both served his father. Lethe's served them *all*. But Azurean was my first, and . . . he wasn't that bad. For a mortal king, you know? I wonder how Celadon's doing."

A gentle soul—Nausicaä had always liked Vesper. Xe'd been a breath of fresh air; young, so very young that she often forgot xe'd only *just* been appointed the bright-eyed new fourth to the Wild Hunt barely a year or so before her expulsion. Famine had chosen xim, had bowed and yielded themself to Vesper the moment xe'd defeated the Hunter who'd previously occupied the role. The same way Death had chosen Eris, and War had chosen Yue. She didn't know how xe'd died, who xe'd been in life, but in death xe'd been a kindness that was rare among immortals from day one, and time hadn't worn that out of xim yet.

Kindness, and a particular fixation on familial duty.

Vesper had always been hyped about that—about *them*, Eris and Yue and Lethe and her; about the importance of looking out for each other and sticking together through good times and bad.

It didn't surprise her that xe was still having trouble adjusting to this recent, complete upheaval.

"Safe to say Celadon's probably feeling like shit right now," Nausicaä supplied, bending to scoop up the latest Viridian and sling him over her shoulder. "Still doing better than this guy, though."

They transported back to the Luminous grounds—yet one more way of Riadne reminding them of their place: unless they were expressly summoned, they were to use the common entrances.

In through the front doors, up Riadne's hideous iron staircase . . .

Nausicaä was used to people shying away from her when she passed. As an Erinys, her role had commanded the utmost respect from her people, satisfying terror in the mortal folk. As an exile, she continued to instill terror in the folk; they recognized her aura as immortal if nothing else, and even a human could sense *something* of her power and know she wasn't someone to mess with, even if they couldn't name why.

She was used to inspiring fear.

Fear had even been her unofficial designation among the Hunters, once upon a time.

But it wasn't fear that othered her now—not fear alone, at least. The palace staffers were all afraid, but more than that they were *disgusted*. It had spread like all-consuming Starfire, the news of who this blond young woman was who'd been trailing Vehan's red-haired friend around the palace this whole time.

Riadne's newest henchman . . . the *Dark Star* made flesh.

In the span of a night, Nausicaä's infamy had finally caught up with her, and she could see it now, every little thing these people bought into about her legend, now attached to a face—*hers*. And the absolute revulsion that stemmed from believing all that gossip . . . stuff Nausicaä had let fan out of control, because what had she cared back when her only desire had been self-Destruction and the Dark Star had been nothing but an anonymous phantom?

Suicidal, therapy had once labeled her mental state. *You don't care what people say about you because you have no intention of surviving their opinion. In fact, the only value you place on your life is that you believe forfeiting it will absolve you of costing your sister hers.*

This was all. So. Hard.

Caring about stuff was such a scam.

Down the gilt-and-marble halls, through the throne room's ivory doors. Eris was already present when Nausicaä, Vesper, and Yue came to a halt at the base of Riadne's pristine white dais; he stood beside her golden seat like they'd been engrossed in conversation before this interruption.

"I'm running out of witty things to say about this," Nausicaä drawled by way of greeting. "Here." She dumped her cargo at Riadne's feet with zero ceremony. "Bon appétit—or whatever it is you do with them, I don't know, but there's definitely at least *one* rumor floating around you've been baking them into pies and feeding them to High Prince Celadon, which is ruthlessly Shakespearean of you, Your Majesty. Kind of badass . . . in a really disturbed way." She paused. "*Are* you baking them into pies and feeding them to your illegitimate, firstborn son?"

Closing her eyes in exasperation, Riadne pinched the bridge of her nose, massaging it gently. "Must we indulge in this repartee *every* time you present yourself to me?"

"That depends—do you prefer aggressive hostility?" Nausicaä replied without missing a beat, despite the blatant warning in Eris's moonstone-white eyes to *stop talking now.* "You only get two character-starter settings to choose from until at least six relation-ship hearts."

Riadne opened her mouth, either to rebut or order Nausicaä taken to the dungeons for a "time-out" (which had already happened twice in the short duration she'd been serving the queen and had done abso-lutely nothing to curb Nausicaä's cheek), but the throne room's ivory doors flung open once more, cutting her off.

Everyone turned to watch, Nausicaä included.

Her first reaction was to roll her eyes.

Theodore Reynolds had proven himself in the last few weeks to be . . . more than the immaculate, cutthroat image he presented.

He'd taken pretty devoutly to Riadne's little competition, which Nausicaä could hardly blame. She would have done the same if she were the mortal fae prince pitted against an infamous immortal legend. With his parents held captive in Riadne's dungeons and dangled over his head like a carrot on a stick, and with the fact that if they *both* didn't put in the effort, Riadne would simply off them and be done with it all, of course Theodore was going to take his role of Queen's Assassin seriously.

But Theodore, as much as he might even wish he was . . . the boy was no killer.

That . . . had surprised her a little, to be perfectly honest.

Theodore had the *air* of one down to a science, and he hadn't con-fided in Nausicaä who he worked for—be it his own family or some other wealthy bored royal, or maybe even one of the Wild Folk; Riadne had to have a billion grudges against her by this point—but she could hazard a guess that he hadn't been planted in Riadne's Court to play only the role of spy and spy alone. Lying in wait as an on-command executioner should Riadne prove too much of a liability to be useful to the one who controlled his actions—this had undoubtedly been a part of his contract too. So the fact that this flashy young prince did every little thing his new High Queen instructed him to do, including kill whoever he'd been sent after—it just made sense. He'd clearly been groomed as a dangerous weapon his entire life.

Except . . .

"Your Majesty!" Theodore greeted, all smiles and elegance as he wafted into the throne room in a cloud of porcelain-white silk and gleaming gold knee-high boots, stark against his deep brown skin.

Except . . .

Riadne perked up in her seat.

Eris stiffened.

Both had noticed something Nausicaä hadn't upon first glance because she'd been too caught up in the memory of finding Theodore after the first and admittedly gruesome death he'd been sent to deliver in Riadne's name—Theodore, bent over a bush in the night-swept gardens, heaving the contents of his stomach onto the tearstained earth below. . . .

His very first mark had included a Viridian babe.

"Nausicaä." Theodore nodded, coming to a halt beside her. He stood at complete ease, radiant, not a single hair out of place or blemish in sight, utterly perfect and *perfectly* composed under the best crafted mask Nausicaä had ever beheld. Truly, if she hadn't witnessed with her own eyes that night in the garden, she wouldn't ever believe he didn't live for this vicious lifestyle.

"Theodore, who is this you bring before me?" was Riadne's softly imperious inquiry, and Nausicaä's eyes snapped from his too-damned-impressive, flawless masquerade to the man held bound in actual fucking *rope* between two nameless Luminous lugs just behind Theodore.

Flaming red hair . . .

Warm hazel eyes that seemed so familiar, if she could just place what was off about them . . . why the color of them fit incongruously with the shape that tugged at her memory. . . .

Theodore beamed at the High Queen. "Rory Jarsdel, Your Majesty," he replied. "Arlo Jarsdel's father."

Nausicaä's eyes widened.

She rounded immediately on Theodore, fury blazing behind her expression.

This deities-damned *snake*—never mind that his whole charade would have been over if Nausicaä had gone straight to Riadne and reported his wuss ass throwing up in her bushes all because it bothered him to murder a young family and their baby on her behalf. She'd kept that to herself, because Theodore was Arlo's *friend*, but here he was handing over the only parent Arlo had left with a shit-eating grin on that pretty fucking face.

Nausicaä was going to bury him.

Arlo's *father*!

"You fucking asshole—"

"I'm confused," Riadne interrupted, leaning back in her throne as she idly picked at a nail. "I care about this human man how? Surely you didn't think this would impress me. Perhaps I should instead be insulted that you think I have need for further leverage over an eighteen-year-old ironborn girl. You . . . disappoint me, Theodore."

Condemning words, but Theodore was already a dead man in Nausicaä's eyes.

"I don't think I do," came Theodore's rebuttal, a flicker of something behind that infuriating mask at last when he looked into Nausicaä's face as she loomed over him. She would almost call it desperation, a plea to wait and hear him out, directed not at Riadne but at her.

The look was gone in an instant, and those sparkling brown eyes were quick to fasten themselves on the queen once more. "At least, I shouldn't. You might not have any need for a human prisoner, but you could, I'm assuming, use a stunningly talented alchemist of a . . . let's call it *legendary* pedigree? Forgive me, my queen—I thought you might like to meet the man Lethe hid from you so ardently that without his express permission, none can even speak Rory Jarsdel's true name."

Riadne stared.

Nausicaä . . . did too.

First at Theodore, then at Rory, who might not look wholly pleased with his situation, but not a *bit* outraged or shocked by such an accusation—or betrayal. Which . . . well . . . it couldn't at all be true, because . . . because . . .

Riadne burst out laughing. "I beg your pardon? This man is an alchemist?" She took Rory in, in his navy cable-knit sweater-vest and his pale khaki pants, graying at the temples, age lines in softening skin. . . . "Lethe has played you for a fool, boy."

"I assure you he very much hasn't," Theodore maintained, wholly unaffected by the queen's scorn. "I cannot speak the family name, but you do know it. We all know it. Once upon a time, it was widely known that this family line had *not* died out as we were later magicked to believe. They live on in the husband and only child to Thalo Viridian-Verdell, the man she'd been tasked to keep under watch, only to fall in love with him instead.

"Once upon a time, we knew that history's greatest alchemist was responsible for more than our rescue from the one who tried to use his life's work to overthrow the Courts. We knew that his own flesh and blood had been the hand behind the attempt. That this flesh and blood had produced an heir of his own."

He paused to let his words sink in, things that if he dared attach to the name they all belonged to would be instantly scrubbed from memory, so powerful was the magic behind what kept it concealed.

A name Nausicaä actually knew.

Riadne wouldn't.

No one did, at least no one mortal, and not in any real sense. *Flamel*—they knew about him in concept, and the magic attached to the name warped the entire history behind it. The folk believed

Nicholas Flamel to be a figure of legend, the man who'd risen to save them from the original restoration of the philosopher's stone.

They'd been forced to forget the truth.

Forced to forget that the family lived on past this one ancient man.

Forced into believing him a bright flame wicked out once his purpose had been served, most likely—from what Nausicaä knew of the incident, which had been well before her time—due to fear that his descendants might inherit even half the talent, not of Nicholas, but of his *son*; fear that ironborn might rally around the heirs that son produced, and those heirs after them.

Because the Flamels had been the admiration of the ironborn golden age, yes. But what folk didn't remember was that they'd been the Courts' worst enemy too. Its greatest, most notorious cult, the head of which had been a mere boy. Mortal history remembered Nicholas as the one to save them—it had been made to forget that it was his own son he'd had to save them from. All immortals knew. Just as they knew that if any of them tried to speak about it, they found the secrets tangled on their tongues, turned gibberish in the attempt to spill them, immediately wiped from the minds of those who overheard.

Nausicaä knew the name.

She knew the history.

What she *hadn't* known was that . . . Rory Jarsdel . . . *Arlo* . . .

"Lethe doesn't toy with this. I know you wonder what he gets up to in his spare time. Rory Jarsdel is part of it, and you very much want him, Your Majesty. Think of how much time you'd save in employing a man so talented at the art you require most that even Magic seeks to keep him from you."

Arlo.

Arlo Jarsdel was . . . couldn't possibly be . . . There had to be some mistake: Theodore had to be wrong; Lethe had to be hazarding a guess . . .

Except . . .

Wildly talented at alchemy—brilliant, frightening even—and all with zero practice. So naturally skilled at what she did that she'd drawn the attention of deities and queens alike . . .

Arlo Jarsdel was Arlo *Flamel.*

There was no way around it now that Nausicaä knew.

Shit.

Shit.

She'd always assumed Arlo's strength had been because of the hint of immortal material to her magic that Nausicaä had sensed from their very first meeting in the Good Vibes Only café—the Wild Card that Fate had made her into, a mortal born with immortal magic and the ability to serve as scion for whichever deity she chose.

But Arlo was a whole-ass fucking Flamel? Descendant of *the* Nicholas Flamel . . . the first mortal to achieve immortality through sheer force of fucking talent—all immortals knew his story; Nausicaä had even met him once, when she'd first been created. Only a handful of days later, his application for Destruction had been Divinely granted, and the whole damned realm had assembled for his funeral, and *what if . . . ?*

No.

No, no, no, no, hells fucking *no,* Fate wouldn't be that bold . . . that mean, to such an innocent, beautiful mortal girl.

Arlo was powerful by blood, sure, but that didn't negate the fact that there *was* immortality in her magic. And Nausicaä didn't want to believe that Fate would have *dared* to use *Nicholas Fucking Flamel's own stardust* to feed right back into his own bloodline, reborn right when it would be most needed—*sought* after—most desperately . . . viciously. . . .

Theodore turned to Rory and snapped his fingers. The Luminous Guard holding Rory prisoner released him to step forward, and Rory did, looking nowhere but up at Riadne Lysterne—the woman who'd murdered his ex-wife and now threatened the safety of his only child.

"I want to make a trade."

Riadne raised a brow. "I don't recall giving you permission to speak."

"I don't recall asking for it."

The part of Nausicaä that wasn't currently wrapped up in horror was amused. Arlo's father had spoken all of two sentences and already she could tell his daughter's occasional flashes of sass weren't fae-born at all.

The queen looked down at him for a hard, long moment before crossing a leg over her knee and smiling brighter than the chandelier overhead. "You'll wish you had. But come, your terms—what can I do for you, my impossible alchemist?"

"It's an insecure tyrant who relies on threats."

"And it's a poor father who loses first his wife and then only daughter."

Don't test her, Nausicaä wanted to warn.

She got it, she did—Rory had to be hurting, furious with Riadne, and it was damned hard to hold your tongue when you had so much to say to the person responsible for all that, but Riadne . . . she wasn't threats.

Riadne was *promises*, and the more cause Rory gave her to be creative with that, the worse it was going to be for him and everyone he ever cared about, Arlo included.

"I want to trade."

"And *I* want to give your charming girl another parent to burn on a pyre, so please, *do* continue repeating yourself at me."

Wisely, Rory ignored the taunt. "I can give you valuable information on the movements of the Assistance," he said instead. "Information you might even be able to make good on *tonight*. And you've started up classes here, training carefully selected ironborn in the darker alchemic arts, in the hopes they'll be able to create your stones."

Riadne had.

Nausicaä hadn't been permitted to sit through any of these classes, but a large portion of the Luminous Palace's southern wing had been converted into lodgings and classrooms for people Riadne had personally selected for her grooming—Arlo first among them.

Not the first of the many shackles keeping her girlfriend tethered here.

"I'm not lying to you. Alchemy runs strong in my veins—I'll perform it now, if you wish to see proof. Nowhere near as strongly as it does in my daughter, but I have knowledge you could only dream of, and I could *teach* you, your students. I could teach my daughter. You let me stay here with Arlo, you let me guide her through learning who she is, and I'll instruct your classes for you. Under my tutelage, there won't be any need for hope; your students *will* craft the rest of the philosopher's stones."

Arlo Jarsdel was Arlo Flamel.

Nausicaä was still stuck on this.

There was no wondering why Arlo hadn't bothered to mention this fact to her, because there was no way she even knew about it herself. Not something like this. Not when so much else had been erased from memory, and Lethe was the only person Nausicaä knew who could have tampered with this information in any way close to what this whole elaborate scheme would require, but it couldn't have been him involved. Just . . . hard no. She didn't want to even think about what that would imply about someone no one really knew all that well; someone they all let bound around this realm like a hyped-up kid in his own glorified bouncy-castle.

Another immortal had to be in on this, an actual god, to be able to full-on wipe Arlo's true ancestry from the whole of the mortal map, because genuine memory manipulation was a legendary-tier fucking talent Lethe should not be capable of. Hunters weren't gods or deities of any sort, powerful as some of them were. Lethe had some talent in the art of manipulation, yes, and the High Sovereigns used this to their advantage, but . . . hard no.

Hard. Fucking. No. Because if for some cursed reason he was behind this . . . that truth changed everything.

Lethe, no longer a piece on this elaborate board but an actual player with actual designs on how this game should end, and the world was a frightening enough place without the concept of Lethe as a genuine power.

But all that aside, much as the rest of them, Arlo absolutely didn't know a thing about who she was.

And by that logic, Rory shouldn't know either—the only way he could was if Lethe or whoever had done this had permitted him in on the secret, and how and when *that* had happened . . . why Lethe would and what it meant . . .

What was even going on anymore?

Riadne, meanwhile, hadn't moved an inch on her throne.

She sat like the room's marble, perfectly still, peering at Rory over her nails in deep assessment of the situation. Did she turn Rory down as a desperate man who'd say anything to be with his daughter and risk letting such a valuable pawn escape her clutches? Did she allow Rory his demands and inherit the downright *terrifying* power of the world's most accomplished ironborn family but risk letting such a danger plant itself in the heart of her Court?

Because Riadne wasn't a fool.

Rory . . . he was here because he wanted to be, had to be gaining something more than proximity to Arlo, and Riadne had to be wondering why this player had presented himself on her board now after all this time.

Memory magic . . . the resurrection of what was basically ironborn royalty, suddenly after hundreds of years . . . Lethe had his claw marks all over this, and Nausicaä could see the stirrings of panic and outrage behind those freezing blue eyes of their new High Queen—what did *she* stand to gain from this?

Was Lethe allowing this man to wander her way to help her plot or hinder it?

Because Lethe had never been her deities-damned *pet*, and it seemed to Nausicaä that what that actually meant for their little partnership here was finally dawning on Riadne.

"You're an alchemist," she repeated at last, her voice as smooth as ice.

Rory nodded curtly. "I swear it."

"Your oath means very little to me, ironborn. If it's true you descend from *legendary pedigree*, then I already have all I need in your daughter." She uncrossed her legs, rose to standing, took her time descending the dais one step at a time. All the while, she watched Rory Jarsdel with a look that could frost over flame. "You thought me perhaps so far gone in my lust for power that I'd allow you to waltz on in here and insert yourself as the clever little spy for . . . I presume whoever *you* serve, my dearest Theodore?" She turned on Theodore, and there was no amount of mask that could hide the way he flinched. "No matter."

Reaching out a hand, she placed it on Theodore's shoulder and squeezed—not hard, Theodore didn't look physically pained by the action, but fear laced barely perceptibly along the fringes of his expression.

"Eris," Riadne commanded in a louder voice, her gaze still holding Theodore's. "Take our guest to the dungeons. He can keep the Reynoldses *and* Bessels company until I decide on whether it amuses me more to string him up as I did his wife or put him through the paces of whatever futile task he's been sent here to accomplish. Get any information you can from him on the Assistance, however you wish to do so."

She turned back to Rory, lifting her hand from Theodore's shoulder to cup the side of his face. "Commander Viridian-Verdell deserved so much *better* than you for a husband," she added in final, biting insult.

Rory returned that ice with a fire that once again surprised Nausicaä in how very *Arlo* it sounded. "And so much greater than *you* for a demise."

...

"What the *fuck*, Reynolds."

Nausicaä had to hand it to Theodore, pinned to the wall by six feet of solid immortal muscle and rage—his mask was just that freaking good. He didn't flinch, didn't cry out, didn't bare his teeth in self-defense or cower in any way. In fact, he almost looked delighted.

"It's a shame you're a lesbian," he said with a waggle of his brow, brown eyes dancing. "This is really hot."

"Save it—what the fuck. What's going on, why did you throw Arlo's dad under the bus like that, and is he *actually* a—"

The name halted itself on her tongue, making her groan in frustration.

"Goodness." Theodore folded himself smaller in the cage of Nausicaä's arms and slipped like a whisp out from under them. With all the self-preservation of a fucking troll, he took one look at the sapphire outrage heating Nausicaä's face and . . . ignored it.

Brushed the wrinkles from his silk sleeves and smoothed a delicate hand over his tight curls to check everything was still in place. "You know what you should be more concerned about? Where *your* points are coming from. Whether or not Rory Jarsdel is my mysterious master's plant, Riadne's thrilled. I brought her a sparkling new plaything—you've just been dumping the same old mice on her doorstep for weeks. Do better than this low-hanging fruit, Nausicaä. Take this seriously. You *do* know it's your heart she wants me to gift her in the end, right?"

Rude that someone so effortlessly blithe could also be so intelligent.

But ah, he'd caught that part, had he? The true intent behind this little "competition"? Good. Nausicaä had worked out immediately what Riadne wanted, and she'd bet her whole immortality on the fact that he didn't understand what this meant she wanted from Nausicaä, but it worked better if they were at least reading from the same book, if not the same page just yet.

"You're the biggest, baddest thing in this entire realm—"

"This really stokes my ego, and I appreciate that, but I regret to inform you that Lethe exists."

Theodore raised a manicured brow. "Lethe exists—but it's still *you* she wants me to hand over. You're a threat to her. Lethe she can work with, because whatever he truly wants, at least part of it aligns with seeing her complete her goal. *You*, on the other hand . . . I don't know if you've heard, but word is you're fairly difficult to work with if one isn't a red-haired ironborn girl by the name of Arlo Jarsdel."

Nausicaä nodded. "Even then, I'm sure Arlo would rate that satisfaction level a five out of ten."

"Exactly. The only mystery is, why don't you just kill Riadne? I have to admit . . . I'm surprised you haven't. Given what I know about you and what she's done to Arlo, if nothing else. You could do it so easily, and it would stop *everything*, save us all. But you haven't—why?"

Tch—this *boy*.

Theodore was clever; Nausicaä actually liked him sometimes. It was a shame, therefore, that he was in well over his head at this point, and whoever he truly served, she hoped to hells they were ready to face what was coming. However much the Immortal Realm had involved themselves in the stakes, the battle soon at hand would be up to mortal blood and mortal blood alone to fight.

Peeling herself away from the wall, Nausicaä deflated a little from her anger. It still pissed her off that Theodore had allowed Arlo's father to become a part of this mess, even if it was maybe what Rory wanted, but this *question* . . . this was all just . . .

Hard.

Caring sucked.

"I can't," she replied simply, shrugging a shoulder. Whether Theodore picked up on it or not, it was more candid than she'd been in a while with anyone other than Arlo. "Flat out. The moment Riadne killed Azurean, the Bone Crown became hers. Do you think I didn't want to? When I transported back to the ballroom that night to all that blood and death and Arlo screaming? But . . . I can't. I'm an immortal. If I kill Riadne, I break the treaty between our realms, and if you think we've all got problems now, thank your lucky fucking stars we don't have the added chaos of my ilk warring around the place, claiming territory, exacting revenge for their exile. If I kill Riadne, it's pretty much immediate game-over."

There was silence for a beat, in which Theodore weighed what Nausicaä had said—and what she hadn't.

Even to Lethe, Riadne was untouchable. There was no one who could help them dispose of her in her mortal High Queen status.

"All right," Theodore conceded, a note of solemnity to his composure now. "Well then, how about: Whose heart are you going to give her? Who are you supposed to hand over to impress your way into her employ? Given your skill, I would think you'd have to aim quite high with your chosen mark. My money's on Lethe, and that doesn't seem like an easy win."

With a scoff, Nausicaä turned her back to him. "Oh, it's not Lethe. Don't worry, she expects the exact same thing from the both of us."

"And what does *that* mean?"

"Later, Theo!" she answered with a wave, already beginning to stalk off down the hall. It was nearing time for Arlo's lessons to let out, and she had . . . an update to share that may or may not go over all that well.

Not that anything seemed to go over all that well, these days.

That didn't stop Nausicaä from trying; that wouldn't scare her away from Arlo's side.

She'd already failed one person she'd loved. She wouldn't do the same again.

"But you can tell Lethe he's a dick the next time you see him!" she added as she went. "He'll know it's from me."

The good news was, if Riadne *did* manage to get her hands on Nausicaä's heart, she wouldn't have to deal with all these maddening feelings anymore.

CHAPTER 6

Arlo

$\sim\!\!\frown\!\!\frown$

N OW, BEFORE I SEND you off for the day"—Leda withdrew from the chalkboard at the front of the room to reveal what she'd completed drawing—"can anyone tell me what *this* is?"

It was more the silence than the question that drew Arlo out of her thoughts. She'd spent most of today's lesson staring out the bay of windows lined along the left-hand wall beside her. The glass looked out over cheerful white and yellow flowers; sunlight-gilded, manicured grounds; the busy gardeners attending to it all; off to that dense, forbidding forest that surrounded the Luminous Palace like bars on a pretty cage.

Out of bounds.

In compliance with her vow to Riadne—her service, her skill, her alchemy, her ability as a Hollow Star, all sworn in a neat little package deal the queen had secured like a happy bonus to the butchering of the Viridian family tree—Arlo wasn't permitted to set a single foot past the hedge that marked the palace perimeter. She wasn't *permitted* to join Nausicaä on any more Hunts (not that the ones that took up her time currently were all that appealing to Arlo) or return to the Palace of Spring to visit Celadon (though apparently he couldn't be bothered to come visit *her*; she hadn't seen even a glimpse of him here in the weeks since Riadne's Crowning). She wasn't permitted to talk about her family or contact her father to at least let him know she was alive and okay, which he had to be assuming she very much wasn't by now after such a long period of nothing—but what was Rory Jarsdel going to do? Her human father . . . it wasn't like he could march right up to the palace he didn't know existed and demand to see his daughter from an evil faerie queen he didn't even believe in.

A daughter he probably wouldn't even want to see at the end of it all, because oops, there was *that* cat out of the bag—Arlo was half-fae; Thalo had been fae as well. *Had* been. If he somehow found it within himself to forgive Arlo for being part of the magic he'd detested enough to leave his family, what would he think of her when he found out she was the reason her mother was now a past tense?

ExhaustionGuiltAgonyANGER—

Leda asked her question.

Arlo shifted her gaze from the world outside the classroom windows to glance at what was on the board.

She didn't need to lift her chin from the palm that cradled it to do so. She didn't really care what Leda had drawn.

Class after class, lesson after lesson, day in and day out, all Arlo was *permitted* to do was study. History, elemental magic, politics—the things their new High Queen felt she was woefully undereducated in as a royal sidhe fae of a Founding family—but those were all just filler for her time between waking and eating and sleeping again.

Between alchemy lessons she probably wouldn't even need, not these basics in the very least once the conditions Magic had informed her about were met. From the sounds of it, once Arlo's stolen memories of her ability were returned, she'd be well above what they sat here poring over, but Riadne had insisted.

Arlo might be compelled to listen, but that didn't mean she had to divulge every one of her secrets.

Let the High Queen think she needed this extra help, that this wasn't just buying time until she could figure out what to do . . . and how best to use her knowledge to her advantage.

Day in and day out, Arlo sat in this quaint little room with dried herbs strung from the ceiling in happy little fragrant bushels; bookshelves crammed with leather-bound, once-forbidden knowledge; cabinets and tables laden with the most curious instruments of science and magic. She sat at her charming wooden desk in a room of bright-eyed ironborn all like her, except *none* of them were at all like her because *they* were actually happy to be here, and Arlo wanted . . .

ExhaustionGuiltAgonyAnger—

Arlo wanted to *scream*.

"No one? None of you can tell me what this is? We've been learning our arrays for half a month now—no one can hazard even a guess?"

Leda peered hard at them each in turn, her lavender eyes flashing when they lighted on Arlo's gaze.

Did she enjoy her new, official role as tutor to Riadne's "prime" batch of alchemist hopefuls? She certainly looked like she did, a flush of health to her rosewood-brown complexion and sheen to her pansy-black hair. But Leda was careful to keep any personal feelings from her lessons; wise.

If she at all regretted the sort of person Riadne had revealed herself as being, the only hint was in the occasional glance she allowed to Arlo, but Arlo . . .

ExhaustionGuiltAgonyAnger—

How little things that would have mattered before had begun to matter so little to her now.

"Anima," Arlo sighed in reply. "That's the symbol of anima."

All her life, Arlo had wanted to fit in with something. To excel at just one thing enough that people would stop treating her like an embarrassment to her name. So many private wishes and pleas to the gods and tears spilled into her pillow, all for it to turn out that she *was* good at something, she did fit in somewhere—and everything about it she hated.

What it had cost her . . .

The many more secrets it wove around her . . .

The pain and confusion of all this knowledge in alchemy, trapped behind blockers in her memory. Between those memories dislodging of their own accord from wherever they were stuck—was time wearing their confines thin, or was there maybe a limit on how long she could be made to forget? she wondered—and whatever Magic had done to satiate the wish she'd made for the ability to save Vehan, bits of half answers to things like what Leda had asked came to her now like pop-up ads on the sketchy websites she and Celadon used to stream their anime from as kids.

Unbidden.

Unappreciated.

Useless, really—like being handed a couple of pieces from a jigsaw puzzle and expected to see the whole, completed picture from fragments alone.

"Correct," replied Leda through a sigh of her own, like she'd been hoping someone other than Arlo would have figured it out. Like she didn't want to make the daily report required of her, directly to Riadne, how each in the class was performing. "And what does that mean—what *is* anima?"

Two hands shot up into the air in Arlo's periphery.

One belonged to a girl she only really knew as a familiar face in the class, without even a name attached to it. A faerie girl with greenish-blond hair and even deeper emerald eyes that watched Arlo constantly—for what purpose, she couldn't say.

The other . . .

"Fyri?"

Of *course* it was Fyri. Fyri—with all her wide, soft curves and that full, heart-shaped face, smooth amber complexion, and big topaz eyes. She was part common faerie, judging by the feline cut of both her pupils and incisors, and the nails like claws on her hands.

She was also brilliant.

It was no wonder to Arlo why Riadne had invited her here along with the twelve others gathered here. Fyri, who from day one had treated everyone else in the class with an arrogance like they were competition leagues below her level—barely worth the contempt she deigned to flash them.

Arlo, though, she seemed to actively hate.

And good for her.

Did none of them realize why they were here? Or did they really not care, so swept up in finally getting to practice a magic their High Queen *graciously* allowed them to learn?

"'Anima' means soul," Fyri explained, sitting just a little taller, satisfaction as radiant in her cinnamon-bark aura as it was on her face. "It's only used in arrays that center living things, like flora and fauna and even people. When an alchemist adds it to the core of such arrays, it acts as a tether between them and their focus, creates a stronger connection, an easier flow of power between host and subject. Essentially, it's the use of the alchemist's own life force to seize complete control of another's."

Leda nodded gently. "Correct. The anima rune is unnecessary in most alchemic practices. It's the . . . *less friendly* branch that delves into its frequent use, because tapping into one's own life force to tamper with another's is dangerous, to say the very least. Powerful results, to be sure, but always at a cost. And if you foolishly underestimate your focus, it could just as easily reach through that connection to seize control of you instead."

Lifting her head from her palm, Arlo looked a little closer at the rune Leda had drawn.

She hadn't been paying attention before. It had been instinct that had responded more than her, her glance at the board jostling loose the answer like an overripe apple on a laden tree.

She paid attention now, though.

The shape seemed like just fancy, squiggly chalk at first, but the more she looked, the more she realized what she stared at—Leda had drawn that deities-darned *butterfly* in the center of the chalkboard.

Loud in her ears echoed the promise she'd made to a certain boy with just such a thing carved on his chest.

> *We'll get this off you, Vehan. I'll help—of*
> *course I'll help.*

> *We're friends.*

*I wish I possessed enough skill and knowledge in
alchemy to be able to remove
the array etched on Vehan Lysterne's chest.*

*But this I cannot grant, for you already possess
the knowledge
of what must be done.*

ExhaustionGuiltAgonyAnger—All Arlo had wanted was to help. She'd wanted to be useful: to her mother, to her Court, to Riadne, who'd been so wonderful to her, and look where that foolish naivete had landed them.

She'd always known she was a burden, but maybe her probably-now-dead cousins had been right when they'd whispered she was a curse, as well.

"That's what's at the center of the philosopher's stone array," Arlo added without raising her hand, and Leda's eyes flashed again in her direction.

"Correct. The anima rune is the core of the philosopher's stone array—the most difficult of all alchemic runes to wield, let alone master, which anyone who wishes to graduate my lessons into Her High Majesty's employ *will* accomplish. This is where our next lesson picks up. This is what you'll spend the foreseeable future learning how to wield. Master this rune, and you'll have alchemy's greatest tool at your disposal. Master this rune, and—"

"And you'll be granted the honor of creating philosopher's stones for *Her High Majesty*. Never mind that in order for those stones to become hers, their creators have to die," Arlo finished hotly.

Leda winced—a sign that maybe she wasn't as happy to play instructor in this as her compliance suggested; that she knew where this was heading, and why she wasn't exactly happy when someone got an answer right. Maybe Leda was just as much a prisoner here as Arlo.

Fyri, meanwhile, groaned.

She wasn't the only one to do so, because for some reason, they just didn't grasp it? Believe it? Or was it that they didn't care? Riadne could murder whoever she wanted, seize whatever power she wanted, destroy the whole deities-forsaken world so long as she decriminalized alchemy along the way?

They were all here because Riadne wanted alchemists to create the last of the stones for her—she'd never concealed that fact from them. Just as Arlo had never concealed from her classmates what her wish had "happily" filled in for her, that if they didn't have to be here, they should pack their stuff and run as far away from this place as they could. Because if they *did* succeed in making their queen a stone, their lives would have to be forfeited before that stone could be hers.

"Oh my gods, would you stop with that? She didn't kill Councillor Sylvain because she had to," Fyri snapped. "She did it because he was scum that pissed her off. *You* kind of piss *me* off—"

"Yeah." Another of Arlo's classmates joined in, a burly half-goblin boy who looked like he might have done well as a redcap if he weren't also human. "I'm sure there's some sort of oath you can vow to transfer ownership. I mean, isn't consent a big part of magic?"

Arlo glared. "Probably why creating philosopher's stones is *less friendly* magic, then, isn't it?"

Dark magic. This was *dark magic*—what about this didn't they understand? Consent had nothing to do with it.

"Leda will know!"

"Yeah, Leda knows—"

"We don't have to *die*—"

Hands slammed on the table.

Arlo was honestly surprised they hadn't been hers.

She looked up in the stunned, ringing silence at Fyri standing braced at her desk. Trembling with anger, glaring at Arlo. "And even if we do, it would be worth it."

Arlo . . . stared.

"It would be *worth it*," she repeated, her voice pitched low in passion. "You have no idea. Listen, I'm sorry. I know you lost your mother because of her; we all know what happened—I'm sorry. But you sit here like this is all beneath you, like we aren't the first people in hundreds of years to be allowed to even talk about stuff that, up until mere weeks ago, would have gotten us *killed* if the wrong person overheard. A spoiled fae princess who's never actually had to live her life as what it means to *be* ironborn—look around you. Look at us!"

She slammed her hands on the desk again, frustration pouring from her in waves.

"*We* are ironborn, Arlo Jarsdel. We're tired, and we're starving, and we're afraid. We've all lost family and loved ones to the Courts. We're all hurting. You have no idea what it means to come from the sort of poverty we're kept in, the fear. You don't get it. The fae stripped us of *everything* when they turned on us, left nothing but punishment and jail and exile and death to the people who try to use magic we were born with just to keep from dying in the streets. So, if some megalomaniac queen on a power trip wants to give us back our fucking lives along the way? Cool. I'd die *a hundred times over* to make sure that this time, we keep them."

Arlo stared.

And then she stood too.

Grabbed her books and her bag in her arms, turned away from Fyri, from Leda, from the class, and strode for the classroom door.

Then she paused. "You don't." She didn't turn to Fyri, couldn't see if she was even watching or cared at all. But the thing is, Arlo *did* understand; she *did* get it. It wasn't just a reward Riadne dangled over the heads of the people in this room—it was *life*.

She got it. But they didn't, not yet. There was no one better than Riadne at plucking the hope from your deepest desperation and using it to ruin you completely.

"You don't get to keep your lives. You don't get to keep any of this. And I promise that you won't want to before the end . . . if you make it that far. I promise—when Riadne's through with us, no one's even going to want alchemy to *exist*. It's what she does."

"Arlo!"

Arlo's gaze snapped up from the ground.

Her posture straightened, peeling her off the wall where she'd slumped as soon as she'd stepped from the classroom and out into the hall.

There was no situation, no reality, no universe in which Nausicaä Kraken would fail to captivate her.

Even now, when Arlo oscillated between abject misery and frightening apathy; when her every waking moment felt as if she were barely able to keep her head above shark-infested, stormy waters, and she was angry—so, so very angry—and so, so very depressed. And then angry *because* she felt depressed. Everything that had happened had been *her own hecking fault*, and she didn't deserve to feel sad about it. . . .

Nausicaä stalked down the hall toward her with a sway on her hips and delight in her sharp silver eyes. "Hello, Red," she purred when she reached Arlo and planted her elbow against the wall just beside her, leaning her head into her palm. "Did you miss me?"

There was pain in Arlo's heart.

There was heaviness in her body.

There were days she could barely bring herself to get out of bed, and talking to anyone about anything at all drained her down to nothing completely.

So much was her fault, and here she was, trapping others in further torment, inflicting even more wounds.

Arlo *liked* this girl in front of her. Nausicaä—her girlfriend—this incredible, incandescent goddess who had so much emotion and kindness and goodness under all that swagger and prickly defense . . . Of course Arlo missed her. She hated when Nausicaä went away.

But the pain in her heart . . . the heaviness in her chest . . . she hated even more every time Nausicaä had to come back.

For *her*.

If it weren't for Arlo, none of this would have happened. If it weren't for Arlo, her mother would still be alive; Celadon would still have a father; Vehan wouldn't ghost around her, wringing his hands, consumed with guilt he shouldn't even feel—for *Arlo*, who didn't deserve that at all.

And if it weren't for her, for her own reckless foolishness, her desperation to be *special*, Nausicaä wouldn't be trapped in Riadne's clutches, pinned to games she couldn't want to play. Forced into ugliness—into murder—all for the permission to stay with useless, moping, miserable, good-for-nothing Arlo Jarsdel.

"You were only gone for the day," Arlo muttered flatly and looked away.

It wasn't fast enough; she caught the hurt that flexed across Nausicaä's features, and Arlo's heart clenched all over again to see it, to know she was the cause . . . but it was better this way.

If things were different . . . if the Solstice hadn't happened, and Arlo hadn't played right into Riadne's hand, and Nausicaä wasn't stuck here just so that Arlo wouldn't be alone . . . in a happier timeline, Arlo would have closed the distance between them the moment she saw Nausicaä approach.

Would have laughed and kissed her, delighted, and kissed her again, and again, because it was still so new to her, and Nausicaä was so *good* at it—left her weak in the knees and light in the head, all fluttery and warm and smiling because she'd never seen anything more beautiful in her life than the girl standing across from her and couldn't possibly believe she was *hers*.

Heavy lashes fluttered closed.

A hand rose to cover Nausicaä's heart, as though she'd been gravely injured by words that were nothing more than play.

"Gone for a day, perhaps, but a day no garish sun illumed—sweet maiden of flower and air—for bereft is life without *your* light, and till soft to me your smile restores it, eternal will those hours loom."

Arlo tried to roll her eyes.

She tried to keep heat from spreading a blush across her face—and failed terribly.

"There it is," Nausicaä purred in amusement. "No one's immune to my poetry."

Damn it, this was difficult. Just so *difficult* to push Nausicaä away.

There was no pushing her anywhere, really, but she couldn't . . . *they* couldn't . . . Nausicaä was in danger because of her, and Arlo had already gotten people she loved killed because she'd been too weak to do what she needed to do.

Push her away—instinct screamed. *Make her go; keep her safe; the longer she's here for you, the worse Riadne will put her through.*

Riadne will find a way to turn your feelings against you both.

"I don't know what to say to that," Arlo replied, hard as stone, determination renewed. Mean now. Nausicaä had been through so much, had worked so hard to recover from all the darkness and death in her life. . . . However terrible she felt for being mean to her, Arlo would truly be a monster if she continued to lead the girl she'd come to care *so much* about right back into what that girl had fought fire and soul to escape.

But she was also keenly aware of how close Nausicaä had drawn to her while speaking, of the finger she placed under her chin . . .

Tilting her head just so, until they were near enough that when she next spoke, Nausicaä's lips brushed ever so slightly against Arlo's. "You could say you missed me. . . ."

Heat shot low into her, making her shiver.

Arlo was only barely aware of her answer, the desperate truth, the instinctual whisper of "I *always* miss you when—"

Bang.

She jerked back so quickly from Nausicaä, her head smacked against the wall. *"Urgh,"* she groaned, patting her injury, peeking through her wince of pain to the source of what had startled her— the classroom door that had burst open, Fyri storming out.

130

Fyri didn't say anything, didn't so much as pause or make eye contact on her way by back to her newly built dormitory. If Nausicaä picked up on any animosity, it was restrained to a curious look between them, and then glaring at the rest of the *pack* that followed in Fyri's tumultuous wake—the half-goblin boy, who waggled his brows at Arlo; the half-dryad girl, who issued an actual yelp when she and the instantly skittish others realized Nausicaä was there.

There was silence as the class filtered out and down the hall.

Once they were past, Nausicaä brightened. "So—making friends?"

Arlo shook her head. "Pretty much the opposite, I think."

"Making *enemies*—even better. I'm very proud."

"Uh-huh, I'm sure you are. So. You're done for the day, then, are you?" *You have to do it*—she didn't want to. "There can't be many more Viridians left to hunt down at this rate."

She regretted it as soon as it was spoken, but it had to be said. It was the one thing that produced the best results, after all—leading Nausicaä to believe Arlo was angry with her over what Riadne had her doing. *Found another of my family for the queen's torture*—it had been a visible shattering, the mask Nausicaä hid everything behind, the first time Arlo had thought to use her hunts as a weapon against her.

It wasn't fair.

None of this was.

If Arlo had only listened to her girlfriend back in the gardens the night of the Solstice, when Arlo had wanted to give Riadne the world, and Nausicaä had cautioned her not to . . .

"Forget it." Arlo frosted, to save them both the pain of Nausicaä standing there, looking like Arlo had just slapped her in the face, looking like she was the one about to apologize for it.

It wouldn't be forgotten.

And that was . . . kind of the point. It was better this way. The less attached Nausicaä was to her, the less she'd feel compelled to do just to stay by Arlo's side.

Nausicaä closed her mouth. Swallowed. Plastered on an extremely unconvincing smile. "Um . . . so, hey." She seemed nervous all of a sudden. "Slight . . . change of subject, but also not really. There's something I have to show you. Or, I guess . . . someone? Some*where* I want to bring you, I mean, and someone's, um . . . there. Are you . . . free right now?"

Narrowing her gaze in suspicion, Arlo nodded slowly. "I am. What's going on?"

"I think this will go better if I show you." She held out her hand, a silent plea for Arlo to trust her.

Which Arlo did; she trusted Nausicaä more than she trusted herself anymore.

She'd follow her anywhere, through any*thing*.

The problem was, Nausicaä would apparently do the same for Arlo, regardless of what it would personally cost her.

So ignoring Nausicaä's outstretched hand, Arlo stepped around her. Sighing again, she called over her shoulder, "I've got some time, but I have another lesson in half an hour. If we're doing this, it'll have to be quick."

"Who exactly are you taking me to see?" Arlo asked, confidence wavering, as she climbed behind Nausicaä, down a spiral of stone steps that led to the Luminous Palace's infamous dungeons.

All the palaces still had dungeons.

Arlo had been to Spring's exactly once in her life, a very long time ago, and it had been a terrifying experience that stuck with her even now.

The palace dungeons were meant for only the worst of the Court's offenders, after all, and the High King's dungeons even more so—that on top of the fact that it was one of the many areas restricted to Arlo during her visits meant that she'd never had any real desire to explore the place. But one day an obnoxious cousin, looking to get a very young Cel in trouble with his father, had told Cel that he'd seen Arlo being coaxed down to the dungeons by another family member. A likely story, as Arlo's cousins had made sport of constantly trying to get *her* in trouble as well. And when Celadon had rushed immediately off to her rescue, her cousins ran straight to Arlo.

Oh, Arlo, how terrible—

The High Prince, he's gone to the dungeons!

In search of you!

If his father finds out, he'll be furious!

So off to Celadon's rescue *she'd* gone, all the way down to the dungeon's lowest deep. She could still feel the way the humidity had suffocated the air in her lungs; smell the pungent mixture of damp mold and scorched stone; see the way the darkness burned an eerie, glowing green in bursts, like the palace's very beating heart. . . .

Something *lived* down there, Arlo had discovered.

Something enormous and scaly, that made the earth tremble when it dragged its body across the ground, lashed at its confines, and sent a roar like thunder that chased Celadon from its hold, straight into an equally frightened Arlo frozen on the steps.

It had been Thalo who'd come for them.

She'd been livid—first with her and Celadon, then with their cousins when Arlo regained enough calm to explain what had happened.

Arlo's mother . . .

It didn't feel real. Every day she woke and felt her heart break all over again, when habit made her check her phone to discover it blank, no message waiting to greet her with little hearts and "good morning sweetheart" or the "I love you" she would give *anything* to receive just one more time. . . .

ExhaustionGuiltAgonyAnger—

"Just a little farther," Nausicaä said over her shoulder. "Trust me, Arlo. I . . . just trust me."

Arlo said nothing. Fought the instinct to press a little closer to Nausicaä's broad back and followed her girlfriend down.

Down.

Down they descended.

There were guards at the bottom of the long spiral—the Luminous variety, Arlo noted, based on their bone-white armor and the importance they wore in their auras.

Their rigid posture and the way they glared down their sharp noses at Arlo as Nausicaä pulled her through told Arlo they would have *definitely* sent her right back up those stairs if it had been her alone, but with Nausicaä . . .

Arlo didn't have a very clear memory of events after the ballroom during the Solstice, but no one had been able to pry Nausicaä from her the entire night, and . . . it was pretty well known now that Nausicaä was their infamous Dark Star legend; she was the High Queen's almost-assassin and an exiled Fury and immortal. Nausicaä was . . . A Lot, but whatever she'd done to impress her permanence on them when they'd tried to separate them before Riadne's Crowning, even the Luminous Guard now seemed reluctant to so much as draw her attention their way.

The dungeon was more or less what Arlo expected to find.

The stairs let out into darkness illumed by only a sparse scattering of torches down a long, meandering hall, which seemed to stretch forever off down either side of her. Tiny cubicles had been stamped into the stone walls, each outfitted with a bucket and small, uncomfortable-looking cot, and sealed shut by thick, pure iron bars that would drive even the strongest sidhe fae to sickness after a few nights of constant exposure.

It didn't surprise her all that much to discover that—for the most part—these cells were empty.

Riadne Lysterne was more of the *take no prisoners* sort of warlord. In fact, it was only . . .

"Oh, thank gods! It's the pretty redhead. This one-star bed-and-breakfast just became a two."

Startled, Arlo turned her attention to her right, just as Nausicaä stepped over to the cell nearest the stairwell and struck the bars with her palm. "Hey!"

It was *Harlan.*

Aurelian's younger brother.

"Watch your mouth, prisoner," Nausicaä growled. "My girlfriend makes this place at least a three."

Arlo dashed to the bars as well, clutching them tightly.

"She'd make it a ten if she opened that door there. . . ."

"Harlan," she rasped, eyes wide. She hadn't met him on more than a couple of occasions before this, but even so, she could tell he didn't look well.

Still dressed in the clothing he'd planned to wear to the Solstice before Riadne had him quietly snatched up: tight-fitted gold trousers and a billowing silk shirt, as if he were some romantic figure on the cover of a harlequin novel. It was torn and filthy and crusted with dried blood—his *own* dried blood. The cuts they'd come from had healed quickly thanks to his lesidhe magic, but bruises bloomed like ugly flowers up his arms, peeking out over his collar and across his face.

Fresh, then.

He'd recently been beaten.

Nausea shot through Arlo at the realization; this sixteen-year-old boy . . . He sat folded against the back of the cage, holding himself in a way that suggested any sort of movement to his ribs caused him pain. His long brown hair was unbound and wild around his tight shoulders.

"Harlan," she repeated. "Are . . . are you . . . ?"

"Okay?" he finished for her, dropping into the exact same gentle manner that Aurelian spoke to her in. It hit her like a hurricane all of a sudden . . . how much she missed his brother, her stoic, steady friend whose presence she hadn't realized until just now had been like an anchor in all this chaos. "I'm okay, Princess. Better than I would be if it weren't for Celadon, I think. The guards like to rumble that if it weren't for the apparent geas he'd sworn my brother for our protection, Riadne would have had us executed outright, so . . . I suppose this is the better option? It'll take more than a few iron bars and *Her High Majesty's* idiot lugs to change that. I do have some suggestions for improvement, though, if anyone wants to toss me a comment card."

Nausicaä sighed, shaking her head. "Harlan has a hard time keeping his mouth shut."

"You can't ask me to stop being a man," Harlan replied through the crack of a pained grin.

"Come on, Arlo. This . . . isn't who I wanted you to meet. Harlan will be okay."

For now.

Harlan would be okay only so long as it amused Riadne for him to live, to entertain whatever Celadon had bargained to keep them safe, and until she figured out how to use them to trick Aurelian back into her web—as little as she seemed to value his worth, Riadne clearly didn't enjoy when her "things" acted out of turn.

At least, this was all what Arlo hadn't actually had a chance to speak to Vehan yet to confirm Aurelian was even alive and well. Mostly because Riadne kept him extremely busy, but also . . . she just couldn't bring herself to.

The care and concern that shone in his eyes every time their gazes met in the halls . . . it almost made breathing harder, for some reason. But Nausicaä had informed her through the trickle-down of gossip that Aurelian had made it to safety. Thank goodness for that, but it wouldn't last long—Riadne had set a *handsome* price for his capture, after all. . . .

Honestly, I don't know why she hasn't tasked Reynolds or me to fetch him yet, Nausicaä had mused upon imparting this information. *Probably she just wants to torment him. Half the Courts are after him now— whoever returns him to her gets to be a newly minted royal family? I think I missed whatever Aurelian did to make her hate him so much, but wow.*

Down the hall Nausicaä led her.

Past the separated cells containing Nerilla and Matthias, Aurelian's parents. Past Mavren and Eurora, Theodore's parents, in theirs.

Past a few others Arlo didn't know and a few more she didn't *want* to know, until finally Nausicaä came to a halt, stopping Arlo, too.

Silence.

Arlo fixed a questioning look at the tension in Nausicaä's back.

Nausicaä said nothing, which made Arlo more nervous than anything else had so far. Arlo looked to her right, but that cell was empty.

Then she looked to her left.

To the man, stunned to silence too, sitting at the far end of his cell just like Harlan had been, though in considerably better condition.

Fire-red hair and hazel warm eyes . . . the man was both instantly familiar and so *un*familiar at the same time, because how could he be here, staring back at Arlo like his shock wasn't at his surroundings but at *her*?

"Arlo?" her father rasped and scrambled to his feet. Lunged for the bars of his cage and reached through them for her. *"Arlo."*

". . . Dad?"

Her father.

Her father. Her father. Her father.

Nothing in her entire life felt real to her anymore—as if she were floating along, bouncing from one event to the next, an observer instead of an active participant.

She took a step forward, and then another—looked at her father's hand as if it were the most bizarre thing in the whole world. . . .

"Arlo, sweetheart—you're *all right*. Thank goodness. Love, come here. Come . . . here, it's okay. I . . ."

"Dad?" she repeated.

Something inside her felt like breaking, and at the same time . . . she couldn't feel anything at all. She stepped into her father's reach, and Rory drew her in. As awkward but fierce as he could, he pulled her into an embrace through the bars and buried his face in her hair.

Hugged her.

Arlo reeled.

"Dad . . . ," she repeated again, slipping her arms through the bars to hug him back just as awkwardly. "How are you *here*?"

Because it was clear why Arlo was. Why Nausicaä, frightening as she was, had been permitted to lead her right where Riadne undoubtedly wanted her to go; to know that she had Arlo's last bit of family in her clutches, as though Arlo needed any more incentive to play along nicely.

But how was *he* here? Had Nausicaä been sent to fetch him? That was the only thing that made sense, because Rory didn't know about magic. Arlo's whole life had been about keeping it secret from him that magic existed, because he'd hated it back when he knew of its existence . . . yet here he was. Hugging her through the bars of a cell that belonged to one of the most powerful wielders of magic in Court history.

None of this made any sense!

"Arlo," Rory said again, and there was something different about the grief that altered his tone now. There was something different about Rory altogether, Arlo noticed.

He . . . *smelled* different to her.

An aura—when before, for as long as Arlo had known him, Rory Jarsdel hadn't smelled like anything, because there was nothing more to him than who he was. Now, though . . . he smelled like *magic*.

Iron magic.

"Love, I don't know how much time we have." He shot a nervous glance to Nausicaä, who'd finally turned around, but Arlo had never seen her so closed off from all expression. "I . . . don't know how much I can tell you."

Oh.

"Nausicaä is my . . ." She paused. Broke a little more inside every time she had to be this way, but *it was for the best.* "You can trust her," she amended. Rory looked at Nausicaä the way most people looked at Nausicaä. He couldn't possibly know who the Dark Star was, but—

"You're . . . friends with the Dark Star?"

. . . or . . . maybe he did?

Arlo pulled back a little farther, enough to look between her father and Nausicaä, because her girlfriend's stiffness now read a little differently, like she knew something Arlo didn't. . . .

"Dad . . . how do you know who the Dark Star is?"

Rory blew out a heavy sigh, dropped back just enough from the bars to run a hand through his hair. "I wish I didn't have to tell you this way. I wish . . . Arlo. I'm so very sorry. You deserve so much better than *any* of this, and I'm sorry."

"What are you sorry about?"

Her heart hammered in her chest.

Fear coursed through her veins, dissolving like acid through the paralytic numbness that had iced them over. He was about to tell her something—something enormous. Something that would shake her very foundations, she could feel it. But the thing was . . . she didn't have any foundations left to shake.

Riadne had crumbled them, ground them to dust with what she'd done on the Solstice, and Arlo couldn't take it. Not one more thing, *not one more thing—*

"Arlo, I know about magic," he said in a rush, like he couldn't wait to speak the words but didn't know how they'd be received. "I know what you are. I know what your mother is . . . was—"

Arlo flinched.

She felt that "was" like a knife to her gut.

"I . . . I know. But I can't explain it. Not until Lethe removes the block I had him put on your memory—"

The *what*?

"—on *all* memory. There's so much I have to tell you, to apologize for, but you have to know we didn't do any of this to bring you pain. We—"

"We?"

She felt like a broken record.

She felt like . . . Honestly, she felt ill.

139

Like everything she'd ever known had been altered, changed, stripped from her, *killed*—

It was Rory's turn to wince. He looked miserable, the very picture of apologetic. Arlo couldn't comprehend it in the least. "Your mother and I. We . . . Arlo, please know above all else, I love you. I have *always* loved you. Just as I have always loved your mother. We didn't divorce because we wanted to. We didn't choose separation or forgetting because we fell out of love. I don't hate magic, or you, or her—she's the love of my life, Arlo, I . . ." He paused again to catch himself, to trip on the crack that Thalo's death had splintered through his heart.

She could see it now.

Rory was *devastated*.

A man who'd lost the woman he loved and was only just holding himself together.

Arlo was going to be sick.

"You both mean everything to me, and you always have, and we did what we had to do to protect our family. To protect *you*."

You, Arlo.

We did it for you.

This is your fault, Arlo.

"Arlo—survive."

ExhaustionGuiltAgonyAnger

Anger—

ANGER—

Arlo turned around.

"I . . . ," she stammered. "I have to . . ."

She had to go.

She had to be . . . somewhere else.

She couldn't breathe, felt as if she were about to shatter apart into a million pieces, and she couldn't even say why. Her father was here. She wasn't alone. He knew about magic and didn't hate her, and somehow, still, this was *all her fault*, and Arlo was going to throw up.

These words he said to her in a language she couldn't even comprehend. . . . Rory Jarsdel knew about magic. Her *entire life* had been a lie. . . .

And for what?

For *her.*

It wasn't until she'd burst onto the main-floor corridor that Arlo realized she'd fled—and once she'd started running, couldn't bring herself to stop.

CHAPTER 7

Vehan

————

I T FELT GOOD TO RUN.

The days following his mother's Crowning he'd been kept in near-constant motion, a draconian routine Riadne had personally devised just for him, designed to strengthen his body, mind, and magical core. She expected him to sit in on council meetings now, to begin in earnest to practice and study in the Court he'd one day rule. When he wasn't in endless lessons and meetings, his time was spent in training: his magic; his ability to wield and carry lightning; his combat skills, weightlifting, cardio.

Up with the sun, down like a heavy sack of extremely tired flour as soon as day sank below the horizon—Vehan had never been so exhausted, not even when his core had been so dangerously low on magic that he'd almost died, and if it hadn't been for Theodore's help in the Lightning Planes, he would have.

But he liked running.

It was just about the only activity he got to enjoy by himself—more or less—that gave him time to sort out his thoughts and feelings, to plan.

More or less, a not-quite-Vehan voice in his mind purred in dark amusement. *We're never* really *alone though, are we?*

He came to a pause in the woods, on the earthen trail that looped around the palace grounds, only barely outside the hedge that marked its perimeter. Bending to brace his hands on his knees, he allowed himself a moment to catch his breath—to *focus.*

No, he wasn't ever truly alone now.

Not since his mother had baldly informed him of her plan to turn him into her host for the resurrected Ruin she sought to summon with the collected Sins. Not since his magic had finally returned, and he'd started making sure to keep himself topped up on electricity at all times, keep the parasite in him well fed; not since, in combination with this consistent fill of energy, he'd actually begun to flourish under his mother's increased severity, and he was too damned tired to shut out the *thing* that had wormed its way into his heart, the darkness that toyed with his emotions, his mind. . . .

Our *emotions.* Our *mind.*

We will accept this eventually, boy, by choice or force—in the end, it matters not. In the end, this body belongs to us—

Vehan hit play on his phone, drowning out the voice in his head with music that blasted through the tiny white devices in his ears, a gift from Aurelian a few years back. He preferred to run in quiet, but with each passing day, this *thing* inside him grew harder to silence— the stronger Vehan's magic grew, the hungrier and more agitated it became with him for his lack of iron blood to sustain it.

Ruin—the voice in his head, Vehan had concluded—couldn't take control of him yet, not until Riadne did . . . whatever she'd planned to do to make him a viable host, but she'd tied them together in marking him with the array on his chest—different, he suspected, from what she'd marked on the others.

As though he didn't juggle enough difference in his life now.

As High Prince, his extended family, his agemates, his former classmates—*everyone*—flocked around him now in the halls, stopped by for unannounced visits that lasted for days on end. Vehan had received dozens of proposals over the last few weeks because Aurelian Bessel was out of the picture, as far as they were concerned, and there was no one more desirable to them now than what he'd become overnight.

Aurelian—

Wide mouth hot on his . . .

Kiss after kiss as though Aurelian meant to devour him.
Biting claims that marked Vehan his all the way down
Vehan's chest . . .
A keening moan that had surprised Vehan as
coming from himself when Aurelian finally, finally pressed
the length of himself inside . . .

Aurelian was one stolen hour of the *best* moment Vehan had ever lived, now completely out of reach, out of contact save whatever message Lethe deigned to drop or deliver in passing.

For the first time since their meeting as children, Vehan was alone in the palace with his mother while his best friend and greatest love was in *hiding* from her, and it was only Vehan's pretending that kept her search for Aurelian from growing vicious.

So long as Vehan pretended, so long as he played along and did what his mother wanted . . . so long as he pushed himself to breaking each night and made no complaints about her experimentation on him—like the entire wineglass of iron blood, for example, that she'd made him drink the other night in hopes that it would be an easy solution to giving the thing inside him what it craved . . .

Celadon—his brother. Whom he hadn't seen once since the night of the Solstice.

Arlo—whom he hadn't yet been able to bring himself to speak to. Not with the way she avoided him as he avoided her. . . .

Everything was different, and he was alone now, so completely alone. Not to mention his Certification exams were coming, so his anxiety was at a constant high, and Vehan hated every moment he had to spend inside that nightmare palace—

He didn't realize he'd started running again, not until he broke into a clearing in the forest's shallows. Panting, wildly out of breath, Vehan staggered once more to a halt—and stared.

He reached up an absent hand, removed the plastic buds from his ears. . . .

He hadn't meant to come here.

Not to this place.

It had taken him a moment to recognize it through the shock of being thrown so suddenly back into awareness of his surroundings. But when he did . . . the small circle of trees around him, the half-crumbled stone figure worn beyond recognition . . .

This was the clearing his mother tended to.

This was where she whisked away to when she wanted to *be alone*.

It was the clearing his grandmother had tended to before her.

It was also where Vehan's father had died.

Vehan *never* came here. It . . . unnerved him, to stand where his father had stood in his final moments, and whatever had happened . . . *officially* he'd been assassinated along with Queen Arina. *Unofficially* . . .

He'd never wanted to believe it of his mother, what rumor said she'd done—that *she'd* been the one to take Vadrien's life along with her own mother's.

Before the Solstice, he'd actually defended his mother's honor whenever those rumors floated past him. But now . . .

Vehan stepped forward.

He hadn't been here since his father's death, no matter how many times Riadne insisted he face his fear of the place—that it would serve him well to patronize the mystery idol the Lysternes had privately kept for generations.

But this was the first time that he was truly old enough to comprehend this place, and it was . . .

Surprisingly peaceful.

All that running had brought him in front of the nameless statue. Reaching out a hand, Vehan traced a creeping vine away from what had once been a face, now weathered blank and pockmarked.

We do not greet our gods empty-handed, Vehan.

His mother's voice surfaced from the depths of his memory, a recollection of the one and only time she'd brought him here in his toddlerhood.

Vehan looked down at himself. He didn't have anything on him currently to offer whoever this was, who'd watched over their family for such a long time—and what good had worshipping this god done them anyway? But here he was, and there was enough going on in his life right now without a spurned deity's anger heaped on top. . . .

He placed an earbud on the small slab of stone, reached into his pocket, and selected a prettier song than what had pushed him through his punishing laps—the gods had liked music when they'd occupied this realm. A song would be better than nothing, surely?

"Vehan?"

Vehan whipped around, falling back from the statue.

More than the voice in his head, more than his mother discovering him here, more than *anything*, he wasn't quite sure he'd ever felt a fear like what trilled through him now, hearing the voice of the one person he wanted so desperately to talk to and at the same time couldn't bring himself to even breathe the air in her space.

"Arlo . . . ," he gasped, eyes widening.

Arlo.

Arlo looking more than a little distressed.

There were leaves and insect bits in her tangled red hair, like she'd *fought* her way directly through those hedges that magic shouldn't have allowed her past, not without Riadne's permission . . . but here she was. Arlo Jarsdel, in a cream-white blouse and burnished gold trousers, because his mother had taken that from her too—her UnSeelie Spring colors. Her wardrobe. Anything she could that Arlo might be able to cling to as a symbol of the Court she truly belonged to.

Everything except those eyes, vibrant jade, which were currently rimmed red with unshed tears.

"Arlo, are . . . ?"

Are you okay? he'd been about to ask, like Arlo was even remotely *okay* after what his family had done to hers.

"What . . . uh, are you doing here?" he amended.

"Running," Arlo replied, a touch defensively, much heavier with unspoken intension.

And Vehan . . . he deflated.

This wasn't the first time Arlo had given him the impression that she wanted to be left alone. That she rightly blamed him for what had happened and wanted nothing further to do with their friendship. "Running." He nodded. "Yeah. Me too." He slipped his phone back into his pocket, reached down to retrieve his earbud. Made himself busy and unassuming, as nonthreatening as possible, so that Arlo would know he wasn't going to stop her.

His mother might.

His mother *would*—she'd definitely track Arlo down and drag her right back to that horrible palace—but Arlo could run. If that would make her feel better. He'd do anything to make one of his very few friends feel better—not that he was sure she'd call him her friend any longer.

More steps forward—this time Arlo's.

Confusion etched in her expression, she approached him as tentatively as a wild doe, and Vehan stood there, still as though she actually were one, terrified that any movement would scare her away.

He'd envisioned this moment so many times—how he'd apologize to her, beg for her forgiveness. In some of those imaginings, she'd been kind in a way he didn't deserve but desperately wanted. Arlo was . . . well, he didn't want to examine it too closely, how Arlo was one of the only real examples of *gentle* female power in his life, and how peaceful it made him feel to be around her. Fodder for all the therapy he'd have to look into later, he supposed. His overwhelming heap of mother issues.

In his less kind imaginings, Arlo turned from him with devastating finality.

He'd spent so many nights fantasizing about and dreading this moment, and here it was, and he wasn't ready, but then again, his readiness didn't matter. What mattered most was Arlo, and through all that confusion, and the barely concealed pain of whatever had been the last straw to drive her out here, Arlo looked at him like . . . *impossibly* looked at him like—

"Vehan . . . are you okay?"

It hit him in an instant—a blast of power.

Vehan wheeled around once more, instinct turning him back to the indistinguishable stone figure.

He had just enough time to stiffen, to reel back in surprise, because that stone figure was no longer incomplete, no longer stone. It was whole and it was real and it was *She*—he knew, without doubt or prompt, the figure that stood there watching him, in silklike pear-white water around her ample curves, hair whiter than stardust shimmering in waves to her hips . . .

Fate stood looking back at him, white eyes all-consuming, and Vehan had a *moment* to comprehend this before dying daylight overhead pitched itself into night.

His gaze shot skyward—first in wonder, then in alarm.

Darkness bled out across the heavens, but there were no stars or moon to illuminate its black. Instead, its inky pitch was lit by *fire*, flame bursting to life in the trees, lighting on branches and scorching through the ring faster than even a waterborn fae could douse them.

"Arlo!" he gasped again, lowering his gaze to search for her, to usher her protectively behind him—but Arlo was no longer there.

What stood in her place . . . Vehan whipped his hand to his side, summoning the lightning that crackled hot and ready inside him. He sharpened his magic instantly into a lethal, long blade, because there was no doubt in his mind what would happen next.

The boy standing across from him, with hair black as the deepest pits of the underworld, skin like snowy death, eyes burning not red anymore but cold as the void of space between stars . . . It was like looking into a mirror, at a reflection he could barely recognize, because it was himself standing there, resplendent in robes of flowing black, a nightmare prince remade—not Vehan at all anymore, but *Ruin.*

Ruin flew at him, a lightning blade of his own materializing—longer and far more wicked than anything Vehan could summon, the way it crackled in the air sounding like screams.

It was all he could do to lift his own lightning blade, to meet the onslaught and block it.

The *power* in what Ruin swung at him, though . . . Vehan was knocked flat on his back, winded by the force of how hard he hit the ground.

"Poor little Prince of Light," Ruin sneered at him, twisting Vehan's expression into something so ugly and foreign to him—hatred . . . the sort he sometimes saw in his mother. He raised the point of his sword above Vehan's chest. "Alone, you were born. Alone, you lived. Alone is how you'll die."

Ruin drove the sword-point down—straight through Vehan's heart.

He screamed, eyes falling closed to the *agony* that coursed through him, to the realization that what Ruin had said was true.

Alone. He was forever and would always be—

"Vehan!"

Vehan's eyes flew open to find . . . Arlo leaning over him, worry stark on her pale face.

The sky was blue washed over in sun-setting orange. The clearing was no longer on fire. He no longer looked up into his Ruined future, but at *Arlo.* . . .

"Vehan, what's wrong, is it your array? Is it your chest? Vehan—please!"

Arlo's hands were frantic on his chest, trying to pull at his hem to check his array, and it was a scene that would have looked so incredibly indecent to anyone who stumbled across them that Vehan wanted to both laugh and cry in relief so profound it actually hurt worse than Ruin's sword had.

"I'm okay," he replied, in breathless wonder.

Because Arlo looked at him like . . . *impossibly* looked at him like—

You are not alone, Prince of Light, a voice soothed inside his head. Gentle for all the power behind it, compassionate for all its immortality. It wasn't Ruin. This voice belonged to the figure he would bet his crown still stood behind them, though fading back into stone. *Remember what it is that truly makes you strong.*

What made him strong . . .

Vehan stared up at Arlo, a little dazed if he was being perfectly honest. Whatever had just happened, whatever vision Fate had just bestowed on him—possibly, what would happen to him if he allowed this parasite inside him to win—had left him in a considerable stupor. But that was okay, because Arlo was looking down at him like Vehan might just still be her friend.

CHAPTER 8

Aurelian

———◦———

DUSK BEGAN TO SEEP through the forest's dense canopy, wrapping trees in ethereal shrouds of steel and burnished gold.

This place, the plot that brought them out here, delayed weeks over by the fae they were supposed to be meeting . . . all of it made Aurelian so uneasy.

It was too close to night, too close to the time when the horrors that stalked the Hiraeth's moonlight would begin to stir. The Wild Hunt—able to transport themselves around only by way of the shadow that filled darkness—would be at its full and ghastly strength. As soon as the sun sank below the horizon, its dampening effects on Hunter powers would be removed; they'd be able to whisk in anywhere night touched, impossible to fend off in this unfettered form, and would snatch Aurelian and Elyas up right where they stood to deliver them straight back to Riadne.

But it cannot be any other time, Melora had insisted when he and Elyas had been brought before her for the details of their first task, at last. *Theodore has played his part, and it's time the two of you play yours; Riadne has to see that Rory Jarsdel's information is good if he's to gain her trust, so the two of you will meet with Prince Alaric where Autumn's portal to the Hiraeth intersects, and you will do so with just enough time for whoever she sends to glimpse you.*

They were playing with fire.

If he and Elyas couldn't make it back to the portal that waited for them—tucked just far enough away that no one Riadne sent would immediately notice it to block them off but close enough for them to actually stand a chance of making escape—they were doomed.

As much as he wanted desperately, achingly, to see Vehan again . . . it couldn't be this way.

It couldn't be by capture.

And he couldn't let Elyas fall into Riadne's bloodied clutches, this little fae boy who'd . . . grown on him these past few weeks. So much like Arlo and Celadon in many ways, but there was something about him so uniquely his own that stood him apart as well.

"I like this place," Elyas observed, peering around at this new patch of forest, not all that different from what surrounded the Market. But they'd been cooped up inside its walls for so long that this change of view wasn't all that bad to Aurelian, either. "There's something very peaceful about the Hiraeth, don't you think?"

"Depends," Aurelian grunted.

The chattering, the questions—these were the ways he paralleled his iconic uncle.

Undeterred and frowning now up at him, Elyas pressed, "On what?"

"How close you are to something that wants to eat you."

Elyas's frown deepened. "You're not very good with children, are you."

"Probably not," Aurelian replied with a shrug. "I wasn't very good at being one." Too quiet, people had always said of him. Too intelligent, too somber, too blunt, too mature—Aurelian hadn't been good at childhood. It hadn't been until Vehan that he even took much interest in *play* with anyone other than Harlan.

Harlan.

Aurelian's heart constricted.

Please let Celadon be taking care of my family like he promised.

"That's all right. Vehan seems like he is. I've only met him a couple of times, but he was very nice and smiling, and he has a good laugh."

"He does."

Gods, Aurelian missed him.

In all the time since he'd moved to the palace, he'd never gone this long without him. It was like waking up one morning to discover half his entirety was simply *missing* and now he had to figure out how to survive without it.

"Celadon does too."

It was a quieter admission, made Aurelian look down at him.

Elyas was earnest; that's what Aurelian liked best about him. Arlo was earnest too, but it was different. Time and hurt had taught her to build walls around her heart, and Aurelian certainly didn't blame that. But it was a little refreshing, this sidhe fae royal who spoke with complete sincerity, other people's opinions of him be damned.

"I'm sure Celadon will—" *find a way to visit you soon without drawing attention,* he'd meant to say, because he had a feeling that was part of what was bothering Elyas lately.

Celadon hadn't been to see them, hadn't been seen publicly by *anyone*, actually.

Rumor that he'd overheard in the Market was that Celadon had been spending the past few weeks *cowering* in shame in his ill-bought palace, but Aurelian didn't believe it for a second. Not of the Celadon Cornelius Fleur-Viridian he knew, and certainly not of a Lysterne . . . which he hadn't believed at first when Vehan had told him, and doubly hadn't been able to repeat to Elyas yet.

The boy was going through enough as it was.

No.

Celadon's silence was somehow part of some brilliant plan that would help them far more than *the Madam* could, and Aurelian had been about to reassure his newest charge of that as well, but a rustling in the brush interrupted him.

Aurelian's gaze snapped toward the sound. Instinct drew him to full height.

Melora wanted him here as Elyas's bodyguard, and that was fine. Aurelian was well practiced at the job and didn't want any harm to come to Elyas anyway. So Aurelian puffed himself up and relaxed his hands to his sides, blue sparks of the spirit magic he controlled live and crackling at his fingertips, much the way Vehan's lightning did.

Was everything going to remind him of Vehan? Was it normal to feel their separation so acutely?

His heart gave a throb.

It was actual pain inside him, not having the surety of his prince by his side, but there was no time for this right now. He had to compartmentalize. Because the rustling he'd picked up on revealed its culprit a moment later—or rather, *culprits.*

Like spirits gliding out from the air itself, they materialized. It was only thanks to Aurelian's lesidhe senses that he and Elyas had had warning of their arrival at all. Because Prince Alaric Vogel—youngest son of King Dinand, Head of Seelie Autumn—was sidhe fae in every respect. He was cutting-bone structure, brilliant amber eyes, warm brown skin that glowed with royal luminescence, and hair so deep a russet brown that it gleamed almost black.

Not much older than Aurelian, by his estimation, and he could see hints of the resemblance between the two gathered families—Vogel had been High King Azurean's maternal relation, making him and Elyas removed cousins.

But however gifted Alaric might be as a fae prince, he would never be able to sneak up on a lesidhe.

The fae who preceded his arrival, though . . . in their earthen-brown and forest-green armor and tight black underclothing, not a single blade or weapon in sight . . . with their slightly sharper construction and pointier ears and varying but similarly blazing gold eyes . . . Aurelian understood immediately why it was Prince Alaric of all people Melora had wanted them to win to their side tonight—and why she'd judged *Aurelian* an asset to this meeting instead of sending someone far more capable of protecting her prized Viridian pawn.

The Earthen Army. Aurelian had . . . completely forgotten.

Seelie Autumn's Earthen Guard, comparable to their Luminous and Verdant kin, was nearly entirely composed of lesidhe fae.

"Prince Elyas." Alaric nodded in greeting as he stepped ahead of the line of guards, which fell to a casual but highly alert observation. "I regret that this is the circumstance of our first meeting, younger cousin. My condolences for your loss—may Night keep your family."

Alaric had a slow, measured way of speaking, deeper pitched than Aurelian would have guessed of such a slight body, and the steady way he watched Elyas as he spoke was more than a little unnerving—extra so, when those jewel-bright eyes snapped to Aurelian's assessment.

"You, I do not know, though the Madam informed me: Lord Aurelian Bessel, oldest of the two boys born to Nerilla and Matthias Bessel. You originate from *my* Court. Cousin, I commend you on your choice of guard; we of Autumn have never believed in squandering lesidhe talents as all the other Courts do. Were your parents members of the Guard, Lord Bessel?"

Pretentious.

A not-so-small part of Aurelian wanted to grab Elyas and turn right back around for the portal. He was so *tired* of being caught up between pretentious, spoiled, royal sidhe fae.

Tired and . . . there it was—his anger, ever lurking and becoming harder and harder to push down, smother, and ignore.

"They were not," he said around gritted teeth.

The lesidhe were built a little differently, Aurelian had always been told. They were stronger, faster, quieter, more agile. They were heartier, performed powerful magic, could stop a heart in more ways than Aurelian could count—but above all else, as was constantly drilled into him from the time he'd been old enough to listen to words, the lesidhe were always *peaceful*.

It was the "lesidhe way."

His father had taught him this—had taught him that *lesidhe aren't meant to deal harm for glory; our strength is for protection only.* For survival. Their abilities were a gift from the Wild for their devotion to the old ways. Yes, they still felt the unkinder things like anger and blood-lust (probably more so, for how deeply they repressed it), but through

155

Aurelian's entire life, he'd maintained what his parents had taught him because he saw no reason his father should be wrong, why they shouldn't adhere to peace—ever-constricting, slowly crushing *peace*.

To the proper lesidhe way.

But still . . . Aurelian was always just so *angry*.

He was angry about so many things, because . . . Well, Aurelian couldn't explain it really. How it felt to be so conditioned to one way of thinking, to what his father and the majority of his people believed, to what the Courts wanted them to believe, to what Aurelian had never questioned before. But the more and more anger he felt . . . the more it all welled up and knotted together inside him, heavier and heavier to carry, and soon this emotion might just well crush him . . . especially since the greater his anger became, the guiltier he felt for feeling it at all.

It was . . . shameful. To harbor this level of hate inside him. His father would be dismayed to know how much of it he kept concealed—how dark his thoughts sometimes turned.

These Earthen Warriors in front of him did, though. No doubt they embraced all manner of feelings. No doubt they acted on them too—caused harm; took lives. They were an insult to everything the lesidhe stood for.

But . . .

Is it insult, or is it freedom? his anger seemed to argue.

"Thank you, Prince Alaric," Elyas said firmly, snapping Aurelian back to the situation. "And thank you for this meeting. At such a high-cost risk, you honor the Viridian family with this display of loyalty. You honor *yours* with this bravery."

Alaric nodded, visibly pleased by this obvious flattery.

It made Aurelian want to roll his eyes—it always did. High fae society and their pointless customs . . . their sycophantic adulations like they didn't all hate each other and would sooner see their darling friend or family member on a pyre just for wealth or rank or whatever else was apparently worth more than honest happiness.

He had to hand it to Elyas, though—he played the part of diplomat well.

Gone was the wide-eyed kid wondering if Aurelian was serious about the whole "monsters are definitely waiting out here to eat us soon as that sun sets" thing. Still there was that earnestness; still Elyas lacked the special brand of guile unique to sidhe fae nature. But there was no denying at this moment that the boy beside him had been High Prince to a powerful family, spare to the throne, by the way Spring's Crowning Gift had already begun to flourish inside him.

Elyas had been raised well to survive Court politics.

Somehow, Aurelian had the impression Celadon had been the one to see to that.

"Loyalty," Alaric mused. "Bravery . . . the Seelie call it 'responsibility'—one of the key traits we value most." He took another step forward.

Another.

"It is the way of things—each Head that assumes the Bone Crown accepts responsibility for what will come. Power will pass, claimed through bloodshed. Our new High Queen, though vicious in her execution, broke no law in what she did. But there is *responsibility* to observe." Alaric paused to cringe. "A woman of Seelie blood, who chose to ignore time-honored tradition. No period of mourning for the fallen, no funeral, no ceremony for her Crowning? Azurean's High, immediate Family—his wife, his children, slain without first given chance to swear fealty to her. Distasteful. *Ir*responsible." He almost looked angry. "You wish for aid in delivering justice, but my father will not be provoked to war, the useless old toss, and you'll find even less help in my simpering milksop of a Crown Prince brother."

This was . . . incongruous with what Aurelian had learned in his Academy lessons. Both of Autumn's Factions were fairly well known for their war prowess. Very few people wanted to mess with the might of Earth, which this branch of Seelie wielded, and even fewer wanted to mess with the UnSeelie's Death. So what did it say about Alaric that he judged an Autumn king so weak?

He could hear Vehan's voice, soft in the back of his head—Vehan, who was far better skilled at navigating the absent spaces between the things sidhe fae said . . .

Be careful, Aurelian.

"Myself, however—"

Even my mother denied Alaric Vogel's request to play my suitor.

Alaric grinned, revealing incisors that were suspiciously sharp, even for a fae, like he'd filed them deadlier himself. Another step forward, and he paused again, this time to extend his hand. "You're in need of assistance—I've got a bit of that to spare, an Earthen Warrior or two who's loyal to my cause that I'd be more than happy to send your way. If *you*, of course, are loyal to my cause as well."

Aurelian's gaze flicked over Prince Alaric's shoulder to the line of Earthen Guards.

All but one had their gazes trained forward, motionless, waiting— the only deviation was the one Aurelian would bet anything was the leader.

He was enormous for a fae. His arms corded with muscle and his body built like brick, sun-tanned and weathered, pure silver hair pulled tightly back in a series of intricate braids—this one stared not forward, not at his prince, but at *Aurelian*. And Aurelian couldn't pin his expression for anything, but whatever the Guard was thinking, Aurelian wanted no part of it.

Elyas, meanwhile, kept his eyes trained on the prince. "What *is* your cause, exactly, Prince Alaric?"

"Probably he wants you to off Daddy Dearest and Big Brother Cock-Block, tiny Not-Celadon," said a voice from the trees that made Aurelian stiffen, more afraid than anyone in this patch of forest had made him all evening. "Or, like, whatever the equivalent of cock-blocking is for *uwu, if it wasn't for my brother, I'd be next in line for the throne!* There's a word for it—is this my cue yet, by the way, or . . . ? Because no one mailed me the script for this, and I'm not really sure when I'm supposed to swoop in and . . . also cock-block! Hah. Wow, I'm *sure* there's an actual term for this."

"Nos!" Elyas cried, turning for the trees behind them, his entire expression brightening. Because of course he'd be happy to see her. Nausicaä was his friend.

But Aurelian paled.

He could feel the way confusion moldered at Elyas's aura when he took ahold of Elyas's cloak to haul him safely behind his back. Of course Elyas would be confused . . . Nausicaä was his friend—*their* friend . . . but there was much Aurelian hadn't been able to tell him yet.

Like the fact that Riadne had managed to trap one of the most dangerous people in this entire realm, a person Elyas considered good, in her service as her personal assassin—an assassin meant to execute *them*.

Aurelian's gaze wandered upward to meet Nausicaä's. His eyes locked with steel.

For a moment, that steel was unflinching, then—

Make this good, Grumpy, he read in a flash. *I have to take you back to her if you can't escape me.*

"Who is this?" Alaric demanded.

His Guard had pulled themselves to the ready in an instant, but Aurelian knew they had to be reeling, furious that someone could sneak up on them without their noticing. They had no idea who Nausicaä was. Not yet.

They would, and it would be too late.

"Your cue to run," Aurelian warned, firm and dire under his breath. "The Madam agrees to your terms. Now go—the Dark Star only has to return with two captives tonight."

"The *Dark Star*?" Alaric suddenly looked much less assured.

"In my defense, they do say you should never meet your heroes," Nausicaä called mournfully. And two of the Earthen Guard, including the leader, seemed almost . . . intrigued; the others stood stunned, staring up at the indolent girl lounging on a tree branch like a panther musing on which prey she'd go for first.

"Aurelian? Nos . . . what's going on?" Elyas struggled behind him, tried to push Aurelian aside. "You don't have to be afraid of her. Nos is on our side—"

"Sorry, kid," Nausicaä sighed. She stood, stepped off her branch to plummet like a boulder to the ground, and landed with effortless ease in front of them.

Alaric, heeding Aurelian's advice at last, took one last sizing look at her before signaling to the rest of his Guard and disappearing back into the woods.

"I really am sorry. I don't actually want to do this—"

Aurelian squared his jaw. "Then don't—"

He doubled over, words cut off by a wheezing gasp of pain.

Elyas cried out, stumbling back. Nausicaä removed her fist from Aurelian's gut and wound the hair on the back of his head between her fingers, and then it was Aurelian's turn to cry when she yanked him back upright.

"Fuck you, Nausicaä," he growled, eyes watering.

"Aurelian," she warned, in perfect composure, not a *hint* of playfulness to be heard. "It's almost dark."

Shit.

Nausicaä had to do this. She'd been contracted to Riadne's bidding in exchange for Arlo's safety, and tonight was undoubtedly a test of that commitment. Nausicaä couldn't just let them go; she had to make it look like she'd tried for the report that would make it back to Riadne if they didn't. And Aurelian had been dreading this, had been hoping Riadne would determine tonight too soon to let one of her deadliest weapons prove herself, to risk Nausicaä's betrayal on what she stood to gain—but of course Riadne couldn't resist . . . just one more jab at her favorite toy.

It's almost dark.

He had to make this good. He had to make it fast. As soon as the

Wild Hunt arrived, there would be no chance of escape—Aurelian had to fight, had to defend himself. . . .

Lesidhe aren't meant to deal harm for glory; our strength is for protection only—

Another fist, this time to Aurelian's back, and he crumpled to the forest floor.

"*Nausicaä!*" Elyas screamed in admonishment, and the next thing Aurelian knew, the prince had thrown himself at her.

Gasping, aching, Aurelian gaped. Nausicaä looked ill. Her orders be damned (thank goodness), she gracefully sidestepped the young prince's fury and let him sail past. "Elyas—" Aurelian groaned . . . Damn it, he was better than this. Nausicaä was even taking it easy on him. "Elyas, stop it. Get back to the portal."

"You better do what he says, my prince—" Aurelian's heart froze at the sound, the voice he knew only for what it meant in its owner appearing here now.

A Hunter.

"Vesper," another voice said, smoother and deeper. Sad. "We no longer serve him."

"I know, I know, it's just . . . we were there when he was born! I can't just . . ."

Nausicaä picked Aurelian upright again, once more by the back of his hair.

Aurelian snarled at her, tried to push her away—the Hunt was here; he had to grab Elyas; he had to run. They wouldn't make it, but they had to *try*, and damn Melora for this. This was exactly what he'd known would happen; she didn't care about her pawns at all.

Aurelian struggled.

Nausicaä, almost completely unfazed, hauled him closer. "One shot," she hissed in his ear, and he didn't need telling twice—he slugged her, hard; harder than he'd ever hit anyone in his life, fear *exploding* through him to drive a strength he'd never let himself access until now.

Was that shock on her face?

Nausicaä actually stumbled back, not because she was playing into the show, but because she couldn't not.

Aurelian had hit her, and she'd genuinely *felt* it, and he didn't have time to wonder after that how he—a mortal—could physically injure her.

"Oh! Nice shot!" The Hunter called Vesper whistled, dropping to the ground now too. "Wow, they don't kid about that lesidhe strength, do they?"

The calm one with black hair joined xim in an instant. He sighed and shook his head. "She'll be a misery now. She's always been a sore loser."

"I can *hear* you two, you know!"

"I didn't say it quietly."

Aurelian darted forward and grabbed Elyas by the middle. Elyas gave no argument this time as Aurelian hauled him up and over his shoulder like a bag of rice, but there was *no time*!

Night had fallen.

The Hunt was here.

They weren't going to make it, couldn't possibly escape, but he had to, had to, had to *try*—

Shrriiieeeekkkkkkkk!

Aurelian slammed to a halt, only steps away from Nausicaä and the Hunters, but what had stopped him had stopped them, too.

Was it possible for his heart to simply give up beating in his chest?

He was breathing too heavily—the forest was too quiet all of a sudden, and all he wanted right now was to *hear*. To listen. For what he both feared and prayed was panic playing tricks on him, but then . . .

"Uh . . ." Vesper frowned. "Do you guys . . . hear that clicking?"

Clicking.

Aurelian heard it.

A sound like enormous insects, testing the air for movement, clicking coordinates at one another—a sound so faint it had been missed for the commotion, but that *shriek* that had followed . . .

Click.

Cliiick.

SHRIEEEEEEKKK!

The forest exploded.

Aurelian threw himself into the trees.

"Shriekers!" he heard Nausicaä exclaim, in deities-damned *delight*, because only Nausicaä would be happy about this situation.

Shriekers.

The name was all they had right now for whatever hells-spawn demons had surfaced in the Hiraeth since Riadne had started toying with the Sins.

Demons, here in the Mortal Realm. Demons no one would be able to control, Melora had explained, until Riadne summoned her final stone or the Sins were vanquished and the rift that was beginning to fissure between the realms was sealed.

It has to be in the Hiraeth, Melora had explained. *This location, specifically. It's been seeing the most Shrieker activity lately. You'll meet with Prince Alaric here, close enough to nightfall that whoever she sends will be able to glimpse you; nightfall because then she might just send the Hunt, and there will be your assured escape. The only directive higher than the High Queen's is Lord Cosmin's order to Hunt any being out of place in the Mortal Realm.*

Fucking Shriekers.

If they survived this, it was going to be thanks to fucking Shriekers, and Aurelian wanted a deities-damned holiday when this was done and over.

"Aurelian . . ." Elyas spoke in *breathless* fear. Aurelian didn't blame him. They barreled through the trees, faster than Elyas could comprehend, because lesidhe speed was perhaps greater than even windborn ability. Aurelian *ran*, and there was no doubt in his mind that what they fled was hot on their tail, filling Elyas's vision with nightmares for years to come.

He ran.

And he ran.

And finally, blessedly, thank fucking deities, there was the portal that would take them back to the Market's safety—where neither demons nor Hunters nor Furies could enter without the Market's permission.

Safety.

It came out of nowhere.

Aurelian had been running, pushing himself harder than he'd ever pushed himself before, until suddenly—*slam.*

A crushing weight tackled him sideways to the ground.

Elyas hit the forest floor hard, head striking against a moderate boulder in their path. He scrambled to try and right himself despite his daze, and Aurelian couldn't help at all, because the *thing* was on top of him, the grotesque humanoid shape that was oozing pustules and open sores and flayed, rotting flesh; broken bones and a skeleton half consumed by some mysterious, spongy black substance that looked a bit like rot but *breathed* . . .

Broken teeth snapped in his face, a jaw that could crunch bone to dust . . .

Fingers like talons shredded his arms, clawed at his chest, that shrieking, shrieking, *shrieking* all the while in his ears.

The others would soon be upon them.

Damn it—*damn it*; he'd promised Vehan he'd be careful. . . .

Bright light lit up Aurelian's periphery, making him wince. For a moment, his fatigue and fright and adrenaline and injury made him wonder if maybe it was his prince.

As the light hit them, the Shriekers screamed in pain and scattered, no meal worth the unbearable agony of what anything other than darkness caused them.

The light began to fade—and Aurelian was a *fool*; he was magic, damn it. He should have used that to save them, but it was no matter now. Slowly, the light retracted, dialed back into the tiny body that had produced it.

Aurelian had all of seconds to blink up at the woodsprite, no bigger than a robin, lowering herself to his chest.

A *woodsprite* had saved them.

Aurelian wanted to laugh.

Instead, he moaned when hands slotted themselves under his arms and *dragged* his battered body across the forest floor. He was heavier than he looked, he wanted to apologize, but his tongue wouldn't move, and when he opened his mouth, it was only to gag on the blood in the back of his throat. . . .

"Come on, lad," the owner of those hands soothed—a voice he didn't recognize, but something about it left him irritated, like in the back of his head he knew who it was. "Come on, keep it together; we're almost there. You'll be okay."

"Okay," Aurelian finally managed to reply.

He would have liked to ask that they stop dragging him entirely, because the ground was sharp and unforgiving on his bruised and battered back, and it had been . . . a rough evening.

But just as unconsciousness began to tug at his darkening vision—

"Aurelian, goodness!"

"Ah. Ivandril, yes? How nice of the Earthen Captain himself to see our young prince home."

"Elyas, baby—are you okay?"

The world around them had changed from forest to warm, glowing wood. Sticks and leaves and stones and earth had been traded for firm and polished planks, and the only clicking now was that of crackling logs on a fire.

This was better—until those hands let go from under his arms and a body threw itself distraught across him.

"*Oof,*" Aurelian groaned in winded pain. In his current capacity, all he could say for certain was that a rib or two was definitely broken, and he hoped Nausicaä's jaw was really hurting her right now.

"You have to be okay, Aurelian! You can't not be okay!"

It was . . . oh, it was Elyas. Aurelian tried to focus, his vision sifting like sand in the wind. Elyas, and he was crying. "You have to be okay! I can't lose anyone else, all right? I don't care that my father's gone, I don't. He was awful to me and he was worse to Mom, especially when she tried to protect me. And Celadon was the *only* person who ever stood up to him besides her when he got violent, and now I've lost *him*, I haven't seen him at all, and you're all I have, so *please* be okay! Please, you have to be okay—"

"Elyas," Aurelian rasped, lifting a hand to the side of his head and giving it a gentle pat. "I'm okay. Don't squish the woodsprite."

Tinkling fury—an outrage of impressively vulgar insults from the woodsprite that Elyas wouldn't be able to understand as a sidhe fae disconnected from the Wild—was the last thing Aurelian knew before finally, blessedly, unconsciousness claimed him.

CHAPTER 9

Celadon

~⚬~

He shouldn't exist—

He's going to ruin us all—

—has no idea what he's doing—

It would have been better for us all if he'd died with
the rest of them;
A mongrel prince with no training in kingship, the
product of madness and bloodlust . . .

Are you suggesting a coup, Councillor?

I simply propose the idea that we've . . . outgrown
Viridian rule;
Wouldn't you agree, Councillor?

Slam!

Celadon slowly lifted his gaze from the dark slate tile beneath him.

It was difficult to make out anything more than watery shapes through the deluge of his freezing shower, pouring from overhead and cranked to blasting from both sides.

Why he'd decided to shower at all, fully clothed and dazed beyond the point of recollection, he couldn't say, other than this ever-persistent desire to get clean.

Clean, like he'd been filthy, sullied, covered in his family's blood, which he couldn't seem to wash off. But nothing he did seemed to make it any better.

How long had he been in here?

How long had it been since frost began to lace his lashes? His black silk shirt and leather trousers clung like ice to his skin; every shallow breath that escaped his lips crystallized in the air, and in the back of his mind, he knew something was off, because despite all this, he couldn't actually say he was cold.

Concerning.

It should concern him, what this meant. Yet more ice crept in glistening fractals out from where he sat. It coated the entire inside of his shower in a very obvious and *very worrying* display of Winter's Gift, but he simply couldn't process it—not right now, not when thought was so painfully sluggish and all he wanted to do was sleep . . . sleep forever.

Up, up, up Celadon's gaze traveled—stiff as though it was frozen, too. But it needn't climb so far, it seemed; his intruder, the one who'd thrown open the shower's glass door so forcefully that hairline cracks spidered out across the pane, bent to crouching. Head cocked and elbows resting on his knees, he peered at Celadon, who presented quite the miserable picture, he had to imagine, with his knees tucked tight to his chest, face buried against them like a frightened child in hiding.

Slowly, stiffly, Celadon wiped water and frost from his eyes.

He had no idea what to make of the flurry of emotion that flashed in the toxic green gaze that watched him before they settled back behind a much more recognizable apathy.

"I'm sorry," Celadon heard himself say in a trembling, husky voice. He cleared his throat—it didn't help. "I'm a little b-busy right now. I-If you're here to c-collect on the whole bended-knee business we discussed outside the throne room, you'll have to—"

Lethe clicked his tongue at him, a pointed command to *silence*.

Expression souring, he reached over with both hands and slipped them under Celadon's arms. "Up," he ordered, speaking for the first time since appearing in Celadon's bathroom—but was surprisingly gentle in hauling Celadon to his feet.

In allowing Celadon to lean his weight against him as his legs relearned coltish movement, and his bones thawed, and his higher functioning surfaced from the black depths of hypothermia.

In helping Celadon back into his bedroom and depositing him by his fireplace, which Celadon hadn't been the one to light, but was grateful to whoever had.

"Dress," Lethe next command.

There was fury behind that tight tone that Celadon didn't really understand. Fury, bewilderment, hesitation . . . a lot like how Lethe had looked at him back during Riadne's Crowning, when he'd seen Celadon completely divested of Azurean's shield for the very first time.

His hands came up quick to catch what Lethe tossed to him—thick, black-and-emerald flannel pajamas monogrammed CFV. It was just as difficult as it had been in the bathroom to comprehend what was happening. He'd known Lethe his whole life—could count on one hand the number of actual conversations they'd had in the past almost-twenty-one years, equal to the number of times Lethe had ever even acknowledged his existence. It was . . . strange, to be so suddenly the focus of his attention, thrice in the span of a month. . . .

Thank you for saving me—

Unbidden the memory came to him, of him and Lethe in that alley outside the Grim Brotherhood's battle colosseum, where Celadon had unwisely contended in a cage match that would have claimed his life if it hadn't been for this peculiar Hunter's intervention.

The memory of Lethe pressed against him, as furious as he was now, concern in his expression, and the way he'd ordered Celadon to never again do something so foolish . . .

The corner of Celadon's mouth twitched.

He lifted his gaze, opened his mouth to comment on the fact that this was the third time now that Lethe had behaved like a boy with a crush he had no idea how to handle, and did he have a confession he'd like to make? But his breath caught in his throat.

Lethe became a blur across his vision.

He stormed from Celadon's dresser to pause before him; growled something low in his throat that seemed to be distaste with whatever he saw. Those green eyes raked him from head to toe and back again, and Celadon—who was never very shy about his body or his looks—felt a little like curling in on himself under this gaze that seemed to *see* him, through every mask he'd ever worn.

Another snarl of disapproval, and Lethe tore away from him, blustering over to the door that led to Celadon's outer chambers, where apparently several attendants stood in wait for his direction.

Every single one of them looked terrified—one had even dissolved into quiet tears when Lethe ripped open the door to fill its space like imposing doom itself made flesh.

"You would allow your king to *starve*?"

Lethe had never sounded more dangerous, his outrage wearing his voice to a breathlessness that made his words near impossible to hear.

It was . . . well, Celadon wanted a little to laugh, because this entire situation was absurd. They'd never been friends, not that Celadon hadn't found him interesting enough for that. Lethe was one of the rare few people he'd never been able to figure out, the Hunter's cunning and motivations leagues above what the sidhe fae aristocracy played at, and Celadon always felt something of a strange pull to him whenever he was around.

But they weren't friends, and they certainly weren't lovers, either.

Celadon was able to appreciate Lethe's appearance, of course. On the spectrum of asexuality, he didn't exactly feel inclined toward desire, not without a solid foundation of significant familiarity between him and his prospective partner. Even then, he'd come to understand it wasn't the same sort of all-consuming need that drove other people. But Lethe was beautiful. A pleasing assembly of otherworldly abstracts that fascinated Celadon. He enjoyed looking at him, always had, and on the very, extremely, *incredibly* few occasions they'd held meaningful conversation, he'd enjoyed that too—it was far from what made a couple, though.

Lethe slammed the door, startling Celadon out of his inner musings. And when he turned back to him, poison eyes bright and expression etched in deep irritation, for a moment the image struck him . . .

Of *Lethe*, not the far-removed immortal, but a young man not *all* that older than he was in appearance . . . absolutely and wholly alone in a world that seemed to hate and fear him just as much as it currently did Celadon.

Why, when he looked at him, did he get the sense of something off? Like there was something about Lethe that shouldn't be . . . something physical: the hair, for some reason. *It shouldn't be black.*

"Why are you here?" he heard himself ask, instead of the numerous other things that warred for escape. "I suppose Riadne sent you?"

"You mean your mother," Lethe drawled, perhaps a touch meanly, but meanness that seemed like a shield more than a weapon.

"Sure. Answer the question."

Stretching his arms up and behind his head, Lethe dissolved entirely out of anger, into insouciance that was much more his usual speed of pretend. "Mmm, but you do have the *tone* of kingship down, don't you . . ." He grinned—a slow corruption that spread across his face, bearing sharp teeth in the perfect portrait of monstrosity.

Celadon sighed.

Soaking wet, exhausted, cold beginning to settle in to make him shiver violently as Winter's protection receded and left him vulnerable to his own poor decisions—he turned.

Set the clothing Lethe had given him neatly on the armchair beside him.

"My own Court thinks I helped Riadne in exchange for my father's throne," he began in a voice barely above a whisper. "They hate me—they *fear* me, because our new High Queen is, yes, my mother, which makes me the product of a profoundly forbidden union. They wonder what else I've hidden all these years, how powerful I truly am—and how unstable. How long it will take me to dissolve under it all. No one trusts me; no one wishes to cede me control. My advisors and councillors squabble with one another right in front of me over which of my father's duties should be theirs to inherit and they're doing me a favor. Under their careful *guidance*, they tell me, I'll learn all I need to know about kingship, and once I'm more confident, they'll happily transfer that power back to me."

He snorted, tracing the silver thread of his initials on his pajamas.

He'd *never* been a part of this family, not truly. His whole life he'd revolved around his parents and siblings, his staff, the aristocracy, all like an outsider looking in through a pane of glass at a world he'd never belong to.

Like the moon, hanging up in the sky, too far removed from the world to ever actually be a part of it.

And no one had ever liked Celadon either. The too intelligent, too opinionated, too bold, too uncontrollable boy who preferred to keep the company of his ironborn cousin to *proper* sidhe fae; the boy who burned just a little too bright for UnSeelie blood and looked eerily twin to his father's youth.

They hadn't liked him then—they *despised* him now. And Celadon was more alone than ever without Azurean's protection, without Arlo's steadfast company; without Elyas, and Elexa, and everything as it had been before, which had felt so stifling to him back then until he'd learned the alternative was this.

How could he bring himself to face the people left to him? The ones he'd already failed so badly in letting Riadne get away with what she'd done.

What did he do with all this anger inside him?

"My own council plots to overthrow me," he continued after the pause. "It's only a matter of time. And I can't even blame them because I have no Cosmin-damned idea what I'm doing. . . ." He dropped his head back, releasing another heavy sigh. "You're here to collect me, aren't you?" he murmured, eyes fixed on the ceiling, on the spidering gold that streaked through the milk-gray marble—it had to be that.

It was finally time.

His advisors must have decided at last on how they would relieve themselves of him, and as a Hunter, Lethe was here to collect his soul, ferry it up to Cosmin for judgment.

At least he wouldn't have to find out how long it would take for his magic to turn on him.

A presence enveloped him.

Celadon couldn't sense auras the way Arlo could, but he could feel Lethe's magic, a sudden, oily weight against his own, cool as death but not *all* that unpleasant, but deities . . . that power . . .

At some point, Lethe had come up behind him, and instinct made Celadon want to turn to face him—but the hand at the back of his neck froze him quicker than the ice in his shower.

A barely there touch.

Fingers tracing down a thread, following what Celadon honestly couldn't guess in the moment, so surprised by what was probably the first time Lethe's skin had ever made contact with his.

Not until—"What's this?"

It took a moment for his brain to comprehend the words, for his thoughts to thaw and connect what Lethe had said to meaning. "A tattoo. Nothing special."

He made quick work of the buttons on his shirt, to part it open and drop the back enough for Lethe to see the upper portion. If he was going to die tonight, what did it matter opening up like this? To Lethe, who surely wouldn't care.

Elegant flourishes flowed down his neck, following his spine, to wrap like whisps of inky smoke—the air he commanded—around the swell of a pearly white moon, all cradled beneath by looping, cursive letters that spelled out:

"Patron of Lonely Things."

Something in Lethe's voice—the way he read out what Celadon had inscribed on himself—sounded odd.

Tight, too light, and too incredulous at once to be nothing, and they creaked worse than ever when he next added, "Why these words?"

Celadon turned to face him.

Taller than average, he didn't have to crane his neck to meet the gaze of many folk as he had to now with Lethe, but that didn't unsettle him—what caught him off guard was the mixture of wonder and fear that Lethe hadn't managed to hide away quick enough to miss.

Shrugging, Celadon replied, "I don't know. They just felt right. Isn't that what the moon is? Guardian of lonely souls." He explained in a near whisper, feeling absolutely ridiculous and not really understanding why he divulged any of this to Lethe of all people, but then . . . Lethe was probably the first person besides Arlo to ask about it.

It had been his eighteenth-birthday present to himself—something he hadn't even consulted Arlo about before doing on a whim he could remember as keenly as though the feeling driving it were still fresh. No one else who'd noticed the ink on the back of his neck had cared enough to inquire anything—just the moon; of course a Prince of Night would have this.

"The moon," Celadon continued, because Lethe just stood there, staring. So white he looked like a corpse and mouth slightly parted, staring and staring at Celadon, and something in the emotion behind it made Celadon feel like breaking even worse than he already did. "It's . . . a constant. It never leaves the sky—day and night it's always there—and . . . I don't know. It's silly now, but I was younger and Arlo wasn't around, and the moon was sort of like . . . not a friend, really, but just . . . familiar."

He shook his head to dispel the memory of that loneliness, which had never actually gone away—in fact, he was more alone than ever now. . . . "The Sun and Moon and Constellations: we still remember some things from the time the gods lived here alongside us, that these symbols we worshipped were more like positions filled by souls with feelings and thoughts and personalities of their own."

Celadon turned from Lethe and walked a step away, putting some distance between them; allowing him a moment as well to recover from . . . whatever past memory it was that Celadon's tattoo had clearly reminded him of.

"I don't know what you care about knowing of sidhe fae culture, but . . . a lot of us still believe that it's the best of the Seelie fae who get to be reborn as the sun, and the best of the UnSeelie fae who get to be reborn as the moon. To live out a cycle as our most beloved deity and be forever blessed afterward." He paused on a memory, choked out a laugh. "Father always said I was the moon reborn. That I'd already answered our highest of callings and was therefore to be rewarded in every life after with beauty and power and a destiny of greatness. I didn't ever actually believe him. I don't think he really believed it himself. He was just trying to cover up why I had all these *special talents*."

Celadon paused again to sigh.

"I'm not the moon reborn. After all, I don't exactly consider this life to be particularly blessed, do you? But still . . . I always liked it. The thought. The *moon*. And it was always there when Arlo was gone at the end of the day. When I was left alone with a mother and siblings that didn't want me. When everything became a little much and . . . well, it was either I latch dramatically onto a symbol by way of a giant tattoo or walk myself off the CN Tower."

For a moment, silence pervaded the room. Celadon felt a sudden flash of embarrassment for all he'd just revealed and opened his mouth again to say something else, anything else, that would erase the way his vulnerability hung in the air. But then—

"People bore me, Celadon."

Celadon . . . blinked.

He turned back around to stare up at Lethe's face, recovered almost entirely from what he'd been feeling just moments prior.

High Prince, Your Highness, Lethe called him a number of things, but not once could Celadon ever recall that creaking, pit-deep voice of his wrapped around his name.

"How curious it was that you had been so unthreatened by my presence, this little boyish *thing* creeping around in my shadow. Peeking after me around corners. Braving the frightening enormity of my brethren to ask after my past. Do you remember the first time you spoke to me?"

Celadon frowned, because yes, he did—and it wasn't until just now that he remembered what he'd said.

Eight-year-old Celadon, whom his father treated like breakable glass; whom everyone gushed and fawned over when the king was around, but out of earshot had even then considered him too much of all the wrong things. Eight-year-old Celadon, who'd already learned enough of his hideous, cutthroat world to feel like he might drown in all the predictability . . .

"People bore me, Lethe. . . ." There, again, was that monstrous grin spreading too wide across that starlight-freckled face. "I don't care much for children; you were no exception. But I couldn't deny you were intelligent, even then. Significantly more after telling me this, and then threatening me not to bore you too."

A wavering.

The briefest of flickers, of something like devastation sitting just behind his mask—Lethe wasn't as recovered as he currently pretended. Why though? Why had his tattoo shaken him this badly?

"You seem to like me enough now," Celadon hedged, because why not—better that they were on the same page in case Lethe was hoping for something between them that Celadon couldn't deliver.

"Do you want me to like you?" Lethe reached up his hand again.

Celadon tracked it in his periphery, the glint of firelight in those lethal adamantine claws. Careful, very aware they could shred through Celadon's skin to bone at a prick, Lethe rested a tip against his jaw. "Romance is not my particular forte, and I can't say I've ever felt moved to it. But you do have my attention. Quite a . . . bit of it now, as much as you will wish you didn't. They always do."

"And yet . . . here you are."

"Here I am." Lethe dropped his hand to Celadon's shoulder. In a careful but firm grip, he angled Celadon back around, this time facing the fire.

It took a moment for Celadon to realize those poison-green eyes watched him intently through the reflection in the golden-framed mirror above the fireplace mantel. "And here you are. I would call this your crossroads, wouldn't you? The world seems to want to paint you as their villain—how easily you could give them just that, and they would rue what they've asked for. You, son to Riadne Lysterne; by blood you could be . . . so *deliciously* ruthless, oh yes. But you could also be more. Anything else. *Every*thing else. You do have to choose though, and Celadon?"

Celadon hummed in the back of his throat, unable to break his gaze from the reflection of Lethe's.

Lethe's head lowered to press his lips to the back of Celadon's neck—not quite a kiss or a bite—and spoke like a prayer against the dip of ink there. "I don't know if I believe your father's words either. I similarly consider my life to lack that kind of blessing. And even if you were . . . the likelihood that you were also the one that . . . Moon or not, Celadon Viridian-Lysterne, whatever you choose to become, don't you dare turn out to be boring."

Wicked steel bit wicked steel, and the sonorous clang of the two blades' meeting cut sharply above the crowd's excitement to even more thunderous delight.

"Little brother—Lethe, please, it *can't* be true, this isn't you! They say you enjoy this—I refuse to believe that."

Lethe. Lethe, please, tell me what you need me to do.

Lethe leaned into the space between him and today's opponent.

It had taken . . . time.

To reinvent himself.

He'd fought against the change at first, a stubbornness King Atlas had seemed to relish for the license it gave his creativity. From that long-ago day when he'd first been dragged into his "father's" special chamber, and every one preceding, Lethe had learned just how cruel human men could be.

What do you need—I don't know how to protect you against this!

Beaten and whipped, chased and tormented, tortured and conditioned—King Atlas had been relentless in his efforts to mold Lethe into the perfect soldier and son. Bones broke faster than they could heal; weeks passed in confinement so cramped he could barely move; starved on a whim; pushed far beyond exhaustion; and worst of all—was it worst of all? It was certainly anathema to him that nights and weeks would pass where he'd been shut away, locked away, kept from the one thing that still mattered.

Lethe . . .

They'd made quick work of shredding his innocence, too—King

Atlas and his men; to desensitizing him to emotion and violence. They bathed him in blood; serenaded him with the cries of mothers whose babes had been ripped from their arms, forced him to mutilate their corpses in front of them; tasked him to cut down the fiercest of warriors and helpless boys alike, to break him, break him, *break him* into Zeuxis—the perfect Atlantean Prince of Carnage.

Zeuxis, who had no need for the Moon.

But he wasn't Zeuxis, he was Lethe, and he clung to the Moon now with desperation, the only thing that mattered that he'd permitted himself to keep.

"GUT HER!" someone up in the crowd screamed down at him, to another peal of cheers.

Their favorite game was this—these arena matches, in which they pitted him against whatever hideous, fearsome creature they could find, all so they could revel in his hacking them apart.

It wasn't until recently that his opponents became his once-upon-a-time sisters.

To break him, break him, *break him* into forgetting he'd ever been one of them. To test him, test him, *test him* in his resolve, his readiness for the world—a world that King Atlas craved to make his own, and Lethe . . . had made a choice.

He leaned into the space between them—him and Princess Esthe.

Lethe, you only need to accept, and it's yours. I'm older now, my power's more stable, and I have enough to spare—reach through our connection and take it! Your sister or not, I refuse to lose you.

How long had it been since he'd seen Esthe last? Years and years and days and nights . . . Lethe couldn't say. Days far too hot and bright. Nights he had so little time to spend with a friend that had become something . . . more, a connection that had deepened to incomprehension.

The Moon was *his*. The one thing Lethe refused to let go of, the one thing that held on to him in return. The Moon was how he kept himself, kept *Lethe* alive where Zeuxis threatened to consume all else.

The Moon gave him power—offered up its own magical core for his use, permitted Lethe and Lethe alone, the honor! The weapon. His own Gift of the Pull might be naturally weak, but with the Moon's command to bolster his . . . He was not ready yet, though, and his Moon was still growing, too. He wouldn't overextend either of their capabilities and risk causing damage to his Moon, but oh, with a little more time, a little more *practice* . . .

He was older now, so much older, and so was Esthe.

And although Lethe's hair had moldered into black decay and his skin had bubbled and burned in flaking patches; although his limbs had grown only more and more warped for all the abuse he'd suffered, and starvation had made his flesh stretch like hide over bare, jutting bone . . . Esthe was . . . *ugly.*

Beautiful.

Painful.

Her hair was wound tight into a flawless braided bun atop her head; her skin gleamed like an oyster's pearl. She was curves and health and bright ocean eyes, love and sanity and proper rest. She was herself grown up, while Lethe was himself left to fester, King Atlas's deadliest weapon . . . but only for so long.

With just a little more practice, and one last obstacle to overcome.

He grinned down at Esthe.

His darling sister, sibling by blood, the girl who'd soothed every nightmare he'd had as a child, who'd taught him how to read, how to play, how to exist in a world that had been soft and safe and wholesome . . . warm . . .

"Please, my brother. *Lethe*—I'm so, so sorry." Tears welled up in Esthe's eyes as she peered through such fine lashes: one, two, three, twenty, he counted the dewy strands. "We tried, so hard. Mother's been inconsolable over our failure to save you from this place. I'm so sorry, but it's been too long. All I can do for you now is release you from your suffering, from the grip of siren's madness. Let me be the one to give you freedom, little brother. This isn't you. . . ."

Freedom.

"Esthe," he replied, in a voice he barely recognized anymore, like the infernal depths where immortals kept their Sins; like the creaking wood of a ship burning in the night that haunted his memory. "Sweet Esthe . . . *tsk, tsk, tsk.* I am exactly who I mean to be."

He was exactly who he *needed* to be.

They could break him, break him, *break him* all they wanted; they could take and take and take. But Lethe had made the choice—to let them think they'd succeeded, to let them think they'd won, to let them settle into false security, their Prince of Carnage under perfect control.

They wanted a legend?

He'd give them just that.

And when it was *their* blood he was licking clean from the blade they'd taught him to wield—too late, they'd realize their mistake. They'd realize that madness hadn't stolen him quite the way it was supposed to for a siren . . . and maybe all their anger, all the pain and suffering and cruelty they'd inflicted on him, had given him a ledge to hold on to . . . just enough grip on rational thought to keep what he needed most . . .

The Moon.

And his name.

"Lethe . . ."

Esthe's eyes grew wide.

She gasped in surprise as Lethe buried his sword point-first into her belly.

The stadium cheered.

Lethe didn't need to look up at his father to know he was pleased— that finally, here was the proof enough that Zeuxis was ready; trusted; *son.*

"It's not too late," Esthe gurgled around the sapphires that spilled from her lips. He watched them rain in droplets onto the dusty earth—precious and cheap all at once, like everything else. Life was worthless. "Mother hasn't given up on you. We *will* avenge you, Lethe. We will save you, one way or another."

"Unnecessary," Lethe snapped, and twisted his blade even deeper.

A crunch of bone—slippery warmth spread over Lethe's fingers, which he held up to the sunlight like a trophy. Then he heaved the sword back out, and Esthe crumpled at his feet. And all the while, his people cheered, ignorant to the fate awaiting them that would come by this very hand.

"Zeuxis! Zeuxis!"

Gulls cried in the distance.

Lethe . . . Lethe . . . the sea crooned in his ear.

Lethe, the Moon mourned, where Lethe himself couldn't.

He curled his bloodied fingers into a fist, drew on the bond between him and his Moon. And *squeezed.*

No eyes saw what happened—this particular arena existed at the city's heart, built under Atlas's request in the palace's own backyard; all attention was focused inward, not out. Lethe couldn't see it either. But he could still feel it. He could still taste it in the air as he pulled on a bond that strengthened his everything.

With the Moon's help, his Gift was getting . . . *better.*

The sea just beyond all those very big walls that the king thought kept him safe pulsed toward the land it encircled . . . shuddered through every moat that separated Atlantis's districts, one after the other.

A singular ripple, oh, but what a ripple could become with just a bit more time. A bit more practice . . .

CHAPTER 10

Arlo

ARLO SHOT UPRIGHT IN bed, her heartbeat like hummingbird wings in her chest.

She couldn't say what had woken her, only that something had. And while bleary inspection of her night-drenched room revealed no source of disturbance—nothing out of place—even after whole minutes had passed, she couldn't seem to shake the sense of . . . *distortion*, like the world had shifted the slightest degree, leaving everything tilted toward unreality.

Lifting a hand to her chest, she tried to massage away her anxiety. She closed her eyes to focus her breathing and center herself in the moment; to find her calm; to remind herself that she was okay. The past few weeks had made Arlo intimately familiar with random bouts of panic attacks. She'd lost count of the number of times she'd been dragged out of sleep by one, in the dead of the night, gasping for shallow breaths, shaking and clammy and cold.

This wasn't like that.

This was different.

Arlo . . .

Standing at her room's bay of windows, which she could have sworn she'd drawn curtains over before collapsing to sleep earlier that evening, Arlo peered up at the moon. In the back of her mind, she wondered idly how she'd come to be here when she couldn't recall having thrown off her duvet and slipping out of bed, but the moon . . . it hung full and bright in the starry, deeper-than-black sky, and curiously bigger than Arlo recalled ever seeing it before. Almost as though the earth had lurched a few feet closer to it while her eyes had been closed.

It enthralled her.

This was *different*.

Arlo . . .

Her attention wandered downward and landed in the gardens below to be immediately ensnared by a silvery white deer, still as a statue, staring back up from its place by the hedge that marked the palace boundaries—a doe, glowing just as pale and bright as the oversized moon above.

The doe was different too, beyond the obvious. It radiated such a potent, ancient power that even though they were so far separated, Arlo could still feel it where she stood. But there was something else about it . . . an inviting serenity that, despite the instinct growing louder in the back of her mind that nothing about any of this was right, made her want to reach out and touch it. . . .

Arlo . . . Arlo . . .

And so, she tried.

Her fingers met the glass between them, but just as they did, it vanished completely—not only the whole fleet of windows, but her bedroom, too. As suddenly as she'd found herself whisked out of bed, she was now in the palace gardens, and however she'd managed that—a dream, she was certain; she had to be dreaming—Arlo was . . . curiously unbothered.

Maybe it was because she knew this couldn't be happening anywhere but inside her head, that regardless of where this strange magic pulled her, she was actually still in bed—safe.

Maybe it was because, of everything that had happened over the past little while, this was hardly the most bizarre or dangerous situation.

Whatever the reason, Arlo didn't fight it.

She didn't waste much time on attempting to figure out what was going on. For one thing, if this *was* a dream, it would take her where she needed to be regardless of what she did. For another, it was strongly believed among UnSeelie folk that the moon's appearance in their sleep was divine intervention. Arlo didn't particularly need any more of that, but the moon had always been considered a good omen when present in a dream, a symbol of peace and success even to the sidhe fae who pretended they were above such old-world nonsense now—whatever it had to tell Arlo tonight, she could use a little good.

Hand still outstretched, she stepped toward the doe.

It was so much larger up close—enormous, just like the moon it resembled. On all fours, it towered over her, and Arlo had the feeling that if it wanted her to be intimidated, she'd feel exactly that. But the power it exuded was nothing but gentle, and so when her hand met the doe's warm pelt ever so briefly, and just as soon, it turned, there was nothing but that distant warning in the back of her mind to stop her from following.

As though answering some unspoken command, the hedge behind it parted—forming an arching gap in its barricade to allow the doe through, into the forest that waited just beyond.

The magic blockade keeping the palace confined—which earlier in the day Arlo's fury had propelled her through—was not sheer and unmovable but rather a firm deterrent one could choose to disobey at the cost of great exhaustion both magically and physically. Storming through that hedge had felt like running a marathon against hurricane winds, and she had retired to bed well before she normally did because of its toll.

Now, though, there was nothing.

The doe stalked forward, making for the forest's shallows, and the hedge's magic deferred.

Arlo . . .

What called to her—was it the doe?

The moon?

She had no idea. All she knew, inexplicably, was that if she didn't follow quickly, the hedge would seal against her; she'd be left behind, and whatever awaited where the doe wanted her to go, her hesitation now would cost her finding out.

Through the hedge Arlo trailed.

Deep into the forest.

Down the overgrown remains of a long-ago beaten path.

Time skipped at random intervals. There were moments Arlo closed her eyes to blink, and when they opened once more, her surroundings were completely altered. She'd take a step, and a new patch of forest rose to greet her. A sound would drag her attention off to her left, her right, behind . . . and as soon as it did, there was the doe, their course now redirected.

They walked what felt to Arlo like the entire night.

The moon never left its place in the sky. Her bare feet gave no protest to the twigs and earth and stone they were forced to carry her over. The doe walked for hours, with Arlo just behind, but nothing in her felt this. Then, finally, almost like no time at all had passed, the doe came to a strange sort of clearing.

"Where . . . ?" Arlo wondered aloud.

It stood a bit like a temple's hall—a throne's unfurled carpet. The path before them widened significantly with soil dark and freshly tilled, cleared of all debris. On either side stretched a parallel of perfectly groomed trees, all lined up neatly in matching rows like twin colonnades of towering, fragrant cypresses.

"Who are you taking me to meet?" she asked, turning her examination on the doe. But the doe made no reply. It merely pressed onward, down the waiting path, and once again all Arlo could do was choose—choose to follow; choose to remain behind. "It's only a dream . . . ," she reminded herself, pushing on.

It was harder to see now.

The treetops had whittled what she could see of the moon down to a misshapen crescent, so that the gloom around them pressed in even darker, and Arlo was forced to stick as close as possible to her otherworldly guide.

Down the path she trailed it, and much like traveling any corridor in any dream she'd had before, the end seemed ever elusive, constantly pushing deeper into the forest, out of reach. If it wasn't for the fact that this was a dream making impossible things possible, it would have been most likely thanks to her UnSeelie fae senses that Arlo could see as well as she currently could, enough that she could make out the shapes of what began to gather in the cypress colonnades.

At first it was only more deer.

Stags and does alike, young and old, watching on as the one guiding Arlo passed. The longer they walked, the more Arlo noticed; other animals joined the throng. Harmless critters like chipmunks and squirrels and buzzing woodsprites, but there were wolves, too. Coyotes. Bigger things that could make quick work of an eighteen-year-old girl and her doe guardian, however giant, and Arlo sent a fervent prayer to the moon's silvery sliver that whatever kept them calm and restrained to observation held strong.

More unnerving than the creatures, though, were the women.

Young women, their hair half in braids and half in wild disarray; dressed in white and furs and pale leather; armed with arrows, spears, and knives—*hunters*, their appearance screamed. At a glance the oldest of them couldn't be much more than Arlo's age, but it was their eyes that gave them away—a depth, a richness . . . Arlo recognized it instantly. Nausicaä wore immortality in the exact same way—youthfulness in appearance, in attitude, in action, in thought . . . but years upon years upon *years* of existence did something to the eyes.

"Arlo Jarsdel."

Arlo's head snapped forward once more.

She hadn't realized she'd been staring so intently to her left, at one of the white-clad young women whose keen assessment had begun to morph into a challenging grin. But when her gaze was dragged back to the front, Arlo gasped at what she saw.

The path was gone.

In its place now was a proper clearing, but not the one in which she'd found Vehan earlier.

A simple clearing, encircled by the same cypress trees that had carried her here. It was the girl at the center who stole Arlo's breath—a girl who needed no introduction even though they'd never met before.

Her clothing was simple, a knee-high tunic of the same white material as her hunters' attire. On her back she wore a quiver full of arrows and a glinting silver bow. Hair as black as the deepest night wound in elegant braids around a crescent-moon crown of silver.

Moonlight glowed in her olive-brown skin.

In appearance she was Arlo's junior by a handful of years, but there in those cosmic black eyes was eternity, and she was *devastating* to behold.

Mistress of Animals . . .

She of the Wild . . .

It was a bizarre sort of instinct, of magic, this instant recognition.

Once upon a time, humans and folk both remembered that *they*—technically—had been the ones to think up their many pantheons.

There had always been the First Ones, titans, and the scant few deity offspring. But it was mortal belief that gave birth to the world's religions—belief that had been so strong it delivered the rest of the gods that belonged to them, gave them purpose and power that increased the more worship fed it.

Eventually, the gods outgrew the confines of mortal wonder, were able to take on shape in the realm and impose themselves as their indomitable overlords, and not until the Eight Fae Founders did mortals learn how to wield belief like a weapon against them.

Time and complacency—most people had forgotten the origins of the gods. Humans fell out of belief in magic; folk spent so much effort trying to blend in with humans that they began to fall out of touch with their roots.

But the heart didn't forget things as easily as the mind.

Stricken, Arlo watched as the pale doe that had led her here trotted over to the goddess—a goddess Arlo knew immediately by a clench of feeling alone in her chest—and began grazing at her feet.

"Lady Artemis," Arlo breathed in wonder and, with no idea how she was actually supposed to show respect here (it wasn't like they'd covered this even in Riadne's comprehensive lessons), dropped into a bow. "I'm sorry, I . . . don't know how to greet you."

Fingers suddenly beneath her chin tilted Arlo's face back upward. Artemis had made no sound when she moved. Much like the passage of time in this dream that Arlo couldn't say for certain anymore was *just* a dream, she was simply there, prompting Arlo upright.

The many deities will seek to make you a scion of their name, Luck had warned her back in the infirmary when they'd finally told her the last of what she needed to know about becoming a Hollow Star.

"There is war on this realm's horizon, Arlo."

There was. Riadne—

"—is inevitable," said Artemis, pulling this thought straight from Arlo's mind. "It is not her war of which I speak." Artemis's hand fell to her side, and she took a step backward, her leather-bound feet soundless as flight, the perfect huntress. "I refer to what comes after. Who fells the mortal Queen of Sin? By Law, if Riadne dies by common hand, the Bone Crown defaults to her crowned heir—Vehan, then, inherits fate. Perhaps, though, it will be her other son who fells her— but would the moon relinquish the power that had so enthralled the sun that birthed him?"

Arlo wanted to argue. Celadon was nothing like Riadne, would never be tempted by the same thing that had corrupted her. But Artemis spared no pause for rebuttal.

"And perhaps it will be the ironborn princess, a legacy reborn . . . what would *she* do, I wonder, if she could choose to keep the Crown of Death for her own. Who would she return it to, if not?"

Ironborn princess? A legacy reborn?

Arlo had no idea who Artemis referred to and again wasn't given a chance to inquire.

Artemis smiled. It wasn't unkind, but the action excited the hummingbird wings in Arlo's heart once more. "There is so much possibility in this realm—it is both your kind's blessing and its curse. I will tell you quite plainly: I'd like to appeal for your favor, Arlo. I request that however this odyssey should end, you see that the Bone Crown is bestowed unto *me*, back into Olympian control. Our pantheon will be made powerful once more. Deliver to me the Bone Crown, Arlo, and you won't go unrewarded."

The many deities will seek to make you a scion of their name, Luck had warned, but it wasn't until now that Arlo actually understood what they meant.

They didn't just want Arlo to side with them; they wanted . . .

"What would happen if I gave it to you?" she asked without meaning to speak the words out loud.

She hadn't wanted to interrupt a goddess, especially one of Artemis's caliber, a no-nonsense girl in fairly every depiction of her, and ancient even by immortal standards. But Arlo couldn't help herself, and again Artemis smiled.

"How proud she must have been to call herself your mother."

Arlo's heart stopped dead in her chest, her breath strangled in her throat.

"So fierce, so intelligent, and as I've witnessed, an excellent tracker—my doe does not present herself to those without the hunt in their veins. Thalo Viridian-Verdell died with great pride for you in her heart."

There was a stinging in Arlo's eyes, which she blinked furiously against to keep back.

> *"You're not at all your mother's daughter, you*
> *know—how ashamed she'd be."*
> *"Arlo—survive."*

ExhaustionGuiltAgonyAnger—

"It was not my ranks your mother's afterlife joined. The Wild Hunt acknowledges very few women, fools that they are, yet not so foolish to spurn *her*—but she denied them, too. Bestow upon me the Bone

Crown, Arlo—deliver to me the lost and last of the Three Crowns of Power; anoint me as successor to Lord Cosmin's mighty throne, lay command of death at my feet; restore favor to the Olympians and make dominant our worship once more—and in return, I will offer you my ranks as well, welcome you in *your* afterlife. Exalted huntress, a warrior just as she has become, but in your very own way."

A huntress . . . a warrior, just like her mother.

This dream was becoming a little too much.

These things Arlo would give anything to hear her mother say to her herself . . . Arlo had no idea what to make of this, the words both said and unsaid, the promises and . . . almost threats behind Artemis's entreaty.

But it was clear to her there would be no leaving this clearing without an answer.

Artemis stood opposite her, haloed in moonlight, those cosmic eyes fathomless, not the fifteen or sixteen she appeared no older than but ageless.

"Can I think on it?" Her voice had grown hoarse for the emotion it choked on, and she had to swallow twice around what it balled in her throat. It wasn't a no, and it wasn't a yes—she knew enough about the Olympian gods not to make any rash judgments either way, not without consulting Nausicaä, at least.

Nausicaä would steer her true. If she'd listened to Nausicaä before, none of them would be in this situation. Arlo wouldn't be tied to Riadne; her mother wouldn't have died. . . .

And it was the right thing to say, it seemed—or rather, not the wrong thing.

Artemis nodded graciously. "You may. There is still time. Time in which the other deities and pantheons will present petitions of their own, and so I will let you go . . . but not without a gift to remember me by."

She brushed a hand through the air, and from nothing at all, in Arlo's appeared a singular arrow.

Beautiful fletching of black-and-white speckled quail feathers . . . arrowhead and shaft made of pure, otherworldly gold . . .

"Without fail, that arrow will find its mark, deliver swift death to any mortal target . . . and destruction to any immortal. I gift you my might, Arlo Jarsdel; may it aid you well in what's to come."

Arlo shot upright in bed.

Her heart beat like hummingbird wings in her chest again. She could hear it like thunder in her ears. And for a moment, she couldn't say what had woken her, only that something had.

A dream, she told herself.

It was all just a dream.

Except there in her hands . . . was Artemis's arrow.

"So. It begins."

Alarm drew breath sharply through her nose. Arlo lifted her gaze once more to find she wasn't alone, but it wasn't Artemis across from her, or the doe . . . nothing of the dream, which was slipping away from memory as quickly as sand through an hourglass.

It was the last person she expected to see, and at the same time . . . her surprise was more in the fact that it had taken them this long to reappear.

"Luck," she greeted stiffly.

A tone that darkened as steadily as her mood, because *Luck* . . . This wasn't fair, none of it was fair, and it was equally unfair of Arlo to blame this titan for what had befallen her. But Arlo was mortal; she was part human. It was natural to want something to blame for her mother's death, for everything turning as sour as it had, and who better to pin responsibility on than the one who'd dragged her into this entire mess to begin with? It had been Luck who'd armed her with that cursed die she hadn't been able to even look at since the Solstice . . . kept firmly shut away in her bedside drawer. . . . "I haven't seen you in over a month."

Accusation.

Hurt.

Anger and apathy both.

How was it possible for a heart to feel so much at once? Such a small organ in comparison to what she felt—how did it keep up with all the things that raged and wept and beat inside her?

Luck was a familiar face.

She was strangely overwhelmed by the sudden, fierce desire to throw herself at them and bury her face in their shimmery robes. Luck had always been good to her, kind to her, protective even . . . and still. And *still* . . .

Silence met her comment, wore on for long enough that Arlo was on the verge of throwing herself back down in her bed and ordering them away, to pretend she was going to get back to sleep any time soon.

"I'm sorry," they finally replied, cutting her off, and sounded so miserable that a little of the anger inside her relented. "I didn't keep away out of dispassion. You grieve, and I wanted to allow you the space to do so, in the little you've been left of privacy. But I have not abandoned you, and as much as I know you may not wish to see me—"

"Not yet," Arlo admitted to her bedsheets, softer than a whisper.

Not yet. She wasn't ready.

"Which is perfectly okay, Arlo. I don't blame you."

And that was exactly the thing.

No one blamed her, not properly.

Nausicaä didn't blame her. Vehan didn't blame her. Her dad didn't blame her. . . . Celadon clearly did, as there was no other reason to explain why she hadn't seen him since the Solstice, but he wouldn't even give her the benefit of telling her this to her face. Which meant the only person to punish Arlo for what she'd done was Arlo herself.

No one would give her their anger.

In turn, no one was actually giving her their true forgiveness, either.

They were all of them in this mess because of what she did, and what she failed to do, and everyone insisted on walking around her on tiptoes like she was breakable glass, cooing, "It's okay, Arlo," and "I don't blame you."

Tossing her arrow on her bedside stand, Arlo whipped her bedding away from her. She slid from her bed, stuffed her feet into slippers waiting just below. "Listen, it's the middle of the night. Yesterday was a long day. Today is bound to be long as well. Please." She cut her gaze to the titan still standing at the end of her bed, all shamrock-green hair and consuming black eyes, too beautiful and perfect and looking at Arlo with regret like a parent who'd wronged the child they loved deeply.

And Arlo just . . . couldn't.

She didn't have it in her for this.

Not right now. Not when she was so angry, and everyone wanted her to blame them—to acknowledge whatever way they felt *they'd* screwed up, and thus give them a chance for penance as a result—but no one would grant her the same relief. "Please, just go away. I don't want to talk to you right now. I don't want *any* of this."

"Lady Arlo—"

Again Arlo startled.

And there it was.

What had woken her, she realized, hadn't been Luck, or the dream's intensity, or the pounding of her heart in her ears.

It had been *knocking*. Quicker than thought, she grabbed her arrow and stashed it in the first place she could think to keep it hidden, under her pillow.

Luck had vanished into a plume of green that rained onto her carpet like crafting glitter, but there was no time to worry about the mess it left behind. They were gone, and Arlo took quick stock of her appearance. There had to be some evidence of her barefoot journey through the forest tonight, but other than what she'd just tucked away . . . nothing.

Relieved, and not really understanding why just yet, only that she wanted to . . . keep as much of what maybe or maybe not had happened from Riadne for as long as possible, Arlo crossed to her bedroom door and pulled it open at last.

The grim and tightly anxious expressions of her attendants—Zelda and Madelief—greeted her, and Arlo knew right away it was nothing good that had them barging into her room in the middle of the night.

"Yes?" she replied through heavy hesitation.

Zelda, in her fluffy pink housecoat and her unbound, bubblegum hair, looked like she might crumble under whatever it was she'd been sent here for.

"Lady Arlo." Even Madelief's voice wavered as they translated what Zelda signed. "We've been sent to fetch you. The High Queen requests your presence at once."

CHAPTER 11

Nausicaä

I T WAS SORT OF unfair that Riadne Lysterne, radiant fae queen of Light and Day, could still look so flawlessly composed in the deep, dead hours of night.

In her white sheer robes and tight leather trousers that looked to be molten gold poured around her shapely legs, her black-ice hair free and unbound to fall to her waist, and her snowy complexion stark against eyes so electric-bright blue they froze, the new High Queen looked more like a painting than a person, and there was no doubt in Nausicaä's mind she could keep them kneeling before her like this for hours yet to come.

Nausicaä, meanwhile, didn't look half as put-together.

Demon blood crusted black under her nails, smeared her face and arms, stained her clothing.

Her hair was a tangled mass around snagged bits of the Hiraeth.

Tired, smarting—it had actually surprised her that Aurelian had managed such a powerful blow, but *good*; she'd been hoping he'd be able to put on a proper show, so that the Hunt wouldn't be forced to report that Nausicaä wasn't to be trusted, and Riadne wouldn't kick her out of her shitty reenactment of the Hunger Games or resort to sending someone who was much less concerned about the safety of two people Arlo cared for immensely.

Still.

It had *hurt*.

She'd been worried for a moment back there that she hadn't been pulling her punches enough. But finally Nausicaä was given a glimpse at just how powerful Aurelian actually was under all the composure he pretended at.

A glimpse at all the *anger* he carried around inside.

She should probably warn him.

She knew better than anyone that anger that had no outlet was just as bad as a magical rebound. A talk for later, though . . . if any of them survived all this. For now Aurelian had won his freedom, had escaped with Elyas back to safety, and no one could say Nausicaä hadn't put effort into what she'd been tasked to do—but . . . it did mean turning up empty-handed before a *mildly disagreeable* queen, who hadn't said a word to them since their arrival two hours ago.

"High Queen, there were demon spawn—"

Zzzt—

Vesper broke off with a hiss.

She hadn't hurt xim, not with any significance at least. If xe'd been anything less than an immortal Hunter, Nausicaä suspected xe'd be a pile of char on her pretty glass floor right now, but the electric bolt she'd shot xim with hadn't done anything more than sting . . .

. . . Considerably.

And Nausicaä didn't need to turn her head to see the reaction; she *felt* the way Yue stiffened, the way Eris's jaw tightened. Her own hands balled on her thighs. The four of them, Nausicaä in the lead and the Hunters just behind her, had been commanded to kneel on both knees as the first and last thing Riadne had spoken when they'd turned up after their "botched" capture-the-flag mission, and she'd keep them there until she was ready to speak again.

It wasn't often Nausicaä wished this, but she wondered whether Riadne would be so brave if Lethe were here, not galivanting off wherever he kept to when he wasn't making dramatic entrances.

Did she know?

Did she know that *Lethe* had handpicked each of the three behind her?

That he might be a heartless, mercurial bastard in dire need of a good punch to his face, but if there was one decent thing she'd ever say about him, it was the fact that he . . . well, he didn't necessarily *protect* his Hunt, but she'd seen him exact pretty nasty retaliation on an asshole or two in her time when it came to the matter of his possessions' mistreatment.

"There were demon spawn in those woods," Vesper resumed in gritted perseverance, undaunted. "As Lord Cosmin's Hunters, first and foremost—"

Zzzt—

Another groan.

Vesper fell forward, palms meeting the floor with an audible clap. Behind her, Nausicaä heard Yue's fury escape in a hissing gasp.

She didn't dare turn her head to check on them. She kept her gaze on Riadne, insouciant in the way she lounged on her throne, but there it was . . . the beginnings of outrage in those bright blue eyes, tension creeping into her posture.

Good.

Vesper had never *once* let a bully intimidate xim.

Xe'd been one of the only people to stand up to the immortals xe'd overheard speak ill of what Tisiphone had suffered. Xe'd been one of the only people to ever sit with her when she cried, while everyone else treated those tears like a disease. One of the only to attempt to cheer her up when Nausicaä was out on duty, to tell her in words Nausicaä hadn't known how to speak back then that there was nothing wrong with her for feeling the way she had, despite what immortal society insisted.

There was very little Nausicaä wouldn't do for Vesper.

Riadne could choke on a d—

"—our prime directive is to hunt down that which doesn't belong here in the Mortal Realm. We *had* to let them go, Your Majesty."

Keep pushing xim, Nausicaä dared with her narrowing gaze.

Keep pushing xim so Riadne could stew in embarrassment when she finally learned that of everyone in this damned place beholden to her cruelty, it was Vesper she'd *never* change to suit her tastes.

Riadne caught Nausicaä's stare at last.

An expression flexed across her face, something Nausicaä couldn't read clearly, and it was there and gone too quickly to spend much time wondering what it had been. Long legs uncrossed themselves, then recrossed themselves in the opposite manner. Riadne shifted—along with her tactics. "And what of you, then, Dark Star? My Hunters' excuse for incompetence doesn't apply to you, and yet . . ." She leaned in closer, paused to look quite pointedly around the room, empty save the five of them. "I don't see what you were sent to fetch."

Nausicaä continued to stare.

The queen wanted their obedient silence? She could make that obnoxious, too.

"Well?"

Hands on her folded knees, fury burning in her chest, *fuck off, you old hag* barely restrained on the tip of her tongue, just waiting for the chance to pop off at her, Nausicaä smiled serenely.

And said absolutely nothing.

Riadne drew in a deep breath of air, annoyance an electric flicker in her eyes. But her exhale was just as delicate as the smile that spread across her face, and those long legs of hers unwound.

The High Queen stood.

"Very well. It doesn't matter."

As she did, the doors at the back of the throne room heaved open, and Nausicaä didn't have to turn—she couldn't scent magic worth a damn anymore, but she'd know the feel of this aura anywhere; it turned her head, regardless.

"No—" she started, leaping to her feet as well. "All right, okay, you've made your point. I could have tried harder with—" Riadne descended the dais steps, waving off Nausicaä's hurried explanation.

Down the steps, across the glass floor, Riadne stalked toward the group that had entered, the pair of guards flanking two palace attendants Nausicaä was well acquainted with—and there, sandwiched between them, gaunt and exhausted and just as apprehensive as Nausicaä now felt, was Arlo.

"Darling," Riadne greeted.

Her arms spread wide as she approached, as though Arlo were her beloved daughter returning home victorious from some long-waged war. When the two of them reached one another, she wrapped Arlo up in a tight embrace and pressed a motherly kiss to the top of Arlo's head.

Nausicaä stiffened.

Not at the situation, which was . . . *kind of* wack and very tense, to say the least.

Not at the fact that the queen's good mood meant she definitely had some awful update to drop on them any moment now.

Nausicaä stiffened because she saw in the gap over Riadne's shoulder the way *rage* snapped its jaws over Arlo's expression—quick, and buried down deep in a flash . . . but rage, the sort that made stars pale and shrink into the night, the sort Nausicaä knew far too well, a fire she didn't want anywhere near her girl. . . .

Because rage like that met only one end.

But Arlo couldn't.

She *wouldn't*.

There was no losing Arlo, not at all, and certainly not like how Nausicaä had lost Tisiphone. Not like how she'd nearly lost herself, either.

"I have a surprise for you."

Riadne leaned back to observe Arlo, shoulders still clutched in her hands. Nausicaä couldn't see the expression on the High Queen's face, but Arlo's had smoothed back into bland wariness, nothing like what had stormed there just moments ago.

And the worst of it, the part that made Nausicaä's heart clench, was that Arlo clearly wasn't holding back through guile. Without a doubt, there was no clever plan, no scheme. Arlo wasn't feigning the mildness she currently wore. *Without a doubt*, she just had . . . no idea.

Arlo wasn't a violent person.

Nausicaä would bet her mangled wings that Arlo was completely oblivious to the fact that there was anything beneath her gentle surface, beneath the blame she was heaping on herself and the grief she was forced to weather. Arlo had no idea that the sort of anger lurking there was like a starving beast, poised and waiting for just one more crack to fissure through the walls that restrained it. . . .

She hadn't known Arlo all that long.

She didn't need to either—Arlo pushed and pushed and *pushed* down her feelings, made them insignificant to all others'. She kept herself quiet and unassuming because her whole life that's what her shitty relatives had wanted from her, but pushing down feelings didn't make them go away. And much like she worried for Aurelian, if Arlo didn't find some way soon to release some of that building pressure . . . She hadn't even had a proper cry yet about the things that had happened to her. It was like Arlo was still in shock about it all.

Make it right . . .

Nausicaä knew this fear.

She'd felt it once before.

The fear that if she didn't do *something*, she was going to lose the girl she loved. . . .

Snap—

The click of Riadne's fingers reverberated around the room, cutting sharply through Nausicaä's spiral and dragging her out of her head.

If she'd been mortal, that sound would have been the only warning she'd receive for the magic trick Riadne could wield: that Magnetic mesmer of hers that was already just a little *too* good—Nausicaä herself could only just shake herself out of its hold—and if she had the power of all Seven Sins behind her . . .

The deities should be more afraid of who they'd decided to back.

"Follow me," the High Queen commanded and, threading her arm around Arlo's, headed for the open doors.

In silence they made their way down the halls, Riadne and Arlo a few paces in the lead, Nausicaä and the Hunt a stalking shadow just behind.

Something was up.

Riadne had let them off too easy back in the throne room for their failure to drop Elyas and Aurelian at her feet. Too easy for what Nausicaä understood of a newly emerged, cutthroat power that would need to take every opportunity she could to impress her seriousness on a world that would otherwise ignore her.

And she was too damned cheerful.

Riadne carved her way through the halls in such high spirits that she didn't need the lights enchanted to spring to life in her presence—her radiance lit their way just fine.

Nausicaä had spent a good deal of her limited free time combing this place, learning as many of its secrets as she could. But there was one place she hadn't been, one place that made even her skin crawl just to pass by, because she might not be a deities-damned Fury anymore, and her powers might be dwindled by her time in the Mortal Realm, but she remembered the feeling of dark magic—the *darkest* magic—and none of it compared to what she felt oozing through the walls of Riadne Lysterne's private office.

"After you, my dear," Riadne cooed, heaving open her office door and signaling Arlo through with the graceful sweep of a hand.

Arlo went.

Nausicaä followed.

The Hunt filed in close behind.

No light sprang to life when Riadne joined them, sealing the door back shut as she did. Her private office was wholly unassuming to the mortal eye, a mild pallet of white and rain-cloud grays, the occasional splash of watery blue. Sofas and bookcases and large windows draped in fluttery sheer.

Comfortable . . . for anyone who couldn't feel that deities-awful wriggling, the sort of deathly wrongness Nausicaä had always felt in Lethe's magic, but different, somehow. Lethe's had always been eerie, but never sinister, never *evil.* . . .

Vesper shivered.

Yue pressed a little closer to xis side.

A muscle in Eris's jaw leaped for how hard he clenched it, against instinct that screamed in them all—to run. To get away.

Only Arlo stood unfazed by what Nausicaä was certain she could feel as well, given the strength of her own magical awareness . . . but then again, Arlo was a . . . *hells.*

If she really was a Flamel, of course she wouldn't be bothered by what she felt.

The Mortal Realm didn't remember it properly; enchantment had muddled their own history. They'd forgotten that the Flamels weren't only legend, heroes who'd saved them from alchemy's misuse. They'd forgotten how steeped in the dark side of alchemy they'd been, the freaking *Sith lords* of their damned community, and whatever Riadne kept behind that wall . . . the Flamels had been the first to ever successfully command it.

Arlo wouldn't be afraid.

That magic . . . if anything, it would be more afraid of *her.*

She had no idea, and until whoever had made this information unspeakable broke whatever magic they'd cast in order to do so, Nausicaä couldn't say a word to warn her. To explain and make things just a little less overwhelming . . . though perhaps even more overwhelming, simultaneously.

Riadne crossed the room to her desk, to the columbarium behind it, those rows of little square drawers built into the wall, where everyone knew she kept the hearts of the people who'd pissed her off one too many times.

"I have good news," she said in the gloom.

Riadne's voice was a silvery thing. Smooth and thick around the vowels, and fluid, like dipping your hand into cool, melted-down silver. Fascinating. More things that were unfortunate: Riadne was kind of an evil MILF.

"The Sins have officially begun their next cycle. The bad news is, the ironborn children marked for hosting them have fallen some-what . . . wayward. Several of them have escaped my tabs—it's time to track down the rest that remain and locate the ones that have gone missing."

At the same time as speaking, she raised her hand and traced over the unmarked graves of her many victims to one of the center cavities.

Nausicaä had only just enough time to spot it before the drawer was pushed inward instead of pulled open—the smallest symbol etched onto the stone of a great serpent winding its way up around seven golden orbs. . . .

Did Riadne even know what that symbol *meant*?

Using it for her little cult . . . the Flamel family crest, designed not by Nicholas but by the son whose name had been so thoroughly oblit-erated from history that even Nausicaä couldn't remember it. The son who'd taken all the enormity of his family name, all the goodness his father had intended, and had turned it into a nightmare she honestly didn't blame the Courts for fearing forever after.

That's your family crest, Nausicaä thought, looking at Arlo—Arlo, who was too good, nothing at all like her legacy, and please, fucking hell, let it be *Nicholas* that Fate had rewoven her from. . . .

Not the son.

Not. The. Son.

One moment, nothing.

The next, the columbarium sank inward too.

Stone scraped against stone, the heavy drag of it loud in the room as back and back the columbarium depressed, then down and down some hollow into the floor that devoured it.

Revealed before them was a dark passageway.

It reeked of dark magic and death and Sins, and Nausicaä didn't want to go in there, not one bit. She was all kinds of badass, hell unleashed on the Mortal Realm, the Dark Freaking Star, and she didn't want to go in there.

But in there she went when Riadne wound herself back around

Arlo and crossed the pair of them over the threshold.

"I made many of them, you see." Riadne launched back into conversation with a very quiet Arlo, as if this were a stroll in the park and Arlo a happy, willing participant. "The first few batches didn't work out. I didn't have the whole of the *recipe*. Lethe came in useful there, and after his intervention, it did go much smoother—paying off parents for their unborn babes, child bearer and child *both* the center of the array, so that right from birth, the infant would grow with the mark on its chest, would acclimatize early on to the Sins it would one day carry."

On they pushed.

Riadne seemed to enjoy her audience, the chance to explain her cleverness at last to people who'd actually grasp what she'd done.

It grossed Nausicaä out.

This was fucking depraved.

If she'd still been a Fury, this woman would have been number one on her list to drag in for the worst sort of punishment, definitely Destruction. As Megaera should have already done, but clearly Law mattered only when it was *Nausicaä* giving it a big middle finger.

"Once the mark matures, the heart begins to call to the Sins it's been tethered to. The cycle is triggered, during which one of three possible outcomes will occur: Ideal is that the host is deemed agreeable by the Sin that's answered its summons. That the Sin takes root in its chosen heart and waits through a small window of time for its array to be activated, stone complete. Less ideal, but still favorable, is that the host is not deemed agreeable to the current Sin in line for creation but still survives the calling and falls dormant again until the next cycle. Least ideal," Riadne sighed, with a heaviness that implied great sorrow—but sorrow for herself, not the people whose lives she so casually destroyed, "is that the host simply isn't strong enough to sustain the Sins at all and dies as soon as it's touched by one."

They came to a stop at the end of the passage, another door blocking their progress.

Riadne turned to Arlo, a gentleness on her face that spoke to her instability far clearer than anything else so far. "I had perfect tabs on all my hosts until recent endeavors against me. *Someone* seems to have taken it upon themselves to be tracking them down, to hide them out of my reach. And we can't have that, now, can we? After all, I've finally worked out why Lethe suggested choosing hosts all with the same blood type as my younger son. . . . How easy it will be, to have my alchemists swap the heart of whichever host survives all seven transformations for the useless one in Vehan's chest. I'll need each and every one of my experiments, you see, if I'm going to right my foolish oversight; if Vehan is to ever come into the power he *deserves*."

She reached out a hand again, tucked Arlo's hair behind her ear. Arlo looked horrified by what she'd just heard Riadne admit aloud in regard to her own damned son. Nausicaä certainly was, herself.

"I know everything that goes on in my palace, Arlo. Nausicaä brought you to see the newest addition to my dungeon's collection. A man who informs me you might just be a little more useful than originally anticipated. . . ."

With that very same hand, she moved to the door and pushed it open—it swung much easier than the columbarium had but revealed a scene so much worse.

A cavernous room, plain, porous stone for floor and wall. Along its perimeter were dozens of tables laden with all manner of wicked-looking instruments, vials, potions, ingredients, and burners. Bookshelves crammed themselves in between. A handful of people buzzed around them, tinkering with this and that experiment, and at the center . . .

Nausicaä blew out her cheeks.

Gods damn.

At the center was a flat stone altar around which an array had been carved into the ground. Blood and gore dripped over its edges and seeped into the array's grooves, and the mangled body it oozed from . . . ribs pried open like a gruesome maw tearing through its chest . . .

"It was unsuccessful," Rory Jarsdel said in a tight, clipped tone by way of greeting.

Red was smeared on his arms to his elbows, stained down the front of the apron he'd been given, flecked on his face beneath his goggles as if he were some sort of mad scientist pulled out of one of those Saw movies she'd watched a whole one of and decided no, she didn't want to be reminded of what mortals were capable of.

Rory pulled his goggles down, blinked first at Arlo, then Riadne, growing visibly horrified—clearly, he hadn't expected the lessons he bargained presence for here to be this.

Shock stepped him back from the body, and the alchemist Riadne had obviously tasked to help with the dirty work slipped in to finish wrenching the failed stone free from the cavity in the poor child's torso.

"Go to your father, Arlo," Riadne commanded in a much firmer tone. "He claims he's much to teach you—with quite the pedigree, too. So add it to your schedule, dear, that each night henceforth you'll join him here and learn what it takes to harvest a stone." She paused to grin. "Study well. I'm reserving quite the honor for you, *Harbinger of Ruin*."

With a push to Arlo's back, Riadne propelled her forward, and Nausicaä made to tear after her, because *fuck this*. Arlo had seen more than enough of Riadne's cruelty. She already barely ate, barely slept, trudged hollow-eyed around the fucking palace, and played at pushing everyone close to her away.

"Nausicaä."

Nausicaä looked down. At the arm flung out to bar her way.

Over—at the woman who played a more dangerous game than she was aware of. Nausicaä would do anything for the scant few people she still called friends—this fucking queen had no idea what she'd do for *Arlo*.

"She's not summoning Ruin for you," Nausicaä hissed. "It will kill her."

Riadne laughed, a low, delicate thing in the back of her throat—irritatingly, it was just as dangerous a sound. "Then bless that she has her *lucky* little die to wish that fate away." She turned her head, at last looking over at Nausicaä. Not many people could match Nausicaä's stare, in audacity or height, but those blue eyes weren't afraid of anything—at least, not yet.

They would be if she continued to torment Arlo.

Nausicaä . . . Lethe . . . Arlo, herself . . . Riadne would learn what fear was if she continued to push, and push, and *push* . . .

"You will collect them."

"Like fucking shit I will."

"Then you serve no use to me. Shall I exile you here and now?"

"They're *children*," Nausicaä breathed. "Riadne, you're a mother. You have to feel something about this—"

"I feel everything about this—*my* children are on the line!" Riadne hissed, surging into the space between them. "I would pull those stones from those bodies myself if it meant keeping them safe—*that* is motherhood. So pack away your theatrics, Fury. I know what I'm about, just as you know yourself. You will collect my ironborn hosts and return them to me. You will continue to do what I ask of you so that you can continue to stand by your sweet little flower-girl you so deeply fear will turn suicidal without you; to stand by her through all the depths of trauma and darkness that you had to go through alone. And while you're at it, you will remind yourself that you're the Dark Star. If it pains you so terribly to do what you must to ensure the people you love survive, if your heart is getting in the way of what you must do . . . I will remind you there's been a way out of this all along."

Whose heart are you going to give her? Theodore had asked earlier this very day. *Who are you supposed to hand over to impress your way into her employ?*

Riadne turned her attention back to the room, lifted the hand that had stayed Nausicaä in dismissal of her and the Hunt.

A hand armed with not just Pride and Greed but also now Lust, and this was all just fucking inevitable, wasn't it? A ticking clock counting down the days Nausicaä had left to make this all right.

Nausicaä wheeled around and stormed for the shadows, to fall against the wall—watching, waiting.

She wasn't leaving Arlo here. Riadne wanted her to track down those children? Fine. But not before Nausicaä could see Arlo safely returned to her room tonight and every other night Riadne subjected the girl *she fucking loved* to this—this mortal horror that had filled Nausicaä's every day as a Fury; this mortal horror that had edged the last person she'd loved to the precipice of breaking.

Not again.

Make it right.

Nausicaä wasn't going anywhere.

Whatever she had to do, she'd do it—even against Arlo's wishes, Arlo was going to survive.

CHAPTER 12

Vehan

~~~~~~

THIS WAS . . . A PATHETIC attempt at reconciliation, Vehan had to admit.

Granted, he had no real idea how to apologize to someone for his mother murdering nearly their entire family in front of them. Probably this warranted a little more than turning up at that person's bedroom with a tray of breakfast he'd made himself and was therefore on its own extremely sad. All the things Arlo liked, at least what she'd been happiest to eat on the days they'd taken breakfast together before the Solstice: clotted cream and fluffy scones and strawberries and bacon, all arranged on cherry-blossom-print porcelain, and around wildflowers he'd collected from the forest.

On a scale of one to he'd-never-made-anyone-breakfast-before-in-his-life, he thought he hadn't done all that badly, but still . . .

You are not alone, Prince of Light.

This was important.

Remember what it is that truly makes you strong.

He'd contemplated long and hard what Fate had revealed to him back in that clearing yesterday. The gods all worked in mysterious ways and didn't always mean well, but there'd been a message in what Fate had shown him, a hint of hope she'd given him.

What made Vehan strong?

What was it people said about him, sometimes in praise, often in despair? What was it his own mother had told him she viewed as his biggest weakness?

Vehan drew a breath.

Cliché as it sounded, what Vehan himself had always held fast to was goodness. *Love; optimism.* And all those things . . . they were inspired in Vehan by his friends, the people he cared for and wanted to protect. He wasn't going to make anything right on his own, not without them to keep him true. And he wasn't going to gain them back if he didn't swallow down his fear and at least try to make amends with Arlo.

Balancing the tray on his arm, he raised a hand, intending to knock, when . . .

"Vehan?"

Vehan froze.

Just like back in the clearing, once again there was Arlo. Coming down the hall toward him. She looked . . . frightening. Dark circles stamped her eyes like bruises; exhaustion weighed her down, made her movement sluggish and a little clumsy. Nausicaä (hiding only slightly better how tired and frazzled *she* was) quickly caught Arlo when she stumbled in shock over spotting him.

There was a rawness to Arlo's skin, as though she'd just recently scrubbed her arms and hands in scalding-hot water.

To human eyes it wouldn't be noticeable, but there, on the hem of the robe she'd thrown on over her pajamas . . . blood. *Red* blood. Her own, or someone else's? But Nausicaä wouldn't be half as calm as she currently was if Arlo had been somehow injured.

Vehan swallowed.

He wanted to ask, and very much didn't at the same time. A part of his courage deflated as he wondered if whatever had happened, this was again his mother's fault.

"Um . . . good morning," Arlo greeted, audibly hesitant, when she finally reached where he stood.

And Vehan still could only stare, overcome by intimidation.

Apart from the clearing yesterday, this was the first time since the Solstice that either of them had actually spoken to each other. Arlo looked at him with a mixture of wariness and bone-deep fatigue, then dropped her gaze to the tray in his hands, a brow quirking in question.

"I . . . Good morning, Arlo," he blurted out in a nervous rush. "Uh . . . I . . . brought you some breakfast? I'm sorry, I didn't realize you were already up, and of course you and Nausicaä probably already ate. I didn't mean to bother you. I'm sorry, I'll just—"

"You brought me breakfast?"

She frowned down at the tray in confusion.

Vehan's fingers tightened around the tray's handles. He took a moment to collect himself, to draw in a breath and remind himself that this wasn't about him; this wasn't about his nerves, or the array on his chest, or anything he stood to benefit from Arlo's forgiveness.

He held out the tray.

"I'd like to eat with you, if you'd let me. Like we sometimes used to? I know a lot has changed. My mother . . . There's nothing I can ever say or do to make up for what she did. But I'd like to eat breakfast with you. At the very least, I'd like to make sure *you* eat. Because I want you to know that . . . no matter what, I'm still your friend. I will always be your friend. And as your friend, I'm not going anywhere. I'm not ever going to leave you alone."

Arlo blinked at him, her expression even flatter than ever.

"You want me to eat with you to . . . what, prove everything's fine? That you forgive me for screwing up at the Solstice? Or better yet . . . that you, like everyone else, don't blame me at all for what happened."

And Vehan couldn't explain it. He didn't know why he even said what he did next, was a little horrified with himself for the words even escaping his lips . . . except . . . he'd been here before.

Was currently here now.

Didn't realize until this moment, looking into that carefully closed expression, that the same thing that kept Vehan up at night might be exactly what *she* was feeling too.

They'd both, after all, been taken in by Riadne's charm.

Vehan shook his head. Drew a breath. "We were both fools, where my mother was concerned. We both did something stupid because of her. And no one blames us, but we both still feel it, and I just . . . want you to eat with me. So that maybe we can forgive each other."

Arlo dropped her gaze back to the tray.

Then buried her face in her hands and proceeded to burst into tears.

Eyes widening, because here it was—this was how he was going to die—Vehan started to panic. He'd messed up, and Arlo hated him, and now he'd made her cry on top of everything else, and he'd done so in front of *Nausicaä*, who would definitely eviscerate him. . . .

Paling, no idea how to calm down a sobbing young woman whose girlfriend was death and torment made flesh, Vehan lifted his gaze to Nausicaä—*help me,* he was sure his expression cried, and hopefully with the added, *I didn't mean to make her upset!*

But even more startling than Arlo's meltdown was the look on Nausicaä's face.

Not promise of punishment.

Not anger.

Relief.

Nausicaä looked . . . relieved; close to tears of her own. Like maybe . . . it hadn't occurred to her too until Vehan had said it, what Arlo actually needed right now.

"Thank you," she mouthed over Arlo's shoulder, and Arlo only cried harder. Nausicaä reached around her girlfriend to take Vehan's tray, freeing up his hands. And then all of a sudden, his arms were full, Arlo's red hair filling his vision.

She smelled of iron and char and stale air; Vehan ignored it. Resting his chin on top of her head, he brought his hands up her spine to the middle of her back and rubbed in soothing circles.

"It's all my fault," Arlo wept.

Vehan's hand maintained its motion. "What is?"

"All of it, it's all my f-fault! It's all my fault, just like you said, except no one else wants to say it. My mom died, and that's *all my fault.*"

"It's not just your fault," Vehan reminded gently. Continuing to hold her tight, he reached around to open Arlo's bedroom door and maneuvered the pair of them into her room.

Still caught up in his arms, she lifted her face only briefly—only enough to nod at Nausicaä and thank her when she set Vehan's tray down on Arlo's sitting room table and informed Arlo that she was going to poke around the kitchens for her own breakfast so that she and Vehan could have a bit of time to talk, just the two of them. One wildly enthusiastic thumbs-up at him later, Nausicaä whisked back out of the room, leaving Vehan acutely aware that he'd prepared himself for pretty much every scenario but this.

It was quiet in Arlo's chambers.

The windows were all open to the early-summer sunshine and heat, and he could hear the sounds of the gardeners outside, well underway with their day. They stood in the silence, Vehan continuing to rub circles on Arlo's back, Arlo's tears beginning to thin out into hiccups and sniffles.

"I'm sorry," she whispered through a watery laugh. Pulling back a fraction, she patted at the damp patch on Vehan's shoulder. "I'm being silly."

"Arlo," Vehan replied, firmly serious. He placed a finger under her chin, tilted her face so that their eyes could meet and she could see just how much he meant what he said. "You never have to apologize for tears."

"Hmm," Arlo mused a bit absently. When Vehan released her chin, her eyes fell immediately back to his shoulder. "I think this is the first time I've cried about . . . any of this. Everything's changed. My mom is . . . and *your* mom's the new High Queen, and Celadon is your brother, and my dad's being kept in the dungeons here because he's also apparently ironborn, and the *entire life* I thought I knew so well, which was underwhelming and pretty boring but at least it was comfortable and safe and . . . now it's . . ."

Her eyes began to water again. Vehan reeled her back in. Her sobs were a little more subdued this time, but he held her through it like he'd done the first time. "I miss Celadon," she said into his shirt. "I miss Elyas. And my mom. And I don't want to be here, Vehan. I feel so *stupid*. I played right into her hand, and everyone told me to be careful, but I didn't listen because I didn't want to believe it. . . ."

"Yeah," Vehan whispered back, his voice grown hoarse. "Yeah, I . . . get it."

How long had Aurelian been trying to get him to see what was right underneath his nose this whole time? And Vehan had ignored it. He could have done something, could have even stopped his mother before things had escalated to this unbearable height that put her so out of reach now, almost untouchable. . . .

"Arlo," he added, tightening his hold on her. His eyes began to water, too. "I'm so sorry. I'm so, so *sorry*. I've always been so proud of myself for acting where others wouldn't, but when it came to my mother . . . I didn't do anything to stop this, and I'm sorry."

Arlo pulled back a fraction again, placing her hands on the sides of his face. It always threw him a little, the way emotion rimmed human and ironborn eyes with red, sent a blotchy flush across their face that wasn't sapphire or silvery but warm.

"I'm sorry it's taken me this long to . . . see it. You're the only other person who gets it, who understands, and I'm sorry for not realizing that until now. We messed up. We messed up, and it's not just our fault, but we were a part of the problem. So now we'll have to be part of the solution. The both of us together, because no matter what, you're still my friend, Vehan. You'll always be my friend. And I know you're hurting too. I know you miss Aurelian, and that you're scared for his safety, but I *promise you* you'll see him again. I promise you that until then, I won't be leaving you alone here either."

Vehan drew his bottom lip between his teeth.

Princes didn't cry; his mother had drilled that into him from the day he'd lost his father. But screw what his mother wanted.

"Oh!" Arlo exclaimed softly, but was quick to recover, to wrap her arms tightly around him as his turn came to dissolve into tears.

They stayed like that for some time, the two of them in the middle of Arlo's sitting room, standing around crying. A pathetic portrait perhaps, but at the end of it, Vehan could tell they were both feeling better, at least a little. There was actual life in Arlo's eyes now, and he hadn't realized how high she'd built the walls keeping everything in until they were lowered completely and she was relaxed, actually animated in their conversation.

They moved with their breakfast into Arlo's bedroom.

Tray set on the end of her bed, the pair of them picked at its contents from the wrapped-up comfort of her duvet and stacked pillows. Arlo had shed her dirtied robe and changed into a fresh pair of emerald pajamas. Vehan had braided her hair back from her face in the way he used to like doing for his mother when he'd been so little that Vadrien had still been alive and Riadne hadn't grown so steeled against *everything*.

They talked, and they talked—about nothing, about all.

Finally, Vehan dared to ask what she and Nausicaä had been up to before breakfast, but the answer he received . . . His fingers stilled in her hair.

"She's . . . what?"

Arlo sighed. "We have to figure out a way to get that array off your chest, Vehan. She's serious. She wants to summon all seven of the Sins and use them to . . . resurrect Ruin, and she plans on using you to host them."

Yeah.

Vehan was aware.

The worst part was, he knew without a doubt that Riadne thought she was doing her son a *kindness*.

"I don't get it. I don't understand." Arlo threw her hands in the air, dislodging her braid from Vehan's hands. "Doesn't she know? Did Lethe not tell her? Two souls can't inhabit the same body. She'll swap your heart with the ironborn who survives all seven transformations and then summon Ruin into you before your body can purge the iron, and it's too powerful. Ruin will *burn* through you, and you won't be Vehan anymore. You won't be her son at all. You'll die—your soul will die. Why does she want this when it also sounds like she does care about you—"

"She cares," Vehan agreed in a stony, far-away tone.

Fingers tracing the unraveling strands of fire-red hair beneath them, he felt a million miles from here, his thoughts flashing back over every interaction between them. "Riadne cares about her children. She's a single mother, a woman in a world that values her less all because of her gender. People have taken advantage of her; shamed her; ridiculed her—many of them actually *love* that she came into the Bone Crown the way she did because they get to turn around and point and cry *look what happens when women get too ambitious*. She's had to fight and claw and scheme for everything, things she shouldn't have had to do any of that for, and from day one all anyone ever bothered to teach her was that power meant survival, and lack of it meant death. My mother cares. Unfortunately, there's only one way she knows how to show that."

"Hmm," Arlo replied, deep in thought about something.

And Vehan hurried to tack on, "I'm sorry. I wasn't trying to . . . make you sympathize with her. There's no excuse for what she's done—to you, to so many others."

Arlo straightened, shaking her head. "No, no, that's not it." She sighed. "Why do you think I was so eager to take her kindness at face value? I know all about the way the Courts treat powerful women. *My* mother was powerful."

"May Night keep her."

". . . Yeah."

They fell silent again.

Arlo played with the remnants of their clotted cream, dragging the tongs of her fork through it.

Vehan was just casting around for a different point of conversation, something lighter, when—

"We're going to get that mark off your chest, Vehan. The wish I made . . . well, I regret to report that it didn't help for anything other than pointing me in the direction of where I'll find the answer."

Vehan peeked his head around her shoulder; Arlo shifted her body to face him. "There's a block on my memories. The first night I slept after making my wish to be better at alchemy, I spoke with Magic. Long story short, they told me that I actually know a heck of a lot all on my own without their help, but there's something locking it away in my mind. And until I find whoever put the block there and get them to remove it, I won't be able to access it. Right now I can only use the pieces Magic has given me."

He'd been around Court long enough, been subject to his mother his entire life; Vehan knew how to read between the lines.

"You have an idea who put the block there, don't you."

Arlo nodded grimly.

"Dad told me he didn't remember any of who he actually was until the block that was put on his memory was removed. How much do you want to bet the same person is responsible for mine? And that this person is Lethe—the Mortal Realm's best practitioner of memory manipulation."

Even Vehan knew—they all did. Lethe was the Hunter who erased and altered memory on the High Sovereign's behalf. He was the one who managed the fallout of Weighings and divorces, who was sent to clean up after magical events that couldn't be contained by the Falchion or Heads of the Courts, wiping the instances clean from human minds.

Lethe was scary in *very* many ways. Chances were, if you ever learned exactly how, he'd erase that too just as quickly.

"Okay," said Vehan, frowning in thought. "But if it *was* Lethe, does this mean the Courts are behind your block, as well? High King Azurean . . . If Lethe was involved, he doesn't strike me as the sort of person to hand out personal favors; the High King would have had to give him the order to do that. Unless . . ."

"Unless my family not knowing something until a specific time benefited Lethe's plans for me," Arlo finished. "I don't know. There's *so much* I don't know, and I shouldn't have run out on my dad when he was trying to explain it to me. I just . . ."

"It's a lot," Vehan supplied. He understood. "As far as reactions to *hey, your entire life is a lie* go, running is pretty mild."

A bubble of laughter escaped Arlo's chest, and Vehan wrapped an arm around her shoulders once more. "We'll figure it out. Lethe will turn up here at some point, and I'm sure if anyone could get him to answer something seriously, it would be you. His mysterious champion of . . . honestly, what does he want from you? Has he ever actually said?"

Arlo shrugged. Falling back, she slipped under Vehan's arm and dropped against her bed. "Nope. Not really. I could make guesses, and I'm sure none of them are actually it, so . . . I've just been waiting for him to tell me. That's pretty much all I can do anymore—wait for things to happen." She bit her lip. "I miss Celadon. I haven't seen him since the Solstice."

None of them had.

Which Vehan also understood, in a way. He himself had been reeling over everything that had happened, but Celadon . . . His life had changed as well. His family had been murdered in front of him, and rumor blamed him for the whole thing. Whatever was true, Vehan knew Arlo enough to know that Celadon couldn't possess the sort of heart that would conspire with Riadne in such a cruel, violent way.

Most likely, Celadon was just as terrified as Vehan had been. He was probably worried that Arlo blamed him; that she hated him now, like everyone else did. And the fact that this place was now a graveyard to the worst night in his whole existence surely played a role in his absence as well.

"He'll come, Arlo. When he's ready, he'll come."

The morning wore on.

They talked and talked until Arlo trailed off, exhaustion overcoming her. Not long after, Nausicaä returned and found Arlo fast asleep with Vehan stretched out beside her, watching her . . . deep in thought. . . .

"Thank you," Nausicaä said quietly. It was probably the first time she'd ever spoken so kindly to him. "I . . . Thank you." A pause; she seemed to be struggling to put something difficult into words. "When my sister died, no one blamed me. They sure as shit lost their cool with my grief, but no one blamed me, no matter how much I wanted them to. Because it *was* my fault; in part, it was my fault, and I just wanted someone to tell me, *Yeah, you fucked up, I see that, but you're still a good person.*" She blew out a breath, raking a hand through her hair in a backward sweep from her face. "I just wanted someone to acknowledge that it was okay I wasn't perfect. I wanted someone to see the ugly part of who I was and what I'd done and still love me anyhow. I don't know why it didn't occur to me that Arlo felt the same way. I thought she was spiraling. Rather, she *is* spiraling, and I was too busy being so damned afraid that this spiraling was going to drag her right down Tisiphone's path that I just . . . didn't see that it was also *this.* So . . . yeah. Thanks."

"Are *you* okay?" Vehan asked, carefully lifting himself to sitting. He could see how worried she'd been in how much her relief affected her. He didn't know Nausicaä as well as Arlo did, but he knew just enough, and it wasn't easy . . . the constant fear for the person you loved.

Nausicaä looked down at him from Arlo's bedside, entirely impassive.

When a full minute passed in which she said nothing, Vehan wondered if maybe he'd made a misstep. Hiding the embarrassment that warmed his face, he sat up fully now and swung his legs out of bed. "Switch me out? Arlo would probably rather wake up to your face than mine, and I have something I need to do."

"Going for a run?"

It was . . . the way she said it.

Nausicaä wasn't great with emotions. He'd learned that pretty well in the past few months of their friendship. She didn't express things as directly as he did, but it was there underneath . . . the way she asked it . . . the barest tilt to her words that angled them toward concern. "You do that a lot. Don't . . . let her wear you out."

Vehan's smile blew wide across his face.

He nodded to her, and Nausicaä bristled; she rolled her eyes and shooed him off the bed to slip into place next to Arlo. "Don't get chummy, weather boy. But also . . . hey." She turned her head to look at him. "I'll make sure he's all right too, okay?"

It was Vehan's turn to stare.

Swallowing around the lump in his throat, the swell of longing to just hold Aurelian again, he nodded once more. "Thank you." Light, simple—Nausicaä nodded back at him, and this was as close as their heart-to-heart was going to get, but Vehan was grateful nonetheless. "Get some rest, Nausicaä. I'll see you both at dinner."

And hopefully, with the help of his new position as High Prince and all the privileges that came along with it, there'd be one more Lysterne at the table with them.

Sea spray and salt—it crusted his skin, his clothing, his hair, sat heavy on his tongue as the appendage darted to chase after droplets that slicked his flaking lips.

Rain and rain, an endless deluge; Lethe almost couldn't recall the feeling of being dry, after a month on this battlefield, in which the gray-clad sky did nothing but weep and the sea's waves raged against their camp's rocky shore like they were trying to reach up and drag them into its depths, where Lethe belonged.

"Are we taking a breather?" a stony voice ground out beside him. "Has the Prince of Carnage had enough for the day, time to pack it in?"

So much noise they made, these people.

Eyes closed, face tilted toward the sky, Lethe indulged in his moment of pleasure, the feeling of water trickling down his body. It mixed with the salt, the blood, the gore, the dirt and grime and sticky wounds. It washed away flesh. Picked him clean like fishbones, and ah, but it was such a *good* feeling, and the crooning in the back of his head that called him called him called him home . . .

A clang of steel—so much noise; the battle raged on around him.

Most tried to avoid the *Prince of Carnage.*

At first they treated him like a challenge, a test of the legend they hoped to secure for themselves, and the strongest would seek him out. The others would circle to watch, to hope, waiting for the reassurance that Lethe would bleed just the same as they, and it was almost as delicious as sinking his blade through a man's warm belly, the way that hope visibly crumbled each time.

"I'm speaking to you, soldier."

This general was new.

"Get back to what we bought you for—"

He made much too much noise.

A flex of Lethe's arm and a slice clean through the general's neck was all it took to silence him.

Atlas would rumble at the loss of this man and the others Lethe had taken from him, and there would be punishment. Lashes and wounds and more salt ground into them; small, dark cages and fish-bones whose provenance he couldn't quite tell—were they feeding him bits of his own self? Would he devour his own tail whole?

Battle was endless.

War was dull.

Men fell at his feet like flies, and none of it was much fun anymore . . . but this was the only time they let him out, let him out—*Lethe . . . Lethe . . . come home, Lethe*—let him out to see the Moon.

But instead, rain for a month. A sky filled only with clouds.

Lethe sighed. He opened his eyes, kicked the general's head to the side, and swept back into death's current.

Some were young, younger than young, little fingerlings, little boys playing little men, and all of them wept just the same in the end. Bowels emptied, guts spilled—flesh was so easy to rend apart, and bones snapped like twigs in his hands, all the same. Life was disgustingly cheap, and Lethe consumed it all like a plague, swept through the armies Atlas set him upon. The more violent he was, the more vulgar, the more depraved he was in cutting them down, ripping them apart, tearing through throats with teeth . . . the happier his *father* was.

The Prince of Carnage.

Future of Atlantis.

King.

A blade at his left—Lethe swung with the force of the sea that called and called and called him home, and he missed the Moon. His only friend, his more than friend; some days it felt like the other half of his soul. Some days it felt like he was the Moon and the Moon was him. Lately, though . . . all he could feel was the fleeting press of their bond.

All this rain, all these clouds. When would he be able to see the Moon again? When would they be able to speak—he missed the Moon; missed its voice; missed the feel of its magic against his.

Lethe hacked men clean in two down the middle.

A swing from his right—he whipped himself clear around, heaved his sword overhead to crack it down through a helmeted skull.

"Gods bear witness!" cried a voice from behind, and as fluid as a dance—a thing he could barely recall from a life that couldn't have ever been his, but memory hinted had been—Lethe dropped. Swept out a leg. Tumbled the next man running up on his rear into the bloody mud.

It squelched beneath them, gave way to their weight.

Lethe pressed the man's face into the wet earth, drowned him in the filth of his brothers, and it thrilled him a little, the way the man struggled. The way he flailed. A storm before the deadweight calm.

And still Lethe pressed.

Until bone began to crack, and gray matter and endless more blood began to squish out through the fissures, trickle warm over his fingers.

Then he was up. Then others and others and others fell down.

And the sea continued to long for him—Lethe longed back, but first . . . but *first* . . .

"I hear you've given us a fair few positions to fill in our ranks."

King Atlas stood in the center of a marble hall currently under construction. All sparkling white pillars and exquisitely lain mosaic tiles, a vaulted ceiling that echoed back his father's wry amusement.

Before him a statue.

A likeness Lethe didn't recognize, a man dressed in Atlantean splendor and towering like a god. He liked the eyes though. Something about paint of the eyes . . .

Cocking his head, Lethe considered the king's broad back. How easy it would be to snap that spine, to crack his ribs out like spreading wings. "I don't have patience for useless people," he heard himself rasp in reply, in a voice he didn't recognize either, a thing that had once been something memory recalled with pleasing melody but creaked and cracked now from lack of use.

No one needed Lethe for words.

King Atlas chuckled. He wasn't the sort who cared for useless things, either, and probably Lethe's reply had pleased him. That, or he was in too good of a mood to care.

Gold and jewels and enslaved and silks, trinkets and spices and seeds and goods—Lethe piled. He piled and piled in mountains at his king father's feet, and Atlas was oh so pleased by it all. Their glorious return from war was now three days into celebration, more land won to Atlantean rule, more things to sparkle in their keeps.

"Do you like it?" Atlas asked.

Lethe tilted his head in consideration.

"The eyes." What had they bled for that color of green—were those *his* eyes? Was this what he looked like? He doubted that very much, but he could always scoop out what he had and replace them with that stone, with a color that burned like livid poison.

And Atlas chuckled again.

Such a merry spirit he was in, a bit rosy in the face and flush with both wine and victory he hadn't taken part in securing, not in some time. Why spend the effort when he had Lethe? "Come now, Zeuxis, don't look so sour! Every king needs a monument—you've fought long and hard for Atlantean prosperity. It's high time my prince gets commemoration."

A temple was a bit much.

Lethe had no idea who that man was in that marble—miserable wretch; fool of fate and fortune.

"If you say so."

Out to the streets, back to day. To screaming and cries of happiness that clashed just as hideously in his ears as their bleating, their weeping, their anger and jeers. Citizens celebrated. Wine splashed over goblets raised to him as he passed. They loved him today.

They'd hate him tomorrow.

A kingdom surrounded him, glittering bright under a blazing sun . . . his Moon, all he cared for, a pale white imprinted against that ghastly blue.

Too pale.

Too weak—something he hadn't noticed sign of before his leaving for this latest in too many pointless battles, so this was a recent development, then. They were closer than ever, their bond so much stronger; the power between them should be stronger, too.

Instead, Lethe would almost swear it had grown weaker, that there was a chill to its usual warmth inside him now that terrified him.

Please, my friend, are you all right? What has happened—are you ill?

Trinkets and glittering and monuments to misfortune, Atlas laid everything at his feet when in the mood for generosity; was just as quick to take it away when irked, and none of that mattered; the ebb and flow of things in his life—they were just things. But if anything ever happened to his Moon . . . his patron . . . his heart, for Lethe didn't know much of love or really feel moved to the sentiment at all, not for anyone or anything, but for his Moon . . . perhaps.

Everything's fine, the Moon pressed back, its voice as gentle as ever, like springtime air Lethe always thought, and it calmed him instantly to hear it. *I'm so glad you've returned unharmed. . . . You'll have to tell me all that happened.*

Everything's fine, the Moon assured, but Lethe couldn't shake the impression it very much wasn't.

CHAPTER 13

Vehan

~⌘~

THIS WAS THE SECOND time Vehan had used the Egress to show up uninvited to the UnSeelie Court's Palace of Spring.

Stepping through the glass that connected Seelie Summer's mirror to this one, he was just as awestruck as the first time he arrived here. All the gleaming black marble riddled with white veins like starlight, the sweeping crystal windows looking out over the Toronto cityscape, creeping vines and lush greenery growing up the walls to span over the ceiling—the room was built like a solarium made tenebrous by its verdant canopy.

"High Prince!" squeaked one of the two guards standing sentry over the star-glass mirror. A young faerie man with blue-topaz hair and silver piercing his eyebrows and septum. His entire demeanor screamed *new recruit*, along with the young fae woman beside him— earth-brown hair and ruby-bright eyes with an intricate sweep of black tattooed across them from temple to temple.

Both looked at Vehan with a mixture of awe and horror.

"Uh . . . hello," Vehan greeted with as casual a smile as he could, attempting to affect a nonthreatening air.

He hadn't really made any public appearance yet in his new *elevation*. There hadn't been much time, much occasion for him to do so besides standing at his mother's side in perfectly silent composure while she delivered her Inaugural Address to the Courts, greeting them as their High Queen and informing them what she hoped to see accomplished during her reign.

It was all mostly air and words.

A tradition even Riadne wouldn't deviate from.

It allowed all her family, her alliances, the aristocracy, and important members of the public to gather in her throne room, where journalists and reporters would transcribe and record and televise their "happy" faces, and everyone would get to see who they needed to cozy up to if they wanted to infiltrate their Sovereign's inner circle—they got to see who the Sovereign valued most.

Vehan had lived his whole life as a prince, Crown Heir to his Court—he was used to attention wherever he went, to catching people short when they realized he was in their midst. But *this* . . . this was different.

"High Prince!" the young fae woman gasped, remembering her voice now too, and it was a flurry of motion from that point on.

They bowed, exalted him, wished him a long life and Light's endless favor, all the things that were fairly standard for the reception of a High Royal, that even Vehan had been taught to perform when the title had belonged to the Viridians. But then, through some signal or other, the door burst open, and more joined the throng. More fae and faeries and folk of various races—attendants, Vehan gathered, judging by their attire.

Some were older but most were young, and none of them Vehan recognized from the first time he'd been here, or from any function he'd ever attended where UnSeelie Spring had been present.

His heart gave a lurch when he thought about why.

How many people Celadon would have had to replace, roles made vacant not because High King Azurean had died but for the manner in which it had happened: the rumors floating around were that Celadon had conspired with his mother to steal this throne for his inheritance, that he was a blood traitor—a coward. Celadon hadn't earned his power, not in the majority of the public's opinion, and his silence, his disappearance from society, only compounded common belief. Even the Falchion was angry with him for Thalo's death. Many had even quit because of it, refusing to move with the headquarters in its transferal to Seelie Summer.

The palace back home was chaotic with change, aristocrats and powers and government officials moving in, whole wings under construction to accommodate them; there were a number of people his mother had inherited from the Viridians' own employment.

Of *course* his staff would have thinned.

But the people he'd replaced them with . . . a collection of scars and broken bones that hadn't healed properly, tattoos and paint and piercings . . .

Where had Celadon found them? he wondered.

Impossibly, they gave him the impression of having been plucked from the Faerie Ring, their service in exchange for clean records.

"I'm here to see your king," Vehan replied, snapped from his thoughts by an orc girl barely older than he was, and considerably more muscular. She'd elbowed her way between the fussing crowd, was far more composed and far less impressed by his status. It was clear she had a job to do. "I'm sorry, I don't have an appointment with him, but I was hoping—"

Straight to business, the girl waved him off.

"Come with me, Your Highness," she grunted, and turned for the door.

They exited the room.

Out into the hall, down its length to the elevator. The other attendants trailed behind in a chattering cloud of excitement and running commentary. Normally, this would all have made Vehan highly uncomfortable—he'd been groomed to live in the spotlight, but this one was so much hotter than he was used to, and he wasn't sure he liked it.

How had Celadon dealt with this?

Just the knowledge that he could turn to any one of these people and compel them to do his very worst bidding—as High Prince, he had a sway that was magic all its own, and they would be hard-pressed to disobey him.

Down the elevator fell.

Out into the grand foyer.

"—still under construction, as you can see."

This room, it was . . . so *different.*

Vehan had been to UnSeelie Spring's main reception at its height. High King Azurean had spared no expense or talent in the display meant to dazzle his guests and impress upon them the might of his power.

The trees, the greenery, the flowers . . . everything was now dead and shriveled.

The waterfall, the magicked canopy, the thunderstorms enchanted to rumble across the ceiling and mist down rain from overhead . . . quiet; still; petrified to lifeless stone.

Folk were hard at work. Whatever Celadon had planned for the place, it was only in its beginning phase, with scaffolding and enormous chunks of raw marble strewn around, lesidhe fae in deep conversation that broke into arguments over whatever plans they huddled around, other folk and fae busy with uprooting and clearing the dead vegetation.

"—day in and day out."

"Everyone wants a peek!"

"It's been a nightmare trying to keep those doors barred to the public, and reporters, and nosy little Seelie Summer spies just dying to bring something to High Queen Riadne to worm their way into her folds . . . uh, no offense. Your Highness."

"None taken," Vehan murmured, distracted by his surroundings.

Onward his guide took them.

Through the grand foyer, to the double set of elevators at the far end—into the one reserved for private Viridian use. The guard on duty here was older than the ones upstairs, another orc, who nodded at his guide and wordlessly shifted to let her by, but the way his eyes widened a fraction when he noticed Vehan and he stiffened a little straighter at attention . . .

Very possibly, they could all hate him.

If they were loyal to the Viridian name, they *definitely* hated him.

But Vehan's mother was the infamous queen who'd slaughtered an entire royal fae family to get what she wanted—he'd be uncomfortable around him too if he were them.

Into the golden elevator they went, only Vehan and his guide.

The grate closed between their severed group, attendants pressing close to goggle at him through the network of metal, trade comments on how they "—thought he'd be much scarier in person." And almost sounded disappointed.

Down and down the carriage descended.

His guide passed their ride folded against the back wall, head bent and eyes closed. He tried to ask for her name, to strike up some sort of conversation between them.

"It doesn't matter," she replied. Then, sighing, tacked on in an afterthought, "Your Highness."

Down.

And down.

And *down* they went.

There had to be some sort of distortion here; only the Viridian vaults and their dungeons were this far beneath their palace—but they couldn't be going *there*. . . .

Except, apparently, they were.

The elevator glided to a stop. Vehan's guide hauled open the grate, extended an arm to sweep him over its threshold. She followed him out, but only a step, into a plain black stone hall, so dark that he struggled to make out much between the pockets of torchlight spilling from the walls.

Judging by the flank of Verdant Guards at post by an inconspicuous door off to Vehan's right, those must be the Viridian vaults. Now emptied of their most dangerous valuables and transferred to the new High Sovereign's protection, there would still be unspeakable treasures within that hoard. Trinkets and gems and priceless artifacts that had been in this family's possession for generations.

At Azurean's defeat, Riadne would have been given pick of whatever she wanted from that trove, but Vehan had learned from palace gossip that she'd taken nothing. It had never been wealth Riadne had been chasing, after all. And why should she be seen "scrounging" through the Viridians' treasures when her son had inherited it all?

The orc guide pointed off to Vehan's left.

"That way—down the hall to the end. There's a stairwell. You'll find His Highness King Celadon at the very bottom."

"You . . . aren't coming with me?"

How strange Celadon's new attendants were. Even if he were an ordinary prince, no one properly trained for this role would have let him go anywhere without accompaniment, to announce his presence at the very least, to ensure Vehan went where he was supposed to go, as well.

The orc snorted. "Fuck no—you couldn't pay me enough. You're on your own, High Prince. I'll be waiting right here . . . if you make it back out."

Well, *that* was ominous.

Vehan sighed.

There was nothing for it—he'd come all this way and wasn't about to turn around now, even though this hall was creepy as the Sins his mother dabbled in.

Even though he'd heard the rumors about this place.

Everyone had . . . of the beast that lurked in the lowest pit of the Viridian palace dungeons . . .

Darkness pressed around him like closing hands, snuffing out even the radiance of his Crowning Gift that would have naturally illuminated his way. The firelight that lit the hall was sparse and far between as well, the impossible black that flooded the gaps thick as tar. It was more the absolute nothingness that bothered him, the hairs on the backs of his neck and arms standing on end, gooseflesh pebbling over his skin. Nothing waited for him in this dark. He wasn't worried anything would jump out at him. More, each time he stepped out of a pocket of light, it felt like *losing* himself. Desolation and abandonment—this horrid brand of crushing isolation overwhelmed him as soon as the darkness swelled in, so that he was almost glad when he reached the arch stamped into the hall's end and the only slightly better-lit stairs that wound down, and down, and so much farther down. . . .

"What on earth are you up to?" Vehan wondered aloud.

To hells with this. He reached for one of the twin torches on either side of the stairwell's entrance and plucked it from the wall.

It was a much more comfortable journey down the steps with fire to guide him, but with the absence of that terrible loneliness, Vehan's worry turned back to what he might find at the end of this.

Down.

And down.

And down Vehan descended.

The steps were steep, and the farther he went, the air wasn't cool as he'd assumed it would be so low beneath ground level but hot. Hot, and *humid*.

Down.

And down.

And down Vehan climbed.

There were minor platforms throughout his descent. He had to be nearing the end now—he could hear the faint murmur of voices, meaning that whatever was going on, Celadon wasn't alone.

The platform he stepped off had to be the last, but just as he did, the flame on his torch snapped from warm red to vibrant green. The torches along the walls changed too, still burning just as hot, but his passing had triggered something, and he hoped green was good, because he didn't fancy running back up these stairs away from whatever came after him if it wasn't.

Panting, very nearly out of breath, he saw the base of the stairwell come into view.

He couldn't see much past the low-hanging lip of the ceiling, had to stoop a little to clear it and step out onto the landing.

Where . . .

"Vehan?"

Vehan stared.

The room was a cave the Viridians had tunneled down to in the palace's construction. Not overly large, but much bigger than the stairwell, and the ceiling was much higher up. There was no decoration, only the torches—blazing their curious green fire—situated on either side of the stairwell's entrance behind him . . . and the one held in Celadon's hand.

"Celadon," he gasped.

Celadon looked . . . better than he thought he was going to find, because he hadn't believed for a moment what people said about him.

It hadn't taken Vehan long to recover from his shock of the Solstice, at least enough to remember that he knew the High Prince . . . knew his *brother*, knew his heart, who he was at his core as a person. Celadon hadn't conspired against his own family, and whatever had kept him from making an appearance both in public and at Riadne's dinner table . . . Vehan had been expecting to find him spectacularly unwell, grieving.

He didn't expect this young man in black leather trousers and open emerald silk robes that flowed so long the hems pooled like water at his feet. Lysterne copper hair burning bright against his onyx crown with emeralds on its spires blooming like flowers. Glittering black makeup smoked around his eyes, one bright jade and the other shocking blue. A deep, sage matte painted his mouth. Rings on every finger; glinting, jeweled chains around a narrow waist left bare beneath a swatch of sage material bound around his chest . . .

Celadon stood so out of place in this cave; he looked a bit like Luck had back when Arlo had been lain up in the infirmary.

Like a *god*.

"High Prince Vehan!"

There were several men in a line before him, huddled slightly to the side. Vehan recognized them, these sidhe fae with their elaborate robes, expensive finery, jewels encrusting every inch they could afford. He'd met them on occasion at Court functions, previous Solstices, high-society parties. . . . These men, they were the king's private council—Celadon's now, and at the moment, none of them looked happy to be here.

It was Councillor Vrain who'd called his name, a short man much around Vehan's height, old by fae standards, with silvering hair and pale skin beginning to sag in the face. Vrain had been Lead Councillor to High King Azurean—only Lord Morayo and Commander Viridian-Verdell had ranked higher than him in Azurean's advisement—but the way he rounded on Vehan in a mixture of outrage and relief . . . Vrain could have been the High King himself.

"Your Highness—I beseech you, *arrest* this man; strip him of his crown! He's in no fit state to command a Court. Madness has consumed him. The High Queen—"

"Is his mother," Vehan finished, cutting the Councillor off midspeech. "And the one who appointed him as your king. So excuse me if, before I do any of all that, I first ask what's *going on here*?" Bewildered, he looked at Celadon. "Your Highness?" he prompted.

Something flexed across Celadon's face.

An emotion—Vehan couldn't pin it exactly, but he'd almost call it . . . fear? Anxiety? Relief, Vehan was almost certain, though he couldn't exactly say why. Regardless, it was quickly smothered back under the porcelain-perfect appearance of ease.

"Of course, Your Highness," Celadon replied with the incline of his head to Vehan. His voice was as steady and smooth and light as the silk that poured around him—every bit the king acclimatized to control. "I was just explaining to my council the special task I've set for them this evening."

He lifted his torch toward the hole in the wall just behind him, which Vehan had noticed upon entry, but only now for the first time with any real consideration.

Nothing stirred on its opposite side.

Darkness again, so thick over its interior he couldn't see anything of what that next room contained. But with that green-flame torch angled in its direction, the flame's light caught on something just beyond its mouth—a glint off an object that was small and round and gold.

"Rumor . . . gossip . . . legend . . . there isn't anyone in the Courts who hasn't heard that deep within the darkest bowls of High King Azurean's palace lurks a beast so old that time itself has nearly forgotten it." This was for Vehan's sake, he realized. What Celadon explained to him now, he'd clearly just finished illuminating to his council, given how their faces had already drained to the silvery paleness of shock. "Captured—some say by my father himself, others say by Thalo. The story has passed over so many tongues that its hero has worn many names. In one glorification, the beast was a menace employed by the terrible alchemist who once sought to overthrow us. In other lights, it was an evil my long-ago ancestors subdued and chained to our eternal service."

Celadon moved a step closer, allowing Vehan to see a bit better into the next room.

Gold.

Those objects weren't just gold in color but gold itself—*coins*. A scattering of coins, trailing off toward a shadowy heap concealed in the gloom. . . .

"It's a rare instance where truth is more fascinating than rumor," Celadon continued. "The sidhe fae swept in to colonize this land, bringing our religions over with it. Creatures followed. It was indeed my father who secured this one's service, but not out of might, not out of cunning or skill or grand heroism. No one captures an Elder Dragon—but they are, apparently, great opportunists."

An . . . Elder Dragon.

Celadon was suggesting an . . . *Elder Dragon* lived in there?

Vehan wanted to laugh, except no one else was. Even at the mention, the councillors' faces had blanched further, and that had to mean something . . . but an Elder Dragon?

Common dragons had nearly all died out.

So tuned with magic, so powerful in the art, most had adopted human or faerie guises as the world grew smaller, as folk began to hunt them into near extinction, turning their ability to shape-shift into a necessity for survival. Over time . . . with less and less space for them to shift back into their original shape without discovery . . . most had forgotten how. Most had forgotten they could, or that they'd ever been dragons at all, their children and their children's children unaware of the truth of who—what—they were.

An Elder Dragon . . . one of the first seven dragons that magic had ever birthed . . . It just wasn't possible.

Celadon turned abruptly back to them, his features cast in acidic severity by the green glow of the flame in his still raised hand. Formidable—but Celadon had always struck Vehan as the sort not to cross, even back before Celadon had realized how to wield this side of him, as apparently he had now.

"Azurean struck a deal with the beast that lies within. For its every desire, a very valuable service in exchange. I ask nothing of my private council that my own father had not when it had been *his* turn to establish rule," he said in unflinching austerity. "Dragons like their gold—apart from their obsession with precious things, it's heat conductive, far more so than copper or silver, making it the perfect place to nest for long periods of time. In exchange for domain in the Viridian hoard, for protection and secrecy and care, Gwyrdd has agreed to serve as a test for those who'd call themselves loyal to my family." His eyes flashed in the councillors' direction. "Lord Vrain has done this before—really, it's a simple task."

Celadon swept out a hand to his right, and it was then that Vehan noticed the pile of unlit torches beside him.

"Take up a torch. Enter the vault. Present yourself to Gwyrdd for judgment. Elder Dragons are uniquely suited to reading what lies in a person's heart; if Gwyrdd deems you true to the Viridian family, true to the legacy and values of its name, he will light your torch, and you will carry it back out here unscathed—just as I have done."

A powerful statement.

Vehan felt his chest swell a little with pride.

Because in one clean statement, Celadon had found a way to disprove the nastiness everyone believed of him—the Elder Dragon, Gwyrdd, wouldn't have lit his torch if he hadn't judged Celadon true to his father.

"Fail to prove yourself—to my family, to *me* as the rightful heir to the throne, blessed by Gwyrdd himself for the role—and it won't be the torch that the dragon ignites." He paused to stare down Councillor Vrain for a moment . . . two. . . . "I can't imagine why you should have anything to fear, my lord? You are, by your own fervent declaration, most devout to my family."

"To your *father*," Vrain exploded. Surging forward in his temper, he crowded Celadon's space, but Celadon didn't flinch, didn't blink. He simply stood, impassive and unshaken, as Vrain spat at his feet. "I supported the man who ruled this Court, not this painted-up doll playing king on his throne—puppet of our greatest rival. I follow *none* of her ilk, and High King Azurean will greet me in the afterlife with open arms for holding strong against his poison of a son!"

Celadon considered Vrain in silence a moment longer, which seemed to irritate him more. The Councillor looked about ready to launch into another tirade, determined to shake some emotion from the boy-king before him, but Celadon merely lifted his free hand and pointed to the stairwell.

"I'll force no one to take up this task who doesn't wish to. You did prove yourselves once, and normally once would be enough. But I find I do not trust my council as a king should, and if you will not renew your fealty to me, if you will not show proof that I am mistaken about the things you whisper behind my back, then you are free to go, Lord Vrain. But know if you do, you are stripped of your office, your rank, and your privilege in this Court. UnSeelie Spring may remain your home, but you have no place in *mine*."

"You're just like your mother," Vrain hissed.

And surprisingly, Celadon grinned. "Then I'd be very careful if I were you. Because neither of them—Reseda *nor* Riadne—would stand idly by while you scream insults in their face. You may remove yourself now, Percides Vrain."

Vehan watched with the other councillors as Vrain's mouth fell closed. As his further vitriol warred with the reminder that Celadon was no longer the inconsequential boy they thought they knew but a proper king . . . and one whose legacy, though only just beginning, was already steeped in considerable blood.

His wariness having won out, Vrain gathered up the mass of his robes. In a flurry of anger, he stormed for the stairwell, knocking against Vehan's shoulder as he went.

"*Pathetic,*" he growled under his breath, and Vehan glared at him, but the former Councillor was nothing more than barbed words at this point.

He disappeared up the stairs.

"You're free to follow," Celadon added a beat later to the remaining councillors, who all exchanged nervous looks with one another.

Two decided there was no way they were coming out of that chamber alive. With diverted gazes, they bowed to Celadon, mumbled their resignations, and fled far more quietly back up the stairs after Vrain.

Four remained.

One was shaking so badly that Vehan wondered if maybe he simply couldn't move to join the others in departure.

"I'll go first," Vehan announced, surprising even himself.

Not with his determination but with how steady and clear his own voice was, like he'd meant all along to do this, the reason he'd come in the first place.

He stepped forward, set the already lit torch in his hand carefully on the ground, and selected another from the pile.

Everyone watched him with wide eyes. Even Celadon seemed taken aback.

"You . . . don't have to," he said in a much gentler tone, dropping his pageantry for all of a second to allow the genuine, not-much-older-than-Vehan boy to show through. "Vehan, that torch you brought down here wouldn't have stayed lit in your hand if you meant me harm."

Ah, that would explain the relief he'd glimpsed in Celadon earlier.

Vehan stared at him—his older brother.

They didn't look all that alike; Vehan was Vadrien's son through and through. But it struck him then—suddenly, powerfully. "Yeah," he murmured, slightly breathless. He'd always, always wanted a sibling, back when he'd been *so alone*, and all through when Aurelian had been caught up in pretending he didn't care. "I'm still going to do it. What's a little healthy competition between brothers, hmm?"

He couldn't describe the flicker in Celadon's expression.

He didn't want to.

It would stay between them; Vehan would carry it to his grave. One lonely, scared heart that just wanted family to another.

Celadon nodded and took a step back. "Very well—good luck, then."

Gripping his unlit torch tightly, Vehan approached the vault.

He couldn't linger on the threshold. If he hesitated, he might rethink what he was about to do. On the one hand, how many people could say they'd ever seen a dragon in their lifetime, let alone one of the near-extinct Elders? On the other hand, Vehan's own mother had been responsible for so much pain in the Viridian family that Gwyrdd might take his approach as an insult and roast him alive out of sheer indignation.

It was fifty-fifty.

By Urielle he hoped he'd made the right choice.

Over the threshold Vehan stepped.

It was so dark inside this chamber that he couldn't say with any certainty how big it actually was. But the echo of his footsteps over-head suggested a *high* arching ceiling and wide-flung walls.

Sound seemed to suffocate as soon as he crossed into this second cavern. Like stepping through into a completely separate dimension, Vehan was wholly cut off from Celadon and the others.

Nothing moved in this cavern.

Nothing breathed.

There was no slither of scales or sway in the air of some great, uncoiling behemoth like he thought he'd find.

The only pictures he'd seen of Elder Dragons had been sketches in research journals, imaginings in fantasies. It had been so long since the folk had ever seen one that most believed they'd never existed. . . .

I promise you, Little Lightning Prince, I am very much real.

Vehan yelped in surprise.

It wasn't at all a dignified sound, especially for a prince who fan-cied himself brave. But the voice rumbled like thunder. It was almost too much, too loud to bear, and he nearly dropped his torch in the desire to clasp his hands over his ears to muffle it . . . but the words had been spoken in his head.

The Elder Dragon, wherever he lurked, chuckled in amusement.

I do like the pure-hearted ones.

Vehan didn't know whether to take that as a compliment or an insult.

He also didn't know if the dragon wanted him to reply.

"Uh . . . hello, dragon. Your . . . Elderness, sir."

Goodness, the dragon lamented dryly.

He was going to eat him.

Vehan drew a breath, dropped his shoulders and straightened his back, and reminded himself of all the frightening things he'd ever done in his life. He could survive facing one more. "Elder Dragon," he announced in a much calmer tone, "I come before you to prove my loyalty to the Viridian family. I offer you this torch for judgment and ask that if you deem my heart true, light it with your fire."

Little Lightning Prince . . .

The ground began to quake. Vehan was forced to widen his stance, shift his weight with each ripple of force through the stone as finally the Elder Dragon betrayed his location.

A massive body unwound before him and slithered across the mountainous heap of gold at Vehan's feet, raining coins with delicate clinking to the ground.

He couldn't see Gwyrdd, but even the air shuddered with its movement, groaned as enormous wings spread wide. The cavern had to be even bigger than Vehan had imagined, and so too was this dragon.

Instinct drew him a step back, made him grit his teeth against the desire to flee when the dragon inhaled a breath like a building hurricane. He could see it then, only a portion, only a shadowy outline, but as the dragon breathed in, heat glowed in its enormous chest—green fire that shone in the fissures between its scales.

The glow was Vehan's only warning.

The next moment, the dragon breathed out, and with his exhale came fire so hot he would almost swear he could feel his skin boil—but the flame curled around him, didn't touch him at all. Instead, it spread to other torches mounted on the surrounding walls, igniting them to eerie life.

Vehan had closed his eyes against the onslaught, but when the heat receded and the green against his eyelids faded back to black, he chanced a peek.

It was not the flaming torch in his hand that immediately snatched Vehan's gaze.

The room, now illuminated, did indeed run deep. The gold piled before him . . . He'd never seen so much in his life, but none of it was what made his mouth fall open.

Gwyrdd the Elder Dragon was . . . Vehan's brain failed at adjectives. The dragon was *big*. Rich emerald green fading to a pale jade belly, he glinted in the firelight, the pieces of gold that had lodged themselves into and melded with his scales catching every leap of the flame.

Teeth the size of a fully grown man lined his open maw. . . .

A tail barbed with lethal spikes curled like a cat's behind him. . . .

You have already passed my judgment—that's not why you entered my chamber. What called you to me has nothing to do with a loyalty you already well know.

Vehan took another step backward.

That curling tail struck wicked fast, slamming to the ground behind him, sealing the exit shut.

Little Lightning Prince . . . Vehan Lysterne. I should be insulted you seek to use me as a test of the mettle you hope to wield against a greater foe. Perhaps one day I will get to meet this mother who so frightens you.

There was no time to pick apart the dragon's words—it lunged for him.

What was he meant to do here? He didn't understand.

Gold scattered, a waterfall of tinkling, as the dragon's teeth snapped in Vehan's face.

Only barely did he clear certain death by throwing himself to the side, tucking himself small to roll out of harm's way. He had to be careful of his torch—if it extinguished by accident, the dragon probably wouldn't light it a second time, and Vehan would be forced to leave the chamber without the proof of loyalty he needed.

But was it his escape the dragon wanted?

Did Vehan have to earn his exit from this place?

Gwyrdd lunged once more, his entire behemoth strength sending him straight for Vehan, and once again all Vehan could do was just barely manage to roll out of the way.

Do you plan on evading your way out of this room?

It was as good a plan as any. Vehan *could* maybe roll his way around this cavern and eventually make it to the exit—but that tail. No matter where the dragon went, that tail remained a barricade.

Another lunge, another snap of teeth—Vehan dove. He dove again. And again.

Gwyrdd's jaw chased him from one side of the chamber to the

243

other. When his teeth proved insufficient, he resorted to fireballs, and Vehan's journey back to the cavern's mouth diverted this way and that to avoid them.

If he could just reach the exit, getting past the tail had an easy solution. He'd been practicing so hard lately, and Riadne kept him topped to full on lightning that *sparked* in his core right now, guzzling adrenaline like fuel. . . .

Kill it.

The Not-Vehan voice of Ruin crooned in his ear, stirring with the excitement.

*Kill it—you could. And maybe then
your mother might love you.
The way she loves your brother.*

Kill it . . .

Vehan rolled to a stop and straightened.

Kill the dragon. . . . That's what it had always been—slay the dragon, emerge victorious, and become the classic fairy-tale hero. But Vehan . . . he didn't take lives. That had never been his strength. He wasn't like his mother, or even like his father, champion of the Goblin Wars.

Vehan was . . .

It flashed before him, the memory of Celadon back in the cave, the way Vrain had snapped his teeth in his brother's face and Celadon hadn't swayed.

Vehan wasn't a killer.

He hadn't come here to become one.

He'd come here to be exactly who he'd always been—a good friend, a loyal person, *brave* when no one else could be, in a way far different from shows of physical strength. He'd come to be what a prince

244

should be, resolutely good in the face of everything otherwise . . . so Vehan turned around.

Aurelian would kill him all over again when they met each other in the afterlife, but Vehan turned.

Just in time to meet the dragon's teeth closing with a deadly *shiiiiink* at the tip of his nose.

Possibly, Vehan fainted.

Possibly, he died the moment he'd entered this room and this entire scenario was his mind's entertainment while his soul drifted in wait for the Hunt's collection.

Impossibly, nothing happened.

Vehan stood.

The dragon stood too.

The mettle he'd need against his mother wasn't the means to become her. . . . All Vehan needed was to be himself.

Remember what it is that truly makes you strong, Fate had told him.

And finally he understood.

Very good, Little Lightning Prince.

The tail fell away from the door.

Remember that in what's to come.

He exited the chamber.

"What are you doing, Celadon?" he asked later, when it was just him and his brother alone in the cave, the remaining four councillors facing their judgment. "With this task . . . with all those new attendants up there . . . the remodeling. Are you okay?"

Celadon nodded. There was a softness to his expression now that it was just the two of them.

"I think I might actually be," he replied. "But first I need to rebuild this Court. First I need a trusted inner circle. To survive life as the Head of UnSeelie folk . . . to survive Riadne . . ." There it was, at last. Confirmation. They served the same side—Vehan nodded his silent agreement.

"If it's people you can trust you're looking for, I'd like to point out that Theodore thinks the world of you, you know?"

Cocking his head, Celadon considered him.

Vehan continued. "He saved your life back at that arena. He was the one who ran in to beg the Madam to intervene, and when she wouldn't, that was *his* dagger that killed your opponent. Theodore actually likes you. I've known him for a while now, enough to say that he doesn't ever give anyone more than a piece of his truth to hold. Bits and threads . . . that's all he lets anyone learn, but when it comes to you . . . it's just, a lot of people have their claws in Theodore. Whatever his full picture is, I think he'd actually *choose* to be loyal to you—that is, of course, if you could somehow get him out of this competition Mother's set him to that he's never going to win."

Still Celadon looked at him, silent in thought. Then . . . "You might be right."

Vehan nodded. "One more thing," he added, firm but low. "Cards on the table, I'm going to help you. Any way I can. I'm in this now. I wasn't before. I couldn't believe . . . but I see it now, and I'm not leaving anyone alone against our mother. And if it comes down to war . . ." He paused a moment, weighing how best to word this.

This thing he'd been keeping to himself ever since he'd begun pushing the depths of what he'd thought had been the capacity of his magical core.

"She expects you've inherited a great deal of power. She doesn't expect that of me. Not yet. If it comes down to war, I *will* be a valuable weapon to you."

Only one Councillor emerged victorious from the Elder Dragon's lair—the one who'd been a quivering mess, and who now looked wholly shocked with himself, as if in disbelief that he'd actually been true.

"Thank you, Lord Kim." Celadon smiled, recovering instantly from his conversation with Vehan and accepting Lord Kim's torch.

And just before the three of them ventured back up the stairwell,

Vehan quite happy to put this place well behind him, he paused. Took hold of the back of Celadon's robe. "She needs you, you know? Don't forget the person who's been by your side from the very beginning."

"I haven't," Celadon replied in soft contrition. "I promise, I haven't forgotten Arlo—and not you either . . . little brother."

CHAPTER 14

Celadon

~⌐~

CELADON BURST THROUGH THE door of his chambers, shedding his robes as he went. He pitched his onyx crown on a table in passing, rained jewelry on the plush sage carpeting. Three fae had died today—three of his council, three men he'd known his entire life—and it had been Gwyrdd who'd delivered their end, but their blood was on Celadon's hands.

Through his main sitting room, into his office—Celadon slammed his palms flat on the wooden surface of his desk and breathed.

Inhale . . . exhale . . . he'd done what he had to. He'd done what his own father would have done. Those men had been conspiring against him, might have just as easily come for Celadon's life . . . and he'd given them the chance to walk away from it all. They could have followed Vrain, but they'd chosen their path. So then why did Celadon feel like throwing up?

King Celadon Viridian-Lysterne—

Celadon's gaze caught on a letter, recently delivered.

It hadn't been here this morning, but he recognized it instantly, exactly the same as the dozens of others he'd received, all from the same person.

Snatching it off his desk, he didn't bother to read it—didn't need to, he knew what it was: a reminder of what he'd won at the Grim Colosseum, where Theodore had tricked him into participation, undoubtedly on behalf of the Madam, the woman in command of the magical underworld's more dangerous criminal organization, the Grim Brotherhood.

—reminder of the audience you're entitled to, as Champion of the Ring . . .

He'd won against Jerald, the troll-sized faerie man he'd been pitted against in that life-or-death cage match he'd practically wandered into off the streets. It had taken *everything* in Celadon to make it out alive, and still he might not have if it hadn't been for an intervention he'd thought had been Lethe's alone.

The dagger that had shot through a narrow chink in that cage . . . He'd thought it had been his father's Hunter, but then daggers had never been Lethe's modus operandi. Lethe was silver claws and a deadly sword.

Theodore, though . . . Could he recall ever having seen him with a weapon?

And if Vehan was right, if it *had* been the Reynolds heir who'd saved him when it had been his fault Celadon had been there to begin with . . .

His original impression of Theodore had been happy subservience to the Madam's whims. But at least something Vehan had said was irrefutable—no one really had the full scope of who Theodore truly was. Bits and pieces, parceled out at his choosing . . . ?

What if . . .

"Do you live here now?" Celadon asked hotly, pulling himself out of his thoughts to crumple the envelope in his hand and pitch it into a nearby bin.

He didn't need to turn to know who lurked on the corner sofa but did so anyhow.

One long leg bent to rest at an angle over his knee, arms flung wide along the sofa's back, Lethe peered at him through unfairly thick lashes even Celadon would have to use fakes to match. "Should I have someone make up a room for you?"

Lethe cocked his head at him. "I've lived here for over a hundred years, kingling. Technically, this palace is more *my* home than yours."

"I'm not in the mood, Lethe." Celadon frowned. "What do you want?"

Ignoring the question, Lethe stood.

Meandered his way around the room to Celadon.

He stopped to toy with the lamp on an end table; to drag his claws through the spines of several books on a shelf, slicing them clean in half. When he finally came to a halt in front of him, Celadon rolled his eyes.

Friendship with Lethe—if that's what this was—was a bit like owning a feral cat that seemed to actively hate you until it wanted something like food or attention, when its disposition briefly turned to begrudging tolerance.

How long before Lethe got bored and tried to trip him on his way down the stairs for amusement?

"What?" Celadon repeated, staring up at the grinning face, all angles and starlight and too-sharp teeth. He looked . . .

It wasn't often Lethe stood this close; Celadon's attention snagged on a curious detail. "Do you wear a glamour?"

It was something about Lethe's ears.

The telltale sign of magic . . . However better an immortal could bend their illusions, there was always a hint of tampering. Lethe's ears, a little more webbed than fae pointed, seemed strangely . . . *dull* in comparison to the rest of him. That was the best Celadon could describe it. Everything else about Lethe glowed, struck, sliced, pierced, but these ears . . . they were just ears. Stuffed into the mold of a fae's.

Quirking a brow, Lethe pressed a step closer into Celadon's space. He liked doing this.

An intimidation tactic so many would flinch from, but Celadon recognized it instantly—he did the same thing himself. Intimidation not because Lethe wanted to pose a threat; intimidation because Lethe himself needed the reminder that he was one.

It was how Celadon had held his ground so long against siblings that hated him and a Court that had always accused him of being *too much* of all the wrong things.

"Of course I do." He breathed an unkind laugh in Celadon's face. "We all do. Even the darling Dark Star. It's part of the treaty—did you really not know? This is for *your* benefit." He fluttered his lashes, drew his grin even wider across his face. "Would you like to see how I really look?"

Celadon sighed.

Nothing productive would come from poking at Lethe in his current mood, in *Celadon's* current mood, which seemed to be angling for a fight that the Hunter before him wouldn't hesitate to give. Maybe that's why he felt like pushing buttons? Miserably, pathetically, he knew Lethe would punish him the way he deserved and absolve Celadon from what he'd just done.

"Will you come with me to the Luminous Palace?" he asked instead.

Lethe paused.

He blinked at Celadon, then wrinkled his nose and withdrew back into his own space and sighed out deeply in displeasure. Was he bored? Apparently, he'd been angling for a fight as well—for *amusement.* Well, Celadon could still deliver on that, if not in the way he'd been hoping.

It was time to return.

Time at last to face what stalked his nightmares.

He couldn't truly rebuild his foundations into something stronger, sustainable, not with this hesitation fluttering inside him every time he so much as thought about stepping through that Egress once more and out into radiant light.

It was time. He hadn't planned on it at all, hadn't intended for this to be the way he ended the day—what he really wanted was to draw a hot bath and let himself soak in perfumed steam until the tension from earlier finally released him. He didn't want to confront Riadne. He didn't want to face Arlo. But Vehan had happened, and it was something about seeing him for the first time since the Crowning down in Gwyrdd's pit that needled at Celadon—an insistence.

It was time.

He'd put this off long enough.

Vehan, his younger brother—that was a new shift in dynamics he still couldn't wrap himself around fully, but seeing him again hadn't been the horrific ordeal he'd been building up inside his head. It had been more like taking a breath of fresh air after weeks of stale confinement.

His world hadn't ended.

There'd been no dramatics—not anything outside of Celadon's own devising, at least.

The wound in his heart hadn't torn open to fatal, bleeding out in a flood of sorrow and pain and misplaced anger.

Seeing Vehan had been good, and it was time.

"Please," he repeated softer. "Come with me."

"To your *mother's*."

"Yes."

Another pause. Lethe continued to look at him like he genuinely couldn't figure out what he wanted to do in this situation. Celadon could sympathize. "I recall informing you I'm not a taxi," he replied at last.

Swallowing back a sigh of frustration, Celadon maintained his ease. "I didn't ask you to take me. I asked you to come along *with*."

That only seemed to offend Lethe more. "I'm not your pet, either," he snarled, and goodness but Celadon was well aware.

"And nor was it a command."

No one had known what to do with Celadon's sudden arrival at the Luminous Palace. They hadn't been expecting him, and even though he was a Head of Court, if it weren't for the fact that the High Queen was his mother, propriety dictated he place the same request for invitation just like everyone else.

He'd been prepared to make apologies. To see to his own needs and not trouble anyone—didn't particularly want the fuss, besides. But stepping through the Egress and out into the enormous white marble room that housed it had taken him immediately back to earlier this summer, just as he'd feared it would.

To before his entire world had changed.

To a time when he had felt so much *less* as if he were drowning.

This chamber was a stark reminder of just how *different* everything was now in so short a space of time—and yet, for all that had happened . . . the marble, the tiny carvings of lightning bolts and suns, the corridors running off through numerous arches in the walls . . . all of it. It was all still exactly the same.

Much like seeing Vehan again, the hurt wasn't as bad has he'd been anticipating. But still . . . Celadon paused.

To acknowledge the feelings. The past. The pain. And finally take the step toward putting it behind him.

It didn't take long for the guards to swoop in. Attendants were quickly summoned. No one wanted to get too close—Lethe might have condescended to tagging along, but he stood like a scowling shadow at Celadon's back, towering over him, promising death to anyone who so much as looked at him too long.

One moment, Celadon stood blinking up at the glass-dome ceiling; the next, he was out in the hall, following a fae he didn't recognize dressed in rather splendid cream robes.

The palace was a flurry of activity. Apparently the Reverdie wasn't the only place seeing renovation.

As the new High Queen, after all, Riadne was forced to accommodate everything that entailed.

Celadon passed by numerous folk busy with mapping out reconstruction for whole wings. Offices would need to be installed, new quarters for the Falchion, and public amenities that put a bit of a smirk on his face to imagine—something about their new High Queen was incongruous with an in-house Starbucks, but these were all things she'd inherited with the Crown she'd wanted so much.

They passed briefly by the main foyer, already thrumming with traffic.

The iron staircase leading up from the entry landing had remained untouched by the construction around it. Soon, though, Riadne would have to come up with some additional form of parlor trick there, to catch the folk's awe upon arrival through an entrance that needed updating, too.

He didn't envy Riadne one bit.

The reason his father had chosen to make the Palace of Spring accessible by street was because setting up official, constantly regulated portals out around the city had been a waste of time and resources and effort—but it was exactly what Riadne would have to do if she didn't want to pick up her palace altogether and move it someplace else.

"High Prince Cela—"

"Your Highne—"

"Please, Your Grace, a . . . a moment . . ."

As soon as they broke out into the corridor that led to the High Queen's throne room, Celadon was accosted by the folk in line for audience.

An . . . extremely long line.

And yes, he'd heard about this, too.

Riadne didn't waste much time on public audiences, not yet at least, which wasn't uncommon. She wasn't the first High Sovereign to take a moment to establish herself in her new role. But as with any change, the people were anxious. They flocked in droves to Riadne's doorstep, for help, for curiosity, for affirmation they'd be cared for at least as much as they were used to.

It was only about midday. How long had these people been standing in line to be so agitated already?

"Stand back," said his guide with great importance; he clearly relished this particular facet of his duty. "Make way for the High Prince."

"Oh!" Celadon exclaimed. "No, I'll wait. These people were here before me."

His guide looked . . . nonplussed, to put it kindly. "Your Highness, that isn't the way . . ."

And like a dam, the people's reservations broke, giving way to smiles and waves and a bursting forth of questions, many not even about what brought them here today, but kinder things of how he was doing; condolences for the passing of his father; votes of confidence in Celadon's rule as UnSeelie Spring's new king. It had absolutely been Lethe giving them pause—the number of times their gazes flickered to his face, only for them to pale and even tremble; one had broken into tears.

But Lethe had done nothing.

Said nothing.

Celadon supposed he was used to such reactions. Instead of interest, when Celadon stole a glimpse at him over his shoulder, he found Lethe using his claw to whittle away at a piece of marble he'd picked up at some point in their journey here.

It was . . . the most mundane the Hunter had ever been in Celadon's presence.

He didn't seem to be paying attention to anything around him at all.

"Your Highness," said a young faerie mother—timid, with dishwater-blond hair and a mouse's ears. In her arms she held a colicky baby, so impossibly small and frail that Celadon feared he might break in her hold. "Please, can I ask . . . my son, he's *so* ill. There's a potion that would cure him completely, but in order to make it . . . I've heard Her Majesty, your mother, was lenient on the practice of alchemy. Your Grace, please . . . He's the only thing I have left in this world. His father passed just this last winter, and I don't want to lose my son, too."

"Citizen, *step back*." Celadon's guide was ruffled. "You are not to accost the High Prince. You will save your requests for—"

"This is what he does."

It wasn't Celadon who'd spoken, though he'd just been about to remind this attendant of his place.

It wasn't any of the other folk around them.

It was *Lethe* who'd intervened. And only when stunned silence wore on longer than a minute did he look up from the smoothening globe of his marble project to find his comment had drawn attention from everyone within hearing.

Narrowing his acid eyes at Celadon, he bristled indignation, as though it were *his* fault for this attention. "Over a hundred years," he reminded Celadon pointedly, harkening back to their earlier conversation of how long Lethe had been at the Palace of UnSeelie Spring. "Unfortunately, I *have* had to witness your disgusting sympathy, skiving off classes in favor of sitting with folk in your father's foyer"—he paused to shiver for effect, pulling an expression of extreme distaste—"*listening* to their inane problems."

He bent back to his carving.

Everyone stared a moment longer.

At last Celadon turned back to his guide. "Thank you, Lord . . ."

"Y-Yarrow, Your Highness."

"Thank you, Lord Yarrow. I'll be fine from here." Between his mother ahead of him and Lethe at his back, whittling away at what looked like some pockmarked orb, he liked his odds against anyone who might wish harm on him here.

Lord Yarrow bowed—looking not all that pleased to be so dismissed but unable to refuse Celadon his wishes—and fell back silent to the sidelines.

Leaving Celadon to wait, and . . . exactly as Lethe had said, do what he'd been doing for years.

One of the few things he actually liked about his position of High Royalty: he *enjoyed* personal connections. Meeting with people his father couldn't, listening to their problems, and if it was within his power (sometimes even when it wasn't), helping to fix them, or at least ease their sting until High King Azurean could lend better aid.

True as he'd assured, when it came time for the faerie mother and her son to meet with the High Queen, she was granted permission to save her boy by alchemic means. *Tell her exactly what you told me, my lady*, he'd said gently. *That you're simply a mother who'd do anything it took to save her son; I promise you, the queen won't ignore that.*

And his mother hadn't.

The faerie woman gushed a tearful thanks to him on her way back out, causing Lethe to roll his eyes and say something scathing about *bleeding hearts* making for short-lived reigns, but Celadon ignored him. It was his turn now, after all—the first time he'd be speaking directly to Riadne since her Crowning.

He drew a breath to steady his nerves.

As it was nearing nightfall now, the line cut off at him for the day, so he hoped his mother was in as agreeable a mood as she could be for what he wanted to speak about. . . .

The throne room doors opened.

Celadon took a step forward only to pause again in surprise.

"Celadon!" Riadne chimed, bright and tinkling and warm.

Arms spread wide, she made her way toward him, already halfway across the room, because of course she'd known he was here—that wasn't what had caught him up short. The slivered points of her high heels clicked on the glass floor like a building war drum. Her eyes sparked with delight. His whole life, Celadon had known his mother mostly through pictures and social gatherings, and she'd always presented a picture of poise, a radiant idol of fae beauty, austere and forbidding as the ice in her heritage.

Never had he seen her so genuinely *happy*.

"My son." She beamed.

When she reached him, she clasped his face between her hands, that smile only growing wider as she looked him deep in the eye. "You're finally adjusting."

He didn't need to ask what she meant. Undoubtedly, she'd already heard about what happened this morning with his councillors.

"I see you've finally deigned to grace me with your presence," Riadne added in a far cooler tone to Lethe. Her blue eyes flashed a warning that despite her joy to see Celadon, she wouldn't spare her Hunter an inch. "Perhaps you might find it within yourself to share *where you've been?*"

She . . . didn't know?

She really hadn't been the one to sic Lethe on him? He'd been popping in and out of the Reverdie so often Celadon did actually wonder if he should set up quarters for him. He'd be sprawled out on a couch reading when Celadon walked into a room; he'd poke around Celadon's things, asking odd and random questions about them, like in all his years here he still didn't grasp the modern mortal world all that clearly and was . . . curious to learn. And it had all been strangely easy—like falling back in with a long-ago close companion.

A part of Celadon had been convinced this was Riadne's way of keeping tabs on him, but if she really didn't know . . .

In a blink Lethe had whisked around him.

Before anyone could act—the guards on the sidelines, Riadne herself—and not that anyone would dare, he had the soft of her throat by the fine point of an adamantine claw.

And Celadon had forgotten . . .

Lethe had been almost subdued around him, as *normal* as someone like him could be.

He'd forgotten how mean this Hunter could turn—how people were right to fear him.

"Remember who you're speaking to, my queen."

Blue welled in a bead over the claw's deadly point, oozed brightly down its gleaming silver.

And several things happened at once—

"Lethe . . . ," Celadon warned.

"Mother?" hedged a new voice behind them.

Riadne knocked that hand away, and Lethe creaked a laugh like

258

old wood, fell back from his queen only to grin at her from the sidelines as he licked her blood from his finger like a threat.

It was Vehan who'd joined them.

His younger brother had looked a little frazzled when he'd turned up at the Palace of Spring earlier. Celadon could see the fatigue in him; whatever Riadne had him doing, there was much on his plate, but it didn't seem to bother Riadne any that Vehan looked exhausted right now, ready to drop, leaner than even a month ago when he was already practically muscle and bone.

His current attire—pale gray jogging pants and a tight white tee, all of it damp with humidity and sweat—suggested he'd just been pulled from a run.

In an instant, Riadne had recovered—oh, she'd no doubt try to find *some* way to punish Lethe for the reminder that there was still one person in this realm she'd never control . . . and maybe Lethe should be a little more wary. If Riadne couldn't break something down and remake it to her use, she'd already proven how far she'd go to wipe it off her board.

"Vehan," she greeted, a touch stonily. "Good. I thought it would be nice if the three of us spent some time together before dinner this evening, as a family. And I have just the activity."

She threw out a hand, snapped her fingers. "Hunter, I require transport."

For a moment Celadon feared that it might have been directed at Lethe.

But a plume of black—not quite smoke, not quite ink—bled into the air at Riadne's back. Celadon knew it as what manifested the Wild Hunt once summoned.

It was Eris who stepped out of the cloud of night, which fell around him and settled into his starry Hunter's robes. As leader, of course it would be; Eris was expected to directly attend the High Sovereign, to keep to their side unless sent specifically from it. All other orders were delegated through him to the rest of his troop.

He didn't pause to acknowledge Lethe, or Celadon even, just swept himself into a bow of greeting at his queen's feet.

And Riadne paid him no attention.

She closed the gap between herself and her sons, clasping a shoulder each and drawing them to her. As she did, Eris dissolved once more; black exploded around them, filling Celadon's senses, cool and fluid against his skin. He had to fight the instinct in his brain that panicked he was suffocating, being buried alive, all manner of uncomfortable things inspired by the way darkness *squeezed* around him.

And then, as suddenly as it had enveloped him . . .

"I will hand it to your father, Celadon." Riadne's voice was quieter than it had been in her throne room, almost hushed, as though to match the pitch of night around them. "As far as human cities go, he could have chosen worse than Toronto."

Wind swept through Celadon's hair, fluttered the length of his silk robe.

He looked out at the city.

Eris had transported them to the very top of Toronto's city hall—two towering buildings built like brackets, each curving toward the other at one end, the opposite end spread wide as though to cradle the courtyard below, where giant letters spelled out TORONTO. Sandwiched between an equally large maple leaf and the Indigenous Medicine Wheel, together their neon-glowing light bathed the sprawling pool of water at its base.

It was nothing like what Riadne would be more accustomed to in Las Vegas, but Celadon agreed—the city *was* beautiful; especially so high up, and looking out across the jeweled darkness that blanketed its spires.

"Mother," said Celadon, before whatever she had planned could waylay any further what he wanted to ask—the reason he'd come to her before *Arlo*, whom he wanted to see infinitely more. "I would like to request something."

He turned to face her, to square himself and stand tall. He didn't know his mother all that well, he realized, but what little he did suggested she'd respect his confidence far more than timidity.

Riadne didn't turn to meet him, but she did angle her chin slightly more his way. "I hear you've been busy. An entire council to replace . . . my." It was the barest curl to the corner of her mouth, but Celadon saw it.

Something he'd never seen before.

Reseda had never embraced him as her son, and even after Celadon had worked out that the reason was that he *wasn't* her son, the rejection had still hurt. But here was Riadne, a terrible woman who'd done terrible things and plotted even more . . . Was he truly so pathetically desperate for maternal affection that the pride in that hint of a smile made him *happy*?

"What would you ask of me?"

"I would like to have Theodore Reynolds."

Riadne turned to him now, her expression instantly shrewd. "Your reason?"

Celadon held his ground, maintained his ease as though he weren't attempting to pull one over on a woman notoriously two steps ahead of any given plot.

From Riadne's other side, and pretending very much not to care, Vehan stiffened.

To business, then.

"Prince Theodore . . . likes me. We get along well. I know you suspect his ties are to the Grim Brotherhood—"

"—an accusation I will not make without irrefutable proof," Riadne cut in sharply, a strategist to the core.

The Grim Brotherhood was capable of many things, controlled many things. Most important to the aristocracy was the wealth that ran through the Brotherhood's channels. Nearly every Head of Court sat in the Madam's debt in some way or another, and Riadne might now possess a magical stone that produced gold, but if she called out Theodore on suspicion alone and it turned out his master *wasn't* the

261

Madam . . . there were a great many ways the Grim Brotherhood could complicate the foundations Riadne was trying to build right now, even more with the public provocation.

Riadne was a patient woman.

There would be no war until she was ready for it.

Celadon nodded. "And neither will I. But Theodore likes me, and as you said, I have a council to replace. I'm also willing to bet it would be much easier to catch him off guard in a place where his walls aren't built up so high."

Chiming a laugh, Riadne regarded him anew—there was that hint of pride again. "You would spy on the spy? You would betray a friend to execution? Oh, Celadon." She reached out to clasp his shoulder, the grip this time a little tighter, fingers digging sharply into his flesh. "We've a long way to go before I earn that sort of devotion from you, and while I commend the strength you showed in pruning the rot from your garden today, you've also a heart still too soft for genuine *cruelty.*"

Gritting his teeth, steeling his nerves, Celadon matched his mother's icy stare. "You mistake me, Mother. I had no plans on handing over whatever information I learn. If it somehow comes to light that Theodore is who we both suspect, it would be a good bargaining chip . . . one Head of Court to another."

Now, *that* made her happy.

"I see. How would you pay for this demand, exactly? You want Prince Theodore on your council, in your pocket? He's mine; it amuses me to keep him around, and he isn't doing a terrible job of making life entertaining. What will you give me for him? I wonder."

"I figured I'd leave the pricing to you."

Riadne considered him.

A moment . . . two . . .

"Do you know why I brought you up here, boys?"

Drawn now into the conversation, Vehan shook his head. Celadon did as well. Wordlessly, she stalked to the rooftop ledge. Wind rippled through her white sheer cloak, tossed it around her snow-white leather-clad legs and knee-high heeled boots.

She lifted a hand out before her.

The air around them *groaned.*

Riadne Lysterne was a powerful fae, was one of the rare few of the electricborn sidhe to ever register as a Class Four wielder. Celadon had grown up hearing what that sort of ability could do, but armed now with her Bone Crown and three Sins to bolster her magical strength . . .

Riadne curled her fingers into a fist, and like a wave was crashing over the city, Toronto dimmed to absolute black.

The streetlights, the sign down below, buildings, cars, anything running, anything producing light, all of it blew out like a flame on a candle.

Out and out the wave poured in all directions, the entirety of the GTA falling at her feet—nearly three thousand miles when even the strongest fae could command only a few hundred.

If it spanned any farther, Celadon couldn't tell from here, and Riadne didn't even seem impressed with herself as she should be— didn't seem bothered, either, by the shouts and cries down below, the crashes and cacophony of accidents and injuries. Those were ambulances caught in her display . . . hospitals . . . life-saving machines humans depended on, and even many folk . . .

"Vehan's Classification Exam is soon at hand," she carried on. "A matter of weeks. He's been hard at practice, and his tutors all agree he's easily a Three. Vehan," she called, dropping her hand. None of the light below was resorted. "Show me the progress you've made."

And Vehan nodded—darted for the rooftop's ledge as well.

It wasn't like he could refuse this command, this *exercise in familial bonding*, and Celadon felt a rush of protective anger flood him. A fool could see how eager he was to please Riadne, to earn her esteem, to be acknowledged by her. It was Reseda all over again, and the kindhearted young man that Vehan had grown to be, despite every-thing working against that outcome, deserved better.

But exactly as his mother had done, Vehan extended a hand.

A moment . . . two . . .

It took just a little longer, but another wave groaned through the air, and power was restored to the city. Block by block, lamp by lamp, Toronto winked back to life on and on and . . .

Stuttered out completely.

All of it, back to black.

"Sorry, Mother," Vehan murmured, rubbing the back of his head. "I'm tired."

Riadne sighed. Irritation flexed in her jaw. "A Three's reach." She rounded on Celadon. "Your brother nearly had it. Show him how it's done. Wield electric magic for me, Celadon, and Prince Theodore will be yours."

Celadon stared.

It was all he could do in the freezing grip of sudden panic.

Fear iced his veins—wield *this* magic? Magic that shouldn't be his, except was. Magic he wanted to ignore, push down, snuff out, hoped would die out on its own like a withered plant denied water and light.

The only time he'd ever shown even a hint of electric control had been in the Grim Brotherhood's Colosseum. Class One wielding at best, that's all he'd ever demonstrated, and even that had been enough to terrify him. Because even that was enough to mark him dangerous, deadly, most of all to himself.

The same as it had come over him during Riadne's Crowning, the thought returned: *How much longer?*

If he used this magic, if he acknowledged what raged deep inside him . . . how long would he have before it consumed him?

He couldn't do this and keep his secrets.

He couldn't do this and keep himself safe.

But there would be no leaving here until he tried, so Celadon lifted a trembling hand, clenched it into a fist.

He couldn't do this.

He didn't want to.

Fear and anger warred inside him just as viciously as his conflicting thoughts.

Mirroring what Vehan had done, he closed his eyes, focused his core. Essentially, it was magic he'd access in the same way he reached for wind, and oh, but he could feel it sparking, down in those depths where he very much wanted to keep it, but Celadon forced himself to grab ahold of it.

Through all that fear and anger, he unfurled his fingers with extreme reluctance, and here it would be, confirmation that he'd inherited yet more power that only made him a liability to his own damned survival. Another step toward death that loomed behind his eyelids like the hanging, limp corpses of his mutilated family.

He couldn't do this—he *willed* that electricity into the tips of his fingers, and tears stung hot in his firmly shut eyes.

A moment passed.

At first, nothing.

But not long after, the air began to croon with the force of what happened next.

Power burst out in a rippling effect—the city ignited back to life, mile after mile after hundreds of miles, thousands, every bit of what Riadne had doused flared daylight bright before settling back to humming normalcy, Toronto in motion once more.

Celadon's eyes widened in shock.

Shock because . . . this . . . It hadn't been him at all.

He kept his gaze trained carefully forward, strictly away from the boy standing oh so innocently beside him, pretending at awe as well.

She expects you've inherited a great deal of power. She doesn't expect that of me.

Not yet.

Vehan's cryptic words in Gwyrdd's den . . . They came back to him now, wove themselves into clearer sense, because this power hadn't been Celadon's at all, and if Riadne had been paying attention, hadn't been so determined to claim Celadon as her prized possession and cast Vehan as *needs improvement*, she'd have been able to track it just as easily . . . the vein of that magic threading all the way back not to Celadon but to his younger brother.

Vehan wasn't at all the Three he'd apparently been pretending to be.

If it comes down to war, I will be a valuable weapon to you, echoed in Celadon's head as finally . . . he understood.

Riadne clasped him on the shoulder.

He let her believe it was *humility* that rendered him speechless, as Celadon's brain connected the final points of what Vehan had been hinting at.

"My son." She beamed again, pressing a kiss to the top of his head. "From day one I knew you'd be different. That *you* would be the one to take this realm by storm—I'm just setting things up for you." Another squeeze of affection, and Riadne sauntered back down the roof toward Eris, who stood back in wait. "The prince is yours," she called over her shoulder.

"What did I say about boring me?" Lethe purred quietly against Celadon's ear, so suddenly there when he hadn't been at all a moment before, and so very unamused. "Are you really going to fade yourself into dutiful mediocrity all to ignore the potential inside you and what you think it means . . . what you've been conditioned to *fear* it means." The tip of a cool finger on the back of his neck traced the ink that disappeared there down his spine. "I could feel it in you. See it on your face. That fear of your own power is far more corrosive than the power itself, Celadon. The Little Lightning Prince has figured this out. How much longer until you do too?"

CHAPTER 15

Celadon

———

FEAR OF YOUR OWN power is far more corrosive than the power itself.

Lethe's words had stayed with Celadon all through dinner— an awkward affair of just him, Vehan, and Riadne, where the three of them played at such overexaggerated pleasantness that they were all fairly glad, he had the suspicion, when the meal was over.

The words followed him to the rooms Riadne had made up for him in his absence—no longer situated in Arlo's wing but an entire section of the palace all his own, a sprawling, golden excess he had little desire to explore.

And those words chased him right back out of this offensive splendor once his escort bowed himself through the door, and Celadon could no longer stand sitting on the edge of his bed, churning through his thoughts.

Because Lethe was right, even if it was easier said than done.

At the very least, his words were a voice that echoed something Celadon had been struggling with for a while, in tandem with his fear. On the one hand, there was no denying that his existence created an imbalance. There was *power* inside him—such a raw, blustering, unfathomable power. Now that Azurean's magic had been wiped clean from him, now that there was no longer this barrier between him and the truth of what he was, Celadon could feel it growing by the day; could peer over the edge of the well of his core into dark, frightening waters that seemed to have no bottom, and *see* it.

And he didn't at all want to touch it.

To acknowledge it.

To draw it out.

Everything they'd ever been taught about combining such potent powers screamed at Celadon to pull away. To let that power wither and decay to death, and then he wouldn't be a threat to the Courts . . . to himself . . . to the people he loved, a number growing slimmer by the day.

If Celadon gave in to his power, and the things they whispered in fear about such a thing were right, then at best Celadon could be the one to die—torn apart at the seams under the inevitable war of dominance between Spring and Summer and Winter, affinities that already showed their hold on him and wouldn't at all play nicely together for long.

At worst, he could survive.

Survive to become that power's puppet, a monster no better than Riadne that only crushed and craved and consumed.

But there had been something else beneath all that—a voice he couldn't quite tune out that *wondered*. . . .

They didn't have much of a control group to work with here; the little they knew about children born of inter-Head union came from less than a handful of samples born so long ago that no one had actually thought to write down the initial account of it all.

Sure, this power growing inside him could be deadly, dangerous, undesirable—but it wasn't impossible that Celadon could also be . . . fine.

That the more deadly, dangerous, undesirable thing was in *not* acknowledging who he was, in letting it rage deep down inside him and never learning how to control it until it burst free of its confines and . . .

". . . and I can't believe I'm seriously contemplating sense from *Lethe*," he groaned under his breath, dropping against a pillar that held up a gaping archway, one of many base-floor openings that led out into Riadne's gardens, where a tiny trio of lemon trees grew.

The night air was warmer here than in Toronto, but the breeze that tumbled past him still felt nice on his face.

He'd been somewhat aiming for Arlo's quarters. An attendant had informed them at dinner that she'd still been asleep, unable to join them, and Celadon hoped that was all it was, that she hadn't overheard he was here and was actually trying to avoid him.

But Vehan spoke true—he couldn't hide away from his cousin any longer. He had to face her, had to explain himself and hope that Arlo would forgive him, as she'd always forgiven him for pretty much everything . . . even though a part of him didn't feel like he deserved forgiveness at all.

Tilting his face to the starry sky, Celadon sighed.

It was impossible sometimes—more than his power, the *feelings* he carried; the guilt and the grief, but also . . . the anger.

Anger that, if left to mix with his fears much longer, would certainly destroy him if his newfound magic didn't.

He needed to take control of both.

It started with facing Arlo.

Another breath to fortify his nerves, and Celadon peeled away from the pillar. He was about to reroute his path back in his cousin's direction, and he couldn't say for certain whether it was instinct or sight that stopped him first, but his attention quickly fixed on it: the shimmer out of the corner of his eye.

For a moment, Celadon could only watch, entranced by the sight—and iced with fear all over again.

It was a recent development, this change in his Gift that allowed him to pick out past conversations from the air. He couldn't say for certain when it had morphed into something more but hazarded the guess that it was another side effect of the dampening magic woven over him by Azurean.

A shimmer out by one of the nearby lemon trees—Celadon watched as spectral shapes took form in swirling, moonlit air, that of a young fae man and a younger faerie girl wringing her hands across from him.

Celadon stared.

The memory began to play out—because that's what this was; his Gift was no longer confined to voices but able to pick up on whole scenes the air could play for him like a private performance—and Celadon *stared*.

Stared, because the young fae man was Theodore, and the faerie girl he stood frowning at . . . Celadon didn't recognize, but she was dressed like palace staff.

It has to be now, Helene—the High Queen is out, and High Prince Celadon's arrival has given us just the right amount of distraction. It has to be now, or I can't get you out until next month at the earliest.

Get her out?

What was going on here?

The faerie girl, Helene, dissolved even further into distress.

I just . . . It's so much sooner than I was expecting. I haven't been able to say my goodbyes, and I don't have any of my things.

It's stuff, Helene, Theodore replied . . . a little tersely, the way one might reply in frustration to someone they knew and cared about, not a random member of the house staff. Celadon didn't balk at friendships between the classes, had made his own friend or two among the people who'd worked for his family. He didn't know why it struck him as odd, that Theodore should have done the same. *It's stuff, and this is Riadne. How long do you want to press your luck? She'll eventually notice the dress you ruined by running red in with her precious white laundry, and she's going to figure out it was you. Look what happened just last week to Alec—she took his eyes, Helene. With a spoon. Right there at the breakfast table, just because he mistakenly put salt instead of sugar in her tea. If you want to chance it and wait until I can make my next run, that's your business, but I can get you out right now, and I think you should take advantage of that.*

Celadon's feet moved of their own accord, carried him into the garden and closer to the tree.

It . . . didn't surprise him—this further evidence of his mother's viciousness—but what Theodore and Helene were discussing . . . It sounded to him like Theodore was offering to help her flee the palace; like this was something the prince did regularly. Gods, but if Riadne ever discovered he was doing this—spiriting people away from her punishments, helping those contracted to her service skip out before that contract was up . . .

Why, though?

What did Theodore stand to gain from this?

Was this another task he'd been set to by the Madam, or was this *him*—the truth Vehan had been hinting at, that putting together all these pieces he scattered among his acquaintances would reveal Theodore as . . . kind. Caring. Brave.

A leg swung down from the branch above, dashing the ghostly memory to nothingness.

Celadon blinked out of his daze, his attention traveling upward.

It really wasn't any of his business if someone wanted to climb Riadne's fruit trees in the middle of the night. Most likely, it was one of the palace staff enjoying a bit of peace and solitude—maybe even Helene, and the last thing she'd probably want right now was him, but something drew him nearer, something he couldn't ignore . . . a compulsion that thrummed through him, like Fate nudging him toward a path in a fork in his road.

Or maybe he was just looking for an excuse not to face Arlo just yet.

Regardless . . .

"Theodore?"

Theodore startled.

Not badly, but apparently Celadon had been quiet enough in his approach that the Seelie Summer Prince hadn't heard him, and his eyes shot open, mild alarm smoothing first into relief when he spotted Celadon . . . then wariness.

"Your . . . Highness. I . . ."

Loose-fitted white cotton pajama bottoms . . . a pale gray T-shirt tucked into the waist . . . no makeup, no jewels, no embellishments of any kind, Theodore was still as he'd appeared in the memory Celadon witnessed—was here just a boy who'd been relaxing in the summer night's air; who looked so at home in this tree that it was now the mental image of him in a palace that seemed absurd.

A heartbeat passed in the silence between them.

Theodore recovered much quicker than Celadon could.

Smiling wide and easily, he bent and extended a hand.

It had been . . . a very long time since Celadon had climbed a tree.

He used to do it a lot with Arlo when they'd go stomping through the woods on camping excursions, in a childhood Celadon couldn't talk about anymore, because everything—*everything*—was so twisted and complicated these days. . . .

"Welcome to my tree," Theodore said when Celadon heaved himself onto the branch as well and positioned himself to face him.

He nodded congenially. "It's a lovely home." Then, melting a little, added more seriously, "What are you doing up here, Theodore? Is . . . everything okay?"

He wanted to ask after Helene—wanted to know what she'd chosen—but asking that was a loaded conversation. Where to even begin?

Theodore snorted.

Because of course things were not okay. Things were so far from okay right now for everyone. For Theodore especially, with his parents trapped in Riadne's clutches; with him tied to the Madam and forced to play spy, forced to play assassin, forced to play so many roles, but who was Theodore *really* underneath?

Celadon knew nothing.

Nothing of his hopes and dreams, his desires, the things he liked and didn't, because everything he'd learned so far had been from the prince, not from the boy . . . and it occurred to him in this very moment that for all Theodore was trapped here, Celadon hadn't asked him if he actually wanted to be rescued.

The conflict of his thoughts must have been evident in his eyes, because Celadon looked up to find Theodore studying him.

Relaxing back against the tree's trunk, Theodore let his gaze travel out to the night. "I feel better out here," he began, in a steady voice like he might be telling Celadon a bedtime story. "Eight years, and it still feels weird to sleep in a bed."

Eight years?

There was something to that seemingly offhand comment.

A thread Celadon wanted to follow and ask after, but this was Theodore's moment, and just as he'd felt the importance of coming out here, something in him told him to hush and let the prince speak.

"You already know who I work for, so there's no point in withholding names—four of those years I spent in the Madam's *program*, trained by her and her elite forces to be whatever she could need—spy, assassin, performer, a future king's consort . . . So much time and effort, even more wealth and resources, nothing was spared in breaking and remaking me, and even after all of this . . ." He paused to laugh. To shake his head and drop his gaze, then flutter it over to Celadon. "Do you know I actually failed? Too soft, she said. I didn't like taking lives, couldn't hit half her marks, and the ones I did made me *embarrassingly* ill afterward. And that was a problem, because my parents were extremely in her debt."

Another sigh.

Theodore turned his gaze back out to the night beyond.

"Not many people remember it, and few of them who do actually know the full details. I'm sure you're fully aware, though, that my father was a commoner, and my grandparents were . . . let's call it appalled when my princess mother came to them, fell to her knees, and begged them to let her marry him. True love, she called it, but the Reynoldses are a very old and very powerful family—a power that was built on a foundation of extreme fortune. A fortune that was beginning to dwindle, so no, my mother could very much *not* marry some nameless common fae boy with no connections and barely any gold to rub together."

Celadon did know this much. Not all the details, mind, and

much more he suspected were lies—his Gift of reading the air wasn't infallible, and just because a person spoke something didn't make it true.

"Except . . . well, my father did have a connection. A grandparent of his own, one his parents had severed ties with a long time prior. But my parents were desperate, and everyone knows if there's something you want, there's always a way, because you *always* have something the Grim Queen needs."

And . . . *that* was new information.

Why was Theodore telling him this? Confessing this. The implications . . . if Riadne knew . . .

"The Madam. The Madam is . . . your great-grandmother?"

"I promise it didn't yield me any favors," Theodore replied a touch acridly. "Yes. My mother and father went to the Madam to beseech her help. They asked my great-grandmother for a title and fortune for my father's name, and the Madam was happy to provide . . . if they agreed to give her their firstborn child. For the first fourteen years, I would be raised solely by the Madam. After that, sent back to them, but for the rest of my life, I'd be in her employ, dispatched to any mission she required me on. My parents reassured me it was the hardest choice they'd ever made, and some days I even believe them . . . that they regret it, regret that my mother didn't just run away with my father and start their family in peace. Other days, though, I'm . . . impossibly angry."

Celadon couldn't imagine.

Except maybe he could . . . in a way.

His parents had put a price on his life as well, had played games with his future without his consent. . . .

"Yeah," he uttered softly, still shocked; empathetic. "Yeah, I imagine you are."

"But they're still my parents," Theodore replied, hardening a little and, at the same time, softening into some resignation. "They love me. I've only really known them for four years, but they love me, and I love them, and they'd already paid this much to get here. So when it turned out in the end that I was spectacularly *not* what the Madam hoped I would be, and the title and fortune were on the line . . . I couldn't do it to them. I'm angry, and hurt, and I don't think there's anything in this entire world strong enough to convey or assuage that, so like hells I was going to let the meager good that came from it all be taken from us too. One last shot—a second chance. I asked the Madam to assign me to Queen Riadne Lysterne. Everyone knew she was going to make a play for the High King's Bone Crown, just as they knew there was a chance she could take those ambitions even further. I was the one to nudge the Madam's attention to what could happen if Riadne likely decided she didn't want to share her power and refused to align herself in the unofficial treaty that has always existed between the High Sovereign and the Queen of the Grim Brotherhood. If she did prove a liability, I vowed to my great-grandmother that I would be the one to assassinate her."

Had Theodore ever shared this with anyone?

And why, again, was he sharing this now? And with Celadon of all people? This was as good as a confession that would see him executed the *instant* Riadne found out about it. All Celadon would have to do was just *hint* at this to her, and Theodore's life would be over.

"So here you are," Celadon said. "Trapped now in a competition against an immortal Fury that only ends with your life." He hesitated a moment, then added, "Theodore. Why tell me this?"

Theodore cocked his head at him, something lurking under the waters of those dark amber eyes that Celadon couldn't name—his "training" no doubt to thank for this. Theodore was an impossible person to read when he didn't want his thoughts known.

"You know, I can't really say," Theodore replied, his tone thoughtful. "There's something about you, Celadon. There's always been something about you. A steadiness, a serenity. I used to sleep all my nights in trees; the stars and the moon . . . they were comforting. You're comforting in an oddly similar way. Steady. Dependable. True. I suppose I simply can't help myself."

275

"Or you can, and my knowing this piece of your background plays somehow to your favor."

And Theodore grinned. "Who can say? Not improbably I just like the sound of my own voice."

"Theodore," Celadon interrupted, and the grin on the boy's face faded. "If I could take you away from here, would you want to go? The Madam can't honestly believe you alone would be able to take out Riadne, not anymore, and Riadne is one shred of proof away from tying you to the Brotherhood. And with the task she's set you to against Nausicaä . . . It's just not safe for you here anymore."

Because that was the heart of it all, he suspected. What was Theodore working toward now that that goal had become unachievable? What did he want? Was it really to be tied for the rest of his life to these politics when right now, in this tree, he looked better than Celadon had ever known him?

A moment passed.

That grin returned—a smile that spread slow as honey across Theodore's face.

"Safety? Sorry, Your Highness, but personal safety hasn't been my concern for quite some time. And let's just say that, as it is for the Madam, it's . . . in my *nature* to guard what is mine to the end. This Court, its people, its wealth, its splendor . . . I'm exactly where I want to be. I don't need safety. I could do with an ally, though. Funnily enough, I think you could, too."

CHAPTER 16

Aurelian

~⤝⤞~

T HIS PLACE GIVES ME the creeps."

Aurelian snorted, casting a glance at Bulruk, the amethyst-toned goblin beside him in enchantment-reinforced leather armor fitted over top of a plain forest-green tunic and leather trousers; a wicked wood-and-silver crossbow rested in his gnarled hands, and twin daggers, long as Aurelian's forearms, were strapped to both hips. He was older than Aurelian by a handful of years and mean enough to match, and it amused Aurelian that his partner for tonight's patrol was more bothered by the remains of some discarded temple than the deities-damned *demons* they'd been tasked with chasing from Market borders.

"Whose is it?" he asked, following Bulruk up what was left of the temple's crumbling stone steps.

Weathered marble winked at them in the waves of shadow and light that rolled through the forest canopy. Moss and vines and wild-flowers overgrew its surface; ferns and trees and thorns jutted from gaping holes in its high-reaching ceiling.

There was nothing outside to suggest who or what had been worshipped within its confines. No statues or busts; any distinctive markings had been worn down by its surrounding elements and considerable time.

Crossbow clutched firm at the ready, head snapping this way and that in constant surveillance of their surroundings, Bulruk grunted. "Couldn't tell you, exactly. Another relic Magic absorbed and spat out here in the Hiraeth—likes to collect trophies, it does. Popular guess is from sites that see significant magic, and who's to say the things it stores here are even from our world to begin with . . . if you believe that sort of thing. It could have belonged to anyone. But we call it the Temple of Misfortune."

"Cheerful."

Personally, he didn't agree. Of the bit of the Hiraeth he'd patrolled so far—because like hells was he sitting useless while everyone he cared about fought for their lives—he didn't mind this place. It wasn't exactly peaceful, since nothing felt peaceful to him anymore, but it wasn't . . . uncomfortable. It didn't give him *the creeps*. Perhaps it was just the stillness, the silence of this space, when his whole world had become movement and chaos and burgeoning war.

"S'not supposed to be cheerful, Bessel. It's where she drops them off," Bulruk added a moment later, just when Aurelian thought the conversation was over.

Shifting his gaze to Bulruk's tense back, he furrowed his brow in confusion. "Drops who off?"

"The babes!"

Aurelian . . . wasn't following.

Bulruk paused.

Confused now too, he turned to Aurelian, his crossbow lowering just enough that it wasn't aimed between his eyes. "You don't know nothing, do you."

Aurelian pursed his lips. "I know you clearly want to tell me what you're on about. What kids—who's *she?*"

"The Madam!" He really did look shocked, like it genuinely surprised him that Aurelian hadn't a clue what he was talking about. But then something flexed over his expression, a dawning comprehension that made him snort and turn back around. "Right, you're practically sidhe. Spent too much time playing house with the *colonizers*—of course you wouldn't know."

It wasn't the comment that irritated Aurelian; he was used to this reaction by now.

As lesidhe—the race of fae that had never left the Wild to begin with—he was still embraced as brother by the Others that called the Wild home too. But Aurelian was one of the growing many whose family had traded freedom for *security* from the sidhe Courts, and insult added to injury was that he'd also been titled a lord of Riadne Lysterne's household.

Bulruk wasn't the only one to have thrown that perceived betrayal in Aurelian's face.

"Tell me or don't." He shrugged off the comment. He wasn't here to make friends. "It doesn't matter to me."

"Hell of a stance to take. Hey." On the temple's landing, Bulruk paused again. Turned back to Aurelian. Pressed the tip of his crossbow against Aurelian's chest, and Aurelian didn't budge, didn't flinch, held his ground—but injury or intimidation didn't seem to be Bulruk's game. "That's the mafia back there. It's not some street gang. It's not some morally corrupt government organization that pretends it cares for its people. It's *the mafia*. It's a woman who takes babies in payment for debt and chucks them into this temple. And if they're lucky, they die. If they're unlucky, Magic claims them the same way it does changelings, and those poor kids are raised by these fucking woods, which ain't a gods-damned party, let me tell you. Ten years they're left to fight for survival, and the ones that make it, the Madam has her minions track them down. Recapture them, all so she can break them down in the ugliest, vilest, most horrific ways possible and remold all their feral, Wild ferocity into poise and sophistication—a deadly little army, abused and conditioned into doing her bidding, because the Madam is *the fucking mafia*."

He pressed his crossbow just a little firmer against Aurelian's chest.

"You've been moping around this place since you got here. Nothing seems to matter to you unless it's to do with your sidhe fae prince. We're so desperate for help against that prince's mother that we let the gods-damned mafia take control of things, but don't you mistake it, boy—don't think for a moment we're one and the same. Those are good people back in that Market. Good people who only want to stand up for what's right; good people trapped in this mess just like you, who didn't really have a choice when the Madam took a shining to using this place as her base of operations. Maybe they don't want to be involved in this, and maybe you don't want to be either, but we are the Wild. We are a family. And family means we're something you fight for—family means we're something that fights for you, as well. You don't have to be a one-man show anymore, but only if you let us in."

The crossbow fell away.

Bulruk turned for the archway that led through to the temple's interior.

A moment passed, then Aurelian . . . swallowed. Followed up the remaining steps to join him.

You don't have to be a one-man show anymore.

How long had it been just Aurelian against the insurmountable odds?

Bulruk was . . . right, of course.

Aurelian was a part of this, whether he liked it or not.

The Madam wasn't good—but then, he'd already known that. It was why he'd wanted so desperately to have nothing to do with her; why it had confused him that Nikos Chorley, leader of the Assistance, and *Arlo's father* seemed to be on such good terms with her, but maybe it was just as Bulruk had said. Maybe it was less good terms and more that she had them in her pocket, the same way she'd taken hold of the Market.

If Aurelian wanted to survive this with the people who mattered, he had to give this new game a proper effort; he'd have to calm this panic inside him, freezing him immobile every time reality set in that Vehan wasn't with him. That other people needed his protection right now, and the Madam was Riadne all over again, but he already had plenty of practice standing up to dangerous queens . . .

He'd have to remember how to reach out for help, because finally there were people who could protect him, too.

"I'd never heard that about the Madam before," Aurelian said, stepping through the temple's entrance and coming up to Bulruk's side. "About the kids."

Bulruk shrugged. "Not exactly something they advertise. And it's mostly the sidhe fae aristocracy who buy into it. All that nasty debt, cleared up in a matter of ten years, and then she sends the kid back to them, all elegance and wit, perfectly groomed for high society, but all the while, a vicious beast on a leash she controls." He actually shivered. "I was a stupid youth. Got myself in a heap of trouble, and the Madam said she'd make it all go away, that all I had to do was join the troop sent to drag in one of those poor kids. I did it. And it was the worst thing I've ever done. Ever hear the sound of a ten-year-old boy screaming for death as every bone in his body is broken just so *she* can teach him her meaning of pain? I'll tell you one thing— Theodore Reynolds ain't scared one bit of Riadne Lysterne, not after everything he's been through."

Aurelian . . . stared.

"Excuse me, *what?*" he heard himself ask in a dark timbre. "Are you . . . ? Are you actually suggesting *Theodore* was one of—"

But Bulruk raised a hand. "You hear that?"

Aurelian was still reeling over the revelation about Theodore, who seemed . . . nothing like what he'd imagine of a child who'd spend the first ten years of his life raised by the Hiraeth's inhospitality. Had he even known how to speak before the Madam had come along to scoop him back up again and . . . and *beat* the image of a pampered, charming prince into him, the only version of Theodore that Aurelian had ever known?

Urielle.

But Bulruk's comment forced him out of his spiral.

He didn't think he could ever walk up to Theodore—on the rare occasion that he saw the prince in the Market, delivering news or new folk seeking shelter—and ask him about any of this, but he resolved to consider the implications later.

When he wasn't on patrol.

"I don't hear anything." Aurelian shook his head. The temple was darker within, with only what light spilled in through holes in its stone to lend illumination.

Again, there was no indication who the place could have belonged to, what purpose it served beyond worship.

It was rather underwhelmingly sparse inside for all the handsome architecture: nothing but more overgrown vegetation and a singular statue of a man on a pedestal at the hall's center. His paint was all but faded remnants, his features worn indistinguishable by time. The Temple of Misfortune—however long ago this was built, however long it had been here, the one thing that glared back at Aurelian as piercing and fresh and *toxic* as it had probably been at creation was the man's set of poison-green eyes.

Eyes the like of which Aurelian had only ever seen on one person.

Bulruk lowered his crossbow once more. "The fucking creeps . . . ," he murmured with a shake of his head. "All right, come on, this area's clear. Just a little farther to the east and we can make it back for dinner."

The Madam's tavern was busy this evening—there wasn't a single table vacant by the time Aurelian was washed and changed, presentable for dinner. The air was thick with excitement, too; something was going on tonight, and he was certain someone had told him *what*, but Bulruk hadn't misread him. Aurelian's mind had been so full of self-pity and worry over Vehan that he'd been little better than a ghost in this place, no real use at all.

On the bottom step of the stairs that led up to the higher floors, Aurelian paused and craned his head in search of Elyas.

If there was anyone who knew what was going on, it would be the young prince. Elyas had taken to life in the Market with *vibrancy*, marveling over its every facet, and despite the fact that he was sidhe fae royalty, was too eager and earnest and damned adorable for anyone to remotely dislike him.

Elyas knew things.

The boy was a miniature Celadon in the making.

And there—he'd spotted him. A familiar white-blond head in the distance, firmly lodged in the midst of a group Aurelian knew only as the new recruits he was being trained with. A goblin girl named Tiffin, the deepest shade of African violet, with long, tightly coiled ebony hair; a faerie boy named Jaxon, so moonstone pale he was nearly translucent, with short, shaggy gray hair and a wolf's tail and ears; a lesidhe girl, Rosalie, with the softest gold eyes Aurelian had ever encountered in his kind, full-figured plump with beautiful blond curls and a vocabulary like a human sailor; an ogre everyone called Ten for the "X" stamped just under their left eye. Only slightly older than Aurelian, they had an undercut and rainbow-dyed hair, were thick as a boulder and towered over Aurelian's height, and had so many tattoos covering their body that they were more ink than forest-green skin.

"Aurelian!" Elyas exclaimed when he approached the table. There was already so little space at it, but Elyas leaped up as soon as he spotted him and snagged an unused chair from behind them, cramming it between him and Tiffin. "And Leaf!"

Brow furrowed, Aurelian needed a moment to figure that last part out.

But then the woodsprite who'd more or less attached herself to him the night he'd been mauled by demons flitted off his shoulder with her green-veined wings fluttering hummingbird fast and flew over to Elyas's food. Elyas adored her, never mind that she seemed to actively dislike the whole lot of them—even Aurelian, despite the fact that she followed him everywhere like a shadow.

Sure enough, Leaf ignored the young prince's greeting and helped herself to a cucumber from his plate without so much as a "please" or "thank you." And all the while Elyas beamed like of course she should be this rude to him.

Rolling his eyes, Aurelian sat.

As soon as he did, food appeared in dishes in front of him—salad and hearty vegetable soup, and a whole loaf of freshly baked, buttery bread, because the magic that tended this tavern's guests had discovered the only other weakness he had, separate from Vehan, and was possibly trying to kill him with it.

"Know what's going on?" he asked, breaking the loaf in half.

After a long patrol, it smelled like heaven . . . and made him miss his parents more than ever.

We are a family, Bulruk had said.

Aurelian bit his lip.

But Elyas brightened even further. "Prince Alaric's troop, don't you remember? He agreed to send some of his private guard to help us train."

"I hope they're hot," said Rosalie, dragging what remained of her own bread through the gravy left on her plate. "I'm balls fucking tired of looking at *your* ugly mugs. Not you, Aurelian. You're very pretty."

Aurelian rolled his eyes.

"I hope we actually get to fight something soon," Ten groused, stabbing a potato the size of a softball and stuffing it whole in their mouth. "They promised fighting."

A piece of chewed potato splattered Rosalie's hair.

"That's fuckin' gross, Ten. Learn how to swallow."

"Wanna show me how?"

"In your wettest fucking dreams, maybe—"

Aurelian glared witheringly. "There's an eleven-year-old boy at this table."

Elyas bristled. "I know what fellatio is, Aurelian," he said, making Tiffin splutter into her tankard and snort ale through her nose. Snickering broke out across the table.

Only Jaxon said nothing, but that was fairly normal for what Aurelian knew of him. He cut into his practically raw steak with perfect manners, prim and straight in his chair. Leaf nibbled her stolen haul by his plate because he was the only one in the entire world she maybe seemed to tolerate—at the very least, he piqued her interest.

"What was it like?" Rosalie asked after a moment, and it surprised Aurelian; it had been so long since they'd tried to coax him into direct conversation, he assumed they'd given up.

He didn't mean to be reticent.

For the last majority of his life, survival—*sanity*—meant ignoring the classmates who crammed around him, the spoiled sidhe fae children who treated him like an animal they'd caged as a sideshow attraction.

Somewhere along the line, he'd forgotten how to make friends.

But for some reason or other—and it wasn't just this ragtag crew of folk, for example; it had been this way his entire life—people . . . gravitated toward him. They cared what he had to say, listened when he spoke.

His mother said it was all in his air, that his calm disposition and zero-nonsense attitude made him a believable, trustworthy sort that was especially appealing in times of crisis.

Like now, perhaps.

Aurelian looked up from his plate.

We are a family.

You don't have to be a one-man show anymore.

Everyone looked back at him—Rosalie half in expectation that he'd blow her off, but with a glimmer of hope that he'd do something more than shrug. Because they cared. What he had to say. And he was the only person at this table who'd actually faced what they were up against.

Damn it . . .

Aurelian sighed. They *were* a family, and Aurelian's family had always, *always* been important to him. "What was what like?" he responded quietly.

No one seemed to know what to do for an eternal moment. They stared at him, bewildered by the fact he'd responded, he suspected, until Ten grunted and stabbed another potato. "So he does talk to us—hey!"

Rosalie had kicked them.

"The demon attack." It was Tiffin who'd picked up the conversation next, sitting a little taller, angling herself to better speak with him. "What was it like? They say those woods are getting more and more overrun by them, but they don't want us out there. Say we're too unprepared—that's why the Madam asked that prince to send us people to help us train. What was it like . . . ? Are they really that bad?"

Are they really that bad?

The stench of gore and decay on its breath . . .

The peeled and flayed and bubbling skin . . .

The mold that consumed them, and black rot that oozed from their sores, and the way they *clicked* at one another . . . the soul-petrifying way they shrieked as they launched themselves at him, dug nails like razors into his skin and reeled him in for the kill . . .

Swallowing, Aurelian nodded. "Worse."

And the Shriekers weren't even nearly as terrifying as the queen they had no chance in hells of defeating if half their army was only learning now how to wield a weapon. But damn it all . . . Aurelian wasn't going to let Riadne just *take* what she wanted.

And it was a new sensation to be surrounded by people willing to fight much the same.

CHAPTER 17

Arlo

~⌒c⌒~

YONGE-DUNDAS SQUARE ROSE UP around Arlo almost exactly as she'd left it.

She hadn't realized how badly she missed home until just now, standing in the center of tall, encircling buildings, sunlight glinting off their glassy fronts, neon signs and televised advertisements flashing down at her from every angle.

Traffic streamed along the sidewalks and streets, flowed from the Eaton Center just off to her right, and poured from every corner of Toronto, and it was strange but . . . in her periphery, everything moved at a blurring speed of rainbow color; whatever she turned her gaze to, though, slowed to almost no motion at all.

Dreaming.

She was dreaming again—this could be the only explanation. Remembering the very last place in Toronto she had been with Celadon, just before they'd gone through the palace Egress and right into Riadne's web.

Even unconscious, she couldn't escape how much she missed her cousin.

Almost as soon as she thought this, he appeared in front of her, bright and happy and whole, the Celadon she remembered best—russet hair like High King Azurean's, matching jade eyes, a warmer complexion, a little less iciness in the exact cut of his features that in the world outside her dream were so strikingly *Riadne* that Arlo wondered how magic could have ever concealed it.

Did he blame her for what happened?

Is that why Celadon kept his distance? How badly she'd wanted what Vehan had given her, someone to acknowledge she'd messed up, to give her permission to feel bad so that she could move on from it in some way. She'd gotten it from Vehan, but in her heart she knew who she wanted it from—but Celadon had retreated so completely from her, and it was almost too unbearable.

Riadne had confiscated her phone, so she couldn't even text him, and she was fairly certain she hadn't taken a proper breath since his leaving after the Solstice; they'd never been separated like this from each other longer than a few days, and even then, they'd always had some form of contact.

Did he hate her? It was all her fault, after all. . . . His family was dead because she'd been so intent on seeing Riadne as she wanted to see her instead of as who she really was.

Almost as soon as she'd summoned Celadon's ghost, others appeared as well.

Other people her actions had harmed.

There was Nausicaä beside him, exhausted and scared and so *dim* compared to her usual fire, because everything Nausicaä did right now was burning her out. She worked so hard to make sure *Arlo* was okay at the cost of her own health.

Her father, Rory, eyes rimmed red and face wet with tears, mourning a wife he'd apparently loved this whole time and had parted from only to keep her and Arlo safe.

Her mother, dead-eyed and ashen; Vehan, black spidering through his veins, red burning bright in his own vacant stare. Aurelian, Elyas, High King Azurean, Lords Lekan and Morayo, Theodore—one by one the crowd before Arlo grew, and as it did, it became harder to breathe.

All these people she'd failed in the course of a night—the act of a singular wish. This was why she'd never wanted to be anyone's hero; just as she knew back in the Faerie Ring, she was only going to let everyone down.

She took a step backward, tried to get away, wanted to run and never stop, never look back . . . like the child she'd never grow up from being.

Another step back . . .

Like hitting a wall, Arlo froze.

There was something behind her—or rather, someone. They radiated power, and for a moment instinct screamed that it was Riadne, because that power was cold—that power was fear, was death, was *bad*—but no . . . even Riadne couldn't contend with this sort of strength. Lethe, then, but . . . Lethe had never felt like this corruption to her, and it lacked that telltale sickly sweetness that clung to his magical aura, a little like dying flowers, a little like rotting fish.

"I would not turn around."

Arlo's gaze snapped back to the front.

She hadn't realized she'd been shifting to meet whatever stood at her back, but the voice before her stole back her focus.

Gone was the crowd of her failure.

Yonge-Dundas Square seemed to be . . . devolving around her.

Time seemed not to wind forward but *back*, the buildings stripping down to their skeletal foundations and crumbling to earth. Trees and grass and wildflowers sprouted in place where those buildings once stood, and finally the world slowed down to an almost tranquil halt.

And there, just before her . . .

Arlo was dreaming—and just like the last time, she found herself with immortal company.

"Your treaty holds no power over the realm of Dreams," the man that stood before her explained.

Not really a man—or not fully one, at least. He had long, powerful legs under thin, pale trousers that hung low on his hips, a beautiful pattern of rainbow thread embroidered clear around the waist. His chest was bare, his arms corded with muscle, every inch of it covered in smooth, tawny-brown skin, but in place of a human head was a wolf's—no . . . Arlo recalled the distinction; not a wolf's but a coyote's. Fur ran down from his narrow snout to his shoulders; his pointed ears sat large and perked atop yellow eyes that *pierced* Arlo with ancient cunning and intelligence. . . . This was no man, no mere immortal.

Arlo had recognized Artemis instantly—who in the West didn't know even a little about the Greek and Roman gods?—but this one . . .

"My children fill the unmarked graves of schools designed to ensure you *wouldn't* know who I am," the man said in a measured tone. "Your Court exists on my land, on the blood of my relations, but you won't find me in any of your lessons or textbooks." He folded his arms over his chest, dull canine teeth—meant for crunching bone—flashing at her as he spoke. "I am the Beginning. I am Giver of Names, of Story, of Song. I am he who made possible holy message through dream; he who sanctified the Sun and Moon your people took for worship. Trickster to some; philosopher to others; omen and sign to travelers. You may call me Coyote."

Coyote—a god significant to many of the Indigenous tribes. Arlo knew him only barely, for exactly the reason he gave; they weren't taught anything about the Indigenous gods that had existed here well before the Courts. Sidhe fae schools glossed entirely over that part of their past, and the human schools did similarly, but it was only through her studies at the latter that she knew Coyote's name at all.

Arlo inclined her head, respectful . . . and wary.

"Wary why?" Coyote asked, like he could read her mind.

"I'm not . . . sure what you want from me," Arlo explained. "Why you've chosen to appear to me."

If this were any other deity, she would assume he was here for the same reason Artemis had appeared to her. For what Luck had warned her about—that one by one, the immortals would start presenting their case as to why she should tie her favor to them.

But the Indigenous traditions . . . their myths and deities and folk . . .

"Your treaty has power over us only by extension." Coyote nodded. "European humans swept over the waters and claimed this land for theirs. They tricked and slaughtered and tortured their way to power, and the folk they brought with them, who followed on those ships . . . some helped to protect my people. Many more dispersed through the Wild to do much the same as their human brethren. And then your great-uncle, the grand High King Azurean—with his shining fae warriors and his head full of ideals, inspired by human colonization—decided here would be the best display of UnSeelie Spring's new rule. By blood and blade, he established his throne here, swallowed our lands into his domain, and so too my immortal ilk."

Because originally, it was only the gods the fae worshipped who'd been banned from the Mortal Realm. As the Courts grew, as more and more fell under its reach, converted to its vision, more and more gods of *other* religions were subsequently banished. Chased to the only place they could exist with any peace and power, the lack of worship dwindling them to nothing.

It was only in the Wild spaces such immortals and deities could still visit, but even then . . . most were now so disconnected from their people, who had turned to worship more modern things, that they simply preferred their separate domain.

Arlo's mouth pressed flat in unease.

What Coyote said . . . It was something most sidhe didn't think about, didn't talk about. It made them *uncomfortable*, despite how much they pretended to be above caring. How the white European humans had treated the Indigenous people was horrible, vicious, disgusting—but how the sidhe fae had treated them and so many others to get what they wanted . . . wasn't much better.

Whatever Coyote wanted, Arlo doubted it was the same thing Artemis wanted—at least, not exactly.

"Very true." Coyote nodded again. "I have no interest in your Courts. I want no power over your people, and words and promises you once gave to us in seeming earnestness turned to betrayal—they hold no meaning to us anymore. I am owed your blood, your pain, quite a lot in reparation you will never be able to satiate. What I ask for instead is something else."

Arlo straightened. "And what would that be?"

Coyote inclined his head. She got the impression from the glint in his eyes that if this had been any other occasion, if that so horribly unsettling presence hadn't been pressing itself against her back, demanding her attention, he would have led her on a little longer, taken his time.

Right now, though, they had very little of it, and Arlo doubted he'd appeared to her now just to waste an opportunity.

"When what will happen comes to pass," he said, still in that steady, measured voice that was low and melodic, and perhaps just on the verge of hinting at mischief. "When one of the many possible fates has been locked in place, should you find a queen fallen at your feet at the end of it . . . what I ask, Arlo Jarsdel, is that you destroy the Bone Crown that tumbles with it. That is what lies in your power. That is the *action* that will prove you're actually capable of listening—that perhaps you really are interested in change." He lifted his hands, extended them out. He hadn't been holding anything before, but now, what appeared in them . . . "A symbol of faith between us. As I understand it, Artemis gave you a gift as well. I wouldn't want to be rude."

Arlo stared at the gift in his hands.

A woven blanket.

Coyote grinned. Those yellow eyes flashed darkly with humor. Philosopher, he called himself, but Trickster as well. "Will you not take it? It's just a blanket. . . . What harm has one ever done?"

Arlo reached for it.

Just as she did, power once again pulsed strong at her back.

The frigid corruption that pressed against her throbbed for attention, and Arlo felt it begin to tug . . . tug . . . tug hers in that direction.

"Arlo, you must not—" Coyote began, only to be cut off by a familiar voice.

"Arlo!"

It was the second voice that saved her from looking at who stood behind her. She couldn't explain how, but knew with absolute certainty that if she looked, she'd be lost, and maybe Coyote had chosen now on purpose . . . had been playing distraction in tandem with capitalizing on the moment, buying time until that second voice could cut through her sleep and pull Arlo from its clutches. . . .

Arlo shot up in bed, gasping.

Hand over her stuttering heart, eyes wide, she looked into Nausicaä's panicked face.

It was once again late at night—she'd slept all day, she realized—and there on the foot of her mattress with the leftovers of the breakfast Vehan had brought her . . . was the blanket Coyote had gifted.

"Arlo . . . ," Nausicaä began, slow and steady, more blatantly terrified than Arlo had ever seen her. Arlo's gaze wandered back to hers. "Arlo . . . you didn't look, please tell me you didn't *look* at him! I felt him—wherever you were in dreaming, he was with you, and I felt it, and just . . . Please tell me you didn't look!"

Confusion weighing heavy on her brow, Arlo frowned. "Look at who?"

Nausicaä searched her face a frantic moment longer. Whatever she'd been looking for, she found no sign of it given the way she deflated and eased to sitting on the bed beside her.

"I didn't realize it had started already."

"*What*, Nos? *What* has started? Who am I not supposed to be looking at—"

"Moros," Nausicaä replied simply.

Just saying the name seemed to shatter her, but it triggered something in the back of Arlo's memory. A past conversation in her bedroom, yes, in which Nausicaä had told her that it wasn't time yet to let her in on the most dangerous person her potential would attract.

And another past conversation in her hospital room, in which Luck had told her that name.

But there was something more to that name . . . something deeper . . . something only barely out of reach in her mind. . . .

Nausicaä looked at her. It scared Arlo worse than anything else so far to see such genuine fear there. "Shit, Red, I'm sorry. I didn't want to put you in any more danger, but I . . . I guess it's time. Whether I like it or not. He's already found you."

Arlo placed her hands on Nausicaä's knees—more affection than she'd allowed herself to show in over a month, but for the moment, she couldn't help it. Nausicaä was afraid; Arlo gentled. "Just tell me, Nos. I don't understand. Who's this person even you and Luck and the other immortals are all so afraid of that you don't even want me to look at him?"

Nausicaä sighed.

"—no one knows their names, you see. No one knows if they ever even had one. They're simply the End, and the Beginning, and who's to say which came first."

It was dark in Lethe's cell tonight.

The room where he was kept when Father had no need for him—nothing to bash, nothing to break, nothing to cut and watch while it bled—wasn't uncomfortable; they'd given him a bed and moonlight for company at long last, and normally that would have been enough to keep him something close to happy, but the Moon, the *Moon*, where had it gone tonight?

Stolen from him . . . hidden . . . clouds again, they were such jealous creatures. They covered its face and, just like so many nights before, for too long. Lethe could only just feel it.

The fading hint—paint diluted by too much water—of his Moon through a bond tied to coldness like lurking death.

Everything was not fine, not like his Moon had promised. Nothing got better. What sat in the sky these days was little more than an empty husk waiting to be refilled, and what did he do with that? What did that mean?

Don't play with your food, Lethe, someone had once told him—he couldn't quite remember who, but it was someone he'd once known. He'd been on land one, twenty, hundreds, and too many thousands of days too long, and this wasn't quite how he'd imagined turning siren would go. By all accounts, he shouldn't be this sane—if this could be called sanity, this thing that came fleetingly and left just as quickly. By all accounts, he should be lost to the water's call altogether, a bloody trail of death and dismemberment on his way to rejoin it.

What was happening to his Moon? What was this almost corpse in the sky?

The sea sang to him.

Some days it was hard to hear anything else.

Others, there was one sound screaming louder in his head, drowning out that watery song—

Don't play with your food, Lethe

Lethe . . .

Lethe . . .

Lethe.

Lethe, Lethe . . .

He supposed that was why.

Why what?

Why he . . . remembered.

Who he was—enough to miss the Moon; enough at least that his cradle-turned-grave hadn't claimed him just yet. He was Lethe, and he still had something to do in this place before he could quit it.

Lethe gave the bucket he clutched between pale, bony fingers a vicious shake and creaked a laugh when water sloshed over the edge; when the two fish crammed inside flapped in distress. With one hand curled like claws, he struck—snatched one of the silvery fish and angled it, wriggling, nose to his nose.

"No one knows the First Ones' names," he continued, regaling his dinner with a story the Moon had listened much better to. "The End and the Beginning—progenitors of not only *our* realm but all. Fate herself fears them; as the immortals tell it, it was she and her titan siblings who put their considerable combined power toward the trickery that tethered the First Ones each to their thrones."

Frowning, Lethe glared at his captive audience. "How should I know why? I couldn't care. Immortals are jealous creatures too. Always after things they can't have—perhaps the real villain was Fate. Perhaps the immortals spun lies and tales and fibs, and the First Ones were actually good. Do you know some stories say those thrones are empty? That the titans *ate* their progenitors, believing it would give them their power. Not a terrible idea . . ." Lethe grinned. "I wonder how Father would taste?"

Metal struck metal—a bang reverberated loudly around his small enclosure, making Lethe wince. With his fish, he reached to cover his ears.

"Hey! Shut the fuck up, freak," a guard on the other side of the bars growled at him. "By Hades, I'll come in there and shove that fish down your throat if you don't *shut up* and eat your fucking dinner in silence."

He struck the bars again, a final warning that was only that: a warning; a threat; nothing of consequence.

They beat Lethe so often, for so many reasons, that it wasn't really punishment anymore. Those iron rods of theirs, this place, those bars . . . a team of them together, and it didn't matter that Lethe was his father's Prince of Carnage. It didn't matter anymore how much glory he brought them. They could and would overpower him easily enough. He was moldering scales and flesh that peeled and flaked in wide-spreading patches, sunbaked and blistered and rotting.

Gore stained his teeth.

Madness and fatigue hollowed his body to skeletal bone, warped and misaligned by constant abuse. He'd been so young when they'd taken him; his magic had done its best to help him survive. His *Moon* had done its best—was that why it currently festered like a carcass in its grave?

He'd been here too long.

Lethe wasn't enough. Not on his own, without the Moon to brace him—and it was dying. No more Moon, and Lethe would become an even easier target for a people who feared his appearance and legend, hated him for things *they'd* made him do, made him become, the things they'd almost loved him for when it had lain gold and jewels and fame at their doorsteps. . . .

The guard spat past the bars at him and wandered back up the hall to check on the enslaved Lethe was caged with.

Lethe watched him go—a moment . . . two . . . then, stuffing his fish between his teeth, heaved himself up off the floor. Up the wall he pulled his body—fingers anchored around the bars of his window, he reeled himself to its ledge to peer out at the view beyond.

He chewed on his fish.

Crunched through the fragile bone.

Flesh and scales and oozing innards spilled down his front, but what was cleanliness anymore? A prince they called him—he'd once been one. Maybe? Of what . . . ? The sea he couldn't see on the other side of that distant wall? It called to him, tried to lure him back to a home that wasn't home.

He wouldn't listen—not yet!

He had something to do.

Lethe.

My name is Lethe. I am Lethe.

Lethe, Lethe, Lethe, Lethe—

Lethe dropped to the ground. His bare feet hit the stone without sound, mashed the errant pieces of his meal beneath their soles.

He reached for his bucket—one more fishy, swimming frantic laps. To eat him or not . . . the Moon was away, was gone, was stolen, and Lethe had to admit . . . it got a bit lonely. All by himself.

"The First Ones grew lonely too." He peered into his bucket at the harrowing reflection of a face he didn't often glimpse and hardly recognized. "That's what I think. Bound to their thrones, trapped with only their misery and anger and madness for company, they broke the rules. Gathered bits and stuffs and molded it all into children—two, named Eos and Moros. Devoted scions whose only purpose was to venture out into the realms and seek that which would free the First Ones from their prison-thrones."

Eos of Dawn, with beauty and charm, the Beginning's fair beckoning that would tempt any mortal. Moros of Doom, terror incarnate, harbinger of demise. With guile and fear and terrible might, the End would swallow all in shadow. Once upon a time, even mortals knew these twins, but immortals had made them forget their names. To look away if something too lovely or dark came to creep across their path . . .

"Eos and Moros have rules to play by too. One look in their direction is all it takes to give them shape. Shape is all it takes to give them power. Power is all they need to seize it—the Crowns of the Great Three. Two are known; one will be kept for last. The missing one first is what they search for. Reunited with these missing pieces, assembled, the First Ones will be rejuvenated—the Crowns are made from their bones, after all. Who knows what they want—their power returned, perhaps? Who knows if the realms would be a better place with them back in control. Eos and Moros are kept so busy, so busy, no sleep, no freedom—but my *own* freedom . . ."

He chucked the bucket onto the ground.

The water spilled over, the last remaining fish pouring out with it to flap and splat and flail, mouth popping open, eyes bulging. . . .

Lethe's freedom would be easier won.

So long as he acted soon.

"I told you to shut the fuck up!"

The guard cracked his rod once more on the bars, and Lethe lifted his gaze—up and up, all the way to the ceiling, tipping his head to follow a snaking fissure there back to the window.

"Are you listening to me, freak?"

Lethe turned, strolled back to the wall, paused to wriggle his toes in the puddle of water.

"Ignore me, will you? Well, I think you don't need any dinner. You're just playing with it anyhow, making a gods-damned mess of the place—like you don't already reek enough without sloshing around in fish guts." As he spoke, the guard rummaged for keys; slotted one into the cage's lock; opened its door with a vibrating creak, and all the while Lethe kept his back to him.

Sword out, rod raised, the guard inched his way into the cell.

It was a brave show they all put on when Lethe was behind bars. When he couldn't reach them, when he was too tired to try, when they'd beaten him immobile and he could only lie there and take what they continued to give, to yield what they wanted from him. . . .

"Don't fucking try anything," the guard warned.

A brave show . . . but they were all *cowards*, especially when it was just one of them alone.

The scraping of wood against the floor signaled the guard had reached the bucket, was scooping the fish back inside. Lethe turned just as he straightened—hands folded neatly behind his back, he towered over the man, stared him down . . . smiled an innocent smile.

The guard stared back. There was fear in his eyes but defiance in the square of his jaw—admirable to some; foolish to Lethe.

"You can have this back when you're done being a creep, you understand?"

Lethe cocked his head. "I'm tired of small fishes."

"Well, that's too damned bad, because fish are all you're—"

Lethe lunged.

Too quick for the guard to escape him, Lethe was atop him in an instant. He tackled him over—soft human bone struck the floor and gave a satisfying *crack* he loved so dearly to hear—and all the while the guard screamed murder. Roared dying rage. Fought and thrashed and kicked against Lethe rolling him easily to his back, pinning his hands above his head, stuffing his nose against the guard's nose—and smiling again. "Let's try something bigger, hmm?"

Lethe *pulled*.

He'd been practicing however he could on his own. His Moon was all but gone, but the bond remained, just enough to keep Lethe teth-

300

ered to the power he needed to give his a boost—tethered, but Lethe had been practicing.

How to work off that power without draining it, without depleting that too-weak life force from the Moon, who needed it most.

Rest, my friend.

Get better, please—I need you, I need *you . . . you, not your power.*

I don't want to be left alone.

Practicing. Storing up energy for nights when the king unleashed him on this or that target, and when no one was looking, he practiced. On corpses no one would examine too deeply as to how he was *befouling* them . . . on fishes he desperately needed, too little food for so much body, but starving meant practice, and practice would save him, and Lethe's time was trickling out quickly; the bond that fueled him had grown so faint.

If he wanted revenge, if he wanted freedom—the chance to escape and track down his Moon, to rescue it in turn—he had to act soon.

Without the Moon for a tether, that familiarity, there would be nothing left in him his magic would recognize.

It would leave him too.

Lifting his hand, Lethe curled his fingers into a fist and *pulled* on the guard's very essence—the water inside him, inside his blood—and at first nothing happened, but then the guard groaned.

He moaned.

He cried.

Red began to well up in his pores—the tiniest pricks of it, all over his body. It welled, and it welled, and soon began to pool in other places: in his eyes, in his nose, in the back of his throat.

The guard began to choke, began to *scream*, and Lethe continued to pull.

He pulled until that welling-up burst, a wet sort-of-tearing, and with bottled-up force through every opening, blood sprayed from the guard's body down Lethe's front; across the cell walls; coated the ceiling and floor.

And Lethe laughed.

He laughed when the other guards turned up, too late.

Laughed when they yelled at him, called him names, flew into the cell and beat him into submission—bound his hands behind his back.

"What did you do to him?"

"You fucking monster!"

"If the king doesn't kill you for this, I'll end you myself!"

Time running out . . .

The pull responded so sweetly to him now, not perfect, but it would do just fine for what he needed. The sea was calling; the Moon was waiting. So without complaint or struggle, he let the men who'd tormented him the whole of his life drag him to his father.

Time running out—but not only for him.

Lethe was finally ready.

CHAPTER 18

Arlo

IT WAS HARD TO focus on her lessons the next morning. With everything Nausicaä had told her the night before, Arlo's mind was far too preoccupied, reeling over the fact that the Immortal Realm wasn't at all afraid of Riadne Lysterne, or the Sins she was summoning, or the creature she hoped they would help her unleash—but they were *terrified* of the End and the Beginning, and because Arlo's entire life seemed fueled by nothing but misfortune anymore, naturally, these nebulous beings of creation and decay were exactly who she'd managed to attract.

They can't hurt you, Arlo. They can't reach you or influence you in any way, Nausicaä had explained, the softest note of hysteria behind her words that made Arlo suspect her calm was an act. *Eos and Moros act on behalf of the First Ones—their eyes and ears and hands in the realms—but so long as you don't look, so long as you don't speak to them or acknowledge their presence, they can't get to you. I'm sorry,* she'd added. *I really did think we had more time? Which was stupid, because of course we don't, you're smack in the middle of the most interesting thing that's happened in this realm since immortals were banished from it—of course they were going to notice you. And I guess . . .* She'd trailed off a moment, gaze wandering to the side and landing on Coyote's blanket—reaching out, she'd traced her fingers over the fabric, a beautiful, intricate weave of colors. Moonlight had glinted off the gold that leafed her wrist, remnant of their encounter with Hieronymus Aurum what felt like ages ago now. *The immortals have started their bidding war over you.*

An accurate summary of what this felt like.

Arlo had explained her dream with Coyote and the one with Artemis the night before, the arrow she'd given to tempt Arlo's choice. *I've met Artemis once or twice before, Coyote only in passing. You were right not to promise either of them anything, Arlo, and I'd be real careful about using their gifts until you've made a decision about all this, but . . .* She'd snorted a laugh. *Points for the sass. This blanket's actually dope as fuck.*

What does it do? Arlo had asked.

And Nausicaä had picked it up, smoothed out its surface, reached to set it gently on Arlo's lap. *Nothing at all. It's just a nice blanket. From someone who doesn't owe you a damn.* And then, with a glance at Arlo's bedside table, she added very carefully, with no inflection of personal opinion . . . *I haven't seen your die in a while.*

"Arlo?"

Arlo startled.

She looked up from her table, from the array she'd been absently drawing out—the same array they'd all been drawing while Leda combed the classroom's aisles, presiding over the task. So lost had she been in her memories and thoughts, Arlo hadn't noticed Leda come up beside her. Their gazes met briefly. Arlo was instantly overcome by the recollection of the last time they'd seen each other, down in the room Riadne kept secret through a door in the wall of her office.

Prisoners—the both of them.

Leda had looked just as grim about that night as Arlo's father.

She had a grim sort of look about her now, too, as she dropped her gaze and peered at what Arlo had apparently finished while her mind had been miles away.

"It's perfect," she said.

Simply.

Disappointed.

Today's lesson had come as no surprise. Given what Riadne had dropped about her plans for her son the other night, and what Arlo and Vehan had talked about after, Arlo had almost expected to walk into class to what Leda had drawn on the chalkboard.

The animus rune could be used in many ways—today, they'd been set to mapping out two mirrored arrays, anchored to two different flowers. Their objective was simple: swap out a feature. Take command of two living things at once and alter an aspect of each with something from the other.

It was alchemy more advanced than anything they'd done under Leda's tutelage. Arlo hadn't been paying attention to her hands, to the magic and science she balanced and calculated, worlds beyond the flashy bits of alchemy she'd performed on chunks of iron. But there on the two sheets of parchment before her . . .

"Which features will you swap between them?"

Arlo considered her teacher.

She dropped her focus to her desk.

The flowers before her: a buttery pale yellow rose with delicate petals soft as satin and an elegant lily, stark as pure, white snow. The animus rune would anchor her life to theirs, her soul to their souls, magic to their magic, as all nature possessed to some degree. As simple a starting point as they could manage, because a flower wouldn't be able to fight back, to dominate Arlo's will and take control of her instead—but even drawing the rune had exhausted her.

She was always exhausted these days.

Which features would she swap out?

Arlo reached, touched a hand each to the arrays before her, and let her eyes fall closed. This was her first time encountering this rune. She'd never done magic like this before—something that allowed her to touch another's life force. . . . It scared her a little, how easy it was. Like breathing, she almost didn't have to think about it, only had to reach out with her magic and take hold of what it brushed against, and the flowers gave a pitiful shudder for a struggle, then fell limp in her mind's hands.

The *power* in that moment.

She'd never before felt anything like it.

Absolute control of another living thing . . . *dark magic*. The warning flashed through her mind, and Arlo released her hold. The flowers' life forces slipped away, retreated like wounded creatures that would never again trust her for what she'd just done, the violation—

"Ooh!" a classmate exclaimed, stealing the room's attention. Both Arlo's and Leda's heads snapped to the side. "Look, Fyri's got it!"

And Fyri had.

"Look, the lily's yellow now!"

"The rose is white!"

But Fyri looked—surprisingly, and for the first time Arlo could ever recall—far from pleased with her performance. In fact, she looked just as horrified as Arlo felt.

Their eyes met briefly.

"Fyri—are you okay? You look like you're going to be—"

Arlo threw up.

She threw up again.

A *flower*, and it had felt awful. She'd held life in her hands, and for the first time she really, truly appreciated why the Furies existed, how important Nausicaä's role had been in making sure no one ever wielded that sort of magic against another person.

Dropping her back against the door of the bathroom stall she occupied, Arlo ran a hand through her hair. Willed her heart rate to calm. Tried to stop trembling—everything, everything, *everything* was horrible, and Arlo hadn't so much as looked at the die she kept sealed in the top drawer of her bedside table, because everything, everything, *everything* was her fault. All she wanted to do was wish it all away, make it all better, but that die was the reason her life had fallen apart, and it scared her.

What if she did try to wish this all right, and instead only made things worse?

The bathroom door swung open.

Arlo had fled so quickly from the classroom that she hadn't even grabbed her things. Most likely it was Leda coming to check on her, or maybe Fyri, because she'd looked like she'd been about to throw up, too. Like maybe, finally, she'd figured out there were far better ways to restore ironborn rights than serving as a vicious queen's puppet. Either way, she didn't feel like talking, but just as she resolved to ignore whoever it was . . . she smelled it.

Rain and cedar.

Without even thinking, Arlo tore open the door of her stall and stared.

"Celadon," she gasped a moment later . . . because there he was.

He'd been gone so long.

A part of her had wanted it that way—didn't at all know if she was ready even now for this, the way her heart thundered in her chest.

Her best friend, her family, the person who'd faced so much by her side, and she hadn't realized until he was gone so long how lonely the world was without him, and she was terrified.

Terrified of his rejection.

Even more terrified of his forgiveness.

Celadon, who was still him—from that green silk robe and even darker lipstick right down to the Lysterne copper hair and blue-green eyes and ice-sharp features so distinctly Riadne now, but all of it . . . together, it was all still *him*.

"Celadon," she breathed again.

And threw herself at her cousin before the panic in her brain could tell her *no, don't, you don't deserve him.* Celadon caught her with a gasp of his own and buried his face in her hair.

"I'm sorry, Arlo," he breathed against her.

How ridiculous.

"Shut up," she scolded, through trembling emotion. "You have nothing to be sorry about."

"I'm sorry for abandoning you here. I'm sorry that, for a little bit there, I lost myself and . . . didn't want you to see. Not you. Not when I knew you'd still love me anyhow, and I . . ."

"Didn't think you deserved it."

Arlo pulled back.

The pair of them . . . So many people commented on it, and Arlo really had to agree—they were so much alike, to a fault, at times.

Like right now.

Arlo looked up into Celadon's face. Over a month, and it felt like forever, like looking at him as though reuniting after years apart. At the same time, nothing had changed. Reaching up, she patted his chest. "Or rather, you wanted blame you knew I'd never give you." She sighed. She'd been doing the same thing. With him, with Vehan, with Nausicaä, too. "I get it. Guess we'll both have to suffer our disappointing love for each other." Trying at a smile—not too sure how to even form one anymore, now that she had to focus so hard on shaping it—Arlo added, vowing on his true name, "Just so you know, there's no one you could become who I wouldn't love, Calix."

No one—because she knew without needing to be told that Celadon would stand by her just the same.

Biting his lip, Celadon nodded, close to tears.

Arlo reached up to tug on his hair. "No one. Remember that. But I swear to gosh if you've cut all your shirts up into crop tops again, like you did in your *last* identity crisis . . ."

She trailed off, because there was something else now—a scent behind the rain and cedar that was Celadon's magical signature, tinged now faintly with ginger.

It took her a moment.

That sickly sweet scent . . .

Grabbing hold of Celadon's hand, she tore through the bathroom door back out into the hall. . . .

"Lethe!" she exclaimed.

"Arlo," he drawled, the man folded nonchalantly against the opposite wall.

Lethe looked . . . different.

She almost wanted to say . . . better?

He'd brushed his hair at least, for the first time in Arlo didn't know how long, and was it her imagination or did it . . . look a bit gray rather than its usual oil-slick black?

It was no longer knotted and tangled, for sure. Free of the insect carcasses and bits of twigs and goodness knew what else that had been caught up in now gleaming silken strands. There were still a few braids here and there, rewoven and tidy. And he must have eaten a meal somewhere, because he didn't look quite as starved as the figure that haunted Arlo's memories of Hieronymus Aurum's factory.

Lethe's poison-bright eyes shifted to Celadon, and she was almost shocked at how . . . congenially he spoke to him. "If you're sufficiently occupied now, I *do* have a life of my own to tend to."

Arlo looked at him.

She looked at Celadon.

Celadon sighed. "It's a long story. In short, he eats my food and sleeps in my palace, and in just a few more months, we'll be able to file for common-law marriage."

The revulsion on Lethe's face drew so grossly sour that Arlo didn't know whether to laugh or take cover back in the bathroom. She opted for frozen alarm.

"Quaint," Lethe said scathingly. Something about it seemed . . . a little *too* repulsed. Like a kid on the playground who'd just been accused of having a crush on someone he very much did have a crush on but would rather chew off his own arm than admit it. "Arlo, darling—" he began in farewell, but Arlo recovered just in time.

To remember that, more than anyone, it was Lethe she actually needed right now.

And she'd rather chew off *her* arm than admit that too.

But—"Lethe?" she called again, and Lethe paused in peeling away from the wall. Cocked his head at her, considered her with those inhuman eyes, the otherworldly warp of his body, those features that were striking and bizarre all at once, and definitely glamoured to conceal some truth beneath, but to the mortal eye . . . he was really just . . . *pretty.*

And Arlo knew her cousin well.

Celadon might be asexual—leaning more toward demi-sexual, as he'd explained it to her when he'd been trying to sort himself out and required Arlo for a sounding board. He might not be all that interested in sex, but goodness knew he'd always had an appreciation for unusual, pretty things.

She and Cel would have to talk.

Later.

For now . . .

"Yes, my dear?"

"You're the one who removed the block on my father's memories, aren't you."

It wasn't a question.

And the way Celadon stiffened beside her—and the way that stiffness was so different from confusion or shock . . . almost more like Arlo had spoken a secret he was in on and didn't know until now she knew.

And . . . oh?

They would have to talk about a few things, it seemed.

But *for now* . . .

Lethe considered her calmly. Those too-green eyes blinked at her in assessment, a moment . . . two . . . then he pulled himself to standing fully, and deities but he was so tall. . . .

"You want me to do the same for you."

Arlo nodded. "Yes. You're the one who put them there, aren't you?" There was no comment, no indication of confirmation or denial, but Arlo didn't need it.

She knew already.

"I . . . didn't get a chance to talk with Dad yet, but—"

"It doesn't matter." Lethe waved a hand. "He can't tell you much anyhow. No one can. He doesn't have my permission to, and until that block is removed completely, my permission he will continue to need." He grinned at her, not kindly, but not meanly, either—amused.

And Arlo bristled. "So you *did* tamper with my memories, then. You, specifically."

"Oh yes. I very much did."

"For the Courts?" Arlo demanded.

And Celadon stiffened further—why?

Lethe shook his head. "No, no. Well . . . in part. Pieces of the truth, yes, but . . . no. What I've taken from you came at another's behest: a desperate bargain to protect you from yourself, my clever little princess. From what the Courts would do if they realized . . ."

"Realized *what?*"

Why did *everyone* know things about her that she didn't even know herself? She was so deities-darn tired of bouncing off events, being tugged this way and that, a doll between people who cared about her, sure, she knew, but would no one give her the chance to act on things herself? Was this what her life was . . . ? Was she really just a pawn to be played on someone else's chessboard?

Clicking his tongue, Lethe bent in and wagged a finger before Arlo's face. "Tsk, tsk, tsk . . . we're getting ahead of ourselves, I think. You aren't ready for that yet, dearest."

"Why?" she demanded again.

Lethe reeled himself back to standing. Peered down his nose, first at Arlo, then Celadon, then back to her. Something in his expression fell away, a seriousness rising to take its place that she didn't even know he was capable of. "You want me to remove the block on your memories so that you'll know the whole of it, everything. Yes, Arlo *Jarsdel?*"

"Yes!"

"Then I'll see you outside in the training arena in two mornings' time, bright and early."

"The . . . training arena?"

She didn't understand. Would she . . . have to fight him for this information back? Defeat him in combat before he'd agree to yield what was already hers?

"Yes," Lethe purred, an answer to both her spoken and unspoken thoughts. And those poison eyes flared deadly brighter, like this was exactly what he'd wanted. Like it was all he'd *ever* wanted. "The training arena. Two mornings' time, and the morning after, and the morning after that—until little Arlo can wield her blade with just enough know-how that she might actually stand a chance of surviving what comes after certain things are returned."

"You'll teach me, too."

Arlo frowned, turning to study her cousin. Lethe considered him too.

Celadon's announcement was firm and commanding, a fire behind his eyes she saw only when he was well and truly passionate about something—something that upset him; something, usually, that pertained to her.

Cocking his head in the opposite direction, Lethe continued his blank assessment . . . then—"I will, will I?"

"Why not?" Celadon challenged. Arlo didn't really understand what was going on, this quiet battle of wills between them, but she wouldn't press right now. This seemed . . . important. "Don't think it would be *boring*, do you?"

A moment . . .

Two . . .

Lethe clicked his tongue—three times, that sound that was almost like a nervous tic.

Then, "Follow me."

CHAPTER 19

Celadon

"P ICK IT UP," LETHE drawled casually as he sauntered for the middle of the room, and Celadon's gaze dropped to his feet—to the sword there hardening into steel from a burst of inky smoke.

The Crystal Atrium had always been one of his favorite rooms in the Luminous Palace. Back when he'd been younger, before he'd even figured out Reseda wasn't his birth mother and Riadne had been no one more than his father's greatest rival, he'd actually admitted this to Riadne in his last ever visit here.

The way sunlight filtered in through fissures cut like streaks of lightning in the rainbow-stained crystal . . . the way everything seemed to run together, fluid, like melted wax . . . It had seemed to Celadon back then like a dreamscape made reality. Celadon finally now understood why she'd been so guarded and uncomfortable around him that whole trip, but when he'd asked her back then—all wide-eyed amazed and embarrassingly earnest—if she'd ever teach him how to duel here, she'd smiled at him, so impossibly radiant . . . *happy* . . .

And handed him a sword.

I understand you just turned sixteen, High Prince. It's Winter's custom to mark such an important milestone with the gift of a blade. I'm sure your father has given you many; I would like to present you with one, as well, if you would have it.

Celadon hadn't understood.

He'd simply been delighted by the present—an elegant blade of spring-green glass and wicked-sharp obsidian, encrusted with emeralds and black diamonds like stars around a moonstone moon inlaid in both sides of the hilt.

And when he'd later shown his father, he still hadn't understood why Azurean had first looked stricken and then angry. He had berated Riadne fiercely for carelessness, and Celadon had assumed then his father had thought she'd been hoping he'd injure himself with the gift, or maybe it had been enchanted to harm him.

His response had been to act out—to show his father he was sorry for being so careless himself, to punish Riadne for putting him in that position. The Pokémon cards he'd used to make a fool of her in front of her Court . . . the genuine hurt in Riadne's eyes when she realized what he'd done. . . . His father had laughed—relieved, Celadon supposed now, that their secret remained undiscovered.

That had been the last time the Viridians had ever been welcome in Riadne's home.

Azurean had confiscated the sword immediately, and Celadon hadn't cared, had forgotten it entirely—assumed it had been destroyed, and that was that . . .

Until now.

Until here it was, winking up at him, on the atrium's gleaming floor.

"We haven't got all day, Celadon . . . ," Lethe prodded, and Celadon blinked, resurfaced from his memories to bend and retrieve his blade.

Just as back then—like no time at all had passed for it; like wherever it had been stored, it had been well cared for—the blade was exquisite. Perfectly balanced in his hand, cool and smooth to the touch, it cut the air with a melodious whistle when Celadon tested its feel with a swing.

"You want me to train you."

His gaze lifted sharply from his sword to find Lethe watching him. Superficial amusement gleamed on the surface of those acid eyes, distracting from the fathomless depths of what he was truly thinking.

Celadon nodded.

"I do," he replied.

And heaving a sigh of great dramatics, Lethe flicked out his hand—the one with claws.

The adamantine there grew and branched out and twisted, until snaked around his hand was a hilt and lengthening to a lethal point was no blade Celadon could ever hope to contend with; it made his own sword look like a toothpick in comparison—small and offensively boring.

Lethe grinned at him. "A test, then. Inspire me, Your Highness—show me I wouldn't be wasting my time, that you won't just run in fear from this, too." His creaking, sepulchral voice dripped with private glee. Those acid eyes danced. "How sad, your adoring Courts used to bleat for you. How sad that Daddy had fallen too ill to train his youngest son. How noble, they would *simper* for you, that you filled your time instead with study."

That grin turned vicious.

Celadon's grip tightened nervously around the hilt in his palm.

"Inspire me, Viridian. Show me what that warlord father of yours taught you in private, where no one would see and start to wonder if maybe they too should be afraid of this pretty, little, unassuming boy they'd so much prefer stay their porcelain doll . . . useless, decorative . . . *boring*."

Celadon struck.

The clash of their blades was like a crack of thunder throughout the atrium, and he heard Arlo's gasp on the sidelines.

She knew.

She was the only person he'd ever confided in about what his father had been teaching him in the protected bowels of the palace; in a darkened room only UnSeelie eyes could see properly in, where no one was allowed but the two of them. Azurean had forbidden Celadon to speak of it to anyone . . . but he'd told Arlo, because as she was the keeper of his true name, no promise could ever bind him from hiding anything from her that he wanted to share. Not even the Hunters were permitted in on what Azurean simply called their private lessons, between High King and High Prince, who was meant to inherit the Court's deadliest secrets as future Councillor on the Head's Committee.

Arlo knew—but she'd never seen with her own two eyes how *good* Celadon actually was with a sword.

How he could strike, and strike, and strike like lightning—bolt, after bolt, after bolt.

Powerful blows they were, too.

Azurean had taught him well, how to bend the air to his aid so he could fly around this arena like gliding; how to angle his strength just so, track his opponent's movements to pick up patterns of how they'd attack.

Celadon was good—he was better than good, and he'd stuffed it all down in fear.

But it was time. Just as Lethe said, it was time to figure out what he wanted for himself. He needed to find a way to relieve himself of all these caged-up emotions that would only drag him down, would only serve to render him useless against further threats to the precious few he had left to love.

It was time to stop running.

Lethe wanted him to prove himself? To prove he was done with cowering from his own shadow?

He lunged, so quick that the crack of their blades was a hair of a second later, and Lethe's grinned spread even wider, as though his face might split in two.

"You don't fight like him at all, you know," Lethe taunted, then lunged right back.

He threw his weight against their crossed blades, and Celadon had time only to register a shift before he was sent careening backward— and immediately assailed with blows.

Strike after strike after strike, Lethe was . . . Cosmin, there was no way to describe it. He wasn't good; he wasn't great; he wasn't best in all the realms. Lethe just *was*—war, battle, death—and all Celadon could do was block; dodge; roll out of the way as night streaked after and adamantine cut clean through crystal where his head, his chest, his leg had just been.

Block . . . but it was clear to him that he was only managing even that because Lethe didn't actually want to kill him; was even now pulling his strength, and Cosmin, he didn't want to be the actual target of this being's genuine ire.

"You fight like *her*," he purred in Celadon's ear when their blades locked again, and Lethe swept his feet out beneath him, slammed his sword into the floor just inches above Celadon's head, and draped himself over his body. . . .

Muscle and bone . . . Lethe was like solid steel against him.

But rather than frightened, Celadon felt calm.

Anyone else this close in his space—this intimately, besides—would rankle immediate discomfort. But not once, not ever, in their whole time knowing each other, had Celadon ever felt like Lethe would actually force something from him that he didn't want.

The touches, and closeness, the indecency . . . It was starting to feel to Celadon like Lethe just had no concept of personal space; had never been afforded the luxury; had at some point had it stolen from him, broken from him, been violently disabused of the right . . . and at the same time, seemed a little bit starved for connection.

Like after he'd been taught that his body didn't belong to him, he'd been cruelly and wholly discarded.

"It's the desperation," the star-freckled Hunter continued to tease, nose brushing Celadon's nose. "How badly you want to prove yourself to opinion that shouldn't matter—"

Lethe cut off—felt it, and stiffened.

It was Celadon's turn to grin, but he didn't.

The dagger he kept on himself at all times now, hidden just up his sleeve. Lethe had been so distracted by his own game, had underestimated Celadon, and that was exactly what Celadon had been taught to take advantage of. Because Lethe was right—the

Courts would so much rather he play the role of a pretty face and nothing else, and Azurean wanted him to have every protection he could.

Pressed just a little bit firmer, the blade at the side of Lethe's throat punctured skin.

A pinprick of sapphire welled up around it.

In the silence that spanned eternity, wherein Lethe simply stared, that blood trickled down that dagger's edge and kissed the tip of Celadon's finger.

"It's not their opinion that matters to me, Lethe."

. . . and continued to stare . . .

"I'm not after opinion at all."

. . . and continued to stare . . .

"I've made my choice. I'm tired of running. I'm tired of being afraid. And I'm especially tired of being just like every other person in your life—for all this attention from you lately, I'm still just a pawn. And I can't really explain why, except that I've never really enjoyed measuring *less* in the esteem of people who've managed to catch my attention, but I would much, much rather be seen as your equal. Or, you know"—he chanced it now, the hint of a grin, of hope that Lethe wasn't about to eviscerate him for playing too close at familiarity—"as equal as a mortal fae and immortal warrior of death can ever be. I would like to be your *friend*."

. . . and continued to stare.

Then slowly, watching him all the while, like at any moment Celadon might take advantage of his hesitance and attack full-force, Lethe withdrew. Reeled back to his knees and continued to stare. Heaved his sword from the ground and continued to stare. Swept back to standing—but it was Riadne he watched now.

Riadne, whose singular clap turned from one to two to steady, reverberating applause.

Celadon craned his head.

His mother had been watching this entire time alongside a collection of people who'd gathered at the doorway and had quietly filtered into the stands that wrapped around the room. She clapped for him, looking beside herself with pride—her son, he'd just bested a Hunter. But there was something else, too, in the way her focus narrowed on Lethe that could almost be . . . smug, like she'd just acquired a shiny new weapon, a valuable piece of knowledge.

Lethe narrowed his eyes back, almost like a dare to wield it against him.

Remembering himself, Celadon scrambled to peel himself off the floor. Cosmin, what a foolish thing to forget, even for a moment, that every single thing he did now stood the chance of becoming a knife at his throat, and Riadne had just gained an advantage.

A knowing.

That Celadon liked the Hunter across from him, the man who felt so oddly familiar to him at times in a far more profound way than someone who'd simply been around his entire life.

And a knowing that Lethe might . . . actually like Celadon back.

The clapping stopped. His mother lowered her gaze to him. "Again," she commanded, and before Celadon could pull himself back together, night lunged itself at him once more.

"—and I bequeath to you my PS5, which I paid way too much for on eBay but will never regret for the stunning clarity of Sephiroth in all his leather-clad glory."

"Yeah," Arlo replied fairly dryly to what was possibly Celadon being a touch overdramatic as he sat crumpled against the atrium wall, trying to force burning lungs to breathe again.

She patted his head, gaze traveling up to Lethe, who was, in Celadon's opinion, unfairly unfazed by the whole four hours Riadne had pinned them both to training—and to her piercing assessment of their relationship.

Not even a bead of sweat on that brow . . . and here was Celadon, half hoping he died soon to escape this soul-deep exhaustion. "Yeah," Arlo repeated, "I'm starting to connect some dots now." Her gaze cut to Lethe. "You do have a type."

Lethe eyed them skeptically. "If I ask what a Sephiroth is, will I regret it?"

Celadon laughed—he very much would regret it, because there was one thing in this world that Arlo would happily discuss with pretty much anyone, probably even Riadne if she took a pause for interest. And sure enough, Arlo's expression brightened like the sun on his mother's skin. "It's a Final Fantasy character—"

"Oh look, I do regret it," Lethe said witheringly.

He was spared the continued explanation, regardless. Riadne appeared before them, the room having drained to just them on the sidelines. She was *very* pleased by what had just happened, but it was a small price to pay, Celadon reasoned. It wasn't like she could harm Lethe in any way, and Celadon wasn't a fool—Lethe liked him as much as he might ever like another person, but ultimately . . . Celadon was replaceable.

The moment she tried to use Celadon against him, Lethe would probably laugh and help her.

Celadon had won far more from this risk than she had; he could tell that by the way Lethe lingered, still here beside him, and a little . . . subdued, instead of bristling and whisking away like he was better known to do.

"Might I inquire what that was about?"

All eyes deferred to Celadon.

Heaving on breath, he attempted to straighten—he was a Cosmin-damned windborn fae; he'd spent whole days in training with his father before, but four mere hours against Lethe and right now he just wanted to lie on this floor, and if he ever moved again, it would be too soon.

"A test to see if we'd be up to the task. Arlo and I . . . we'd like to train. With Lethe, if you'd allow this, Mother?"

Because that's what this was about.

This was her palace—there was no way Riadne didn't know what was going on already. But there was protocol to follow and a reminder that the decision to allow this was entirely hers.

"It does neither of us any good to occupy our current roles without the physical means to defend ourselves. Myself against assassination, which I'm certain will soon be attempted; Arlo against much the same, when the wrong people figure out her importance to you."

"My clever boy," Riadne mused, not quite gently, only barely a threat. "Your father taught you a silver tongue too—he was quite skilled at that, back in his prime. You will be careful how you use it on me." To Lethe she said in a clipped voice, "You will train them, and my other son, too. Vehan is to be included in these lessons. It will do him good to strengthen under proper force. I fear I've just been too soft on him, as a mother tends to be."

Celadon recalled his brother's exhaustion.

How haunted Vehan looked behind sunshine and grace, by a lifetime that didn't come anywhere close to the definition of "soft," he was sure.

Riadne knew where to draw the line . . . didn't she? She wasn't so far gone in her quest for power that she'd forgotten that Vehan was flesh and bone and fragile life that could, and very well might, just extinguish rather than fan into the wildfire she hoped for . . . right?

Lethe snorted and turned just as abruptly to leave.

It was as much of a reply as she was going to get, and not an outright no, which Celadon had come to learn meant that he wouldn't turn Vehan away if he showed up in two days in the training arena with them.

"Mother to son, what are you hoping for here, Celadon? Truly."

Eyes not once leaving Lethe's retreating back, Celadon struggled to standing. Arlo helped. Did her best to ignore Riadne altogether—good. Riadne had no idea what she'd bitten off in holding his cousin hostage here. Arlo was no one's perfect doll, either.

"Just making friends," he replied with all the air of charm. "Don't worry, Mother," he added, tearing his eyes at last from Lethe to drop Riadne a winsome wink and wrap his arm around Arlo's shoulders, hugging her close to his side . . . for support . . . for strength . . . for a quiet thank-you. "I promise that, in the end, you'll be *very* proud."

CHAPTER 20

Nausicaä

~⟡~

F OR LAW, I WAS made. As Justice, I serve. To duty, I surrender all—vigilant, impartial, resolute . . ." Nausicaä stabbed her slice of cake clean through the middle and proceeded to shovel an entire half into her mouth, earning one or two worried glances from the others at the tables around her.

Vigilant, impartial, resolute . . . what a joke her life had been.

These were the words she'd sworn upon assumption of her role as Alecto. This was the promise every Erinys made, that she'd been close to bursting with pride over when her turn had come to speak the oh so glorious Oath to Order . . . like it had meant fucking anything, in the end.

Justice, Law, duty . . . these were the things she was meant to devote her entire existence to, to ensure the realms upheld themselves. And then her sister had died, and she'd taken her frustrations out on a miserable waste of a mortal and half his disgusting crew, and justice, Law, duty . . . these were all so quick to play their part, to punish her for breaking the rules; to expel her from the only home she'd ever known, the only family she had; to banish her here—but where was all that justice now?

Law, duty . . . Where were the Erinyes? Where was Megaera, who'd always been so deities-damned perfect? And now, when a mortal queen was using hells fucking *pitch*-dark magic to stir up actual capital *E* Evil . . . nothing.

Silence.

Not even a slap on the wrist.

Nausicaä had been so pleased with herself. She'd really thought back then that she'd stood for something, meant something, was doing good in the realms—that her actions mattered, even in the smallest of ways. Of course, that mattering hadn't made the things she'd been forced to witness any better, but it had been . . . bearable, because of it.

The things they'd seen, the horrors people were capable of inflicting on others . . . it had broken Tisiphone; it broke a lot of them. But Nausicaä had been so damned naive, so embarrassingly proud of what she did, and none of it had *ever fucking mattered.*

She stabbed the other half of her cake so violently that the elderly couple beside her jolted in their seats.

Nausicaä sighed.

Tried to reel herself back in.

Nothing was as it should be.

Over a hundred years later, and she still carried a soul-wrenching grief around inside her.

The Mortal Realm was going to shit.

None of the immortals would intervene, because all of them, even their damned bloody Law, were grasping at straws now for their freedom.

And Arlo . . . the first person to fight their way through all of Nausicaä's barbed wire and barriers and snarling defenses to see the hollow, pathetic remains of who Nausicaä was beneath—really *see* her, and not shrink away in secondhand shame . . .

Arlo.

The first person to make her remember love was more than the pain she carried, the scars she wore like a warning to others. Arlo was at the center of everything right now, and Nausicaä just wanted to protect her at any cost . . . even this one.

Even the one that had her sitting here in this quaint little café hacking apart cake. Eating . . . quietly watching . . . waiting . . . as the ironborn boy she'd been tasked with following today sat hunched over his cup of plain black coffee at a table of his own.

The nostalgia of it all made her want to bark a laugh.

Maybe she would have, if she could say for certain that laughter wouldn't turn into something else. Because this could almost be the Good Vibes Only café all over again, but . . . Nausicaä wasn't here out of curiosity this time. The embers of duty to a way of life that *no longer mattered* weren't what compelled her actions now.

She'd worked so hard to be the person who deserved to be with someone like Arlo, who was all things beautiful in this world, so passionate, steadfast, and good to her very core. Nausicaä had really tried. . . .

The boy at the table across the way heaved himself back to an upright position.

Nausicaä's gaze cut briefly to him.

Thick brown hair, a cherubic face only just beginning to sharpen in the jaw and cheeks—he couldn't be more than seventeen, but life hadn't been all that kind to him either, by the looks of things. There was muscle to his alarmingly thin frame, but the sort cut from day after day of hard labor and night after night of too little food and proper sleep. His clothes were just a bit too large for him, old and faded. Nausicaä had only just taken up tracking him, but she didn't need it spelled out for her, the tragic backstory of heartbreak and neglect of a kid at the mercy of a foster system that bounced him from one overcrowded home to the next.

She didn't know his name.

It was definitely easier that way.

Puppy, she called him in her head—like *that* made things any easier, but he reminded her of a sad little dog left abandoned on the side of the road in a pathetic little cardboard box in the middle of a rainstorm . . . and none of this helped what she was here to do.

Regardless, he was Puppy—and Puppy was finally on the move.

Standing from his table, he threw back the remaining contents of his cup, pulled a face like it had been whisky. Without a glance at his surroundings, expression grim as if he were marching off to war,

Puppy made for the café's exit and out into the busy New York streets.

He had no idea.

None of them did—and for their lack of training, their lack of awareness, none of them ever saw it; and if they did, not until it was too late.

But Nausicaä did . . .

The glowing green that flashed in his veins just as he took his leave.

Sighing, Nausicaä stood. Shoved the last piece of Emotional Support Cake in her mouth and swept from the café as well.

New York was a . . . place. Nausicaä liked cities in fits and bursts, had lived in many when the mood struck her to be surrounded by noise and people and distraction. Increasing was the appeal of disappearing into the woods to live her life as a hermit in blissful solitude, but she couldn't deny there was something about the severe reality of human architecture. Romantic in some lights, austere in others, but simple compared to the obnoxious grandeur of what was found in the Immortal Realm.

Down the streets Nausicaä trailed.

Puppy had somewhere specific to be, she could tell by his hustle, the purpose in his stride, and he cut through the sidewalk thoroughfare with ease; who needed invisibility when the world would much rather look the other way than acknowledge a person they'd failed?

Down the street, around the corner, sharply into a narrow alley . . .

Nausicaä was careful to give him his space, to allow him a moment or two to himself in that narrow sliver of gloom before she followed him in—and paused on the threshold.

Facing her now, arms folded across his chest, an adorable picture of cross the way he glared at her, Puppy eyed Nausicaä from head to toe and back again . . . and glared just a little harder for the assessment. "If you're looking to jump me, I've got nothing to steal."

Oh well.

They would have had to cross this bridge at some point—it wasn't like Nausicaä could just scoop him up unawares and deposit him at

Riadne's doorstep, clean as that. At least there was some privacy now.

"That's a matter of perspective, I guess." Shrugging, she stepped into the alley. "Listen, Puppy—"

Puppy stared. "I . . . What?"

Nausicaä waved him off. "It's nothing personal, okay? I'm just doing my job. But you're going to have to come with me—by choice or force, that's up to you—"

"Oh my God, you're trying to *steal* me?"

His frown drew deeper, and there was wariness now. He took a step away from her, retreating just a little farther into the alley, but embers sparked in his deep brown eyes. "Are you working for them, then?"

It was Nausicaä's turn to stare. She cocked her head, considered what the boy implied.

"Is this what you do?" Puppy snarled, those embers in his eyes catching fire. "Is this how you abducted my brother? You're sick, you know that? A bunch of disgusting pedophiles—"

Something . . . wasn't adding up here.

Nausicaä raised her hand.

"Question, because I felt like we were maybe on the same page up until the whole pedophile thing: Hi, I'm Nausicaä. You can call me the Dark Star. I work for the High Queen of the Eight Great Courts, and she's sent me to bring you in so she can perform all sorts of No Beuno dark magic on you to resurrect one of the Seven Sins she's injected into your heart and definitely murder you in the process." Dropping her hand, she peered a little closer at her puppy. "What are *you* doing?"

Puppy's eyes widened with disbelief before narrowing sharply with suspicion. "You don't work for the Fang Gang?"

"I . . . kind of want to set whatever the Fang Gang is on fire for having such a stupid fucking name, but no."

Puppy snorted, his suspicion turned withering. "You just called yourself the Dark Star."

"Which is a great name!" Nausicaä defended hotly. "I don't have to explain myself to someone named Puppy."

"No one calls me that! You call me that! That's not my name, *Dork Star*."

"Oh, wow, I didn't realize I was kidnapping a five-year-old."

"Whatever," Puppy sighed harshly. "I don't have time for this. If you're not one of Fangtasia's lugs, help or get out of the way."

This was going . . . decidedly not how Nausicaä had pictured this going. And Puppy had already turned from her to make his way toward a dented, peeling red door stamped into the alley's grimy, pockmarked left wall. She had to admit . . . she was curious. The kid wasn't getting away from her, and Riadne hadn't put a time stamp on his due date, so she had some time—she'd bite. It wasn't like she actually wanted to lead Puppy to his sacrificial slaughter, anyhow.

You're getting too soft, she mentally berated.

If your heart is getting in the way of what you must do . . . I will remind you, there's been a way out of this all along, Riadne's words echoed in her ears.

"What's Fangtasia?" she heard herself ask, and there she went, following Puppy. . . . She should get this over with, and quickly, before she formed any further attachment.

Together, the pair of them stood before the door.

There was no indication it was anything more than a side entrance to the smoothie shop that the front of the building labeled it as being. But Puppy looked firmly convinced this was . . . Well, by the name, it sounded like some sort of club getting up to no good. The question was, was this just a bunch of shitty humans playing at intimidation? Or was it actually vampires . . . and did Puppy have any idea?

"It's a club run by vampires."

Okay. Puppy had some idea, then.

Which wasn't surprising, because he was ironborn, which meant even if his foster families were human and therefore not capable of training him in folk ways, he still possessed something of the Sight—

not nearly enough, if the Courts hadn't brought him in for even the pretense of a Weighing, but some.

Eyeing him sidelong, Nausicaä kept her tone ambiguous. "Vampires, huh?"

Puppy sighed. "Whatever. You don't have to believe me—"

"Not saying I don't—"

"Just . . . you're spouting off about working for some High Queen and . . . the Sins, and whatever else, and I'm not stupid. I know that's all code. But those are actually vampires in there—or at the very least they really play up the part. Whatever you want from me, fine, you can have it, but first you have to help me. They took my little brother. They take so many kids—it's gross, it's vile, it's . . . They *feed* on them. Literally feed on them."

. . . Oh really.

Nausicaä turned her focus back to the door. Vigilant, impartial, resolute . . . the old ways, they died hard, and those words might not matter a lick to the rest of her kind these days, but to Nausicaä . . . "I'm assuming you have some sort of proof?"

"Nothing physical." Puppy's voice was close to breathless now, anger clinging in tears to his lower lashes. "The police wouldn't listen. They called me *crazy*. I'm just some stupid throwaway to them, to all of them, and no one cares . . ." He winced, reaching up to massage his chest, and Nausicaä . . . felt her own heart clench, just briefly. "But I snuck in. I have to find my brother, Dark Star, I have to! We're all we have left in the world—who's going to look out for him but me? I have to find him, and I did—here, with a bunch of . . . of fucking *monsters*, and I don't care if they kill me, I'm going in there and getting him out, today."

You mean the world to me, Tisiphone.
I love you.
Who's going to look out for us but each other?

Fuck.

"Yeesh. It's getting harder and harder to live, laugh, love in these conditions. All right. So, I guess we're kicking some vampire ass, then. Never liked them anyhow—vampires are all dicks."

Puppy looked at her like she'd just invented Christmas.

The door was open—because of course it was; vampires were so dull. They entered the building, and as soon as they did . . .

Nausicaä wrinkled her nose.

"Yup. Vampires."

It was the smell of the place—the coppery tang of human blood, the sickly bittersweetness of folk blood, all of it layered with fear and death, because apparently Fangtasia didn't play by the "rules" either. The *Fang Gang* was rogue. Nausicaä didn't need to see any corpses lying around—which she undoubtedly would if she poked her head in enough of the doors they passed in this dimly lit, cement stretch of hall. She could smell them. Bodies—decaying, fresh. Like a flood she was hit by the memories of one of the more gruesome horrors she'd ever had to tend to; of Noel—Pallas Viridian's infamous lover—and the madness he'd fallen to, the darkness that had stolen him, broken him, and used his shell for slaughter and pain.

It had been . . . bad.

She recalled Tisiphone after, despondent for weeks.

So bad even the Divine Council had deemed it necessary to give the Erinyes a night's "reprieve" from their duties, which Nausicaä didn't really remember, because that night was also the first she'd ever drank enough to black out whole hours of her life.

Whole hours, but never this—not the way it smelled.

"You hang back, okay, Puppy?" she whispered at him when they came to the end of the hall and paused at a plain red door. The kid had all the right words, but she doubted he actually believed it himself—not fully, at least, but he would. Those were *vampires* in there. As little as Nausicaä thought of them, they were nothing any mortal could simply laugh off.

"The hell I will," Puppy growled under his breath. "Do you know what my brother looks like?"

Rolling her eyes, Nausicaä conceded that, "No, fine, I don't—but you let me do all the fighting, toothpick."

"Has anyone ever told you you've got the creative depth of a teaspoon?"

It was a shame Puppy was going to die. No matter what Nausicaä did, the array on his chest she knew was there without having to see, given that she could sense the dark magic for miles off . . . He'd succumb to it, somehow or another. But it figured that Puppy was . . . all right.

Luck, Destiny, Fate—whoever; whichever; none of them seemed to like her all that much.

"Just keep behind me till the room is clear, okay?"

"Fine."

Nausicaä opened the door.

The words to describe what they walked into . . . they were all just *words*. They didn't suffice. The room sank down a flight of crushed-velvet stairs to a cavernous pit without windows. Light was the barest flicker of candles—on tables; mounted on the wall; perched in the overhead chandelier that hung from the high-lifted ceiling, where strung up around it were cages of bone and corpses half decomposed.

Very small bones.

Very small corpses.

Very small bodies that were nearly dead but too dazed to notice, too drained to care, propped up on the richly upholstered sofas below.

I'm not a murderer, Nausicaä tried to remind herself again and again, and she never believed it, because moments like this—descending the velvet stairs to a symphony of hissing, and snarls, and shouts, her wings flaring open wide, her glamour fading; Erebus, her sword, materializing in her hand—moments like this, she'd choose death every time.

Fangtasia rose as one and lunged.

Four . . . seven . . . fifteen strong, an entire horde of vampires, rogue of their Conclave, of Pallas and the founding others who'd committed the original sin, and now in punishment served as a puppet government to all those who came after.

How had they been allowed this freedom for so long?

This was Riadne's own backyard. . . . She had to have known—did she simply not care? Or was this more a reflection of how horrible everything was devolving that there just wasn't the capacity to keep track of it all anymore?

Riadne would owe her, regardless.

"You called the police?"

Nausicaä slipped her phone back into her pocket. "They'll take it from here."

They stood in the alley afterward, Puppy white and trembling, his far-too-young little brother unconscious but alive in his arms. Nausicaä could already hear sirens in the distance drawing steadily near—*slot it away; deal with what happened later.* She reached out. Carefully disentangled the sleeping brother from Puppy's arms. Turned and placed him gently on the alley floor, propped against the wall.

"They'll find him, right?" Puppy worried, inching a step forward like he couldn't help himself. "He'll be okay?"

Sighing, Nausicaä unfurled back to standing. "As okay as he's ever going to be, I suppose. This kind of thing, it . . . sticks with you."

"Will you . . . check on him, once in a while?"

Damn it all.

This was not how this was supposed to go. She'd gotten too involved, too attached. Fine, yes, Nausicaä had no problem delivering death to horrible people—in fact, she'd locked it in as a character trait and happily moved on. But she didn't like murdering innocent people. She didn't like what she'd have to do to this kid.

But if she didn't do it, Arlo would suffer.

"Listen, Puppy—"

"Jordan."

Nausicaä stared a moment . . . two . . . exhaled annoyance through her nose and nodded curtly. Fine. "Jordan," she amended. "Don't get the wrong idea, okay? I'm not a good person."

"I'll give you that. You're kind of shit, yeah? But the world isn't split into good and bad, and people aren't either."

"Life advice from a five-year-old."

Puppy—*Jordan*—ignored the dry remark. Raised a hand to his chest, rubbed at the muscle there. "I didn't really believe it, you know. The vampires . . . all of it. I kept thinking there had to be some sort of explanation, that monsters weren't real, that Kyle was just . . . Damn, is it fucked-up that I hoped he'd just been abducted by human traffickers that catered to weird fetishes?"

Nausicaä shrugged.

She was more preoccupied with the green that was beginning to spread through his veins again, slower this time, and thicker—like the steady pour of molasses.

"It's just," Jordan continued. "It was real. Which means . . . whatever the hell you are is real, too, and maybe you *are* here for exactly what you said you were. This . . . this queen of yours? What does she want with me? You mentioned something about my heart."

"Giving you trouble, is it?"

Slowly, Puppy nodded.

"Once in a while, does it ever twinge? Clench in your chest and feel like it might give out altogether or squeeze itself into dust?"

He nodded again.

"Ever catch a glowing in your periphery? Gold . . . red . . . green? Nothing distinct, nothing you find around you when you look, just . . . you could almost swear it was coming from *you*?"

There was silence this time.

Puppy looked grim.

And it was all the answer Nausicaä needed. "I don't know what happened, kid. Your parents must have been down on their luck.

Riadne must have made them an offer they just couldn't refuse, to use their newly conceived child in a dark magic experiment they didn't really understand, and ever since you were born . . . there's been a strange mark on your chest, right? You can't quite make it out—you haven't been trained in anything, and your Sight's probably next to nil. But there's something there—it's called an array, and it's tethered you to the Seven Sins. One by one, they're popping in and trying out your heart like a pair of shoes that are either going to crap out under their pressure or, worse, they'll obliterate your soul and take over your husk like a parasite." She shook her head at him. Riadne had damned him—seventeen years of hell for nothing. "Either way . . . you're going to die. I'm sorry, Jordan. I really am."

Jordan looked like he might cry.

His face was still white with shock and fear.

A good, strong breeze might kick up and crumble him to the ground, but he stood in front of Nausicaä, and there was still that fire in his eyes. That deities-damned fire nothing was ever going to put out . . . until Riadne got her hands on him.

"She wants you to take me to her?"

"What can I say, I'm a glorified shepherd, rounding up sheep."

She wanted to be sick.

Slot it away; deal with what's happening later.

Make it right.

"Can I ask you a favor?"

It was Nausicaä's turn to affect bravery, nonchalance; she pursed her lips and folded her arms over her chest. "Oh, just the one?"

Again, Jordan ignored her.

"Will *you* do it?" he asked in a small but resolute voice.

Vigilant, impartial, resolute . . .

Nausicaä didn't need to clarify. "I . . ."

"Please, will you do it? If I'm going to die either way—if my only options are death by heart attack or death by obliteration, please . . . give me the dignity of choice? Let me choose here . . . with my family."

"Jordan, I—"

"Please?"

Fuck.

Shit.

HellsGodsDamn.

Those fucking eyes.

This fucking life.

Nausicaä wasn't a murderer, she wasn't, she *wasn't*, and all she'd ever wanted was to protect the people she loved. Arlo mattered so much, and Nausicaä would do anything to keep her, to make sure she didn't abandon her like she'd abandoned Tisiphone in her time of need.

But this kid . . . this *fucking kid* . . .

"Thank you," he breathed, in a wet bubble of laughter.

Belatedly, very distantly, Nausicaä could feel his blood trickle warm and slick over her fingers, her blade buried to its hilt in Jordan's chest. "You're a good person, Dork Star."

He crumpled to the ground.

Nausicaä stared.

And stared.

The sirens grew closer.

"She isn't going to be happy about this," Yue said softly, peeling away from the shadows to begin his work collecting Puppy's soul.

Her face was wet.

Yue could see.

If your heart is getting in the way of what you must do . . . I will remind you, there's been a way out of this all along.

"She can join the fucking club," Nausicaä snarled at him and, in a burst of smoke, dissolved down to nothing . . .

And reappeared in the midst of a vacant throne room.

Through the palace she carved her displeasure, tracking down her quarry with a singular focus that made guests and staff and government officials alike dart quickly out of her way.

Down the halls, straight into that cursed private office, where Riadne might not realize the full gravity of what she played with yet, but soon, oh, one day soon . . . in fact, the very moment Arlo's memory of who she was returned, and Riadne learned about all who would happily bow to the Flamel legacy . . .

"Fuck. You."

Riadne looked up from paperwork she'd been perusing.

She took in the copper-red slick still on Nausicaä's hands, the blackened sapphire of vampire blood splashed across her torso, down the front of her legs, staining the strands of her hair.

Bending, Nausicaä slammed her sticky hands on the desk, pressing handprints into valuable documents. "I'm not doing this."

"I see," came Riadne's delicate reply. She lifted her gaze from the blood on her desk to meet briefly with Nausicaä's eyes.

Then, with a sniff, turned back to her paperwork.

For a moment, two, there was nothing but silence. Riadne had genuinely turned back to her work—which only pissed off Nausicaä even more.

"Put me back on garbage duty, get one of your many sycophant lackeys to collect your stones. Hells, you could probably get one of the immortals to do it, 'cause it seems they don't give a shit about—"

"I said I see. You are dismissed, Nausicaä Kraken." Riadne cut her off like a deadly blade, eyes not leaving her paper. "I accept your resignation and, under the outlined terms of your failure, give you the night to collect your things and say your goodbyes—by morning you will remove yourself from my palace and Courts."

"I'm not going anywhere. This wasn't—"

Riadne breathed a laugh as light as wind chimes—it was just as dangerous a sound as the clip of her previous order. "You refuse my commands, cannot even lay before me the heart of someone with no connection to you at all. What use have I with an assassin such as you, so willful and weighed down by morals?"

Forcing her jaw unclenched, Nausicaä restrained her temper to the curl of her nails scoring lines through the handsome wood beneath them. "I'm the *Dark Star*. You could have me do anything, but you'd rather my immortal skills wasted on playing collection service for your free-range experiments?"

A flash of electric blue—Riadne's gaze met hers again at last, and she looked far from amused.

"So where is it?"

"Where is what? The heart crapped out, a failed stone."

"But still a stone, and still with power, and still mine to possess. You were sent to collect it, successful or otherwise, and though by your own words the task was far beneath your capabilities, where is the heart, Nausicaä Kraken?" She waited a beat; another; three. And in this contained eternity, Riadne glared; Nausicaä glared right back. "So I repeat: you are *dismissed*."

Another slam of Nausicaä's hands on the desk made the object groan, threatening to crack in two down the middle. "I have until the Autumn Solstice. Give me something else to do."

Riadne rose from her seat.

Placed her hands on the desk as well.

Pressed with all her fae strength, the added support of her Crown, and the three Sins she controlled . . . and then the desk really did crack, like Riadne would rather tear everything she'd worked for apart with her own two hands than let anyone else be the cause of any amount of destruction.

Control.

Riadne was always, *always* about control, and Nausicaä had always, *always* balked at any authority other than her own. . . . Their conflict had been inevitable.

Neither of them pulled away.

Inches from each other, Riadne smiled, slow and sharp and cruel. "I gave you until the Autumn Solstice"—she spoke in a fan of breath across Nausicaä's face, spiced by the rich wines she favored at any hour of the day—"should you manage to sustain my amusement that long. But so far, and with so much at stake, you've only managed to act like a spoiled child, stomping around, pouting over your own miserable self-pity. You don't want to do this; you don't want to do that; you thwart and refuse me at every angle. You don't take this game of ours seriously, and oh, but that's far more disappointing to me than failure, not when I'd expected so much better sport from you, *Dark Star*."

Leaning in, she pressed a motherly kiss to Nausicaä's brow, which Nausicaä felt like a bucket of worms poured down her spine. "You are dismissed," she said, like granting a boon. "As High Queen in command of the treaty between our people, you who have been exiled to my protection have until morning to remove yourself. Failure to comply with *my* exile will be in breach of the treaty between our realms—grounds for Destruction, which I think you no longer want, but your immortal brethren now very much do, for all you've tampered with their plans. . . ."

Riadne . . . knew?

Of course she did.

Lethe had most definitely told her what the Immortal Realm was hoping for in quiet support of her aims, and that she still went ahead with this despite that. . . . This was all a giant game to her—and Riadne called *Nausicaä* a child.

"It would bring me great joy, as Sovereign of this realm, to give them permission to come and collect you. And then where would darling Arlo be? All alone, in so much darkness, so much grief, so much to propel her to the same tragic end as the one you loved before."

For all she claimed to be bored with her, there was a great deal of delight in what she added next: "In fact, I think the only thing I would like more now than to hand you over is *you* handing over what would have won you this competition from the very beginning . . . what would have spared you from all these useless, tender feelings that prevent you from living to your full potential."

337

And there it was . . . Nausicaä was out of time.

"You have until the morning," Riadne sealed. "Now remove yourself from my sight."

Out of time, caught between Destruction and worse, with only until morning to figure out which option frightened her more—or rather, which would protect Arlo best . . . and which would she hate Nausicaä the least for choosing?

CHAPTER 21

Vehan

———◦◦———

THE REFLECTION STARING BACK at Vehan in the glass of his standing mirror might as well have been a stranger, for all he couldn't recognize himself right now in the least. "I look ridiculous," he moaned, tugging at the far-too-little fabric of his porcelain-white . . . Whatever this was that Celadon had forced on him, he had no idea, but it hardly classified as a shirt.

The only solid bit of material on it was the zigzagged bolt of lightning cut to stretch from his shoulder to the jut of the opposite hip. Gossamer mesh made up the rest, not that there was much, and the whole of Vehan's abdomen had been left exposed to flash off the series of fine gold chains strung with a waterfall effect against his tan skin. Paired with dark bronze leather pants so tight they might as well be painted on him and bright gold riding boots despite the fact it wasn't a ride he was off to tonight and Vehan feared that, rather than resembling the stunning fae models on the covers of their fashion magazines, he looked like a kid playing dress-up.

Gold and shocking white smeared his eyes.

Powdered gold dust had been brushed through his hair, along with some magic or other he suspected, because never had it looked so black it *burned.*

Celadon didn't so much as glance up from his phone he was scrolling through when he replied, "Ridiculous would actually be what you planned on wearing before my intervention; your Court would have eaten you alive."

More sighing. Vehan wrinkled his nose and tried to tug his shirt a little farther down his torso.

He'd been a crown prince his entire life, and still this all seemed so daunting to him, how extreme the difference truly was in what their people expected of High Royalty. And then there was Celadon, also born into this life, these rules and expectations that were like steps in a deadly dance no one had taught him to perform, but one wrong move would cost him everything.

Stretched on his stomach across Vehan's bed, Celadon didn't look even a fraction concerned about . . . anything.

In similarly tight, liquid-tar leather painted onto his long legs; some airy swatch of black sheer wound about his frame in the semblance of an open blouse; black eyeliner sharp enough to be a blade and shadow smeared like soot around his eyes—the only bit of color to his older brother was his molten copper hair, bright as the core of the burning sun, and his stiletto shoes that were such an acidic green they could rival Vehan's least favorite Hunter's eyes.

Celadon was made for this.

Celadon *was* fashion. Most of his life he had been setting the standard for sidhe fae trends, and he was good at it, excelled at it, genuinely seemed to love the indulgence.

Celadon was still a High Prince, Vehan thought bitterly, so why had that mantle fallen to *Vehan* now, just because he was crown of the ruling Court?

"You look good, Vehan," Celadon added, still engrossed in his phone. "You're also making this harder than it has to be—you're the High Prince. *The* High Prince. Whatever you wear is going to be what they strut down next season's catwalk and cycle through our stores. Literally anything, Vehan. I just refuse to turn up to a revel with someone in khakis."

It was then that Vehan's bathroom door burst open.

And Arlo stepped out in a huff.

"I look ridiculous," she moaned.

"See!" Vehan cried.

"This *family* is ridiculous—no one appreciates me." Shaking his

340

head, Celadon finally clicked off his phone and slipped it into what had to be a void in space and time, because Vehan honestly didn't know how he even got *himself* into those pants, let alone anything else. Unspooling like a cat, he crossed his legs and eyed Arlo critically— and it panged Vehan a little that there was so much familiarity in the feigned disdain that was actually pure, warmest love.

He'd always wanted a sibling.

Now that he had one, he didn't really know how to go about bridging the gap that time had created between them.

"You look beautiful, Arlo," he said instead.

She did, in her fluttery emerald pants slit up to midthigh on both sides and a crop top bound across her chest in the same exact shade.

Arlo was still far from her usual self. There remained a wall between her and everyone else, a stiff reservation, like she couldn't quite keep herself from her friends but didn't dare get too close again. Not yet. Not until they proved to her that letting them close didn't put them in any more danger than they were already in, Vehan suspected.

But there was plenty of time for regaining the grounds of their relationship later.

For tonight, it seemed Arlo had relented a little more; had missed the closeness of her newly returned cousin. Enough, at least, to let Celadon curl and pile her fire-red hair like a series of roses that draped off over her left shoulder and twist around her arms and waist in moon-bright bands of silver, jagged and studded to resemble thorns.

Their first Court revel, both Arlo's and his.

Vehan had been dodging this for weeks now—ever since his mother had been Crowned High Queen, and his peers he'd attended school with were all crucial people with whom he was expected to make and maintain connections. After all, these were the one-day sidhe elite of Seelie Summer, the aristocracy that would keep their horribly corrupt system running just the way they liked it.

Fina, Kine . . . the fae he'd grown up with, seen every day since toddlerhood, and he couldn't stand the majority of them, but if Vehan wanted protection in this world, if he wanted to survive, he needed them, and they needed him. A vicious circle of cutthroat contempt masquerading as smiles.

Revels were a bit of unspoken tradition.

Like the games they'd played in school, zapping each other with lightning until one emerged the victor, revels weren't . . . strictly allowed. Revels were exactly what they sounded like—fae youth let loose in all their hormonal monstrosity, indulging in powerful wines and narcotics to celebrate, explore, party with one another, forge unions, and break hearts to a backdrop of decadence and vice.

Vehan had gone his whole life without ever being roped into one—Aurelian had been a good deterrent to hide behind whenever his peers had tried calling on him.

But he was High Prince now, and his mother had actually insisted when she intercepted the invitation slipped to him during this morning's breakfast.

You will attend. They expect you to attend. Droll as they are, those children will be your advisors, your government, your eyes and ears when the time comes for you to sit on this throne. Anything you gain now will be vital leverage later against their collected power. But do take Celadon with you, she'd added, handing him back the folded bit of paper and picking up her wine once more. *Goodness knows, if there's any veracity to our tabloids, he's a little too well versed in this particular sport. And Arlo will go along as well—she can't learn all there is to being fae by studying out of books.*

Arlo, who also struggled with the amount of skin her clothing revealed, given the way she held closed her pants as she walked, moved to Vehan's side to assess her reflection as well.

A moment passed . . . two . . .

"You don't have to, you know," she said to him quietly—not so quietly that Celadon couldn't hear, but clearly the conversation was meant for them alone.

Vehan's mirror gaze sought hers. He raised a brow. "I don't have to go? Unfortunately, I do—"

Shaking her head, Arlo clarified, "No, I mean, you don't have to wear it. The outfit. You never have to wear anything Celadon picks. It's just . . . I mean, *I* didn't really understand it until recently—like, the reason he's so into clothing. I think it's how he protects himself, you know? His armor against the world. And it used to annoy me, how he'd always want a say in my wardrobe, even though what he picked was always way better than anything I chose, but . . . knowing how much he associates his outfits with security, I think it's more . . . this is how he protects the people he cares about as well. But you don't actually have to wear it if it makes you uncomfortable. For all he whines, he won't actually be upset. I've told him to shove off *so* many times." She nudged his side, her smirk deepening. "He was serious about the khakis, though."

Nudging her back, Vehan smiled in return, small and slowly blooming, a confidential thing between them.

How he protects the people he cares about.

That . . . made Vehan happy.

To hear. To know that Celadon hadn't been despairing of him and his poor sense of style, annoyed that Vehan needed his help; to know that his assistance had been an olive branch of sorts—and okay, maybe he didn't look terrible right now; he could show up in worse things tonight. Vehan spied Celadon in the glass, bent back over his phone, hiding that bit of sapphire in his face that betrayed embarrassment because he of course had heard every word Arlo said, and the more Vehan got to know Celadon, the more he realized how shy Celadon actually was underneath all that confidence and poise.

It was worth a bit of discomfort, he decided—the small but significant acknowledgment that as much as Vehan wanted to reshape their dynamic as the family he never had, Celadon might want the same thing too.

A knock at the bedroom door—startled, all three of them whipped their heads toward the sound, then relaxed when the wooden barrier cracked open an inch for Nausicaä's head to peek through. "Is my princess in this tower?" she asked, hand over her eyes, in the chance that Vehan was in the middle of undressing.

She didn't look . . . well.

Vehan studied her a moment before replying. Between Celadon and Arlo, one or both had obviously texted her about tonight's excursion given her outfit, which entailed black knee-high boots pulled over black tights and a tight, leopard-print halter crop top that was pretty much just a bikini, pinched together at the center by a rhinestone-studded onyx ring.

Black matte lipstick painted her bold lips.

Gold glitter rimmed her eyes.

The glamour Nausicaä wore was so attractive it was almost absurd—all immortals had something extra about them, and their overwhelming beauty had been just as much a weapon against mortal kind as their power. Whatever lurked beneath all that distraction, on the outside, she was perfect to look at.

But there was still something off about her tonight.

Vehan couldn't pinpoint what.

Arlo, who could read her far better, seemed to notice as well. She frowned a moment, then recovered quickly and crossed the room to plant herself directly in front of her.

There was even more distance between the two of them than usual. Arlo had somewhat let Vehan and Celadon back in, but it was Nausicaä—had always been Nausicaä, for at least as long as Vehan had known them—that Arlo protected more fiercely than she did anyone else, including herself.

Whatever she was still holding back from Nausicaä, Arlo clearly couldn't resist the banter, and added in a huff of fond exasperation, "You know you're definitely Bowser in this situation, right?"

And Nausicaä unfurled a grin down at her girlfriend.

Vehan dropped his gaze—the intimacy at the moment seemed . . . indecent for him to intrude on.

"Pretty Petal, you have no idea."

...

"This is us."

Vehan rolled up the tinted window of his mother's white Tesla Roadster. From her large collection of vehicles, they'd chosen something a little flashier than what Vehan normally drove around in—mostly at Celadon's insistence. A quick enough journey down the Las Vegas Strip, and they were soon nestled in a parking garage, the entrance to which had been visible only to those with the Sight.

The garage was packed.

Stepping out into the narrow sliver of space he'd been waved into by one of the revel's attendants, Vehan was hit with the night's humidity, cooler and fragrant with some concoction he was sure to encounter in much greater concentration when they actually got to the party.

"Weird that it's underground. . . ."

Vehan had been to precisely zero revels, but he knew enough about them to know that they were usually outdoor events in lush, open spaces and hosted among the trees.

"This isn't a *faerie* revel, Vehan," Celadon replied upon exiting the vehicle too. He straightened to standing, immediately made to open Arlo's passenger side door and help her out, and once everyone was assembled, drew them into a close huddle at the car's back bumper. "None of you have been to a sidhe revel before—"

"False," Nausicaä stated, but rather than be annoyed by the interruption, Vehan noted a flicker of relief across Celadon's expression.

"—So I'm going to need you to listen." He pointed his gaze at Vehan. "You're full-blooded sidhe, Crown Prince of your Court, and Ruling High Prince of all Eight. You will be the focal point of that entire party. They will expect you to indulge them, indulge in their dance and food and drink and various other forms of intoxication. I advise you to partake only in the sliver amount that will appease them, because just as your . . . Just as *our* mother no doubt intends you to gain from this experience, everyone here is looking for something to hold leverage over you later on down the line. One wrong

345

word, one glance that lingers too long, who you choose to keep company with—everything here tonight is a test designed by your peers to gauge where they stand with you and how best to get their claws in you. So just be *careful*, Vehan. What happens tonight sets the entire foundation of your future rule."

Vehan swallowed.

No pressure, then. Gods, he wished Aurelian were here—and then had to bite the inside of his cheek to keep from nervous laughter as he imagined how thoroughly Aurelian would *hate* if he actually were.

To Arlo now Celadon turned his focus. "You take this." He popped the trunk of the car, handed Arlo the water bottle from the pack he'd pitched there before they'd set out. "I know you don't really drink alcohol, but anything you put in your mouth"—Nausicaä interrupted to purr suggestively—"you chase it with a drink from that bottle."

Ah, so it was holy water.

Different from the human version, though it was created and used somewhat similarly. Spring water drawn from a natural source and purified with salt, mixed together and blessed with a fae prayer of protection. Much like faerie braids, it worked only if the prayer was spoken by someone who cared for the person they were giving it to, and as simple as it was, holy water was one of the best ways of cleansing malicious magic from the system.

Celadon had come prepared.

"Don't let that out of your sight, okay? If any of us needs it, please use it, but Arlo keeps it with her. And I wouldn't advise dancing with anyone, Arlo, unless it's with Nausicaä, Vehan, or myself. This works basically like a Faerie Ring."

Tugging on one of the braids in the mass of Arlo's hair, Nausicaä bent closer to her, whispered something in her ear that made Arlo blush and swat at her arm, and Nausicaä barked laughter that echoed off the garage's low ceiling.

"Are *you* going to be okay in there?" Vehan asked. Celadon was older and far more experienced when it came to these things, but that didn't mean he couldn't use their protection too. Arlo had woven a braid into his hair, had woven one into Vehan's too, and he'd blushed and been rather embarrassingly touched about it all night, because the only person to ever give him one had been Aurelian, years ago, back before they'd been caught up in pretend. Still, Celadon was . . . even more the focus of gossip these days, and even more of that gossip unkind.

Was this his first social outing as king of his Court?

Would he be in danger, considering what folk whispered about him?

Celadon winked at him—a brave face, all the air of composure and confidence. "I'll be just fine. I don't plan on straying much from you, in fact. Riadne was . . . rather direct in her expectations of me tonight. I'm to keep an eye on you and make sure you make it home in the morning."

It was Arlo who snorted, taking Vehan by surprise.

"Remember that time when you were seventeen and we were all in a panic because you were missing for three days, and everyone thought you'd been kidnapped, and we were worried sick until a random Falchion officer found you high off your butt hiding out in High Park—for *three whole days*—because someone at a revel dared you to drink an entire bottle of cough syrup mixed with Pixie Dust? I'm still not convinced you didn't die that night and we just found a really good changeling to replace you."

"I . . . remember being found," Celadon replied a touch sheepishly. "And being very, *very* sick for three more days."

"Yes." Arlo pursed her lips, gave Celadon the meanest, most disappointed-mother look anyone had ever given, and thrust her water bottle out to him. "*You* keep this. I'm not the one who makes poor life choices." She then proceeded to march past her cousin for the archway just opposite them, where two burly fae dressed solidly in white stood playing bouncer. Nausicaä trailed with a chuckle after her.

Vehan looked at Celadon. "You . . . drank a whole bottle of cough syrup and Pixie Dust."

"I don't recommend it," Celadon replied, closing his eyes and effecting a shiver. Opening them again, he clutched his water bottle close and proceeded to sling an arm over Vehan's shoulders. "Consider this your first piece of sage wisdom passed down from your older brother—don't take anything that has Pixie Dust in it. Probably don't take anything with cough syrup in it either."

Instantly, Vehan recalled how ill he'd been back during his first visit to the Hiraeth. When the goblin gang had chased him through the forest right into a Sleeping Hollow—a patch of earth that had known such awful, dark magic that all that could grow there after were the poppy-like flowers with ash for petals, the key ingredient used to make Pixie Dust, the most potent drug the folk had ever concocted.

He remembered the hallucinations, how he'd felt like dying all through his dinner with the late High King Azurean . . . how he'd spent that entire night curled up in his bathroom, throwing up to the point of blood, all of this even when he'd had the rowan wood Lethe had given him to dispel the worst of the damage.

When Vehan shivered, it wasn't for effect. "Don't worry, I won't."

Why had he never reveled before?

Why had Celadon made such a fuss on their arrival?

This was *lovely.*

They'd descended from the parking garage into a massive, hollowed-out cavern, and whatever magic the revel's host had done to get it here, at the center grew an oak so thick that three of Vehan linked hand in hand would only barely be able to close a circle around its trunk. Faerie lights fluttered and hummed where they'd been enchanted to dance like flames, illuminating the cave in washes of pale blues and purples, rosy pinks and softest white. Carved into the far wall was a bar stocked with things both human- and folk-made, manned by fierce fae pouring even meaner drinks, and anything else one wished to order.

This was no faerie revel—Celadon had been correct.

The musicians that played from a small chamber orchestra were some of their sidhe fae best. The revelers dancing around the tree were a mixture of sidhe fae nobles and celebrities. The groups that lounged together in the pockets of cushions, smoking and drinking and laughing and talking—Vehan recognized every one of them, and they'd recognized him, too, but it was Fina and Kine and a few others from school he'd joined with Celadon, Arlo, and Nausicaä, because as his mother had said, his best bet was to get close to the people his own age, the ones he'd grow his Court with.

At first it had been awful, uncomfortable, terrifying—Vehan liked social interaction well enough, considered himself good at it. But this revel threw him into a whole new world he'd never before navigated. For the most part, he'd followed Celadon's lead, tried to relax into his purple crushed-velvet cloud of a cushion, allowed his school mates to dictate conversation and spoke only when spoken to.

Then the faerie wine happened.

He had to partake in something, as Celadon had warned him earlier. It was rude to show up to a revel and not eat or drink or otherwise imbibe what was offered, and Vehan was the High Prince. He understood what that meant. That his people wouldn't trust him if he couldn't *unwind* with them, and of all the forms of inebriation he could choose, faerie wine was the least offensive.

Now four or five glasses in, Vehan couldn't fathom why he'd never done this before.

Had he mentioned it was lovely?

It really was.

If he lolled his head back and just let himself *be*, the twinkling lights overhead looked like stars, and he felt like he could sink and sink into the comfort of his cushion, so perfectly relaxed like he hadn't been in so, so long.

And this faerie wine—this decadence, a concoction that tasted like sweet black current, nutmeg, and cinnamon and rolled silken across the tongue as he drank. It was powerful stuff—there was a reason even the fae didn't consume this on a regular basis, why humans were warned against even a taste—and more dangerous was the fact that he couldn't taste its potency at all.

Each glass he threw back was like drinking juice, each sip a burst of flavor on his tongue, like biting into a perfectly ripened fruit.

Vehan wasn't new to being fae, had already experienced the horror of a faerie wine hangover, and felt he was doing a decent job of pacing himself given the excess to which others around him were drinking, injecting, snorting, and eating a wide variety of much worse things. It was only four . . . five . . . Was this his sixth glass? The cavern spun any time he moved his head, and he'd quite forgotten how to stand—but what did any of that matter? This was *lovely*. . . . Quite possibly, he'd never felt this good in his entire life.

"What do you think, Your Highness?"

It took him a moment to realize the question had been directed at him. "Hmm?" he hummed, lifting his head. Blinking his sight back to stationary, he pinned the voice to Fina. Fina, who was a little bit closer than before—a lot bit closer than he liked, especially considering he didn't like her, probably at all, and was fully in love with Aurelian, whom he wished was here.

On the cushion now beside him, she draped herself over its puffy back. Angled on her side just so, facing him . . . and that's what that tickling was on his arm. Her nails traced a lazy pattern on his skin. It was difficult, required all the effort of heaving a boulder, but Vehan shifted himself out of reach; he was still firmly Aurelian's, and not interested besides, even if in the eyes of the Courts he was once again an eligible bachelor.

"What do I think about what?" he repeated thickly.

"Theodore," Fina purred, undeterred from him in the least. "We're taking bets, silly—has all that wine gone to your head already?" She giggled at him. It sounded like breaking glass in his ears. "How do you think she's going to off him when he loses his bet to *her*?"

Her—Nausicaä.

An eternal moment later, Vehan's focus shifted to the opposite side of their circle.

Fina beside him, Kine beside her, a brown-haired boy named Mabric, a black-haired girl name Yarja, and a green-haired boy they called Sage for obvious reasons—but there, just on his other side, Celadon sat closest to him. Tonight he'd earned some forgiveness, it seemed, or at least the people had been forced to remember how disgustingly pretty he was and therefore, even if he had conspired to murder his family for the throne he now occupied, were now happy to overlook it for a bit of his attention.

All genders of fae pressed a little closer in behind Celadon, passed intentionally by in the hopes for a word, a brief chat, a glance in their direction. He'd been flitting in and out of these revolving conversations all night, but at the moment he sat alone. Watchful. Nursing the same glass of wine he'd taken up at the beginning of the night—how? Hadn't anyone told him the wine was lovely?

Arlo beside him—water bottle in hand.

Nausicaä beside her.

The group had tried so many times all evening to draw the Dark Star into conversation. They'd been alarmed at first, but their curiosity got the better of them quickly, as well as their spitefulness and cruelty born of aristocratic boredom. They'd asked all sorts of questions, tried all sorts of tricks to coax a response out of her, but Nausicaä ignored them. She'd ignored them all night. Got up and danced with Arlo a few times, sat with her neat glass of spiced faerie rum, stared them back into silence with a gaze that burned molten hot whenever she was tired of them trying for her attention.

Was Nausicaä having fun?

Revels seemed like her thing, but at the moment she mostly looked mildly pissed.

What had Fina's question been, again?

"My money's still on electrocution," Mabric chimed in. "The

power move that would be—I just want to see her do it. Theodore's a Seelie Summer prince; electricity runs in his veins. The amount of that element your mother would have to use to make him pop like a microwaved cherry . . ."

He exaggerated a shiver of excitement, earning a slap—and amused laughed—from Yarja.

"What in hells is a microwave?" Kine remarked dryly, raising a brow.

"Urielle, Kine, they brought one into Human Studies—do you ever pay attention in class?"

"I do believe my father would disown me entirely if I came home with an A in something so offensive to our pedigree."

"Didn't your mom have that human fuck-toy?"

"Oh my gods, I remember that scandal—Kine, your mom's a—"

Right. They were discussing what would happen to Theodore, when—not if—Nausicaä won the competition for the role of his mother's assassin. But Vehan had already taken care of that. Theodore would be safe, as safe has he could be, at least, under Celadon's protection. And now he was remembering why Theo didn't attend these things either—this conversation, it was decidedly *un*lovely.

It was Fina who interrupted the digression, lifting herself on her elbows.

Something glinted in her eyes—a hint of dark amusement, of meanness, of retaliation against Vehan, because of course she hadn't taken his rejection of her without insult, after all. "What do you think, Arlo?" Her voice was melted tar—silken smooth and vile. Nausicaä and Celadon both sat up straighter. Fina had to be beyond intoxicated for her to miss the way their auras snapped to immediate threat of death depending on what she said next.

Vehan stared.

Arlo stared too.

She took a sip of her water, replaced the cap, remained perfectly calm—steady. Fixed Fina with an unflinching gaze. Goodness. Again,

Vehan was reminded how alike Arlo and Celadon could be and how foolish anyone was to assume she was the easy target they mistook her gentle nature for.

How quickly they forgot she was part fae, and a Viridian besides.

"I think you remind me a lot of the people I went to school with."

Mabric snickered. "She's calling you thick as a human, Feen," he explained to the dirty look Fina shot him.

But it wasn't Mabric that Fina spat at.

"Will you cry for them too?" Her focus pinned itself on Arlo, and gone was the mockery of pleasantness. "No, wait, you didn't cry at all for your human-fucker mom. That was your cousin . . . or is he your lover? I can't really tell the difference with the two of you."

Vehan . . . stared.

Urielle.

It was the faerie wine. It was the Pixie Dust. Fina had been consuming both—the Dust in moderation, an additive to the cake they'd all been snacking on, just enough to dull her edges into probably the worst decision she'd ever made, given the way Nausicaä unfurled to standing like doom itself.

Everyone watched.

Nausicaä just stood there, glaring, frightening as all hells, but she made no move for Fina. Like she was waiting for Arlo's permission to act on her behalf. But Arlo just sat there too, and one blink . . . two . . . Fina relaxed. Vehan's classmates dissolved into laughter, and oh, but that had been blood in the water; they'd become sharks, and none of this was lovely at all anymore. . . .

"Have you ever seen something so pathetic, though?" Fina asked their classmates.

"One of the staff filmed it—Rodigar sent it to me, the whole embarrassing thing. The way she dragged them out into the Court-yard, with the High Prince blubbering the whole time!" Mabric trailed off into a pageantry of wailing that was supposed to be Celadon, Vehan assumed.

What the hells was happening?

But then . . . this wasn't all that surprising, was it?

Celadon stiffened. No one did anything. Because this was a test. Even Vehan—sobering quickly—could tell it was. A test for their allegiance—Celadon's, Arlo's, Nausicaä's. A test for *his; to* see how each of them would react to things that wouldn't bother someone genuinely aligned with Riadne and the Summer Court; to see who Vehan would choose to protect against an inevitable retaliation . . .

Vehan looked at Arlo.

Arlo looked back at him.

It broke his heart a little that she recognized it too. Arlo had spent her entire life being baited by fae royals; this behavior was nothing new. She expected him to side with his classmates—his future cohort.

He also saw the way she clutched her water bottle just the slightest bit tighter.

"Oh gods, this is so boring," Vehan complained loudly, kicking his legs out in front of them and doing a good job of drunken disturbance, the way his foot made the table screech askew. "Are we just going to sit around *talking*? Fina." He snapped his fingers at her, much like his mother always did when she wanted attention, and Fina perked up instantly. "Dance with me."

It was this or subject Arlo to further torment. Aurelian would understand.

Fina practically launched out of her cushion. Lunged for him. Wrapped herself against Vehan's side and batted her eyes prettily up at him.

Made to follow him down the platform that elevated them above the dance floor . . .

And paused.

"No, but truly." She turned back to Arlo. "I've been simply dying to ask. Seriously, do you and your cousin ever . . . ?" She made a crude motion with her hand toward her mouth, tongue in her cheek. Kine burst out laughing, and the others echoed glee once again.

"I mean, it would explain a lot."

"He's probably not even asexual; his preference is just between her legs."

"Ew, I'm picturing it now. Make it stop!"

Laughter . . . vulgarity . . . Vehan's classmates were choking on both now, Fina beside him all the while smiling at Arlo like vinegar.

And Arlo stood as well now.

Spoke directly to Vehan, and Vehan only, light and conversationally, like Fina didn't exist at all. "We should probably get going, eh? The three of us have training in the morning."

"Oh!" Vehan exclaimed brightly. Oh, thank goodness—why hadn't he thought of that? He'd forgotten entirely what his mother had explained would be added to his roster of too many things, but that was the perfect out from dancing. "Of course, that's right. Fina, we'll have to dance another time."

"You're a disgrace to your family." Fina ignored him. Her target was Arlo, and like any proper fae elite, she wouldn't yield until she got the tears she craved.

Arlo turned to Celadon and offered a hand to help him up.

"The Viridians were pure until you came along, one of our oldest houses, and your filthy human blood *infected* it. Just like you infect him."

Celadon took her hand and stood. Arlo turned next to Nausicaä and placed a hand on her arm, and Nausicaä melted instantly into a softness just for her. Bent to whisper something to Arlo, who smiled tightly and nodded . . .

"Is that why you did it?" Fina stepped forward. "I mean, it's quite obvious. Poor little ironborn bitch, nobody likes her, family's mean, and Mommy neglects her. I can't imagine why the High Queen would let someone so grossly pitiful as you survive the Solstice unless you were in on it too."

"Good night, Fina," Arlo replied, making for the stairs and snagging Vehan's arm from Fina's grasp along the way.

"Arlo?"

She paused.

Turned back around.

Raised a brow at Kine, who'd spoken, drawling her name from his cushion. And Kine smiled handsomely at her, raised his glass in toast between them. "No hard feelings, sweetheart. It's all in fun. We love you to *pieces*, you know?"

Mabric, Sage, Yarja—the three of them jumped at the cue. To gag and scream and pull horrified faces, reenacting with gleeful exaggeration the way the Viridian family had been hacked apart, piece by piece, by Vehan's mother's revenge.

And Fina positively squealed with laughter.

She laughed . . . and she laughed . . . and turned to Arlo to put on her own gross impersonation of Thalo's face before she died, lifting her hands as though to fling a nonexistent sword—

Just for her head to snap painfully backward as Arlo's fist connected firm and square between her eyes.

CHAPTER 22

Arlo

～⌒～

EXHAUSTIONGUILTAGONYANGER—
Fina's head snapped back in the air, and Arlo couldn't breathe.

"Your allegiance, Arlo.
"You, and your little die, and all that alchemy
you just wished on yourself.
"I demand all three . . ."

"Arlo—survive."

". . . and in exchange . . . I will spare one of
your family tonight.
I will even let you choose."

"Arlo—survive."

"Speak the name of who you wish to save.
Decline, and I will kill
every single one of them."

"Arlo—"
"Arlo—"
"Arlo—"

In a world slowed to molasses motion, Fina's head reeled upright
once more.

Arlo had struck her hard.

Hard enough to crack fae bone. Hard enough that Fina's nose was definitely broken. Arlo watched—such slow, slow motion—as Fina raised a hand in shock to her face, felt around her injury, and drew back her fingers to look down in horror at the sapphire blood there, sticky and warm.

Arlo couldn't really hear it; as though through some long-stretched tunnel, Fina began to cry.

"You . . . you hit me!" she wailed through tears. "You—"

ExhaustionGuiltAgonyAnger.

"Arlo—survive."

Fina's head snapped back again.

Arlo struck another blow—something inside of her had cracked, and everything, all of it, the exhaustion, guilt, agony, anger spilled out through the gaps.

Everything bottling up for so long had exploded, and not into the sobs these nasty people wanted, though her face was wet, so maybe her own tears were falling too. But it was anger that drove her, hot as the blood on her fist.

Rage.

She couldn't breathe.

She couldn't see.

She couldn't feel anything but rage, which made her want to *scream*, to split open wide and devour this world she hated with every fiber of who she was.

Fina fell to the ground, and Arlo lunged to straddle her.

There was commotion all around her, Fina's friends no doubt leaping to her rescue and Nausicaä stepping in to flare her wings and cut them off, and again Arlo struck. And struck. And *struck* . . .

She struck until her fist squelched.

She struck until the bone she pummeled gave way to the *pieces* they'd been mocking.

ExhaustionGuiltAgonyAnger—she couldn't bear it anymore!

She struck, and struck, and struck, and—

"Arlo."

A voice spoke gently, steady against her ear. Private conversation, just the two of them. Heaving breath; pain splintering down Arlo's hand stemming from her knuckles. Another hand held her wrist, stopped it in midair. Her lungs hurt too, she realized belatedly, from how harshly she'd been panting . . . and still she was so, so angry.

So impossibly angry . . .

"Arlo, I'm not going to stop you."—*ExhaustionGuiltAgonyAnger*—"In a moment, I'll let go of this hand."—*Arlo . . . survive*—"You get to choose what happens when I do, but I want you to know . . . Arlo, do you hear me? Nod if you understand: your next blow is going to kill that girl."

No hard feelings, sweetheart. It's all in fun. We love you to pieces, you know?

It was the happiest day of my life when I gave birth to you, and I am proud *of the person you've become.*

"Red?"

Arlo nodded understanding.

True to her word, Nausicaä released Arlo's hand.

It remained in the air a moment . . . two. . . . The revel had screeched to a halt around her, silent and staring in fascinated horror. Vehan and Celadon stood just behind her, frozen along with Fina's friends, waiting to see what she'd do.

If she really would give in to this thing inside her, this monster that ate and ate away at her heart . . .

And Fina motionless beneath her.

Deities . . . Oh gods . . . *Fina*, limp and unconscious—

Gasping, Arlo scrambled backward, right into the fold of Nausicaä's arms. And immediately those wings wrapped around them. Her vision blurred, but not just with her growing hysteria, her nausea—oh gods, what had she almost done?

There was a pull at Arlo's core—the world dropped out from under her.

For a moment she couldn't say what had happened, because a part of her wondered if she'd just had some sort of mental break, but then Nausicaä's wings retreated. Furling up closed, they withered into black smoke and vanished on the night breeze.

They were suddenly back in the perfectly groomed, gorgeous palace gardens that Arlo had come to despise.

Nausicaä had brought them back . . . well, it wasn't home, but it was all Arlo had now.

This *place.*

"I'm sorry," Arlo gasped. She rasped. She trembled.

Hands in her hair—her own; they pulled. She wanted to be sick, could still feel the way she'd almost broken clean through Fina's face. . . .

Nausicaä stepped forward—Arlo retreated another step away, something feral snapping teeth inside her. *The release of it all, it had felt so good.* She wanted to be sick.

Hands up—Nausicaä's, wary, putting space back between them. "You have nothing to be sorry for."

"I almost killed someone tonight."

"And chose not to."

"But I *wanted* to."

Arlo laughed.

Well, she wasn't sure it was laughter. Quite possibly it could have been that screaming pent up in her head. The night closed in around her; all this fresh air, but Arlo still felt trapped.

Fingers gripped her hair even tighter. "I wanted to. I want to. I hate this place, Nausicaä—I hate it! I hate everything! I hate pretending I don't want to be with you. I hate that you have to do all these awful things just because of *me.* I hate that still, after everything, I'm nothing but a liability to my friends and family, and I'm so angry all the time, and I want to . . . I don't even know—I just want to *break* something. Anything. All of it. I've never felt this angry in my life. There's some days I can't even breathe for it, I can't even move, and I just want . . . I just want . . . I just want to *scream*, and—how do I live like this, Nos? How do I keep carrying this feeling around inside me?"

At some point she'd bent into a crouch, like curling in on herself would help keep some of that anger in. But she looked up at Nausicaä now.

Pleadingly.

How? How was she meant to be someone she couldn't even remember anymore, the Arlo who could bear the things people said about her, thought about her, who never raised her voice or hand to anyone, who let the world trample her.

The way Nausicaä looked down at her . . .

Arlo felt her eyes grow hot with tears.

"Hey," Nausicaä said, folding up small in front of Arlo, still not touching, still giving space, but watching Arlo with such tenderness she didn't deserve, not after what she'd nearly done, and certainly not after how terribly Arlo had been treating her. "Can I tell you something? Can I . . . talk for a moment?"

Arlo nodded quietly.

"It's not exactly a secret that I've struggled with anger my entire life. Even before what happened with Tisiphone, I was . . . an angry person. Hot-tempered. As an immortal, it was celebrated. As an Erinys, as Fire, they said it made me fierce. But I was angry, and the things I was forced to see and do and be . . . It didn't help. So, you know, unsurprising confession: I got into a lot of fights." She paused to snort, to feel out Arlo's mood with a tentative smile.

Arlo couldn't return it, but she was listening, and Nausicaä seemed content with that. "Granted," she continued, "you can't really kill an immortal—not without very specific means and intention, at least. But I did get into fights, and once with one of my agemates, before I earned my Erinys rank. It was . . . pretty bad. I messed her up pretty good. And everyone cheered, and told me well done, because immortals are all sorts of fucked-up, but meanwhile they had to *scrape* that poor girl off the floor. It took her a whole month just to recover enough to sit upright again. My mother threw me a party."

Nausicaä didn't . . . talk about her mother. Ever. Arlo tried to recall, but she didn't think there'd been even one instance beyond a general reference.

"It was so bizarre. I felt awful—that girl, I'd *broken* her, and I could hardly believe I was capable of that. I didn't like that I was capable of that. But it was . . . something I was apparently supposed to pride myself in? I was like . . . barely a couple of years newly made. Fresh and hot off the Fire, so to speak. What did I know about anything? So hey, maybe violence *was* the answer."

She shrugged.

Frowned.

Dropped her gaze to the grass and clicked her tongue at something private. "It was Lethe who pulled me aside at the party. *Lethe.* My whole life since, I've never had a genuine conversation with the asshole, and he *is* an asshole, even if there were . . . moments. When he wasn't. He's a shit, and all sorts of fucked-up too, but he pulled me aside that night and told me something I haven't forgotten. Every day I remember it, and only recently—yeah, it took exile and so much hurt, but it finally clicked."

Lifting her gaze once more, Nausicaä softened. "Anger is the first and only power we're born with. It grows with us, is shaped by our experiences, just as much as we are. It serves and protects us, gives passion to life, strength when it's needed most. It's not something we bear. It's not an evil inside us. It's not something to be ashamed or afraid of. Anger is power, and power is life, and pretty simply, Arlo, like any other living thing, it requires purpose."

"So, you're saying it was . . . good to hit Fina?"

"No. Again, it took me a bit to figure it out, too. Lethe sort of dropped this shit and dipped, and I was half convinced at the time he'd been playing sport with me. But . . . no. What I'm saying is that you're never going to separate yourself from anger. It's not something you carry inside you. Anger is just as much a part of us as our heart is. And like all living things, if you don't treat it right, if you don't give it guidance, if you abuse it . . . Anger is what you make of it, and if you try to make it into nothing, it finds its own way to give itself purpose . . . like beating an all-around genuinely horrible piece of trash to a sapphire pulp."

"Ah," Arlo replied quietly. "So you're saying I need to take my anger for walks."

Nausicaä winked at her. "Something like that. But seriously . . . there are ways of managing how we feel, Arlo. And I'm here to help you with that. To talk things out, to spar if you need to release some energy. To remind you that anger itself doesn't make you a bad person, and neither does what happened tonight. You know who you are. Trust that."

"It was nice of Lethe to . . . tell you all this."

"I suppose," she sighed. "To be honest, it probably served some nefarious purpose, so don't get *too* starry-eyed about him. Digression: Are he and Celadon, like, a *thing*? It sort of seems like they are. Which is . . . wild. I have never known anyone brave enough to consider Lethe a . . . thing to be thunged."

It was Arlo's turn to shrug, picking at a blade of grass. She wondered too, but Celadon would tell her when he was ready, if there was anything to tell.

"Arlo?"

"Hmm?" She lifted her gaze.

Between them, Nausicaä had extended a hand, reaching for Arlo. A silent plea, a call for a truce. Arlo had been building up walls and pushing people away, but ever since Vehan with that plate of breakfast in the bedroom, the words acknowledging her guilt, she just felt . . . exhausted.

Arlo was tired.

She was so tired of being alone, and she was tired of pretending she didn't want Nausicaä beside her.

Arlo reached back, their fingers brushing together—she could still protect her friends, her loved ones, the people she had left, without cutting herself off from them completely. She just had to be smarter now, had to figure out how to rely on *herself*, not hide behind others. . . .

And goodness, but how long had it been since she'd let herself marvel in this feeling? The warmth of Nausicaä's magic curling around hers. The tingling that danced over her skin at any contact, and the way it made Arlo bite her lip when those steel eyes raked over her.

It was so . . . strange.

A good sort of strange, but still a coming-to-terms.

All her life . . . Thalo had never discouraged her from interest in other women. In the Courts, however much they'd adopted certain human ways to survive in a changing world, gender and sexuality were free and fluid things. No one cared who you liked or didn't. No one cared who you were. But Arlo had spent the majority of her life more entrenched in the human world than any other—in their prejudices, in their culture, in their set way of thinking, and while no one there had ever come out and said *thinking about girls is wrong, Arlo*, they'd never said it was *right*, either.

Her whole life, spent in a society built around the binary construct of man and woman, where proper was the union of one of each, not two or more of the same.

It was like . . . relearning who she was.

Relearning how to think.

She *could* look at Nausicaä and think about her the way she thought about attractive guys. She could linger on how much she liked the shape of her. She could wonder what it would be like to trail kisses down her chest, feel those thighs wrapped around her, to want—*oh*.

Her thoughts had wandered, and she felt like laughing, because that in itself was such a wonderful feeling, that she was getting comfortable enough with who she was that her mind had chosen to wander in that direction at all.

"There's no one you could be who I wouldn't love," Nausicaä finished—quiet, reverent, the pads of her fingers tracing down the inseams of Arlo's. It was a thing Celadon had said to her before, and yet it felt . . . so very different. Appreciated the same, but coming from Nausicaä, who wasn't family, had nothing, really, to tie her to Arlo but this one, enormous feeling . . . "A dark and hollow star . . . remember?" She threaded their fingers together and squeezed. "I promise, no matter what happens, no matter what I have to do, I am doing this because I want to. For me, and my love for you, and nothing *you* say or do will drive me from your side. I'm with you to the end in this, Red. I'm not leaving you, and I'll never stop loving you. So you can be angry; you can hit as many shitty sidhe fae brats in the face as you want. I'm *not going anywhere*, okay?"

Eyes watering, Arlo squeezed back. "Okay," she whispered.

She hated it here.

She hated what Riadne was making her do, was making her father do, her friends, the people she loved. She hated what was happening and how it all made her feel, like a monster straining on a leash that Arlo couldn't get proper hold of.

She wanted to go home. . . .

She missed her mother. . . .

And it occurred to her then, exactly how much and how specifically Nausicaä could sympathize with this. Grieving the loss of her sister . . . cast out of the only home she knew, from every friend and family member . . . so many years spent alone with her anger in a realm that called *her* a monster.

"A dark and hollow star," Arlo whispered back. "Nausicaä?"

"Hmm?"

CHAPTER 23

Nausicaä

$\sim$

THE BEDROOM DOOR SLAMMED shut beneath their combined weight, and Nausicaä could barely think past the feel of Arlo pinned against her. She should turn the lock—but there were soft lips at the hollow of her throat, a delicate tongue tracing the sharp lines of the black star tattooed there.

They should . . . probably talk more, right?

Had they done enough talking?

But sin and stars and the fucking hells between, those clever fingers traveling her spine spread fire through her, straight for her core.

Teeth bit lightly down on the curve of her collarbone—Nausicaä's head dipped backward, and the groan that spilled from her open mouth . . . No, think, pause; wait.

"Arlo?" she asked, breathless, panting.

She pulled back a step, lifted her hands to Arlo's shoulders. Deities, the way desire had darkened those big, jade eyes . . . Nausicaä wanted.

She had no idea what, but she *wanted*.

Well, she did have some idea. She hadn't spent the past 117 years in celibacy, had worked her way steadily through a blur of pretty women in the first couple of years of her exile. Sex wasn't a wide-eyed new concept to her. She liked to imagine it was something she was good at; great at, even. But in 117 years, and a hundred-some-odd before that, Arlo was the first girl she'd ever wanted in any way that mattered, and she couldn't—*wouldn't*—fuck this up.

She wanted everything with this girl, who was fire and life and beauty and so deities-damned intelligent, so fierce, so strong, so *good*, so . . . Arlo.

She was Arlo, and Nausicaä had never met anyone like her, and the things she wanted to do to her . . . how wicked lovely she could make Arlo feel . . .

Nausicaä shook her head to clear her thoughts, desire clouding them much like Arlo's eyes. "Arlo, we don't have to do anything."

"I know we don't," Arlo replied like a challenge, her voice pitched a husky octave lower than usual, and that difference alone—so slight, barely anything, but a shiver lighted down Nausicaä's back to hear it. "Do you want to stop?"

At the moment, she'd never wanted anything less in her life. "I don't," she returned, retracting her step away to close the distance between them once more. A breath was all that could fit in the space between them now. Nausicaä's hand brushed across Arlo's throat on the way to her chin, tilted it to bring that jade back into view. "I don't want to stop, Arlo. What I want is *you*. Since the first time you yelled at me back in that café. In the Faerie Ring. When you slapped a Fury to defend my honor, and squared off against a Reaper, and followed me into that deities-fucking elevator even though it was dangerous and I shouldn't have meant anything to you at all to risk your life like that . . . I've wanted you this entire time. Regardless of what we do or don't do tonight, that won't change."

Arlo looked up at her.

Those fucking eyes . . . that mouth . . . Nausicaä only just managed to catch herself in time and growled low in the back of her throat when those too-close lips brushed featherlight against her own.

Arlo spoke: "How long have you loved me?"

Nausicaä didn't even need to think about the answer.

"I've loved you, Arlo, from the very beginning. I'll love you until the end."

"I love you, too," Arlo breathed in reply—finally. Finally! Nausicaä's heart leaped in her chest. This was . . . It was enormous and nothing all at once. Of course she loved Arlo—how inadequate a word for what she felt, and yet . . . it meant too much. It meant everything. Because she *loved* this girl, and Arlo . . . Arlo loved her back. "This is

367

what I want. But I . . . just so you know, I haven't done this before," she added, softer, smaller, diminished, like the admission could possibly make Nausicaä change her mind. "Not with anyone. It's what I want, but I . . . I might be bad at it."

And Nausicaä laughed, low and rich.

Because Arlo was farthest from bad at this, the way Nausicaä felt a *winding* inside her, a coil already beginning to tighten . . . and tighten . . . all for the way their lips weren't even touching yet, and deities . . . she fucking wanted this girl.

The tip of her nose traced along Arlo's jaw, traveled the line of the side of her throat.

Fluttering kisses—little more than a brush of skin—pressed their way down to the hollow between life and bone. . . .

Arlo's pulse beneath her teeth—she laughed again, deeper, huskier, a promise of the devil she'd be in taking Arlo apart.

Slowly.

Inch by trembling inch, until Arlo *begged* to be undone, a writhing suppliant under Nausicaä's mouth . . . her fingers . . . her tongue . . .

"Don't worry, Red . . ." She chuckled like sin and began her journey lower.

Sank to her knees.

Kissed her way down Arlo's breast, bit her way down her exposed stomach.

Traced her tongue along the hem of her pants.

"I promise to be very, very bad as well."

And curling her fingers over the waist, as slowly as she'd bent to worship, she pulled the clothing down. Pretty green underwear and pants alike . . . dipped her tongue lower . . . buried it deep between Arlo's legs, and the way Arlo gasped . . . Oh, but she was going to be *so* very bad to this beautiful, sweet-as-honey girl. . . .

I love you, too.

You're a good person, Dork Star.

368

Immortals didn't require much sleep. Really, it was pure indulgence they even did it at all. A way to pass time, and normally, Nausicaä was happy for anything she could spend her excess of hours on.

But not last night.

Not this morning.

Nausicaä hadn't closed her eyes once. In reverence, yes. In passion, most definitely. In joy, relief, peace she hadn't known perhaps her entire life—but not to rest.

Arlo had fallen asleep in her arms, and Nausicaä stayed awake simply watching. She watched moonlight drape itself over those curves, watched as morning rose to claim possession, stretch warm fingers across their sheets to where the two of them lay, legs intertwined. . . .

The steady rise and fall of breath.

The way the sun turned those red locks to blazing fire.

Each of the many freckles down the length of Arlo's arms— Nausicaä watched, committed every detail to memory.

I've loved you, Arlo, from the very beginning. I'll love you until the end.

I love you, too.

Nausicaä had never been one for words. Her emotions tended toward physical displays to make themselves best known. But she watched Arlo sleep, and the hours ticked by, too quickly for what she liked. In that brief eternity, she composed her thoughts, and finally . . . It wasn't enough; it would never be enough. There were no words in any language that could express what Nausicaä felt. To be here, after everything. To be in love when she'd thought her heart broken beyond repair.

To be Arlo's, and Arlo hers.

If your heart is getting in the way of what you must do . . . I will remind you, there's been a way out of this all along.

I love you, too.

Make it right.

You have until morning . . .

The only thing I would like more now than to hand you over is you handing over what would have won you this competition from the very beginning.

I love you, too.

Make. It. Right.

Make it right—and Nausicaä would.

For 117 years, she'd been trying to do just that, and now she saw . . . this was the only way.

Shifting slowly, carefully, quietly, Nausicaä slipped from the bed.

Tucked the blanket around Arlo's body—slowly, carefully, quietly, despite the way her heart broke and her fingers hesitated, trembling against the skin they brushed by accident.

This was the only way.

Her time was up, she was out of options, and she'd do anything for Arlo, for this love like a burning star in her chest—cataclysmic in its intensity, but also the purest, brightest light she'd ever had to guide her true.

Arlo needed her to stay.

Riadne needed a heart.

Nausicaä needed Arlo. So she drew away. Dressed. Searched out a piece of paper . . . and wrote. The truth. Her story. Everything. But most important, how no matter what, Arlo would always and only and ever be *love* to Nausicaä. And Nausicaä would always and only and ever be Arlo's in return.

"I love you," she whispered, pressing a kiss to Arlo's temple, and she stirred a moment—stretched a hand across the bed, even in sleep seeking Nausicaä, because they were . . . simply meant to be.

Together.

Nausicaä hesitated.

She wanted to stay—unfortunately, it was this exactly why she had to leave. And do what was probably the hardest thing she'd ever done . . . but it was the only way. To make things right . . . and to keep her promise.

Sliding her folded note onto the bedside table, Nausicaä exited the bedroom.

Out into the main chamber. Out into the hall beyond.

Down and around and forward Nausicaä strode, hands clenched at her sides, jaw squared, aura *fierce* with violent temper, sending all who encountered her skittering back for the walls.

Down and around and forward—to the throne room, where already folk were gathering to meet with their High Queen.

People scattered.

Nausicaä didn't ask; she didn't have to. The line parted like spooked fish for the beauty melting away to horror—to tattered wings like the sails on a gutted ship; to flesh pulled taut over skeletal bone; to razor-sharp claws and white-fire hair and steel like knives for eyes.

The guards at the doors acted quickly, let her through without her breaking stride.

Heaved it closed behind her . . .

"Ah," Riadne drawled from her lofty chair of jewels and gold, seated and primed to begin her reception, and wisely her handful of attendants fled for the shadowed sidelines. "Come to say your goodbye?"

To her credit, she made no comment on Nausicaä's appearance.

Nausicaä didn't give a single shit.

Down the sea of glass she carved; up the sharp-cut steps.

Riadne's brow pinched—first in confusion, then alarm, but Nausicaä didn't give her a moment's chance to call for help. Help wouldn't save her. This was what she wanted? She'd have to pay the price. Hand shooting out, Nausicaä grabbed her by the face, sealed her palm over her mouth, and *shoved* that fragile mortal head back against the throne.

Again to Riadne's credit—she didn't cry out, but there was murder in those electric-blue eyes. It was . . . adorable. She really thought she was oh so mean.

Nausicaä almost wished she'd care enough to laugh in Riadne's face when this was all over, and the queen realized she'd bitten off far more than her voracious appetite for death could chew.

"If Arlo dies, I'll gut you," Nausicaä hissed in Riadne's ear.

Head bent, so close her nose brushed the shell of that sensitive skin, she thought it might be worth this entire thing for the way Riadne's flesh pebbled in fear.

"I don't need my heart to act on betrayal. Justice, Law, duty—these things have been ground into the very fabric of my being, no heart required to know when they're wronged. So if Arlo dies, if you harm her in any way, I'll *gut* you, and this contract is null and void. I'll give you what you want, the power you crave and can't ever satisfy, all with my willing consent. You'll make me your assassin, but wherever Arlo goes, I get to follow, and *if she dies, if she's hurt*, I'll ensure you suffer two times worse."

It all came down to consent.

Because Riadne possessed Lust, and Lust was the Sin that inspired loyalty, love, and desperation to do whatever the possessor wanted. A compulsion harder to ignore the weaker one's will, and inescapable and all-consuming to whosoever was foolish enough to vow Lust their "heart."

In the end, all Lust needed to strip her of full and permanent control was consent.

Lust was one of the finicky stones, Nausicaä had learned chasing long-ago curiosity. Without consent, without its target yielding themselves willingly to Lust's effects, Riadne could control her victims only one at a time. Temporarily. Would be forced to release them back to themselves as soon as the next was needed.

But when one willingly surrendered their free will in clearly defined terms . . . the contract made would bind *both* participants.

Snapping her teeth at the shell of her ear, Nausicaä withdrew, locked their gazes, and held that sparking stare a moment . . . two . . . then slowly peeled her hand away from Riadne's mouth.

She watched as the queen worked her jaw.

She watched as *delight* made her sunny glow flare.

"Such grim vows so early in the morning," she breathed hungrily.

Eyes wide, chest heaving, straight on the edge of her seat. She thought she was getting what she'd been after all this time. She thought she was coming into power.

Riadne Lysterne was ill prepared for what she'd receive instead.

Nausicaä withdrew another step . . . two . . .

"I have and always will be the one to decide my own destiny," she replied, and on the edge of the dais, Nausicaä lowered herself to her knees; glared down those too-blue eyes—so pleased with herself, so laughably naive.

The Dark Star of legend, at last in her grasp . . . but the Dark Star had never been real; had always been Nausicaä reduced, by grief and rage and feeling. The Dark Star wasn't what Riadne would get from this. What she'd get would be *so much worse*, so much harder for her to control, even with Lust strengthening the reins.

It would bite her in that perfectly sculpted ass, and the old Nausicaä would be delighted to know how deeply in over her head Riadne really was. But like everything else now, that didn't matter, either.

"Riadne Lysterne, I present you the heart of the fiercest monster this realm contains—I give you *my* heart in exchange for the role of personal assassin and continued stay at Arlo's side. I give this to you with my consent—but in consenting, you agree as well to uphold the terms of this trade. My heart for Arlo's safety."

The queen unfurled from her throne.

She strode to Nausicaä and bent.

The red haze of Lust's power glowed around her fingers. She'd been waiting prepared, that stone red as iron blood concealed somewhere on her person, to be able to utilize its power right now. The glow was all the warning Nausicaä received before magic plunged that hand through her chest. Through flesh and bone, but nothing tore, nothing broke—it was Lust that closed those fingers around what was not

373

really her heart, but it was certainly as painful as though it had.

Nausicaä gasped.

She groaned in barely restrained agony.

It felt like dying, her life being tugged on, summoned, drawn into a pool in the basin of Riadne's palm.

"Deal," Riadne whispered at Nausicaä's ear, before wrenching that hand back out. And Nausicaä *shuddered*. She couldn't describe it—words weren't her thing—but it was pain like nothing she'd ever felt as everything that made Nausicaä *her*—not her soul but her essence, her likes and dislikes, her morals, her convictions, the things that inspired and drove her on . . .

Riadne pulled, and Nausicaä felt the things that gave her substance tear away from the fragile organ.

Everything . . .

Everything . . .

Until Nausicaä was nothing at all but light dimmed to black. Feeling doused in ice. Peace that wasn't peace but paralytic poison—apathy . . .

Freedom.

Riadne stood.

In her pristine hand was no blood or gore, just a ghostly, glowing, sapphiric ball—the core of all that Nausicaä was. Strange . . . that this should all be so underwhelming.

"Oh, the things we'll achieve together . . ." Riadne drew a breath, relished it like fine wine. Released it back through her nose, and *smiled.* "I can hardly wait to begin."

Hands shoved him roughly to his knees in the sand. Fingers dug into his hair, wound themselves tightly around greasy strands to yank back his head and bare his throat.

With his arms bound painfully behind him by iron that burned against his flesh; with the sea right there, so close he could hardly hear his own thoughts over the way it crooned such tempting things to coax him back to water . . . it was so hard to focus, to struggle, to fight back—but that was exactly King Atlas's intent in dragging him all the way out here, in doling out his punishments on Atlantis's glistening white shores.

"Tsk, tsk, tsk, Zeuxis. . . ." Atlas crouched before him.

His father was older now.

Age had worn lines in his handsome face, pulled on his suntanned skin.

Gray streaked his hair. Muscle had begun to atrophy. And yet he was still as deadly as ever, a glorious war-king whose appetite had been whetted on the splendor and might piled like gold and rubies and diamonds on his name. Stunning jewels Lethe had been the one to lay at his feet, but not enough, never enough . . .

Atlas took Lethe's jaw in hand.

Tattoos and rings, calluses and scars—it turned Lethe's face this way and that for his inspection.

"You killed one of my men tonight."

Hardly worth fanfare—Lethe had killed many of them, and if it had been in the heat of battle, if it came with a chest of riches or land won to the Atlantean banner, Atlas wouldn't have cared at all.

375

And Lethe was oh so tired of all these hands, all these faces, all these broken bones and bruises. He was ready. It was time. He only needed an inch. . . .

Atlas dropped his hand with a sigh.

He reeled himself upright, looked down at Lethe with a father's heavy disappointment. "You have such potential, my son. If only you'd yield. If only you'd realize how great you could be, content by my side. Not against but *with* me, a willing prince. This kingdom you helped build through sweat and blood and death—it would all become yours if you'd simply behave." Steel hardened that disappointment; anger darkened the king's expression. "Prince of legend—together, you and I could spread the borders of Atlantis far beyond this island. Together, we could become not *one* of history's great empires but its *greatest*. And yet . . . there you sit, preferring the role of feral dog. Do you know what I do to dogs that won't listen?"

The sound of tearing cloth filled his ears—hands again, this time at his back, cutting through and ripping his sweat-stained, fouled tunic.

Pale skin, sunburnt and scarred and bubbled, laid bare to the night. . . . Skin stretched over bone and knobs of spine protruding far too sharply beneath, the Moon tattooed in ink down his spine—his only friend; his long-ago and desperate attempt to cling to the one thing about his life that was good; to what remained of who he'd been. Atlas himself had brought in someone to perform the inking, had allowed Lethe to choose the image as a reward for easy compliance with this latest test of his desensitization to pain, because that's what it had been.

The Moon, and Lethe.

Friends.

Lovers, in the sense that their souls had been bound, would forever be bound and known with an intimacy by each other that Lethe couldn't imagine anyone else ever knowing the same way.

"Do you know what I do to dogs who bite, and bite, again and again, at the gracious hands of their masters?"

Agony lit through him with a crack like thunder.

Lethe stiffened but made no sound.

Another *crack*—the guard behind him wielded his whip, hard and true, scoring more lines on Lethe's abused flesh like they hadn't tried this tactic before.

It was time, he was ready, and if he didn't act now, he would never have this chance again. The Moon was going, going away. He could say that for certain now, what remained of their bond little better than residue that wouldn't linger between them much longer.

What had happened?

It was so hard to think! Funny, how the mind tried to purge the memory of pain as though it helped to forget.

As though it hurt any less, as that agony burned through him fresh again. And again. He was ready; it was time; this body meant nothing. It was bones and breaks and tired, so tired, and didn't that water look nice . . .

It sang so sweetly.

The water, Lethe . . . come to the water. The water is your home.

He wouldn't listen—not yet! He had something to do.

Lethe, come.

My name is Lethe.

Lethe, Lethe . . .

Lethe, Lethe—

Behind him, Lethe's bound hands curled into fists.

Father would go first. Loving, kind Father, who'd taught him so much, too well—he would be the first Lethe used his Pull to drown. With what remained of his Moon, he would coax the sea beside him to gather itself. To rise in a wave and sweep to the shore and drag the whole lot of them out to their death, and only once it's done would Lethe be free to return home.

He would drown them all, but Father first—in his own blood, just as he'd done to the guard that made this ending possible.

Lethe curled his hands into fists and focused his Gift, his connection to the water. On the fumes of the only thing to ever matter, that bond he could feel beginning to unravel like a fraying blanket, faster and faster and faster—a race against time—Lethe pulled.

And pulled.

And Atlas began to twitch. To groan and frown, and oh, how that handsome, scarless face morphed into the sweetest confusion that bled into pain . . .

And he *pulled.*

"No!" Lethe shrieked, when suddenly the whip fell away, and rough hands returned to rip his iron shackles from skin that melted off in meaty chunks with it, dripping sapphire. . . .

Lethe gritted his teeth.

He thrashed against hands.

The action had disrupted him—frightened his Gift back into the depths of his core like a tiny, spooked minnow, and no, no no!

His bond with the Moon . . .

He felt it worse than the cracks of that whip, the way it broke, finally spent, and withered to dust between them.

The Moon . . .

Their bond . . .

What had happened, *what had happened?*

The last thing Lethe had left, and not until this moment did he realize how terrifying, how painful it would be, no! No, this couldn't happen . . . to lose his Moon. . . . It was truly gone now; what had once been life and warmth and *love* tethering them together was nothing but cold and absence now.

He was all alone.

And given no time to mourn this.

The death of his most beloved friend . . . and that of his long-planned revenge.

Choking on sand, Lethe was forced facedown to the ground, his hands yanked from his sides and splayed out in the sand above his head.

His father's heel pressed against the fingers of Lethe's right hand—sudden, hard, and sure.

Snap.

Lethe screamed as they broke under that vicious weight. Gagged on bile and pain when that boot came crunching down again and again, until the bones were splinters and the flesh bloody pulp.

"Next time, Zeuxis," King Atlas growled, as he reached down to wind his fingers into the back of Lethe's filthy hair and wrench him painfully upright enough to spit his next words directly into Lethe's face. "I'll *cut* that hand off—you only need one, after all, to wield a sword."

It was too much.

Too much.

The Pull, the Moon, his revenge, everything—it all fell away like his only lifeline slipping out of a grasp that could grasp no longer. No hands to hold on to it, no mercy, just pain . . . and the swelling of rage.

Rage so hot and bright . . . like all that sapphire on the sand.

"Lethe," he wheezed, and it was almost as pretty as the song the sea sang, that darkness in his father's face moldering to purple.

Lethe.

My name is Lethe.

Lethe, Lethe, Lethe, Lethe, Lethe, Lethe, Lethe, Lethe, Lethe, Lethe, Lethe, Lethe, Lethe, Lethe, Lethe, Lethe—

Atlas struck him across the face, spilling Lethe onto his side, like little toy blocks tumbling over, and Lethe . . . laughed.

Because it was funny.

Because now on his side, he could see that barren, hideous sky, and what were those stars in the night above going to do?

The way they watched, would they save him? Lethe laughed. They hadn't saved the Moon, so what could they do for him? And they were the ones to put him here. *Cosmin* had put him here. No one would do anything. Lethe had only and ever been a toy for others to play with and smash when he no longer suited them.

"Is this what you wanted?" he rasped to his sire, all the way up in those unfeeling heavens. "Does this make you *happy*?"

Where was the Moon?

He was lonely now that it had gone away. . . .

King Atlas aimed his next swift kick at Lethe's head, and then Lethe went away too, sinking into darkness, where he hoped he'd find it, the Moon who was his friend. . . .

CHAPTER 24

Arlo

⤛⤜

ARLO STRETCHED THE LENGTH of her bed, luxuriating in the feel of soft cotton against her skin. The early-morning sunlight streaming in through the open windows was undiluted, bright and warm, and already she could tell today's heat and humidity would be high. But today it didn't matter. She felt . . . good—better than she had in some time, and remembering why tugged a sleepy smile onto her face.

Shifting onto her side, she felt her heart leap in her chest.

She'd spent nights with Nausicaä before, had woken up to her more mornings than Arlo could count now, but this was different. This was . . . *more.* And the euphoria blooming in her chest was so pure, so immense, so relieving to feel something other than grief and anger that she wanted to laugh—she'd had sex with Nausicaä.

She'd slept with a girl, and it had been . . . perfect. The most natural thing in the world to her.

Her eyes fluttered open . . . and her smile dimmed.

"Nos?" she called, sitting up and drawing the sheets along with her. Arlo scanned the room.

There was no sign of Nausicaä anywhere, and her clothing was gone from the floor. . . . Maybe she was fetching breakfast? Maybe she already had and was waiting for Arlo out in her sitting room.

Swinging her legs out of bed, Arlo crossed her room to a chair in the far corner where she'd slung her soft pink housecoat. Slipping it on, she turned for the door, just in time for the knock that sounded on its wood. And there was the blossoming euphoria again—it had to be Nausicaä. She flew forward, turned the

handle . . . and once again wilted in disappointment when opening it revealed . . .

"Arlo!" Celadon greeted, almost too brightly, which meant his
thoughts were definitely still on what she'd done last night. The
false cheer took a noticeable dive when he registered her expression.
"I'm . . . just checking up on you. Is everything all right?"

Arlo nodded.

Riadne kept Nausicaä busy, so of course she already had elsewhere
to be, and it was ridiculous of Arlo to feel this . . . doubt. This fear
that Nausicaä had gotten what she'd wanted and left or, worse, that
Arlo had been so terrible a bed partner that Nausicaä had cut her
losses and fled.

Ridiculous.

Nausicaä had said she loved her, and as impossible as it sometimes
seemed that someone like Nos could like someone like her, the way
she'd said it . . . it hadn't been a joke or something uttered in haste. It
wasn't passion in the moment. Nausicaä had meant it, and Arlo would
just have to trust that.

"I'm fine." She waved him off, looking him over, because the real
mystery right now was: "What are you wearing?"

Celadon raised a brow at her.

In his plain black tee and black cotton jogging pants, this was the
Celadon she knew as just the two of them, together. On lazy Satur-
day mornings holed up in her bedroom. Planted on the couch, her
glass coffee table laden with food, burning away the hours on anime
and cartoons, switching to video games when the day wore on, until
her mother came home at dinner, and she'd scold them for not even
changing out of their pajamas. . . .

And suddenly Arlo's eyes stung.

Which Celadon seemed to notice—his brow smoothed out with
concern.

"Training with Lethe, remember, Lo?"

Arlo bubbled a laugh. He hadn't called her that since they were kids, Arlo trailing him around like a duckling, held fast to the back of his shirt. And then there was horror.

Oh gosh—she'd forgotten! They had training with Lethe!

"Oh my gods, I have to change! We're going to be late; he's going to *murder us.*"

But Celadon caught her arm before she could dart back into her room.

Pausing, Arlo looked at him—searched his face in silent question for a hint of what he was after. . . .

"Are you sure you're okay?" he pressed.

And Arlo nodded. "I am, Cel. Really, I'm okay."

"All right," he replied lightly, and released her arm. "Do you know you have a mark on your neck that looks suspiciously like a hickey? And also . . . in the most delicate way of mentioning this, you smell like Nausicaä."

Heat flared bright and hot in her face, and her immediate reaction was to slam the door shut in his face.

"Oh my *gods,*" Celadon half screamed, half cackled, all of it muffled behind the wood between them. "Arlo! My little girl, all grown up . . ."

Arlo heaved the door open once more.

She glared up at Celadon, whose hands shot for the air in immediate surrender, but the glee in his mismatched eyes . . . "Not a word," she growled, still blushing.

"I wouldn't dream of it," Celadon humored.

For a moment.

For two.

And then just as Arlo had expected, he collapsed under the impossibility of reservation. "Was it good?"

"We're not having this conversation," Arlo hollered, perhaps a little loudly, but that was the embarrassment talking.

Celadon looked like he might cry. "What do you mean? Who else would you tell this to? Has someone replaced me in the hierarchy of your confidence? I'll fight them—is it Vehan? I am *not* above kicking my own brother's—"

"It was good, okay?" Sighing heavily, Arlo rolled her eyes. "We had lots of fun. It was an A-plus time. Nausicaä is . . . very talented. Ten out of ten, would visit again."

"There, was that so hard?" He grinned down at her, but the playfulness melted into something softer when he added, "I'm glad. I was worried about you after last night. That girl, Fina? She said some horrendous things, and one hundred percent got what she deserved for it, but you were so angry, and those blows had to hurt just as badly emotionally as they did physically, and . . . I just wanted to make sure you're okay."

Arlo nodded again—this time gentler, this time with much more feeling, however small and tucked to her chest the action had been. "I am."

"Good. That's . . . good." He lifted a hand to her shoulder. "All I want is for you to be okay. To be happy, Arlo. And safe. And cared for."

Peering up at her cousin, Arlo frowned. They'd veered into a different subject—spurred, perhaps, by what had happened last night at the revel—but once again Celadon looked close to tears, and it tugged at her heart to see even this glimpse of how much hurt he tried to keep buried so far down. "That's all I want for you, too, Cel."

She pressed forward.

Wrapped her arms around his waist and held him in a hug. "How are *you* doing with everything? You always ask me. Everyone's always so concerned about me—but you lost your family too. And gained a new one. It's a lot. For anyone. Even a prince who's been made a king, and I just want you to remember you can talk to *me*, you know? That I'm always going to stand beside you, no matter what."

It took him a moment to return the embrace, but then his arms were around her, reeling her in so tightly against him that she huffed a breath, laughed, but tightened her own hold too.

"I'm going to get you out of here."

Arlo opened her eyes.

"You're not staying here. Neither is Vehan. Neither is your father. I'm getting all of you out of here. Do you trust me, Arlo?"

It was effort, but she pulled herself back—looked up into Celadon's gaze, which had hardened around a fiery resolve; when Celadon made his mind up about something, hells and high water couldn't hold him back. "Of course I do."

"I'm getting you out of here."

"I believe you."

His grip on her shoulders clenched with the ardency of this vow.

"I haven't abandoned you. I will never abandon you. I'm sorry it took some time to pull myself back together, but I promise you . . . I'm rebuilding our Court. I'm putting things right. I'm going to get you out of here and bring you home—I just need you to hold out for a little bit longer. Just a little longer, Arlo . . . Can you do that?"

Eyes falling closed once again, Arlo squeezed another hug around her cousin's middle. "I'll be okay, Cel," she reassured him. "I can hold out as long as you need, and *help* you, too. I'm not defenseless. Not anymore . . ."

"No," Celadon mused, his tone ambiguous. "In so many more ways than you realize." Whatever he meant, he didn't elaborate. "Now please go put some clothes on—I don't imagine you'll want to face whatever Lethe's going to drag us through today in just a robe."

Arlo groaned.

Already she regretted this bargain she'd entered. . . .

Bright, cloudless sky . . . dusty, hot earth . . . Arlo had been in this arena before, during that fateful day when Luck had shown her how to use her die to chase after possibilities like side quests to her main journey.

She'd come here then, had found Riadne, had unwittingly learned what the queen had been after in inviting her to the palace for the summer. If Arlo had only been paying better attention . . . if she'd understood what Riadne had meant in her talk of betrayal and trust, the prodding into what made Arlo so *special* . . . Riadne had known all along that there was something more to her than just some silly ironborn girl, and recognizing that might have actually made Arlo stop. Reassess. *Question*—what-ifs, could-haves . . . Would Arlo ever escape this guilt?

Out into the circle of wooden fence around flattened earth, Arlo followed Vehan and Celadon.

Lethe was already present.

He stood tall at the ring's dead center, dressed unlike Arlo had ever seen him, in black leather that clung to his legs and a simple, long-sleeved black shirt. His paling hair was roped into a singular, long braid over his shoulder; all piercings and rings and silver fastenings were gone.

It was . . . Lethe looked . . . Arlo wanted to gape.

He looked like a young man. Just an ordinary young man, nothing deadly or frightening about him in the least—save that menacing air to his aura, the wriggling, writhing, sickly sweet rotting of death that clung to the scent of his magic.

Lethe tracked their approach with those antifreeze eyes—or rather, tracked Celadon, and Celadon watched him, too.

She had absolutely no idea what was going on there.

Lethe didn't strike her as the romantic-attachment sort, and Celadon was demi-sexual, so his attraction to others relied first and foremost on boundaries and a deep, long-established emotional bond. She knew her cousin. He wasn't there yet. But something about the way the two looked at each other . . . Arlo had never known Celadon to take an interest in someone to the degree of what stretched between that acid and mismatched stare.

It wasn't Celadon Lethe spoke to, though, on their arrival.

When the three of them came to a halt before him, it was Arlo Lethe turned to. It was Arlo to whom he spoke. And it was straight to business. "You want your memories back, Arlo Jarsdel? You're going to have to earn them."

It wasn't the first time Arlo had felt that this was a little unfair.

He was the one who'd stolen her memories from her—she shouldn't have to pay anything for their return, but this was Lethe. Lethe might like her cousin, might be doing all of this for her, in some twisted way, but she didn't think he'd be all that . . . receptive to her demanding anything.

So Arlo sighed.

And nodded her head. "I know. I agree to your terms."

Lethe creaked a bemused laugh and took a step toward her. And another. And another. "In these lessons," he drawled as he weaved to stalk around them, "I'm not going to teach you to fight like your noble warrior mother. You won't learn to fight like your vicious queen beholden. Nor even like the realms-wide infamous Fury you've taken for a lover." He surged for her from behind so quickly, Arlo didn't realize he was there until his breath skated cool across her throat, making her skin pebble and posture tighten with tension. "You agree to my terms? Are you sure about this, lovely, sweet Arlo? I will ask you only just this once to consider what it is you're doing—and should you answer yes . . ." He snapped teeth at her ear, creaked more laughter when she startled, but Arlo held her ground enough at least to keep from falling away. "Answer yes, and you should know that all the things I break in you will be rebuilt as *me*. Is this what you want, Arlo?"

So be it—she couldn't walk around incomplete any longer, and the sooner she remembered the things she needed to know, the sooner she could save Vehan. Stop Riadne. Put all this mess back to rights . . .

"Yes," she replied, firm. Unflinching.

Lethe leaned in.

"That's my girl," he hissed in her ear, and then, in a blink, pulled away.

Curled back around them . . . back to the front. . . . In the wake of his retreat, Arlo's legs felt like their bones had been replaced with Jell-O.

"This is going to hurt," Lethe announced, returned to the ring's center. His tone dipped into wicked delight that Arlo didn't like at all, and yeah . . . she'd figured. She'd already made peace with the fact that she was probably going to ache for the rest of her life, if she survived these lessons at all. "I'll take personal insult if it doesn't. And let me disabuse you now, in case those pretty little heads have already started wandering toward weapons—we won't even look at a sword until you've built up your endurance. I assure you, as it is, it's lacking for what I'm going to put you through."

All three of them stood a little taller, none of them wanting to give the impression that he'd scared them already.

"This morning, you run. Tomorrow, you run again. And tomorrow, and the next day . . ."

Vehan snorted—then caught himself in horror when he realized what he'd done, and to whom.

"Is that funny, Princeling?"

"No," Vehan hurried to amend, vigorously shaking his head. "No, I'm sorry. I was just thinking how lucky it was that my mother already had me doing this daily. An advantage, at long last . . ." He chuckled weakly in the hopes that humor might save him from however Lethe chose to respond.

And Lethe smiled.

He smiled, and smiled, and it stretched into something quite vicious. "Oh, you think so?"

Vehan paled to sickly, and Arlo dreaded to find out how Lethe was about to prove him wrong.

"See, because I'm not your mommy dearest. And . . . well, there's quite the difference between your morning jogs and running for your life."

Arlo raised her hand into the air. "You . . . don't mean that literally, do you? You're joking, right?" Because it begged clarification. What he'd said.

388

And when Lethe turned to her, already she knew the answer.

"Do I strike you as the joking sort?"

Behind him, something amassed in his shadow. It swelled from the ground, ripping and snarling, grew and shuddered and twitched until it settled itself into the shape of an enormous hound. Skeletal under thin, taught flesh, with oil-slick fur the pearlescent color of film on water, moldering teeth, and acid-bright eyes . . .

Each of the Hunt had a familiar that could take different shapes, but most commonly that of a giant dog, Arlo recalled Nausicaä saying during one of their meandering late-night conversations.

Lethe's was Pestilence.

"I would get going, if I were you," Lethe taunted in singsong glee. Pestilence stepped forward, snapping at them, those green eyes *burning*, spittle flying from its blackened mouth. "Vehan knows the way I'd follow him. Since Mommy was so kind, let's see if that advantage helps him, hmm?"

He gave a whistle.

Pestilence lunged.

Vehan's hand in one of hers, Celadon's in the other—Arlo had never moved so fast in her life.

"I want to diiieeee," Arlo moaned hours later, collapsing on her bed.

Her body felt simultaneously featherlight and coltish and like the heaviest block of lead. Her lungs were fire. Air went like knives down each inhale. There were stars in her vision, and her ankle throbbed where Lethe's familiar had bitten her painfully the only moment she dared to let her exhaustion slow her down. She still had a full day of alchemy lessons, and Vehan—retching in her bathroom right now, where he'd taken to attend to his own warning bite—still had further training.

He probably wanted to die as well.

But it was he who found it . . . the note on her bedside table.

"Arlo, what's this?" Sweat slicked his hair to odd angles, his shirt glued to his back, Vehan handed her a folded bit of paper addressed to her, and Arlo had no idea what it was.

Until she opened it.

And read.

> Arlo,
> I've never asked forgiveness from anyone in my
> life—I'm begging for yours. . . .

CHAPTER 25

Aurelian

⟨⟩

I 'M TIRED—"

"My arms feel like balloons—"

"Is this dying? Is this what that feels like? Just leave me here in the dirt, you guys. Go on without me, save yourselves. Remember me fondly at dinner."

Aurelian frowned at the moaning group that dropped like flies at his feet. Curled from the outside over the railing that designated the Market's training arena, out behind its only barracks, he hadn't participated in today's exercises, as he hadn't in yesterday's, either, but Tiffin, Rosalie, Jaxon, and Ten were making good use of their new, illustrious mentors—or rather, from Aurelian's perspective, the Earthen Warriors that Prince Alaric had sent to hammer them all into better fighting shape were making good use of them.

"And you wanted them to let you help fight demons," he commented dryly.

It was a good evening for being outdoors.

Summer's warmth had settled in sticky and hot on a near-daily basis now, but the Hiraeth's dense canopy and ever-shifting landscape alleviated the worst of it. This evening, there was a decent breeze, cool on the back of Aurelian's neck and gentle through his hair, and while the days wore long this time of year, the first hint of dusk was finally beginning to rouge the edges of light that filtered through the forest.

Baked and buttery goods, fried vegetables and spice—the air had taken on mouthwatering fragrance. On a post just beside his arm, Leaf munched on a piece of lettuce that was bigger than she was while she watched their companions get whipped around the ring.

Aurelian was getting hungry too.

He could have gone to the tavern himself, but somehow or another, he'd acquired even more responsibility, this group like baby ducklings that had imprinted on him. As much as they were loath to let him do anything on his own nowadays, Aurelian was finding more and more . . . maybe it wasn't terrible.

To have friends of his own again.

Ever since he'd made the mistake of engaging in conversation with them, they had made it their mission to draw him into their circle and their lives, which at first he'd chalked up to his meager amount of fame in having seen and survived the demons in the woods. But lately . . .

He did begin to wonder.

Because it wasn't only his self-appointed friends that seemed to act a little differently around him. Aurelian couldn't explain it, but it was almost like he held some sort of allure. The sort Riadne possessed, and Theodore, and Vehan—the electricborn fae who'd always been impossible to escape once caught up in their magnetic field.

For as long as Aurelian had been aware of it, he'd never had any trouble attracting attention. He was decently attractive, and quiet, which people liked to view as a challenge, and it all seemed normal, so he'd never thought twice about it. Not when Vehan had a pull about him that was almost *physical* in its strength, and Aurelian's wasn't anywhere close to that. Not at first.

But recently . . .

It was hard to explain.

He'd almost been able to *feel* this invisible shift in things, where sometimes now that attraction was keyed up to an unnerving intensity in random people he didn't even know.

Folk in the Market would stop when he passed to gawk after him, would even place themselves in his path to stop him for a chat. He couldn't for sure say they were behaving unusually, but any time it happened, they sounded a touch dazed, and he got the impression they couldn't explain why they were doing this themselves.

Some even seemed to time their errands to match exactly with his to create opportunities for these conversations.

But while all of this bothered him, his makeshift group of friends here . . . they were all right. Their noise in his background. Mostly bickering and showing off to one another, but to the tune of something more wholesome than what he'd trained himself to ignore in the sidhe fae that flocked after Vehan.

So, despite the fact that he was starving and everything smelled like food right now, like the responsible parent he'd apparently become, he wasn't about to take off without them. And he told himself it was really the fact that Elyas was still out in that ring that stayed him.

As though Ten could read where his thoughts had wandered: "He's a braver man than any of us," they remarked in withering dramatics, brushing a hand off in Elyas's direction. "Gods' speed, tiny sir."

Tiffin, pulling herself up the fence to sit upright beside Ten, stared after Elyas in wonder. "How young do they start teaching them this stuff?"

"Young," Aurelian grunted. By accounts of palace staff, Vehan had only just learned to stand on his own when Riadne had shoved a practice stick in his little hands and trotted him out for training. There'd been speculation for some time about how diligent High King Azurean was being with his heirs—that his building mania had impeded both Elyas's and Celadon's training, and neither were all that skilled for it. But it was clear the way Elyas kept pace with the man leading him through the last of the night's exercises that this hadn't been the case after all. The boy *had* been taught how to fight—and well.

"Do you think he'll last to the end—"

A collective *oooh* broke out through the group, and all six of them winced, Leaf included, when the instructor at last took the upper hand and knocked the prince flat to his back.

"I could feel that."

"Better him than me."

"Ivandril looks pleased."

It was Jaxon who'd pointed it out, speaking for the first time this evening. Pausing in picking out the debris from his bushy gray wolf's tail, he regarded the lesidhe who'd been training Elyas with more interest than Aurelian had seen him take in pretty much anything so far.

And Aurelian had to agree.

He'd recognized Ivandril instantly—though the name he hadn't learned until his arrival at the Market. This lesidhe was the Earthen Warrior he'd noted back in the clearing. The one Prince Alaric had brought with him. The one who'd dragged Aurelian to the portal after he'd been attacked by a Shrieker.

Back in that clearing, Aurelian had immediately pinned Ivandril as the leader of the troop, and he'd been right. On arrival the enormous lesidhe had been introduced as Captain, and the way he walked, the way he held himself, the self-assurance and confidence and grace with which he moved and spoke and acted . . .

"Ivandril could totally get it," Rosalie sighed from the ground.

"Too bad you're dead, then," Ten remarked, kicking their boot out at her leg and earning a growl.

Aurelian shook his head.

For some reason, Ivandril just rubbed him wrong, and he couldn't exactly say why. Perhaps because Ivandril had devoted his life to violence, and everything he was teaching the others was spitting in the face of lesidhe culture as well. Or it could be because of the calculating way Ivandril looked at him . . . like the lesidhe knew his heart better than Aurelian did himself. . . .

Elyas bounding toward them drew him out of this line of thought.

Visibly pleased as well, the young prince was all sweat-rucked white-blond hair glowing fire bright in the dying day, and sapphire flushed in the face with adrenaline.

Happy.

Elyas seemed far more comfortable here than any of them, and that was good. The boy deserved some peace. "Ivandril said he'd teach me how to kill a man in one blow!"

Aurelian groaned. "Elyas, I don't think—"

"We've a ways to go before that, little prince," said a deep voice, rich with mirth, and the entire group but Aurelian perked up instantly. Ivandril stalked over to them, grinning at Elyas all the way. "But I admire your passion—we'll make a warrior out of you yet."

His words were thick around a German accent, which meant Ivandril wasn't using magic to translate language—much like Aurelian, he'd taught himself the hard way. Perhaps unfairly, even *that* irritated Aurelian.

Glaring, Aurelian straightened. "Time to wash up for dinner, Elyas. Let's go find your mother."

He held out an arm to wave Elyas ahead, turning already from the ring.

But Ivandril stopped him. "Will you really not train with us?"

"I don't engage in violence unnecessary to the defense of my prince," Aurelian reasserted for the millionth time, because no one wanted to respect that Aurelian's resistance didn't come in the form of physical blows. He'd gather as many armies as the Madam could send him after, but Aurelian wasn't picking up a weapon, and he wasn't training with these lesidhe who embraced what he'd vowed to never acknowledge—it was dangerous; too dangerous.

He already held such shaky control over the reins of his anger. He didn't need to prod it into any stronger a struggle.

"Yes, that. A personal choice, is it, Aurelian? Or is that the rhetoric of your Courts talking?"

Rosalie, Ten, Jaxon, Tiffin—even Elyas and Leaf, everyone watched in silence, their eyes darting back and forth like following a tennis match.

Aurelian narrowed his eyes, but Ivandril continued, undaunted. "Is it the garbage they've all been feeding you that I'm speaking to right now? The outdated code our people used to live by—that lesidhe are just tenders of the forest and should be only timid and nurturing until absolute necessity allows us to be anything else? Is it the filth the Courts latched on to, romanticized, used against us to teach our young that the strength inside us is something to be feared? That our power is violent, uncivilized, all because it's different from theirs?" Ivandril advanced a step on him, heat pitching his voice even deeper. "There's so much talent in you, Aurelian. An electric current that's wrapped around you, feeding into your strength. Have you really not guessed it? Do you really not know what's happened between you and your prince? Do you truly choose *peaceful* inaction because it's what makes you happy, or do you choose it because the only way they have of controlling you is by convincing you that your anger makes you wrong?"

Aurelian reeled a step back.

Do you really not know what's happened between you and your prince?

He didn't need this.

The pent-up, vicious creature growing larger and meaner inside him, he didn't need Ivandril poking it any more than he needed him arming it with the knowledge of how to draw blood.

His *anger.*

It wasn't until Riadne happened in his life that this thing he'd been carrying around for some time took shape as definable anger. Once he acknowledged it, he could no longer ignore it. Once he named it, he couldn't stuff it back down as completely as he'd done as a child. All the little aggravations, frustrations, and injustices he'd picked up and carried around like stones had suddenly become much heavier in weight—a weight that seemed to have grown unbearable. Had required locking up tighter, in sturdier boxes, buried further deep, deep down inside because he just couldn't risk it . . . because it wasn't who he wanted to be. . . .

Because Aurelian had no idea what Ivandril was hinting at—that his strength was unusual even for a lesidhe; that his appeal was an echo of Vehan's electric magnetism, growing more powerful the more

Vehan did himself; that the strange but sure *feeling* that he could reach out and meet Vehan's touch in the air was something more than his own wishful thinking, and . . . *no.* He had no idea. And if he *did* have some idea, well . . . he'd shove that down too.

Because it was dangerous.

It was all so dangerous . . . so alluring in its own way to the building *rage* he felt over all the ways he'd been wronged in his life, stuffed into molds and pushed around like a piece on a board, and denied, denied, forever denied, the one thing—the one *person*—that made all that anger quiet.

And this was most likely the heart of it—why Ivandril rankled him so much.

This man who was so comfortable with himself, at one with the feelings inside him—anger didn't bother him, opinion didn't bother him, and what use did he have for the Courts? Aurelian might . . . might a little bit wish *he* could be like that.

Free of burden.

Free to actually contemplate what he'd choose if the choice were really up to him.

Free to be and be *with* whoever he wanted without any of it being used against him.

"You don't have to understand it," Aurelian said, whisper quiet. "I am exactly who I need to be."

"But not who you want to be. Which is *what*, Aurelian? Do you even know yourself at all? All these people surrounding you, flocking to you, watching as you come and go—they look up to you. Who are they looking at?"

Wasn't that the question, though.

And Aurelian didn't like this anymore. He wanted to be left alone.

"Elyas," Aurelian commanded, dismissing the conversation here. "Go find your mother." If his voice trembled, he ignored it. If it bit a little harsher than usual, Elyas would forgive him. "I'll meet you at dinner."

He needed . . . space.

He needed to breathe.

Hilarious.

He had more freedom now than he'd known in a while, even penned up inside the Goblin Market, unable to leave because Riadne would snatch him up in an instant if he did. More time to think, despite how much he was becoming deeper and deeper entrenched in Riadne's web—attached to a boy even more caught up in danger than he was.

Riadne had said it before, something Aurelian had even wondered in his darkest hours—*was* it possible his attachment to Vehan had been born out of trauma, a bonding of necessity because he'd been so alone, and it was Vehan or nothing?

But Ivandril had just hinted something very different, something Aurelian himself had been wondering over more and more lately, with all this distance to make what existed between him and Vehan more pronounced. . . .

As soon as the word for it flashed through his mind, Aurelian snorted. He was being a fool.

Romantic legend, that's all it was. And Riadne was equally far from the mar—all he had to do was remind himself of the way it tasted to swallow one of Vehan's breathy gasps of pleasure. . . .

The way it thrilled Aurelian just to be near him . . .

How precious every moment had ever been, even before things had turned from questionable to bad to gruesome worse . . .

Vehan had his soul entirely. His heart had surrendered itself on volition to the Crown Prince of Seelie Summer, but *not* because of some fantasy folk whispered about fairy-tale true love.

Aurelian had fallen in love with Vehan the moment he and his mother had turned up in his family's bakery, the quiet boy with big blue eyes and a smile like the sun after a lifetime of rain. . . . It was love, pure and simple.

Love as it should be felt, for someone so wonderful, and . . .

"I'm pathetic," Aurelian chided aloud under his breath as his feet carried him toward the Market's high walls.

"Hi, Aurelian!"

"Are you heading to dinner soon, Aurelian? I was just on my way, myself. . . ."

People called after him.

Stopped to smile, or wave, or just watch, and Aurelian barely registered any of it. His hands curled around the bars of a ladder, and one by one he climbed them up to the battlement.

He knew there were much more important things going on, but if he could just see Vehan one more time . . . It had been over a month, and Aurelian was intimately familiar with withdrawal—this felt uncomfortably close to that.

So . . . maybe he was a little dependent on Vehan.

He did have an addictive personality—could he really expect any more of himself?

This time apart was . . . good for them. Right?

Vehan wasn't growing apart from him—hadn't forgotten about him, had he? Enchanted by one of his many new admirers, as his new High title would undoubtedly draw. Deep down he knew Vehan loved him, but it was just that they couldn't text, they couldn't write, and Lethe hadn't visited the Market in some time to bring an update. . . .

"It's quiet out there," said Rovert, one of the goblins on sentry tonight. "Always means it's going to be a rough night." Aurelian grunted in reply and dropped to his elbows on the lip of the wall's wood.

The days were quieter and quieter with each that passed since the Hiraeth's usual inhabitants had fled to deeper hideaways to escape the new creatures moving in. Now it seemed like the greater the stillness, the higher the chance of demon activity once day fell to night.

"Can't train 'em up faster, I'd say," Grisson replied, another of the goblins on duty. Both he and Rovert had their crossbows armed and aimed in line with their sight at the trees. "Could have used the whole damned Earthen Army . . ."

He allowed the murmur of conversation to fade, focused instead on the forest ambience. The rustling of leaves that sounded like water rushing over stone . . . the twittering of small birds in the trees . . . the crack of detritus underfoot as one of the patrol groups swept in from the woods, another exiting through the Hiraeth's front gate in the trade-off.

Breath in.

Breathe out.

Hold—repeat.

Pink deepened to rosier red through the canopy; he should probably head in for dinner before the tavern stopped serving. There was nothing to occupy him at the moment, no further task yet from the Madam, and they might need every body they could get out there to hold back the press of creeping evil, but there were only so many partners who were willing to take him on patrol when Aurelian wouldn't carry a weapon.

Dinner . . . then he'd roam the Market a bit more, pick something new to learn about it, maybe stop in the library and find a book to pass the night with. . . .

He peeled away from the wall, intending to leave the goblins to it and slink back to Elyas, when in unison, Grisson and Rovert raised their crossbows higher.

Aurelian, curious, drew back to look at their target.

A crunching—a crashing.

Something stumbled out of the woods, and Aurelian immediately stiffened.

He knew that figure, that familiar hard body and all that black leather and shoulder-length blond hair that was just a bit longer, like she hadn't had much time lately to keep it trimmed. . . .

"Don't shoot!" Aurelian commanded. "Don't shoot. I know her!"

To the figure he called, "Nausicaä?"

And Nausicaä's gaze lifted to him.

It hit him in a swell—the wrongness in her aura. Nausicaä's magic had always been violent, been needles and knives and broken glass, smelled of fire and smoke and melted steel. Nausicaä was anger in its purest form; it was . . . half the reason, he suspected, why they just didn't get along. Because Aurelian was anger too. And they both recognized it in each other—the part of themselves they didn't want to see reflected back, impossible to ignore.

But he didn't actually hate her.

Nausicaä was . . . a friend.

So his immediate reaction when he picked up the note of something so desperately *off* about her aura wasn't fear but concern.

And the second thing he registered was that she was bleeding.

"Nausicaä?" he called again, a little more panicked. Nausicaä, *bleeding*—what in the hells could have hurt her? She clutched her side, some wound there spilling sapphire down her front. Her face had gone pale; there was a grimace like humor thrown over pain, because of course she'd hold on to her bravado even now.

She stumbled to a halt at the Market's perimeter, just enough back that the goblins wouldn't feel threatened to shoot but close enough that Aurelian could see much clearer the strain under her expression.

"Hey, Grumpy. Wanna let me in?"

"Don't shoot," he begged again of the goblins, raising a hand to Rovert's arm. "That's Nausicaä; she's a friend, and she's injured."

Wrong.

It shocked through him like lightning—the warning.

Something was wrong.

Yes—that something is whatever injured Nausicaä! Aurelian shook his head.

Rovert didn't seem convinced. "She's the High Queen's assassin, and a Hunter. She's not stepping foot in here. We let her in, and she can invite in whoever she wants once inside."

"She's *hurt*," Aurelian growled, repeating himself. "And she's on our side." Louder, he added, "Nausicaä, what happened? What did this to you?"

"Aurelian," Nausicaä rasped—she paled further, sank to her knees; sapphire gushed out over her fingers. "Please . . . let me in. It's Vehan . . . he's . . ."

His heart clenched to frozen in his chest.

Nausicaä collapsed on the forest floor, and Aurelian forgot how to breathe.

"Open the gate," he begged. "OPEN THE GATE," he hollered much louder when no one moved to comply.

Rovert looked at him . . . then at Grisson . . . and dropped his crossbow back to his side. Flagged a signal to the goblins down below. "Open the gate, and fetch a medic—we have one to come through for healing."

The Goblin Market gate creaked open at last.

CHAPTER 26

Celadon

CELADON EXITED HIS EN suite feeling infinitely better. His body and lungs still ached, of course, but steam and hot water had soothed the worst of his pain. And peeling off those sweaty, salt-crusted clothing and trading them for casual black linen trousers and a formfitting surplice tee the deepest shade of sage . . . He felt like a person again.

A person who had a Court to run, much to do, despite how deeply he wanted to sink into that king-sized bed of his and sleep away the rest of the day. . . .

Celadon sighed.

It wasn't until hours later, a slim shadow falling over him at his desk in his private office, that he looked up from his work for the first time since sitting down.

"What *is* all this?" Lethe asked, selecting a sheet from one of Celadon's many piles of paper as he speared a strawberry on the end of a claw—from the bowl an attendant had delivered around lunch and Celadon hadn't touched—and bit into it as he read.

The fruit was never for Celadon, anyhow.

It was always for Lethe.

Lethe, who didn't like sweets all that much, or breads, or poultry, or the majority of things they had to eat, but any time seafood was served for a meal, there he was at the table. And it had taken about a week of fruit disappearing from the kitchens for Celadon to start requesting it on a regular basis.

If Lethe had noticed the uptick in mangoes, in pear slices and peaches, kiwi and melon, and above all else, strawberries . . . he didn't mention it. But he was around much more frequently.

This really was like befriending a feral cat.

Celadon blinked at him—Lethe, sans his Hunter's cloak, about three belts strapped around sharp, leather-clad hips, and a series of fine-link silver chains fastened to the buckles waterfalling in a swoop down his right thigh.

As Lethe was immortal, Toronto's summer heat wouldn't affect him at all, so it wasn't the tight, long-sleeved black shirt that sparked Celadon's curiosity. It wasn't the odd and inexplainable way his hair had begun to pale from that gunmetal black to this salted gray.

No, it was the curl of black ink up and around the back of his neck, in exactly the same placement as Celadon's own, that he had never noticed before . . . most likely because all that hair was still tied back in a braid instead of down and wild like usual.

A tattoo?

Of what? Celadon wondered. And why hadn't he mentioned having one in the same place when Celadon had presented his.

With a strange sort of immediate fixation, he found himself desperately wanting to know.

Lethe glanced up at what probably looked like Celadon's vacant expression; he shook the paper between them.

Right—Lethe had asked a question.

"Our Laws," Celadon explained, returning his attention to the paper beneath his stilled pen. "If I'm to rebuild this Court, I'm going to do it properly. Not just the palace . . . not just our territory. . . . Everything from the foundations up needs to be inspected, gutted, and overhauled."

"And approved by your new High Queen, of course."

"Mmm," Celadon hummed noncommittedly. Because this wasn't a plan that hinged on Riadne's approval. What he had in mind, she'd have no say in its execution—which was fortunate, as he doubted she'd be at all supportive of what he'd been working day in and day out lately to devise. "I'm almost at a good place to pause. Are you staying for dinner?" He looked up again, snorting a soft, dry laugh. "Would you be offended if I told you that, other than Arlo, I think you're probably my best friend now? Or rather, my only friend . . . so that's best by default, and again, there's still Arlo, but . . . Lethe?"

He trailed off, sobering instantly.

They'd been . . . whatever they were for over a month now, and Celadon was a quick learner, observant. Lethe wasn't all that clever at disguising his emotions either. They did seem to cycle mostly between anger, revulsion, contempt, and wicked amusement, but over the past little while, Celadon had been allowed to glimpse more and more the *other* things Lethe felt as well.

Like concern—and just now, it was clear on his face.

His gaze was still trained on the paper he held, but it wasn't the words he was focused so intently on. His attention had drifted just past its edge, and clearly this was something internal—when Lethe's eyes shot to meet his, Celadon startled in his seat. "Lethe?" he pressed again, and set down his pen; rose from his seat. "What's the matter?"

Lethe's brow furrowed, that concern deepening. "I'm being summoned . . . ," he replied, the words coming as slow as tree sap. That acid-green stare drifted to the desk, focus retreating back inward.

"Where? By whom?" Celadon prompted, striding around his desk for Lethe's side.

A moment . . . two . . .

Lethe never made a fuss about summonings. If they were together when Riadne wanted him, he simply left if he felt like going and returned when he was through with whatever she'd tasked him with. None of it fazed Celadon in the least. But this confusion . . . the worry . . . It made Celadon feel both of those things as well.

"To the Goblin Market," Lethe replied at last, eyes lifting back to Celadon. "By Nausicaä . . ."

Something had happened.

Something was wrong.

Lethe looked shaken, and there was something he wasn't telling him, and if it was Nausicaä . . . the Goblin Market, where Elyas was—

"I'm coming with you."

Slapping his sheet of paper back on Celadon's desk, Lethe drew himself taller, more menacing, and glared down his nose at him. "You are *not.*"

"I *am.* Whether you take me or I have the Egress spit me out in the Hiraeth and I wander around until I find it, if something's happened at the Market, I'm going. Elyas is my nephew. Nausicaä is my friend. So is Aurelian, and he's there too."

The hand not tipped in lethal claws shot for Celadon's chest, gripped the front of his shirt, and reeled him in, and Lethe looked livid. Scared, almost. But certainly angry, and Celadon couldn't tell if it was because he was being cornered into doing something he didn't want to do, or because . . . for whatever reason . . . he didn't want Celadon to follow him into potential danger.

Most likely, he didn't want the burden of responsibility over another person.

But Celadon was a king now—he could take care of himself just fine.

Lethe leaned closer. "You will not leave my side," he hissed at him, and before Celadon could react, before he could even agree, black-like-tar swelled around them, rose up, swallow them whole . . .

Then drained away to fire.

"Celadon."

Lethe gasped his name.

Hand still balled in his shirt, Lethe recovered quickly from the shock of their arrival to heave Celadon back—because *fire,* and Celadon, who'd instinctually tried to dart straight toward it, felt his heart burst into flames as well at the sight.

Struggling against Lethe's adamantine hold, he cried, "Let me go! Let me go, Lethe—Elyas is in there!"

Fire.

Fire, *everywhere.*

Lethe's magic had deposited them outside the Market, because even invited, there was no power in any realm that could transport them inside—the Market had to be physically entered, through the front gate or not at all, and right now it was all on fire.

Fire that lapped at the wooden fence wrapped around the Market's borders, the scout towers, the buildings, the trees all within.

It roared, and groaned, and consumed down to breaking, down to crumbling, to ash.

Tremors rocked through the earth as homes collapsed, as trees cracked down the middle and crashed to the ground. Folk fled in droves through the Market's flaming gate—they ran screaming, crying, flailing, panicked. Some were doused in flames as well, and rolled and writhed on the ground as they tried to crawl their way to safety, other folk attempting to help put them out while scrambling for their own escape. . . .

"Elyas! Nausicaä! Aurelian!" Celadon called over it all—he struggled, struck out, growled threats at Lethe, but those impossibly strong arms just wouldn't let go, only wrapped him up tighter and pulled him farther away from the heat that had already started to bubble at his skin. . . .

"Stop it," Lethe snarled back. "Stop! That's Fire, you fool. *Fire*— the element itself, not the fledgling flames smuggled to your world. That *is* Nausicaä—listen to me!"

He hauled Celadon around to face him. Celadon went as easily as a doll, but not because he wanted to; Lethe was simply that strong.

Their eyes met.

Celadon felt half wild with fear and desperation to get to his nephew. Elyas, whom he hadn't been able to see at all in over a month; he'd had to rely on others to keep him apprised of his well-being, because setting foot in the Madam's territory would mean a confrontation that he hadn't yet figured out how to handle.

This would be his first time seeing Elyas since the Solstice, and Celadon could hardly breathe for how afraid he was right now that it would be his last. He didn't at all comprehend what Lethe was saying, but a moment passed between them . . . followed by another.

One breath . . .

Two . . .

Slowly, reason stealing over panic, Celadon asked, "What do you mean that's Nausicaä?"

"Something's wrong." Lethe shook his head; looked back to the flaming sky. "Nausicaä's summons . . . Her magic called to the Hunt, inviting us into the Market. But it wasn't *hers*. It didn't feel right. I've known that girl her entire life, and that magic . . . Something's wrong with it. Something that feels like . . ."

He trailed off—again there was that confusion, that concern.

Fisting the front of Lethe's shirt now, Celadon dragged his attention back to him with a pitiful attempt at a shake. "It feels like what?" he demanded to know.

And Lethe looked at him.

Lifted his clawed hand.

Brushed it through the air, and in the wake of the stroke, black-like-smoke billowed and curled and wove itself into a cloak.

A cloak that Lethe draped around Celadon's shoulders. Sickly sweet, musty earth, and a hint of briny air, dampness, and coolness like in a sunken grotto—Lethe's scent. This cloak was his Hunter's garb.

"Stay behind me," Lethe commanded, low and between them. "That cloak can only protect your mortal body from so much—do not let those flames touch you."

Celadon nodded.

Together, Lethe firm in the lead, they made for the Market's entrance.

He was immediately glad for Lethe's cloak. Keeping as close to the Hunter's back as he could, he did his best to stay out of the fire's reach, but the heat would have been excruciating were it not for the material surrounding him, magicked somehow to keep him cool.

In they plunged.

Down the path they bobbed and wove, carving their way through the frightened mob that threatened to dislodge Celadon's hold of Lethe at every jostle, every rough collision.

At one point, an ogre man fleeing with a young girl clutched in his arms knocked so firmly into Celadon that Celadon stumbled back, as at the very same time a burst of oxygen shot flame scorching across their trail—and it had been lucky.

Had Celadon not fallen, he would have been caught in its blast.

Quickly Lethe paused. Eyes wide, he ripped back around for Celadon, snatched up his wrist, and they were hand in hand now, combing the streets for signs of a little fae boy, no better than looking for a pin in this chaotic flaming haystack.

"Elyas!" Celadon called. "Elyas! Elexa! Nausicaä!"

Lethe slammed to a halt so suddenly that Celadon collided with his back.

An arm shot out instantly, and Celadon knew why: it was to keep him back. Lethe had found something that would upset him, and Celadon's heart clenched, his blood ran frozen. . . .

He curled himself around Lethe's arm to scream, because there—"Elyas!"

There was Elyas, unconscious. Slung over Aurelian's shoulder. Neither of them looked in the best of shape, streaked with soot, gashes bleeding, clothing scorched. . . . In the middle of the Market's central square, the tavern they'd been holing up in just beyond, Aurelian held his ground admirably—legs spread, hunched over panting, and golden eyes bright with his own confusion, his own anger, his own fear.

Where was Melora?

This was the Madam's territory, her place to defend, her people she no doubt had sworn to protect in being allowed to establish her mockery of a Court here.

And she was nowhere in sight.

Instead, there was a lesidhe man built like a mountain, with silver for hair and a sword in hand, standing firm in front of Aurelian and Elyas. Beside him stood Elexa, the pair of them acting as shield, and good for them—Celadon didn't think there were many in this realm or any other who could boast enough bravery to stand between prey and . . .

"Nausicaä?" Celadon breathed out in shock.

Nausicaä like he'd never seen her.

"That is not Nausicaä," Lethe warned darkly. "Or rather . . . that is not Nausicaä controlling her actions." He took a step back, ushering Celadon farther away from where he needed to be, and no! "*Celadon . . . stop.* That's a Sin."

Celadon . . . stopped.

He stared at Nausicaä.

White hair billowing in actual flame around her skeletal frame; black, tattered wings flaring wide; veins glowing bright as red-hot coals beneath her skin. Wherever Nausicaä stepped, flame sprang to life at her heels, licked at skin that wouldn't burn, leaped for her surroundings. Those steel eyes scalded, that mouth full of razors bared at the night. . . .

"Come on now, Grumpy—it's just me. We're just going home. Don't you want to see Vehan?"

"Nausicaä!" Aurelian growled around his lesidhe protector. "Nausicaä, this isn't you!"

Because of course Aurelian could sense it too, with his lesidhe magic more attuned with the spirit. Whatever had happened, Nausicaä had fallen prey to a Sin's power—one of his mother's stones, he was sure of it, and oh gods . . . Already the pieces were slotting together.

"Nausicaä!" Celadon shouted, so loudly his voice cracked. Lethe stiffened, didn't appreciate the attention that snapped their way, but no . . . this couldn't happen. "Nausicaä, please! If you take them to her, she'll kill them! Aurelian . . . Elyas . . . they're your friends!"

Nausicaä examined him with wholly inhumane eyes.

There wasn't so much as a trace of the girl he knew behind them.

"Lethe," she called in a booming, dark voice. "Control your toy, or I'll roast him, too." She turned then back for Aurelian and slashed a hand through the air. Fire bloomed in a bleeding gash directly across Elexa and the lesidhe in front of him, dropped them both crying in pain to the earth.

Nausicaä advanced, one sauntering step forward at a time. . . .

Lethe retreated.

Pulled Celadon even farther with him.

"Stop it," Celadon barked. "Stop. I'm not going anywhere—"

"*She* isn't going to kill them." Head angled to the side, speaking to Celadon but keeping track of the threat before him the entire time, Lethe actually . . . sounded as if he were pleading. "Celadon, we must go. I . . . I don't know what's going on. The High Queen has done something, I don't know what, but Nausicaä is no longer in possession of a heart. Her actions aren't hers. We need to get back, or we'll miss it—"

"Miss *what?*" Celadon snarled, barely able to tear his gaze away either, as Nausicaä shot a hand to grip Aurelian's face, and Aurelian cried out like those fingers were a hot brand held against his skin. "Right here is where we need to be. You have to stop her! You *can* stop her. Don't even pretend with me you can't—"

"I can." Lethe turned to him. His lip curled over his teeth, painting him the most frustrated Celadon had ever witnessed, perhaps, but he didn't care.

"*Help* them!" Celadon begged, tears in his eyes, hands splayed on Lethe's chest. Desperate. "Please. Riadne will kill them. . . ."

Lethe gripped his elbow like a man who might be drowning in the current of whatever warred behind those acid eyes.

"Celadon," he said in a deathly voice, and leaned close enough that his breath fanned Celadon's lips. "In all the millennia of our lives, when have I ever refused you anything?"

Then they were gone.

Gone before Celadon could make sense of that statement.

In a mad dash, Lethe had taken hold of Celadon's wrist once more and fled for the exit, and Celadon could only stumble along—trusting this man, whom he didn't actually know at all, who never called Celadon by his name, and had now multiple times in one night. *Please,* Celadon begged in silence. *Please, not Elyas. Please let him live. . . .* Please let Lethe be true to his word.

Elyas . . . he was just a kid.

The sweetest kid he'd ever known, despite the fact that his mother had been forced into marriage with a man who didn't deserve to call himself Elyas's father—a man who both verbally and physically abused them. Celadon's older brother had been a swine, a worm, and never had Celadon ever been so bold in his defiance of Reseda's oldest son as when his brother had raised his hand to Elexa . . . as when he'd bullied Elyas and Arlo both to tears. . . . Elyas had never been just his nephew. In all ways that mattered, Celadon had been raising the boy like his own brother, and he couldn't . . . not Elyas, he couldn't lose him, too. . . .

Outside the Market, Lethe heaved Celadon into his arms, pressed him close for the darkness to swallow them up once more—and throw them out into the Luminous Palace's front gardens, where the two of them stumbled—entangled—and fell in their hurry.

It was the most undignified Celadon had ever known of Lethe's usual, loping grace, and he didn't care—they had to hurry. He had to get to his mother, to stop this, somehow, *anyhow.* . . .

More black smoke bloomed in the air over the palace front lawn and took shape.

Nausicaä appeared beside them, Aurelian bound in an iron chain, Elyas still unconscious, thrown over her shoulder like a sack.

She regarded them—Celadon and Lethe where they lay strewn— dully before she tugged on the loop of Aurelian's chain, heaving him forward on unsteady footing. A grimace of pain crossed his face; that iron had to hurt . . . Nausicaä's rough care of him, as well.

And then more figures.

One by one the Wild Hunt assembled on the lawn: Yue, Vesper, Eris. A mass of prisoners was held between them ranging from as young as fifteen to no older than twenty—ironborn, all of them. Undoubtedly, they were the children the Madam and her forces had been hiding from Riadne's grasp, the children who'd been Riadne's experiments, her incubators for the stones she hoped to make, and *where had the Madam gone throughout all of this?*

Where had she fled like a cowardly slug?

With all her might, why hadn't she tried to stop this at all . . . or had she, and Nausicaä had simply stricken her down the way she'd done that lesidhe man?

Celadon growled—lunged forward for Nausicaä without thinking; Lethe caught the back of his shirt just as Nausicaä's head snapped in his direction again, a promise of quick, painful demise in her eyes that faded to razor threat when she realized he'd been neutralized.

The Wild Hunt and their catch started forward once more, making for the palace's front entrance.

"We follow and observe," Lethe instructed, pulling himself close to Celadon's back. "What would you do with your little prince if you even managed to snatch him away from her? Where would you run? This requires intelligence. I did think you possessed that—was I wrong?"

Breathing harshly, glaring at Nausicaä's retreating back, Celadon took a moment . . . then snorted disgust. "Fine. Let's go." And taking Lethe this time by the wrist, made for the palace as well.

They trailed the Hunt like a grim, silent shadow, and everyone they passed froze, stared, then yelped and shrank to the side. Even the guards took one look at this party and held themselves flat to the walls. Riadne's triumph had already proven itself a vicious thing; these were dead fae walking, in their eyes, and no one wanted to get in the way.

Certainly not with Nausicaä leading the procession, still a frightening horror, but the flame she ignited with every step extinguished as soon as she passed.

Down the halls, through the throne room's entrance . . .

A crowd had been gathered to greet them. Fae who Celadon recognized, gathered to the side much as they'd done for Riadne's Crowning—the Council, courtiers, Vehan's vile agemates, among them Fina, and Celadon felt a surge of pride noticing that magic had yet to heal her completely; the bruise on her face swelled an ugly, blotchy, blackish green.

At the head of the room, splendid on her throne, a rare sight in a dress of stark-white gauzy material, Riadne sat in *blazing* radiance.

Beside her—pale, stricken, horrified—stood Vehan, Theodore . . . and Arlo.

"Nausicaä!" Riadne greeted, standing as soon as the procession reached the foot of her dais. "My assassin returns." Her face was all dazzling smile.

Nausicaä dropped Elyas in an unceremonious heap. With one strong yank, she proceeded to haul Aurelian forward next, kicked the back of his knees to fell him at her feet. And Vehan flinched, but it wasn't him who flew down the steps, who threw themselves at Nausicaä. Celadon couldn't see any expression from where he stood, but Nausicaä . . . there was something of her still inside; whatever had happened, it had stolen control of the Fury, but nothing in this realm, it seemed, would compel her to harm Arlo.

"*Nos,*" Arlo breathed.

Heedless of the fire, the death, and the danger writhing in that aura, Arlo made for Nausicaä and wrapped her arms around the Fury's middle.

And Nausicaä . . . extinguished.

Like a candle blown out, her fire receded, and her glamour reasserted itself; in an instant, she was leather and charm and *Nausicaä* once more . . . but she didn't hug Arlo back.

As though incapable of action, Nausicaä merely stood there, head cocked slightly and body curved on instinct to make room for Arlo, but she didn't touch back.

"Nos—Nos, I read your letter. *Please*, I don't understand. . . ." Arlo glanced around, first at Aurelian, then at Elyas, then beseechingly back at Nausicaä. "Please, what's happened? What's going on? I don't understand!"

Nausicaä looked down at Arlo. Took her by the arm. Detached Arlo from her torso and guided her firmly to the side, out of the way. "Not now, Red. Don't worry; everything's fine."

"It's *not* fine, Nos; you're acting—"

"Please!" It was Riadne who spoke.

Smirking, she descended the steps of her dais slowly, like a cat advancing on some unwitting bird.

"It's no trouble, Arlo, darling. Nausicaä, we really should tell them. Would you like to do the honors, or should I?"

Nausicaä turned her gaze to Riadne.

Celadon felt just as ill as Vehan and the others looked.

Riadne had won something—and there it was. What she'd been after since her Crowning, since she'd set Nausicaä and Theodore to that sham of a competition, and Celadon had known as soon as she'd tasked it what she'd been after. But how . . . why . . . what had made Nausicaä give in *now*, when there'd still been time?

When it was clear Nausicaä wouldn't speak—defiance; Nausicaä was still in there, and she wouldn't speak to Riadne unless speaking was necessary, it seemed—Riadne's eyes flashed to notice this too.

"Our competition has found its winner," the queen continued. "Nausicaä has presented a heart. Her own, in fact—and I value that above any other. Though Theodore, dear . . . the children you squirreled away from me, my experiments I worked so hard on?" She paused to speak to the Reynolds prince, tilting her head but not quite looking at him. "How have you been doing this? That's quite the collection, almost every one I haven't been able to account for these past few months. I was rather hoping you would have had it in you to bring the lot of them to me in trade. I might have forgiven you your betrayal if you had—would have been happy to send you off to Celadon's budding Court. He asked for you personally, after all, and I'm a woman of my word. But it seems your Madam didn't break you properly when she pulled you from those woods." She turned to him fully then.

Theodore—his complexion had drained nearly bloodless.

"Oh yes. Did you think I didn't know that, either? That I wouldn't at least guess what the Madam was doing with some of my own subjects, given the secrets I spent a lifetime gathering?" She snorted. "I really was hoping. You had such *opportunity* to prove to be better than you turned out. No matter . . ." And then Riadne turned back around. "Congratulations are in order. For this morning, Nausicaä came and bent her knee, and on such a pittance of terms, yielded her heart to my control."

Riadne held up her hand.

In her palm was a misshapen chunk of oval rock, crimson red as iron blood.

The stone pulled from the chest of the serving boy back in the ballroom on the night of the Solstice . . . the stone, Celadon had since learned through careful investigation and late-night conversations with Lethe, known as Lust—whose special gift allowed the wielder to manipulate free will.

Damn it all.

He'd been right. He'd guessed it back at the Crowning when Riadne had first set this task to them, and Celadon had seen immediately how much she'd wanted to add this girl's power to her own.

Riadne had been after Nausicaä this whole time, and the stone had given her exactly what she wanted: a Fury, violent and powerful and dangerous; an immortal all hers to control.

Celadon gritted his teeth against the growl that wanted to rip from his throat.

"My new assassin—and already, my greatest asset." At the bottom of the steps now, Riadne came to a halt.

Right in front of Aurelian.

Where she bent, took him by the hair, and wrenched his head back to smile even brighter down at him. "Hello, *Lord Bessel.*"

"Mother, please—" Vehan cried.

Aurelian spat in her face.

The whole room inhaled, held itself on a breath. Riadne lifted her hand and in a delicate motion wiped saliva from her high, sharp cheek . . . and grinned at him.

But it was Celadon who felt his soul sink through the glass-and-marble floor.

It was Nausicaä who stiffened . . . and Lethe, too.

Because it was *Arlo* the room turned on its axis to watch, as in one swift movement, she'd armed herself with a dagger pulled from somewhere in the folds of the training clothing she still wore from earlier that morning.

A dagger . . . and clever Arlo, brave Arlo, his immeasurably precious cousin, who understood too much of cruel things . . . a dagger she held not to anyone in the room but to her own throat.

"You'll let them go."

The words were pitched in such threat that the tone surprised even Celadon.

Arlo took a step back from Nausicaä, who'd turned as though to grab and disarm her—but clever, brave, precious Arlo was windborn; she darted too quickly away and pressed frighteningly harder against her jugular.

Nausicaä froze in place. She wouldn't risk it.

Not Arlo—whatever Nausicaä's terms, whatever controlled her, Arlo would not come to harm. Celadon was certain of it.

"You will let Nausicaä go. You will let Aurelian go, and Elyas, and Theodore. My father, too—anyone who wants to leave, you will allow to do so, or I swear to you, I swear it on my mother's life that *you* took, that I'll spill my own life right here on your throne."

What a position to be in.

Celadon couldn't tear his eyes away from that blade, already drawing a score of red on pale, fragile skin. . . .

Riadne watched too. As did Nausicaä. As did Lethe. What would she choose, when also watching was the Court she'd gathered to witness humiliation.

"I know you need me," Arlo added in additional warning when Riadne didn't move. "You let them go, and I'll stay. I'll help you. But I *swear it*, Riadne Lysterne, if you don't, I'll end it all right now—everything you've worked for."

"Riadne," Nausicaä drawled, and it was probably the most dangerous sound Celadon had ever heard.

Riadne blinked. She straightened further from Aurelian. Raising a hand, she snapped her fingers loudly at Arlo, and in a calm, measured tone that Celadon recognized instantly as the Magnetic Gift she'd hid from the Courts for so many years, said, "You will put that knife away this instant, child."

"I will not," Arlo returned in a bite of triumph.

. . . oh.

Celadon felt like laughing.

Riadne's expression flickered to murderous.

Rage began to boil under that steadily glaring light in her skin. Riadne had pushed it too far in the ballroom that night, had poured too much of herself into compelling Arlo's obedience. And because of that, Arlo had built up a resistance. No longer did that Magnetism hold enough sway over her, not when Arlo's defiance was so high, her will so strongly rallied. Not when she'd been ready for it. . . .

"Lethe needs me too," Arlo continued, taking another step back. "Whatever you've done to Nausicaä, it doesn't seem like she wants me to die. Two immortals you very much don't want making you their target, *High Queen*—you'll have bigger problems on your hands than training a new alchemist replacement if you force me to go through with this."

"Mother," Celadon rasped. Pushing past Lethe's defenses, he stepped forward. And didn't need to clarify. Didn't need to explain. Said simply, and pointedly, "You owe me."

For everything she'd done.

For everything she'd stolen from him.

For everything she'd committed in his name that he'd never asked for.

Riadne's blue eyes gleamed. Made a fool in front of her people tonight . . . there would be punishment, but for whom? The queen rounded back on Arlo. "You can have one. I will spare *one*."

"No, *all of them*!" Arlo yelled—Riadne's words a trigger of sorts. Lethe had filled him in on what had happened between them, that Riadne had forced Arlo to choose which family member to save, and the guilt Celadon carried that she had chosen *him*. . . . The words Riadne just said had clearly pushed Arlo too far back into that memory, and that dagger pressed harder, and skin broke to blood, and Nausicaä whirled on Riadne, fire igniting in hair and at heel.

"All of them for me—that's my only deal."

"Mother!"

"Riadne . . ."

"YOU CAN HAVE WHAT I ALLOW," Riadne boomed over the crowd.

Breathless with ire, eyes like ice, electricity snapping around her in threat—a bolt of it shot for Arlo's blade, and with a clatter Arlo dropped it to the ground.

She shook her fingers with the way it must have smarted, and Celadon watched with a further sinking feeling as she realized the flaw in her plan: the underestimation that Riadne could ever be backed into a corner. "You can have what I say you can have," Riadne said frostily, inflating like a massing storm. "Nausicaä I exempt from nothing—she gave herself willingly, is free to leave whenever she pleases. Your father came to me willing too, and the door is not barred against his exit either, should he declare his decision to leave. They are here for *you*. I prevent no one from leaving but *you*—because you are right, Arlo Jarsdel; I do require your skills. And I do require them surrendered of your own volition, so all your stunt here tonight has bought you is a reminder. A lesson, which I dearly hope you learn from, as I will not bend to teach you it again: what it means to make yourself my enemy."

Striding to Nausicaä, she took hold of her shoulder and propelled her forward with a shove. "Nausicaä, you will arrest Arlo Jarsdel, Aurelian Bessel, and Prince Elyas Viridian. Take them to the dungeons and lock them up." Turning, she rounded on Theodore. "Two lives I've spared, two more that were never in danger to begin with, but this *is* what she wanted, so Theodore Reynolds, I release you, too. By impassioned request, I let you go. Though I'd urge you to run very far, very fast . . . for I also denounce you."

Celadon gasped—he wasn't the only one to do so.

"I denounce you for the crime of treason against your High Queen; for sedition; conspiracy; attempted assassination. I strip you of your ranks and titles, deny you home in my Court. I spare you my blade, and release you from my home, and you have one hour, as tradition goes, to get yourself gone from my sight, and never again set foot in my Courts. I denounce you . . . and Mark your life for death."

Lethe, Vesper, Yue, Eris—each stiffened to attention. There were more gasps now around the room; Celadon could hardly breathe.

Marked was the Hunt unleashed at their full, brutal power. If captured—which the Marked always were, in the end—it would be unbearable torture that ended their life, with no chance of an after when the body gave out; no chance of rebirth, either. The Marked were hunted, and caught, and utterly destroyed.

It was a fate worse than death—and when Riadne had just promised Theodore to him, to Celadon's protection! No. He didn't deserve this; Theodore was many things, but he'd saved Celadon's life back in that arena, and Celadon couldn't let this happen.

Theodore, meanwhile, seemed unable to move.

Shocked.

Unsure of what to do.

It was Vehan who bent in—whispered something in his ear, pushed him forward with a glance to Celadon. And it was Celadon that Theodore's gaze met, pleadingly, as he stumbled down the stairs.

Out of the room . . . into the hall . . . tore off out of sight . . .

"Nausicaä, Rory, Aurelian, Elyas, Theodore—my dear, that makes five." Riadne's tone had grown silken and dark; the air around her buzzed. "Five named lives . . . as requested. I've been nothing but accommodating to you this entire time—caring. I gave you freedom to roam my palace, to eat my food, to study with my sons, to sleep and pass time in luxury and comfort. But still you beg knowledge of what it truly means to be my enemy, so with five lives spared, that means five to take their place, you foolish girl. To the dungeons with you!" She snapped her fingers at the Luminous Guard in a line behind her throne, and five men resplendent in bone-white armor poured down the dais to her attendance. "Prepare for the morning," she said icily to the men at her back. "At dawn, we execute Mavren and Eurora Reynolds, and Matthias, Nerilla, and Harlan Bessel."

"*No!*" Aurelian cried.

"Mother!" Vehan exclaimed in shock.

"LEAVE MY SIGHT IMMEDIATELY, ALL OF YOU! I AM YOUR QUEEN! YOU WILL DO AS *I* COMMAND, NOT THIS IRONBORN NOTHING GIRL!" Riadne burst in a flare of emotion, a bolt of hot electricity zipping through the room and scorching the wall.

The room began to empty in an instant.

Eris, Yue, and Vesper made to usher the whimpering, trembling, stunned ironborn children contained between them for a door at the back of the room—an offshoot that would lead directly to Riadne's private offices.

Nausicaä busied herself with immediate, Spartan compliance.

And through it all, Celadon could only stare.

"OUT!" Riadne raged.

"Lethe," he murmured, reaching down to take hold of Lethe's wrist once more and squeeze a plea. "I need you."

He needed his help, rather desperately.

The Bessels . . . Theodore . . . they were all under his protection. Aurelian had done his best to keep Elyas safe—it was Celadon's turn to make good on that promise they'd sworn each other at the start of the summer; the geas that clenched in Celadon's chest and rode his heartbeat like an untamed horse.

Celadon turned to him.

And raising a brow, creaking a chuckle of dark insinuation, Lethe transformed entirely in the sinful way he purred, "Oh, *do* you?"

CHAPTER 27

Aurelian

~⌒~

IT WASN'T UNTIL AURELIAN came to that he realized he'd been knocked out. The last thing he remembered was struggling against the hands that hauled him up from the ground—his parents, his younger brother, condemned to death in his place; *no*, he couldn't allow this—and then a blow to the back of his head, and his vision burst into stars that fizzled into black. . . .

"The nerd's awake."

A jolt shot down Aurelian's spine. He straightened too quickly; groaned when the action made the back of his head throb. Slower, he pushed himself up to sitting, back plastered against the stone wall behind him.

Dim lighting . . . stale air that smelled like body odor, damp cement, and mold . . . bars to his front, and at his sides—a cell, he concluded, and not a very big one.

"Harlan."

"What? We're spittin' straight facts here, Mom. He is a nerd. He is awake. Morning, sunshine—you look like shit."

Aurelian stared.

Gods . . . his brother . . . in the cell opposite his, Harlan was definitely worse for the wear, rail thin and blotchy with bruises that had to be fresh, and too frequently beat into his skin for his lesidhe healing to smooth it away. His hair had gone greasy and was lumped in a haphazard bun, his clothing torn and bloodstained and soiled.

"Harlan . . ." Aurelian's voice wavered with emotion. His little brother—shit, had Celadon done anything at all to protect him? He'd *promised. . . .*

Swallowing, he extended his legs in front of him and did his best to clamp down on frustration and tears, to hold himself together like Harlan was doing. "You look like worse shit."

"Aurelian!" Nerilla called from a cell just a little farther off down the line. "Could you boys just once *behave yourselves!*"

"Sorry, Mom," they called in unison back at her, and Aurelian breathed a laugh that most certainly wasn't at all a sob.

He'd done this.

His family . . . This was all his fault. If he'd just fought back; if he'd just listened to the voice in the back of his head telling him something was wrong. That Nausicaä wouldn't just turn up like this, and nothing—nothing—could possibly injure her enough to peel her from Arlo's side, to chase her to *Aurelian* for help with the one thing that would made him act irrationally: Vehan.

He'd been a gods-damned fool. Of course she'd been lying, and now his family would pay the price. And this was exactly why he'd been trying to ignore it for so long—the truth; what people used against him thinking he just *loved* Vehan . . . The things they'd do, be able to use, if they ever figured out it was so much more than that . . .

It took him a moment to realize the wriggling under his shirt wasn't a random muscle spasming. Pulling at his collar, he peeked down the front—"Leaf?" he murmured, and fished her out.

Quaking, terrified, clutching fast to his fingers was indeed . . . Leaf.

Oh—right, he remembered. Leaf, she'd refused to leave without him, had been tugging him by the back of his shirt the whole time in the Market, trying to pull him in the direction of the exit, away from the fire. He'd snatched her out of the air and stuffed her down his shirt, all the protection he could really offer the kindling she'd be to those flames.

"Sorry," he apologized. "Forgot you were in there."

"She is rather fond of you."

The voice made him stiffen.

424

Aurelian's eyes shot up from his hand to the figure that had been curled insouciantly around the front bars of his cell. Lethe, all shark-sharp grin and acid-bright eyes, hair that was noticeably paler than how he'd seen it last, almost like it was fading to white; no cloak, but those silver claws gleamed in the firelight; no weapon, but Lethe didn't need one.

"The fuck do you want?"

He wasn't in the mood.

This was Lethe's fault too—if he'd just left Aurelian alone at the Solstice, Aurelian could have been here, could have at least tried to get his family to safety, saved them from these cells. . . .

"She lost her children to fire," Lethe continued, ignoring his question. "A storm, some lightning, you know how it goes when you build your home in tall trees. *Zzzt*, and then flames." He pulled an expression of exaggerated sorrow. "And poor, lone, little mother was out collecting food and came home to no children, only ash. . . ."

That was . . . heartbreaking to hear. If at all true. "And you know this how?"

Lethe peeled back from the bars to dangle his weight backward. "Memory, Aurelian. My power is memory—I did show you. Moon and stars, you're oh so tedious. Tiresome. Dull . . ." He snapped himself upright, all trace of playfulness gone. "Predictable."

How much of Lethe was genuine instability? How much of it was an act—a defense, a shield, a mask he wore, because the world looked at him and expected an unhinged monster, and it was easier to play into that image?

It had to be a blend of both, Aurelian suspected.

The way Lethe watched him—this Hunter was clever. Careful. In the brief time they'd spent together, Aurelian had learned how excruciatingly precise he was, how everything he did and said was tied to deeper meaning.

"A good thing for you he's predictable, too." And then, with nothing else, Lethe turned like the crack of a whip; the pair of guards at the

425

stairwell's base snapped to frightened attention. "You and you—fetch tomorrow's entertainment."

Aurelian flew to the bars. "What are you doing?" he rumbled, but Lethe brushed him off without so much as a glance.

The pair of guards cast a hurried, wary look between them.

"Uh . . . ," one began, timid and clutching his royal spear like a shield to cower behind. "S-sir? We're not meant to bring the prisoners until morning."

Lethe raised a brow. "Did I ask for conversation?"

"Uh . . . sir—no, but . . ."

He lifted his clawed hand to study his nails. "Your queen is mistaken to believe I'm a pet. The rabble argues with me. Perhaps they require . . . reminding of who I am."

"S-sir!" The other guard rushed to comply. "Forgive us—right away!" He slapped his companion across the chest, and the two of them scurried like terrified mice, hands shaking as they searched out their keys to unlock Harlan's bars and pull him from the cell's innards.

Aurelian's parents were next, then Theodore's, all held to the point of a spear that might not be Lethe's adamantine claws, but enchantment had sharpened it to more than deadly.

"Lethe!" Aurelian shouted after the Hunter's retreating back. "Lethe, what are you doing? Where are you taking them—please, what are you talking about? I don't understand! Lethe!"

His family shuffled past him.

Aurelian reached through the bars for his mother, his father, his brother, and in his desperation, the iron under his weight began to bend. . . .

"Do take care with my things," Lethe called from the stairwell where he waited. "I'll be most predictable too if you break him."

Him?

But then Lethe turned . . . to nothing. A bit of empty air beside him. Snorted, "Good luck," and whisked himself up the steps after the guards, and Aurelian was left to ringing silence.

Damn it!

No—

"He means Cel," said a quiet, flat voice from the cell beside him, and Aurelian startled; she hadn't spoken once since he'd awoken, and in the chaos of everything, he hadn't even noticed her there. But tucked up small against her patch of wall, knees to her chest, eyes red, Arlo sat hunkered in abject defeat. "His him is Celadon. *Your* predicable him is—"

"That was easier than I thought it would be," Vehan gasped, tugging away a piece of fabric that had been draped over him. Invisible, but when he bunched it up and passed it to the taller, copper-haired fae beside him, it burned black as the holes in space and glittered like starlight.

A *Hunter's cloak.*

Aurelian gaped a little.

"Vehan?" he whispered in sheer disbelief. "Celadon?"

Vehan, meanwhile, was paused in a frown. "Honestly, too easy. We should probably speak to someone about this afterward. I mean . . . hooray for us and all, but there *are* people we keep down here who actually shouldn't be—"

"It was easy because of Lethe," Celadon said dismissively, taking . . . What in every deity's name had the two of them paid to have *Lethe's* cloak?

Aurelian's brain reeled.

Darting forward, Celadon latched himself onto the cell next to Arlo's—dropped to his knees, called to Elyas—and Aurelian's heart stuttered, because he hadn't heard from Elyas yet either, and gods . . . please . . . The boy had inhaled so much smoke, had gotten so close to those flames. But whatever passed between them, Aurelian's attention was drawn like a magnet to the boy who rushed to clutch the bars in front of him.

"Aurelian," Vehan whispered, wonder and misery all at once.

And Aurelian couldn't help it—he broke. Hands through the bars, he grabbed for Vehan's front and pulled them as close as they could get. Nothing touched—it didn't need to. Eyes falling closed, their foreheads resting on iron he registered only faintly as pain, Aurelian breathed for what felt like the first time since their parting, and that gingery, floral scent of his prince . . . how quickly he lost himself, how difficult to think. . . . "Vehan, what's going on?"

CHAPTER 28

Vehan

———◦⌣⌣◦———

FOR A BRIEF MOMENT, everything fell away.

The scheming, the danger, the bite of the iron against his skin—there was only Aurelian, the warm-autumn scent of him, his best friend and fiercest love. For a moment he was back in the Market tavern: Aurelian's hard body against him, bare skin to bare skin, that mouth sealed over his own. . . .

"Vehan, what's going on?"

Vehan's eyes fluttered open. He sighed and pulled back a fraction, only enough to think clearly again and surface from the pull inside him that was *Aurelian, Aurelian*, almost constantly. Drawing a breath to steady himself, he replied, "We're getting you out."

A wince pinched the corners of Aurelian's expression. "I'm not leaving here without my family."

"And I wouldn't make you," Vehan reassured, slipping from the bars. "Lethe's bringing them to the Market as we speak. I guess the Madam returned and they were finally able to put the fire out? They'll need to rebuild pretty much . . . everything, but the Market's still the Market—Nausicaä, the Hunt, none of them can get back inside without invitation, even Lethe. He's dropping them off at the gates, where they'll be safe. Where we're taking you."

"And you, with me."

It was the sharpest demand Aurelian had ever given him, and Vehan felt his heart sink. Luckily, he was spared a reply.

The dull groan of warping metal cut through their conversation, and in less than a minute, a hole opened up in the front of Aurelian's cage large enough for him to squeeze his way out—

another groan, and the bars of Elyas's cage bent similarly,

"*El,*" Celadon cried, nearly lunging for the younger boy in desperate flight to wrap him up in a tight hug.

Elyas fell into his uncle's arms gladly, a sob wrenched from his throat that was quickly swallowed by Celadon's chest, where he planted his face and murmured something. Celadon murmured words back, smoothing out his hair, holding him *so tight*, and it was all too much to witness.

This was the first time his brother and . . . well, Elyas was sort of Vehan's nephew too, in a way, but this was the first time Celadon and the youngest surviving Viridian had seen each other since the Solstice.

Feeling as if he were intruding on a moment not meant for others to share, he blinked away the emotion that made his eyes sting and turned his attention instead to Arlo.

"You're getting very good at that, you know?" Vehan observed, moving to stand in front of Arlo's cell.

Still curled up back against the wall, a stick of chalk in her hand that Celadon had rolled to her. Once again Vehan was glad to have such a talented alchemist on their side.

Aurelian followed to his side, trailed by a woodsprite who seemed rather shy of Vehan, clutching to Aurelian's shoulder to hide the way she peeked out at him—and when Vehan gave her a wink, a halo of bashful green lit her wings before she could dart out of view.

Celadon took up his other side, Elyas still wrapped safely and puffy-eyed against him—all of them already knew how this would go.

"Nausicaä would want you to come," Vehan tried, regardless.

But Arlo shook her head. "I'm not leaving her here. We made a promise—it's the both of us together, or neither at all. If she can be stubborn about that, then so can I. I'm staying here . . . until the end."

The last bit made her eyes water, and Vehan's too, because he got it.

The conviction, the desperation.

Vehan wouldn't be leaving, either—he'd made a promise as well. Not without Arlo, and Arlo not without Nausicaä, and Aurelian was going to be so angry with him, but he would understand. "Besides. You heard her, right? Your mother . . . she needs what I can do. If I go with you, there isn't anywhere Riadne won't follow to steal me back. You're safer with me here."

"Arlo?"

The way Celadon's voice cracked . . . Vehan wished they could give the two of them privacy, that they had more time to spare for goodbyes. But the longer they spent here, the greater the risk that his mother would notice something amiss, and Celadon . . . Lethe . . . they were paying such a dear price already, just for this much.

Arlo lifted her head. Vehan turned his back so at the very least . . . they could have this.

"This isn't goodbye."

"Of course not."

"I'm getting you out of here too."

"I know. I believe you. It's okay, Cel. . . . Get them to safety."

"Arlo . . ."

"Hmm?"

"This *isn't* goodbye . . . but I won't be able to see you again. Not for a while."

Not given what this was going to cost when Riadne inevitably learned not only what Celadon had contrived here tonight but, as a result, his true intentions this entire time—that Celadon was not on her side at all.

"Please," Celadon added, breathing the words like a prayer. "Please be careful. Please don't forget I love you, and I'm coming back."

Arlo huffed a laugh that sounded quite wet, but Vehan wouldn't judge. "I love you, too. Now get lost, and . . . thank you. For letting me choose."

It broke his heart a little to leave Arlo down there, when she was so obviously frightened and miserable and alone in the pressing dark. However wretched Vehan felt about it, Celadon's aura was a sour, congealing mass of depression, but he'd done the right thing; so many people had stolen choice from Arlo for so long that it mattered that he didn't force her to escape.

Vehan could tell how much it pained him, though.

Don't worry, Celadon. I'm going to protect her, he vowed in silence to his brother as they climbed.

Up the stairs, out into the hall—

"Please tell me the next part of your plan doesn't involve all four of us crowded under that cloak. . . ."

Vehan beamed at Aurelian, who looked back at him with such flat dismay he almost wanted to laugh. "It stretches to fit," he reassured instead, as Celadon passed the ball of material to him to shake it out. "Seriously, this thing is incredible. I would trade the entire Lysterne fortune for one of these! On a scale of one to violently dismembered, how much trouble would I be in if we just . . . didn't give this back, you think?"

Rolling his eyes, Celadon flicked his shoulder. "Put it on, Vehan. We don't have time."

Throwing the cloak unfurled, Vehan slipped it over their huddled group—an awkward fit, but it could have been worse; so long as the cloak was touching them, their entire form was concealed from view, even the bits that stuck out.

The quick rundown Lethe had given was that this magic would work only with his permission for their use of it, and only so long as invisibility was what they willed from it. *It has many other functions,* Lethe had added. *None of which you'll utilize tonight. Abuse my magnanimity, and I'll exact its worth in pounds of your flesh.*

"How are we getting out, then?" Aurelian inquired, and added with a snort, "Don't say the front door."

"No," Vehan replied. "The Egress. Lethe's given us fifteen minutes of uninterrupted access to get there, and we're to go through to the Hiraeth. Our destination's the Market as well."

Nodding, Aurelian relented. Fell in behind Vehan, holding sure to his waist, and the contact sent a thrill of heat through Vehan . . . but there was no time; there wouldn't be time for them again, not until this was over.

How badly Vehan wished he could go with them . . .

How much danger he'd put them in too, if he did, with the ghost of Ruin haunting his heart, and his life hinged so unfairly on his mother's machinations. Riadne would chase him to the ends of this earth as well. He couldn't go, but . . . *Urielle*, he missed his boyfriend.

On they walked, at a much slower pace, to keep from making too much noise.

They skirted the halls, made for the Endless Corridor, where his mother kept the magic mirror that would allow them transport anywhere they could picture.

They passed by the Grand Ballroom and . . . Vehan paused.

Issuing a quiet *oof* of surprise, Aurelian knocked into the back of him and stopped short as well. "What is it? Guards?"

He couldn't say.

At least, not until he heard it again. "I'm doing this for *them*! But they don't understand."

It was . . .

His mother.

Vehan stilled.

His gaze fixed in horror on the gap in that ballroom door, where no one had entered since the Solstice; since Arlo had cut down her family and buried them, and whispers began to circulate that it was haunted.

His mother . . . standing there holding her Crown, speaking to it like it was another living person.

Crying.

What a . . . horrible sensation, to realize how deeply that shook him. Riadne . . . his mother.

"—a monster," she hissed through choking emotion. "The world can think what it wants about me, but I'd do anything for those boys—*our* boys, and they just won't see. . . . They don't understand. . . .

Azurean, I didn't mean it. What I said that night. After all this time. I really do still love you—"

A hand on Vehan's shoulder.

Celadon looked . . . affected as well. But more capable of slotting away whatever he felt about this startling revelation, this thing Vehan had forgotten—that his mother had . . . feelings.

Feelings that she had *lied* about.

"We have to move."

And those feelings turned him instantly into the boy he'd once been. Quiet, attached, protective—he'd been fast at his mother's side after his father's passing. He'd always loved her too, snapped at any insult or disgusting rumor about her that crossed him. His mother . . .

Creak—

The door he'd been pressed against opened a bit farther, not as soundlessly as he would have liked. Not quietly enough to escape Riadne's notice, as her tears cut themselves abruptly off and her head swung in their direction.

"*Vehan,*" Celadon urged, and grabbed him harshly by the front of his shirt, hauling him physically onward. Aurelian's hands behind him, gentler, pressed him on as well.

They were quicker in their flight now.

Far more reckless with the noise they made.

Maybe Riadne had heard him, maybe she hadn't—they couldn't linger to find out. He berated himself for the lapse in his judgment. He could feel what he felt about this later; Riadne was going to *kill* Aurelian if she caught them.

They had to move.

Down the halls, at last to the Egress. They burst into the glaringly white room, and Vehan ripped off the cloak from around them as Lethe, lounging against the mirror's frame, tracked their approach with a piercing, bright gaze.

No guards—he'd been true to his word.

"Here," Vehan called, throwing the bundled-up cloak at him. "Celadon, you first with Elyas."

Celadon nodded.

Paused at the mirror's threshold, as its glass rippled like the surface of water, and the Hiraeth's image swam into view.

"Thank you, Lethe," Celadon murmured between them.

It was curious, to see the way the things that made Lethe *him*—that terrifying aura, those acid eyes, all that bite and threat and glinting silver—all of it just seemed to . . . soften. A little. Enough that maybe Lethe was an actual person, too. A person that liked Vehan's brother, more than very much. . . .

"Don't be insulting."

Celadon breathed a laugh. "I'll see you soon."

Lethe nodded, and Celadon stepped up to the mirror and through its glass with his nephew.

Vehan turned to Aurelian, to his woodsprite, who took one last starry-eyed look at him before diving back for cover under Aurelian's shirt.

Odd thing.

"You two next," Vehan urged.

But Aurelian merely stood there—staring. Looking at Vehan like he'd already figured it out. "You aren't coming either."

One step forward . . . two . . . Vehan closed the distance between them. He placed his hands firmly on Aurelian's chest and surged up to Aurelian's mouth, sealed his lips in a kiss that sparked through him to the bone.

Vehan groaned in the back of his throat a little when Aurelian's hand slipped behind his head.

It was desperation that drove them, a goodbye he couldn't put into words.

I'll see you again, he promised by way of a nip to Aurelian's bottom lip.

I'll see you again, Aurelian promised in return, by way of his other hand slipping down to Vehan's hip and drawing their bodies closer.

With dramatic, very pointed sighing, Lethe turned away.

And when Vehan pulled back, he felt his resolve take a hit. . . . How dark the gold in Aurelian's eyes had turned in desire. Desire for *him*. It was still so new, so wonderful, that he could have any of this boy's affection, this man whom he had loved what felt like his whole life. . . .

"It'll be okay, Rel. I'll be okay. This is what I have to do."

"I love you," Aurelian whispered, the words so ardent Vehan could almost feel them like tangible things. "I love you, Julean Soliel Lysterne. The next time I see you will be our last reunion. I'm never letting you go again."

Vehan melted.

He bit his lip against the swell of his heart.

Aurelian loved him. "I—" *love you, too,* he wanted to say, but couldn't.

Couldn't . . . because he'd noticed too late.

There, just over Aurelian's shoulder, was Riadne, standing in the corridor's doorway.

Riadne, incandescent with rage.

At her hand built a great charge of electricity, so much more than what she carried in her core, but drawn from the room as well, which already had begun to dim. And as though time had slowed to an impossible crawl, Vehan's world became one . . . two . . . three.

One—Lethe whirled, his eyes grown large in genuine surprise; so this hadn't been at all part of his plan. He surged as though to jump as shield between his mistress and them.

Two—Vehan grabbed hold of Aurelian's front and *pushed* him back toward the Egress, where he stumbled but sailed through.

Three—too late; she'd only just missed him. Lethe, who'd been just a sliver too slow. Aurelian, who'd been her intended target.

Three, and the bolt of lightning Riadne had sent straight for Aurelian's heart collided . . . but not with Aurelian.

Not with what mattered most to Vehan in the world.

He could almost laugh.

But he couldn't do anything.

It was too late for him to move as well.

Three—but not too late to see Aurelian sink through the glass. Golden eyes grown wide in shock. Riadne's bolt had found a mark to substitute the one it had lost. And Vehan's heart stopped dead in his chest the second after its impact.

CHAPTER 29

Arlo

~⌒~

IT WASN'T UNTIL HER breath began to frost a visible cloud in the air that Arlo noticed how unnaturally cold it had grown in so short a span of time—she'd been too wrapped up in her misery.

Misery, because she was so damned tired of living through one historical event after another.

Misery, because once again—and perhaps more crushingly, given how this time she'd actually tried, and still her effort hadn't made a difference—Riadne had gotten the better of her.

Misery, because here Arlo was alone in the dungeons of a murderous queen, and maybe the Reynoldses and Bessels would get to safety; maybe Aurelian and Elyas and Cel would too, and they'd locate Theodore, tuck him somewhere out of harm as well, and despite all that hope, the world would still be far from perfect because Nausicaä . . . *Nausicaä* . . .

What had Nausicaä done?

For her—what had Nausicaä been forced to do for *her*?

This was exactly what she'd been afraid of. Nausicaä would do anything for her, and Arlo had known that, and despite her better judgment, she still went ahead and allowed her foolish, soft heart to lead her actions instead of her head.

Arlo should have turned her down.

Last night, before she let herself get wrapped up in the most wonderful thing she had to hold on to lately, she should have *pushed Nausicaä away* just like she'd intended before she let herself believe that maybe she could juggle her own happiness with doing what was right.

Why was she so useless in every situation?

All this power they kept telling Arlo she had, all these special gifts, all the hopes continuously pinned to her that she would be this and that and this . . . some formidable alchemist, a Hollow Star, a warrior, a savior, a hero; a Viridian sidhe fae; the lynchpin of immortal devise . . .

Arms wrapped around the knees Arlo tucked to her chest, she clenched her hands into fists.

Anger swelled in her chest just as viciously as it had massed itself at the revel. It unfurled like some noxious bloom, a vile plague that spread through her heart and trickled out into her veins.

Another form of supposed power, but right now . . . it was just another way that Arlo felt useless, because what purpose did this anger even serve? Against immortals and Sins and hundreds-of-years-old queens who were so much better equipped for this level of intrigue, Arlo was—quite embarrassingly, and more evident than ever—a nobody mortal child.

She was Arlo—just Arlo—and her destiny, it seemed, was whatever Fate wanted it to be; not up to her at all.

Arlo breathed.

She breathed again, and finally she noticed that icy cloud before her face.

Had it always been this cold down here? She looked at her feet, at the black fabric of her running shoes; frost clung to her laces, curled over the round of her toes.

Frowning slightly, she reeled upright against the stone wall at her back; examined her surroundings a little more critically.

Cold, and it had dimmed strangely darker, too. The torches scattered down the hall were brighter farther on, but the ones closest to Arlo's cage had dwindled considerably. Their flames leaped with pathetic struggle against the air's chill—but it wasn't just that; something else sent them quivering to their wicks.

Palms pressed firm on the wall to guide her, Arlo felt her way up to standing—stepped to the front of her cell and latched on to the bars;

peered harder at the unnatural darkness creeping slowly but steadily toward her.

What was . . . ?

Arlo Jarsdel.

It was instinct for Arlo to stiffen. Ice licked its way across the floor, wound itself in delicate fractals up the length of the iron bars. Her breath froze like sharp needles before it even had the chance to escape her lungs, but Arlo wouldn't turn around.

She'd felt this presence before.

Most notably when she'd met Coyote, and something moldering, dying, and bleak had pressed and pressed for her attention . . . to just turn around . . . to *look.*

They can't hurt you, Arlo. They can't reach you or influence you in any way.

So long as you don't look.

So long as you don't speak to them or acknowledge their presence, they can't get to you. . . .

"Arlo Jarsdel," said a voice that was now a very present, real thing against the shell of her ear.

And how to describe that voice at all—deeper than the darkest pit that sank below the ocean floor. Rounded vowels whisper-accented by a language she'd never before heard. When the voice spoke, it hit her to the core like thunder, and yet the quality of it was gentle, peaceful like the grave.

Don't look.

This had to be some trick, and Arlo wouldn't let anyone—or any*thing*—else get the best of her naivete.

Head firmly forward, she immediately cast her eyes to the ground. Pressure built around her with a force that made her ears pop and stars spark off in her peripheral vision. Darkness reached fingers for her over the ice, sticky as spiderwebbing, black as fresh-poured tar.

Moros, scion of the End—portent of Doom—closed in all around her, and Arlo drew a breath to calm herself; to hold herself still; to

440

keep herself from closing her eyes or skittering away or screaming . . . anything that would acknowledge Moros as real.

A dark chuckle rolled through her. "The Fury teaches well—but there is much the young don't understand. Much that tongues and time have altered. You won't look at me, child? Your friend did not instruct you wrong—only those who acknowledge my presence would be vulnerable to my speech. . . . So what does that mean, then, that you can hear me now?"

Don't look—and Arlo wouldn't.

Not as the cold made her begin to shake, and the darkness oozed up the backs of her legs, and that voice filled her *wild* with fear.

She wouldn't look, and she wouldn't listen; he could tempt her all he wanted, play to her curiosity, do his worst. . . .

"You really won't look? I've been with you your entire life, through everything you've faced. Eos and myself, we've both watched over you for so long, but not until your meeting with Coyote did you show signs—signs of starting to remember."

Starting to remember . . . remember *what*?

"You will not look?" Moros oozed out the words in a voice that both mourned and mocked. "A wasted effort, especially when I could be of such assistance, Arlo. When the ones I serve could ease this heavy burden you carry. Who else, after all, to aid in putting misery to end than the End themself? Who to aid you in taking control than she who is the Beginning, inspiration of all?"

Don't look, don't look, don't look, don't look! It was all Arlo could do to keep her fingers from clenching around the bars.

"Perhaps you need a bit more time . . ."

Don't look.

"Do you like my tricks, child? The frost and chill and surrounding darkness; of course, it's all in your head—*illusion*, but what is truth but a matter of perception?"

Don't look.

Don't look.

"And perception is an amusing thing. So very dependent, weak on its own, but immeasurably powerful when utilized correctly. I'll give you a taste of what you could do when perception is bent to your will. Don't worry—this is a gift that comes with no attached strings; those already exist between us. . . . You will remember soon. You won't even have to accept it until I'm gone, and accepting does nothing . . . but ah, what a thing perception becomes when what was believed has been altered, and maybe what you've been taught all your life were wrongs they wanted you to *perceive* as right. Maybe . . ."

A tinkling on the ground—something small and made of glass clattered at Arlo's feet and rolled to a stop at the base of her shoe, and only because she'd been looking there already did she know it was a vial.

Such a tiny thing, crystal-clear liquid sloshing inside, only enough for a swallow at most.

"Maybe your perception will change when you remember what you've been forced to forget. Nothing is more dangerous than a fairy tale, Arlo Jarsdel—save to the one who tells it. When you're ready to talk . . . when you *remember*, you only need to call."

When she remembered *what?*

It was hard to distinguish what happened first.

At the top of the stairwell, just across the way, a resonating *bang* echoed down to her cell. And perhaps at the very same moment, or as a result, Moros withdrew himself back into the shadows and vanished.

The cold receded.

The torches reignited fierce and bright.

Arlo's cell was Arlo's once more—but the vial at her foot remained.

She released a sigh; with the tip of her shoe, she kicked the vial away and sent it tinkling across stone . . . just in time for Nausicaä to come stomping into view.

Arlo surged against the bars. "Nos—"

"It's your lucky day, Red! All hands on deck—I've been sent to fetch you."

The way she said "Red," as casually as she'd ever said it before, and yet so different. There was no heart behind the term, no passion, none of the fondness that had always accompanied its saying before, and this was closer than Arlo had come all day to tears just to hear it. Something about that word, so clinical, detached, made what had happened real, and she wanted to cry.

Eyes watering, she refused to budge. "Nos . . . please. *Please*—what happened?"

Nausicaä reached her cell and paused.

Frowned. Cocked her head at Arlo. "Like, to me? Arlo, listen, honestly, I'm fine. Kind of better than fine; I'm actually thinking clearly for the first time in . . . shit, way too many years. I still love you. You're still my girl—"

"But you say that like you're speaking to a brick wall. Not me."

"Maybe I like brick, too. Hey, I know, it sucks, I'm not big on letting other people call my shots, but I did what I had to do to keep my spot here—you did read my letter, right?"

Arlo . . . nodded.

That heartbreaking letter . . . almost as difficult to process as this stilted, unfeeling conversation.

"Then relax, Red. I gave Riadne permission to use her philosopher's stone to 'take my heart,' and she's going to use it to send me off on stupid little tasks until good triumphs over evil and you guys win, and Riadne has her toys taken away, easy peasy. Best of all, none of what I have to do will bother me at all because, hey, I don't feel upset about things anymore! Nothing. It's like a vacation from *me*, and I don't know if you've met me, Arlo, but me is a person a *lot* of people would like to take a vacation from."

"Not me," Arlo whispered, dropping her head against the bars. "I love you, Nos. I didn't want this. I don't want this."

Nausicaä nodded matter-of-factly. "Again, I love you, too. It'll be all right, Arlo. I mean . . . all right for you. Less all right for a certain dark-haired lightning prince if we don't mosey."

443

That caught her attention.

Arlo straightened, lifting her head again from the bars. "I . . . what?" Dark-haired lightning prince . . . "What's the matter with Vehan?" she asked in a rush, connecting those dots and feeling her veins ice over again colder than even when Moros had been right beside her.

"Oh!" Nausicaä answered brightly. "Wild story. Vehan's dead—"

Arlo flew.

Vehan's dead.

Riadne shot him with lightning and stopped his heart.

She flew up the stairwell, down the hall to Riadne's private office.

Through the open columbarium at the back of the room, down this next winding set of stairs . . .

Vehan's dead.

This was dread unlike anything Arlo had felt. It was her mother all over again, but different. It was everything that kept her awake at night, the fate she feared for all the people who mattered to her—she had to get to Vehan, but what would she find when she did?

They burst into the chamber under Riadne's office, the one she'd built and outfitted for alchemic experimentation.

It was chaos with everyone darting around, running from table to table.

At the center of the room, on the altar where Arlo had witnessed her father tear through the chest of an ironborn child, Vehan lay prone . . . rigid . . . unmoving . . . pale as the death Arlo couldn't, wouldn't contemplate. . . .

A halo of glowing light around him: magic spun to preserve a body that would have otherwise started decomposing. Alchemists including Arlo's father gathered around, keeping that halo powered, all of them attempting to restart a heart that just wouldn't beat—

And Riadne, bent over Vehan's chest . . .

The look on her face . . .

Focus composed the Seelie Summer High Queen; with painstaking care and incomprehensible precision, Riadne seemed to be extracting her magic from her son's, siphoning the electricity she'd apparently shot into him, so devastatingly *much* that it had blown his capacity well past a Surge, right into immediate and fatal failure.

Strand after white-glowing strand she pulled . . . untangled her magic from Vehan's very life force with the steadiest hand . . . absorbed it back into her, and replaced what was his, just to reach for another strand and repeat.

"—have to move faster!"

"—have to siphon more!"

"—can't restart his heart until you do, Your Majesty; just a little more!"

Leda was in front of her in the blink of an instant. "Arlo," she breathed, her own face pale and wild, but bright with clear purpose. "Arlo, listen to me."

It took a moment.

Arlo couldn't think past the shock of the sight in front of her—one of her best friends, dead. Dead! Vehan was *dead.* . . .

"Arlo?"

Leda took her by the shoulders and gave a careful but firm shake back to attention.

Arlo gaped at her.

"This is . . . beyond a delicate procedure. You shouldn't even be attempting this at all, I wouldn't ask you unless it was dire, but you need to be the one to restart the prince's heart."

. . . and continued to gape at her.

Another shake. Leda's eyes grew brighter. "Alchemy works better the closer the connection between the two anchors. Remember from class, Arlo? Between alchemist and subject—between you and the prince. Of anyone here, you have the best shot of pulling this off. Riadne will siphon the excess current from her son's magic, and you will power the array we've etched on him. Sulfur, Arlo. Remember Sulfur."

Sulfur also represents spirit, but in a different way than our element—it's the vital force of a thing. Through Sulfur we can transmute intention, craft a potion that heals grave injury—or, far darker—reanimate the dead.

The words Leda had spoken during their very first alchemy lesson together came back to Arlo then, the memory of the three key components to every array: Salt, Mercury, Sulfur. But this was more complicated than anything Arlo had ever attempted. . . .

This was Arlo, reaching down to the very core of what Vehan was, taking hold of his life, and forcing it against its will to attach back to its host.

Dark magic.

Worth it.

Let the Furies who governed the use of such things come at her. Arlo had never done something so difficult, ever, but she'd give it her all.

"Right," she replied, coming back to herself and pushing past Leda.

She crossed the room to the central altar.

The gathering of Riadne's alchemists parted to make way for her, Rory coming up behind her to murmur gentle consolations . . . and instruction.

Vehan looked . . . horrifically peaceful through it all.

That black hair was far too dark against his icy complexion. Blue-tinged were his lips. . . . He was more like a doll made of porcelain as he lay there, not flesh and blood and heart. "Vehan," she breathed—she wouldn't let him die. It was unfathomable to let him die.

Riadne didn't look up at her, didn't acknowledge her in the slightest; continued to extract the damage she'd done with a singular-minded focus, like nothing else in the room existed but saving her son's life.

Good. The anger inside Arlo bit.

And a part of her—a small and ugly and, oh gods, not-at-all-kind part of her—hoped Vehan wouldn't wake. That Riadne would learn how it felt to lose someone *she* loved.

"Arlo, place your hands here."

Another array.

Arlo looked down at Vehan's chest.

His shirt had been ripped open down the middle to bare his chest, and revealed was the black-and-blue philosopher's stone array, now paired with another just beside it. More dark magic on a boy who was one of the sunniest, purest people she'd met.

Lifting her hands, Arlo touched them to the array's outer circle . . .

And tried her best to perform a miracle.

CHAPTER 30

Aurelian

———✦———

SLAM—AURELIAN HIT THE GROUND.

Dried twigs and decaying leaves crunched under his back. The Hiraeth was an unforgiving, painful break to his fall, but he didn't notice; he didn't care. There was only one thing that mattered right now, only one thing that *ever* mattered, and he couldn't feel, couldn't think, nothing but—

"VEHAN! NO!"

Aurelian fought to scramble upright against nausea, against his own smarting body, against the disorientation of what had transpired and travel through the Egress. Eternity passed in the time it took to haul himself back to standing on legs that shook like the rest of him and turn back to the portal.

It was just in time.

It was far too late.

It was excruciating, this feeling inside him, like his heart unraveling at the seams. Like all that had been holding the both of them together was a singular thread spanned between them, and Aurelian had felt it *snap.*

Snap . . . the moment Vehan pushed him toward the glass.

Snap . . . the moment that bolt of lightning made contact.

Snap, and Aurelian couldn't breathe. He felt as though he were falling away, shattering apart. No matter what he did to scramble after that slipping thread, Vehan's half, no matter how *desperately* he tried to clutch it . . .

The air before him shimmered, a tear in the space he'd just stumbled through that reflected where he'd come from—the other side of the Egress.

Shrinking smaller, fading by the second, sealing itself back over as the Hiraeth—Aurelian and Vehan irrevocably separated—it had all been just in time to witness as though in slow motion Riadne screaming and darting forward, eyes wide in a mixture of fury and fear.

To witness Lethe whirl around, alarm on his face that might actually be genuine, and Aurelian didn't care. Didn't care because it was *all just in time.*

And far too late.

To see.

The way Vehan stood there, shocked in place. Blue eyes . . . vacant of their usual light.

The way he collapsed to the floor like a marionette cut of its strings, and the Egress closed up before Aurelian could reach it; could throw himself back through its gap; could get back . . . back . . .

To see the very moment Vehan's life blew out like an overwhelmed circuit board—the very instant Vehan . . . *his* Vehan, his light, his prince . . . his soulmate . . . simply died.

"Aurelian!"

"Aurelian."

"Boy, we have to go!"

"Aurelian, stop, you're hurting yourself!"

The sounds—it took Aurelian a moment to realize the guttural anguish was his. These things that were moans, that were agony tearing out of his mouth the same way his nails scored through the fabric of his shirt to claw and claw and bloody his chest, to reach for his heart . . . to grasp for that thread . . .

"Let me go," he managed between those awful sounds. "Let me go—Vehan! *No!*"

There were hands on him, pulling him back, away from where he needed to be, and Aurelian struggled against them.

"I can't hold him!"

"Tellis, boy—we can't do this right now!"

Aurelian snarled.

449

It was a sound he'd never heard from his mouth, and it surprised him to hear it wrapped in his voice, but he just didn't care. "Let me go—*let me go!*"

He struggled and flailed and writhed in the hands pulling and pulling him away from where the Egress was no longer. There was no going back . . . but that wasn't possible. Vehan could not be dead—there was *always* a way back.

A way back to him.

He would not accept this as real.

A man came before him, boar-black hair, olive-brown tan—Nikos Chorley—and placed his hands on Aurelian's shoulders. "Son, I'm sorry, but we can't stay here—"

"Get the fuck out of my way," Aurelian snapped at him and threw his whole weight forward.

They wanted a lesidhe's rage? They wanted to see what Aurelian's anger could do? He heaved his arms forward, and like those hands had belonged to rag dolls, Aurelian swung and flung their owners violently to the ground—Celadon and . . . Harlan? They toppled with a cry.

More people rushing forward.

His mother, his father, others he didn't care about—not right now; not with them in safety and Vehan collapsed in a heap on that floor. . . .

He surged into Nikos's space, took hold of the front of his shirt, swung him to the ground with Celadon, too.

"Aurelian, you can't get back! I'm . . . I'm *sorry*—"

"*Fuck off,* Celadon," he growled out. There were tears in Celadon's mismatched eyes; he was sorry, was he? Did Celadon hurt? To have witnessed as well the moment Riadne killed his younger brother? Good—he hoped it agonized him. Why didn't he understand? How could he not feel *this*? This gaping hole widening in Aurelian's chest, bleeding anger . . . and unspooling after this thread that had tied him to the *only thing that mattered* had been cruelly severed with one single snap.

"I'm sorry, but we have to go before Riadne sends her Guard after us—we have to get to the Market. Don't let . . . Don't let Vehan's sacrifice . . ."

Celadon choked on the words.

Aurelian bared his teeth—*don't say it.*

He ripped away from the group, flew to the place where the Egress had just closed.

It was still warm; the residue of its magical signature still hummed in the air, and if Aurelian could just figure out a way to grab onto it . . . to force the portal back open before it disconnected from the Egress entirely . . .

More hands on him now.

Again, they pulled.

But he wouldn't leave Vehan there.

He would kill Riadne with his own two hands. Her son—he hadn't been her target, but that had been *her* son, and she'd murdered him right in front of Aurelian's face, and he felt . . . he felt . . .

"Grief" was a pale term for this feeling.

He felt . . . *wrath*, as pure as the Sin itself.

More hands—"I apologize, Aurelian."

Ivandril.

Then the Earthen Warrior's hand was wrapping over the back of Aurelian's shoulder, close to the hollow of his throat. And Aurelian cried out when that hand gave a squeeze and his vision filled with stars and then finally, blessedly, faded to black.

CHAPTER 31

DARKNESS ALL AROUND HIM, as far as he could see. An abyss that wore on endlessly in every direction, and he had no idea where he was—*who* he was, for that matter. And more frightening than all of this was that he was also wholly alone.

Alone with himself, quite literally it seemed.

Something pressed against his back where he sat on a glassy black surface, his knees tucked up against his chest, his head bent.

He was cold, and he was frightened, and he was so very alone with something—some*one*—that felt like him. Him, without a heart. Him, without good. Him, the very worst of who he could be, darker than the absence of light around him.

"A pity this place is only bearable now that you are dead."

That voice—was it his?

He had no idea, couldn't at all remember what he sounded like, but if it *was* his, there was something quite wrong with it, as wrong and unnatural as this place he was in. A place that should be the brightest warm light and stained-glass color, a place where he knew exactly who he was but had faded now, moldered now, withered to black and black and fear, and cold that chilled him to the bone.

"And to think how fond I'd become of this body, this pure heart that posed such a *challenge* to corrupt, so well and uniquely protected against my influence. . . ."

He could see it in the barest outline of shapes, the things the glass he sat on depicted.

Smiles and laughter and love preserved, moments made images

laid out like a stained-glass window of all the things, all the people, that gave him hope—not absent of grief, or hurt or anger; these things had been etched in the glass as well, but in a way that tied all the good together, led from one happiness to the next.

None of it should be drowned in this darkness.

"Oh well, I suppose. Such as it goes. Rest now. Relax. Let oblivion welcome you to blissful release. Let it all fall away as you give yourself over. While the glory of serving as my vessel will not be yours, rejoice in knowing that your power, your life, your everything belongs to me and will still serve as fuel for my return. I appreciate your sacrifice."

"Ve—"

"—han, *no*."

He gasped with a start, pulled out of the lull of sleep he'd been fading away to.

That voice—he knew it.

Knew it like air, like his very reason for living, for loving, and—"Urgh!" he cried out, a hand to his chest. It felt like a bolt of lightning had shot right through it, but when he looked, he noticed . . . the thin thread of gold, so pure, so bright, so impossibly *strong* as it trailed off into that darkness.

As though someone had grabbed ahold of it and given the thread a firm yank, he felt it. Felt it like stars bursting behind his eyes and electricity through his veins.

"Yes, I did quite like that too," said the someone not him behind him. "A curious pride, to claim a heart that has managed a soulbond. I had truly been hoping it would be you. Then that lesidhe boy would be mine as well, and two would be won over by one. Oh well, as I said. A pity, but . . . oh?"

The someone behind him paused.

Straightened as well, attention focused below them . . .

Jade poured out from where they sat, glowing veins that grew and grew, steadily spreading to illuminate the abyss he was trapped in.

"Nostalgia," the someone sighed, and almost sounded reverent, happy. "A different color, but you know what they say: you never forget your first." They reached down to touch their fingers like a lover's caress to the light just beside his thigh. "It seems we've been given a second chance—"

"*Vehan!*"

He gasped again. His gaze snapped up just in time, and he could act only on instinct as a hand shot out of the darkness—his sliver of opportunity, gone for good if he missed this one chance he had to reach out and grab this lifeline . . . not of a miracle, but another person that mattered oh so very much, whom Vehan had always believed in, loved, known would be the one to help him where no one else could. *"Arlo . . ."*

CHAPTER 32

Arlo

~ 〜 ~

AND ARLO TRIED.

She studied the shape of the array she'd try to activate: every curve, every symbol, every complicated equation. Closing her eyes, she repainted the array in the black of her mind, envisioned it powered to glowing life.

Just like with the flowers, it scared her how easily this magic yielded to her. Once again it was like breathing; she didn't have to think about it, only had to reach out with her magic to take hold of what brushed against it with the array of a steady, luminous glow, humming power.

This life force was considerably harder to *keep* hold of, though.

It lashed and struggled, fought her every way, shocked and struck out at her, snapped and zapped and roiled . . . like it was afraid of her, didn't recognize her as friend yet and therefore didn't trust what she wanted to do with it.

It also wasn't alone.

Something else wrapped vine-like around it . . . something oily and black as sludge, a parasite . . . *the philosopher's stone array,* she realized. That something was the dark magic Riadne had tied to her son, and it throbbed, inextricable, constricted as though it would rather choke out the life that fed it than yield it to Arlo's command . . . but there was also something so incredibly *familiar* about it.

And Arlo didn't have the time to wonder.

She clamped down on it—Vehan and the dark magic both.

With a firm push, she sent all her might into her magic, and Vehan's life force—still so impossibly strong, but faded down to the rags of death—suddenly and fiercely complied.

Complied, almost as though for the whole span of a second, Vehan recognized this reach as *her*.

Complied, and then fell limp in the mental image of her hands. And Arlo shuddered.

It was . . . terrible. So much worse than holding the soul of those flowers. This life wasn't hers, and Vehan might trust her, but his life was also its own entity, and it resented her deeply for what she was doing. It lay powerless to stop her, and loathed her for it, and all she could do was hope Vehan would forgive her for what she had to do. That when he awoke, he wouldn't hate her as fiercely and wholly as his soul did right now.

If he did . . . that was the price she would pay, and gladly.

Arlo tried.

And tried.

And *tried*.

With his life quite literally in her hands, with her magic wrapped tight around his, Arlo guided her friend back to himself; willed his soul to attach once more to the flesh and blood and heart it belonged to. She tried her best. . . .

Vehan gasped.

"She did it—"

"Incredible."

"Your Majesty—he's awake!"

Arlo's gaze locked with Vehan's. She shook, down to her own soul, terrified. . . . Would he hate her?

Those blue eyes were wide and looking back at her. . . .

Riadne immediately peeled away from Vehan and stormed around her son without comment, without checking him over or expressing gratitude for what Arlo had done, seemingly without care that her son had lived through what *she'd* done.

She stalked around the altar, took hold of the alchemist most unfortunately closest, and heaved him even closer. "My son's Classification Exam is in three days—rain or shine. You will ensure he doesn't miss it. *You*," she snarled, dropping her victim to round on another: Rory. "Time to earn your keep. Prepare my ironborn. I am done with the time you're all wasting. Get me my next stone, *now*."

"Hey," Vehan meanwhile whispered, his voice a touch hoarse. The fingers at his side twitched, and instinctually she knew what he wanted; she reached out a hand to link their fingers together. "Thank you . . . I think. I don't really remember what happened, but I . . . remember you. *Thank you*."

"You're welcome," she breathed.

"I wouldn't mind a vacation when this is all over. What about you?"

Those blue eyes on hers . . . as fond as ever; nothing had changed.

Arlo bubbled a laugh that turned into tears. "A vacation sounds nice," she choked out before throwing herself in a hug across his chest. "I'm so glad you're okay. And I'm sorry for violating you on a really gross and soul-deep level that I never want to do again."

Vehan's hand slipped into the back of her hair. "I'm sorry it always has to be you."

CHAPTER 33

Aurelian

AURELIAN CAME TO, SHOOTING upright in . . . his bed? The air smelled like smoke and char, water and damp, burnt wood. There were noises outside—shouts; commands; the sounds of people clearing, rebuilding, preserving what remained of what they'd lost. The Market still stood so long as even a single post of its perimeter did and even one soul remained within to invite the rest back in.

The tavern had fared all right, it seemed.

Aurelian felt . . . hazy, lethargic.

Ivandril had delivered a nerve pinch that had knocked him out for a good long while, he guessed from the way the sun outside had risen to midday, but that didn't account for the way his body moved like lead—like he'd been sedated.

"Hello."

Like wading through fog, Aurelian slowly turned his head to examine the chair at his bedside and the person sitting there who'd spoken to him.

A young man sat vigil over him. Copper hair tousled and tangled and matted with sweat; twilight-glowing complexion paled to waxen; one eye jade, the other too painfully familiar a blue that Aurelian's heart constricted and—in self-defense, protection against this despair, this agony blooming like mold in the hollow where his heart had been—he shut the thought away.

He made a sound.

It was meant to be "hey," but it sounded a little like garbled nonsense.

Celadon didn't seem to mind.

There was a man at his side, standing just behind his shoulder. Recognizable in many ways, not least by the Hunter's garb he wore . . . as well as that long hair, once black, now taking on so much white it could only barely be labeled as gray . . . and those poison eyes.

Lethe seemed to be holding himself in a curious way.

Stiffly.

Like it hurt him to move overmuch—and what did that mean? Had Riadne punished his involvement in what had happened? In aiding Aurelian and Elyas's escape, in his family's, and Theodore's, too . . .

What in hells could Riadne do to someone like Lethe, even armed with three Sins, a Bone Crown, and her considerable natural talent?

Lethe was still an immortal.

Aurelian didn't want to think about it—preferred to imagine Lethe was rather just uncomfortable with playing caretaker at his bedside.

"Vehan's okay."

Aurelian . . . looked at Celadon.

Possibly, he'd just sprouted another head. It was difficult to tell—had the sedation really been necessary? His mouth felt like cotton, his head like empty sky. "What?"

Rolling forward to rest his elbows on his knees, Celadon peered at him intently. Aurelian's heart gave a throb. Had Celadon really said . . . ?

"Vehan is okay," Celadon repeated. "Arlo saved his life. Riadne siphoned just enough energy from his core to stabilize it, which allowed Arlo—through use of extremely impressive alchemy—to reach in and restart his heart. Vehan is okay, Aurelian. He lives."

Aurelian buried his face in his hands and wept.

There was murmuring. Lethe's creaking baritone bristling against Celadon's alto pitch. Emotional displays made him uncomfortable, it seemed, but Aurelian didn't care.

Vehan was *alive*.

He could feel it now if he concentrated. He hadn't been allowing himself to check, to focus inward on that thread he'd felt sever, and would fear ever feeling such a traumatic thing again, but there it was . . . *there it was.* The thread back in place, healthy and warm and glowing and electric with *life.*

That was just as unfathomable as the opposite—unreal, until he held Vehan in his arms again; until he could feel Vehan warm against him, his heartbeat under his lips; until his head filled with those breathy gasps, that laughter, his honey-warm voice . . .

"Theodore's okay, too, you might be happy to know," Celadon added. "Lethe brought him in a short bit ago. He's outside with your parents, your brother, his parents . . . Elyas. All the people who wouldn't have been okay if it wasn't for what Vehan did. You should be very proud of him."

"And you," Aurelian choked between sobs he tried to swallow back to calmness. Lowering his hands, he knew he looked quite the sight right now, but if that bothered either of the men beside him, they probably shouldn't have drugged him into not giving a damn. "You saved them too. And *Arlo* . . ."

He would spend the rest of his life repaying what Arlo had done for him—and gladly. She'd saved Vehan's life. He was . . . she was . . . Tears welled up in Aurelian's eyes all over again, and Lethe snorted before looking away.

Celadon leaned back in his chair once more.

"Yes, well . . . a team effort. None of which would have been possible without Lethe." Lethe, who stiffened even further upon the mention, and there was a wince of actual pain on his face when the movement jostled too much. "Which brings me to our damage report. I don't have long to linger; the Market doesn't extend its welcome to Hunters right now, so we're here on borrowed time." Because Celadon wouldn't send Lethe away, and neither would he go where Lethe wasn't, it seemed. The two of them . . . Aurelian hoped whatever was going on, they were at least happy; it wasn't his place to wonder much more than that, and he understood—how it felt to be separated from someone deeply cared for.

"As I suspected, Riadne has placed me on house arrest until she can decide how to interpret my involvement in your escape. Arlo and Rory remain in her grasp; Vehan lives, is mending well—quickly. His exam is in two days' time, and Riadne will not permit him to miss it."

That woman . . . that *monster.*

Aurelian wanted to . . . With his two bare hands, he wanted to . . .

"A morning event had been promised, and Riadne still delivered—by way of public punishment, a whipping which Lethe bore the brunt of." Ah. That . . . sort of explained the pain. Aurelian had witnessed Riadne's wrath in this way only once before.

Public *electric* lashing.

And with the Bone Crown behind her, with three of the seven Sins at her disposal . . .

How many times had she whipped him, though, that he should still be sporting the ache of it now?

"We are at the point where things will devolve quite rapidly, I'm afraid. Riadne is going to get much more dangerous, is going to force things along at a far quicker pace. Her stones created, I'm told she intends to use Arlo to transfer the heart of the ironborn who survives all seven callings to Vehan, then summon Ruin using Vehan as host. We don't have much time now, so we'll have to act accordingly. I have things to do, to prepare for that. Things I would ask of you to make that possible."

Riadne was going to use Arlo to summon Ruin into her son—yeah, Aurelian had . . . figured that out, more or less. And he didn't need to ask how Celadon knew this. Lethe had to know . . . and now there was even less love between him and his cruel queen to stay his tongue.

"I intend to establish a Court, Aurelian. Separate from the others. A *new* Court, with new laws, new ways of handling things. It will need a foil, among other things, but in order for my vision to stand reality against Riadne's forces, there are certain . . . assurances I need to put in place." He lifted a leg, crossed it elegantly over the other, flattened his palms on the arms of his chair like it was his throne— Celadon might not have come into power by natural succession, but he was clearly born for the role, and he seemed to be growing aware of that, more and more.

Each time Aurelian saw him, it was like meeting a different person.

"Vehan has already sworn me his support. I am certain Theodore and Elyas can be persuaded. I would also like to have *your* allegiance for this trusted inner circle. Can I count on you, Aurelian?"

Aurelian studied the King of UnSeelie Spring.

It was odd to stare into a face he'd always ever known as the late High King Azurean's. Now it was tempered with features clearly Riadne's in the cut of his cheekbone, the delicacy of his nose and jaw. That electric-ice eye . . .

Celadon was almost *too* beautiful. Maybe because Celadon was Vehan's brother, it explained a little why Aurelian had softened toward him, and he could admit that if things were different, if he weren't so entirely in love with Vehan, he'd have been just as enamored as anyone else was with the young man across from him.

But there was Lethe at his back, glaring coolly now at Aurelian as though he could read his thoughts—sometimes he suspected he really could. Good luck to anyone who sought to turn the young king's head with the likes of that Hunter around . . . and Lethe seemed to know that.

For better or worse, whatever that meant to him, Lethe seemed quite secure in the knowledge that he had as much of Celadon Viridian-Lysterne's attention as Aurelian had ever known him to give someone other than Arlo Jarsdel.

"I'll think about it," Aurelian replied. "We get Vehan out of there. Arlo too. Her father—everyone to safety, and I'll think about siding with you."

Rather than showing displeasure at his response, Celadon's mouth twitched in the hint of a smile. "I expected no less. We'll talk again soon, then." He made to stand, then, "Oh—and, Aurelian?"

Aurelian blinked at him.

The fog was beginning to dissipate. He could smell food just beyond the door, sense the magical auras of his unlikely crew of . . . well, not quite friends—he didn't know what to call them—but Jaxon, Tiffin, Ten, Rosalie, Elyas, and Leaf were all out in the hall, waiting for Celadon to give them permission to enter.

He lifted a brow.

"It's time to decide on the role you would like in this coming war. As a lesidhe raised in sidhe society, which has never been very kind to anyone other than *us*; caught up in Riadne's clutches; forced into many different roles, into many different sacrifices, to live years in fear and threat of death . . . there is anger inside you, and that emotion will not shrink itself simply because you will it to. You've seen enough of what it's capable of when disabused by power to know that penning it up will be just as useless to you as letting it get away from you like it did back in the woods. So start training with Ivandril. Give yourself an outlet. No one's asking for your wanton violence, but you can't protect anyone—not Vehan, and least of all yourself—with no idea what to do with all the strength inside you."

Dropping back against his pillow—remembering in a flash the rage that had scorched through him earlier back in the woods—Aurelian sighed, neither agreement nor otherwise, but yes. He could use with training.

His rage had been building for so, so long. Giving it an outlet for release wasn't the worst idea.

And if all their planning failed, if they didn't get to Vehan in time, if Riadne won like she always did in this game rigged to her favor, his outlet was going to be her death, passivity be damned.

CHAPTER 34

Celadon

W HY DID YOU DO it?"

"Why did I do what?"

It wasn't until Lethe replied that Celadon real-
ized he'd asked his question aloud. He blinked, and his awareness
focused on where he'd stopped, at the top of the stairs that would
carry them back down from Aurelian's bedroom to the main room
of the tavern.

A quiet hall, and only the press of Lethe's presence at his back . . .

A muffled clamor of voices below . . .

Aurelian's family had been quick to take up his bedside on their
departure, and wherever Theodore, Elyas, and Elexa had gotten to,
they were no longer here. It was just the two of them, him and Lethe,
and Celadon's mind was a tempest of thoughts, but the one thing that
blustering couldn't shake him from, the one thing that stood with
consuming permanence in the fore of it all . . .

Celadon's hand tightened on the banister.

He didn't think he could turn around.

He hadn't meant to ask it, but Lethe had replied, and now there
was no letting it go. "That punishment was mine. I was the one
Riadne intended for public humiliation, not you. I was the one that
lashing was meant for, and it would have been awful, it would have
hurt, but she wouldn't have used the same force on me that she did
on you for threatening her into letting you take my place." Celadon
swallowed. He could still see it, still hear it, still feel it—how *angry*
Lethe had been, frightening in his vitriol, like a trigger had set him off
the moment Riadne declared her sentence for Celadon's actions—to

the point that even Riadne had balked and eventually agreed to his terms. "Why did you do it?"

If you so much as raise that whip to him, I'll end your life where you stand.

For a moment, only silence met his question, and Celadon wondered if Lethe might not explain. Honestly, he didn't really expect him to, so when a second moment stretched the silence even thinner, more awkward, more weighted between them . . . Celadon sighed.

He shook his head, tried to pull himself together.

"Never mind," he said gently. "It doesn't matt—"

"You asked for my help. I did tell you there was nothing I would refuse you."

And finally Celadon turned around. "Your help, yes. I asked for your *help*, not your injury, your martyrdom." How quickly his own anger heated his voice, leaped to command his emotions. This . . . It infuriated him. It scared him. It confused him!

He had no idea what they were becoming, what Lethe truly wanted from him. And on top of all the things he had to deal with, to sort through, to relearn and manage about himself was this constant insistence . . . this feeling, a sureness, that whatever they were growing into, they'd once been quite a lot to each other.

Lifetimes ago.

Whole *people* ago.

Lethe mattered to him. And Celadon couldn't explain it, just as he couldn't explain why it had locked his breath in his throat, his heart in a vise, had flooded his veins with poison and frost to witness Riadne order her guard to tear open the back of Lethe's robes and whip him to a sapphire pulp.

Why he'd so very much wanted to tend to that wound, make it any amount better that he could.

Why it hurt each time Lethe denied him that request.

"I didn't ask you to take that punishment for me. I would *never* ask you to do that, and it wasn't at all what I wanted—"

"How unlucky for you, then, that you aren't my master. I don't care what you want." A lie—Celadon was sure he would have seen a wince as proof if Lethe had been fae. "I did what *I* wanted and don't have to explain."

At some point in this building argument, the two of them had drawn closer.

Celadon's chest heaved with all this frustration inside him, everything at war in his heart and his mind, and this almost maddening *tether* between them.

He was a sidhe; his magic wasn't attuned to his soul the way it was for the lesidhe, but he would swear on his life that there was something there, something warm and alive that Celadon could reach out and touch, grab hold of like a line. . . .

Did Lethe feel it too? It was impossible to say, especially with the way he loomed over Celadon currently, glaring down his nose at him, daring him to press the issue. Emotion warred behind those acid eyes as well. Something quite profound struggled beneath his apathetic surface.

Lethe clearly had so much more to say, but right now he bit his tongue against this one act of contradiction to his claim—there was one thing he would deny Celadon: the truth.

Lethe, who never held back what he thought about something, and Celadon wished he would just tell him.

Tell him what was going on.

"I don't like it when you're hurt, Lethe." Hands slipping up of their own accord—he was still angry, but that anger was subsiding to this strange pull between them, a connection that didn't make sense at all—Celadon's palms smoothed out the fabric over Lethe's chest. His fingers splayed, seeping warmth into what felt like cool stone beneath. "I like it even less when it's my fault. It *scared* me, Lethe. For a moment, I thought she might go too far and I would . . . lose you."

Seconds ticked by . . .

Ticked into the next . . .

It was the greatest shock of this entire event, more than Vehan's death *and* resurrection, that slowly . . . hesitantly . . . not at all sure of himself, Lethe lifted a hand as well.

And placed it over the one Celadon rested on his heart.

Slowly . . . hesitantly . . . with more feeling than he'd ever spoken anything to him so far, he added to Celadon's wonder with his reply: "You could live a thousand lives, be reborn a thousand different people; take countless lovers and forge endless friendships. You could have everything, and then it all stripped away, again and again and again . . . and still you will never know what it felt like. To just once be the one to lose *you*."

"What?" Celadon gasped, a touch breathless. His fingers curled against Lethe's chest to fist the cloth beneath. "Lethe, I . . . I don't understand. I don't understand *you*. I don't understand this thing between us—what is it? Why does it feel like I've known you far longer than my entire life? Why does it feel like I—"

Lethe suddenly hardened to ice. "Can we help you, princeling?"

It took Celadon a moment to catch up with the proceedings.

He stood there, blinking up at Lethe, who'd already hidden himself entirely under his colder, haughtier, usual mask he walked around wearing. Celadon drifted his gaze past Lethe's shoulder to notice as well now the young man at the end of the hall, caught between pretended ignorance of what he'd just interrupted and no small amount of terror that Lethe might gut him for it anyhow.

Swallowing, doing his best to right himself and pull his thoughts into order, Celadon released the Hunter.

Took a proper step back.

Cleared his throat—"Theodore. I was actually hoping we might run into you before we took our leave."

"Uh . . ." Theodore continued to stand there, even more stunned than Celadon had been.

An entire minute fit into the gap of his vacancy, while he clearly struggled to remember what had brought him out into the hall. All

467

the while, Lethe stood in fixed place too. Staring down at Celadon. No trace of the moments-ago affection, but apparently that vulnerability wasn't as easy to recover from as he feigned. "Sorry," Theodore continued at last. "I didn't mean to interrupt. It's just that . . . well, I think we should talk, Your Highness. Our cards on the table. I'm not sitting sidelined just because your mother exiled me."

Right.

Yes, that's what Celadon needed to focus on right now.

Not the way Lethe felt against him. Not the confusion of their present and past. Not the thing inside him beginning to lift its head in interest of something that he worried, always worried, would never be enough for what the subject of that interest might want, except . . .

Now was not the time.

Celadon had a Court to establish, a High Queen to keep ahead of.

And Theodore could be a key facet of what he'd begun to plan.

"Of course," he said smoothly, a smile on his face that might be a little more sapphire flushed than usual, but Theodore clearly wasn't going to comment. "Is there a room free down there?"

Theodore nodded, waved off to the door he'd just come from, and stood aside to make room for Celadon, who stepped around Lethe and headed in.

"You saved his life back in that arena."

Just inside the modest bedroom—a small but clean space of a singular window, a white-draped bed, and a table with chairs stuffed into the corner—Celadon turned.

But the comment wasn't for him.

Lethe filled the doorway, his back to Celadon. The creaking drawl of his almost offhand statement was for Theodore, whom Celadon could spy in gaps between the Hunter and the doorframe was frozen in place, tense with fight-or-flight instinct.

"Uh . . . ," he replied like before.

And Lethe sighed. Clicked his tongue. Probably rolled his eyes, knowing his habits as Celadon did now. "That knife that felled his opponent in that cage. That was you. You saved his life."

"Um. Yeah. You're . . . welcome?"

"*You're* welcome. It's what saved yours, just now."

It was Celadon's turn to roll his eyes. Lethe melted away from the door, slunk off to the table to take a difficult, stiff seat on its surface, which had Celadon's panic fluttering once more, that need to take care of him flaring hot—but no, this wasn't the time.

Theodore entered at last, closing the door behind him, and Celadon's gaze snapped forward once more.

"Okay then, to business—"

"I want to be King of Seelie Summer. I want the Radiant Throne."

Celadon paused.

"You asked before," Theodore explained, taking another step closer. "A few nights ago, you asked what I wanted, and I told you the truth. I've been keeping as close an eye as one can on what you're getting up to in private. I know you're rebuilding more than just your palace. You have some vision for the future of the Courts. Would this vision be amenable to including mine?"

Celadon considered the boy across from him.

He was absolutely correct—Celadon had been busy with more than remodeling his home, and he'd already mentioned as much to Aurelian; what he had in mind would require support, a light to play foil to his darkness, so to speak. A Seelie throne in hand with UnSeelie's.

But . . .

"You would actually be a good king, I think," Celadon said, after a beat. "You've been working quite hard in the background, I've noticed, caring for the Seelie people the way a king should. I know you've been helping those who want free of Riadne's clutches. You're a prince, you know how to play the game, and more than this, you're good at it. But," he added, his tone dipping ruefully, "Vehan would be just as good a choice, and as the crowned heir of a Seelie throne already . . ."

469

Clasping his hands delicately in front of him, Theodore smiled, affected every air of charm and a taunting of private knowledge. "You're rebuilding, and I'm fairly confident I know how, just as I know you're going to need more than a Seelie sovereign beside you. You aren't a fool; you haven't overlooked that the Wild will need to be brought into this for it to really work. But you can't want my great-grandmother for Head of that Court. *I* don't want the Madam for that Court. And I don't want to be the one to take her place. No offense to the Hiraeth, but I've had my fill of the place for several lifetimes to come, and I feel my intimate knowledge and camaraderie with the Wild would be put to better use from within the Courts directly. But there's someone else who could fill her vacancy, isn't there?"

His smile grew sharper.

"Someone on whom the Wild was not inflicted as I was but born with it in his blood. Someone the folk there seem happy to gravitate to. Someone who stood when the Madam fled, while the Market crumbled to ash and flame. Someone likewise to my relationship with the Hiraeth—an outsider raised with the knowledge of royal Court life."

Aurelian.

Theodore was talking about Aurelian—and Celadon had considered it. Reports on Aurelian's welfare in the Market had sent him down that train of thought, and Aurelian *would* make a valuable asset as Head of the Wild. Aurelian would be his first choice, after Theodore. But this was entirely dependent on what the boy chose—whether or not he decided to take a more active role in this war; whether or not he wanted to become the person he would have to be for the Wild to acknowledge him as its ambassador.

"Aurelian would flourish in this role. He'd hate being a Seelie king, as he'd become if you chose Vehan. And I've known Vehan a bit longer than you have, on a personal level. He was born for leadership, he'd be a good king too, and he adores the Seelie people—has fought harder than perhaps any of us for them, in many ways. But Vehan's true happiness is at Aurelian's side. He's happiest when Aurelian's happy. And he'd be just as good on a Wild throne."

True.

This was all true.

But . . .

Celadon sighed. "We'd have to speak to them about this. And no matter what they say, first and foremost, the Madam needs . . . dislodging. There's no reordering anything with her holding the Market captive—it's the Wild's heart, their capital."

"Oh, I quite agree." Theodore nodded, but his smile began to dim. "I won't be able to help you there. It's . . . well, I'm . . . not allowed to say. I'm sorry. A family secret I've been sworn to keep. All I can tell you is that, while I can't act against our matriarch, while I can't turn my power against our *elder*, you're uniquely positioned with loyalty from one of the rare few who can and actually would win." His gaze cut to where Lethe sat, watching this all, no doubt already well aware of who Melora really was and what he'd need to do to unseat her.

But Celadon wouldn't ask.

He wouldn't rely on Lethe for everything.

Not when Lethe enjoyed Celadon's cleverness as much as he did— and for some Cosmin-damned reason, it mattered to him: making Lethe happy.

"All I can tell you is that you know her kin; employ one in your service, as a matter of fact, if rumor is to be believed. Remove the Madam from her nest, Celadon. Do this for me, and I'll give you my full loyalty, as Head of Seelie Summer or whatever else you devise, but I promise you, one way or another, that golden throne will be mine."

Dawn broke over the watery horizon in shades of sour yellow and steel. Carried on the white-crested backs of gentle morning waves, it spilled onto the shore where Lethe had been discarded, did little to warm his battered face and the ragged flesh of his exposed back.

They'd left him here—to heal or to die, whichever Lethe chose; two guards sat waiting on the heap of rocks just up the way, tasked with reporting back to King Atlas with Lethe's decision: either his waste of a prince had chosen to surrender himself to the call of the sea and the seafoam he'd become, or he'd chosen survival—and the further *conditioning* that came with it.

How wonderful it would be to simply cease existing and disappear.

Lethe was tempted; he was always so tempted. The water sang so sweetly of relief from the torment his life had become, and the Moon was gone, taking with it his only source of companionship; his only remainder of feelings; the only real chance he had for revenge.

He was so very tempted to roll himself into the sea and be done with this all. What other use was there in lingering? To be tortured and bloodied and broken to splinters until the day he died, regardless. It certainly wasn't to hope for a power that would now never strengthen on its own.

Lethe, Prince of the Seas, stolen too early . . . before he'd had time to learn the things that were his by right, the Gift that all these years on land had no doubt diluted.

Of course the Pull wouldn't answer to him; of course the tides had turned on him. Who was he to them? A long-forgotten child who was more of the earth than of water by now.

Shifting was painful.

Movement made his body scream.

He was screaming already in his head—a keening, a mourning; it was agony worse than anything his father had ever inflicted to feel that bond he'd clung to for so long sever completely in two—and every muscle, every bone, formed a choir of suffering inside him.

Regardless, he turned onto his back.

Salt in the wound—sand in the wound—Lethe breathed a cry that was half tears, half bitter laughter, and the guards on their rock echoed laughter back at him to realize he was at last awake.

His friend.

His only solace.

The sea was singing to him, and all Lethe wanted was one last look at the Moon's pale face; to remember what comfort felt like, family, peace . . . even if the Moon could no longer gaze on him back.

Even if . . .

. . .

Laughter and tears took hold of him again.

The sound squeezed from his throat with a sapphire splurge, forced Lethe to turn his head and spit his piddling life onto the sand beside him. Teeth and blood . . . ravage and rage . . . Lethe grinned knives at the man who stood suddenly at his side and hovering over him where nothing had been standing just before.

"Father," he wheezed through a sneer, and spit again.

"My son."

Hilarious.

Quaint.

That *Cosmin* should stand there and call him such a disgusting name. Son to a man who'd handed him over to torture and death and suffering? Son to the Night that had forsaken him. That had stolen everything from him, even his Moon.

Lethe was no son.

Had no interest in being one.

This time, he spit blood at the god, and given that the guards watching him hadn't fled or shouted or come rushing over meant that Cosmin had appeared *only* to him. Likely the guards were merely amused, thinking Lethe was throwing one final tantrum to himself.

Regardless, Cosmin allowed his disrespect—sapphire sprayed the hem of his long robes, made of navy and black and cosmic dust, stars that melted and shivered and churned. He didn't step back out of range, merely looked down at Lethe wearing what he probably thought was a look of remorse.

"You may hate me," Cosmin said, voice full of sorrow, words full of things Lethe didn't care a *shit* about. "That is your right. I have given you much cause for scorn."

Lethe glared at him.

Cosmin bowed his head. Such displays of contrition, when it no longer mattered—of course he was sorry now! To see the one he called his progeny so miserable, a pathetic reflection of his failure . . .

He continued to speak in words Lethe couldn't care less to hear.

"I am no more privy to Fate's machinations than you, Lethe. I do know this much: I was instructed to grant the child that presented himself that night on the ship and did not for a moment think it would be you. But to Fate I am beholden—a son I had to deliver, as much as it pained me that the son was you."

Stuff and words.

He was oh so tired of nonsense and stuff and all these pointless words.

People spoke too much, said too many things with too little brain. Struggled and clawed and plodded through life and filled it with *stuff and words*.

Cheap.

They were as cheap as their trinkets. As cheap as their thoughts. Meat and minerals and water, packed into flesh casing—nothing.

Cosmin was cheap too.

"A son who, no matter how much I loved you, was not actually mine."

Cheap and . . . what?

Lethe stared.

And Cosmin sighed a most solemn breath, continued to look down at Lethe with all that grief.

"You see, my partner, Luck, is a titan, one of the children of the First Ones, and they operate under restrictions of their own. Titans are free to indulge in much that the rest of us immortals cannot, but at our Crowning, they were stripped of the privilege of further reproduction so that no more gods could be made. I love my partner, Lethe. I love them so much more than I could put into the word. I love them so much that when the opportunity presented itself . . . me, incapable of fertility, and your mother pleading for a child to Crown when every try but one produced death . . ."

Stuff and words and nonsense and *what*?

What was Cosmin saying?

That Lethe wasn't his child? But then, if that was true . . .

"I would give Luck anything, including this. Together we conspired to betray the regulations, to give my partner a child, to give your mother her legacy, and we hid it all under the pretense that Luck had simply bent favor in *my* fortune, made you the product of *my* loin."

Lethe wasn't Cosmin's son.

"I love you, too, Lethe."

But he *wasn't Cosmin's son.*

Was that better or worse—did he laugh, or cry? So many parents, it seemed, and none of them at all cared about him.

"Your parents beg my intervention. Neither wishes to see you like this, and your mother has paid great sacrifice to the darkest deep to aid you in your revenge."

His mother.

She'd meant something once as well.

Sisters had too.

Family all and nothing now.

"It was none of us Fate heeded though. In the end, what bought her permission to assist you was paid by the Celestial one of the Moon."

. . . what?

Cosmin's expression crumpled again into sorrow that meant nothing, and Lethe couldn't think, couldn't breathe—didn't at all want the god to continue, and at the same time if he did not tell him what his friend had sacrificed for this moment . . .

"What transpired exactly between your Celestial friend and Mother Fate, I cannot say. But the Moon paid its life, traded its Celestialhood, so that I might be sent to give you what you crave most."

What Lethe craved most?

And the Moon had thought that was *power*? Had valued its life as meaning so little to Lethe? He couldn't breathe; that misconception had been his fault. He'd been so obsessed with revenge, with inflicting himself on Atlas and his kingdom, and the Moon had thought itself second to it all, when it wasn't, it wasn't, it *wasn't*.

"How charming to know," Lethe replied around the sob that wanted to tear from his throat. He'd lost his friend, and it had been all his fault. "I want nothing from you or anyone else. Leave me be, no father of mine."

"Lethe . . ."

Cosmin didn't understand.

His friend—what that word meant to someone like Lethe, who'd had nothing at all where Cosmin had everything.

Lowering himself to a crouch, Cosmin regarded him with all that ugly regret, that shame. Nothing for Lethe, all for himself. The gods didn't feel what mortals felt, and Cosmin had never been his father in any way, it seemed, so what did it matter?

"You *are* my son, Lethe," he continued to bleat. "In every way that matters, you are mine as well. These people have mistreated you. King of legend you were meant to become, and I did hope . . . I know you want nothing from me. From any of us . . ." His eyes fluttered closed, and he breathed a steady breath of calm. Would it anger him terribly if Lethe spit on him again? What did a god's wrath feel like? he wondered. His human father's had only ever been pain. "I know you don't want our help, but I'll give you the offer regardless. The Moon, which had kept itself alive on pure ardency of feeling for you, paid dearly for this trade, and I mean to make good on what it bought you."

Those swirling, dark eyes opened again.

He reached out a hand, took up Lethe's—the one that had suffered such damage that it would never be functional again.

"Bought and paid for. The Moon demanded it, and Fate permits I yield a birthright—one that you would have inherited from your mer lineage if fortune had ever been in your favor, if all had gone according to our plan, and you'd been allowed to grow in safety and love and guidance. If the other thing you were didn't war with that blood."

The pit in his chest filled with bile, with rage, with confusion and bared teeth and *what was Cosmin talking about?*

"Fate allows me to grant you full prowess in every mer power that could be yours. The Pull you wished to use last night, it will be yours completely, to the most devastating degree. But the cost of its use will be to wipe godhood from your veins—you, Lethe, the offspring of the only titan to break immortal stipulation, and birth an heir. For the revenge you plan, Fate will permit assistance, and the cost of it will be your truth." He smiled grimly. "Her way, I suppose, of setting her board right—of clipping a thread that shouldn't have been added to her divine tapestry—but even Fate is soft when it comes to her Celestial children. She honors what the Moon wanted."

So gently Cosmin held his hand, like glass that might break, like bones that were already smashed to splinters could shatter even further . . . like the pain meant anything.

He turned it this way.

He turned it that.

Lethe had no idea what about it had caught his attention, but a moment of Cosmin's silent inspection, and then there was glittering like smoke.

Black as Cosmin's robes, the plumes of it wrapped around Lethe's hand, sank beneath the skin, the most curious of sensations—until sensation became more pain, and Lethe gritted his teeth against it; so tired, too tired, but not enough that he'd let this man who wasn't his father witness how truly he was injured.

Bone wove together.

The glittering smoke slithered, settled into and around the breaks in his fingers. . . . Lethe could only watch as it hardened, as it shaped itself like claws; cooled into impossible metal far deadlier than anything the Mortal Realm could produce. . . .

"Fate ordains my assistance, gives her permission—but you are not only your mother's son, and I love your titan progenitor enough to have disobeyed divine order once; let me prove my love to *you* with disobedience too."

Cosmin turned Lethe's newly repaired hand palm-up. The metal he had no name for shimmered in the rising day and was oh so lovely to behold. Wicked glints of light; claws that would tear deliciously into flesh . . . not that he craved much of anything, at this point.

The God of Death pressed his palm to Lethe's, and when he pulled it back, Lethe could only stare once again . . . at the strangest die he'd ever seen, black as consuming darkness, etched with numbers so bright a poisonous green they reminded Lethe of the eyes in the statue Atlas had commanded made for him.

"Let me deliver a birthright—or rather, a choice between two; it'll be up to you. What Fate has ordained will deliver the revenge you wish through to completion. But you are not only a mer. You are Lethe, a *god*, son of Luck, and they will not allow you to suffer all the indignities of your life without something to show for it. Without *power*, bound not by mortal confines."

Lethe looked down at the die.

Son of Luck, was he?

"You can choose Fate's path and follow it through, giving up your afterlife as a god in exchange, or with this die, you can choose a different inheritance, one that will allow you to carve a path of your own outside of Fate's reach. This die is half of Luck's power—a conduit of sorts; direct link to control over fortune. Whatever you can think up, that die will help make it reality."

And Lethe . . . laughed.

Falling back in the sand—he laughed and he laughed, as though he'd never found anything so amusing in his entire life.

Son of *Luck*?

Carve a path of his own, should he . . .

Lethe *laughed*, his fingers closing tightly over the object in his hand. "Son of Luck . . . yes, that does make me a god—but don't all gods have a mantle?" He raised the die up to light and inspection, pinched between two glittering claws, and oh, he laughed.

No one else would be laughing soon.

The Moon had bought this trinket for him; this was thanks to his friend alone. Cosmin, Fate, Luck . . . Lethe meant so little to everyone else that they'd felt moved to his assistance—him, one of their own—only once his soulbound friend had traded in their life for him to have it.

The immortals wanted to help Lethe exact his revenge on Atlantis? Then they were fools. They should have turned the Moon away, should have offered help of their own accord; for now, revenge wouldn't *possibly* stop with Atlas.

Son of Luck—and still all this time he'd been nothing but a pawn, nothing but a check in the tally of things others wanted, toyed with and discarded at will.

Betrayed, tortured, all these years of neglect and pain and wishing. That path he would carve . . . oh yes, all the way up to those divine thrones, where the gods who toyed thought they sat in safety, but Lethe was a god too. When he died, he'd ascend to immortality. Fate wanted to prevent it, wanted to keep her board *hers*, but . . . she should have acted sooner, shouldn't have let him learn who he was, and didn't all gods have a mantle?

A specialty.

Cosmin, Lord of Death and Night.

Luck, Titan of Fortune.

"Son of Luck . . . but I would say Misfortune's more my throne. . . ."

They would *all* regret what they really, *really* shouldn't have done in taking away the last thing he had to remind himself of anything other than cruelty.

CHAPTER 35

Nausicaä

I
T WAS CHAOS IN the palace this morning—everyone seemed to
have something to do of the utmost importance, tasks that sent
them scurrying from room to room, snapping at one another over
every interruption and inevitable collision.

If Nausicaä still possessed the ability, she'd lament this wasted
opportunity, this perfect climate for the mischief she would have been
quite happy to instigate under normal circumstances. Ah, but alas, in
these *new* circumstances, she just didn't care.

And didn't care about not caring, either.

Stalking down the halls, Nausicaä didn't pause to angle a wolfish
grin at the folk who scrambled out of her way, as she'd liked to do
before; she didn't nip at them playfully, didn't make any comment or
acknowledge them in the least, again not in the way she used to.

It was a curious sensation inside her—or rather, she imagined it
would be curious. Without her heart, she didn't feel any which way
about this lack of emotion, but if she could, what would it be?

A freedom, of sorts, she had to assume.

All the anger she'd been carrying around inside her—gone. All
the grief, the depression, the frustration, the pain . . . gone, gone, as
completely as though it had never existed, leaving her weightless in its
absence. And she didn't even have to stress about who she was without it, either, because worry was gone as well. And happiness, relief,
compassion . . . love.

But then . . . Arlo still meant something.

In the bounds of her contract, Arlo still meant something. Nausicaä was still Nausicaä, even without her heart—there were simply

things she'd been made to be, right down to the very fabric of her existence. Justice, Law, duty . . . Detached from sentiment as she was, she still had memory, knew why she'd chosen to yield herself like this to Riadne's use: that it would be far easier to do what Riadne would have her doing if Nausicaä didn't have to cry about it afterward; that in order to secure her place here with Arlo, this had to happen.

It would all undo if Arlo died, and that stipulation meant something.

Arlo *meant* something.

That knife to Arlo's throat in the throne room a few nights ago . . . yeah, that girl still meant something; had imprinted herself on Nausicaä so completely that the shell of her hollowed-out soul remembered, if not what love felt like, that it belonged entirely to that red-haired girl, and losing her would be . . .

Whatever "bad" was.

Down the halls she stalked for the throne room.

It was really fucking busy today—more than what Nausicaä had anticipated.

Bits of the fuss she understood. The prince had healed up from his resurrection as good as he was going to get with only three days for recovery; his Classification Exam would therefore take place as scheduled later this very evening, not pushed off for another year's time.

There was also the fact that the Luminous Palace was now the central focal point for the Eight Great Courts, and folk now flocked in droves to bring their problems to their High Queen. Complaints of demon activity grew more and more frequent—had to be what brought at least a handful of today's supplicants to the line that stretched all the way out to that infamous iron staircase.

But the craning heads . . .

The whispers Nausicaä cut through as she strode to the front of the queue . . .

"Dark Star," the guards on door duty greeted in unison. Fear snapped them to attention, made their eyes widen to be standing so close to a figure who was more or less their fairy-tale boogeyman. "Th-The High Queen is in a meeting; she will not be disturbed."

"Uh-huh." Nausicaä nodded. "With who?"

They looked between them.

Clearly, if it had been anyone else asking, they would have told her to piss off and get back in line. But Nausicaä was still Nausicaä, and even without her heart—*especially* without her heart—she could tear their heads clean off their shoulders like ripping a sheet of paper in half.

"She meets with the Queen of Seelie Winter."

Nausicaä blinked her surprise.

Was silent a moment . . . "Aslaug's here?" Then she waved a hand at the matching doorstops. "Move," she ordered succinctly.

"But Her Majesty—"

"Make me repeat myself. See how that goes."

Wisely, they moved, and Nausicaä pushed her way through to the throne room—stopped just inside, doors swinging quietly closed at her back, to study the scene before her.

Interest? Confusion? These things swept across her awareness with no real meaning, only the knowledge that if she could feel them, that's what they'd be.

This was the reason for the commotion.

This was what had put the entire skittish palace on high alert.

Who in the Eight Great Courts didn't know Queen Aslaug? The battle-axe sidhe fae woman who'd single-handedly disposed of Seelie Winter's entire ruling royal family; the commoner who wielded such magic and strength that she'd then risen up to take over their throne by force—the first nonroyal to ever do so.

Aslaug recognized no family name; they called her Of Winter and bowed at her feet, and she was damned good at what she did, so her people rejoiced in her reign.

Wheat-blond hair and eyes like pale water . . . a thick build and robust voice to match . . . Aslaug was a beauty Nausicaä hadn't even tried to resist back in the early days of her exile, and they'd passed a few Winter Solstices warming her bed, trading laughter and war stories by a great roaring fire.

What Nausicaä liked best about her though—or had, but probably the sentiment remained—was that Aslaug didn't give a single shit about the Court's way of doing things. She minded only what was strictly enforced of her, but otherwise kept to her own affairs.

She didn't attend parties and refused to consort with the other Court Heads.

That she was here, that she stood in greeting, clasped in arm with Riadne at the base of her dais . . . yeah.

Nausicaä understood the tension now.

Aslaug didn't leave her Court for anything less than war. The question undoubtedly on everyone's mind: Was she here to join Riadne or pit herself against her? And could Seelie Summer afford either, when joining would mean siding with another queen who'd already taken one throne by force, and not joining meant the possibility of declaring that queen an enemy?

"Nausicaä," Riadne observed dryly, withdrawing a step from Aslaug. "I did not summon you."

"Nausicaä!" Aslaug cried—boomed, rather, in delight.

She whirled around, her smile brightening, but it quickly dimmed to a frown when all Nausicaä did was nod back at her. Aslaug was a lifetime ago, and Nausicaä simply didn't care.

"I see." She turned back to Riadne. "This is half the reason I came, you know? Our new High Queen—hah! The balls on you; these milksop men must have shit themselves when you dangled that fat sack in their faces. And I said to myself, *this* is a Sovereign I'd like to meet. Then you went and collared yourself a Fury."

Riadne didn't appreciate vulgarity, would have recoiled and ended the conversation right there if it had been anyone else. But to Aslaug she inclined her head, the perfect show of humility. "Yes, well, I am honored you'd come all this way, Your Highness."

"Oh ja, honored, I'm sure; curious more—like me. They say you're building an army."

As casually graceful as anything else Riadne did, she quirked a brow. "And if gossip rings true?"

Aslaug shrugged, expression bland. "It would be smart. An army builds itself against *you*. The world doesn't like when women have anything—even less when they've taken it of their own accord. It would be smart to be ready."

"And smart to entreat your assistance in that, I'm assuming. Is this why you've come, Queen Aslaug of Winter?"

Nausicaä crossed the room to Riadne's side, if for nothing else than a closer seat to the conversation. This didn't exactly get her going like it used to, but old habits died hard, she supposed. Nausicaä knew herself well enough to accept the fact that she was nosy, and here were the two most powerful mortal women in current times.

Nausicaä had lost her heart; she wasn't *dead*.

Angling herself to face Riadne fully, Aslaug watched the High Queen carefully. Her thoughts still concealed, she spent a moment on silence . . . another . . . three . . . No one but she could have wasted this much of Riadne's patience without consequence, but Riadne had to feel it too—this meeting could change things, for detrimental better or worse.

And then . . .

Aslaug lowered herself to a knee she'd never taken for anyone else.

"High Queen Riadne, I won't play with words." Her voice was firm as stone. "What you do is your prerogative. What other things I hear are none of my concern—you being Sovereign, a leader, a Woman of Mab, I will not intervene."

Mab—patron goddess of ambitious woman. Nausicaä had never come across any idol, any tribute, any visible sign that Riadne paid worship to this faerie goddess that the Courts had basically outlawed. For such-and-such blah-blah reason that all boiled down to Mab having been a shit-disturber queen in her mortality—one of the first fae sovereigns—and much like the Courts didn't like alchemists to have any reminders they were once powerful, they turned a heavily suspicious eye on any woman in power who looked favorably on the one who'd gone and carved her bloody path all the way up to immortality.

She'd seen nothing like worship of Mab around this place, but if there were anyone Riadne might actually admire, it would definitely be her.

"I come to swear allegiance," Aslaug continued. "To this war that brews in your making; ask only that in the world you reshape, Seelie Winter remains my domain."

Ah.

So in other words, even Aslaug was scared.

A pretty big fucking deal, and clearly showed how dire their situation really was if it brought Of Winter to scraping.

Riadne considered the younger woman for just as many moments as Aslaug had taken from her. Then, extending a hand, she bade Aslaug accept it and rise to her feet. "I do not take it lightly what you yield to my service, Aslaug. As you too are a Woman of Mab—and indeed, one I much admire in accomplishment and steel—I will grant this proposal consideration. Posthaste will I deliver my answer, and terms if that answer is favorable. Until then, rise and return to your Court with the comfort of knowing you have demonstrated deep wisdom in the side you've chosen."

Aslaug stood.

Nausicaä could tell she had other things to say, more to add to her plea. Misgivings to voice—what would be delivered if Riadne's answer was no? But pressing the issue would get her nowhere, and all these things that had trickled to her . . . She had to have heard how *unpleasant* Riadne could be when provoked to a mood.

"Very well," she replied, and nodded a bow of farewell.

In gray wolf furs and heavy robes of silver and blue—the colors of Seelie Winter—Aslaug swept to the throne room's exit and pushed unceremoniously through the doors.

Riadne watched her leave in silence. "What do you think, Nausicaä?" she asked when the quiet had worn on long enough that Nausicaä considered that boredom might be the last feeling left to her.

"What do I think about what?"

"Queen Aslaug, my dear."

Nausicaä shrugged. "I don't know. Aslaug fucks—I'd take her help, if you want. Might be a good time . . ."

Pursing her lips, Riadne let her vulgarity pass in favor of turning back to her throne. "I have considered it, thank you," she murmured as she climbed to her seat, and Nausicaä got the impression that the comment . . . hadn't been to her.

There was no one else in the room, but that Crown was full of tethered souls, and the mortals had no idea how close to right they were when they whispered that their Sovereigns were cursed—haunted by all the ones who'd worn the Crown before them.

Louder, Riadne called over her shoulder, "Was there a reason for your interruption, assassin? Again, I repeat, you were not summoned."

"Oh!" Nausicaä snapped taller, back straight at attention. "Yeah," she replied. "I was sent to tell you—the next cycle's started, and lucky ducky, you've already a winner."

Pause.

Turn.

Riadne smiled, and while Nausicaä couldn't feel things—not a single thing, at all—seeing someone take that much delight in the death of a child . . . she knew the queen definitely didn't feel things right either.

CHAPTER 36

Arlo

—◦◦—

"I S IT POSSIBLE TO use the animus rune to separate dark magic from someone's soul?"

Arlo hated being here.

The bowels of Riadne's laboratory . . . there were almost no words for it. The amount of dark magic that stained this place gave it the permanent aura of death and rot and wriggling-maggot *wrongness*. As did the blood and gore that no amount of scrubbing would ever cleanse from the floors or the altar where actual, living people were dissected for alchemical experimentation.

Children and teens were caged up in the far back left to watch it all, their terror spiking sharply every time one of Riadne's alchemists so much as walked past their hold, always fearing when their turn to die would come.

And on top of it all, having to be here with her father.

She hated seeing him in a cell. The one he was kept in when not set to task here was a little better outfitted than hers had been, before her release after saving Vehan, and brighter lit during the day—the floor swept of debris, the stone washed of grime, and however small the bed in the corner, it was an actual mattress with clean sheets, a modest bedstand beside it for what little Rory was permitted to bring down there.

The guard delivered three meals a day, nothing special, but nourishing enough to keep his mind sharp. They walked him around the palace grounds, an hour in the morning, an hour before nightfall. No one beat him, no one abused him, but this was Arlo's father, and he was in this place because of her. It bothered her to know he was down there, all alone; it bothered her to see him in this lab—her father, this person she'd thought she'd been protecting from the truth for most of her life. That she couldn't protect him from *this* . . . It all left her feeling miserably useless.

Rory frowned—this was as much indication he showed of hearing what she asked.

Arlo wasn't down here to chat.

She was rarely permitted to be so close to her father unsupervised.

But the alchemists were all in a tizzy now, flying around the place to try to speed up every process to appease their queen. Riadne usually liked observing her in this setting, liked keeping a careful watch on their interactions, hoping for . . . something, Arlo supposed, but goodness if she knew what. A slip? Proof that Rory had been lying to her in whatever he'd said to secure his stay, or worse, maybe . . . that he'd been right. As careful as Riadne had been so far to give them no time together to speak about anything beyond the things her father had to impart, today she'd been detained.

Her duties as High Queen had prevented her from overseeing the current activity.

And finally—finally—was Arlo's opportunity at last.

There was no one else she could ask what she needed to know who wasn't in some way bound to report her questions back to their queen.

Gently, as quietly as possible, Rory set down the graduated glass beaker full of ironborn blood he'd been examining and reached for his journal. Pretending to be writing something down in careful steps for Arlo, instead he inquired, "What do you mean, Arlo?"

Trying to ignore that all this blood had come from the motionless body on the altar behind them—to block out the memory and flashes that plagued her of Vehan lying dead there as well—Arlo sighed. "When I used that array to force Vehan's soul back into his body, I could feel the life force of the philosopher's stone array wrapped around it. Since the animus rune is used to make it too, is there a way to like . . . hack into it, and force it to let go?"

It was a look Arlo knew with profound familiarity, Rory's expression shifting from confusion to deep contemplation.

Eyes bright, mouth pressed into a fine line, he considered her question the way he pondered the theories he used to sort through at home—the way he pretended now to ponder what he'd written in his journal.

Instantly, she was transported back there: to the armchair in his study; to the crisp fall outside and cozy warmth within, a cup of cocoa between her hands and Rory fixed in front of a green slate chalkboard, a spiral of equations before him.

Another instant, and Arlo was transported even farther back—to a place she didn't fully recognize beyond the feeling that this had been home as well.

Another study.

Far more books.

Rory standing in front of a chalkboard here, too, but the equations were different . . . were balanced with alchemic runes. And Arlo, so young, on the floor with crayons and a piece of paper. She saw it in slow motion, as her father turned—just to check on his toddler daughter, make sure she was doing all right—but he saw what she'd been drawing . . . cried out in panicked alarm . . .

Arlo startled, his cry of her name throwing her back to the present, where he stood much older, looking over at her with growing concern.

"Sorry," she murmured, shaking her head. "What did you say?"

"I said it *is* possible. Fairly anything's possible, Lo. That isn't the question—rather, *should* you use the animus rune to save your friend? And to that I would caution no."

Lo—she could almost laugh at how incongruous this all was, how absurd to be standing in a faerie queen's lair, trading alchemic theory with a man who used to wrap her up in a bundle of blankets and sit with her on their patio to watch thunderstorms roll in; Lo and Dad.

"Why not?" she pressed.

It was Rory's turn to sigh. "Simply put, the effort would kill you.

It would require you to anchor to the Sins themselves, not to your friend, and you're a powerful girl, Arlo—I wish I could tell you how truly gifted you really are—but currently you aren't up to that task. Leda did warn you in your lessons, didn't she? The dangers of anchoring yourself to another living thing and opening a channel between your cores . . . The Sins are too strong, love. They'd reach through the link and overpower you instantly, extinguish your soul like the flame of a candle." He frowned even deeper. "Even if you somehow managed it, I wouldn't trust its effect on Vehan. He's grown with that magic inside him since birth—it's likely just as much a part of him now as any other organ."

"But if the only other option is to let him die . . ."

"Almost done, Rory?" one of the alchemists called from across the room.

"Just a few more minutes," Rory called back, not taking his eyes off Arlo.

Setting his journal back down on his worktable, Rory reached for a pen. Began to draw out something—an array, Arlo realized. She watched him form lines, form runes, form equations . . . slowly, but soon it was just enough to piece together what he'd been doing.

This array . . . it was everything balanced that comprised the human body.

Paired with that container of blood, as soon as the array was activated—Arlo knew without doubt; something inside her just *knew*—it would activate the blood within, too. Blood that had come from an ironborn with the philosopher's stone array, which meant it would glow—and how much was Arlo willing to bet that the stronger the glow, the longer it lasted, the more likely it was that the heart it had come from would be able to withstand a Sin?

Riadne would be armed with a tool that would allow her to functionally bypass the natural process altogether, would allow her to test out her subjects one by one and summon her Sin right then and there.

She wouldn't have to waste time on searching.

She'd have this array etched out on her floor, and as soon as the next cycle was set into action, she'd trot her experiments to its center and in a matter of moments be able to sort out from the batch which of them would be her prize.

Oh gods . . . her father couldn't—he couldn't arm Riadne with something like this!

"Is it ready?" asked one of the supervisors, coming over, another part-fae alchemist with blond hair and maybe a handsome face, once upon a time, but here it was tired and stamped with so much death it had forgotten how to look alive.

Rory nodded.

He stepped aside to allow the alchemist clear view to assess his work, and Arlo only just saw it—the tip of the pen he'd been pushing against his index finger the whole time, as though in nervous thought, nothing to think much of if it weren't for the way he removed it so quickly.

Reached out with that ink-stained finger to tap one of the symbols he'd drawn—a firm, singular press of its pad.

Pretended to be explaining something, and the alchemist nodded, and others came over, and no one noticed . . . but Arlo did, that when her father removed his finger, a dot had been stamped into the symbol.

Rendering the whole thing useless.

That's all it took.

When the alchemist tried out what Rory had done for them—when he pressed his hands to the array and poured his magic into it, it wouldn't activate.

Nods turned to head shaking, sighs of dismay. The blond alchemist patted Rory's shoulder and moved off back to what he'd been previously occupied with—"You'll get there soon, just keep at it."

Arlo stared.

She'd been wondering—what her father was really doing here. Sure, she believed that he wanted to protect her, to watch over her

here, but there had been something else—something else that someone had set him to, and maybe not Lethe necessarily—for her father
to suddenly remember all this stuff about his past and turn up at the
palace. . . .

"There's another way, Arlo," Rory said, so quietly she could almost
dismiss it as all in her head. Her father reached for his notebook;
flipped to a new page; set about the next stage in his mission to,
apparently, to do anything he could to slow down Riadne's progress
and buy her opposition time. "There's always another way. You just
haven't thought of it yet, but you will. If anyone can, it's you, sweetheart. I believe in you."

Easy for him to say.

Easy for everyone else to say—to look at her with hopeful eyes
and assure her they had every confidence in her ability to save them,
but in the end, it was all up to Arlo. They could believe in her all they
wanted; she still had no idea what to do.

A little unfairly, maybe—he *had* tried to tell her things, and she'd
shut him down—Arlo bit out, "You still haven't told me why you know
all this stuff. You still haven't explained anything important to me."

In fragments and stolen moments aside, he'd filled her in on some
parts.

That Rory had always been ironborn.

That the Jarsdel family was a long line of ironborn alchemists, the
magic in their blood stemming from so powerful a source that even
this far along, its strength hadn't diminished—was unlikely to do so
for generations after.

He'd told her the Courts had been keeping an eye on their family
for quite a while; that this was the reason he and Thalo had met, when
she'd been drafted to watch him, and they'd fallen in love instead. A
whole mess had occurred in the wake of that, but High King Azurean
had given his blessing for their union in the end, under the provision
that Rory renounce his ties to his family and their art altogether and
adopt the surname Jarsdel.

He'd also explained that the same person who'd sealed his memory had sealed Arlo's as well . . . erased what he claimed had been common knowledge from mortal history altogether.

And it was that same person whose permission he and anyone else who learned the truth needed to even speak it to another. Without that permission, this had been all Rory could tell her—bits and pieces, nothing useful beyond the fact that Arlo had absolutely no idea who she was now, and that somehow this all tied back to Lethe.

Her father's face softened even further, and he paused with his pen in his hand and turned to her. "Arlo," he said gently. "I really do wish I could give you the answers you deserve. I'm *sorry*—so sorry—that when you *do* regain your memory, as I think you soon will, you'll remember too the decisions that we made on your behalf. Not by your choice. I'm sorry for taking that away from you. Your mother and I . . . we only wanted to protect you."

"From what?" she pressed.

"From the Courts," he answered cryptically. "I can't explain any further than this, Arlo. You know who you need to talk to. You know what you must do. I can only tell you that it served Lethe's purpose to awaken me fully after so long . . . but I'm here now, and all I can do is swear to you that I won't let you do this alone."

Arlo relented, deflating a little. "Thanks."

She was still angry with him for the years of lies. But at the very least, she understood—he'd done whatever he'd done because he'd really thought it had been the right thing to do. "Okay, well . . . I mean, are you . . . all right? I guess I haven't asked that yet. And I'm sure you're not, but . . . is there anything I can do? To make it better."

Rory smiled at her, a touch sadly, but still with fondness that made her heart clench. He shook his head. "You don't need to make anything better, love. I'm your dad—that's *my* job to do for you. But thank you. And . . . thank you for allowing me back into your life."

The clenching clamped tighter.

"Oh, yeah, well, you know—it's pretty glamorous, isn't it? Bet you're really glad I did."

He laughed at her, a quiet thing that was no less fond, and reached over to ruffle her hair. "She's been good for you, I can tell."

Confused, Arlo looked at him. "Who?"

"Your girlfriend! Your . . . mother told me about her, actually. Just before the . . . well. We'd had a decent conversation about it over the phone—reminded me a little how we were before . . . necessity changed things. But . . ." He shook his head, and Arlo didn't know how much more of this clenching she could withstand to see the flash of grief in his eyes just talking about her mother.

About the family Arlo would have had, the three of them, that she'd been cruelly robbed of.

"Anyhow, it's hard to explain, but you seem . . . surprisingly, for everything going on, like she's brought you out of your shell a little. This Nausicaä, she's helped you start to see what I've seen all along in you."

"Ah." Arlo nodded sagely, swallowing around swelling discomfort. "That black is my color."

"That you've got *fire* inside you," he ignored her to say, smiling at her with so much pride that Arlo had to look away. "And woe betide whoever tries to put it out."

Stopping on the stairwell's top landing just inside Riadne's office, Arlo drew a breath; released it slowly through her nose.

Emotionally exhausted was her perpetual state of being these days, one thing after the next pulling and tugging at her heart, flooding her veins with adrenaline or icing them over with fear.

Time was running out, in so many ways.

Arlo had to get her father out of here; had to save Vehan from his mother's plot; had to stop Riadne and find a way to return Nausicaä's heart to its rightful place. . . .

And now she was back to square one, no closer to removing Vehan's array than she'd been this whole time.

She couldn't dissolve it without more training. . . .

She couldn't reach into the magic itself and force it to let go. . . .

There had to be a way, something she was missing. The answer was right in front of her—she just didn't have all the pieces she needed yet to see its completed picture.

"Red! Hey—there you are."

Arlo's gaze snapped up from the floor.

It was cruel that Nausicaä should look so wholly unchanged by the loss of something so significant. It was so strange to be around her now—these past three days of a Nausicaä who didn't growl at things or try to fight them; didn't rage, didn't laugh, didn't engage much in conversation or terrorize the palace staff.

Nausicaä wasn't *herself* anymore—all the passion inside her, her own brand of fire, had been smothered down to smoke. She just sort of . . . existed, often in Arlo's space, and at least there was that—Arlo still mattered to her somehow—but it was strange and upsetting, and weirder still was that she *looked* the same.

Black leather, tight-fitted clothing, her jacket even though it was summer, and those heavy black combat boots. She still smelled like woodsmoke and ash and steel when Arlo hugged her; was still warmer than the average person to touch. Still Nausicaä . . . and at the same time not.

"Hey . . . ," Arlo greeted, however hesitant. There was purpose in Nausicaä's stride that carried her from the office door and planted her in front of Arlo, which meant only one thing, and nothing good.

"I've been looking for you. Come with me."

No preamble, no prodding, no flirtatious remarks.

Sighing, Arlo followed her girlfriend as she led them back down the hall. "Nos," she asked after a few minutes of uncomfortable silence, because now was as good a time as any, and what her father had said . . . that there was always a way . . . Nausicaä had done this for her; the least Arlo could do was *try* to save her. "What are the terms of your contract with Riadne, exactly?"

Nausicaä came to a halt.

She looked at Arlo—true to her new normal, there was no hint of feeling in the expression angled down at her, but she seemed to be thinking something over. Maybe whether telling Arlo broke some sort of rule.

At last she replied, "Pretty standard. Riadne gets my heart and subsequent control of my will. In return, I get to stay with you. If you die or she hurts you for any reason, the contract is null."

Right, well . . . preferably, Arlo didn't want to have to resort to such drastic measures. Nausicaä wouldn't thank her, either, if Arlo sacrificed herself to rescue Nausicaä from what *she'd* sacrificed.

There had to be another way.

And something inside her—a weird half feeling she couldn't quite grasp, like these broken bits of memory that came and went as they pleased—told her this other way was the answer to everything.

"There's . . . nothing else?"

Nausicaä shook her head.

"What if I destroyed it? That stone."

"Oh, you'll definitely have to destroy it. That's kind of what I was banking on when I made this deal in the first place. Kind of what this has all been about. Stop Riadne, break her toys—in the meantime, come on. We have somewhere to be."

The Endless Corridor.

They came at last to their destination, the room that kept Riadne's Egress. It was glass and stark-white marble and sparkling fissures of gold, carved pillars, and so many archways, halls shooting off from the room like arteries flowing from the palace's heart.

Much like the first time Arlo had been here, Riadne stood by the mirror to receive her.

"Arlo," the queen said frostily, no smile in greeting; she hadn't yet forgiven her for her disrespect in the throne room, even if her ire had yielded a little for the part Arlo had played in saving her son. "Nausicaä—shall we?"

She moved aside to sweep out her hand, indicating Arlo through first.

"What's going on?" Arlo demanded, but Riadne made no acknowledgment she'd spoken. Nausicaä, with her orders issued, had already taken ahold of Arlo's shoulder and began to steer her for the Egress's watery glass—

And out the other side onto a patch of windswept cliff.

At her back unfurled forest, rolling down the land like a verdant cloak. Before her was dull gray sea. Rock jutted out over the waves that crashed against the cliff, reaching for the murky horizon. The Egress had led out to an unremarkable slab of stone and crabgrass and thistle, fully exposed to the elements and damp with the fine mist collecting in a promise of rain.

It was the array that made her pale.

It was the teenage girl standing blank-eyed and sour-green glowing at its center, and the other girl standing at its rim with Leda bent close and whispering instructions.

It was the half of the alchemists that had been missing from the usual full cohort in Riadne's lab, in chattering groups around her— and there, huddled in their masses, concealed in a plain brown cloak with its hood drawn as though against the elements, Arlo noticed in the brief but sure moment their gazes met . . .

Fyri—her classmate, her rival of sorts in a competition Arlo wanted no part in.

A competition she'd thought Fyri quite happy to have a place in, herself, but that look in her eyes . . . the fear, and confusion, and stubborn determination to witness once and for all just what Riadne was made of . . .

A brief nod, and Fyri quickly peeled her gaze away. Faded into the group, away from Riadne's attention.

Arlo shrank an unconscious step back—and was met not with

Nausicaä's hands on her shoulders to pin her in place but the queen's.

"I did tell you," Riadne began, in a rhythmic, low voice as smug as it was delicate, and Arlo felt her fists clench at her sides. "The Sins require summoning in a very specific order, with very specific conditions met before they'll answer a call. To win over Lust, Briar Sylvain sacrificed what he loved most: the sham of his full sidhe blood status. Tonight, we welcome Envy into the world. A rather difficult stone; I spent quite some time tracking down this particular stage, for Envy must be the star of our show and will not be summoned to any place that has known a single instance of magic or remarkable feat of any kind."

She walked Arlo forward, pushing her closer to Leda and the girl on the edge of the array—why couldn't Arlo remember her name? This was clearly a classmate: Arlo had seen her in lessons with them, but she could barely recall her ever standing out enough to warrant her selection for the evening.

The girl seemed to know Arlo, however. She glared down at her advance, the barest trace of shock in her eyes, followed by a flex of anger, like she hadn't wanted to share her triumph with Arlo in any way.

Like she'd been shadowed all this time by Arlo and finally thought, here tonight, that she'd cast a shadow all her own.

That anger quickly morphed into stubborn pride, and that glare into a smirk. "Hello, Arlo. So glad you could make it to my graduation."

The girl knew her name.

Arlo didn't know her at all.

Oh gods . . . how horrible was she? This girl was going to die— Riadne would use her to create her next stone, then kill her just as she had all the others, and Arlo didn't even know her *name*. . . .

"So much time wasted," Riadne sighed, continuing with her story. "The earth is very old, has known so much, and finding a truly untouched space was harder even than expected. . . ."

She steered Arlo just off to the side and parked her on the windy ledge.

"Are you surprised to see me, Arlo?" The girl at the array peered around Riadne's back, not quite done with the opportunity she'd decided this had become. "You haven't said hello in return. . . ."

The girl was part faerie, with greenish-blond hair, the underlayer of which fell in a veil of leafy, dark ivy. Even deeper green eyes, freckles all over, and a face that would have been sweet if it weren't for the way she sneered . . . but Arlo had never paid much attention to anyone, really, and only a few of them she knew by name.

But maybe she did recall something . . . that sometimes, there had been someone other than her and Fyri to raise their hand with an answer—someone who'd always been passed over, whom Leda had barely seemed to acknowledge herself, with Arlo and Fyri to claim her notice.

"H-hello . . . ," she returned.

"Ephelia," the girl—Ephelia—supplied in a tone like a dagger's edge. "It's all right. I suppose you thought I was too beneath you to take much interest in. But here I am, and there *you* are, and it looks like Fyri wasn't the one you had to look out for after—"

"Comfortable, Arlo?" Riadne grinned.

Anger flexed again across Ephelia's face—warred with a flash of jealousy that read very clearly as irritation at being talked over, and that if anyone should have their High Queen's attention right now, it was her.

But there it was.

Riadne knew what she was doing—could pick out weakness like a hawk hunting mice in a field. She would have sensed this competitive envy immediately in Ephelia and known just how to use it.

Envy for an envious Sin . . .

"Wonderful," she cooed without waiting for Arlo's response, and withdrew when Nausicaä stalked into place at Arlo's side. Turning, Riadne lifted her hand and, with no ceremony, bade Ephelia begin.

It was just as horrifying an experience as what she'd been forced to witness in the ballroom the night of the Solstice.

Ephelia bent swiftly to the array, placed her hands on its shell. A moment . . . two . . . Bluish-white light poured through its outline on the third beat of nothing; carved its way into the equations and runes.

When it reached the girl in the array's center, she snapped rigid.

Her eyes rolled back into her head.

The green glowing in her veins began to intensify, and as it did, her muscles began to spasm, twitch. The Sin in her chest had already taken over most of her, but the groan of pain that escaped from her mouth as her soul started dying inside her . . .

It was a sound Arlo would never forget.

It was a sound that stuck with her as the girl dropped motionless to the ground, and the blend of blue-green light receded. As Ephelia stalked forward and plunged the dagger Leda had given her clean through the girl's chest—and with inhuman strength reached into the wound to rend it wider by hand.

"Very good," Riadne congratulated when, minutes later, Ephelia presented her stone.

And *zzt*—it was over that quickly.

Ephelia crumpled lifelessly to the rock as well, Riadne stepping around her corpse with as little care as though she were a weed.

The cluster of alchemists looked away quickly.

All except Fyri, wearing an expression that both relieved and grieved Arlo—one that read she finally understood.

Riadne was not and had never been a friend to any of them; she would never be good for or further the ironborn cause, and every one of their class were *all* in line for Ephelia's exact same end.

Hours later . . . how long had she been lying in her bed, staring up at the ceiling? That groan of pain was on repeat in her head, soundtrack to all the impossible things that were up to her alone to do. Hours later, Vehan entered her room, and Arlo scrambled upright.

His Classification Exam—she'd completely forgotten.

He moved to her bedside, pale and trembling slightly—though he was always pale now, never fully steady, like his coltish body was relearning every basic function, couldn't quite believe it was alive still either.

Hovered a moment, simply staring.

"How . . . did it go?" She'd feared to ask. Too powerful, and Riadne would only push harder. Not powerful enough, and she'd push harder still.

Vehan said and did nothing long enough that Arlo swung herself out of bed, panic taking control of her action—deities, it had been too soon! He'd *died* three days ago, and even that hadn't excused him from his mother's expectations. Too much too soon, and now Vehan looked like he wanted to vomit all over her floor. . . .

But slowly, he grinned.

CHAPTER 37

Celadon

~⚬~

YOU'LL BE HAPPY TO know the prince scored an unremarkably acceptable Three on his Classification Exam."

Celadon looked up from his desk to find Lethe prowling toward him. He hadn't heard him enter, and while that wasn't uncommon for his ghostlike ability to appear and vanish at will, this time Celadon suspected it had more to do with the chessboard he'd been contemplating for . . . well over three hours now.

Urgh.

Drooping moodily back in his chair, he exhaled sharply—tried to pull himself out of irritation to focus on something else for a moment and give the dull throbbing behind his eyes a chance to settle.

Between all this planning and his private training of late in the chamber where he used to train with his father, where he now spent those hours alone practicing, practicing, practicing all the magic he'd been locking away for so long, this headache seemed an eternal thing.

"Vehan demonstrated far more than a Three's capability on that rooftop a few weeks ago. He's downplaying his ability for our gain, a secret weapon Riadne won't have any chance to prepare for."

He appreciated the effort.

The fewer tools at Riadne's disposal right now, the better, because Vehan registering at anything more powerful than expectation would only be used against them. Riadne didn't press too much with her Magnetic Gift where Vehan was concerned, hadn't bothered with Celadon (despite believing him to be the one to make that impressive rooftop display) because she'd clearly been under the misconception he could be won to her side.

But if she knew what either of them could really do—what Celadon had inherited from both his parents and that on the rooftop, Vehan's natural power had been almost frighteningly equal to hers bolstered by the Bone Crown *and* her collected Sins—she'd ensnare and deploy them in an instant.

"Unfortunately, I've still to work out a way of actually *getting* him to our side."

Lethe splayed his long-fingered hands on Celadon's desk, bending himself over the board Celadon had been staring too long at with no success.

"Your brother has started a scheme of his own," he agreed in what was almost a silken tone for him. "One that plays very nicely on his mother's underestimation, because Riadne expected nothing less in his grading, but nothing more, either. Commendable—I honestly didn't think he had such deception in him." Acid-green eyes flickered up to Celadon's face, searched him for something, then without explanation, dropped back to his parody of a chessboard. "This is you, I take it."

He reached out to touch the piece at the back of the board—the black king.

Celadon sighed to be reeled back into this but nodded confirmation.

"You will have to explain the others."

Straightening in his seat, Celadon divulged the state of his war board. "This is Vehan." He touched the piece to his king's left—the white queen—tucked up in the corner. "This is Arlo," he added, finger skating to his piece's other side—the black queen. "My generals. Both powerful, both uniquely poised for significant damage. Vehan knows Riadne better than any of us and, despite everything, has the most of her trust as well. Arlo is . . . easily my most valuable piece, but she's at the center of a lot of attention and has yet to come into her full potential. It's her Riadne fears more than anyone, though, I think. And it's her that she's hinged a great deal of her success on."

He pointed out the rest—his rooks, his knights, his pawns. Lethe already knew where Celadon sat with his plans so far; without Arlo to confide in, the Hunter had become his sounding board.

Dangerous?

Perhaps.

But Riadne was pissed at Lethe too, after what had transpired with her prisoners' escape; had demoted him to grunt work and clipped commands, had barred him from most of her meetings right now and refused him on her council.

Still, understandable or not, Celadon had been livid with his mother for the public humiliation she'd subjected Lethe to even before all of this—*livid*.

The whole of whatever this was between them, why sometimes he could swear he knew Lethe on a level he shouldn't, why he'd so quickly gone from bare awareness of his existence to a near-gravitational pull drawing them closer and closer—regardless of all of it, Lethe was one of his closest friends these days, and Celadon had always been protective of the few friends he had.

He suspected, though, that his house arrest had more to do with the second screaming match between them, the one after Lethe had been released back to him, bloody and stiff and snarling in a foul mood, when Celadon had told her in no uncertainty that if she ever did such a thing to Lethe again, he'd throw his crown at her feet and renounce her as his mother.

Which hadn't gone over well.

Riadne had sneered at him; had warned him to take his own punishments next time instead of hiding behind others; and had banished him to more or less a time-out while she decided on what her new use of him would be. Now the whole of the Courts were undoubtedly twittering that Celadon was fucking the big, scary Hunter that rumor had him often in company with.

A Hunter that, despite her anger, was still Riadne's—Celadon really shouldn't confide so much in him. But . . .

He gave himself a gentle shake. This wasn't where his thoughts needed to be right now. It consumed Celadon just as incessantly these days as the finer workings of this plot he'd undertaken—what, exactly, he wanted from Lethe; what, exactly, Lethe meant to him; and vice versa. But that was something they could figure out later . . . maybe.

When this was all over, if things turned out favorably, and if Lethe was . . . still around after he got what *he* wanted.

"I see."

Looking up from the board, Celadon studied that inscrutable expression he was beginning to associate with deep contemplation.

Lethe reached for the piece Celadon had designated as Riadne: the white king at the opposite end of the board. With his other hand, he swept the remaining pieces aside, all but the matching black king that represented Celadon.

Celadon cried out in alarm when his carefully arranged players toppled and clattered against the wood, a few skittering over the surface to drop to the moss-green carpet.

But Lethe ignored this.

Instead, selecting one of the fallen white pawns, he replaced it in Riadne's position. "You overestimate your opponent's worth." He spoke very quietly, his tone very pointed, and held Celadon's gaze the entire time. "The High Queen is not the threat you think she is, though yes, she is your main priority right now. Ruin isn't either. Nor any of the other immortals. All are capable of causing destruction, of ending your life and the lives of all you care about, and the Mortal Realm on the whole if they wished it . . . and yet they're *still* not what you should fear the most—the rot that's been building beneath you all this time . . ." He shook his head. "You already know some of it; you're the only person who's ever been immune to my manipulation of memory. But you don't know the whole story. You have no idea what you're up against, Celadon, in what you're daring to attempt with this new vision for the Courts."

And Lethe paused.

Focused such intensity on him that Celadon couldn't look away, couldn't breathe, couldn't think. . . .

Ardent and low and so incredibly dangerous, he added, "You're forgetting your most important weapon." Reaching again, he selected something from his pocket this time—a tar-black die etched with acid-green numbers, so much larger and heavier than Arlo's. "Where would you put *me*?"

Celadon swallowed as Lethe held out to him the strange die pinched between his fingers.

For a moment, all he could do was look down at it. Eventually, though, he straightened.

Matched the flint in Lethe's eyes with steel. "I wasn't under the impression you were mine to have anywhere at all."

"Oh." Lethe dipped into purring, a smirk winding up in the corner of his mouth. "Then you haven't been paying attention, it seems. For this piece recalls it quite obvious how *much* yours he's been for some time, in any way you'd claim him."

What did he even say to that?

What did Celadon *want* to say to that?

Lethe was . . . some variation of demi-romantic; Celadon demi-sexual. What did it mean for them, that they fit so . . . remarkably well together? What was this relationship between them? Because Celadon *was* starting to feel it—not the curious strengthening of the bond between them, but the curl of actual desire for this man.

Nowhere near what others described it as, and he didn't know if he could ever live up to what Lethe was probably accustomed to as a bed partner, but . . . the way Lethe looked at him; the way he spoke to him; the way they teased each other; and how relaxed Celadon felt with him . . . how comfortable Lethe seemed to be growing with him in turn . . .

Unsticking his tongue, Celadon replied, "What is this, Lethe? You never answered me back in the tavern, and you've been almost avoiding me ever since. What do you want? What would *you* like to do in all this?" How did Lethe want to be . . . *claimed*?

Lethe considered him, a moment . . . another . . . those toxic eyes bright as ever, and at the same time so dark with things Celadon couldn't name. Then, quite suddenly, he unfurled upright from his curl over the desk.

And Celadon stood too.

He walked around his desk, holding Lethe's gaze all the way.

Brought himself before his Hunter, closer than decent, hand up again—just as last time—and tentative before taking the plunge and pressing it to the firm muscle of his clothed chest. "Why do I feel this way toward you? This bond between us . . . Has it always been there? You never seemed to care before."

Lethe looked down at him.

His hand rose too.

The Hunter deep in thought, those cool fingers traced up the length of Celadon's arm, over the exposed skin of his wrist, and Celadon had to repress a shiver at how sensitive he was right now to that touch. . . .

"It took a while for me to notice too," he replied in that creaking, low voice of his, pitched into intimacy Celadon barely recognized. "I'd closed myself off from it for so long that it wasn't until back at Riadne's Crowning, when I saw you again for the first time since you were stripped of Azurean's magic, that I realized a certain . . . familiarity to it, to what had been hidden beneath."

Up his arm, down the underside—those fingers traced a looping pattern, absent of intention, but Celadon couldn't tell whether this or that voice was more enthralling right now.

"And then I saw what you'd tattooed on your back. And the more I reached, the more I touched, the more I was around you . . ."

He sighed.

Celadon might have echoed it.

It was hard to tell, hard to focus on anything other than the lightest caress of skin, the barest scrape of nails.

"I should have realized, though. You asked about my book, the one your name had been written in, and how I've crossed it out every instance—snatching your name back from death each time it was slated for taking. You have no idea the amount of danger you're constantly in, even more so for my meddling. Fate doesn't like when one plays with her toys, but I don't much care for Fate, not after what she did to me . . ." Another pause. "To us . . ."

The fingers stilled.

Celadon looked up into Lethe's bright gaze—even brighter right now with impossible things he shouldn't be feeling at all . . . things Celadon didn't deserve.

"I didn't understand, not at first. Why I couldn't bear letting Fate claim you again. I didn't realize who you were. At first, I'd only stricken your name from that book because, against all frustration, you amused me, and I do enjoy taking from her, besides."

But Lethe's explanation stopped . . . as he took note at last of what had snagged his fingers' exploration.

"What's this?" Lethe murmured.

Peeling Celadon's hand from his chest, Lethe held it out for examination. Not his hand but his wrist, Celadon noted, when he was able to lift himself out of his fog.

Lethe was smoothing his thumb across the bit of braided thread looped around it.

Sage and black—the colors of UnSeelie Spring—strung through a singular, flat bead with the symbol of a flower stamped on one side, a crescent moon on the other—their sigil.

Arlo had made it for him, forever ago.

They'd been kids, wrapped up on her sofa, streaming anime on her laptop, weaving friendship bracelet after friendship bracelet purely for the joy of it. The one on his wrist had broken several times over the course of the years, but Arlo always rewove it for him.

Lethe stared at it.

He stared at it long enough that Celadon wondered if he'd done

509

something wrong, if the bracelet offended him somehow or stirred up a painful memory that made his focus withdraw inward. But then Celadon realized it wasn't the bracelet he was staring at; it was the bead.

Faceup on the moon.

"Arlo made it for me," he replied. "Nothing fancy. It used to be hidden under my . . . under . . ."

Under the Viridian bangle he'd been given at birth. A bracelet enchanted by ancient magic that all Viridians were gifted and that, once activated by its current sovereign, would transport them to safety if UnSeelie Spring was ever threatened.

You're a child of Spring, Celadon had told Arlo on their way to the Seelie Summer palace, back before their lives had devolved into death and chaos. *So long as even one Viridian stands to call this place our home, you will always be safe here.*

The Circle of UnSeelie Spring.

Termonn—that's all you have to say, while touching the stone, and it will take you . . .

Celadon gasped.

Blinking through the remnants of fog, distraction from all the profound things Lethe had just been hinting at, Celadon resurfaced.

Lethe's attention snapped back to him—concerned but furrowing quickly into confusion that deepened as Celadon stepped away.

"I've just figured it out," he whispered, excitement bubbling under his tone. He surged back in, placed both hands now on Lethe's chest. "I know how we're going to do it. I know how we're going to get Arlo out of the palace, and Vehan, too. And . . . Lethe, can I ask another favor of you? You've held your cards so close for so long, and I won't demand anything from you, but if you could . . . would you tell me what exactly *you* need from *Arlo*? Will you confide in me your plan so I can form mine?"

Staring . . . and staring . . . and something very painful was occurring behind that look; Lethe almost seemed to be . . . debating something.

Something frightening and real and at a great personal cost to him, and before Celadon could repeat his question, Lethe pulled back.

Drew away.

"At first I didn't understand," he began once more. "Then I started wondering."

He turned his back to Celadon and shed his Hunter's cloak to the ground, speaking words all the while like actual torture had ripped them from him . . . but then, maybe it really was that painful for Lethe to trust anyone enough to tell them his private thoughts. "Why do you have that mark on your back, those words that had once been another's—that particular image, same as what *I* had branded myself with in a long-ago attempt to hold on to the sliver that remained of me as I'd been, before misery, pain, and *misfortune.*"

Long-fingered hands sought the hem of his shirt.

Began to lift it up and over his shoulders, and Celadon could only watch, a little stunned, as revealed was tight muscle and sharp bone and groves his fingers itched to trace . . . swollen wounds yet to be healed, jagged bolts of pearly scars from Riadne's electric whip, and he very much wanted to soothe his touch over them, as well.

But what captivated him most was that tattoo.

"After all these years, after searching for so long, for that soul I'd once shared mine with—the Moon that had once been my only friend—I'd given up hope of our meeting again and closed myself away."

That tattoo.

The one he'd noticed a hint of before and had been wondering about himself, and now . . . wondering further, because that tattoo . . .

It was *exactly* the same as what was on Celadon's back.

Down to the most minute detail, and in exactly the same place, too. And neither of them had any idea its copy existed on the other.

"Fate does seem to enjoy her sport." He sighed the weariest sound— the most *mortal* sound—Celadon had ever heard him make. "You can ask anything you like of me, Celadon." And he spoke Celadon's name like reverence, a vow, but still didn't face him—like speaking at all was already hard enough without looking Celadon in the eye while he did it. "Whatever you need. I will tell you my plan, but in order for you to . . . understand, as I hope you will—as you did once, before you were taken from me—I'll . . . have to start at the beginning."

Before you were taken from me.

Wordless—so many things he wanted to say, things he had no idea how to express, and that incredible pull of that strange bond between them . . . It took him a moment; he swallowed. And there was that feeling again, welling up inside him, like he'd known Lethe his entire life—really *known* him, not just as a Hunter . . . and well before that word had held any meaning.

"Whatever you wish to share with me, I'll gladly accept," Celadon breathed, taking an instinctual step closer. He didn't understand, not anything, but: "Whatever you *need* to share."

Another sigh.

"It's been a long time since we've spoken . . . my friend. So much has happened . . . so much to beg forgiveness for." Lethe turned around. Those poison eyes . . . *his friend* . . . "It starts, I suppose, the same as it ends—with meddling gods and horrific sacrifice, and a king so obsessed with earning his place in legend that he forgot most legends weren't good."

Laughter roiled in Lethe's chest, spilled like bile from his mouth onto the sandy shore he'd been left to.

Cosmin had no idea what he'd done in granting him this alternate option. This piece of prettily shaped glass, a gift from his true parent, that warmed in his hand as soon as he'd claimed it.

Cosmin had explained it just before whisking back to his heavenly keep.

This die grants you access to fortune's pool, the well of magic belonging to Fate, from which only Luck has been permitted to draw, until now. They devised the tool themselves—the first of its kind, made especially for you—and by it, you will be able to perform whatever you wish. Whatever you can think up to inflict in your revenge, chance will decide its intensity; the number it chooses will correspond with the potency of your desire's effect.

The pretty glass would grant him power—and power was exactly what began to fill him the moment he made his first demand of what his titan progenitor had gifted. Power that trickled, worm-wriggling and cool as the bleakest of sunken grottos, through his veins; that had infinite possibility, bound only by the well of Lethe's anger, a thing that ran *so deep* . . . a deep that knew no bottom, fed by years upon years of agony, torment, torture, neglect, humiliation, desperation, and the slow decay of madness that ate away at everything he'd ever been.

Nothing but years upon years of *rage*.

Luck had given him death at his fingertips; destruction. Accessing

Fate's pool of fortune gave him the ability to inflict all his terrible *lack* of it. The *mis*fortune he'd suffered his entire life, finally turned on those who deserved it.

On the mortals, thought the gods who sat watching him high up on their thrones—but it wasn't the *mortals* who'd made Lethe a jester, plodding around their miserable stage; it wasn't the *mortals* who'd taken the Moon from him.

The immortals wanted entertainment?

Lethe would happily deliver.

He was destined, after all, to make glorious legend. Foolish would be the ones who thought it ended, not began, with a fall.

His entire body shook with laughter.

"What's so gods-damned funny?" asked one of the guards left on the beach, now standing over Lethe.

Lethe could taste the guard's fear mixed with his revulsion, because when King Atlas wasn't around, and it wasn't a full phalanx of soldiers gathered against poor only him, they didn't have a fraction of the bravery they pretended to with one another.

They remembered Lethe had always been dangerous—had no idea what he was now, but as Cosmin would learn, as Luck would learn, as Fate and all the others who played with their children like little rag dolls, so too would they.

The one crouched over him checking his vitals pitched a handful of sand in Lethe's face.

"Ugly fuck," he ground out, rising to his feet. "The king's finally beaten the brains out of him. Come on, let's leave him to bake and be rid of him."

And Lethe only continued to laugh as he raised a hand, closed it quickly to a fist around his die, and made his first request of it to bolster his Pull.

The pretty glass flared even hotter.

Lethe watched light bound around between his fingers before slowing to a stop on a number, and almost as soon, the guards popped like overripe fruit where they stood; burst into a fine mist of salt and red that scattered on the sea breeze.

The Pull was swift and sweet to him now, because he wouldn't accept just one aspect of what he was; he would have it *all*.

Nothing in Lethe ached anymore.

Was that the anger sweeping through him or this wriggling, cool, sedating power that didn't so much course like blood through his veins now but had seemingly replaced that vital substance altogether.

No matter—Lethe rose with ease.

The sky clouded darker, like the heavens gathering to witness what would never occur again.

Yes, Cosmin would learn, Luck would learn, *they all would learn*—Fate would not be so lenient twice, would never again permit this sort of intervention, but that would all come too late. For now they could only watch and tremble in fear when they finally realized this rage would be turned on them.

Up the beach he carved his way, in through Atlantis's front gates.

Guards, drunkards stumbling home, urchins on the street—these were the next to join the first; screams that gave way to the patters of rain, of salt and red and mist on the air; flesh and bones that withered like his scales had under the too-hot sun.

Families tucked up sleeping in beds, farmers, shopkeepers—youngest and oldest alike. Wealthy, poor, important, forgotten . . . as Lethe walked, hand splayed at his side, his die clutched tight in the other, Atlantis bled for their sins against him.

After all the misfortune of his life, the die delivered what was long overdue to him: extraordinary luck to balance it out, and Lethe would make them all *suffer.*

Bleed like he'd been whipped and beaten and cut and broken to bleeding for all of them; *he* had made possible the comforts and securities they enjoyed, and in return they spat at him, called him crude names, chained him up to rot on their land, deprived him of the only joy he'd had left . . . until even the Moon was taken from him.

It was nothing—like breathing.

The Pull hardly needed direction now. Lethe simply had to will it, to give it free rein; his command had been to destroy everything inside these walls, and everything it claimed.

Like a pestilence sweeping through the land, as Lethe advanced through every tier, it began to flood with screams, with the death of its people.

Darker and darker the sky grew overhead.

Something amassed behind him.

He could feel it like what pressed against the backs of his eyes, and knowing what it was made him grin.

A grinning that grew sharper as he strode over the bridge that connected to the palace district; as Atlas's elite poured out of their nests like streams of busy little ants; as one after one after many after all dissolved into mist like every other before.

Darker and darker . . . higher and higher . . .

Lethe climbed the palace's front steps, sauntered in through the gaping wound of its entrance, which oozed a cascade of blood thick as oil down all that glittery marble. His bare feet tracked prints through the puddles of it that squelched between his toes. The world without grew quieter—blessedly quieter—but within Lethe's head it was song.

The sea called out to him.

Soon, he crooned like a promise back.

Up and up.

Darker and darker.

The pressure built behind his eyes.

Lethe climbed to where he knew Atlas kept. Pushed effortlessly into his room.

A strike of steel. Lethe caught in his glorious new metal claws the blade his father had been waiting with by the door, had swung at him in a roar of very admirable but insufficient . . . Well, Lethe wouldn't call it anger. Such a mild thing, a minnow swimming next to the shark that would swallow it up in a—Lethe snapped his teeth at Atlas; ripped his sword by the blade from his grasp.

"You foul, ungrateful, feral *beast*—" his father spat.

Forward Lethe stalked.

Backward Atlas scrambled.

In this dance they wove through the white sheer curtains and out onto his father's balcony. More marble and gold, exotic plants potted in bright blue clay, sofas and cushions and trollies laden with Atlas's favorite delicacies—oh, poor father, he'd been in the middle of enjoying his trove of flesh, a young woman and man in a state of disrobe, now collapsed in yet more puddles.

What a beautiful portrait they painted in death.

How poetic—like the view of this city, like the shadow of what rose in a terrible wall around it. Up and up, darker and darker, a circling tidal wave of Lethe's rage loomed, poised to crash down around them, all at Lethe's command.

"You look thirsty, Father," he drawled in a parody of exactly what Atlas had said to him all those years ago.

In that room where Lethe had asked for nothing but mercy, and Atlas had given him only pain.

Eyes wide, wild and darting around at the water that walled them clear up to those trembling clouds . . . "You'll die too, you know. If you do this—you can't return to the water. If you do this, you'll die. I know how it works, you moldering sack of fish guts!"

How wonderful it would be to die—to simply cease existing and disappear.

One day, perhaps, but not tonight. Lethe had no plans of dying—or rather, he did, but no death that would rob him of himself, as nothing ever had before. Atlas hadn't forged all this rage alone, but for his full revenge, Lethe would need to trade his broken mortal body for something new.

"Enough, Father," Lethe soothed. He took hold of Atlas's face gently with his piercing claws. "That's enough tears. You want to be remembered at your very best, don't you? In the legend you oh so craved . . ."

"Zeuxis—"

"*Lethe!*" he snarled.

And the wall came crashing down.

Lethe—as the earth trembled. *Lethe*, as Atlantis crumbled under the crushing weight of all that water atop it. In an instant, the world's greatest kingdom dissolved into obliteration, and Lethe into foam.

And down, down, down they both sank, pulled by the churn of waves to settle at the sea's dark floor.

Lethe. Lethe. My name is Lethe—

He hoped the Moon would forgive him the next time they met. For Lethe would find it . . . Somehow, he'd find his Moon again.

And the pair of them reunited at last . . . how afraid the immortals should be.

"Arise, my son."

Lethe's eyes opened.

Where he was, he didn't know—he'd never been here before. Gleaming black sand cushioned his back, a shore that stretched for a none-too-distant cliff. All around, shimmering cosmos, streaked with swirls of pinks and blues and purples and oranges and greens. Studded with stars and suns and planets, moons that weren't . . . something. His?

Ah, that's right. He'd had a moon once.

Where had it gone?

Lifting himself to sitting, Lethe noted several things in quick succession. The first was that he felt . . . indescribably incredible.

Oh, there was rage—no such thing as peace for him, even in what he suspected was his afterlife—but . . . no aching. No stiffness. No pain of any kind.

He looked down at his hands, his arms, his legs, wrapped in a thin swatch of black like a shroud. He could make out his body with little obstruction. Still driftwood warped, still crooked angles, but smooth alabaster skin, remaining scales that were glossy pearlescent.

He reached up to his hair—silken and clean. He touched his face—soft, unmarred. Nothing burnt, nothing scarred, nothing ripped or torn or shredded . . .

"You wonder where you are—have no memory of where you came from or what happened to bring you to this place. Fear not, my son, that was all part of Fate's plan; all part of how this goes for newly awakened immortals—"

Lethe snorted. "I'm at the Starpool." That halo of silvery light beyond the cliff's ledge . . . it couldn't be anything else. Lethe . . . remembered the stories told about it.

He *remembered.*

The voice . . . the man it belonged to, standing before him: cosmic black eyes, hair like deepest night in some angles, moonlight bright in others; in robes of melting and stardust and rot . . . "Hello, Not Father."

Cosmin paled. "You—"

Lethe, Lethe, my name is Lethe!

The sunken prince of Atlantis—well, he supposed it was sunken *king* now, with him surviving when Atlas had not. . . .

Lethe remembered *everything.* He remembered his life; he remembered his rage; he remembered what this man had done, and what he was owed for the doing—him, and the other immortals that had stolen his life and his Moon from him.

"Lethe—you . . . remember yourself?" It amused him that Cosmin looked genuinely frightened. "You were not meant to. It is dangerous that you do."

"Mmm, but here we are." He rolled to his feet, and oh, but sanity, clarity—how long since those things had been his? Deities and stars, it felt good to be able to think in a linear progression again. And silence, the quiet of it all . . . of the sea no longer crooning for his return day in and day out, years upon years of its song in his head.

Confusion flexed across Cosmin's face.

It didn't take long for realization to dawn there.

His gaze dropped to what Lethe clutched in his hand, and oh . . . right, the die he'd been given, still very much his. "So desperate to cling to yourself all those years . . . It seems immortality has gifted you memory."

A Gift—every immortal of importance was owed one, and Lethe had been the supposed demi-god son of Death. Not his fault he was actually a titan's offspring with so much more to inherit. He'd still ascended to immortality and was still owed by magic's law a reward, and memory was fitting.

What else could he do with it? he wondered.

"And you named yourself, used the die to take up the mantle of Misfortune. . . . Lethe, you must give it back. We'd intended you to give it back when you remembered nothing of what it meant. Keeping it will forge itself to you, half of Luck's own power. . . . That die is first of its make; nothing like it has existed and nothing will again, not in the same way. It's too much to control, and what it allowed you to do . . . You were *never meant to keep it*; you were supposed to forget, to yield it and surrender your ties to godhood too, and live out your eternity in peace as an ordinary immortal—I beg you, my son, please give it back."

"Not your son," Lethe teased, holding the die up, pinched between his shiny new claws. "And I think I'll have to decline your proposition. Half of Luck's power? It *should* be mine."

Sighing, Cosmin softened to a sorrow Lethe couldn't care any less for. It mattered nothing to him. "You *are* my son, Lethe. I love you as good as a father. And as a father, I beg of you, please reconsider! Fate will not allow you to exist like this. She will command your Destruction. The Divine Council will consider you a threat; you, no mere immortal but a newborn god when no more were to be made. Yield the die, Lethe. Take up the freedom of simple eternity and live your days as you deserve after all you have been through."

The Divine Council?

Threatened by his power . . .

Oh yes. They should be.

Lethe considered the tired, ancient god before him. "Let's stop pretending you don't have a fail-safe should I refuse you even in vulnerable forgetting. You love me like a father? Let's hear it, then, the plan you've contrived to circumvent my Destruction." What would it be? What would Lethe have to sacrifice now to buy himself time once again?

Time for planning his revenge . . .

Time for finding his Moon . . .

Cosmin sighed again, weariness old as all the very many years he'd lived. "I've been given leave to reward select mortals—those who in life become legend through battle will be permitted immortality if they swear their service to immortality's cause. Return your die and submit your godhood; yield yourself to Destruction; or if you choose it, take up the position as General and First of my Wild Hunt, but do not keep that power for yourself, Lethe. You do not want to make an enemy of Fate, as you will if you press her magnanimity any further."

An enemy of Fate?

Lethe would not submit anything to anyone any longer—and neither did he wish for obliteration.

But he would, if he might say so himself, make a spectacular Hunter.

While he waited for time . . . and his Moon . . . and revenge . . . to show Fate that perhaps she should fear making an enemy of him.

CHAPTER 38

Arlo

◀──❦──▶

IN THE MONTH THAT followed Envy's summoning, September rolling in with one final heat wave that scorched through a week's worth of days, Arlo's life had become singularly focused on training.

Training in alchemy, which had taken a darker turn into complexity that left her mind swimming in intricacies.

Training with Lethe, now dwindled to her and Vehan, which had pushed to a grueling pace she could barely keep up with, a wooden practice sword placed in her hands and Lethe a vicious, unrelenting onslaught of maneuvers that she stumbled through the parody of copying.

Every evening after dinner now, Arlo was sent to Riadne's private laboratory for even more lessons with her father. At his side, she was made to observe as the queen's appointed alchemists worked their way through dangerous, obscure experiments, putting their knowledge to use in ways that wouldn't have ever occurred to Arlo, but steadily found she followed quite . . . easily.

Envy collected—four stones down—it didn't take long to pull Gluttony from the ironborn stuffed in her prison. And soon after Gluttony, Riadne had managed to summon Sloth, too, which meant one mere stone was all that stood between them and Ruin—the High Queen's triumph and their defeat.

Lying on her bed, Arlo contemplated what was left of her options.

It was the still of night.

She should be sleeping.

Tomorrow morning would dawn too early, would pull her from

her bed exhausted and throw her back into that unrelenting training. Her muscles ached, her head hurt, her heart felt pulled in so many directions, and she should take advantage of any rest she could, but every moment brought them closer and closer to losing.

Losing Vehan . . .

Losing Nausicaä . . .

Losing the war . . . and Arlo couldn't explain it, but she knew so assuredly that Riadne would get to enjoy her spoils for all of a blink before what would befall them once the queen inevitably lost control of Ruin and they consumed her along with everything else.

One stone left, and Arlo still hadn't figured out how to get that array off Vehan's chest.

One stone left, and she was no closer to rescuing Nausicaä from the contract she'd signed her heart away to.

One stone left, and Arlo had no idea what was going on with this supposed army amassing in the Hiraeth, or with Celadon's plans to save them, and Arlo still didn't have back her memories—the most crucial part to everything, the only thing that would make her powerful enough quickly enough that she might be able to simply dissolve the mark on Vehan's chest . . . even if that wouldn't stop Riadne from transferring her goals to someone else.

Sighing, Arlo rolled over on her still-made bed.

In her overlarge tee stamped with Taylor Swift's face—which belonged to Nausicaä, and Arlo had stolen it from her room because it smelled like woodsmoke and steel and was pretty much the only thing that offered her any calm right now—Arlo curled in on herself. This all felt so impossible; Arlo, just Arlo, against insurmountable odds.

I haven't seen your die in a while. . . .

Arlo glared at her bedside table.

At the die she'd kept shut firmly away in its drawer.

She hadn't even looked at it since the night of the Solstice—hadn't wanted to. That die was the reason they were in this mess. She'd been such a fool, had been so easily manipulated by the false sense of importance it had filled her with, like with it maybe Arlo was in any way equipped to contend with immortals and queens. That die was evidence of all her failures, and so she'd shut it away, and almost as long as it had been gone, Arlo hadn't seen or spoken to Luck, either.

It was unfair of her, she knew.

None of this had been their fault.

But Arlo was just so angry, and sad, and tired, and she just wanted help. She was so fed up with trying to solve everything on her own, just wanted someone or something to jump out at her with flashing lights and clear neon writing telling her what she should do. . . .

Arlo blinked.

Slowly, she sat up on her bed.

You can channel your luck to trigger certain events.

She remembered her lessons with Luck—specifically the one that had taught her how to use her die to expose possibilities like side quests to whatever main objective she tasked of it. Ask the die to help her, and it would point out the various current paths she could follow to lend her that aid.

The solution to her problems had been right there beside her all this time. . . .

Arlo lunged for her bedside table and yanked open the drawer— then paused.

I would caution you to be very specific, though, in what you ask— magic operates in a peculiar precision.

Keep in mind: just as with your wishes, doing this might force certain other things to happen that you might not like.

Biting her lip, Arlo recalled the other things Luck had warned her of in their lesson.

There would be consequences.

Luck trailed misfortune, and misfortune trailed close to Luck; she might not like the results of utilizing this power.

How quickly she'd abandoned her resolution to do this without the die's help—when had she become so reliant on it? And more importantly, what would she run the risk of sacrificing this time? Her first experience in manipulating possibility hadn't been too awful. Nowhere like the cost of using a wish. Her path that day had led her to Riadne, who'd given her lessons with a sword, a new skill-tree unlocked that she'd been able to use the die later to bolster in combat against the ice wraiths. Exhausted and, yeah, after the ice wraiths she'd been poisoned, but Arlo had survived; no one had died. If she chose her words right . . . if she didn't use a wish to make this possible but merely nudged things along . . .

Arlo reached into the drawer and extracted her die.

Cool at first, such an innocent bit of pretty jade and vibrant gold, but in her palm it warmed almost instantly. Those numbers flared hot and bright—like it had been waiting for her all this time to pick it up, was primed and ready to go. Really, it might be Arlo's imagination, but she could almost feel a sort of reaching from it, as though it also . . . missed her.

With a sigh, Arlo closed her fingers around it.

Was she going to do this?

She'd promised she wouldn't. Her mother, at her funeral—she'd promised she wouldn't use this again. But if it was the only way to save them from the corner they'd been backed into . . .

"Lead me to what will help me stop Riadne from winning this war."

In an instant, the world shuddered to a halt.

Color drained to whites and grays, all but Arlo, and the writing that appeared in glittering gold scrawled across the air.

Roll . . . Assist . . . Escape . . . Three.

And just above these options, the glowing red of the number seventeen—what she wanted to do tonight was considered quite difficult, but given what she'd asked, that didn't surprise her.

"Roll," Arlo firmly announced, and the glittering dissolved in a shower.

The world regained its color and unfroze back to motion, and Arlo looked down at her die one last time. "All right," she sighed. "Here we go, I guess. Good luck to me . . ."

Arlo rolled her die.

It clattered to the floor, rolled over the carpet in tiny bounces—knocked against the leg of her desk and tumbled backward a rotation . . . two . . . then rocked to a stop. She flew to where it landed and bent to examine its number.

What sort of blowback would she suffer if it didn't land on the minimum of what she needed? How would she rephrase her question. What would she ask for instead to force similar results?

But her worry was for nothing.

Arlo stared down at the die.

"Twenty," she murmured under her breath, awed. A critical roll, like the die was playing nicely with her out of apology.

What she'd asked for should reveal itself perfectly to her—no hitch in its execution—and perhaps even more than what she'd need.

She watched as golden clovers formed themselves in a sparkling gold trail that led from her die out through her bedroom. Heart hammering in her chest, she stooped to collect Luck's gift to her. This was the moment of truth; if she did this, it would actually work. No blowback. And no terrible consequences, she had to believe. Arlo had asked, and this time, fortune was in her favor.

The young woman standing before me . . . It was the happiest day of my life when I gave birth to you, and I am proud *of the person you've become.*

Arlo moved.

One step . . . two . . . foot in front of foot in front of foot, Arlo followed the trail of clover from her room.

Out into her sitting room.

Out into the hall.

It was just as quiet in the rest of the palace as it had been in her bedroom. The only people she passed were guards on patrol, the occasional night-shift servant making their rounds from room to room, ensuring all was clean and prepared for a new day.

No one stopped her to ask what she was doing.

No one questioned the High Queen's *guest*. So long as Arlo didn't try to leave, wasn't running around shouting plans to assassinate Riadne, no one had any cause to think she was up to anything other than a midnight stroll.

On the trail of clovers led her, the ones she passed dissolving behind her to reassemble ahead.

As she walked, she tried to imagine where they might be leading her.

What *would* help her defeat Riadne? Would it be a person, a weapon, some errant bit of information she'd been missing all this time, like the final puzzle piece that would complete her picture?

The clover turned down a darkened hall.

In the Luminous Palace, it was never truly night. Glass and crystal and jewels caught every flash of light; will-o'-the-wisps and fairy lights glowed ever luminescent like fireflies buzzing around their appointed fixtures.

But down here was . . . different.

Arlo had gone on many walks through Vehan's home, sometimes now even with Vehan when he had the time to spare after all his training as well—yet never had they gone here.

Marble for both floor and walls, a pale gray carpet running down the center of its length, the hall had no windows; the ceiling wasn't enchanted to reveal any sky; nothing illuminated what this hall contained, but between Arlo's UnSeelie fae eyesight and the soft glow effused from the clover, she walked down the hall entranced by what she was able to see in near perfect clarity.

Pictures.

This was a hall of portraits, but none depicting the Lysterne family line. Portraits . . . murals . . . landscapes . . . they looked like they could be human paintings hung in some grand museum.

And the *things* they showed . . .

Otherworldly settings; creatures she had no name for. One showed a city street that could have been from anywhere, but certainly not this realm, not with the futuristic bend to its layout, and people who looked half-cybernetic.

They weren't portals. . . . They didn't have that particular hum and scent of magic about them, but they were alive with something. Arlo could feel it, as if she were standing at a window peering out into a glimpse of . . . other worlds?

She wondered idly if Vehan even knew this was here at all—if this place wasn't somehow enchanted out of view to anyone except Riadne and whoever she gave permission to view it. Arlo wouldn't have found them either, likely, if it hadn't been for the clover.

How had Riadne even come into possession of these—and why keep them hidden?

Nothing Arlo passed moved. Nothing she stopped briefly to inspect gave a flutter to indicate that what she saw looked back.

But there—the trail of clover came to an end, right in the hall's center. The last pair of clovers blinked in waiting for her in front of a painting on the left-hand wall, and when Arlo stepped into place, they vanished.

She could feel exhaustion already beginning to settle in.

Nowhere near as intensely as it had the first time she'd done this— the strength of Arlo's magic had progressed significantly since then— but a new ache joined the usual dull throb in her bones, and she didn't care, didn't give it any more than passing notice.

Because there on the wall . . .

Arlo stared.

She'd seen this painting before. She knew what this was, why Riadne kept it hidden from sight.

Her mother had had one exactly like it, and she probably hadn't known that Arlo knew, that Arlo had found it one day in poking around her mother's home office, where she wasn't allowed to be. The painting depicted a throne built right into the forest that grew around it, wood and vines and flowers twisted to support the woman who commanded it.

That woman stared back at Arlo with such fierce intensity, just as she had from the smaller image Arlo had discovered in her mother's accidentally unlocked desk drawer. Wild, boar-black hair; olive-brown skin; eyes the color of melted silver . . . spider silk and chain mail for dress, great gray wolf pelts hanging from her shoulders; around her throat was strung a necklace of clouded eyes preserved by magic, trophies from all the men who ever dared to pit themselves against her.

This woman . . . the symbol of rebellion for much of the folk.

This woman turned patron goddess for those who sought to *take up space* in a way that men would have them not, Celadon had explained when Arlo had asked him in secret.

Mab, the first faerie queen, before Courts, before factions, before Bone Crowns and fear of what women in power could be—magnificent; competent; ferocious.

Possession of these portraits, of idols or even tokens of Mab, was more or less illegal in the Courts. Arlo had no real idea why, other than they didn't want too much power routed back to a woman even time couldn't extinguish, who'd taken goddesshood for her own and would definitely return with a vengeance if she could.

Arlo suspected they were just afraid.

That women like her mother . . . or like Riadne, it seemed, would draw too much inspiration from her.

When the faerie world started to take on human prejudice against genders, Arlo suspected it correlated with rooting their Courts in the hearts of human cities instead of keeping to the Wild. And Mab—Queen of Nightmares, men had taken to calling her—was too much a reminder of how far they'd strayed from what they'd once been.

It didn't surprise Arlo that Riadne kept this, a much bigger and far more exquisite rendition than the bootleg print her mother had kept framed under lock and key. If Riadne admired anyone, it was bound to be Mab.

No . . . what caught Arlo's attention . . .

"Mom?"

Arlo stepped closer to the painting—so close her nose almost touched its canvas.

Mab was always depicted with a host around her, the majority women. Her most dedicated warriors, who'd devoted their lives to her service, and when Arlo had looked deeper into this obscure vein of worship, she had found the common belief to be that any who lived and fought in Queen Mab's name, who died with devotion to her in their breast, would be offered to join her ranks in the afterlife.

Arlo's mother . . .

What had Artemis said?

A warrior just as she has become . . .

Her fingers reached of their own volition to trace a face she knew *so well* . . . a face that could belong to no one but her mother. It was Thalo. It had to be—

As soon as Arlo touched the paint, it began to melt.

Startled, she took a step back, watched in growing horror as colors ran together in streams for the frame's bottom. The paint spilled over the gold and down to the floor, a pouring so much more than the amount of paint on that canvas, and Arlo's veins iced over in fear.

Taking another step back, she tried at first a careful escape, as if rushing things would make the paint gush faster. Pools of color spread across the floor, crept for Arlo's feet.

She'd done something—set something off—and gone was the reassurance that her critical roll would protect her.

Arlo tried to flee.

The color crashed after her, a flood at her heels that spread up the walls around her, closed over the exit, and stopped Arlo's flight in its tracks, and she braced herself; the wave of paint rising up behind her would fall on her any moment, and whatever would happen, there would be no preventing it. . . .

But the wave parted to flow around her.

Up the walls, down the hall, colors remade the space into something else entirely. Stone became earth became trees became . . . Mab. The hall expanded; the Queen of Nightmares' throne spilled out, and in moments, Arlo found herself on the other side of this window-like portrait . . . inside the very painting.

Forest around her—there was twittering in the distance, an ebb and flow of breeze through leaves like rushing water. . . . Pine and cedar and soil hit her senses.

Holy crap, she was inside the painting!

There was Queen Mab's throne—Queen Mab herself upon it— and an army that fanned out around her in the clearing, a group that stood so thick Arlo couldn't even see how far off they sank into the trees.

Living and real—Queen Mab looked down at her. Heart picking up frantic pace in her chest once more, Arlo could only stare back a moment . . . until she remembered what had drawn her initial interest.

"Mom!"

Arlo flew.

Thalo stood in the very front lines, among women dressed in varying ages of ancient garb. Her mother looked resplendent . . . perfect . . . with her wavy russet hair, a flush high on her cheeks, her jade eyes bright and fierce. Arlo threw her arms around her mother's waist, buried her face against her—trembled with tears she was actually too shocked to cry—and Thalo said . . . nothing. But she lifted her arms as well and wrapped them around Arlo's shoulders, hugging her back.

"It is the way of mortality reborn immortal to sever that life from memory."

Queen Mab spoke with a tone that was velvet wrapped around a sharpened blade. There was nothing cruel about it, though. Firm. Cuttingly clear. But . . . with a certain amount of almost motherly fondness.

But Arlo stilled, regardless.

She pulled back her head—what had that meant? Severed from memory . . . Did Thalo not . . . remember her own daughter in the afterlife?

But the way her mother looked down at her, proud and fond and a little glassy-eyed, too.

It was Queen Mab who spoke again. Rising from her throne, she stole Arlo's focus. "There are benefits to detachment; I find, however, that ferocity burns brighter when heart gives it meaning. I am a goddess, Arlo. Immortality is what *I* chose it to be, for me and those I embrace. Your mother remembers you, and you are most welcome here, daughter of such fierce blood."

There were no steps to separate her from her Court. Mab strode forward, her silk and chain mail dragging through dirt and debris in a train behind her. It was impossible not to note another thing the Courts disliked the reminder of: that the fae didn't have to slot into this singular image of slender, wispish beauty—that beauty took on other forms too, and Mab was a big woman. Stunning to Arlo, Mab made her feel like Nausicaä did, that her own larger size wasn't something to be ashamed of but powerful and beautiful, too.

Mab extended a hand, curled her finger to summon Arlo closer. Arlo was loath to separate from her mother, but Thalo released her and nudged her forward.

"I am glad to meet you, Arlo Fl_____."

Arlo winced. Her hands flew to her ears.

Something strange had occurred in her hearing—a flare of loud white noise that swallowed Queen Mab's words—and she looked back at Arlo like she knew whatever she'd just said had been wiped from the air.

Which was . . . strange.

What had Mab called her? And why had something tried to prevent Arlo from hearing it?

"Destiny has spun itself into quite the jumble around you," Mab continued congenially, ignoring Arlo's reaction. "I am always interested in meeting historically significant women. I would be deeply honored by devotion from one such as you—a formidable addition to my ranks—but to speak quite plainly, it is not me you will choose. Worry not, my daughter. This doesn't offend me; I like even better significant women who carve futures of their own."

It was always a little bit painful, speaking with an immortal.

Nausicaä had been in the Mortal Realm long enough that her pattern of speech had adjusted, but the way the others spoke . . . they were hard to keep up with. They all seemed to know things she didn't and delighted in dangling that knowledge just visible but out of reach.

But luckily, this wasn't Arlo's first time trying to pull sense out of their particular brand of riddles.

"You haven't called me here to convince me to give you the Bone Crown," she concluded.

Mab shook her head. "I have not. How fine it would look on my head, and legend does leave much to wonder. But I have not summoned you for it, though, no. In truth, I have not summoned you at all."

"Then . . ." Arlo looked around her. "Why am I here?"

"A very good question—a very intriguing accomplishment. To transcend the veil of death between us . . ."

Arlo considered this. If Mab hadn't called her, but the clover had most definitely led her to *this* painting . . . "Are you . . . able to help me, then?"

"That would depend entirely on the situation. With what do you require help?"

"Riadne." She drew a breath, pulled herself up tall. "I need to find a way to stop Riadne from summoning Ruin and winning the war she's so close to launching. If it starts, I don't think we're going to survive it, not any of us, and all she needs is one more stone. . . ."

Queen Mab's eyes flashed at her, a look passing over her expression—one of longing and excitement. "Riadne Lysterne."

Arlo nodded, hesitant.

Mab's gaze turned fierce. "A daughter stolen—Riadne is *mine*. Her death should belong to me! How I wept the day that Crown touched her head and sealed her afterlife to its eternal tomb. And here you come to me asking for help, when, Arlo, I would beseech yours instead . . . and ask you to save her."

"I . . ." Arlo faltered. "Sorry, what?"

Mab stepped even closer, those silver eyes brighter, and took Arlo's hands in her own. "The Bone Crown does not relinquish the soul that contracts its power. In death, Riadne will know no peace, no afterlife but torment, trapped for eternity in the Bone Crown's clutches. How, do you think, has it grown in such strength? Why, do you imagine, has Lord Cosmin—that vile, plotting male—allowed it to fall in the Mortal Realm, where death is so swift, and life after life consumed grows its power?" Fervent now, Mab seemed overcome with what had been stolen from her. It sharpened her features, frightened Arlo a little, but there was no pulling out of the way she clutched her. "Very clever of him. Or perhaps, clever of him to hide behind this obvious bit of distraction. His immortal ilk wouldn't think him traitor if led to believe this true. Perhaps he desires what others have asked you, will ask you, but . . . it is time. To destroy the Crown—release Riadne's destiny back to me. In asking, I would arm you. . . ."

Mab released her, withdrew a few paces, but Arlo's hands weren't empty.

A shimmering between them, and then solid weight dropped into her hold. She scrambled to clutch it . . . her mother's sword.

Arlo stared at it.

This was Thalo's sword, the very same one she'd flung to Arlo in the ballroom, and Arlo had recovered only to stash it away in her closet much like she'd hidden away her die. Not because she hated it; because even looking at it reminded her how greatly she'd failed her mother and continued to do so.

This was Thalo's sword—she knew every nick and grain of it—but now it hummed with new life, looked somehow . . . sharper, in higher definition. The marks Thalo had taken pride in were still etched in its steel, but everything was polished and vibrant and throbbing with a reinforced magical current.

"You will not thwart Riadne before Ruin is summoned. You can, however, survive what comes next; and in surviving, you may just stop her. I ask that if you do, *when* you do, you use my gift to destroy the Bone Crown."

Arlo lifted her mother's sword to balance it flat on the palms of both hands.

"Arlo?"

And promptly lowered it to spin around.

Thalo stepped forward; crossed the distance between them; brought herself before Arlo, took her by the shoulders, and looked her firm in the eye. A look that watered . . . and Arlo felt hers begin to water as well. "I didn't say it enough. I am *so* proud of you. No matter what happens, that won't change."

Emotion bubbled out of her in sobs. Clutching her mother's sword to her chest, she bent around it, gasped out, "I'm so sorry, Mom. I'm so *sorry.*"

Sorry for not being a better daughter.

Sorry for the fights, for the dramatics, for pulling away from her and being so petty; for getting upset when she couldn't make a parent-teacher conference or had to change vacation plans—such small things; such ridiculous things to throw tantrums over.

Sorry for being the cause of her death.

"Arlo," Thalo repeated, a hand under her chin, lifting Arlo's gaze back to hers. Tears streamed down both their faces. "You have nothing to be sorry for. You have only ever been the joy of my life."

It began like a spreading of ice through her core—it ended like a hook through her belly. Something reached for her, yanked firmly on what had tethered them together, and far too suddenly, Arlo was . . . back.

Torn away from her mother—and that hurt more viciously than what had ripped her away—Arlo once again found herself in the dark hall of paintings. Mab was back on her throne, the painting still once more.

A palace guard was beside her, and the way he looked at her . . .

Ah, Arlo was still clutching the sword Mab had magicked from her closet and gifted back to her, reforged.

That might explain the look. She hurried to tuck it behind her back, searched her brain for something to gloss this over, because she didn't want him thinking she'd stolen this and confiscate it or, worse . . . hand it over to Riadne.

"I . . . uh . . . this isn't—"

"What in the *stars* were you doing?"

Uh . . .

Arlo stared.

Because the guard had started to *melt*, much like the painting, really, and maybe Arlo had consumed something off at dinner, and the meeting with Mab and her mother had been all in her head, and she should lie down, because the guard was dissolving . . . but in a very peculiar way.

His *image* dissolved into glittering stardust that heaped in a pile at his feet—a pile that swept itself up and back around him, reassembling and settling into a cloak black as night on his shoulders.

And then it was Lethe staring back at her.

He looked . . . just as confounded as she was.

Then—"Oh my gosh!" Arlo screeched, nearly tripping backward. "It's *you!*"

"Stop shouting!" Lethe said, startled, hands shooting out to steady her. "Arlo, do you have any idea—"

"You were a guard, and then you weren't!"

"Focus, please—"

"How did you do that? Have you always been able to do that?" Arlo withdrew again, scandalized. "Oh my gosh, can you turn into anyone? If you've ever pretended to be Nos around me, I swear I'll kick you between the—"

"Arlo," Lethe growled, then drew a breath. Drew another. Summoned whatever composure was left to him, and Arlo didn't think he had the right to be glaring at her in such a way, not after this revelation that Lethe could shape-shift. "Nausicaä has a Hunter's cloak—has she not divulged what one can do? Yes, it allows the wearer to shape-shift into any form, down to their magical signature. No, I have never once felt moved to experience the *disgusting* affection between you."

"Ah, affection's only not disgusting when it's Celadon, hmm?"

"I repeat myself: Do you know where you just were? Do you realize you just activated a gateway into the Immortal Realm? Stars, we're running out of time; your magic is getting away from you—and what have you got in your hands?"

"Oh." Arlo frowned. Shifting her sword out from behind her back, she held it between them.

A critical roll, and the clover had led her to the painting, had armed her with the tool she'd need to destroy the Bone Crown, but was this really everything she needed to put a stop to Riadne's war?

With a start, she realized there was a trail of clover behind Lethe, shimmering into disappearance—but *her* clover had already disappeared when she reached this painting. So how . . . ?

"I asked my die to help me find a way to stop Riadne."

Lethe transferred his confusion to her sword. "To stop Riadne," he repeated dully.

"Mab—the die led me to her, and she said there wasn't actually a way of stopping Riadne, not yet; that I couldn't stop her before she summoned Ruin; that I could only survive it."

"Could only survive it . . ." Lethe repeated her words once more.

He seemed to be processing something quite important, and Arlo held her breath in hope.

This had to be it. This had to be what she needed. Lethe seemed to know so much, and maybe now that he realized the lengths to which she was willing to go, he'd give her back her memories, and Arlo would be complete—would have everything she needed. . . .

And then Lethe's acid eyes traveled up to meet her gaze.

"Arlo," he said in a voice pitched cool and whisper light. "Cosmin does wish the Bone Crown returned. Powered by so many years of mortal death, it would return to our realm now an object of unconquerable strength—a strength he means to use to keep the order of things as they've been since the immortal banishment. Order with him and his sisters in control. I have been tasked with convincing you to see this return come to pass in your lifetime. In exchange for your favor, Cosmin offers you a place in his Hunt." Lethe swallowed, straightened tall to peer down his nose at her, expression inscrutable. "To guide and instruct you, convince you to support his aims, to give you means to win in combat against me, and the place you'd be offered would be *mine*—my freedom at last in exchange for yours."

His.

Lethe was doing all of this so that Arlo would take his place . . . and free him from the Wild Hunt?

"But," he continued, "I've never much enjoyed playing to other people's whims. Would you like to hear what I've devised instead to earn freedom my own way? What I've been working so hard toward? Why I've kept you safe all these years in the hopes you'd be willing to choose?"

He grinned at her. "Would you like to know what will actually stop *both* wars you face, Arlo Cyan Flamel?"

CHAPTER 39

Nausicaä

~~~

S O MANY YEARS SINCE she'd last been here, but when Nausicaä
stepped through Riadne's Egress and into Seelie Winter's palace, it was almost like traveling back through time.

*They stood, the two of them, facing the mirror, its image reflecting
a sprawling foyer made entirely of handsome, dark-stained wood—of a
high-flung and peaked, multilayered ceiling; angular archways and sturdy
pillars with carvings of beasts and the battles against them depicted along
their lengths.*

*"I admire Queen Aslaug's accomplishments greatly," said Riadne, blue
eyes fixed on their shimmering location.*

The Luminous Guard had preceded her arrival, stood still at the
ready, fanned out and flanked on either side of portal the Egress had
torn open in the air. The spluttered surprise, the anger, the horror of
dawning realization at what such an unannounced and well-armed
visit could only mean—not visit but *invasion*, and Nausicaä could
only imagine what their reception had been. By the time she walked
out to join the modest army Riadne had employed to help deliver
her verdict to Aslaug's proposal, the guard Seelie Winter would have
had stationed at its front entrance had already fled, were undoubtedly
already well on track to delivering the alert to their queen.

*"This is nothing personal—in fact, it grieves me to lose such a worthy
contemporary. But I do not make pacts with people I need nothing from,
Nausicaä. And allyship that wasn't offered before my ascension to power*

means very little to me now." Riadne didn't falter, didn't shift in place or glance in Nausicaä's direction for a sign or lack of approval. As sure as anything else she'd ever done, Riadne stood poised at command and perfectly composed. "Nothing personal," she repeated, and Nausicaä didn't glance at her, either. "Aslaug's request has simply made her a liability I won't ignore. How easily I can slot into her place a much more docile puppet . . . Nausicaä?"

The High Queen turned to her at last.

Those blue eyes burned like nitrogen ice.

Nausicaä unfurled her wings. She shed a bit of her glamour, allowing the monster beneath to bleed through her softer image. White-hot flame scorched down the length of her pale blond hair, replacing it with a crackling cascade—her as she'd been when she'd first come to this realm, before she'd taken to hiding further and further behind a face no one would look twice at. When Aslaug had first hunted her down, trapped her out in the snow, and convinced her back into these halls, that had become the first good thing in Nausicaä's life since the passing of her sister.

Home, when hers had been taken away.

Family, when her own had cast her out.

"I will ask you only once, Nausicaä. There seems to be camaraderie between you and Seelie Winter's queen. I keep your heart, you are mine to control, but what I task you to tonight . . . You will not waver in your duty."

Not exactly a question, but Nausicaä understood what she wanted, regardless.

When she got her heart back, if she ever got her heart back—if this war was resolved in their favor and Nausicaä was freed from the contract that bound her—this was going to hurt. What she did here tonight was going to stay with her for the rest of her life, and it would hurt. But would she waver? Would she falter in the slightest? Would memory and sentiment prevent her from performing her duty?

Nausicaä cocked her head at the queen.

She didn't smile, didn't smirk, didn't quip anything she'd usually have felt inclined to do in a situation that would have made her beyond uncomfortable before. Nausicaä merely nodded and blandly replied, "Ready when you are, Your Majesty."

Riadne Lysterne was the last to sweep through the Egress. In armor of magically enchanted glass, jagged cut and fit to overlapping—so similar to the dress she'd worn to the Summer Solstice—in lethal glass boots shaped to fit snugly up to her knees; in a draping like chain mail underneath the armor, where the links were all fizzling, angry electricity, Riadne was resplendent as ever as she stepped into Seelie Winter's foyer.

Her infamous glass sword angled at her side, she strode to the room's lead, her guard peeling from formation to fall into line in her wake, Nausicaä at her side.

"We'll make short work of this," Riadne said in a clipped tone. "Aslaug is mine—kill the rest. Leave none who do not kneel in fealty to your High Queen."

They poured from the foyer, into the hall, and there their siege began.

Nausicaä knew these people.

She knew so many of the warriors she cut down, one after the other. It had been many years since she'd been here, but many still lived, and to die like this was an honor—the belief in this Court had always been that only those who did not die *glorious* deaths would be reincarnated, and glory was achieved only by physical conflict. For the brave people she slayed, however, their afterlife would be an eternity of glittering gold halls and banquets and battles. This was how they all wanted to die. . . . But the betrayal on their faces when they realized who they fought . . . It would hurt later. For now, though, Nausicaä knew only duty.

Seelie Winter gave impressive opposition.

Aslaug had to have been expecting something along these lines for so many of her warriors to be so quickly armed and ready to go, and they poured from the woodwork, rained down from balconies, echoing great roars and shouts and vulgarities as they came.

They knew they were doomed—Nausicaä saw it in every pair of eyes she clouded over—but still they fought; no one shrank back from their own call to duty, and no one cowered in her shadow.

A Fury upon them, and a High Queen armed with a Bone Crown and Sins, but none of Aslaug's guard so much as flinched to contend with their likes.

Yes, this would hurt later.

Riadne sliced through the final barrier between her and the throne room where Aslaug kept. With the wipe of her blade on the sleeve of one of the fallen, she drew herself upright—such severity; so poised; unaffected in the least by the sapphire blood that splattered all her pretty chain and glass, flecked her pale face, matted bits of her hair.

If circumstances were different, if Riadne hadn't been the cause of so much personal pain and Nausicaä still cared, she might have actually been . . . proud to wage war beside someone so fierce.

Stalking forward for the throne room, Riadne pushed through the dark pinewood door.

Close on her heel, Nausicaä followed.

"So this is the might of our *eminent* queen," Aslaug bellowed, rising from her enormous throne of wood and pelt and bone. "A coward whose strength relies on deceit! For a fae of light, how quickly you slither to shadows for cover."

The throne room was massive—nearly twice the size of Riadne's—but most of it was unusable space. Water circled the room's perimeter, built into the wood like a moat, fed in some endless, magical loop by the wraparound curtain of water that cascaded down the pale stone walls.

It was a modest room, all things considered.

Another high-peaked, multilayered ceiling dangled a singular but large chandelier, its candles not illuminated by flame but churning, watery light. Apart from this, a silver carpet cutting straight down the room's blue agate-stone floor, and the throne Aslaug had occupied, there was nothing else to remark on. Aslaug was the feature here—as impressive as her control over the Seelie Winter element of water was, no one came to her palace to see it; they came here to see *her*.

Still poised, still tall, Riadne walked down the trail of silver. "An interesting summation of my character," she replied, airy light, but somehow still threatening as the encroachment of dark clouds. "Yet . . . I did not see you out in those halls. Where was all this bravery when it was your warriors falling at my feet? Such prowess, such might—such *reputation*. I led my own battle—you seem to be nice and cloistered in here, unscathed . . . hiding. . . ."

That seemed to rankle.

Nausicaä didn't have much to comment on this verbal repartee. Two queens before her, and only one would survive, and Nausicaä wasn't foolish enough to place a bet on anyone other than Riadne.

This was just her luxuriating in her kill.

Toying with her food.

Riadne had won the moment she decided Aslaug was too much risk to leave alive, and Nausicaä just . . . well, she wouldn't say "hoped," but the sooner she got this over with, the better. She could use a bath.

Movement in her periphery—it came viper quick, a blur of blue-and-silver robes, of streaming black hair; a glint of steel. Aslaug wasn't the only impressive woman this Court had to boast, and if it hadn't been for Nausicaä, things . . . might have been different.

Riadne's back was turned to the threat.

Even she hadn't rounded in time to catch the blade that swung for her head—sure and true, in one fell swoop, it would have cleaved it clean from Riadne's body.

But unfortunately for their assailant . . . Nausicaä was faster.

A blink.

That was all the time it took her to whirl about with her own blade. The sharp whistle of Erebus slicing through the air, and then there was a dull, wet *thud*. The sturdy trunk of Councillor Synnøve's body stood a full minute after its severed head rolled to Nausicaä's boot.

Instant death preserved the fury in her expression.

Synnøve Halversen.

You'll feel this laterfeelthislaterfeelthislaterfeelthis—

Aslaug sank to her knees with such a guttural cry of grief that Nausicaä's attention snapped up once more. Synnøve Halversen: representative of Seelie Winter on the Fae High Council, retired war general, and Aslaug's right hand.

Her wife of several years now.

Nausicaä had been personally invited to their wedding but hadn't gone; she'd been too mired in depression to join any celebration, even though she'd been happy for them.

Synnøve had made her rabbit stew once, and it had tasted awful—rabbit wasn't Nausicaä's thing, she'd decided then—but it had been the first bit of softness from someone since Tisiphone.

Another cry from Aslaug came like a punch to Nausicaä's chest, something she felt the physical force of, even if it didn't hurt.

"What have you done?" Aslaug rasped, attempting to claw her way down the carpet toward her fallen wife. "What have you done? What have you *done*?"

Who the question was for, Nausicaä could only guess. Aslaug seemed wild in her sorrow, barely able to comprehend her surroundings—the only thing that mattered was getting to Synnøve.

Riadne raised her sword.

"Wait." It took Nausicaä a moment to realize the command had come from her.

Turning, Riadne raised a brow at her. Skepticism darkened her face—was Nausicaä under her control or not, she clearly wondered, and Nausicaä . . . in this very beat of a second . . . honestly couldn't confirm or deny anything. But Justice, Law, and duty . . . they thrummed inside her, demanding, "Wait." She strode forward.

Reached down.

Hauled Aslaug to her feet.

Shoved Erebus into her hands and turned her about to face Riadne.

"Not on her knees. Not with her hands empty."

Not when her people so firmly believed that glory was the only way to achieve eternal happiness, and cutting her down defenseless and weeping would deny her where Synnøve was bound.

But Nausicaä didn't say that last part aloud.

By the look on Riadne's face, she didn't need to.

Aslaug recovered only enough that agony latched on to rage. She flung herself forward, straight for Riadne, but it wasn't with anywhere near the skill she would have needed to pull this off. Too distracted, too heartbroken, she was cut down easily by Riadne.

"You will explain what that was," Riadne demanded, clipped and to the point, as she handed her sword off to one of her Guard for proper cleaning.

Luminous soldiers milled about, dragging survivors into the room and at blade point offering them, "Bend to fealty, or fall to death?"

Not a single knee touched the ground.

Nausicaä watched as Aslaug was carried from the room. She shrugged. "Principle, probably." Whatever it had been, if Riadne suspected Nausicaä might be regaining independence, *feeling* . . . she might be tempted to test it out by using Arlo. But why did that matter so profoundly?

"You are loyal to me." It wasn't a question.

"And I didn't stop you—I don't care; it was just a matter of principle. You may control my heart, I might have to bend to your will, but there are things about me that will always just *be*, and I was created for principle."

It actually sounded believable when she phrased it like that, but it didn't lessen the suspicion she felt with Riadne's eyes fixed on her back clear out into the hall.

CHAPTER 40

Aurelian

❧⟶

A MONTH SINCE AURELIAN HAD last seen Vehan—day after day spent in training. From the first glint of sunlight through the trees until the last flickered out under nightfall, Ivandril had him running laps, lifting weights, learning hand-to-hand combat and mixed martial arts and how to not only properly swing a sword but use it to cleave a grown fae in two.

I'm almost sickened by how naturally all this has come to you, he'd told Aurelian one afternoon after Aurelian had successfully flipped him onto his back and pinned him under the weight of muscle even he had been surprised by how quickly his body had developed—like he was always meant to be bigger than lean. *When this is over, if we survive this war, you should know I'm making it my life's mission to recruit you to my ranks.*

On "rest days"—at least one a week, which Ivandril demanded he observe to help all this bulk of his heal properly—Aurelian chopped wood; practiced his magic; put all the things he'd learned out of books to use in helping the Market rebuild; ran patrol through the Hiraeth; and ate meals with his family and friends.

So many meals—Aurelian was pretty much always hungry now, had never consumed so much protein powder in his life, a staple since he didn't eat meat but needed to give his body *something* with which to repair itself.

The stubborn side of him that hated when someone was right about something he didn't want to admit to was sickened by the results of just a month of this lifestyle—how much calmer he felt, more in control of himself, no longer stuffing down rage and afraid it would burst out of him at any moment.

He felt good, better than he'd felt in quite some time.

The only thing was . . .

"You never change."

Aurelian looked up from the dumbbell he'd racked, surfacing from his thoughts to realize he'd probably been standing there staring at the row of weights for a good long minute or two.

The Madam had outfitted their cause with a gym, had filled it with all manner of equipment at Ivandril's request. His new mentor would have a fit if he caught Aurelian here today—this was his day off from training, but Aurelian had been too restless, because the only thing was . . .

For a heart-stopping moment he'd feared that intruding voice belonged to Ivandril. But his gaze lifted, and the haze of deep thought dissipated, and it was his younger brother he saw beside him, arms folded over his chest.

Aurelian raised a brow at him. "What?"

"Always fucking brooding. Brooding at breakfast, brooding while you punch those big old bags of sand over there; brooding while you piss, probably. It's your favorite sport. Has been since you were born—will be until you die."

"At the risk of sounding five," Aurelian threatened, "if you don't watch your mouth, I'm telling Mom."

Harlan waved him off, unconcerned.

He looked so much better after a month of proper nutrition and sleep.

A month of no more beatings, with all this fresh air and distance from iron and the Hiraeth's peculiar wildness to sooth him.

Harlan was a city boy—he'd liked Vegas and palace life—but there was a flush of health in his face Aurelian hadn't seen since they'd run through the trees together back behind their childhood home.

"You miss him," Harlan stated a little softer, some of the teasing draining from his tone. There was something misty about the way he looked at Aurelian that made Aurelian look back to the row of dumbbells. "You know, I was a little jealous of him at first."

And then his gaze snapped immediately back. "Of . . . Vehan?"

"Who else?" Harlan snorted. "You were like . . . my idol when we were kids. My big brother and best friend, who'd beat up the human kids for making fun of me on days I couldn't bear another minute of pretending to be a girl. You hated goofing around, but that never stopped you from taking me trekking through mud to catch snakes and frogs; building tree forts in the woods with me. I didn't understand your obsession with weird science things, and you always made me participate in experiments, and they were stupid, but it made you happy, so it made *me* happy too. Then Vehan happened."

Aurelian remembered.

Harlan had always been his favorite company back then.

At least, until Vehan.

"Riadne stepped through our shop with her son, and that was the first time I'd ever seen you look at someone the way so many someones have looked at you. I mean, you're my older brother. Age was bound to take us down different paths, and we like different things— even when we were kids, I didn't think it would be forever that you'd want me tagging along after you. Didn't want that, myself. But Vehan happened, and it was like your entire life just *bam*—shifted. Entirely focused on big blue eyes and a sunny smile and weirdly magnetic personality . . . kind of exactly like yours."

Harlan laughed, as though the memory of what had hurt during the time was nothing but funny to him now.

"We moved because of you. Do you know that? I heard Mom and Dad talking it over the night before they sent their acceptance of Riadne's request. They didn't care about a royal warrant or the glamour and fame of being the Seelie Summer Queen's chosen pâtissiers. We moved because Vehan happened, and for the first time since ever, you talked about something other than taking computers apart and fucking Star Trek Wars."

Aurelian sighed. "*Star Trek* and *Star Wars*—they're two different things!"

"*Regardless,*" Harlan continued, "Vehan came, and you looked at him as if he were some sort of god, and then he left and you, like . . . withered. Do you remember? When their vacation was over and Vehan had to go home, no more playtime together and snacks and chasing through the woods just the two of you—Riadne took her son home, and you withered up like she'd stolen the sun. Weren't even brooding, just full-on tears for two days straight, like your heart had actually broken. Mom even brought you to a doctor to make sure you were okay. You were *still* crying when the two of you came home with a clean bill of health and warning of dehydration."

He remembered this too.

It *had* felt like breaking. He couldn't really put it into words, and it had been so long ago that the feeling had worn softer for the time. But Aurelian did recall how devastating it had been, the first time Vehan had been taken from him.

A flutter in his chest—Aurelian twitched, and he felt a bit of the panic that lurked under his skin, a constant itch he couldn't scratch that had started since Lethe had taken him from the Solstice and had abated only in the hours he and Vehan had been reunited.

"The lesidhe believe a lot of things. Used to be that one of those things was that everyone had someone their magic aligned with. We were caretakers of the forest, one with the birds and trees and shit. Our souls were meant to reach out for things, to connect, and yours . . . I don't know. I don't really believe in the whole soulmate thing, but you and Vehan just vibe, Aurelian. In a way most people will go their lives wishing they could feel just a fraction of. So no one's all that surprised that you're barely keeping it together right now."

"Ah," Aurelian somewhat rasped, his throat unsticking.

Vehan had died; he'd nearly lost him, and it wasn't the first time he'd wondered if there wasn't something deeper to the connection between them, but whatever the truth, it didn't matter. What mattered was that Aurelian loved him, and although the Market made him feel whole in a way nowhere else had . . . it was still missing the most important thing: Vehan. "You're worried about me. I promise I won't start crying for days."

"Nah." Harlan laughed again, but there was sadness at the edge of the sound. "I mean, I was worried about you at first. After the way you were in the woods when you'd thought Vehan had died, and then having to be separated from him even after finding out Arlo had saved him. But since you started training . . . seeing you in your new environment . . . Dad means well, and there's nothing against abstaining from unnecessary battles, but I never once bought into the whole *lesidhe don't do violence* bs. And I think, deep down, neither did you. Because it's not all violence. Standing up for what's right, protecting what's important—that isn't violence; it's *fight*, and fight is a necessity of survival. And it's people who are guilty of actual violence who are quickest to tell you that fight is wrong."

Aurelian stared.

This kid.

When had Harlan grown up to become this man?

It was true, what he said. And something Aurelian had been thinking more and more about. The less he bared his teeth at Ivandril's opposing ideology, the more he realized how much the Courts *had* taken the lesidhe's naturally mild disposition to an extreme; had definitely used the image they'd crafted to keep the lesidhe beneath their thumb and under their control. No violence, no weapons—it's not the lesidhe way to indulge in either, but it was certainly the way of the Courts.

Aurelian would always be against strength where it wasn't due, but just as Harlan had pointed out . . . there was violence, and there was *protection*. Ivandril wasn't completely wrong to want to live his life outside of a stereotype Aurelian hadn't ever bought into himself, not fully.

Not if he really thought about it.

A loud bang on the glass between the main workout room and the newly built addition made Aurelian startle.

He and Harlan both looked up to find Rosalie plastered to the window, grinning like a cat who'd just caught several pixies and flailing madly to get Aurelian's attention. Once he saw her, she gestured back at Ten, in the process of setting a personal record of bench-pressing ten full reps of sixteen plates—eight forty-five-pound weights stacked on either side, for a total of seven hundred and twenty pounds, plus the forty-five pounds of the Olympic standard bar.

Faerie strength at its finest.

Aurelian was still stuck at six plates on each side.

Jaxon and Tiffin stood cheering beside them. Leaf flitted around, a flurry of excitement in the air just above.

"I like your new friends," Harlan said softly. "And I'm even more glad that it seems they've helped you finally remember that, as awesome as dark-haired fae princes are, there's more to life than romantic love; more to *fight* for than one boy."

. . . Yeah.

Aurelian liked his new friends too.

"Come on," he rumbled, face a touch warm, which had nothing to do with embarrassment if anyone asked. Slinging an arm around his brother's shoulders, he walked him toward the door to the new room, where Ten had just racked their bar to thunderous applause and whistles. "They'll be expecting attention for this. But please don't tell them they're my friends—I'll *never* get them to leave me alone if you do."

"Your secret's safe with me, nerd," Harlan replied, with more laughter that Aurelian could never hear enough of—another thing to fight for, too.

CHAPTER 41

Arlo

⌒

THE LUMINOUS PALACE HAD one observatory—one more than Arlo had expected of it, given that Seelie Summer didn't pay their worship to night and its stars—but much like anything else here, Riadne had spared no expense or flare in its design.

A bulbous room domed by pale stone that turned crystalline-transparent from twilight to dawn, it was outfitted with moon-white cushions for reclining on to look up at the sky, and enormous telescopes Arlo would more expect to find in an actual astronomer's lab.

There were glass cabinets with curious, complicated instruments for divining and astrological study; there were shelves stuffed with books; the floor was a wide-blown mosaic of white and teal and black tiles arranged to depict the most stunning, highly detailed celestial chart; and at the very center of the room, a basin sprouted like a birdbath supporting a discus full to the brim with silvery, perfectly still water.

Arlo didn't know what the basin was meant for.

She'd paused on her way to the observatory's open balcony to peer in briefly at the reflection of the moon within, clear as though she were instead looking up at the sky but didn't linger on contemplating why.

Her thoughts were already far too occupied.

"I've never much enjoyed playing to other people's whims. Would you like to hear what I've devised to earn freedom my own way? What I've been working so hard toward? Why I've kept you safe all these years in

the hopes you'd be willing to choose?" He grinned at her. "Would you like to know what will actually stop both wars you face, Arlo Cyan Flamel?"

Arlo stared at him, speechless in her confusion.

What had he just called her?

Flamel . . . but that didn't make any sense. The Flamels had died. Everyone knew the story, that they'd been the ones to save the Courts from the alchemist who sought to turn Flamel's own work against them—but doing so had cost Nicholas Flamel his life, and he'd died without an heir to succeed him.

Lethe was just toying with her . . . wasn't he?

Very slowly, very carefully, Arlo asked, "What do you mean?"

And Lethe's grin grew even sharper. "You want your memories back. I've been training you quite rigorously this past month for that very cause, planting the seeds of potential in you, because if you want those memories back, Arlo, you're going to have to spend a wish and win against me in combat, and that wish will have less chance of exacting cruel payment if you already possess a fraction of the skill you'll need in order to achieve this victory."

That did make sense, and Arlo recalled Luck explaining something similar to her back in her beginning lessons.

The bigger the request, the greater the toll would be. If Arlo had a decent footing in combat, as Lethe had been trying to instill in her, then this impossible ask of skill enough to defeat the greatest Hunter of all time—an ask that, without that training, would probably cost an arm and a leg in later recompense—would come to her a little easier.

"Just as Cosmin would have, I want you to challenge me. By rule, any mortal who defeats a Hunter in battle usurps their place in Cosmin's esteemed troupe. A usurped Hunter also loses their place in immortality; they die—but ah, fear not, not me. My immortality was inherited, not granted. I'd revert back to the same position I was in when I first ascended to it—a liability, a threat. Cosmin believes that after all these years, my temper is now better suited for me to make the right choice in what he asked of my rebirth all those many years ago, that my anger has been exhausted by time—and that belief is his mistake to make."

And here they'd arrived at last—what Lethe would get from this, more than just freedom from a position that Arlo knew he could have found many ways out of by now, if it were freedom alone he was after.

More than that, was this what Arlo even wanted?

Immortality . . .

If she won against him, she'd earn a Hunter's conditional immortality. She'd get to spend the rest of eternity with Nausicaä, and since Nos was an unofficial member of the Hunt as well, they'd get to work together too.

All of a sudden it was like she was back in the Good Vibes Only café again, talking possibilities with her father. She'd been so worked up about whether or not to go to university in the fall, and Arlo wanted to . . . well, she wasn't sure if it was to laugh or cry at the moment, when she compared that to what she struggled with now. . . .

"If you can beat me, it's your choice entirely what to do with what you'll have earned, but if I could make a suggestion . . ." Lethe held out a hand.

Arlo stared at the flat, open palm now, a second . . . two . . . until it clicked what she was looking at.

A die, just like hers, except . . . completely different: bigger by half, as acid green as his eyes, and etched in numbers blacker than tar. There was something about the power radiating from this object as well—far more than the muted fraction of hers, frightening in its raw potential even just to behold.

And what did it mean? That Lethe had this . . . a Hollow Star's die all his own?

"If I could suggest—and though much reassurance was needed, your cousin and I have aligned in this goal, and we hope you'll see it as we do—spend another wish, Arlo. Trade your role as a Hollow Star for Vehan's role as Ruin. Vehan's soul will disintegrate the moment Ruin is summoned into him—bless our new High Queen, she believes so fiercely that he'll be strong enough to survive it, but he won't. You would—your soul would be tethered to immortality, keeping your essence alive until we vanquish Ruin within you, and though your mortal body would die, you would be reborn right into the position of Hunter you'll have won from me. Your death would also release your darling Nausicaä from her contract with Riadne . . . and although typically immortals awaken with no memory of their previous lives, perhaps I could be moved to use my Gift and make yours a permanent thing, not dissolved by immortal Law."

He closed his fingers around his die, retracting it to his chest.

"Two wishes, Arlo," he continued in a whisper-thin voice. "That's all it would take. You'd get immortality, and you'd be saving your prince. I was going to use another means, but that sword of yours will work nicely, too. Already imbued with years of battle experience and with a mother's love, and now enchanted with power by Mab herself? It will do more than nicely against dark magic. Once Ruin is in your immortally reinforced heart, your binding promise to Riadne won't apply anymore after this death of sorts; we'll whisk you away, use Mab's blessing to plunge right through you and vanquish Ruin. All that will be left is destruction of the Crown, and once done, the distraction that immortality has been fighting over breaks; another war ended before it begins."

It was a lot to take in.

And Arlo was still stuck on what it meant that he possessed one of Luck's dice as well.

"You never told me what you really get out of this, and I'm not sure what you're even asking. You want me to choose Cosmin, to align myself with him—"

"Oh, no." Lethe creaked a laugh. "That's what he wants. You on his side to help him regain his Crown once Riadne is thwarted. You to choose his ranks, become one of his Hunters, his power to control and no one else's. What I want is what I have always wanted, and never once hid—quite simply, it's you, Arlo."

And yet that had never felt very simple, to her.

Arlo pursed her lips, her expression furrowed. She didn't see what she could do for someone like Lethe that no one else could.

"I would like you, Arlo," Lethe continued. "I would like you to ascend to immortality and spit in my father's face, and tell him thanks but sorry, you'd much rather join my house. To truly inherit what I'm entitled to, I need a few things first. A mortal shrine, for one, which a long-ago father so fortunately gifted, and a queen has been unwittingly sacrificing to for quite some time."

His tone curled deeply around some private humor, a reference to a life Arlo had no idea about and probably never would.

"A cohort, for another—immortal backing. Even one to my name will give it standing, claim to a throne as a permanent fixture, safe from the Divine Council's Destruction. I want simply what's mine, Arlo, for no more nefarious purpose than what's mine will help me exact a payment I've been owed millennia over."

He squeezed his die, and it evaporated into a cloud of black smoke, much the way the things Nos banished to nonexistence did.

"Our dice aren't the same. Yours is a product of control. Mine is the reason yours comes with rules—it's bound by none and can grant me whatever misfortune I wish on another, including that dismal curse of immortality, which would otherwise be stripped from you for denying the Hunter's position . . ."

What Lethe had told her.

What he wanted her to do . . .

It did sound rather straightforward when he spelled it out like that. And the more she thought about it, the more his actions seemed to line up now with his purpose. How pleased he'd been that she'd chosen to become a Hollow Star; how long he'd been protecting her; how deeply he'd entrenched himself in Riadne's plot to keep an eye on her progress with the stones and take control of a situation that would have happened one way or another without him.

But was any of this what *Arlo* wanted?

As an immortal, she wouldn't be allowed here anymore; would never get to see Celadon again. Maybe, once this was all over, they'd be able to renegotiate terms between the realms, but it wouldn't be the same. *They* wouldn't be the same.

Not to mention that her entire life had been a lie, if Lethe hadn't been playing with her about the *Flamel* of it all. And worse, her entire life had been dictated by others, led and pushed and waltzed around from one event to the next, never in her control, subject always to other people's whims.

Her memories taken because someone else wanted them gone.

A deferred Weighing because she wasn't enough of someone else's standards.

Become a Hollow Star . . . become an alchemist . . . give this person the Crown and become their champion; give it to that person, and become theirs; destroy it; trade wishes for victories and become a Hunter instead, then trade Hunter for something else. . . .

Arlo had never wanted to become a hero.

She didn't *want* to play main protagonist in this tale of good versus evil.

Yet here she was, the center of so much, Fate traded for Luck and still she felt like her life was entirely out of her own control. Still others made the decisions for her.

You made a decision once—look where it got you, an unkind voice in her head reminded her. *Your mother dead, and Riadne in power . . .*

But at least it had been her choice.

I've never much enjoyed playing to other people's whims, Lethe had said to her.

His words echoed in her head.

Would you like to hear what I've devised to earn freedom my own way?

What would *Arlo's* own way to freedom be . . . ?

"Your thoughts are loud tonight."

Arlo stiffened.

Clutching the balcony's railing in one hand, she whirled in place to face who'd come up behind her. In complete silence, wholly undetected, but then . . . Luck was a titan; what was there to hear, when a being could simply appear from nothing?

"You know," Luck continued, moving to drop beside her, posture bent and arms folded to rest on the railing. They looked up at the sky. . . . "From our very first conversation in the Faerie Ring, I had a feeling you would be the first to follow in his steps, to take your destiny from Fate and Luck *both*."

Arlo merely looked at them.

It was Luck in their true appearance—all shamrock-green hair and fluttery robes and fathomless, cosmic black eyes—but dialed to a more human setting. They didn't tower much more beside her than Nausicaä did, and if it weren't for the curve of their great black horns from their crown to their jaw, they could almost pass for an ordinary young man.

Months.

It had been months since Arlo had seen or spoken to Luck, who'd been a near-constant companion for a short bit of time.

She'd been too angry with them, and ashamed all at once. Scared to summon them back because a part of her blamed them for abandoning her to power she clearly didn't know how to use yet, but she also couldn't shake the feeling that she'd disappointed them. That they might be angry with her too, for how she'd chased them away the last time.

But Luck didn't look anything other than at ease right now—tired, perhaps, and was it her imagination, or was that an apology weighing on the fringe of his expression?

"Whose footsteps?" Arlo hedged, soft and a bit like a verbal olive branch.

Luck's mouth didn't lose its smile, but the curl of it turned rueful. "I love my husband. The good and bad, no one is fully without either, and Cosmin is a rare joy—funny, for one who governs the dead. He has done much for me over the millennia, as I have done for him, but I do regret . . . We were terrible parents when it came to Lethe."

Arlo . . . stared.

She had no idea what to say.

Lethe was . . .

"I let down my son. Allowed my faith in the order of things long overdue for reconfiguration to rule where my hearts should have led me. I wanted so much for him; it will be my greatest regret for as long as I live that I failed him so grievously." Luck glanced at her. "Your heart wishes to take the lead, too—where would it have you follow?"

Arlo didn't need to explain. She knew they knew—a titan of fortune, and apparently Lethe's parent? There was no way they didn't know what Arlo currently weighed.

"Will it work?" she asked, instead of *I'm sorry.*

"It will," Luck replied, instead of *I'm sorry, too.*

Challenge Lethe—regain her memories.

Defeat him and achieve immortality.

Spend a wish, make a trade, and Vehan would live; Nausicaä's heart would be returned. It was what she should do, and it made the most sense. Here at the end of the line, it was their only real option, and if Arlo agreed to do it, she knew Celadon already had the particulars planned out, but she needed to talk with him first.

Needed to know how he truly felt about this.

Needed to hear it directly from him that he would be okay if she went through with it.

And there was something, *something*, in the back of her head telling her to do it. To take Lethe's position in the Hunt and get back her memories. Something, *something*, telling her that once she did, it would all become clear. . . .

What would?

A missing memory—something specific; this something whispered she'd have to remember what it was that had condemned her to forgetting in order to . . .

What?

She didn't know, and it was frustrating! This was all so frustrating, but it was the very same thing she'd been feeling all along, she realized.

The *what-ifs* from the very beginning.

The *what-if* that urged her to extend her Weighing.

The *what-if* that propelled her after Nausicaä and into Hierony-mus Aurum's lab.

The *what-if* that led her through every obstacle to here—hope, yes, but a very specific kind: *What if there was something important she needed to do?*

"It will work," Luck repeated. "If you have the strength to see it through." They caught her eye at last, and their expression softened. "I did mean it, what I said before. I am . . . profoundly sorry, Arlo. For what occurred at the Solstice. For what you've lost and suffered that I couldn't protect you from. For what you'll go through yet. I would spare you from it all, but you've seen the way wishes work. Nothing without a price."

And Arlo . . . softened too.

She turned back around so that they stood side by side now, arms pressed together. "I never said thank you."

"For what?" Luck asked, quirking a brow.

Arlo exhaled a deep breath, deflated a little in what felt like relief for finally saying these words out loud. "For giving me the means to take charge of my life? Not that I've done a great job of that yet, but if it weren't for meeting you, if you didn't give me this die, I wouldn't be here. And yeah . . . here kind of sucks right now, but for the first time in my life, I have *people.* Friends. And the things I've learned about who I am and want to be? Just . . . thanks. For being a part of that."

It was quiet between them now.

A moment passed in which Arlo stared straight ahead but was keenly aware of Luck's eyes on her.

"I liked you from the very beginning," they said at last, very quietly. "You're the first Hollow Star I ever sought out myself, do you know? Normally, it's the other way around. But it's been . . . refreshing—your acquaintance; your heart. You possess a great deal of goodness, and for all you couldn't see yourself before, there's little

I did, or Nausicaä, or anyone else, to make you who you are now. You have always known yourself; you have always and resolutely been Arlo Jarsdel—an honor and privilege to know."

Biting her lip, Arlo tucked in on herself, unprepared for how much she'd needed to hear something like that. "Could be Flamel."

"Will always be Arlo."

"I'll miss you," Arlo breathed. "If . . . if I go through with it."

And Luck nodded. "I will miss you, too." Then, with a flourish and exaggerated brightness, they added, "And you are owed the assistance—just this once, a bit of a favor with no strings attached: a reminder that what Moros gifted you is still down in the dungeons. A vial you kicked to the back of your once-upon-a-time cell, that upon consumption of its contents will transform the drinker into any imagined and perfect likeness for the set course of an hour."

It was Arlo's turn to quirk a brow, staring up at Luck with no real comprehension of what they were on about.

"So that's two things, now, is it not? That you possess, or will come into the possession of, that will transform shape into something else . . . *someone* else. A vial, and a cloak—if you can win it from the Hunter that owns it. Just as a reminder. For what you'll need to go through with Lethe's plot . . . for what you'll need in case what you learn when your memories are returned is something that might give you a plot of your own."

All the way back to her bedroom, Arlo thought about what they'd said.

It sounded like a hint—Luck wouldn't spout off ramblings that served no purpose to her—but Arlo had no idea what use to make of knowing she could have one or two or a thousand ways of altering her appearance into something or someone else besides pulling one over on Riadne and swapping out her appearance as well as her fate for Vehan's.

What plot of her own could she devise from any of this information?

What would trading appearances with Vehan serve in addition to trading for his role as Ruin?

If not Vehan, who would she choose to become? Who would she *need* to become in order to help Vehan and Nausicaä and everyone else?

Into her room, through to her bedroom, Arlo stared at her bedside table deep in thought—at her cell phone lying innocuously on the polished wood, and beside it, two bracelets like the one Celadon had given her just before they'd come here back at the start of June. One that would whisk Arlo to safety as soon as she spoke the enchanted command . . .

"Uh . . ."

. . . Wait.

Something wasn't right.

Lifting her wrist, Arlo examined the bracelets there. The friendship bracelet of thread Celadon had made for her years ago . . . and the thin bit of polished slate that protected Viridian blood.

So where had this second and third come from . . . and now, more importantly . . . ?

Riadne had taken her phone from her after the Solstice—she was forbidden to have it, to contact anyone—and had locked it away most likely in her private office. Who would be foolish enough to both scour that highly secured place *and* return their findings to her?

The screen lit up.

Arlo yelped in surprise, dove in for a closer look, and tapped the thread of messages on her screen. Hundreds of missed texts and calls, it seemed like, but the newest from Celadon.

Her eyes read:

Asked Lethe to return your phone to you.

You already have your bracelet, but these two others, one is for Vehan and the other for Rory. They can't use it themselves unless I'm the one presenting it to them, but so long as they HAVE it, I can issue a mass summoning, and anyone under Viridian protection will be pulled to the Circle. All Nausicaä has to do is teleport. She'll go wherever you are.

She tapped the screen to expand the message.

I'm sure by now Lethe's filled you in on our plan and . . . there's so much I want to talk to you about before this, so much I want to promise you. Please, when you get this, will you call me? Or at least text. The one thing I don't want to lose in this is you, and I promise you I won't; no matter what I have to do, I'll make it so that we'll still have each other. But I will not force your choice in this, so please . . . let's talk. Let's lay out our cards and figure out what we want to do.

What she wanted . . .

Three bracelets.

Two cloaks.

One destiny traded for another.

And Luck's reminder like a hint . . . that maybe whatever she decided now would change once she *remembered.*

What if . . . ?

What if where she needed to be wasn't back in her cousin's safety . . . ?

"Arlo!" Celadon fairly cried in relief, answering her call on the very first ring, and Arlo felt tears well up in her eyes.

"Cel . . . ," she replied, and though her heart broke to do this, her tone was steady.

What if where she needed to be was right where she already was.

"Cel, I . . . I'm going to need another bracelet. Just one more—for one of Riadne's alchemists in training we're going to want on our side."

CHAPTER 42

Celadon

~~~

YOU DO ENJOY PRESSING your luck," Lethe observed in a drawl. "How many more times do you think the Madam will let you come and go right under her nose before her *requests* for your attention become a demand?"

"Then it's a good thing the Madam is exactly who we're here to see." Lethe turned to face him.

A grin lifted at the corner of his mouth.

"So you've worked it out, then? Who and what Melora is?"

They stood, the two of them, just outside the Goblin Market's newly reforged and firmly shut front gate.

Dawn hovered fresh on the horizon; mist curled damp and low through the trees. Lethe in full Hunter's garb, his silver fastenings and clasps and chains glinting in the ever-shifting slants of light; Celadon in black to match—tight-fitted trousers and a plain black top, silk and sheer spilling from his shoulders in a cascading cloak, his obsidian crown on his head.

As a pair, they painted a formidable picture, and Celadon . . . liked that. The togetherness. How they looked side by side . . .

The story Lethe had shared with him . . . Celadon didn't know whether or not he could call it truth—it was certainly truth to Lethe, but to believe he'd once lived a lifetime as the Moon . . . it was almost too much. But there was no denying how incredibly similar their origins were, with Lethe brought up to believe himself one thing only to find out cruelly late that he was actually someone else.

To be tossed around by family and fate, alone and afraid with nothing but the Moon for a friend.

It was hard to believe that soul had been *his*, and yet . . . impossible to ignore the rightness of it.

Togetherness.

Arlo was his best friend, and for the longest time he'd thought of her as his missing other half. But maybe he wasn't meant to be split only two ways but three.

A moment longer of inscrutable silence, of acid eyes dangerously bright and fixed on Celadon's face, and Lethe finally spoke in that same steady, creaking drawl of his—at once as deep and cool as water. "You've worked it out. You were always the clever one. But before we go any further in this . . . In life I was taken prisoner, abducted from my home and forced into servitude, bound to a cruel king. In death I was shackled by something made out to be a boon that became instead eternity spent on the end of yet another leash. Control was passed to all but me. I will say this only once to you, Celadon Cornelius Fleur-Viridian Lysterne: I will never again allow another such power over me. Not even you, whatever should happen from here forward."

Celadon looked back at him.

Up into those toxic eyes.

At this man who, in the past few months, had become so much more to Celadon than he could ever imagine possible, both of Lethe and of anyone in general.

A man who'd somehow or another, and with great patience, made it past Celadon's defenses and planted himself in Celadon's heart. Whatever existed in their future, whatever happened between them, however long Lethe chose to stay, it didn't matter. Lethe and Arlo: these were the people Celadon wanted to face his present with.

So he took a step closer.

Closed the distance between them by laying a hand on the Hunter's chest, and this time, pressed his lips to Lethe's in a soft, brief kiss.

"I will never again allow another such power over you either," he said, speaking the words against Lethe's mouth, shivering slightly at the sensation of fluttering touch to such sensitive skin. "Not even myself. Come as you like. Go as you like. Stay as long as you wish—anything you do by my side from here on out will be at your choosing, and no other's."

And Lethe bent in.

Claimed another kiss that left Celadon fairly breathless after, his lower lip swollen by the bite of sharp teeth. "Good," Lethe said, slowly and carefully, pitched so deep his voice might have sounded deathly frigid to someone who didn't know this god as well as Celadon now did. "Lucky you. Today, I *choose* to lay a kingdom at your feet. Anything at all for you . . . my friend. My Moon."

It was only Celadon requesting an audience with the Madam that permitted them both through the gate.

Well-armed and watchful goblins conveyed them to her tavern, up to her office, and it had been quick across her features, but Celadon had caught it—the flicker of triumph, because of course the Madam had assumed she'd won.

After all this time, all her effort—after longing so greatly for what Celadon and his Gifts could do for her—he was finally here, seated in a wooden chair opposite her behind her desk.

Melora, Queen of the Grim Brotherhood; she was taller than he'd expected.

Stronger . . . beautiful, especially in all that melted gold and encrusted with rubies. She also thought she had the advantage, that Celadon hadn't yet figured out what she was. . . .

"King Celadon," the Madam greeted warmly, smiling widely at them—a look like a predator sizing up prey. "I have to admit, I was beginning to worry you wouldn't show. After that performance in my arena, I've been dying to meet you. . . . What brings you to me now after all this time?"

The Madam's den was warm, a fire lit behind her despite the final vestiges of summer's heat. With so many glittering possessions hoarded around her, this space reminded him strongly of Professor

Feng's office whenever she'd pulled him aside to remind him of his duty, his responsibility to get along with his cousins, at least during her lessons.

"I think you might have some idea," Celadon replied easily. "Perhaps we might have even crossed paths before this if you hadn't been noticeably absent during the Market's incineration."

The Madam folded her hands on her desk and leaned in a little closer, a touch more intimate. "A tactical retreat—you know how it is. Humor me, Your Highness. I'd like you to say it."

Celadon watched her a moment . . . two. . . . She'd be humored, all right, by what he was here for.

"Riadne grows too powerful," he began. "Any day now, she'll have her final stone, and we won't be able to thwart this. We can only plan accordingly to contend with the fallout." Crossing his legs, Celadon paused. He let the Madam linger just another few seconds longer on believing she knew where all this would go: Celadon agreeing to play her spy in exchange for her support.

The Madam watched him, smile never slipping, only growing sharper.

"Undoubtedly, you've heard I've been busy—rebuilding my Court, remaking it the way it should have always been."

And sharper still . . .

"This bastion against Riadne's reign will stand only so long as it has power enough to rival hers. On my own, that power is insufficient. With allies . . ."

And here they were.

The Madam was practically half across her desk in eager anticipation of what she'd wanted for so long.

Celadon placed his hands on the arms of his seat—sat up straight, took command of the room in a single, elegant shift of posture that he could now see was all Riadne. "Melora, Queen of the Grim Brotherhood: I issue you a challenge."

The Madam . . . stared.

She stared . . . and then she laughed. "Boy, this isn't the Bone Crown. Don't waste my time with frivolities, I'm a busy woman—"

He continued, undeterred. "I challenge you—my strength against your own; to defeat, not death, and if you win, you will get my full service. I will be your spy, the king in your pocket, to use however you please. But if *I* win . . ." It was Celadon's turn to smile like a threat. "If I win, you must take yourself and go. The Grim Brotherhood may remain in your control, whatever is left of it through the coming war, but the Wild will not give it throne any longer. If I win, you remove yourself from the Market and yield these folk to their own government. Deny my challenge, and it will be the last I ever put myself on bargain to you."

One shot at something she'd craved for so long, at the risk of losing all.

Celadon knew who the Madam was.

He'd learned as a boy how to deal with dragons—that they liked their homes warm, kept their treasures close, and couldn't resist a challenge that offered up rare rewards.

Melora unspooled.

She rose from her desk like a growing shadow, anger flexing behind her expression, tight in the muscle that clenched beneath her skin. Most dragons didn't even know what they were anymore; after too long spent in hiding, they'd forgotten their truth. The majority of the few who did remember still couldn't recall how to shift back. It was a handful at most in this big, wide world who both remembered and possessed the ability to ease between shapes—and Melora was one. Celadon had suspected, and now, with the terrible way she rose in front of him, had the confirmation.

If looks could incinerate, Celadon would be ash.

Lethe sat quiet and poised through it all—really, it was as though he weren't paying attention, more engrossed in polishing his adamantine claws with the hem of his glittering cloak.

And wasn't *that* a threat . . . possibly the only one that kept the

Madam from reaching across the table and swiping deadly claws of her own across Celadon's throat.

A moment passed . . . followed by another. . . .

The Madam drew a breath, then released it in a baleful huff of another laugh. "Such meager terms between sovereigns. Your ambition exceeds my expectations, I'll give you that, Child of Spring and Summer. You've more of your mother in you than I thought. But don't come to me with pittances when you can give me troves. Your strength against mine?" Her next huff fanned fire-heated breath across the gap between them, right into his face. "My Court, then, for *yours*. I'll take your challenge, but it will be for crowns. If you win, the Market, the Wild, the Brotherhood, all will be yours to utilize as you wish. But if I win, UnSeelie Spring falls to me . . . and you along with it."

Lethe's polishing paused.

He sat very still, listening intently, watching Celadon for offense.

But really . . . this was exactly what he'd imagined would happen. Dragons were greedy beings.

"My strength against yours. Court for Court," Celadon echoed, and rose to stand as well. He held out his hand to her. "I accept your terms."

Melora clasped him; they shook on the deal.

And in a singular, fluid motion, Lethe rose to standing too.

As Melora looked between them, fear flickered quickly across her face, then was shoved even more quickly behind defensive viciousness at the way Lethe's gaze was fixed on her. . . . "The Grim and Sunken Kings," she spat; their titles, Celadon assumed, if he should win her crown.

Celadon clenched his teeth. "The Sunken King" was what Lethe had told him many of immortalkind had taunted him as before they'd learned to hold their tongues. Melora spoke the brand like an insult as well, and that rankled Celadon enough to glower.

"Of course," the Madam continued, inspecting this entire exchange. "Rumor has it the two of you have become indecently involved—of course he would call on you to fight his battles for him, Lethe. And what did he vow," she added in building ire, "to tempt one such as you to this contract? It doesn't matter." She turned her meanness back on Celadon. "Our bargain was clear—by your very words, my strength against *yours*, Celadon."

"Oh yes," Celadon agreed, rising to stand as well, adopting a cheerful manner—she had every right to not want to pit herself against Lethe, and after all, Lethe had warned him.

Don't you dare turn out to be boring.

"My strength, yes. For the longest time, you know, I did consider that to be the connections I make all too easily. . . ."

Lethe cocked his head at him, blinked thick, dark lashes over big acid eyes. Lethe had been expecting it too—Celadon to call on *him* to win this fight, but how boring would that be, how utterly . . . predictable, and Celadon was anything but.

He'd forgotten this fact in the swell of his own fears and shaken foundations, but not anymore.

Celadon had never been, and never would be, predictable; it was this that would win them Riadne's war—a woman twelve steps ahead of every plot. . . .

"But it was recently pointed out to me that I had considerable potential—and how much more dangerous it would be to ignore it than to give in and learn how to properly wield it."

It was worth it, the risk, for the way Lethe's glee unspooled across his face, the farthest away from bored.

And Celadon only continued to smile—"So let's see what's greater"—as Summer's electricity crackled in his eyes and Winter's ice licked its way up his arms; as Autumn's earth began to tremble the foundations of Melora's tavern; as Spring began to churn darkly in the sky outside her window. "Your strength against mine. I'll even let you choose the venue."

Melora roared her fury.

"It seems, at the moment, that my strength set against yours is pretty evenly matched," said Celadon, standing in front of where Melora had gathered her hulking crimson form. She towered over him, her golden eyes blazing down at him, the both of them just as exhausted as the other. But to Celadon's credit—to Lethe's pride—there was nothing like fear in his Moon's expression.

"I don't want your crown, Melora. I don't want your Court. You are cruel and manipulative and just as ill-suited for power as Riadne, and the Grim Brotherhood stands for nothing I wish to be myself. The choice is yours—we can continue to chase each other around this arena . . ."

"Or?" Melora rumbled, no less a threat for her fatigue.

"Or we end this here, and you take your leave. You keep your title— the Wild keeps themselves."

"Your back is still hurting you."

Lethe dropped his gaze from the ceiling to the youth who stood beside him. Arms folded over xis chest and yellow eyes bright with accusation, Vesper stared back at him with all the defiance of a mother waiting for her son to confess his wrongdoing.

Clicking his tongue against his teeth, Lethe shifted his sprawl.

Retracted his legs from where they'd been flung over the arm of the couch he'd been resting on, and thought he'd done admirable work of concealing the way the movement made the muscles in his back twinge—he was immortal, a god, near invincible, but not impervious to pain. However much higher his threshold was for violence, Riadne's little flogging session . . . It would take a bit more time yet to recover completely from punishment powered by Sins.

Annoyingly, Vesper wasn't to be fooled or deterred.

"Come on, let's see."

Lethe bared his teeth in a mockery of a hiss. "I am *fine*."

"You think you're so damn scary," Vesper sighed, ignoring his teeth and darting a hand to snag his leg before Lethe could tuck it away. "Stop struggling—don't make me get the spray bottle."

They were all so . . . familiar with him.

These people who'd somehow or other become . . .

Eris, off in the corner of this ostentatious sitting room, all pale yellows and splashes of white, cream carpeting and gleaming gold fixtures and silk-upholstered seating. It was the room in which Riadne like to conduct her weekly *debriefing* of them over tea, and she was late this morning—her prerogative, Lethe supposed. To pass the time, Eris had stuffed his nose into one of the books from the glass-encased shelves against the far wall.

Yue, seated on the couch opposite Lethe, serene and ignoring them all completely as he tended to his twin adamantine daggers.

Vesper buzzing incessantly around him, like death had given him the personal task of looking after Lethe where Lethe couldn't be bothered.

. . . these people who'd become his family.

Not that he'd admit such an offensive term aloud.

They were infuriating enough as it was, checking in on him, talking with him, seeking him out for this and that—Vesper when xe wanted a game of hunt through the woods; Yue when he wanted someone to mediate with; Eris when he wanted to talk over what he'd learned from all those damned books he was always reading.

It hadn't been his intention to form an attachment to his chosen *companions*.

They might comprise the Wild Hunt, might be the elite of all the current Hunters Cosmin had gathered over time, and not the first of this collection either—but their positions were open to any who could get a familiar's bow of approval, then defeat their master in combat. Lethe hadn't cared overmuch about the ones who'd come before, but for *some reason* . . .

Eris—a fae man who'd taken on an entire pack of werewolves after one had killed his daughter in the woods during a full moon.

Yue—an ironborn prince born to a Chinese emperor, whose concubine mother had been sentenced to death for amorous interactions with one of the Imperial Guard, and Yue had taken out nearly half of the emperor's force before they managed to *subdue* him as well.

Vesper—a faerie kid. A street urchin. Nothing all that intimidating, a bleeding heart that smiled too widely and shared too much with the other children orphaned to the streets, always willing to choose hunger if it meant another mouth got fed. Vesper, who'd died trying to protect a sex worker cornered in some grimy Parisian ally, beaten to death by a mean group of much bigger, drunken men.

Lethe had collected all three of them himself.

Unlike the others who'd ascended to the Wild Hunt, he'd also trained them personally as Hunters and primed them with what they'd need to be chosen by Famine, War, and Death.

Perhaps that was it.

He'd put too much of himself into this project. Thankfully there wouldn't be a next time—he was determined to be done with this soon, no matter what it took.

Ssss—he breathed in a hiss when Vesper's struggling to inspect his back wrenched him painfully hard. "I said it was fine!"

"I just want to look!" Vesper replied just as defensively. "Maybe we can put something on it to help it heal faster!"

"I'll put *you* in a—*oof.*"

Vesper toppled, xis inconsiderable weight just enough to knock the air from Lethe's lungs, which he didn't feel all that much, but the nerve of this waif—it was constant! Vesper touched and crowded and tugged at his attention. It was what he imagined owning a puppy would be like.

Yue sighed. "No roughhousing indoors," he warned.

"Riadne won't thank you if you break something again, you two," Eris chimed in.

Again.

This was all such nonsense.

These people were ridiculous, and he was glad to be rid of them. Celadon didn't crawl over him like this, didn't force himself into his space, didn't—

"Wow." Vesper whistled low under xis breath after hiking Lethe's shirt up to his chest, baring his stomach to the room. "You're not half-bad under all that leather and chains, Leeth."

Lethe growled. "Call me that *one more time*—"

Where Vesper produced a spray bottle from, he had no idea and didn't much care. Staring down its nozzle, Lethe glared; squared his jaw; poured every ounce of threat he possessed into his aura; and simply dared Vesper to pull that trigger.

"Let me help you."

His glare intensified. "Absolutely not—"

Ksssst.

Lethe froze, water dripping down his cheek. Yue glanced up from his dagger. Eris peered over the rim of his book—both of them no doubt wondering who would be chosen to fill Vesper's role when Lethe *eviscerated* xim for xis audacity. . . .

But just in time—a knock at the sitting room's door.

Vesper fled, trailing laughter behind xim, bouncing over to open it.

Revealed on the other side was Arlo, pale and grim. She didn't need to say anything; Lethe had been too preoccupied, but the way Eris and Yue rose slowly to standing . . . They could feel it now just as he did.

A shift in power.

The final stone was ready for extraction. . . . Riadne was late, and apparently for very good reason.

Arlo's gaze swept the room, searched out Lethe specifically; once finding him, she drew herself tall. And again, she needn't say anything. Lethe already knew what had brought her to them—and ah, but he did enjoy a hard-won triumph.

How long had he been working toward this?

How many years . . . how many threads . . . how many seeds planted and pawns primed? All the patience he'd had to observe to wait for this one small moment of—

"I accept your deal, Lethe," Arlo announced to the room's confusion, but oh . . . not his. Lethe unspooled from his couch; he rose with a grin—which stretched even wider when she added, "And I want to do it now."

———————————————————————

CHAPTER 43

Vehan

A KNOCK AT HIS DOOR—VEHAN sat up in bed.

It was well into the night, verging on morning, but he hadn't been able to sleep a wink yet. There was too much rolling through his mind for rest, a constant rotation of plans and concerns.

The dark magic that had been growing inside him, leeching off his core, had begun to throb on a constant basis; to flutter and squeeze even tighter around him in panic, as though it could tell the last stone had reached completion, and without a source of iron, could sense its course was nearing its end too.

How he'd managed to conceal from Riadne just how strong he'd become, he'd never know, but he was constantly topped up on electricity now to accommodate for his parasite. A few months of intensified training with that magic primed and running hot—it didn't take long for Vehan to realize, once feeling the difference, that he'd spent his entire life until now unwell and dangerously low on current, but that disadvantage had proven useful.

Because Vehan wasn't a Class Three wielder.

Vehan was easily a top-tier Four with promising elements of a Five, and a lifetime of mediocracy had probably helped him deflect his mother's attention in that department.

It would be useful later—the real strength of his magic—but this depended entirely on there being a later. Because his other concerns were the fact that they were *one frightening ceremony away* from his mother having all she needed to summon Ruin, and her array was still etched on his chest.

She would either succeed in swapping his heart for whichever of her surviving ironborn captives was unfortunate enough to be selected for the sacrifice—Vehan would become Ruin and then die—or she would fail, and Vehan *wouldn't* become Ruin, but like every other inviable host come the final summoning, he would still die.

Neither option sounded great, honestly.

Not to mention that dying would mean leaving Arlo behind on her own, and Aurelian . . . Vehan's death would *destroy* the boy he loved.

He didn't want that . . . but did he want Arlo to die in his stead?

She and Celadon and Lethe—they'd had a bit of a conference call about it, and Arlo had seemed somewhat hesitant, like she wasn't *completely* sold, which meant Celadon wasn't either, and Vehan even less so.

Arlo . . . swapping his role as Ruin for hers as a Hollow Star . . .

If it all went smoothly, it would actually work—but when had anything so far gone without a setback or a hitch? And he just couldn't get past the idea of Arlo dying in his place, no matter that she would be reborn as an immortal and that Celadon assured that, in his new reform, he'd establish a rule that would allow her to visit whenever she wished.

"Vehan?"

The door creaked open a fraction for a small, gentle voice to whisper through.

And Vehan blinked, sat up straighter, then threw his legs over his bed and crossed to his bedroom door in quick strides. Pulling it open revealed Arlo, and . . . someone else just behind her whom he didn't know. Dark brown hair and soft curves and big topaz eyes. She was part common faerie, whoever this was, judging by the feline cut of both her pupils and incisors, and the nails like claws on her hands. All he could say was that he was fairly certain she was a classmate in Arlo's lessons.

Ironborn—an alchemist in training; fodder for his mother's goals.

Both girls were in their pajamas, Arlo in pink silk, the other girl in green-and-sapphire plaid. Neither looked to have slept at all, though. In fact, Arlo looked somehow . . . different from the last time they'd spoken a couple of nights ago.

She was bright-eyed wild with a self-awareness he'd never seen in her, a burning intelligence in her gaze and the sort of exhilaration like she was on the edge of something either terrible or immense or both . . . and that made him snap to sharper attention. "Arlo . . . ," he breathed, then stepped aside to permit her through. "What's going on? Is everything okay?"

Arlo swept inside his room, pulling her friend along behind her.

When he closed the door, she turned, and it was then he noticed a tiny, clear ampoule of silvery liquid in one of her hands.

"I need your help."

Vehan frowned, not daring to even guess at what those words might mean—not daring to hope, as he did a little, that they meant she wanted to get out of what they had planned. "Help with what, Arlo?"

"I'd like to know the same myself." The girl behind her folded her arms over her chest and eyed Arlo with wariness, and a little bit more dislike. "Why have you pulled me out of my bed and inflicted us both on the High Prince? What's going on?"

And Arlo just stood there, staring up at Vehan, trusting him in a way people didn't often trust him—all Vehan had ever wanted was to be as great as their Eight Founders, as heroic and brave and good, but to Arlo, it was like he was already those things.

She ignored the girl's question, invoking a snort of irritation.

"We're friends, right?"

"Always," Vehan assured. "No matter what. Arlo, whatever's going on, whatever you need, it's yours. What can I do?"

"Something monumentally stupid, I think."

"Good thing that's my specialty." He looked at her closer—*something* was *different.* . . . "If this is about Lethe's plan . . ." He cut his gaze to the unknown girl, hesitant, not sure what he should say in front of her. "If you need an out—"

"Close," Arlo replied, as light as it was heavy with underlying meaning, and pressed her tiny vial into Vehan's palm. "If I asked you to trust me and not question why, would you do it, Vehan? Could you?"

She reached into her pocket, opened her other hand to reveal two more slate bracelets like the one she'd already given him back when they'd first discussed this plan; like the one she'd snuck to her father; like the one she currently wore that would take them all to safety. "Your mother succeeded in summoning the final stone. It's only a matter of hours now before she has everything primed to call Ruin, and our plan will have to be set in motion. But there's something I need to do before this is all over, and Vehan . . . I need you and Fyri both to keep this between us until our plan's seen through."

To Vehan she extended one bracelet.

To Fyri, who looked increasingly more confused the more Arlo spoke, she extended the other.

"A slight alteration. Will you hear me out?"

CHAPTER 44

Aurelian

~⌒~

WHEN THE LETTER ARRIVED, Aurelian had known that whatever cards Celadon had been keeping close—the reason his palace had been shut to the public for months; why rumor whispered a mere two days ago that he'd shown up unannounced in the Market again with Lethe in tow, and ever since the Madam had been equally closed to the world as well—whatever the new king of UnSeelie Spring had been planning, it was finally time to reveal his hand.

And Aurelian had no idea what he'd been expecting.

The letter—an invitation on thick pearl-white stock with deep black ink—requested his presence for the grand reopening of Celadon's Court; that should he accept by nightfall, a portal would be arranged for dusk the following day that would convey him straight to the palace reception for a private meeting of powers.

He wasn't the only person to receive one.

Precisely as outlined, come dusk Aurelian was joined outside the Market's front gate by Theodore, Ivandril, Nikos Chorley, Elyas, and Elexa.

A portal was opened, they all went through, and he had no idea what he'd been expecting . . . but it sure as hells wasn't this.

His first impression was that of darkness; it took his eyes a moment to adjust.

When they did, it was to the discovery that the Reverdie was gone—what replaced it was now something else entirely.

The floor was a solid ocean of obsidian glass, black and fathomless as the night, and stepping out onto it left Aurelian a bit disoriented at first, like his brain couldn't quite comprehend that he wouldn't sink right through it to drown in its depths. The only break in this illusion was the bold white sigil at the room's center: an enormous crescent moon with points as sharp as the bite of fangs, wrapped around a small white sun, that sun hollowed out to contain two things: a singular leaf and the ancient rune for *iron*.

Once upon a time, that rune had belonged to the ironborn when the Courts had embraced their alchemy.

This sigil, then . . . a unity of powers: UnSeelie, Seelie, ironborn, and . . . that leaf, what would Aurelian bet that leaf was a symbol of the Wild?

What was Celadon up to?

As below, so above—the ceiling that before had been enchanted to a moving forest canopy now reflected the shimmering sweep of night, the room's main source of light the hundreds upon thousands of stars twinkling against its deepest black, occasionally streaked by passing comets. On and off, stars fell in a shower, raining down a glittering dust that fizzled to dissolving as soon as it touched Aurelian's skin.

Gone were the statues of previous High Sovereigns.

Gone were the trees for pillars.

Gone were the offices, the business fronts, the Falchion headquarters.

The walls were solid black marble and moon-white archways that led off to Aurelian could only guess where. Twin elevators that used to be gold were now silver. The door to the throne room stood as massive as before but carved entirely out of gleaming moonstone and giving off its own luminescence.

It was a rather simple display for how pretty it also was.

Aurelian supposed he'd just been expecting *more*—and judging by the people around him, already gathered just ahead of his arrival, still arriving behind him, he wasn't the only one to feel this way.

"Is that a *vampire?*" Elyas whispered beside Aurelian, tugging his attention immediately off to his right.

Russet hair and high-flung cheekbones and a deeply familiar structure, the man folded against the far-right wall, alone and speaking to no one, looked like he could be a Viridian, was *definitely* a vampire, Aurelian concluded, when those claret eyes briefly met his inspection, and Aurelian was overcome with a swell of dark magic and death and an aura that smelled like blood.

So many others Aurelian didn't know—all manner of folk had been summoned tonight—but also Prince Alaric . . . Vehan's Winter-born cousin Dmitri. . . . Noticeably absent, though, was anyone from the Fae High Council, and what did that mean?

Motion broke him from his consideration of Celadon's guests.

The throne room's door eased open slowly.

No one exited to fetch them or signal them forward, and by the murmurs that rolled through the crowd around him, Aurelian gathered no one was very impressed by this—these people were clearly used to a certain amount of fuss, and it was a risky move to deny them their pageantry when Aurelian could only assume they were here because Celadon wanted something from them.

"Does he expect us to escort ourselves in?"

"Are we dogs to be called to attention at a whistle?"

Aurelian rolled his eyes.

He wasn't the first one to step forward though—Elyas beat him to it with his white-blond head held high, and just behind him, his mother.

The possibly Viridian vampire snorted, shook his head, and peeled off the wall, striding for the throne room too.

And once he did, the rest of the room seemed to take this as a challenge, where losing was anyone left behind when those doors swung closed again.

Sighing, Aurelian made to follow, fell into line behind an enormous man with the head of an elephant, his torso dressed in a crisp white suit and every appendage laden with gold jewelry.

He heard the gasps before he saw what caused them.

Celadon's reception hall was modest—beautiful but underwhelming by the standards of his reputation.

His throne room well exceeded them.

Aurelian entered a boundless expanse. More obsidian glass like black water for the floor, which stretched off on either side of him and poured like actual water in a cascade over the edges. There were no walls; instead, the floor narrowed off into a stretch of walkway seemingly suspended in the night sky. Wide-open space loomed overhead, swept with blacks and blues, silvers and whites of glittering stars, like the ceiling of the reception—but somehow, in here, the illusion was better, like they were actually out in night-drenched heaven.

And the halo glow from somewhere below . . . Aurelian didn't stray from his path, but from excited exclamations of those who'd crept to the edges, it was the burn of city lights far, far beneath them.

"The tower—look!"

"There's the palace!"

"We're standing above *Toronto.*"

In a marveling group, they walked the stretch of the room, passing massive columns of pure selenite, which held up nothing, but were enthralling in the way they shimmered and flashed at every angle.

In the beginning, Aurelian hadn't been able to see what they walked toward, only that the procession was moving to some end. Thankfully, the floor was wide enough for their mass to fan out once they reached the opposite end, a base of yet more obsidian steps.

One, two, four, eight levels elevated above them was Celadon's newly fashioned throne.

Made one moment from humming electricity, it morphed into glistening ice the next, then blustering wind, before hardening to earth that bloomed spring, those cheerful, fragrant flowers sparking to catch fire and flicker back into electricity to begin the cycle again.

An intentional nod to what had happened to his family? Aurelian couldn't say. Was a little too caught up in the young man seated on this throne to ponder it much at the moment. . . .

Celadon, smeared in shimmering white makeup, kohl dark around his eyes. Matte black lipstick and heels like liquid tar to match.

His robes were airy light, starlight white and flowing around him, laid over black leather pants and a matching shirt, onyx in a circlet atop his head . . . of hair enchanted as deep a black as the void of space above him.

It was almost like looking at an alternate-universe Riadne Lysterne.

Of its own accord, his gaze slid off to Celadon's left and traveled down to the man lazing in an insouciant sprawl on the gleaming steps. It took him a moment, threw Aurelian to register this man at last as Lethe in something other than his Hunter's attire.

The cloak was gone.

Lethe was . . . different; Aurelian almost didn't recognize him. It was simple magic to change the color of one's hair as Celadon had done. Folk did it constantly to keep up with trends and whims.

Somehow, he didn't think that was what had happened to Lethe's hair. It had seemed to be fading of late, and now it was shining as white as the moon that was suspiciously nowhere in sight in the enchanted sky . . . almost as though they were to infer that this symbol of strength was Celadon himself.

Still in tight-fitted leather and knee-high boots and so many silver buckles and chains and fastenings he looked like a character from one of Arlo's Final Fantasy games, Lethe was resting his weight on his elbows and looked . . . Aurelian would almost say he looked . . .

Happy.

Yet those acid eyes as they raked the crowd . . . Lethe was still deadly.

Celadon rose from his throne, and the moment he did—and Aurelian was sure most in the crowd didn't understand why since they couldn't feel, like Aurelian and the other gathered lesidhe could, the immense pressure of Celadon's aura, all that magic he'd inherited and had apparently been restraining, unleashed and on full display—the room bowed at his feet.

This.

This was what they'd tried to prevent in establishing the law that Heads of Courts couldn't procreate with other Heads. This was what the Courts feared would happen if one such offspring survived to adulthood.

This power. This command.

Slowly, Aurelian knelt as well—the last to do so—and once he did, Celadon finally spoke.

"Thank you all for your attendance tonight," he began in a smooth, clear voice. "I am sure, by now, you've heard quite a number of rumors. Questions of my character . . . my mental state . . . and I'm happy to divulge that, for the most part, the gossip you've all been spreading is true. Yes, I am the son of High Queen Riadne Lysterne and the late High King Azurean Lazuli-Viridian. Yes, I've inherited both their Crowning Gifts of Spring and Radiance. Yes, I've inherited those of Autumn and Winter as well. Yes, I am coming for your Courts."

That drew attention.

Several pairs of eyes darted up from the floor, and people began to rise in outraged shock, mumbling to themselves and their companions.

"We belong to a system built on corruption and deceit, on blood and stolen land, a hierarchy designed to benefit sidhe fae alone, often at the expense of our fellow folk and *certainly* of the ones who called our spaces home before we did. We belong to a government of manipulation and lies and horror the likes of which you couldn't begin to guess at. We've progressed admirably in many ways, achieved much in our years of unity, some of it even good—but we are long overdue for change. Change, therefore, will be my aim."

He paused a moment to let that statement take hold.

"Before I can turn work toward what's needed, though," he continued a moment later. "Before we can overturn our *esteemed* High Council, we first need to survive what's at hand. And so, before your powers as witness, I, Celadon Cornelius Fleur-Viridian Lysterne, declare war on High Queen Riadne Lysterne and set myself separate from her domain."

More murmurs now, more outrage . . . alarm . . . disbelief. A rustling like they couldn't believe what they were hearing, and one or two huffs of laughter like they refused to take Celadon as anything more than a boy shouting words he didn't understand.

Aurelian remained kneeling.

He was keenly aware of Lethe's gaze, the way he tracked every single person . . . and their reaction.

Meanwhile, Celadon continued undaunted—stronger, almost, for the room's growing doubt.

"This new system will require new leadership. Seelie, Wild, and ironborn thrones . . . these are the spaces I intend to fill, with folk who believe as I do that the Courts cannot be left to function as they have for all these years. For those of you who wish to reserve your judgment of me and my ambition; those who want no part in this; or those who would rather side with your High Queen . . ." He brushed a hand outward, and the door to the throne room swung open once more, but the space between reflected the room back at them like the glass of a mirror . . . or rather, the Egress. "I invite you now to take your leave."

A murmuring broke out in the crowd.

Heads turned and craned to survey reaction, dipped into low conversation with partners. A moment of tension, another, three—several folk broke off from the congregation. Cast wary nods to Celadon as they backed their way to the exit.

Aurelian, who knew none of them really, not beyond the superficial information he'd learned from his time as Vehan's steward, watched as one hesitated on the threshold—a fae Aurelian had seen before at parties in close company with Head Councillor Larsen. They bowed to Celadon, and Celadon inclined his head in return, and then just like that their group had whittled to considerably less, but Celadon didn't seem surprised or unhappy.

"Those of you who choose to stay," he began again when attention swiveled back to him. "Those of you who stand with me in support." Aurelian watched him open his arms, a smile blooming lovely across his face. "Welcome to the new Court of Night."

"You promised me Vehan's safety."

The words were out of Aurelian's mouth before he'd even recognized they were his. But he knew without looking that Vehan wasn't among this group.

There'd been no word of what was going on at the palace, and Riadne had to be close to creating her final stone, if she hadn't already. Celadon had *promised him* he had a plan to get Vehan to safety, but where was he right now?

As unflinchingly as Celadon peered down at him, Aurelian held his gaze. He rose back to standing. "You gave me your word, Night King, and I won't bend—neither does the Market, none of us. We won't kneel to you until you prove you can make good on your word. Tell me how you plan on delivering what you owe."

A bold statement.

Aurelian didn't exactly have the muscle to back that up—the Madam was suspiciously absent from this gathering, which had to mean something, but the Market was still hers. It didn't answer to Aurelian. Melora might have abandoned them to Nausicaä's wrath, but she was still the only one spending their money and efforts on supplying much-needed necessities right now, like food and training and medicine.

Aurelian couldn't offer any of that—or say why he even envisioned himself in her place of command at all.

Thankfully, beside him, Ivandril squared himself.

Shored up Aurelian's foolish claim by folding his arms over his chest and glowering up at Celadon. Theodore remained still, unmoving, but . . . perhaps in support of Aurelian's claim as well, he continued steadfast at his other side.

And Elyas . . . took a step backward to plant himself firmly in front of Aurelian. "I want Arlo and Vehan back as well," he said, his words like a challenge up at his uncle.

Celadon descended his throne.

CHAPTER 45

Arlo

*I*T'S STILL THE SAME *plan as before.*"

Arlo stood in the small, darkened study—a carpeted room with its curtains drawn, lined wall to wall with bookcases, nothing else in it but a quaint little group of armchairs upholstered in gold brocade arranged around an unlit marble fireplace.

It was strange to be staring at her exact likeness in something other than her mirror.

Fire-red hair, a soft smattering of freckles, jade-green eyes—Moros's vial had done a frighteningly good job of transforming Vehan into her, from what he'd been wearing right down to the aura of his magic, which had now completely vanished (and she had to hope this was because it now resembled hers too perfectly for her to detect). The moment Vehan had thrown back the contents of what she'd given him, he'd become Arlo Jarsdel entirely.

"We don't have much time," Vehan said hurriedly, casting a nervous glance at the closed door . . . then frowned in concentration. "Wow. I forgot how dull everything was back before Maturity; your hearing and eyesight are awful, Arlo."

Arlo rolled her eyes. "Thanks," she muttered, as she reached over to . . . a slight pause.

Now that the moment was at hand, she faltered.

How silly. She'd wanted nothing to do with this thing in the beginning; now it felt like tearing off a limb to give it away.

But there was no time to waste.

She could mourn this loss later.

Quickly, she stuffed her Hollow Star die into Vehan's pocket.

"Remember the plan," she warned. "Riadne promised I could use a wish to ensure I wouldn't die in summoning Ruin. Pull it out when she gives you the go-ahead, and I'll activate its magic from the altar. We'll use the pretense of wishing for safety while the die isn't yours yet to waste a wish on, and that's when we make the swap."

She shook out her cloak as she spoke and threw it quickly around her.

Arlo stood across from Vehan, who was holding her vial in one hand and one of the Viridian bracelets in his other; Fyri came up beside him with its twin. After convincing Celadon to use his status as king to make one last additional bracelet, and a good deal of tries, Arlo had replicated a spare all on her own.

A difficult alchemical task—it was flawless in every other way, perfectly unrecognizable as fake against the others if held beside it.

But fake nonetheless.

Her one act of betrayal.

She hoped one day they'd forgive her.

"We still need to wait for Ruin's ceremony. As far as I understand from my lessons, any of the ironborn still alive after the final Sin's been called into being will be viable candidates for Ruin. All that needs doing is to wait for them to begin to glow with calling to the titan, and as soon as they do, she's going to have us swap one of their hearts for yours.

"Honestly, if your magic were weaker, you'd probably die immediately from the shock of iron blood through your system so suddenly like that. But you're strong—she made sure you were strong—so you'll be okay, but your magic will start to fight back. It'll work to try to neutralize what shouldn't be there, which I'm sure Riadne has taken into account and will therefore combine both ceremonies into one—the transfer and the final summoning. I give us a couple of days, tops."

Even stranger than staring into a perfect replica of her face was the sensation of her own beginning to shift under her new cloak's magic.

Not hers yet, technically—she'd have to die to assert that claim—but Lethe had yielded it to help with the plan he *thought* she was following, and its alteration of her appearance began like a trickle of cool water poured over her head; washed down around her body; and turned to warmth in the spread of its wake, which seeped through her skin to her very bone.

Arlo gasped as tingling crept through her to grow and elongate her bones, to cut and narrow and trim and straighten different parts of her body. She caught a glimpse as Vehan's eyes widened to witness her features morph right in front of him—and it didn't hurt, but it felt . . . unusual. As quickly as it began, it ended, and Arlo reached up to feel her jaw.

"Did it work?" she whispered—and startled herself; goodness!

Her voice was much deeper now, not hers at all but Vehan's to exactness.

As soon as he made to reply, they were interrupted by the guards. The study's door was wrenched open, revealing the fae who'd been sent to escort them down to Riadne's laboratory. The guards looked thoroughly unimpressed and, just as Arlo had been counting on, not surprised in the least by what they clearly assumed was a poor attempt at a last-ditch effort to escape.

"You'll take this vial. It's the one Moros gave me. The one we already planned on you drinking to transform your appearance into mine for a short period of time. We'll still wait for the guards to come to collect us both and bring us down to Riadne to start Ruin's summoning. We'll still stage a brief escape attempt and head for the same designated place if we can—if not, then we'll find somewhere private on our own to swap our appearances."

Fyri watched them speak with a closed-off expression, her thoughts entirely her own, no hint of whether she'd agree to any of this, but Arlo had faith.

They didn't know each other all that well, but she understood on a fundamental level what her classmate wanted.

The same thing that Arlo wanted—to survive; to protect.

Vehan studied the vial a moment longer, his reservations heavy behind his expression, and Arlo could tell he was still trying to figure out a way to spare her from this.

He would be so upset with her when he realized her deception, but there was no way else around it.

This was what she had to do.

What she'd always been meant to do, her entire life. Furthermore, it was what she chose to do.

"Yes," Vehan said at last, lifting his gaze to hers. "That's all the plan . . . but I still don't like trading my life for yours. And I know you and Celadon have talked this over, but he can't be as okay with this as he's pretending. He could rewrite as many laws as he wants to make it possible for you to visit when you're immortal, but you're still his cousin. . . . He still loves you. . . . I love you too, Arlo."

Sighing, Arlo took a step forward like approaching a wounded animal in the woods. "You can absolutely refuse this, Vehan. I'll text Celadon, he'll whisk us out of here using these bracelets, and we'll find another way. But this is our best and most immediate solution—who knows what else we'll lose to any more wasted time. It's my choice, too. I'm the one who has to do the dying. Vehan . . . please? I'm asking you to trust me."

"Come on, you two," said the guard on the left, jerking her chin in the direction of the hall, her companion clearing the way to let them through.

Together, Arlo and Vehan exited the study.

"Did you really think that would work?" the other asked, punctuating his question with a snort, because surely they couldn't have been that foolish. "There's no running from your mother, Your Highness. What she wants is what she gets. You're better off giving it without a struggle; now, are you two going to behave, or should we escort you both in chains?"

"Apologies," said Arlo, doing her best to sound and act like Vehan, since their question had really been aimed more at the prince. "That won't be necessary."

Vehan dipped his head as well, murmured a quiet, "Sorry," as she would have done, and their journey continued.

She swallowed her reservations, the part of her that didn't want to do this, because this lie she had to tell next . . . It would come with heavy consequence.

But tell it she would have to do to bring this all to an end.

"Please? I won't pretend this plan isn't dangerous. I won't pretend I'm not scared. There's a million ways this could all go wrong, and even if it goes right . . . But I still want to do it. I still want to trade my role as Hollow Star for yours as Ruin, Vehan. Once Riadne gives the go-ahead, I'll make the wish. Your array, the dark magic, all of it gets transferred to me. You'll be touching the array on the floor when the swap is made. I can easily make it look like you performing the magic. And same for when the summoning happens—I won't need to do much but picture it all in my head to get it going."

Ruin would then be summoned.

As Lethe's plan went, Arlo's soul, bound to immortality, was now made of stronger stuff and would take more effort to extinguish—effort Ruin wouldn't have just yet, so newly reborn into the world. Unable to be forced from her own heart completely, but equally unable to ascend to her Hunter afterlife until she officially died, she'd linger long enough in her body for Celadon to summon them all back to UnSeelie Spring, where he and Lethe waited with her mother's remade sword that Arlo had given them, just in time to run her through with it, killing both her and Ruin inside her in one fell swoop.

Vehan was studying her, hesitating on something. Suddenly, his mouth fell closed, his expression turned grim, and he placed his hands firmly on Arlo's shoulders.

"You remember, don't you?"

Arlo nodded softly. "I remember. I challenged Lethe and I won, and he returned my memories to me. No one else knows the full truth of what he sealed away yet; Lethe gave power over that to me, and to break the spell over that knowledge, all I have to do is verbally claim my name. Which I'm not doing, not just yet, because . . . Yeah. I remember, Vehan. And I remember there's something I have to do before this is all over."

It was Fyri who broke the silence that had swelled up to take over the conversation.

"What are the bracelets for?"

She held hers up to glint in the light, and it was now or never—Arlo had to take the plunge.

To lie, and hope no one noticed.

"My alteration. The thing I want you guys to keep secret without questioning why. I asked Celadon to make two more for me. Vehan, when we swap appearances, I would like you to give that one to Nausicaä. Riadne has her so occupied right now that I can't do it myself, but she'll be at the ceremony, and I just need to know that Nausicaä will be okay, will for sure be safe from anything Riadne might do before Nos could manage to teleport over."

Almost all of the plan was still the same.

Once Arlo succeeded in summoning Ruin into herself, Vehan would touch his bracelet. Would focus his magic on reaching for Celadon and speak "termonn," and that would be all the signal Celadon would need to act. To pull them to safety, Nausicaä now too.

But who they'd be leaving behind . . .

"Fyri," she said, turning now to her classmate. "Celadon's trying to reorganize the Courts. He's trying to make our future better, but to do that, we need to have a say—we, the ironborn, who've been neglected and abused by the system for so long. I would like you to take this bracelet and escape with us back to Celadon's protection. You told me once that you knew what it meant to bear the ironborn struggles. You've been trained by the best, seen the worst, and you're incredibly powerful. Nikos isn't strong enough in alchemy, and Leda doesn't want the position—she barely wants to be involved in any of this. I can't think of anyone better to be the one to *stand as our leader, in what's to come, than you. I've already told Celadon that you're my choice for the role, and he's agreed to bring you in to talk possibilities."*

Down the halls . . .
Into Riadne's private office . . .
Through the already open columbarium . . .
A part of Arlo was terrified.

It was one thing to entertain this plot in her head and another to walk into Riadne's laboratory, where everything—the fixtures and tables and instruments and books—had been cleared from the room, leaving only the altar and the philosopher's stone array etched into the floor around it.

Power thrummed in her veins.

Knowledge fed answers to questions she'd barely finished forming in thought.

Arlo was terrified about what she planned to do, but she also felt for the very first time in so many years like she was finally *awake.* Like a film had been over her eyes, and at long last it had peeled away to reveal the world in stunningly clear high-definition, hers to rediscover.

"You want me to give this bracelet to Nausicaä, and you don't want me to say anything to anyone about it. For some reason, it sounds like you're asking so much more than just that."

Vehan looked down at her.

Arlo looked up.

They held each other's stare for a minute that felt like an hour before Arlo nodded—once, but resolute. "My whole life I've been a side charac-ter to my own story. I was made to forget who I was, shut out from my family, led to believe I was powerless, weak, that I couldn't do anything but keep my head down and follow along, hope to keep out of the way of better people. This is what I choose, Vehan. This is me taking back control. Please, just trust me. Just this one secret, only for a short while."

There was something she needed to do—something only she could do before this was all over. And if she needed to become what Magic had suggested back when they first came to her the night after the Solstice . . . that hint that it took just as much bravery to be the villain . . . If that's who Arlo had to become to get this done, then so be it.

A look passed behind Vehan's gaze, soft and sorrowful and . . . understanding. To a degree. At least of what it was like to want just once to have control of one's own life.

"What do you want me to say? When I slip this to her."

Nausicaä wouldn't be happy about any of this when she came back to herself. But she'd done what she needed to do and trusted that Arlo would still be there for her when it was over. Arlo could only hope for the same in return.

"Whatever you need to say to get her to take it and put it on." Fishing a folded-up piece of paper out of her pocket, she handed it to Vehan—Nausicaä's letter, the one she'd left on Arlo's bedside, with a small addition to the end: Arlo's reply. "But if you don't mind, you could also remind her that we started this together; we'll finish it together, too."

"Vehan—to me," Riadne commanded from her place across the room, on the opposite side of the array they'd entered to.

"Yes, Mother," Arlo replied. Back straight, head held high—one last look at Vehan, who nodded softly back at her—Arlo complied with the High Queen's command and took her first step over that line of bravery straight into the realm of foolishness.

"Arlo, you may make your wish."

CHAPTER 46

Celadon

H E'D NEVER ONCE BROKEN a promise he'd made—he didn't intend to start now.

Celadon descended from his throne, gaze pinned on Aurelian's molten-gold glare all the while. His robes trailed in a train down the steps behind him; the enchanted night's sky dimmed darker as stars shrank back as though cowering from his passing. All for effect—he was good at putting on a performance when it was expected of him; even better when it wasn't.

Fae thought so highly of themselves. They didn't often bend to people who didn't intimidate them out of an inflated sense of self-importance. Aurelian had no such temper; Celadon could run at him teeth bared and sword poised, and the young man wouldn't flinch from what drove him, kept him steady. But none of this had been to impress *him*, anyhow.

There was only one path Aurelian would follow, one person who'd ever hold any sway over him.

And Celadon admired that, really.

Aurelian had always known himself; through everything, he remained the same.

But it did mean that Aurelian—an important piece, both Theodore and Lethe agreed, for how naturally others followed him—would be rather easily won over.

"I promised you Vehan," Celadon agreed and, when he reached Aurelian, paused.

He flung his hand in the direction of the exit, currently connected to the portal of his Egress, and the image it reflected changed.

Cityscape and bustling traffic, pedestrians weaving down the sidewalks in great packs—Yonge-Dundas Square. The Viridian Circle, where Sentinels stood, always at the ready, primed to protect Celadon and his blood.

If only there'd been time . . . If only his father would have pulled his family to safety, things might not have gone the way they did, but there was no use dwelling on what could have been. Celadon was king now, attempting to launch a new Court, and if he showed even the slightest bit of weakness, the ones standing in wait for him to fail would eat him alive with glee—and that would be the least of his problems.

"The final stone has already been summoned—"

The carefully selected powers he'd gathered broke under this announcement like a dam, flooding the room with yet more murmurs, but Celadon paid attention to nothing but the shock-turning-fury on Aurelian's face. "I've been informed that, as we speak, Riadne begins to summon Ruin."

"You *promised*," Aurelian snarled, launching forward.

Clearly he'd intended to take Celadon by the front of his robes, to snarl something else in his face, but Lethe was faster—Lethe, who'd changed so much in the short span of time since he'd come to accept that Celadon hadn't been lying; that he was safe now; that within these halls, he would *always* be safe; and it wasn't just his hair's return to shimmering white that reflected this.

Lethe, armed with Thalo's sword, which he pointed at Aurelian's throat from over Celadon's shoulder . . .

That rumble of a fae growl sounded deep in Aurelian's chest. He stood . . . so much more intimidating himself these days, with all that muscle and sharper awareness of how to use it. "Call off your dog," he spat at Celadon.

Celadon lifted his head.

Squared his jaw just a *bit* unfriendly. "Lethe's no pet. Mind how you speak to the God of Misfortune. And I never said I wouldn't deliver what you want from me, Aurelian. Ruin is being summoned, and our plan is underway. All you need to do at this moment is trust *them*—Vehan and Arlo. Arlo, who, after all she's done for you and your prince, I do think you owe belief in right now, if my word has come to mean so little."

Aurelian's anger extinguished in an instant.

It didn't snuff out without a trace—hints of it lingered like smoke from the wick, and he continued to glare at Celadon.

"Do you trust her?" Celadon repeated, firmer.

And Aurelian nodded like defeat. "I do."

"Good," Celadon said, clipped. "Because it's time we make for our final stage. We don't want to be late."

CHAPTER 47

Arlo

~⁓~

HERE WAS NO HESITATION when Arlo arrived at the altar in the middle of the array and quietly proceeded to lift herself onto its flat stone surface and lie down.

"Are you ready, Arlo?" Lethe asked, turning in place to face her.

They stood, the pair of them, at the center of their practice arena, the only place in the Luminous Palace she'd spent more time in lately than the classroom and Riadne's lab.

No, Arlo wasn't ready, and doubted she ever would be. Yes, she was ready—as much as she was going to be, because this had to be done, and she'd come this far; there was no way she'd turn back now.

Not with that what-if *burning inside her and the sense that this was where she was meant to wind up all along.*

Unable to speak, Arlo nodded.

Planting his boots in the dusty earth, Lethe widened his stance. "Have you made your wish? With the clear parameters that you desire to beat me in physical combat and claim my position in the Wild Hunt?"

Arlo nodded again. She had—as soon as Lethe had sent her to her rooms to gather what she'd need, with instructions on what specifically to ask the die for before meeting him in the arena.

"Very good." Lethe grinned at her. "Then all you have left to do is issue your formal challenge. Speak the words, and the fight begins—but one last warning: I won't be pulling any punches. By rule, I must defend my mantle to the best of my ability, no holding back. Are you sure this is what you want?" The grin sharpened into something a touch deadlier and infinitely more frightening. "Wish or not, defeating me will be no easy task."

Lifting her chin, straightening her posture, planting her stance a little surer as well, Arlo replied, "This is what I want. Lethe, I challenge you to physical combat for your place in the Wild Hunt."

"Lovely," he purred, and slashed his claw-tipped hand through the air.

On the down of its swing, those claws elongated, melded together, fashioning themselves into a long, deadly blade that sliced through the earth like butter.

"Arlo, you may make your wish—only the wish that I approved, mind; Nausicaä will be watching to tell me if you stray."

Disguised as Arlo, Vehan approached the outer rim of the array.

Reached into his pocket.

She could tell he was nervous—there was so much about this plan that could go wrong, and nothing about the room that was at all comforting. Ironborn and alchemists and Riadne's personal council stood in the shadowy offing, dressed in dark robes and holding candles, burning incense, and droning in low, creepy voices, "*mors tua, vita mea*"—your death, my life.

There were Arlo's classmates, the ones who hadn't been used to summon stones, pale in their silent terror and situated at strategic points around the array. No saving them; this would already cost so much, and Arlo couldn't bear it, but at least . . . she didn't see Fyri.

Riadne would take it as cold feet, Fyri fleeing, and probably had guards already sent out to find her—but it would be too late. Fyri was talented, could keep herself hidden long enough for Celadon to summon her to safety, so long as their plan kept on track.

She wished she could have done something for the others—more bracelets, but they weren't meant to be doled out like that, would stretch the magic that fueled them too thin. She wished they would have done something for themselves, left while they still had the chance, but there they were, and there was Arlo's father standing apart from them, watching along the wall. There was Nausicaä, arms folded and gaze fixed on Vehan, as though she could tell something was off about him—or rather, Arlo—but couldn't quite pin what.

On her wrist glinted the slate bracelet Vehan had successfully slipped to her.

Arlo had overheard in passing as Nausicaä had taken hers with a dull thanks. For a brief moment, Arlo had worried that she might simply pocket it, but—a bit of luck—there it was, dark against the gold that leafed her skin, and her father wore his too.

Then there was the array itself—Riadne's seven stones had been set into seven slots in the floor, all at strategic points of the array's main ring. Ironborn blood filled the grooves that carved every single ring and symbol and equation of this darkest magic.

"Arlo?" Riadne prompted, raising a brow at her pause.

On the altar, Arlo cleared her throat, snapped Vehan out of his thoughts and into action to pull out Luck's die.

At the same time, Arlo closed her eyes, pictured the die in her mind.

The world clunked to a standstill, faded to gray.

Luck had assured in their conversation that this would work, that Moros's gift would be strong enough to fool even fortune. None were left in motion to witness or hear what happened at this moment—none except Vehan, disguised so deeply as Arlo that even her die was confused about who to respond to, and of course Nausicaä, watching Vehan oh so closely for a sign of the something she suspected was off.

A good thing, then, that Arlo had been practicing that function she'd learned in the grotto on her first-ever date with her girlfriend.

How to use her die without physically holding it.

In the air between them, their options appeared.

Roll, Assist, Escape, Two.

If Nausicaä thought anything of Arlo's wishes having dwindled by one more point than she last recalled them being, she didn't say. Only watched, and continued watching, as aloud, Vehan said, "I wish to survive the toll of summoning Ruin."

In her mind, Arlo forced her will to seize the die in full from Vehan and declared instead, I wish to swap my role as Hollow Star for Vehan Lysterne's role as Ruin's vessel.

Vehan reached out, pretending toward the number two; Arlo pictured selecting it. The number shattered into a shower of glitter, and she couldn't describe this feeling, the sudden sensation of something beginning to drain from her very being.

On the altar, she wanted so desperately to shiver with the chilling sensation. Wanted to cry out in pain as a searing began to cut away at her chest, just above her heart.

But she had to hold herself still, as still as she'd tried to keep throughout the whole exchange. It hadn't taken much to coax her cloak into fading her out to gray as she should have been if she were really Vehan, but she couldn't move until the world clunked back into gear.

Hold it . . .

Hold it . . .

Tears gathered in the corners of her eyes when the last of Luck's favor left her completely and transferred itself to Vehan; when the philosopher's stone array finished carving itself on its new mark. But Nausicaä was watching, and she couldn't let her see. . . .

At last the world regained its color, its motion.

Riadne turned a look to Nausicaä—Nausicaä nodded her head.

All was well.

Their first hurdle passed.

"Relax, my son," Riadne called across to her. "This will all be over soon."

Like Vehan would have survived this.

Like she truly believed her son's soul would have been strong enough to contend with Ruin, leaving any bit of him alive to be anything of what he'd once been.

"Arlo," she added, turning her electric gaze on Vehan. "When the prince is in position, you may begin."

For a moment, it seemed like Vehan had forgotten everything he was supposed to do.

He stood there, wide-eyed in shock, staring back at Riadne as though he couldn't comprehend what she'd said. And Arlo felt a panic tug at her nerves.

"Arlo," she called across to him. "You've got this. It's okay."

Vehan stared another moment . . . then thankfully came back to himself. "Right." He nodded and, without hesitation, lowered himself to the floor.

Lethe came at her like the whole of the cosmos crashing down over her head.

She'd seen him fight—sparred with him numerous times, and the mock bit of battle between him and Celadon in Riadne's Crystal Atrium had been impressive. But all of it paled in comparison to what flew at her now, leaving Arlo suddenly and completely *aware of why even Nausicaä, so skilled with a weapon herself, was afraid of him.*

A wish spent on boosting her ability great enough to overcome his and still all *Arlo could do at the moment was raise her own sword to block him.*

Not the one her mother had given her and Mab had enchanted—this was an ordinary sword from the armory; her goal hadn't been to kill him. But now she wondered if maybe she could have used that extra edge against this, an immortal who fought like the god of war, or rather instead like the god of greatest misfortune—hers. He was wholly unconquerable.

Lethe lunged.

He struck.

He jabbed.

He feigned one direction just to swing to another faster than Arlo could blink.

All this time he'd been grooming her for this, teaching her his moves, and Arlo had been so foolish to believe that would be enough, but seeing them in proper action—the speed and dexterity and deftness with which Lethe moved . . .

Arlo dove.

Arlo blocked.

Arlo attempted to parry.

Their blades clashed in the air between them, and Lethe leaned in between the cross of them to snarl, "You're fighting it. You won't even last, let alone defeat me, if you keep fighting against your wish."

Relaxing into it was easier said than done, though.

Instinct made Arlo's heart flutter, made her reckless, made it so hard to focus on anything other than this sharp bit of metal flying at her from every direction, and now she realized the other reason Lethe had made her train.

Less impact from what she'd wished for, sure, but also . . . familiarity.

It was so difficult to trust herself right now and let her wish take effect—it would have been impossible without any inkling of what to do.

Lethe threw his weight against the swords, and Arlo stumbled backward—tripped, fell flat on her back, sprawled breathlessly on the dirt, sweating profusely, pale and trembling and exhausted to the bone.

A Luck-given wish, and it hadn't been enough.

Barely minutes into this challenge, and with all the help in the world, Arlo still couldn't contend with the enormity glaring down at her.

"You really won't try? Is this who you are, Arlo Jarsdel?" He crouched over her, reached his free hand to ball the front of her shirt in his fist and heave her upper body closer to the disgust that soured his features. "With all my effort and every advantage in your corner? Then I guess Arlo Jarsdel really is no one. She prefers to spend her life safe and tucked in the shadows of other people's greatness—poor, defenseless, pathetic Arlo." A sneer tugged at the upper lip of his wide mouth. His antifreeze-green eyes pierced her like daggers. "How long you've been moping around the palace," he spat, "convinced that responsibility for your mother's death fell on your shoulders. You know what?" He pulled her even closer, so close that their noses touched. "This is the first time I actually believe it."

And something inside Arlo roared.

Vehan placed the fingers of both his hands on the array's outer ring, primed and ready to go at command.

The chanting grew louder.

Arlo cast one last look at him. At her father. At Nausicaä—where it lingered, and something inside her cracked, because this . . . would be upsetting to her girlfriend. This would scare her. This was dangerous, and Nausicaä had worked so hard to keep Arlo safe, but here Arlo was, throwing herself headfirst into death.

Please, she begged in her head to any deity listening. *Please let her forgive me when this is all over.* And. *Please let this plan work.*

And.

I love you, Nausicaä Kraken.

Arlo lay properly back on the altar, allowing her eyes to close.

She tuned out the chanting, pulled herself from the dizzying cloud of smoke and incense meant, she realized, to relax nerves and mood.

And waited for this horror to begin.

With force that could belong only to magic, Arlo threw herself against Lethe, knocking him off from on top of her.

She didn't spare any time to watch him roll to his feet and arm himself bright-eyed and laughing once more.

Arlo snatched her sword from the ground—felt magic pulling at her like her body was connected to a host of strings. Before, she'd been too anxious to give herself over to its tug, but now . . .

Arlo swung a blow Lethe only just dodged in time.

He swung back, and Arlo blocked it with a resounding clang—spun in place to kick him in the side and crumple him to his left, where she spun again to meet him with her blade.

More and more, it became Lethe only barely keeping up with what Arlo aimed at him.

She lunged . . . struck . . . jabbed . . . feinted, every one of Lethe's moves pitted against him, and she could see how it delighted and frustrated him in turns, because this was what he'd wanted . . . but how long had it been since Lethe had last tasted defeat?

One of Riadne's alchemists approached her on the altar.

He raised a hand armed with a scalpel and pulled aside what appeared to be Vehan's clothing to reveal his chest.

The cloak's magic was a marvel, really. Arlo's disguise remained firmly intact, precise down to the angry sapphire it painted the newly carved array on her chest with instead of iron red.

Two more alchemists approached the altar to pin Arlo's hands at her sides. One more at her feet. The alchemist with the scalpel leaned in, and agony spread like fire through her, tensing in her muscles.

She couldn't conceal her cry this time as a fresh array was added to her skin—the one that would allow them to exchange her heart for that of the ironborn boy they tugged from his dwindled ranks.

She had to act fast.

The alchemist lowered his scalpel, and Arlo blinked herself through the pain, focused her thoughts—there was no time to spare. She had to counteract what the alchemist was doing before he could complete the transfer. She wasn't compatible, not with the boy they'd chosen for *Vehan's* blood type and not for what she intended for after.

A swell of blue light—the alchemist activated her array, and the boy began to squirm, to cry, to clutch his chest.

Arlo felt the effects as well. Not nearly as acutely as she'd felt that carving on her skin, but it certainly wasn't comfortable. She had to act fast, but it was a balance in performance—too fast, and they'd be suspicious; too slow, and her heart truly would be swapped. Then she'd die as soon as she removed this cloak, its magic reverting Vehan's blood type back to hers.

A moment became two, ticked into three . . .

Finally, Arlo pressed back.

Closed her eyes and, just as she'd done to the array sealing Hieronymus Aurum's factory, pictured the second array on her chest dissolving, overriding the alchemist's power to wipe it clean from her skin.

For another moment, there was only confusion.

Riadne stepped closer. "Did it work?" she asked, peering around her alchemists to her son's chest, bare save what had always been there.

The alchemist frowned in thought.

It hadn't worked, of course. Undoubtedly he knew something was off, but they had only minutes to spare before impending heart failure. Before the iron blood in the boy's heart ran its course through Vehan and was replaced by a sort the organ wasn't accustomed to dealing with, and vice versa for the boy. Not enough time to examine anything too closely . . .

"Your Majesty, I'm not sure . . ."

And it was too easy.

To let up on a bit of her disguise. To allow her own black-light glowing beneath to start filtering through, light that had flared to life inside her the moment she'd switched her fate with Vehan's.

"A success," the alchemist declared with relief, and Riadne nodded her own.

Stepped back in line.

Called to Vehan across the way, "You may begin, Arlo. The prince is ready."

Good luck, she willed to Vehan as she watched him close his eyes.

She allowed her own to close once more as well.

How easy this was too. Arlo pictured Ruin's array in her mind, its every detail down to the exact shade of the blood that filled its grooves, the way candlelight glinted off the Seven Sins planted around its edge. She trusted Vehan to do his part, to make a good show of pretending it was him activating the array—gritting his teeth and stiffening under the drain of such terrible magic like everyone expected she should feel.

But really . . . this was laughably easy.

Arlo reached for her magic, and it leaped to meet her fingers—to bend to her bidding, placing itself in full trust of her knowledge and control, because Arlo was master of both now. Between memory and the wish she'd made back in Riadne's Courtyard, what had started this all . . . Arlo didn't have power, she *was* power, and she didn't blame her father for what he'd done to try to protect her, but there was no denying how good it felt to be completely *her* again.

Still Arlo—still herself—but an Arlo who now knew exactly what she needed to do . . . and wasn't afraid to face it.

Because this . . .

This was all *familiar.*

Arlo pictured the array in her mind, basked a moment in its blue-glowing light, then reached out with her magic; she touched it to the array. As soon as it began to hum with life, a voice—baritone rich, sepulchered in dark amusement, so great it vibrated through her like rumbling thunder—spoke into her mind. "Hello, Flamel," it purred, it chuckled, it dripped like poisoned honey. It was so very, very amused—and happy. "What a long time it's been. I was hoping it would be *you.*"

Arlo stood over Lethe, who lay sprawled on the dirt, her sword pointed at the soft of his throat; he looked up at her with pride . . . with relief . . . with tears in his eyes that made him a little too real for her liking, less like some aloof, untouchable god and more like a young man not all that much older than Cel.

Like he'd been waiting all this time for someone to help him.

"It will hurt," he rasped when Arlo removed her sword and held her hand out to him instead; pulled him up to standing, panting just as harshly as he.

She looked up at him, confused by the statement. "What will hurt?"

Lethe's claws separated, retracted back to their usual form. The hand he'd used to take hers lifted to her temple, and an expression fluttered too briefly across his face for Arlo to be certain it was any one thing, but she thought perhaps it might be an apology.

"Close your eyes, Arlo. It's time to give back what was taken from you. I'll also let you choose: I can return your memories but keep concealed the truth that the Courts had expunged from common knowledge until you desire it revealed at a more . . . opportune moment; all you'd have to do to release the knowledge to the world is verbally claim your

name. *If you'd rather, though, I can yield my keeping of both right now.*"

Oh.

Her memories . . . Lethe was going to give them back; she'd finally remember whatever he'd taken, and why, and . . . it frightened her a little. What if she didn't like the Arlo Jarsdel she really was?

You've got fire inside you. Woe betide whoever tries
to put it out.

It was the happiest day of my life when I gave birth
to you, and I am proud of the person you've become.

You're something else, Arlo Jarsdel. But you're also
weird as fuck.

I'm still your friend. I will always be your friend. And
as your friend, I'm not going anywhere.

"What do you choose, Arlo?"

And Arlo lifted her chin.

She was Arlo Jarsdel, and whatever that meant, she'd been through so much already—had come out the other side of it changed for sure, but despite it all . . . she was still her. All she could do was trust in herself.

"Just the memories for now, please." No sense in letting Riadne in yet on what she could do and run the risk of foiling her own plan.

Lethe nodded. "Again, I apologize. It really will hurt."

He pressed his fingers harder against her skin, and Arlo's mouth opened to . . .

Screaming—it tore from her; this was pain unlike anything she'd ever felt.

It ate at her vision, threatened to drag her into the safety of unconsciousness. She felt her body arch off the stone, twist and writhe and tremble against the pure agony of dark magic sweeping through to claim her.

Dying was agony.

She couldn't tell what was happening around her.

There were voices, there was commotion, there was a lot of black-tinted light, and the baritone laughter in her head was beginning to lighten, to take on the lilt of *her* voice.

It was all she could do to keep herself conscious, breathing; to not let go of the array in her mind and picture it, picture it, picture it glowing.

But it hurt so bad, and tears streamed down Arlo's face—something warm and sticky trickled from her nose, crested the groove of her lips and tasted like bitter copper.

More voices—more commotion; Arlo cracked an eye.

She could only just make out through clouding vision her classmates dead—their energy all used up to withering in order to power such a powerful array. Vehan standing, his disguise holding strong, and he looked back at her with a mixture of agony too, of pain and sorrow and fierce determination to see this through to the end.

Because he was Vehan Lysterne, and she was Arlo Flamel—and no one decided their destinies but them.

See you soon, she bade to him. Tried to say aloud but didn't really know if the words made it past her lips.

She smiled—more a grimace through screaming—when commotion exploded into confusion as Vehan simply *vanished,* as though pulled by some invisible hook. And Nausicaä staggered forward, just to vanish as well . . . Rory next, and Arlo kept smiling . . .

And screamed, and screamed, *and how had none of this drawn attention? Or maybe it had, she couldn't tell; she was in such shredding agony that Arlo could hardly keep conscious.*

Memories upon years upon years upon memories—it all came flooding back.

Arlo and her parents . . . the beautiful home they'd lived in together, tucked away in one of Toronto's old-money-wealth suburbs.

Arlo and Rory, a wildly intelligent man, so bright with passion and always returning home at the end of the day with some scrape or another, Thalo scolding him in all her fondness for getting up to no good with Nikos again.

Arlo and her mother . . . all of them together . . . cozied up as they read to her; Arlo sprawled on the floor with her drawings . . .

It was agony that had torn these things from her, like pages from a book. It was agony that stitched them back into the binding. It was—

"Arlo, no!"

"GET BACK—GET AWAY FROM HER! ARLO, COME HERE, DON'T LOOK AT THEM, NO!"

It was—

"You may call me the End."

"And I the Beginning."

"GET AWAY FROM MY DAUGHTER!"

It was—

"We're only asking she chooses—"

It was everything leading up to that once crucial moment when eight-year-old Arlo learned that nothing indeed was more dangerous than a fairy tale . . . especially the ones the Courts had invented to keep them from the truth.

All the people she cared about, they would be safe. Vehan; her father; Fyri, the ironborn future in her hands, with the additional bracelet Arlo had asked Celadon to make; Nausicaä with Arlo's original bracelet, swapped out for the fake that Arlo currently wore on her wrist.

Everyone safe who could be saved—that was what mattered.

Arlo smiled through her screaming, and screaming, and screaming; smiled despite all her pain and rage; felt even more conviction for what she had to do.

Smiled . . . and screamed, like song; like a grim vow no longer hollow but sunken—right down to Riadne's level.

"You want a war, Riadne Lysterne?" she gritted out through her teeth, and knew without a doubt that Riadne heard. "I started the greatest war this realm has ever seen, and now I'll be the one to end it—me. Arlo Flamel."

It fell like a cloth dropped to the floor—unceremonious, wholly, instant.

Arlo had claimed her name aloud, and the magic concealing the truth . . . it fell.

Unceremonious.

Wholly.

Instant.

And Arlo *screamed.* At last, the chance to make this right, everything that woman had done; everything the Courts had done; everything the Immortal Realm had conspired for their return . . .

Arlo would make *all* of it right.

She remembered now, what it was the End and the Beginning had asked of her future, and Arlo would be the one to put it all right, would take destiny into her hands and change it.

But first, for Riadne, who thought this was what she'd wanted . . . who thought things like the Bone Crown and Sins and Ruin would be anything but tools to wield against her; who'd spent all this time underestimating what it meant to be Arlo's enemy . . .

Arlo would make things right, oh yes, but first, she'd make them so much *worse.*

EPILOGUE

Arlo

Flamel Residence—Toronto, Ten Years Prior

PLACING HER PIECE OF chalk on the ground beside where she knelt, Arlo stood at long last to examine her creation.

It was perfect—at least compared to what she kept seeing in her head. An array that would get her into a lot of trouble for drawing it out like this; Dad hadn't been too happy to see it that one day back in his office when she first began to doodle its outline, and he'd forbidden her from it after.

She didn't like doing things she wasn't supposed to.

She didn't like making Dad upset.

But this array, it just wouldn't leave her alone. It was there every time she went to bed. It was there when she woke up. She'd seen it in shapes in the books she read, on the playground, at school. On the days Lethe would turn up, and she always liked when he did—he was funny, and not at all good with kids, and she didn't like getting into trouble, but sometimes he would let her get away with things when her parents weren't looking, give her a pat on the head when he caught her and then pretended it hadn't happened.

But he didn't like her thinking about this array either.

You put that away, Arlo. That's not a thing little alchemists should be playing around with.

But Arlo wasn't playing.

The array was all drawn out—there was a reason she kept seeing it, that it wouldn't leave her alone. Ever since stumbling across its components in Dad's many books, the ones all written out by some unknown hand in a code that made perfect sense to her now that she'd figured out its key, a key he hadn't yet learned.

It was finished. It was perfect. She just wanted to see what it would do. The book called it a portal.

Not a dangerous one, just something that would act like a magic mirror in that Snow White movie her parents had watched with her—or that's what the books made it seem like. That's what all these symbols suggested. Nothing could get through; something just wanted to talk!

It would be rude to ignore it.

Her parents would have to understand. They'd been the ones to teach her it was impolite to ignore someone when they were speaking to her, as sometimes happened when she got caught up with symbols and reading.

Wiping her hands on her coverall dress, rolling her sleeves up to her elbows, Arlo repositioned herself at the very base of her array and got back down on her knees.

Mom and Dad were busy upstairs, in some meeting with other grown-ups that she wasn't allowed to join, and normally she would still try to spy, but this was her only chance.

To find out what whoever this array let her speak to wanted from an eight-year-old girl.

Carefully she touched her hands to the outer ring of chalk—carefully, because if she smudged it in any way, it wouldn't work.

Closing her eyes, she pictured it glowing, willed her array active; poured her power into the most complicated runes and equations she'd ever encountered.

It took a moment, but soon enough, the world outside her head began to glow as well.

Arlo opened her eyes, watched as a line of light split through the air in front of her face. It lengthened, then widened, pulling the space apart like a parting curtain, revealing a shimmering, deep navy . . . nothing.

Nothing, no matter how hard Arlo looked.

Frowning, she leaned a little closer—maybe it was dark in there, and she should get the flashlight. . . .

Crack—

Arlo startled, jerking back.

She looked down at where her hands had been . . . the fissures in the basement stone, in the laundry room she'd tucked away in, because it was the only bare surface down here she could draw on.

Crack—CRACK—

The fissures spread.

Movement upstairs said her parents definitely heard it, and they were going to be so upset with her—she dove for the array, tugged at her sleeves and tried to use them to scrub the chalk from the stone. Disrupt the array, break the connection; it was one of the first things she'd learned about alchemy, but it didn't seem to be working right now.

Her magic had scorched it into the floor—she'd just have to use that power, then, to shut it down the hard way. But as soon as she closed her eyes once more, she *felt* it beside her.

Darkness pressing in on her left.

Light pressing in on her right.

A chill and a warmth, safety and fear—tracking ran strong in her mom's family, and Arlo had inherited the ability with considerable ease, just like her alchemy; she could *smell* these auras as well as feel them, sense them in every way, and while there was nothing in them that seemed to want to hurt her, what they were . . . the *strength* in the way they closed around her . . .

"Arlo," the voice to her left purred, and Arlo wanted to look, but instinct screamed at her to keep her eyes closed.

"Arlo," smoothed the voice to her right.

"It's okay, child." They spoke in unison. "You've nothing to fear from us."

"You may call me Moros, scion of the End—"

615

"—And I, Eos, scion of the Beginning—"

"—Together we serve the beings of unity. Balance. All, start to finish; the First Ones; alchemy. You, my darling girl, have nothing to fear from us or our progenitors. We wish only to talk."

The cracking didn't stop; Arlo's home began to tremble.

"Arlo?" her mom called down the stairs. "Arlo, what's going on down there? Is everything okay?"

The sound of footsteps—she was going to be in so much trouble, and she didn't want to open her eyes, didn't want to see; wanted this all to be a bad, scary dream.

But then a hand on her shoulder . . . and Arlo looked up.

Looked over into Eos's indescribable face, so beautiful, so warm, so . . . entirely unreal.

"We only wish to talk with you, Arlo Flamel."

Moros placed cool fingers beneath her chin and tilted her gaze to him. Another indescribable sight, frightening . . . cold . . . equally unreal . . .

"We only wish to warn you."

"The Crown in this realm is no friend to you. Will bring about in your time unimaginable destruction."

"Arlo, no!"
"GET BACK—GET AWAY FROM HER! ARLO,
COME HERE!"
"DON'T LOOK AT THEM, NO!"
"GET AWAY FROM MY DAUGHTER!"

Arlo stared.

This felt like a dream.

This entire house might crumble around her—the power spilling out from wherever Eos and Moros had crept through might crush them all, her and her family, under its terrible weight—but she couldn't look away.

Could only barely register her parents trying to force their way through the current keeping them back, their shouting a distant sound.

"You, Arlo, the reincarnation of time's greatest alchemist," Moros said in his voice like silk. "The Courts have been lying to you, have lied to all; it was never your family who wished to use Ruin's power to conquer realms—this one, and others, all of them would have fallen to the Courts' control if they had had their way."

"Your family tried to stop them," Eos sighed. "The Arlo you were, the fallen son, alchemy's greatest master. He did his best—but not enough, not in time. The Courts wiped him off their board as surely as they'll wipe you off it once they realize what you can do."

Together: "Once they remember who Arlo Flamel is."

Eos bowed her head. "We beg your assistance as we did the man whose magic lives again inside you—a man whose sacrifice made him a villain in the eyes of all but truth. We beg of you, loath as we are to ask it again. One final time—"

Moros lowered himself to a knee. "We ask for help."

Together once more: "Help to make this right. Help to put an end to this cycle and destroy not just the Crown in your realm but the other two as well. Destroy all the Crowns. Take power away from what festers in both realms so that healing can begin. So that balance and unity can be restored. . . ."

Something *tore* Arlo away from the . . . well, Arlo would call them gods, but she wasn't really sure what they were.

Blinking . . . slowly . . . she craned her head, looked behind her and into Lethe's face; Lethe, who stood there, pale in a way that frightened her more than anything else going on.

"I concealed that truth for a reason," he hissed. "You have no idea what promises I was forced to make to wipe the Flamel identity from all but the High Sovereign. They will *kill* her for what you've just spoken back into existence. . . ."

Lethe sounded . . . not happy. It made Arlo even more afraid, and before she could stop it, she burst into tears.

Eos cocked her head at him. Moros smirked. "Conceal it again, Misfortune," they said back in unison—in balance, like they were one entity, not two. "After all, you've already decided on the role of villain, yourself. . . ."

"We're only asking she chooses villain, too."

ACKNOWLEDGMENTS

This book, like the others before it, would not be possible without the love and labour of so many people. As such, these particular pages are aways the hardest to write because they never feel like enough in terms of my gratitude, but here we go.

As always, I am thankful to my incredibly supportive family, who think what I do is very cool and glamorous. I'm not very much either of those things, especially on a deadline, but your enthusiasm still means the world to me.

To my agent—Mandy Hubbard—who remains the same fierce champion of this story as she was when she first took it on all those years ago. Who always has my back, and never fails in her kindness to make sure I'm okay while writing.

To my "irl" friends Kyle, Jess, Jeryn, Juli, Colleen, Laura, Jee, and Shana; to my writing community friends Liselle, Priyanka, Brittany, Koren, and Nicki.

To Zack, my cat and constant companion.

To the entirety of the S&S teams, US and Canada—the editors, the publicists, the marketers, the roles I don't even know about, all the great many who work so hard to make sure these books are polished and pretty in just a year's time to hit the shelves. To the Canadian Council of Arts for the grant that allows me to dedicate myself entirely to this career. To my fellow LGBTQ+ creators laying groundwork for future queer and trans joy.

Thank you all.

And I don't mean my thanks any more or less for anyone, but I do want to focus this next part on a few specific people.

On my editor, Sarah McCabe, who worked her ass off on tighter deadlines so that I could have whatever time I needed to fall asleep at my laptop, combat morning sickness, write so much slower than normal, and require much more help managing plot, and in the end, for all her care, deliver a whole, healthy baby. Sarah, who has always understood the assignment; who loves these characters as much as I do and never fails to see what this story needs to make it next-level.

On Cayley Pimentel, Mackenzie Croft, and Arden Hagedorn, who have been such an incredible team to work with, always so loving and supportive. I consider myself very lucky to have you all with me and these books.

On the Book Bloggers; the TikTokers; the Instagrammers; the booksellers—the people who are such an integral part of this community, who not only move the things authors write but make this community so much fun with their creative displays and content. I have endless amounts of respect and appreciation for all of you, and while I try to keep myself on the author side of the fence now, and let readers have their space to love or hate what I do without pressure, there are a few people I'd like to thank for their support of the Hollow Star Saga: Zeal, Amy Poirier, Chloe (theelvenwarrior), Tae (taebereading), Angelina (library.of.lina), Star, Meghan Mazzaferro, Kate Oliver, DJReadsBooks, J.J.Fryer, Cass (kaznyp), and the entirety of the ACAFL Street Team.

Thank you also to my partner, Kade. The love of my life. My best friend. The guy with all the tattoos and quiet broodiness, whom I thought hated me all those years ago because he wouldn't say more anything more than "thank you" when he came through my till, but was actually only coming into my store so he could see me. You might not like reading, but you've always been my biggest fan, and I'll always, always be grateful for you.

But I lied before. I do mean this next thanks more than any of the others. Nyx, my baby boy, currently sound asleep on my shoulder because I'm writing this during our afternoon contact nap. I started this book when I was pregnant with you, and finished it when you were born. I cannot thank you enough, just for being you. Just for existing. Before you I was so incredibly heartbroken by loss. I was tired and hurting, and losing the spark I'd always felt for telling stories. Because of you, I rediscovered my joy in creating worlds from words, and my biggest hope now is to write one you'll someday want to explore; that will inspire you to discover what brings *you* joy.

And last, but certainly not least, thanks to you, the reader. Without you, there is no book. Without you, this story only exists in my head. It has been an honour and a privilege to take this journey with you all—I look forward to concluding it with you at my side.

Meet you at the finish line <3